SAFFRON AND HONEY

HOW SHOULD I KNOW YOU?

1st edition 2024.
ISBN 978-1-7380438-0-4 (trade paperback)

1. FICTION / Romance / LGBTQ+ / Bisexual.
2. FICTION / Disabilities.
3. FICTION / Erotica / Science Fiction, Fantasy & Horror.

Saffron and Honey

How Should I Know You?

Aphy Ray

This one's for everyone who's sewn belonging into a name that always meant being alone.

To the friends who stretch our best weeks out into years, and especially to the partner who dragged me grumbling and swearing out of my own dark and peaceful sanctuary, I couldn't have told this story without you. Thank you.

And a very special thanks to the best and brightest at Milk+Tea. This book is 90% green tea and pomegranate syrup by volume. Don't lick the pages.

Also hey heads up, this story has some spicy scenes in it, so, you know, watch out!

∽ *Part I* ∽

Let's Just Say It's Growing on Me

Ravi's coworker at the warehouse, Erwin, pulled a little mason jar out of his pocket like a secret. The warped glass made it hard for them to make sense of the pink blob floating inside.

"Tumor," he explained with a toothy smile.

Ravi brought their hand to their mouth in disgust and took a big step back from the old man, nearly dropping the box they were trying very hard to put on the right shelf as soon as possible to silence the automated voice in their earpiece for five whole damn seconds.

"Oh, what are you being such a baby for? It's just meat. A miserable little lump of meat."

Ravi tried to calm themself down. He was right. Just meat. We're all just meat, right? It's fine. But, no, it was all for show. They couldn't settle their stomach, no matter how cool they tried to look while they examined the jar. They refused to touch the glass themself, of course, so in Erwin's hand it remained.

—Oh god. Did it just... move...?

"*Where* did you get a tumor from?"

"It's mine! They carved it out last week. Missed three whole days of work for this little piece of shit." He gave the glob of flesh a little shake and a menacing smile. "You'll pay for that," he threatened the thing, like it knew what it had done.

Ravi got the feeling Erwin was the sort of person who put his furniture in the corner after it had stubbed his toe – you know, to think about what it had done.

They grinned at the thought of Erwin dressing the little wad of flesh in a uniform and putting it behind the wheel of the forklift for a few days, as retribution for the lost wages.

"Do you think anyone will notice?" they asked idly.

"Notice what?"

"When the tumor takes your job."

It took Erwin a moment to realize he was being insulted, "You shit. You've been here nine months, kid, you're lucky I don't give it *your* badge. It'll get more work done. Might even pass a performance review for once. What'd you get last time, Butterfingers McGee? 'Absolute shit'?"

Needs work. Close enough, though. Ravi was supposed to be a little more crushed by that evaluation, based on the grave look on their supervisor's face when she delivered the report and presented the sum total of every cent they'd cost the company by dropping boxes. But the review felt more like a matter of fact. A state of being. *Ravi needs work.*

"I should get my own pet tumor," they said, grinning at Erwin. "Take a little vacation. Get a raise. Get a girlfriend. Hell, it could just live my whole life for me. The latest model. *Ravi 20XS+:* New and improved. Less bullshit."

When the two of them bumped into each other later that day during a rainy, frigid, harried smoke break, Ravi had to ask why. It had been on their mind all day. Who keeps a hunk of cancerous flesh? He wasn't going to eat it or something, was he?

"Don't they burn that stuff?" they asked, attempting to flick their lighter's flame on for emphasis – but, sputtering as it was in the wet weather, it was much less dramatic than they wanted. Worse, their cigarette refused to light. This was going to be a complete waste of the only break they were going to get all day.

"They sure do, but I told 'em I wanted it. They still said no, so I grabbed it out of the guy's hand when he was showing it to me and bolted out the door."

"You bolted out the door," Ravi echoed in disbelief. "After surgery? No sedatives?"

"You think a little tranq is going to stop me? Kid."

Ravi remembered the first time they accepted Erwin's insistent weekly offers to join him for a bottle at his place after work. It turned out an 'Erwin' bottle is about the size of gas can – and the stuff in it smelled about the same. And somehow, even after getting through all that and then finishing off Ravi's beer, he was still on his feet. He even walked them home in the rain, wearing a smile and dancing like a lunatic the whole way. So, yeah, no doubt in Ravi's mind: Erwin could probably run a marathon on a whole barrel of ketamine.

"You're just going to keep it?" Ravi really didn't want to ask about it directly – the whole auto-cannibalism thing – but they were aching to be rid of all the images their mind was conjuring of Erwin preparing his excision for breakfast, lunch, and dinner. They practically had a whole cookbook of body horror in their mind, ready to be burned.

Erwin was graciously not shoving his unsettling pet in Ravi's face anymore, but he was clearly fiddling with it in his coat pocket while he spoke.

"Our *business* is not complete," he assured Ravi. When they failed to nod with understanding, he launched into a hypothetical situation that quickly turned into some kind of parable: "If you killed a bear before it killed you, you'd spend some *intimate* time with the thing after, yeah? You'd sit with it, feel it out, *know* it – figure out where it was going and why it ended up there, *with you*, angry and scared. It's a force of nature you can hold in your hands. And if one hair were out of place, that bear would've won, Rav." He could no longer resist the urge to draw out the metaphorical beast from his pocket to glare at it. "I haven't sat with that long enough yet."

That conversation played through Ravi's mind while they waited in line in the chilly late September air for their turn at the clinic.

They wondered if they too could bolt out of a hospital hopped up on anesthetic. But it wasn't really worth considering. There was no surgery for what they had going on, and the nurses never used anesthetic for this thing. Out-patient, they called it.

The sign on the front door promised in-and-out in fifteen minutes.

They'd had quickies longer, with more tender aftercare and less awkward eye contact, too.

But back here, a hundred feet from the front door of the clinic, there was a standing sign on the sidewalk that proudly pronounced – in stark contrast to the *other* sign's promise of a mercifully short engagement – that the wait from this point in the line was 'only' one hour.

Both signs were untrue of course. Unless clocks and time were fiercely warped around here, or maybe there was some hidden asterisk somewhere in the signage.

No, this was always a day-long adventure.

It never healed, they were told when they were diagnosed, back in the second year of their undergrad. It could never heal. The deep, cystic wounds would fill with black agony over the course of every month, then the nurse would take the horrible black stuff out, put it in a jar, and burn it. And that was it. They'd get another month. And they'd get several hundred months fewer on Earth than the people lucky enough to avoid getting sick with it – though what exactly that blessed crowd were doing differently than the infected was still a medical mystery, apparently.

The line was the worst part of this whole experience – is what Ravi tried to convince themself. That gymnastic mental exercise was better for their soul. Focus on the clinical *annoyance* instead of that knife-twisting ache piercing their back and shoulder. —And it wasn't too hard a lie to believe, since there was just a whole lot of annoyance to focus on out here.

In the last year, the line had been growing longer every month. An article – maybe even a reputable one – strongly suggested that the infected were migrating to the city, sent there by small, overburdened community clinics. The author wrote a merciless and heartless indictment of the little underfunded towns for 'making their problems our problem' – because they simply 'refused' to put their scant resources towards treating their ill. The article chastised them for 'burdening' all the province's largest and most important hospitals. It was very much the kind of article that could only be written by someone who had never lived outside the city limits.

Whoever's problem the swelling of the population of the ill was, it was their problem today trying to keep their spot in line in the uneasy crowd.

Ravi used to be a lot scrawnier, a lot easier to knock over, but eight years in warehouses paying for rent and research supplies and private student debt had bulked them up a bit, toughened their skin. But still, as a dispirited little meatloaf of a postgrad student, they didn't take up much space, and they were far too soft-hearted to push back when some sick person pushed forward, which seemed to be an invitation for the occasional impatient guy to cut in line, or for some young woman to insist that she was suffering more severely than they were. 'Kids at home.' 'Kettle on the boil.' Whatever scant excuse came to mind was always enough to shove Ravi aside.

And as soon as one person saw them concede their spot, the rest saw an easy mark.

Ravi wasn't going to argue, though. Getting in a fight in their current state was way too risky. Might just tear the tender leather of their sores right open.

But whatever. What was another hour? Not like they were doing anything else this weekend. Not until their pain got sorted out by the unenthusiastic in-and-out from the nurse at the end of the line.

It was pretty painful to lose a whole weekend of overtime, though, stuck waiting in the cold like this. Did it compare to the pain of leaving their wounds untreated? It was always a tight race, but the physical pain won every month. As much as they wanted to be spiteful enough to power through it, they could barely stifle the scream that came from having to lift their arm over their head right now. Even slipping their binder on in the morning was impossible, never mind hauling an endless stream of heavy boxes.

But the line and the wait and the pushy people... Today was the worst it had ever been. Ravi felt like they were actually getting shoved backwards by the unjust swelling of the line in front of them. And most of these people were too sick, too frail, and too achy to fight back against whoever had the audacity to shove ahead.

If this kept up, they'd end up pushed all the way back to the *two-hour* sign by the time the clinic closed.

And, as if it weren't bad enough having to stand and freeze in a stagnant line with a couple hundred grumpy people, there was suddenly an overbearingly sweet floral scent coming from somewhere nearby, like someone was emptying a can of air freshener into the air.

Who the hell brings air freshener to a clinic? And who the hell sprays air freshener *outdoors* at a clinic?

"Amy Bee!"

Ravi's shoulders tightened at the sound. No one had called them by that cutesy, childish nickname in almost a decade. They didn't recognize the voice, but it must be someone from a past life.

How the hell do you even run into someone you know in a city this big?

"Amaira Beausoleil! It *is* you!"

An absolutely jubilant and towering young woman – big flowy hair that shone like amber and sun and honey in the grey weather – ran up to Ravi, beaming, making them feel like a sheepish, distant cousin at a family gathering: Spoken of too well behind their back, but entirely out of the loop and stuck owing this would-be stranger a fake smile and a pleasant tone.

"Heyyy, it's... *you.*"

—*Name. Name please. Brain? Help? No?*

Ravi had no idea what to do here. This woman's face should be hard to forget. Cute freckles on cold-blushed cheeks, an impossibly bright smile peeking out over a big knit scarf, sparkling greenish blue eyes that felt like a spell even under the overcast sky. And she was... *tall.* Sturdy. Big. Big energy. Big charm. Just, everything about her was big in a way that made Ravi feel even smaller than usual.

"Oh my gods," she said, putting a gentle, considerate touch on Ravi's arm. "I can't believe you're still wearing this old jacket! Lucky me, though! I recognized it a whole block away. —Of course you would, though. It's *so* you—"

Their denim jacket. The ratty old thing was falling apart at the seams now. They had only grabbed it out of the closet at all because they somehow forgot their real coat after spending all last night at a bar trying to get drunk enough to forget their pain. Apparently, they managed to walk all the way home in the cold, oblivious.

They glanced down at the jacket and conceded that it was pretty distinctive. Slashed up sleeves and chest, covered in cracked, hand-painted, anarchy-flavored graffiti, and decked out with faded, once-vibrant, stapled-on patches for their old favorite bands and naïve teenage politics, and a collection of colorful pride pins that were a lot more relevant when they had time to fuck anyone.

They had no idea it was so iconic to their look, though. The damn thing was probably ten years old by now. An artifact of a past life, like the name this woman was so enthusiastically dragging out of its grave to slap them in the face with.

But that undead name saw a lot more light of day than the jacket. The *name* followed them to every professional and bureaucratic engagement, sadly. No one who *knew them* called them Amaira anymore, but paperwork doesn't really try to flirt or take you home for a fun evening of getting to know you.

The jacket, though, even before the seams started coming undone, they saved it for special occasions – like whenever they wanted to look unapproachable at a bar – which, apparently, didn't work so great last time, since a bar was the very place all the seams got torn apart in a fight. Cracked a few of their ribs too.

And, apparently, it wasn't working so great today either.

Ravi's new mystery friend didn't want to throw them into a brick wall for being a 'fucking mouthy antifa paki terrorist dyke', but she did make the extremely aggressive move of leaning in *far too close* to inspect one of the patches on Ravi's chest pocket.

—Marigold. Apple. Sunshine.

It was *her* – the source of that floral scent, which was already unreasonably powerful in the breeze somehow. Now it was intoxicating, heady and thick with her right under Ravi's nose like this – though, admittedly, the aroma wasn't so suffocating now, now that they knew it wasn't coming out of an aerosol can.

Kind of nice actually.

Reminded them of summer.

—How the hell do you capture the smell of the sun in shampoo like that?

"This is *Kittle Skisses*, isn't it?" she asked, pointing at the band's colorful faded patch. "First album?"

Even Ravi had to look down to doublecheck, but sure enough, it was. "That's... right. Are you a fan?"

"Uh, yeah? Only since they were still scaring all the old guys out of the room at all those cute little open mic nights around here. They're still one of my favorite bands. Wish they'd release another album already. Four years! How long are we supposed to wait?"

"Just *one* of your favorites? What number?"

"Oh. Mm. Near the top, I think. 70ish?"

—70's near the top? Exclusive list...

"How many favorites do you *have*?"

"Oh, a *lot*. I know a lot of bands, though, so even 70 is a *prestigious* position to be in. Even the ones down in the hundreds ranks are top tier, I promise."

"Huh."

Awkward pause.

The woman was still smiling at them. Sharp teeth. Waiting? What was Ravi even supposed to say here? They wanted this conversation to be over as quickly as possible. Talking about their teenage nostalgia was not on the agenda.

—Speed this up, please.

If it went fast enough, they could get out of this without ever revealing that the woman's name had been forever lost to the sandstorm of time between them.

After a few seconds of silence that felt like a hundred years, they asked: "So uh, how have you been?"

"Not great!" she replied, surprisingly cheerful about her 'not great' situation – and, unfortunately, she was apparently one of those people who was willing to be 100% honest about that question, instead of just replying with a 'fine' and moving on. "Not great. My buddy just got evicted. Well, more like the landlord changed his lock. No notice, even! That should be illegal, shouldn't it?"

Ravi nodded. "Yeah uh. That's... definitely not allowed."

"Just because the guy had a little party – and not even a *party* party! You wouldn't call a few friends hanging out and playing games all night a party, would you?"

"*I*... wouldn't? I mean, I would need more details. Like, how loud were these 'friends'?" From a quick, discerning analysis, Ravi felt pretty confident that this woman had the energy of a 'friend' who might just be loud enough to be mistaken for a whole crowd of rambunctious partygoers.

"So I don't even have a couch to crash on anymore," the woman continued without addressing the question.

And then Ravi saw their social assailant's machinations.

"Yeah," they tried to cut in, "Hey, that sucks. I wish I could help—" Maybe they could preemptively excuse themself from the giant ask that was about to be dropped on them.

"—So I *can* stay with you! Oh my gods, thank you so much, you have no idea how much trouble you're saving me. I'll stay out of your way, and I can be gone in a week, for sure. You probably won't even notice I'm there."

Ravi's mouth opened slightly in awe. They tried to say no. They tried to crumple up this beaming, summery woman's optimistic smile and leave her out in the cold with nowhere to go. They really, truly, honestly tried to get a *no* to form on their lips, but somehow it came out *yes*.

"I knew I could count on you, Amy Bee. You were always sweet as honey."

Ravi tried to stifle a cheerful little scoff at that fraudulent assessment. They did a quick mental fact check on that one and came up nil on the 'times dear little Amaira was sweet as honey' scan. This woman was clearly mistaking them for someone else.

Oh well. It didn't matter. This was the right thing to do, putting her up in her time of need, as miserable as it was to admit that.

Their shoulders sunk, but they still put on as friendly a grin as they could muster and started rearranging their apartment in their mind to make accommodations for this woman – who was *allegedly* an old friend – to sleep on their couch.

—*For one and <u>only</u> one week.*

"It's just an old loveseat though," they tried to explain. "Terrible for your back." Maybe if they made it sound uncomfortable enough.

"Perfect," the woman replied, undeterred, to Ravi's dismay. "It's not full or rocks or iron rods, is it?"

Ravi shook their head. What an odd question. Where the hell had she been sleeping until now?

"Just nice soft cushions?"

Ravi nodded reluctantly. It was pretty comfortable, honestly. They loved that couch.

No point lying now.

Their fate was sealed.

"No, really," the woman continued with exuberant gratitude, "that's totally luxurious. My guy's couch had some very aggressive springs in it. I had to get all twisted up just to avoid getting stabbed all night. But normal cushions on a loveseat? Perfect. I'll just curl up in a cozy ball, pretend to be a little cat, you won't even notice me."

—*A stray.*

An extremely tall stray. Even curled up, Ravi couldn't imagine her fitting on the couch. She must've had at least six inches on them. Hard to tell with the hair and the boots. So, what, six feet and a few inches?

The woman – whose name still hadn't returned to Ravi's mind, so... 'Nicole'? Why not. Too late to ask now, and she had big 'Nicole' energy – 'Nicole' leaned back on the heels of her boots and took a long look up and down the stalled and miserable parade of patients waiting to get their monthly treatment.

"You sick?" she asked. Then she finally woke up to the reality of

Ravi's situation and the possibility of them being contagious.

They weren't.

She covered her mouth with the cuff of her coat, but instead of stepping back like a normal person would, she leaned in and eagerly asked, "What is it?" Her voice was muffled by the impromptu mask. "Broken bones? Fever? *Rabies?*"

She looked Ravi up and down trying to diagnose their ailment at a glance, which shouldn't have been possible. They prided themself on being able to hide it. And they were lucky enough to have their wounds in an easily concealed location. Well, lucky for pride's sake anyways. They hurt just a whole bunch worse rubbing under their clothes. And forget wearing a binder when it got bad like this. This whole last week every month, they were stuck tits out for the whole world to gawk at and get them wrong.

"Oh no," she continued with her guessing game. "It's not that tar thing, is it?"

—How.

"That's kind of personal," Ravi replied, trying to avoid the answer.

But 'Nicole' must have managed to put all the clues together – the clues being that most of the people in the line had their ugly black cysts on display, and also that the clinic had big signs on its exterior advertising its tar treatment services today.

The place did other normal medical stuff too, but these clinics got a lot of funding based on the number of these black 'tar' cysts they treated every month. Ravi had even seen nurses turn other patients away, just because they weren't 'sick enough' to justify the cost of taking up an examination room that could otherwise be used to extract a bit of the black, goopy cash crop out of someone's cysts.

'Nicole', during her brief investigation of the scene, had also made note of the sign indicating the hour-long wait time from this point in the line. The look on her face said that that was entirely unacceptable. She paused for a moment to think, very intently, even rolling her head side to side a bit to consider her options, then she told Ravi she'd be right back before rushing to the front of the queue, intently searching for something.

Ravi leaned out of the line as far as they could get without losing their spot, but they couldn't really see what 'Nicole' was up to.

A few minutes later, with an imperative, "Let's go!" from their new roommate, Ravi was ripped right out of their precious spot in line and dragged up to the front. They did their best to protest, but there was apparently no stopping this woman, and by the time they even had a chance to look back, their place was already filled.

—Heartless.

"Here she is!" She showed Ravi off to an older woman near the front of the line, who was acting overjoyed to see them. 'Nicole' turned to Ravi and gave them a not-so-subtle wink. "Your 'mom' was worried about you! Don't wander off anymore, okay?"

Ravi had no idea what was going on, but they weren't about to complain about being thrust to the front of the queue like this. They gave a stupid nod and joined the elderly woman in line.

Before she left, 'Nicole' leaned in and whispered in Ravi's ear, "Thank you, really. Look, I'll meet you at the coffee shop on the corner over there," she pointed. Then gave Ravi a cheerful wave and jogged off.

After she left, Ravi gave their new mom a quiet thank you and what was almost certainly the most awkward smile the features of their face could arrange themselves into.

"Oh, honey don't be shy," she laughed, then gave Ravi a very much unsolicited hug that made them flinch and hiss and wince with pain, barely suppressing an agonized groan.

After mercifully letting go – without an apology – their 'mom' glared at the guy behind them in line, who looked about ready to swear at Ravi for cutting ahead of him – which, honestly, would have been entirely deserved. And not just because it was extremely rude. 'Nicole' had come up with an entirely implausible scheme here. The old woman didn't even have brown skin. They didn't exactly look like a matching pair.

But the guy's ire was quickly deflated by either the woman's threatening glare, or the realization that he'd be yelling and swearing at a sick old woman, and he ended up backing down without a word.

Once Ravi's 'mom' had successfully defended the challenge to the legitimacy of Ravi's stolen spot in the queue, she asked, "So how do you know Danica?"

Ahh, right. *Danica.* Yeah, that was her alright.

Ravi had never actually been friends with her in high school, but she did always seem to be involved in anything they were doing, and everything they weren't. Every club, every sport, every vocation, even student council and the GSA. They tried to remember: Was there even *one class* they didn't share? It definitely wasn't out of any special coincidence though. She was just one of the handful of people in school who seemed to have the energy and fortune to do *literally everything*, while Ravi just kind of fucked around and did whatever felt right.

But in all that time, the two of them never once worked together, or even sat together. They'd only ever had a few conversations at all, and Ravi couldn't remember any of them. The two of them lived in different worlds. And Ravi had a hard time believing they'd made a strong enough impression on her as a twerpy little faux punk kid that she'd remember them after eight whole years. Maybe Danica was just more weirdly attentive to her classmates than they could've imagined.

—Or maybe you're just an asshole, Ravi.

"From school," they replied slowly. "We were in the same year. How do you know her?"

"Oh, she helps me with little errands sometimes, and we have some common interests. She joins our little stitch-and-bitch once in a while – though the little puppy is mostly there for the stitching part." The woman put out her hand. "Angie."

"Ravi." Because why not. Couldn't hurt to be honest. They'd never see this woman again. It didn't matter.

"Pretty name."

—Pretty. Sure.

"Thanks. Picked it myself."

They liked the ambiguity of it. Sounded a little femme in Canada, but it was a boy's name, pulling from some distant relative on their mom's side, for the god of the sun. Felt like a good match for their surname. If they weren't going to get rid of their dad's name, they might as well let themself rule over it, right?

Angie looked sad to hear about Ravi's decision, like it was her business at all. She shook her head with disappointment and chastised Ravi, "Names are powerful gifts. Shame to throw away a treasure like that."

Ravi wasn't planning to get into the storied history of their name with a stranger. Instead, they changed the subject by commenting on the charming colors in the woman's scarf, which got her talking about how it was a handmade gift from one of her girlfriends, and that was enough to keep her attention off of Ravi until the two of them were split into separate rooms for the procedure.

The nurse did the two large cysts over the corners of Ravi's shoulder blade first – after scolding them for the scar in between them there, the scar that was left over from the site of their very first infection, the first cyst that got *extremely* unprofessionally excised with a hunting knife right after their diagnosis... six years ago now?

They didn't need to be reminded how stupid that was. As if the three new cysts that popped up afterwards – and the resulting tripling of their pain – wasn't enough to set them straight about it.

They flinched when the needle went in. They would've liked to pretend that they had made peace with the feeling of the treatment by now, but nothing felt peaceful about the extremely sharp, jaw-clenching, hiss-inducing sensation of having that thick black gunk forcibly displaced from their body.

'Tar' was a fitting nickname for it.

Each extraction filled a small glass vial, which the nurse placed into a rack that contained dozens of others just like it from other patients.

Profitable day for the clinic.

For the final cyst – the one that was just below the soft part of the shoulder on their right arm – they twisted their neck to watch the nurse. They always watched that one. They figured they might have to do it themself one day. Better to know how to take care of yourself, they figured. Ravi didn't enjoy relying on doctors for their body's *upkeep*. Bad experiences with the medical profession. But sadly, love them or hate them, doctors were the ones with the equipment and the prescription pads.

The device the nurse used to administer the treatment was simple enough. It looked a little like a glue gun with two terrifying needles sticking out the front. A wide shallow needle attached to the vacuum-sealed sample vial just barely pierced the thick leathery surface of the cyst to collect the tarry discharge, while the other thinner syringe got nestled *deep* into the abscess to inject some thick, clear, medicinal gel from behind. The gel forced the tar out, to take its place in the cavity of the wound. Then, over the course of the month, the gel would get supplanted, replaced by dozens of tiny black florets that eventually accumulated into the thick, painful globs that went into those vials.

The last vial rattled into place with the others in the rack. Ravi looked at it intently. Erwin's words still rang in their mind. This was their bear, wasn't it? Lots of people died from this. Ravi had been lucky. They continued to be lucky every month. But just one hair out of place, and it could take them. They definitely had some questions for it.

In the moment the nurse had her back turned to discard her gloves, Ravi silently plucked that final vial from the rack and pocketed it, unnoticed.

Their heart was racing when they got out of the building and into the parking lot.

Why did this feel guilty? They deserved this. They owned this, didn't they? After spending a whole month laboriously... *growing* it.

They held the vial up to the bright light of the overcast sky. *Amaira Beausoleil* was printed in thermal ink on the label, along with every number and symbol the clinic could think of to describe what 'Amaira' meant to the world. None of it meant anything to them, but there was one number printed in the bottom corner that gave them a little reason to be concerned: 3/3. It should have been obvious the clinic would be keeping an inventory of the vials to get their handsome funding, but how did they know ahead of time that Ravi only had enough tar for three of them? Kind of presumptuous. And... if they were counting them so meticulously... would they miss this one?

Well, no point worrying about it now. What's done cannot be undone.

They hid the vial in their pocket and started for the bus stop.

They were already three steps onto the bus, mere inches away from tapping on their fare, when they remembered they had forgotten someone.

The walk back to the café where Danica was waiting for them was full of stuttered steps. They came to a full stop every time the thought crossed their mind that they could just walk away right now. Danica had no idea where they lived. She didn't have their contact info. How could she possibly find them? More than once, that thought turned them around, back towards the bus, towards a peaceful home with no noisy guests sleeping on the couch, intruding on their sanctuary, pretending to be harmless as a kitten.

But every turn brought them right back around again towards the café, to the exuberantly patient, dutifully waiting Danica.

She waved them over excitedly, inviting them to sit at a table that felt far too small for two people. But it had two chairs, so it must've been deemed large enough by the café's stingy owner, and by Danica herself, so they didn't really have a choice.

There was no good spot for Ravi's feet under the table. It seemed everywhere they tried to put them, they were stepping on Danica's toes, so they gave up on relaxing and just sat up stiff and straight to keep their feet tucked neatly under their own chair.

This already felt exhausting.

"How was it?" Danica asked, excited to hear the answer. "I hear it hurts."

Ravi's long-lost 'friend' looked down at their face with such interest and intensity that it was hard to look away without feeling rude. The light in the café caught her irises in a way that made them shine like gemstones. Entrancing. Sapphire? Tourmaline? It was hard to tell. The color seemed to shift somehow. Ravi wished their eyes could be so captivating. The abyssal brown that looked back at them in every mirror just didn't do it for them most days.

"It does," Ravi confirmed. They didn't know what else to add. It did hurt. No one really wants the details, and anyone who does just wants them for some perverse, false sense of empathy – as if to hear the words describing the pain was enough to understand what it meant to feel it, to live with it.

"And they make you wait out in the cold all that time! Can't they just get more doctors? Or at least get a bigger space for everyone stuck waiting? It's just cruel!"

Ravi shrugged. "I can't pretend to know how that part of the process works. I'm just lucky it's free. Down south it costs an arm and a leg. So, you know, surprising no one, a lot of people let it grow until they lose their arms and legs."

Danica shook her head sadly. "Gods," she whispered to herself, in awe.

This wasn't new or quiet information though. Like most people, Danica clearly just hadn't been looking out for it. Ravi was always vaguely aware that no one really cared about 'the tar thing', as Danica put it, unless it was directly affecting them.

But it was kind of painful getting hit in the face with it like this.

"That's so dark," she said to Ravi after considering it for a few pensive seconds. "I'm sorry you have to deal with all that, Amy. If there's anything I can do to make it better, please let me know."

"I'll keep that in mind."

They tapped out an uneven, syncopated rhythm on the tabletop, staring at their finger as it rose and fell like a blacksmith's hammer, shaping the answer to an unasked question in their mind – whether or not this annoyance was worth bringing up. Was it worth the trouble for just a week? Or maybe *because* it was just a week, and they didn't care about this woman…? It was *their* home that she was intruding on. She should use the right name. But it was always such a *thing*.

After a dozen slow, heavy impacts, they made up their mind.

"It's Ravi, by the way."

"Huh?"

"No one calls me Amaira anymore," they lied. It felt nice to say it though.

"Oh! 'Ravi'. *Raw-vee*." She tried the name out in quick, quiet whispers to herself, "*Ravi, Ravi, Ravi…*" then returned her attention to them with a cheerful thumbs up. "Okay! Got it."

—*That easy?*

"…And I'm non-binary. So. Gender neutral… *words*."

"Oh, neat! They and them and such, right? Yup. No problem."

—*That easy??*

Ravi shook the shock out of their mind and asked, "What do you go by these days?" It seemed like the courteous thing to do. Ravi's 'mom' called her Danica, but old people always seemed to pick out the least comfortable form of anyone's name.

"You call me whatever you feel like, *Ravi*." She was practicing now.

That was an odd offer. Ravi thought about it for a second before playfully suggesting, "How about 'Nicole'?"

" 'Nicole'… That's pretty cute." She beamed at them, "Alright, let's give that a try, see how it fits!"

Ravi smiled softly at that sentiment. An experiment. A trial. 'Name' science. There was something nostalgic and warm about that. It wasn't that long ago that they were doing the same thing – with the occasional disastrous result. …Okay, with frequent, practically nonstop disastrous results.

Hopefully Ravi could make it a little easier on her.

"Nice to meet you again, *Nicole*," they said, holding their hand out for a playful little handshake.

The newly christened young woman beamed, then dragged Ravi up to the counter to pay for their drink of choice.

The two of them spent a lot longer at the café catching up than Ravi expected them to. Nicole's energy was kind of intoxicating. And Ravi had a lot more patience for it now that they weren't suppressing just a *whole lot of pain* in a miserable line in the cold.

They learned that Nicole had tried her hand at college but found it unsatisfying. Then she spent a year travelling for fun. And another few years on a voluntourism campaign. That was where her heart was at, she said. But 'somehow' she ended up back here.

She glossed over why she didn't have some permanent address to return to, so Ravi invented a fiction in their head that she'd been kicked out of her parents' home for partying too hard or something.

And then she shamelessly informed Ravi that she'd been couch surfing with her friends ever since she returned, chipping in whatever rent and favors she could afford while she hopped between gigs.

"I have a bit saved up though if you need it! I'm not some deadbeat drifter. I always pay back a favor," she asserted, a little indignant at the entirely unspoken suggestion that she wouldn't.

Ravi shot her a playful smirk. "How about you do the dishes, and we'll call it even."

Nicole shook her head. "That's way too little! You're saving my life. I'll find some way to make it up to you properly, okay? I promise."

The 'one week' Ravi had initially offered seemed to last an awfully lot longer than seven days. In fact, it seemed to be composed of multiple weeks that just kept chaining themselves together indefinitely.

Ravi had no intention of bringing that up, though. Living with Nicole wasn't nearly as terrible as they had imagined it would be. Actually, it was kind of nice having her around. She always seemed busy, and she always had stories to tell about her life – both her travels and her daily activities.

And just like a cat, she often left small gifts at Ravi's bedroom door. A clay pot. A scarf. A flowering plant – more of a curse than a gift, those poor plants. Ravi's apartment was where houseplants went to die. An elephant graveyard for ferns, flowers, and succulents. None would be spared. Each cheerful, doomed little plant lived out its miserable little life next to the skeletal remains of its desiccated little cousins on the windowsill in Ravi's bedroom – where Nicole would hopefully never see their shameful bones.

All of Nicole's crafty gifts were handmade by her. She even offered to bring Ravi along to the studios and workshops where she made them.

"They'll love you," she said. She had been on a campaign of trying to get Ravi out more. After her first week there, she had clearly been both surprised and disappointed to find the way Ravi spent their evenings. By the end of week two, there was no end to her encouraging words and... 'gentle' pushes.

She didn't seem to understand how much their work and research at the university took out of them. The night shifts and overtime at the warehouse took more. They were barely home. It was hard to imagine going out during the few hours they had left every week. When were they supposed to relax?

"But it *is* relaxing! Working with your hands, making something. It connects you to the universe, Ravi, shaping it into something new."

"Yeah, something horrifying," they teased her. "They'll write stories about it, call it an eldritch artifact. I'll be strung up as a mad scientist for consorting with demons after Faustian bargains."

But as more and more weeks went by, their '*absolutely not*'s turned into '*maybe*'s, and their '*maybe*'s turned into '*okay fine*'s, where Ravi reluctantly consented to go out with Nicole once in a while, just for a drink or two.

To Nicole's credit, Ravi did enjoy the nights out, despite the resistant fuss they always put up about being too tired to leave the apartment. Nicole was a joy to spend an evening with. Ravi wasn't very social at bars, but the way Nicole drew people in, and held their attention, and somehow made Ravi feel like they were part of the conversation without ever making them participate, it felt like magic. It felt like even stronger magic that she somehow both attracted and deflected dozens of unsolicited phone numbers with that sweet disarming smile of hers. This woman was some kind of wizard.

❦

The next month, Ravi stole another vial from the clinic. It was their secret solace now. They couldn't do anything about their illness, but they could hold it in their hands, growl at it, ask it why.

It did not answer. But they'd keep asking. They felt like *something* important was in there.

In all the time Nicole was there, they'd never revealed their wounds to her. They even dug a plushy, forgotten, out-of-season, new-in-box house robe out of storage, tore the store's stickers and tags off it, and started wearing it around the apartment to keep their affliction hidden – behind reindeer, snowflakes, and candy canes.

Their sores were gross to look at, but there was another reason to hide them, a reason that nagged at Ravi. They remembered Nicole's words when they met, when she found out they were sick. She said she wanted to do something for them, to help with their illness, to pay them back, and this thing just wasn't something she could do anything about. No one could. And it would just hurt her to see it all the time. That's not the kind of burden you put on a stranger. It didn't even feel like the kind of burden they could put on a friend – not that they had a lot of those left to burden these days.

But Nicole couldn't contain her curiosity about the vial when she spotted it in Ravi's hand. It would have been easy to explain it away, but they couldn't say no to Nicole. And they couldn't see any harm in letting her take a look. Conceptually, it was just far enough removed from the reality of the sores on their back. It could be *any* black ooze.

"They have your name wrong," Nicole noted, disappointed. She wasn't ready to hold the glass in her hands – a little too weird – but she was fine idly rolling it around on the table with a pen.

"Among other things, yeah," Ravi confirmed.

"Ah I see, yeah." Nicole spotted the erroneous 'F' on the label. "I guess they don't have a letter for that?"

"They do. They have to change it to an 'X' if you ask."

Nicole got animated hearing that. "You should ask!" She clearly thought this was some self-confidence thing, that a little encouragement would make it better.

Ravi shook their head. "It puts an X on your *head* too. I've read a lot about it. Real bureaucratic horror stories. A lot of things get very hard when you put yourself out there like that. Healthcare gets complicated. Legal stuff is a nightmare. And forget travelling with something weird like that on your passport." They gave Nicole an encouraging smile, to let her know it was fine. "It's just not worth it."

She took a deep breath and tried to accept Ravi's explanation gracefully. Then she returned her attention to the vial.

"There's really nothing they can do?"

"Well, you hear about research and little breakthroughs here and there." Ravi sighed. "I hate to be that weird conspiracy guy, but I don't think there's any profit motive in curing it. The company that makes the treatment doesn't have any competitors. If someone made a real cure, they'd lose a lot of money. It'd get suppressed for sure. Hung up in medical trials forever or something."

Nicole shook her head. "Unbelievable. It's the 21st century, damn it. Why are they treating this like all they've got is fancy leeches? We've got like... so much cool tech... —Gods, we trapped a little *sun* in a *jar* just to keep the whole city lit up at night! But no one can fix something this important when it hurts so many people? It feels like such a little problem! Haven't they got rid of diseases like this before? They totally have, right? I'm not crazy? Something's really wrong with the world. Priorities are all messed up."

Ravi couldn't argue with that. But they *did* have to accept it, and they told Nicole as much, to her disappointment.

But whatever. She'd get over it. They already had.

Well, That's Just Unacceptable, Isn't It?

(*Long Before Dawn, Tuesday, 1st November*)

—*No. Absolutely not.*

Danica's tired mind was stuck on that thought tonight, tossing and turning restlessly thinking about that vial of tar – that vile condensate of all Ravi's pain, wrapped in a label covered in *lies*.

She was incensed at the injustice of it, that Ravi worked so hard and had such a good heart, and still they had to suffer and hurt and hide. It was all so much, and she was sick of watching helplessly.

The worst of it was the stuff was... weird. Untouchable. When Ravi showed it to her, even through the glass, it felt oppressive and dangerous to her in a way nothing ever had. She'd never felt so powerless to help before.

But she wasn't ready to accept it. Dear sweet Ravi Bee was stuck suffering like this for the rest of their life? No way. And if Danica with all her power couldn't solve this, then what was the point of having any power at all? More importantly: If she couldn't help them, then how was she ever going to pay them back for all the kindness they were showing her?

But no matter how much she fretted over it, no matter how badly she wanted it, try as she might, nothing was coming to her. No amount of tossing and turning in her loveseat of a bed, or staring at the dark ceiling or the still TV, or listening to the muted sound of urban traffic below Ravi's apartment, or even tracing the cracks in the paint on the walls with her eyes in search of insightful arcane patterns – none of it was helping at all.

In a dramatic huff, she kicked her blankets off and halfway across the room, uncurling herself and leaving her long legs dangling off the armrest of Ravi's extremely cozy, ratty old loveseat. It was the most comfortable bed she'd had in years – a bed of her own – a bed with no strings attached.

She ended up splayed out like a tragic painting, huffing and sighing lamentably, putting on a good show in the dark for no one.

Ravi wouldn't be back from work until after the sun came up, tired and sore, transmuting pain into rent. Danica didn't envy that life, and it only added to her guilt, to her debt, that she couldn't do more to help out. The little fraction of rent Ravi would let her pay, and the cleaning and the groceries and the little gifts she cobbled together for them, that stuff never felt like enough. Not even close.

It wasn't fair. They didn't deserve to suffer through this awful sickness like this, alone, helpless, hopeless. They'd already suffered *enough* just getting here. Easily top ten among any humans Danica had met in the past century.

She sat up straight and tapped frustrated fists on her knees.

It wasn't fair.

And maybe nothing about the universe was fair, but, gods, Danica was sick of letting the universe get away with that.

After a few more impatient sighs, she decided these dramatic breathing exercises weren't accomplishing anything.

She needed to clear her head a bit. There was no point getting frustrated.

She got up and went to the foyer closet to grab Ravi's old denim jacket. It was still full of pins and needles from when she had last worked on it.

She sat back down on the couch and got to work to distract herself from the miserable thoughts that were plaguing her.

The seams were easy. Danica already made quick work of them when she started on this project. She knew a lot of clever stitches that would hold even better than the sewing machines that put this thing together in its first life. They'd never come loose again.

But some of the damage was beyond just mending torn seams. A bunch of large holes were torn out of the fabric – and clearly not from young Ravi's punky artistry of pointedly slashing up the sleeves and chest. If Danica had to guess, it was probably from drunken stumbling and bar fights. She figured Ravi wouldn't mind hiding some of that. So she had to get kind of creative with it, and ended up darning in pretty hand-stitched thread to fill the gaps, and decorating the borders with colorful abstract floral embroidery.

Ravi didn't hate it, they said with a weird grin when Danica had shown them.

She was tempted to sew Ravi's patches down while she was at it. Wouldn't take much work. A lot of the staples were coming loose. Some patches had clearly already been lost from the faded outlines they left behind.

But maybe that was the point? Celebrating the transience of passions and affections? It's hard to tell what's going on in the head of a teenage rebel. That might have been part of the artist's *vision.* So she did her best not to mess with any of Ravi's own modifications and just focused on restoring the integrity of the fabric to how it was when they first put it on.

The one and only modification she was making was to replace the threadbare lining with a very special one of her own design, one that she was still working on, quilting some spells and seals into in, subtle magic that should do at least a *little bit* to ease their pain whenever they wore it.

It hardly made up for everything they were doing for her, but every little bit helped.

Unfortunately, trying to focus on the charms in the lining wasn't turning out to be much of a distraction when it was forcing her to focus on Ravi's pain. Every stitch just made her hands shakier and her blood hotter with rage at how awful it all was. Why should it even be this bad? That she had to resort to magic to help? Why couldn't the humans just take care of themselves for once?

She cursed at herself under her breath, then stood up and put the coat and her sewing materials away in a huff.

Gods, if she was going to be using magic anyways, she might as well lean into it and go all out.

...Just this once?

Just this once.

It would be fine. No one would get hurt. She could make it work this time. Hell, she could probably even find something useful already on Earth. She wouldn't even have to resort to sketchy deals with her cousins if she could figure something out that way.

Yeah. It'd be fine.

Okay. Time to focus.

She returned to the couch to think, tracing meditative circles and charms on her bare thighs, leaving trails of faintly glowing and quickly disappearing white ink on her skin, trying to jog her memory, to summon some hidden forgotten knowledge of the universe that might help here. Surely someone had solved this before. A curative spell? A recipe for some miraculous panacea? Even just some vague legend of a remedy in folklore? *Anything?*

But there was nothing there. Not in her memory. Not in her hidden and woefully incomplete trove of human knowledge. Not in any library she could remember the location of to caress the covers of their books with ethereal fingertips in her mind's eye.

Why hadn't she spent any of her long life studying medicine? Why only *now* did she have to figure out how important it was to know a little more than basic first aid?

With nothing at her fingertips to even start her off, she was left on her own to just... *figure it out* – and figuring out this kind of stuff was not exactly her strong suit. Her well-meaning plans and machinations hadn't been coming together at all lately. So, with 'careful planning' off the table, she'd been leaning on her *instincts* to guide her this time around – but instinct doesn't do well for these tricky sorts of problems.

Gods, and if she was being honest with herself, even her instincts kind of sucked lately.

The discouraging words of an oh-so-sagely old confidant rang in her mind: '*Don't meddle. Don't meddle, don't meddle, don't meddle. It always makes it worse. You know it does. Just stay on the path. Let the world burn. Let it smolder, or you'll end up spilling oil on the fire, and throwing water on the oil, and turning a <u>problem</u> into a <u>disaster</u>—like you <u>always do</u>.*'

It was probably good advice. But she couldn't help it, she couldn't help who she was. And she never listened to good advice anyways.

She stood up and slowly meandered over to the kitchen, taking a few laps around the coffee table on the way. While she did, she continued drawing half-plans and incomplete calculations in the air. The glimmering white lines lingered briefly before disappearing into dust behind her. She was so distracted that she bumped her head right into the corner of the cupboard that had her tin of *slightly* contraband green tea in it – leaves surreptitiously liberated from some faerie's cupboard in the Faelands by her 'dear' business associate – that oh-so-wise and discouraging confidant of hers.

She rubbed the bump on her forehead and tried not to be mad at the cupboard for the assault.

While she waited for the kettle's whistle, she sat on the counter and admired the colorful knitted tea cozy that swaddled her teapot. She had been bringing it with her everywhere in this lifetime, to every couch, on every adventure. It was a 'gift' from Angie, enchanted to never let the tea go cold, no matter how long it sat in the pot. Danica had a habit of getting distracted and letting her cups go cold, so it was nice always having something hot to return to. Comforting.

Gods, it was just such a *thoughtful* trap of a present, though.

That woman sure looked like a sweet old lady, but she would never accept a gift in return, never let Danica pay it back. Danica's deficit of favor with the woman was growing out of control – despite her best efforts to pay it down running errands of varied *ethical merit* for the witch – and it made Danica extremely uneasy to think about what cruel job she may have to do for that treacherous loan shark if she ever came to collect it all at once.

She snapped her fingers suddenly when it hit her.

"Oh! Angie!" she shouted, pointing at the cozied teapot.

That crafty old witch had been extending her wretched life by trapping fae in her thrall for ages now – and definitely for a whole lot longer than Danica had been stuck wandering the face of the Earth in this body. She must have survived tons of horrible plagues by now.

Yeah. If anyone would know how to trick magic and twisted logic and the cruel will of the universe into staving off an incurable illness, it would be that fox of a woman, the bane of naïve fae, the nigh-immortal queen of cunning and deceit.

Ugh, but how to twist it into a *favor...*

If Danica could somehow come up with a convincing explanation for how she was actually doing Angie a kindness by asking for help...

Maybe spin it as 'Danica taking some of Angie's secrets off her hands'? Or even just 'Listening to a lonely old lady'? It wouldn't be *much,* but it'd at least be a *start* towards getting her debt under control. The trick was just *not to ask,* wasn't it? That's how Angie always managed to trick Danica, anyways – getting favors for free because she never *technically* asked for them in the first place.

"*Naïve faerie,*" she cursed at herself under her breath.

It was more than a little embarrassing that Danica kept falling for it. —No, it was actually *extremely* embarrassing, and dire, and out of control, and she needed to stop it already. Danica was far too old to be falling for these tricks. And she used to be so *good* at making sly, crafty deals. Like, the *best*.

How far she'd fallen – the irresistible Grinning Dagger, the terrifying Black Dog of a thousand names, the fae king's cruelest cleverest prodigal pride and joy. To be so owned by a mere human...

She wasn't proud of the dark exploits of her past – not anymore anyways – but it was still frustrating how out of practice she'd become. Her *sanity* depended on brokering good deals, to keep this eternally aging prison sentence of a body young and sharp.

But this time, the stakes were even higher: Dear Ravi's future was in her fumbling hands.

Danica set out to visit Angie immediately.

She was surprised to find the woman wide awake when she appeared in her cruel debtor's antiquated apartment. The dusty old witch was lively as ever, bright-eyed like a fox toying with a mouse, seated at that lovely and ancient circular oak dining table of hers. A cup of hot tea was already waiting across from Angie for her expected unexpected guest.

Somehow the confounding woman always did this to her, no matter how spontaneous she tried to be when she visited.

Danica smiled and appeared a cup of her own freshly brewed tea in her hand, to make it clear that she had no intention of taking any of Angie's 'kind' offerings today.

"One step ahead," the old woman chuckled, then she poured the cup that was meant for Danica back into the pot. "How unusual. What brings you around so late, my dear? —In your nightie, no less, my goodness."

Danica didn't apologize for her casual state of dress. She just silently pulled out a chair and sat across from Angie.

She had to be very careful with her words here.

While she tried to conjure up the perfect phrasing in her mind, she traced her fingers along the ornate arcane carvings in the table's surface. A seal, probably. The wood always felt lively on her fingertips when she visited, like the tree had never died, like the ridges and valleys were its song, and Angie... the grim conductor of that performance, wasn't she? What grand favor had the poor oak asked for to warrant this servitude in payment, she wondered. Or maybe eternal life as a table was the twisted reward for something it had traded away. Whatever it was, Danica would never get an answer.

Whatever Angie did to it had silenced its voice.

That kind of cunning, that kind of power, that was what she was facing off against tonight – and every other time she sat down with this woman.

After a lot of pensive thought, Danica settled on giving Angie a cautious, "I have something for you."

Then she summoned Ravi's black vial out of the air from its spot in their desk and let it drop gently on the table in front of Angie with a dull clunk as it settled.

But, as Danica should have expected, Angie didn't accept it as a gift. Instead, she just smiled at it warmly and said as a matter of fact, "*Danica Llewellyn Doyle,* this is not yours to give."

Danica cringed and clicked her tongue at Angie for misusing her name like that. *Rude.* She knew what that did to her – hearing her *averit* out loud with that kind of cruel intent. Those were the Earthly syllables of her true name – one variation, anyways – held in consignment alongside hundreds of others in the witch's collection. They were an oppressive force against her in the wrong hands. And when Angie wanted to be cruel, she could make her name sound like shards of glass scraping the inside of her skull.

It was a power Danica had too. She knew Angie's true name, even if she didn't hold the woman's *averit* in her hands. She could still make the old woman beg for mercy. Twist her mind into agonies no human could imagine. But it was a dirty trick and she had promised herself a long, long time ago to never use it again. Never.

"Angie, I thought we had a truce on name-calling."

"We had a truce so long as you made a timely payment, my dear. Instead, you're here for another favor, so I think you'll agree that arrangement is over?"

Danica lowered her head and grumbled, "Fine. Fine, but you don't have to be so shitty about it, do you? Can't you just flick me in the forehead? You don't have to drive a chainsaw into my skull. Gods."

Danica gathered herself and tried to let out a calming breath to shake the indignant tone out of her voice before she continued: "And yes, you're right, the vial's not mine. It's nice to look at, though, isn't it? You don't have to take it. I just thought you'd like to look at it. And uh. Maybe I could... do you... the *favor* of listening to your thoughts on it."

"Someone's turned you to glass, my dear."

"What?" Danica looked down at her hands to check that she had not in fact been transformed, and was relieved to find she was still made of the same old meat and bones as usual.

"You're very *transparent*," Angie explained her meaning, like Danica was a child, like it wasn't entirely possible that Angie had decided on a whim to call in some faerie's favor as a spell to turn Danica's body into living glass.

Still, despite seeing through her, the woman seemed willing to play along with this poorly thought-out trap of a game. Without touching the vial, she inspected Danica's gift. After a moment of careful thought she said, "You shouldn't be playing with this, dear."

"I know! Stuff skeeves me. I never want to see it again," she explained. "That's what I'm here to... to *offer you the opportunity* to talk to me about. Ravi's sick, and it's not fair. They don't deserve it. —Ravi's my roommate now by the way. *Please* leave them alone. —And they don't deserve to be sick. And this looks so simple! Just a bunch of black spots on their skin, right? But the doctors never get rid of it. Just... string them along for some reason. I'm not sure if they're even *trying*. It doesn't make sense. The world's seen worse than this, right? I'm not crazy? But maybe not, I don't know. Maybe human medicine just isn't there yet somehow. But if even all this super advanced modern medicine can't do it, well, it sure makes you wonder what kind of power it *would* take to fix it." Danica leaned back in her chair and put a finger on her chin thoughtfully. "Yeah wow just thinking about it, it just... it *really* makes you want to just *talk* and *talk* in detail about *any* solutions you can think of, doesn't it? —You can go first if you want."

Angie laughed at Danica's feeble attempt, then she stood up slowly and stepped aside the table for Danica to get a look at her. She lifted the hem of her dress to reveal a few large, leathery, slightly deflated clear cysts, each clearly recovering from a recent puncture – just like Ravi's would be today.

That was why she was at the clinic that day? Danica figured the old witch would be immune to any serious illness, considering all the enchantments on her body. She had assumed Angie was only there for some routine maintenance or to get a prescription for fun or something.

Danica noted the skin around Angie's cysts was strangely aged compared to her otherwise magically youthful complexion. Must be a hell of a powerful illness to do that to her.

"If you find a solution, do tell me, and we'll call it even between us."

Danica's eyes went wide – not just at the revelation that her debtor was just as sick as any regular human might be, but at that unbelievable offer. A deal like that... It felt like she was swindling the old woman. It had to be a trick. She was so gods damned tricky, this one.

"Really?" Danica cautiously tried to clarify, "*Even* even? Square? Debt-free? No catch?"

"No catch." Angie sat back down and gave her solemn word, "I promise."

She really meant it. Holy hell, she meant it. Danica was hot with excitement. Her heart was pounding just thinking about her freedom. No more shitty errands. No more *chainsaws in her brain*. No more *Angie*.

The crafty witch interrupted her daydreams to continue in a sympathetic tone, "I'm sorry my sweet little puppy. I know you wanted an answer, but I'm as helpless as your new pet. This vile thing—" She gestured at the vial. "—it's cursed. Made with powerful magic, born of the gods, shaped by iron and malice and greed. I can't do anything about it. And sadly, neither can you."

Danica protested Angie's insulting insinuations, "They're not my pet, they're my *friend*. And I'm *not* your puppy! And... I'm not..." She crossed her arms and chided Angie, "I'm not giving up just because some grumpy old *hag* says it's too hard."

In response to Danica's toothless insult, Angie shot her a cutting grin and jabbed at her, "So this new mortal of yours, your new fascination, you're not going to let this one roam the streets like all the others? Not going to let them out of your sight to get eaten up by your vindictive cousins, dear? Going to keep them safe and captive in your arms night and day?"

Danica grimaced at Angie's reminder. She was right. She didn't have to put it so cruelly, but she was right. Danica had to be careful about getting too close to this one – to Ravi.

Maybe even... maybe even calling them a *friend* was too much. But whatever. She wasn't going to let anything happen to them. Not this time.

Angie continued cruelly prodding at her, "How many innocent humans have we lost to your selfish, careless affections, my sweet little puppy?"

...Too many. But Danica didn't want to admit that here. Not to Angie. The old witch clearly had enough dirt on her already from all the gossip she'd gathered up from her captive cousins.

Angie didn't wait for an answer before she continued, "Don't delude yourself, *Danica.*"

Another painful jab with her averit. Gods. Why, even? There was no reason to be so mean to her.

"Even pets can be friends," she continued with her oh-so-wise rambling. "And you'll always be a puppy in my eyes, dear. And... I'm counting on you never giving up. If anything can save us, it's that stupid stubborn bleeding heart of yours. All that guilt swelling it up in your chest – it's stronger than your head now, stronger than a lot of heads."

Angie made it sound like a compliment, but it sure felt more like she was being patronizing. And frankly, the old woman had no right to treat her like a child. Danica might only have been walking the Earth for half a dozen centuries, but even before that, she'd been around a hell of a long time. Countless time. She might be young among the fae, but still, she knew a lot, a lot more than any mortal *witch* pretending at eternity, and she was a whole lot stronger than Angie seemed to think she was.

That was the trouble with growing old, Danica figured. It seals your mind to possibilities. To the possibility of being wrong, to the possibility of knowledge beyond your understanding waiting out there to be discovered. It's a big universe, and forever is a long time. Bewildering that Angie wanted to live that long, since she had already shut her mind up in a comfortable little box.

What's the point?

It wasn't exactly inspiring to hear Angie so disparaging about Danica's prospects – especially hearing how confident she was in offering that unbelievable deal of hers – freedom for a cure? Danica's heart was still racing at the thought – but crushed too, knowing Angie would never make an offer like that if she really thought Danica could pull it off.

But there was a glaringly obvious omission that she wasn't ignoring: No pact. All Danica had was the old witch's promise. She'd never broken one before, but there were always loopholes the size of galaxies in unsigned promises.

And that meant the woman was afraid to commit.

Which meant she might be afraid Danica would actually win.

Maybe Angie was serious about the incredible power of her stupid heart.

Danica had nothing more to say to the old woman. Time to wrap this up. She really lucked out here. Not only did she manage to avoid getting drawn further into debt, but it actually sounded like she had *sort of* managed to turn all this into a kind of favor for the old witch. A hopeful promise at least. So, big win.

Danica waved her hand through the air to disappear the vial from the surface of the the table and slip it back through the Aether to Ravi's desk drawer. It was a relief to get it out of her sight. As soon as it was gone, it was like a dull roaring whisper in the back of her mind was suddenly silenced.

Before she could vanish herself and her cup of rapidly cooling tea back to the apartment, Angie's arm darted inhumanly across the large ensorcelled table to grab her wrist. She spoke in a stern voice: "Danica. Understand me. You should *not* be playing with this."

As if she needed to be reminded.

She pulled away without a word, then silently disappeared from the witch's home.

Back on her beloved borrowed couch, Danica found herself rotating a comfortable cup of now-cold tea in her hands. A few tea grains had escaped the infuser when it was steeping, and those little bits and pieces drifted gently in the flow of the swirling water. She focused on those slow-dancing specks while she thought about her life. Her debt. Her troublesome affections.

Her pet.

Angie's words haunted Danica in a truly supernatural way, like she was still there, bothering her ear with a forked tongue.

She shook herself free of the illusion that Angie would ever hold up her end of that too-good-to-be-true bargain. And it didn't matter. It didn't. When she thought it through, even if the witch *was* being sincere, the only way Angie would be so generous in the first place is if she were desperate – on her deathbed, taking last resorts.

And if that were true... Maybe finding a cure would be *worse* for Danica. She could just let the old woman die of the illness. Finally. And with her death, all of the debt Danica owed would die too – *and* all the debt countless others back home owed to Angie, debt accrued over at least a dozen centuries, debt that Angie shuffled around like a magical Ponzi scheme. Hell, if Danica played it right, letting the woman die and freeing her cousins might even be enough to finally earn back some scraps of favor with her family again.

Yeah.

Let her die.

That would be best, right?

Really, there was no point fighting this sickness, was there? It wasn't Danica's problem. She had enough to worry about. Too much. And Ravi had clearly made peace with their situation, with their pain, with their short life.

—Short-*er* life. Gods, this sickness felt like a bad joke, a blight on a flower that was already wilting with all speed into grey death and dust in the unblinking eyes of the eternal.

No.

No, she could feel it, some hope, some spark of hope. She could feel it when she worked on their jacket, or when she glanced cheerful fingertips on their wrist. There were long, long futures with Ravi in them, where Danica still might brush on the silk of that unbreakable lining again, where she could touch her fingertips on their wrist again and feel the warmth in them. There were flashes of life among countless possibilities of darkness. Rare. So rare. But they were there. She could save them. Somehow. Somehow, she could do it.

And she would.

Her heart ached to imagine abandoning them now. There was no way she could just *accept* Ravi's fate. She didn't know how to make peace like that, like they did. She only knew how to kick up a fuss and turn the world upside down.

She'd already thrown away so much of herself, desperately trying to stay true to herself, and she wasn't about to stop doing that now. Not when she had a chance to pay Ravi back for their kindness. Not when she had a chance to do something right for humanity for once.

And *this time*, she'd get it right.

Missed Connections

Ravi had been seeing an ad on the metro's intrusive electronic signage lately:

New Parts New You!

There was a surge in the past few years in demand – or at least in marketing – for these fully integrated prosthetics.

Limited release! AugMe™ Tensor X™ with Saffron Red™ Tech – only from InThetics. AugMe™: When you need the Real Human Touch™.

The 'A' in the logo there was styled like an 'H' – 'Hug Me'. With robot arms. The real human touch, huh. Brilliant what these companies can get away with.

There was of course nothing limited about the release other than the fact that in six months, they'd be on to the Tensor XI model. But the charismatic spokesperson for the corporation – Miriam Ortiz, supposedly brilliant engineer and revolutionary entrepreneur, prodigal inheritor of the InThetics legacy – was very good at making the tech sound important to have *today*.

She also made it sound essential to a brighter tomorrow. To stand against her was to stand against progress, to stand against the future, to stand against *humanity*. She often spoke about her vision for the Singularity – immortality, replacing all the mortal bits and pieces of humanity with eternal parts – manufactured by InThetics, of course.

Persuasive as she was, not everyone was on board.

The bulletin boards at Ravi's university always had one or two poorly photocopied, liberal-minded posters decrying the frivolous prosthetics. They called it 'disability tourism'. Lop off an arm, put an immortal machine in its place. All the sci-fi body horror with none of the trauma of getting your bones and muscles ripped to shreds by a horrible accident.

The posters were also always happy to point out that InThetics is a prolific war profiteer: *AUGME ARMS FUND SAUDI ARMS*. Ravi checked about it themself and sure enough, InThetics combat tech armed a whole lot of terrible war efforts around the world.

A criticism that was both catchy and true? Hard to argue with.

But Ortiz, the glittery icon of every InThetics product on the market, had a charismatic smile and a disarming wit that would never let those shameful truths hurt the brand.

Funny that for all Miriam's pushing of these miraculous products, she wasn't using any of it herself.

Still, the prosthetic tech was compelling. Ravi considered it sometimes. Once in a while, when some new feature came out, they popped into one of the chic InThetics showrooms, populated by living and breathing and beautiful young models, themselves pointlessly augmented with the latest version and showing off the capabilities of the limbs. Customers could even give the tech a test ride with a little bundle of electrodes strapped to their skin. Of course, when it was installed properly, all the electronics were hidden beneath the surface. Has to look good to cost that much, after all.

In fact, the only thing that gave an installed InThetics augmentation away – aside from the obnoxious, prestigious, designer logo tattooed right into the synthetic skin – was a paper-thin seam at the bone-mounted, hot-swappable interface – that and the slightly stilted movement. *Just slightly.* Almost imperceptible, but it was still too much, too inhuman.

No, this AugMe gear wasn't ready. Not really. Not for Ravi. But wanting gear like this was part of the modern human condition, wasn't it? To be part of the cutting edge. To belong to the new class of 'real' modern humans – the *homo novus* – cars, electricity, glowing screens, and all the magic unlocked by our command of the full spectrum of electromagnetic radiation. Lag behind and you stop being human at all. Suddenly you're in a third world, 'developing' your humanity.

Ravi wasn't there for the trendy aesthetic upgrades, though. The AugMe virtual catalog included some of the more complicated solutions InThetics provided to people with actual disabilities – including custom-made replacements for arbitrary skeletal and muscular 'challenges'. They seemed to be afraid to use the word 'disabilities'. Probably didn't test well in marketing.

But the gist of it, from Ravi's assessment of InThetics' offerings, was that Ravi could get their arm chopped off and all their tar-afflicted shoulder meat removed, and get a fully functional InThetics-branded replacement – if they could afford it. But that kind of tech would cost more than a house. And the cysts would just pop up somewhere else in their body a month later anyways – probably even more plentiful – and maybe even deeper under the skin.

Disability tourism was a good way to put it.

The wealthy, fully functional elite became even *more* functional, just for fun, while people like Ravi... Well, they did their best.

Ravi's peculiar coworker Erwin had an old AugMe hand from InThetics – a mere humble 2A model from a few years back when the tech was uglier and the biological interface still got rejected by a good percent of bodies. These old ones required a daily dose of proprietary InThetics maintenance medication after the installation, with a few side effects of course – like Erwin's tumor, probably.

That was the selling point of that fancy new 'Saffron Red' tech – the incredibly small, one-in-a-million chance of implant rejection, and weekly medication instead of daily. Plus, Saffron Red? Just sounded kind of posh and cutting edge showing it off at parties. It was *premium.*

If Ravi could believe Ortiz's enthusiastic assertions, the secret was peppering the ceramic biointerface with InThetics' proprietary super-material – Saffron – an engineered mystery substance that was improving and evolving every year through the entire rainbow spectrum as it became more and more 'reliable'.

Ravi suspected it was more likely that the *substance* never changed, and instead the company was just slowly refining the manufacturing process of the ceramics in the biointerface to be more pure and less toxic.

But that was just a theory. You know what they say about hammers. When all you have is an eccentric postgraduate-level familiarity with neoceramics, everything looks like engineered clay.

Erwin's prosthetic didn't have any Saffron in it at all. No wonder he needed to take meds for it.

The false hand was a little worn out, but it was enough to confidently grip the steering wheel of the forklift and maneuver around the warehouse, enough to hold a beer and light a cigarette and flip a coin to decide who paid for the next round – a flip that *somehow* landed in Ravi's favor at least twice as often as it did for Erwin. Some nights Ravi was so 'lucky' that they didn't even pay for a single drink.

The old guy was way too kind to them.

They'd pay him back one day.

He never actually talked about the hand usually, and Ravi never asked, but he got pretty vocal about it one night at the bar. Apparently one of the fingers started crapping out on him.

Erwin was rather animated when he showed Ravi the twitching pinky digit. The two of them were relaxing after work over a pint at his favorite pub – an activity Ravi was being strongarmed into getting comfortable with, since Nikki had started locking them out of the apartment on their few nights off, refusing to let them in until they sent her photographic evidence that they had spent some time out on the town 'doing something fun'.

Not that they couldn't just... get in anyways. They had the key to the backup 'boyfriend lock' – the massive deadbolt they installed after a *very* unpleasant experience with an ex breaking in with an illegally copied spare key and trying to steal their extremely important research laptop. Lucky Ravi was there to kick his ass out the door and down the shaky terrifying stairs of the fire escape. But it was a valuable lesson: *No one* gets the key to the boyfriend lock.

Still, even if they could just open the deadbolt, it was kind of fun to pretend to be locked out for Nicole. Made her smile.

They liked it when she smiled.

And honestly, being out with Erwin was fun enough to be worth it even without Nicole pushing them. He was usually good for a smile – and a few unconventional topics of conversation.

"Microservo's cooked," he explained about the finger with a grin, like he was proud it was broken. "Must've dropped a butt in some moody snowed-in faerie ring in the park or something, 'cause I take better care of this thing than my own sweet mother's grave."

Ravi always had to grin to themself whenever Erwin's superstitious side peeked through. He genuinely believed in faeries and curses and magical gateways to dangerous secret worlds. There was no point trying to talk him out of it. In his eyes, every great fortune and misfortune that hit him was some doing of the fae, some consequence of his courtesies or offenses of some faerie court or another that Ravi could never remember the name of.

They had to admit, there was occasionally a twinge of jealousy in them for it, for the whimsy and the vibrancy and the absolute *certainty* of Erwin's world. As much as they loved the satisfaction of the scientific pursuit of the purest truths of the universe, it sure took a while, and cost a hell of a lot of money along the way.

Ravi asked if they could look at the eccentric old faerie lover's mechanical miracle of a malfunctioning hand. They'd always been intrigued by the technology, even though they'd never be able to afford any of it.

Erwin happily agreed and unhooked the prosthetic for them to poke and prod at until they were satisfied there was nothing that they could learn from it or do to fix it.

The ever-boisterous old man locked it back in place and curled his fingers with a charming, flamboyant flair – except the little finger, which he said he was certain would never move the way he wanted it to again.

"No one can fix it! That shit company, they lock down all the little bits and pieces in there. If you so much as peel back the skin, the whole thing shuts down forever."

"They don't have some in-house repair service or something?"

Erwin laughed. "You bet they do! It's a racket! Costs more to repair it than replace it. The older it is, the more expensive it is to fix!"

"Huh. That is quite fucked."

"Oh, *quite*," he replied in a mockery of a posh accent, sipping at his beer. His malfunctioning little finger stuck out like his pint was a proper cup of English tea. A perfect gentleman.

When Ravi wasn't spending the night locked out for a good time or mindlessly lifting boxes at work and listening to the mechanical voice in their earpiece that puppeteered their body and hands around the warehouse, they were at the university's chemistry lab, working on their postgrad research.

The electronic security locks on the science wing were a magical gateway into the haven fortress that kept their passions safe from the rest of their life.

"Well," they always asked the mindless old kiln at the back of the lab when they came in, crouching down to open its well-insulated steel door, "How'd it go today?" They would inspect the freshly baked inch-thick rectangular plates of ceramic one by one as they pulled them out, and try to give the terrible machine some encouraging words. "Mm. Mhm. Well, little wyrm, I don't want to reward bad behavior, but you only cracked two of these today, so, uh. Better than a complete failure I guess? Good effort, buddy. You'll get it one day."

It did not reply. It wasn't listening. Old tech was good that way.

These weren't the sort of ceramic plates you'd eat off of – something they had to explain to almost everyone who asked. These were thick, slightly curved rectangles, meant to serve as armor for a variety of purposes.

And crafting fancy new-age armor sure sounded cool if you stopped there, without mentioning all the details of the daily work involved.

They'd been spending the last few years on this work, trying hundreds of variations, manually measuring out ingredients and carefully applying the new mixtures in the plate mold one layer at a time. Normally, an automatic printer would do this work, but the school didn't have one that could work with the viscosity of the materials they were mixing.

The rest of their work was in an engineering lab, testing performance, recording results, throwing numbers in the computer, collating data into graphs and tables and reports.

Explaining it at parties always left the poor person foolish enough to ask nodding off to sleep.

Not that they attended very many parties these days. Time and energy and affection for the human race were at an all-time low for them after a string of bad luck with people in general.

But no matter how boring it sounded to anyone else with a pulse, to Ravi every moment of it felt exhilarating. Every step in the tedious process brought them closer to an answer to a question no one else had thought to ask. They *knew* what they didn't know – that precious gap in human knowledge begging to be filled – and no one else in the world could see that hole in our understanding of universe as well as they could.

—Even if that hole was just, "What exact composition of substances might work better than the stuff in the ceramics we've already got?"

Their meager wage at the warehouse paid for the privilege to answer that question when the grants came up short. As they often did. Apparently, it wasn't a very exciting question to the rest of the world, except the military, whose offers were always promptly shredded.

InThetics made a tempting offer once in a while too, but considering the whole war profiteering thing, Ravi felt obligated to drop those ones in the shredder too – though not without a long, pensive minute of consideration about what exactly their morals were worth.

Tough as it was to keep their work funded, they didn't really mind the lack of interest. This quiet, incremental kind of science suited them. No one cared. No one was watching. No deadlines. No headlines. They would just make the world better – slowly, surely, even if no one would know who or why or how. It was better that way. The last thing they wanted was to have their name tied to some crazy paradigm-shifting breakthrough.

&

"Mm. Wow." Ravi's date was doing her best to feign interest while staying honest. "I had no idea it was so… I mean that sounds important."

Beth. Or Gail? Annabella Rosemary-Lou…? Ravi didn't care honestly, they were just going through the motions here, reaching out to see if there was some something in someone somewhere worth their time. They'd get the name on the second date if it mattered.

And to be fair, it's not like she was ever going to get *their* real name. She knew them from university, and their university ID still said 'Amaira', just like their undergrad degree, and their driver's license, and their loans, and their lease, and their birth certificate…

And this woman, too, would only ever say Amaira. Ravi didn't want her that close. They didn't want anyone that close anymore.

This Annabella Rosemary-Lou was the lucky young woman who had been looking at Ravi with bedroom eyes whenever the two of them shared a meal in the staff room at the university. A fellow TA, though she was in some form of social science – the kind that might have something important to say about disability tourism.

And she certainly had *something* to say about it.

"It's awful! Corporations just sucking the blood out of the poor."

"Is it… I thought the problem was fetishizing prosthetics while dehumanizing the disabled?"

—Though it was literally 'de-humanizing', wasn't it? Replacing real

human flesh with synthetics?

What is a human?

"Right, all that is bad too," Annabella Rosemary-Lou said with a dismissive wave of her soft, well-manicured hand, "But the way they treat their workers is the real problem! Wage slavery. Makes me sick. You know how much their warehouse workers make?"

Ravi was of course intimately familiar with how much warehouse workers make. Annabella Rosemary-Lou seemed to have forgotten that bit of Ravi's bio from earlier in the night.

This confounding woman seemed more interested in the union busting and salary disparity at InThetics than the *far* more exciting topics Ravi wanted to talk about, so they were kind of stuck half listening to their date and half talking to themself in their head about exactly how much of the Ship of Theseus could be replaced with parts off a space shuttle before it stopped being a boat.

—As long as it still floats, right?

"Yeah, it just sucks," Annabella Rosemary-Lou said in conclusion to an impromptu essay that Ravi had been spending the last few minutes nodding along to and pretending to ask questions about – questions they already knew the answers to – about the portents of the socioeconomic apocalypse.

Her closing remarks: "Nothing you can do though, right? I don't know."

—She doesn't <u>*know*</u>*? What the hell is she studying this for, then?*

Certainly, as dedicated, hardworking postgrads, the two of them must at least have a shared special interest in joyously tedious research and writing reports. But she couldn't be satisfied with *just that*, could she? Mere theory? It seemed to Ravi that studying the crushing failings of mankind should probably inspire some sentiment a little more passionate than, '*Nothing you can do.*'

But before Ravi could finish mentally admonishing the lovely Annabella Rosemary-Lou, she gave them a very attractive, playful grin that tickled the back of their brain. She leaned in – close enough that Ravi could smell the sweet cocktail on her breath, the pastel makeup on her cheeks, and the chemical cherry in the balm on her lips – to whisper to them with a teasing, raspy voice that sent a wave of shivers and heat through every inch of their body:

"Hey, do you want to get out of here? I have a nice bottle of tequila back at my place. Watch a movie? *Fool around?*"

The way she said the last two words, that wasn't a question. That wasn't even a suggestion. That was a prophecy.

Ravi smiled at their date's frank optimism. They were more of a beer person, but they weren't going to say no to a few free drinks and a little human contact.

"I'm all yours," they said, pounding back the last of their pint to put just enough indiscretion in their step to leave the bar.

The tequila was tolerable. The movie was one Ravi had already seen a couple times before when they were young and that they had since fallen out of love with. And the fooling around was... how to describe it... *humorless?* They felt a bit like an achievement for the woman, a conquest, from how Annabella Rosemary-Lou was taking them – hungry and hurried and almost *hostile* in the way she grabbed them and moved them around her bed and body.

She liked to bite Ravi's lip.

They did not kiss in the morning.

You Can Just Feel It, You Know? Don't Make It Complicated

In the afternoon after their disappointing date, Ravi shoved the coffee table out of the way and took over the little living room to take apart their bike and put it back together again. For fun. 'Fun'.

Before they got down to it, they cracked open the lid of the crackly old record player and put on an old hangover recovery record of theirs. They had to get up every few songs to wipe the grease off their hands, flip the record over, and refill their cup with ever-staler coffee.

With every errant pop of the old speaker, Ravi scowled at the ancient stereo receiver and made a silent threat that it was next, after the bike.

Nicole had been hanging out in the living room sewing when Ravi, in a grumbly half-conscious manner, displaced her with no explanation other than, "Bike fix time."

She had been working on that sewing project of hers for weeks now – fixing up their old denim jacket. It absolutely confounded them why she cared so much about it. And it looked done already. All the seams were flawless again. Even the random holes were patched up with some colorful artistry of hers, weaving different colored threads across the gap in attractive patterns, and outlining each hole with pretty floral stitchwork that made it look like the hole was a *feature*. It was a hell of a way to honor their lost fights and stumbling fuckups.

It looked done. She was just fussing now, with some stupidly intricate, stunningly beautiful embroidery on a new quilted silk lining to replace the threadbare original. It was super overkill for an ancient shoplifted and heavily vandalized jacket – a jacket that Ravi barely wore and that they abused to tatters whenever they did, but it clearly made her happy to work on it, so Ravi gave her their blessing.

Honestly, it made them feel a bit shy to talk about it. The jacket had a price tag big as a semester of university when they stole it, but after all the care Nicole was putting into it, they felt like the thing must be worth a whole doctorate by now.

After quietly working away at her stitching for a while, now curled up in the corner of the loveseat with her materials, pretending to ignore Ravi while they were working, Nicole was apparently so overcome with curiosity that she had to set aside her work for a bit to join them.

She sat cross-legged on the floor nearby, with her usual *frustratingly* bare thighs, humming along to the music, playing with the dozens of greasy bits and pieces that make a bike a bike, occasionally asking what they were for, and regularly refilling Ravi's coffee and her own cup with honeyed green tea – her favorite drink.

Ravi wasn't sure they'd ever seen her drink anything else, actually, other than those flamboyant cocktails at the bar.

—Does she even drink water?

"It's a little cold for biking, isn't it?" she asked.

"It's never too cold to destroy something and put it back together slightly worse than before," they replied in a tired voice that they hoped would be enough to tell Nicole they had no intention of offering any actual justification for what they were doing.

—Fixing a bike only makes it worse...

Ravi grinned wryly to themself at the realization that they might have just uncovered the Universal Law of Amateur Bike Repair Entropy: *Every twist of the wrench and adjustment of the cables' tensions will only make things incrementally worse until the bike is incapable of carrying a human being.*

"Rough night?" Nicole asked, seemingly in response to nothing more than their melancholy tone.

Ravi offered a dry, perfunctory synopsis of the date, leaving out the more disappointing and salacious details – which might have been a mistake, because Nicole's reaction was not at all appropriate considering how unfortunate the evening had been.

In fact she nearly threw her cup across the room with an elated gesture at the news that Ravi had spent a *romantic evening* at someone else's place. She gave them a big hug and what felt like an extremely patronizing cheer, acting as if she thought Ravi had never slept with anyone in their entire 26 years on the planet.

She meant it kindly, though. She always did.

"Chill Nikki. God, you like having the apartment to yourself that much, huh?" they teased her, trying to push her away gently to get out of her powerful embrace. "I see how it is now. Lock me out. Have a little *Nicole* time. Maybe a party. And if Ravi's not here in the morning, bonus, walk around in your underwear all day," Ravi nodded at Nicole's scant, extremely home-casual outfit.

"No! And I walk around in my underwear all the time anyways, you know that—"

"*—And every time I tell you to put some pants on.* Jesus Christ Nikki I'm a human being not a braindead dog."

"Aw, are you embarrassed?" Nicole splayed herself out dramatically like a ballet dancer and stretched out a bare leg in a mockery of a seductive pose to taunt Ravi. "These long beautiful legs too irresistible for you?"

Ravi grinned and gave her shoulder a playful shove, knocking her off-balance and getting a little yelp of indignation out of her.

"Can you *please* just wear some fucking pants! God, who raised you?"

Nicole ignored Ravi's plea for decency, as usual, much to their consternation, and continued with her train of thought.

"I'm just happy for you! I hate seeing you all miserable all the time. And now, at last, to hear that you've *opened the veil of your dark heart* to let some light and happiness in? How could I *not* be overjoyed?"

Her glowing grin was infectious enough to spread to Ravi's cheeks. They did their best to hide it by diverting all their focus to wiping the old grease out of the axle of one of the bike's wheels.

While they averted their eyes from Nicole's smile, they shook their head and complained, "Nicole, I swear to god. You're making me sound like the villain in a Christmas cartoon."

"Yeah! Yes! Gods, that's it exactly, you nailed it. A cold unfeeling miserable old monster hiding every night in their ice fortress in the mountains, scheming—"

"—Stop. Please. I'm not hiding. I have no schemes. And I have a bunch of feelings. Secret feelings."

"Oh I already know all about your secret feelings, *Ravi.*"

"Then please stop knowing immediately."

"Can't help it. You're terrible at hiding them. Despair. Loneliness. Boredom. *Hatred for your fellow man.*"

"Wrong. I love people."

"*You love people,*" Nicole echoed dryly. She was not convinced.

"Yes. I do. —Some people. Some people are great. —And I'm *not* miserable."

"Ravi."

"I'm not! I'm tired. I'm just tired and I never have time to do anything fun. —And whenever I *do* have time to do anything fun it ends up being a huge waste of time like this fucking date."

Nicole tilted her head to the side slightly with a confused look. "Ravi I think the whole point of 'fun' is that it's *supposed to be* a huge waste of time."

"Fun should still... *enrich* you. I don't feel enriched spending a night talking some beautiful, intelligent, *passionless* woman's ear off and then getting *consumed* by her all night like I'm a twelve-ounce steak."

" 'Consumed'...?"

"Nicole, I don't have any better word for it. Look, it was very fun. Like, very... *very* fun... But I was barely there. Just meat on a plate." Ravi plucked a pensive melody on the spokes of the wheel in their hands before they gave in and broke that most sacred Universal Law of Social Etiquette – Don't Kiss and Tell. "She was *very* bitey. Claws in me like forks. I'm lucky my sores were drained the other day or she'd probably have torn them open on me. Kept trying to get my binder off too. She just couldn't contain herself, god. I was swatting her hands away all night. I'm telling you: *voraciously consumed.*"

"Is this that TA who's always flirting with you?"

"God and she's so hot, Nikki. Here, look," Ravi pulled out their phone and showed Nicole a more-than-slightly suggestive picture that *Annabella Rosemary-Lou (???)* had messaged them after they left. Nicole agreed she was very nice to look at. "I thought it was worth a shot. Fellow academic might be worth talking to, you know? She seemed interesting enough at school."

"No?"

"I don't know, she just didn't care about anything I care about. She was so bored with everything I had to say. I wanted to talk about something interesting and all she wanted to do was complain – in great detail – about the evils of capitalism, and then admit that she doesn't know how to fix it, or even want to try. Like, Nicole, what the fuck is that about? That would be like if I devoted my life to studying... I don't know, the toxic effects of lead in paint and then decided to just sit on that with a cute, dumb smile pretending I can't do anything about it."

"What would you do about it?"

"More than fucking shrug and say it's not my problem! God, I don't even know why she took me home. I mean, *I know why she took me home*, but I don't know why, in general, she would take a person home when she doesn't even care about them."

"You did go home with her, though," Nicole said, as if that were enough to make some kind of point.

"What about it?" Ravi asked defensively.

"Well, you're sure making it sound like you don't care about her. Why did *you* go?"

Ravi stopped reloading the bearings into the axle's cup for a moment of consideration. Nicole always poked them in the softest spots.

They shrugged and offered an unconvincing half-truth to appease their interrogator: "She had some nice tequila."

Nicole raised an eyebrow and gave Ravi a skeptical smirk. "You only drink beer," she said, a lawyer presenting evidence in a court. Then she took a satisfied sip of her tea without breaking eye contact, like she'd just won the case.

"Yeah. Well. Last night I drank tequila and got fucked by a woman I don't care about who doesn't care about me or the world – and I don't know which thing is making me feel worse in this, the beautiful radiance of the morning sun," Ravi said, gesturing at the living room's window and at the dull ugly overcast afternoon sky beyond.

Not exactly an inspiring sunrise, but this was the earliest their hangover could get them on their feet and back to the apartment.

"Why choose?" Nicole said. "Spread the blame. Swear off tequila *and* one-night-stands."

They smiled and joked with her, "Let's just quit the tequila for now. The fucking doesn't usually make me throw up."

Nicole playfully informed Ravi it was her turn with the record player, then put on one of her many, many old favorites – some modern math jazz trio taking on a classical suite of music Ravi was only vaguely familiar with.

Ravi had no idea where she was even storing all these. She didn't have any boxes with her when she started sleeping there. Just a big backpack. But somehow, the catalog on the shelf just kept swelling and swelling every time they turned their back on it.

She returned to the couch to continue working on that bewildering sewing project of hers. Ravi smiled when they noticed that even with the strange unpredictable melody, she was still humming along pleasantly. Music fanatic? She probably really did have hundreds of favorite bands, didn't she? Thousands?

The bike was turning out – as Ravi expected – a little worse. Their attempts to straighten out the spokes on the front wheel had left the rim completely misshapen. They'd have to swap it out if they wanted to use the brakes – and they very much did want to use the brakes. But getting rid of it felt wrong. It was the original wheel. It just wouldn't be the same bike if the rims didn't match.

—*Still be a bike though. Better than no bike.*

While they debated whether never stopping again or having an ugly bike was the greater misery, they remembered a question they never got the answer to last night:

"Hey Nikki, if you replaced all the parts of a sailing ship with parts from a space ship, is it still a boat?"

She looked up from her work to give Ravi a sincere, thoughtful reply: "Does it still float?"

—*Yeah. Nicole gets it.*

"Okay, so if a boat floats to be a boat, what does a human do to be a human?"

"Ask questions about boats," she said with a knowing grin.

Ravi smirked right back. "That's it, huh?"

"Why? Are you planning to swap your arms and legs out for rockets and wings? I'd still call you a human if you looked like a space ship, Rav, don't worry. Humanity is deeper than both skin and whatever fancy stuff they put on those shuttles."

Ravi shook their head at Nicole's bad joke. "Cool as that would be, no. I was just thinking about all this stuff with synthetic body parts. That stuff InThetics is always peddling. You know, sci-fi cyborg tech. The Singularity. The immortal merging of man and machine. When does a human stop being a human? Like, brain in a jar: Still human?"

"Does it ask boat questions?"

"Robot brain in a human body?"

"Yeah, I'm sticking to my criteria here. A robot brain with a curiosity about the existential nature of boats is still a human in my books."

"It's just the body that's made of human though. Meat and bones. A shell. At that point you could just put the whole robot brain in a steel box and still get questions about boats."

"Hm." Nicole looked a little troubled by Ravi's challenge.

"I think your checklist might need a few more points," they said with a playful smile.

Nicole's jokey demeanor faded away for a few moments of serious thought. She pensively fiddled with her stitchwork a bit while she put her thoughts together.

"Don't hurt yourself there," Ravi joked with her when they saw how hard she was thinking.

She didn't respond. Lost in her thoughts?

After a few long seconds of still silence, she started frustratedly undoing stitches in her work, and was suddenly far too focused on fixing some mistake she spotted to notice anything else.

Ravi almost got the whole bike back together while they were waiting for a response. Nicole's record was skipping on the staticky silence at the end of the side by the time she finally had an answer for them.

She jabbed the needle into the jacket with a sense of doomed finality and morosely set the unfinished work on her knees to give Ravi her answer:

"Mortality," she said with a solemn, serious look on her face. Her gaze was focused on the jacket, though that wasn't where she was looking. Seemed like she was far, far away. "Knowing your mortality," she continued. "Hating your mortality. Fleeing it. Trying and failing to find a way to live with it. I think everything human comes from that."

From their comfortable seat on the floor beside their upturned bike, holding their grease-stained cup of cold coffee, Ravi casually asked, "Including the boat questions?"

"Especially the boat questions. That's not about body parts, Ravi Bee, that's about people changing forever into something you don't recognize anymore. It's a special kind of death, a special kind of fear. Dying to the people you love. Being some living dead horror, unknown to the people you most want to be known by. It's about the pain of watching someone you love die like that, over and over and over again."

"Right. Like, ego death? And you think only humans can die like that?"

"I think only humans can be afraid of that."

"I don't know about that. You can probably program a machine to be afraid of upgrading to the latest version or something."

"Alright Ravi you're just being difficult now," she replied with a little huff. Apparently this was serious business now.

So Ravi had a serious question of their own.

Ravi leaned down to try to catch Nicole's eye. "Did I die?"

She looked up from her knees with a curious look. "What?"

"You didn't see me for eight years. I've changed a lot. You didn't even know my name. I'm dead, right?"

"I don't... think you're dead. I still recognize you. You're the same old lovable Ravi Bee in my eyes."

"Mm... I wasn't really Ravi B back then, though. That's not what you called me."

"You know what I mean..."

Ravi paused for a moment to consider what to say to challenge her here. At last they settled on a provocative little jab:

"I want to be dead."

"No!"

"...Not <u>literally</u>. *Nicole.* I don't want you to recognize who I was anymore. I want her to be dead to you."

"Why would you want that?"

Ravi crossed their arms and raised an incredulous eyebrow at Nicole. "Why do you think?"

Nicole thought about it for a long pensive breath before trying to explain what she meant: "I don't know how to say it properly, but you're still you, to me. A boat's still a boat if it floats, right? I don't know what it is that makes you float, but everything that's changed about you, it's just wings and rockets. You're still you. You're still going to be you – still going to be everything good I remember about you – even if all your parts get swapped out." She paused for a moment of thought before she offered Ravi an alternative: "Or maybe you just... always were Ravi with me? Always have been? Maybe I just never really knew the person you were before you died?"

—*Nicole.*

Ravi was trying to pick out if she was just trying to flatter them somehow, trying to find just the right words to make them feel good about their transition, like so many people had done before, but honestly, if that's what she was doing, she was doing a terrible job of it. She clearly didn't have a firm grasp on what it meant for Amaira to be dead in Ravi's heart.

No, she was just being sincere. She really just... genuinely liked something in them that managed to carry over from one life to the next.

Ravi was vaguely aware that this wasn't quite the way most people did their transition. For a lot of people, the point was to be recognized correctly, to be seen, at last, as someone they *always were,* someone they were prevented from being.

But Ravi, they generally thought of Amaira and themself as two different drivers of this body of theirs. She wasn't great at it back then. Tried her best though. Tried to make it work. Tried to be strong and be true and be accepted for who she was. She even tried to find a way to live happily in that body. But it wasn't working. Things needed to change, drastically. New name. New self. No more fucking around trying to get anyone else's approval. They just weren't going to be a girl anymore. Period. Just, clean slate.

—Sort of. That was... the *plan* anyways. They still had to drag Amaira's name around everywhere for bureaucratic reasons, but that was all it was. Ravi was at the wheel now.

But... who knows, maybe Nicole was right about them being 'Ravi' with her. They didn't really remember how they were with Nicole back in high school. They didn't really settle on the idea of transitioning and changing their name until second year of university. But... maybe some bits of them had already been taking shape in their head, even back then? Peeking through in little ways?

This all got Ravi thinking about another question they never really got a good answer to.

"...Hey, why do you remember me so well?"

"What do you mean?"

They put their coffee down and leaned back on their hands to give Nicole a discerning look while they grilled her. "You picked me out of that huge line of people without even seeing my face. You had that cutesy nickname for me. I barely remembered you. I don't even remember what we talked about back then."

"Oh. Really? We talked about like... war and history and technology and the end times and big stuff like that. You were always very animated about the troubles of the world, I liked that."

"That's who I am to you? Someone who's animated about the troubles of the world?"

"*Yes!* Yeah, that's got to be it. You care. That's what makes the Ravi boat float. Part of it, at least. You also still have that nice smile and you've still got a good sincere laugh. No bullshit. You make me smile, and it's the same kind of 'making me smile' it always was."

Ravi raised an eyebrow at her and shot her an uneasy smirk. "Thanks. I guess." That was such a corny thing to say, and she said it so *shamelessly*. It was almost enough to make Ravi blush. They made a quick recovery though to try to burst her bubble: "But I have some very bad news for you."

Nicole laughed to preempt them: "Ha! What, that you don't care anymore? *Please.* Ravi, you're not fooling me with your jaded too-cool-to-care act."

"You sure it's an act?"

"You basically just told me that a beautiful, intelligent woman – who took you home and gave you free drinks and a *great* time in bed, all things considered – is a degenerate for not caring about saving the world from the horrors of capitalism with her unfinished master's degree."

"I don't think expecting other people to care is the same thing as caring."

"You think whatever you like, Ravi Bee. I see you."

"Okay well please stop seeing me immediately."

Nicole dutifully closed her eyes and gave a salute very intentionally in the wrong direction.

"Smart ass."

"Who said that?"

Ravi threw a greasy little wad of used paper towel at her and whined, *"Stop."*

After that playful distracted conclusion to the heavy conversation, the two of them went back to their respective projects.

Ravi looked up from their wrenching once in a while to find Nicole working silently now, with a stern look on her face. Seemed like something had taken the wind out of her sails. Even when they flipped the record for her, she didn't seem to have it in her to hum along anymore. They tried to shrug it off, tried not to worry about it while they finished off their own peculiar project, but it was kind of nagging at them the whole time.

Once their bike was finally back together, Ravi was amazed to find that there weren't any leftover nuts or bolts or bearings on the ground. Aside from the fucked-up wheel, this may have been a huge Sisyphean success.

Hopefully they wouldn't have any more terrible dates to hate-fix things over.

The stereo receiver got lucky this time.

When Ravi got back from stuffing their poorly conceived project back in the storage closest in the apartment building's basement, they found Nicole standing by the living room window, looking out at the grey autumn sky. Her sewing was tidily folded up on the armrest of the couch, her tea: Cold on the table.

A new record was under the needle. Something old, from the tinny quality of the recording – something Ravi had never heard before.

Ravi joined her at the window, leaning on the sill to the right of her. She didn't seem to notice, her mind off in the distance again.

She was almost certainly thinking about all that depressing stuff from earlier.

—Probably shouldn't bring it up, right?

They'd feel bad leaving Nicole stuck with a bunch of heavy thoughts like that, though – especially after they were the one who put those heavy thoughts in her head in the first place.

They bumped their shoulder into her arm and asked if she was okay.

"Oh." She was numbly startled by their gesture. She responded slowly, her words clearly heavy on her tongue. "Mm. I think so. Just thinking."

"About that mortality stuff?"

"About that mortality stuff."

She didn't add anything more to that.

Ravi stood next to her looking out the window in silence, hoping she would say something.

She didn't.

So Ravi had to.

"Did you lose someone?"

She replied like someone else was using her lungs and throat. "Lost, been lost. You know, it's surprising how many times you can die in one lifetime."

"Ah. I'm sorry." Why did they even ask? Ravi hadn't ever helped someone deal with this kind of existential melancholy before, and very few people were comforted by the promise of eternal oblivion that put all *their* ontological troubles to rest at night.

Well, too late to back out now.

"If it makes you feel any better, I'm pretty sure I've died to enough people to earn at least a dozen funerals."

She smiled a bit at that and half-heartedly joked, "That's going to be expensive."

"Not for me. I'm dead."

The joke didn't land.

The silence returned.

Ravi didn't feel right just leaving her with this, so they did the only thing they could and stayed with her until she was done.

Both of them stared out the window at the slowly shifting canopy of clouds – though Nicole was certainly looking at something else that Ravi couldn't see. She leaned into them a bit, resting her arm against their shoulder. It was the closest she came to acknowledging them until she left them there a long while later to get dressed and go for a walk that lasted until well after Ravi had to leave for work.

They spent the whole shift worrying that they hadn't done enough, but she thanked them later, when they got home, for standing with her, so apparently they had somehow managed to do a good job at being a shoulder to lean on.

They told her with a soft smile that they would be happy to stand next to her any time she needed. And they meant it.

Ravi hooked up with the degenerate Annabella Rosemary-Lou a few more times after.

...Okay, more than a few times.

Turned out her name was actually Valerie, but, as Ravi suspected, it didn't matter. The more they thought about it in the mornings after, over a solemn, lonely cigarette on their suitress's balcony, the less they wanted to be wanted by her – a woman who was content pursuing an *affaire du cœur* – or, more accurately, an *affaire d'estomac* – with a 'lover' she didn't care about at all. And the more they let their heart linger on it, the less they wanted to be wanted by a woman who was content to shrug at the world's suffering no matter how deep she buried herself in the study of it.

—Newly discovered Universal Law: Don't smile at the TAs in the social science department, no matter how cute they may be.

Ravi starting hiding in some dark corner of the university's least popular café for their lunches, and tried their very best to come up with convincing, creative new ways to excuse themself from spending any more nights with What's-Her-Name. These excuses were generally neither creative enough nor convincing enough to keep Ravi out of her bed.

—Free drinks and human contact, right?

Enough for Now

(Afternoon, Monday, 21st November)

A reverberating clap shattered the silence of the reference section in the university's library – the sound of Danica dropping a couple dozen medical journals on a quiet table tucked away in some back corner hideaway between the stacks. She sheepishly peered around the end of the shelf to make sure no one else was there. Empty, as far as she could see. Lucky.

Once she was sure she hadn't sullied the sanctity of this cavernous academic shrine, she got settled in with her notebook and a colorful bundle of pens.

This table was perfect. Old wood. Real wood. Complimented the earthy smell of the old pages in the stacks. Reminded her of home. This spot was one of the few places in the library that wasn't subjected to cold, buzzing, fluorescent light. Instead, there was a warm little lamp with an old incandescent bulb in it. It felt very natural. Almost like reading by candlelight – which was how books were meant to be read. Especially in a big library.

In her ambitious fugue, she had entirely ransacked the medical science journal shelf. But she had only been sitting down with one of the journals for a few minutes before she realized she only understood about half the words in it. So she added to her collection a tall pile of biology textbooks. And then when she realized she had no idea what any of the numbers or graphs in the journals meant, she grabbed a couple of statistics textbooks as well.

By the end of this session, she'd basically be a qualified medical researcher, she figured.

She was disappointed to find that very few of the journals she read had anything to do with Ravi's sores – which, after some remarkably difficult searches, she managed to find the proper name for: *melanotic sarcoid cysts.* According to the glossary of terms in her pile of books, she cobbled together that the name meant something like *'dark fluid-filled sacs that can show up anywhere in the body'* which was both extremely descriptive and entirely useless in capturing exactly what it was doing to ruin Ravi's life.

The symptom was first recorded about a decade prior, and the illness that caused it seemed to have spread fairly rapidly, but only to a small percentage of people on a global scale. A lot of papers were written trying to correlate the illness to some viral or genetic factor, but nothing ever came up conclusive.

Research on cures was pretty badly hindered by the fact that they couldn't figure out how it was transmitted, or get the disease to grow in lab animals. Seemed like it would only attach itself to a human. And since experimenting on humans wasn't acceptable in the public eye these days, all of the recent research was just desperately looking for ways to spread the illness to things that *weren't* human, just so the field could get moving forward on real research.

The best humanity could muster was a treatment. A monthly injection of a medicinal gel. A company called *InThetics* was the only manufacturer. It was patent protected. They funded and published all of the research into the efficacy of the stuff, and they sure made it *sound* effective. And somehow, they'd managed to persuade the Government of Canada to waive the rigorous medical trials that normally precede approval for such treatments.

It was sketchy, when she put it all down on paper, that was for sure, but there wasn't much to do about it. That's just how pharmaceutical companies did sometimes.

Danica finished another journal and closed it with a sigh. She couldn't help feeling extremely alien while reading all of this.

She didn't usually have to care too much about her own body. It hurt, but it healed quickly. She needed to feed it to keep the pain of hunger away. If she didn't sleep, her mind got delirious and achy. And if she got too old, everything hurt and her mind started slipping entirely. She did all the basic upkeep, but didn't really have to give much consideration to the trickier stuff, like illnesses and injuries. She would never be sick – just human. It was kind of miserable for the fae, but a blessing for a lot of mortals. And honestly, unlike her cousins, she enjoyed it, suffering and all.

She felt tired for the human race. There was a weight to it, an injustice that made her heart ache, to be sitting here next to a stack of journals and textbooks, thousands of pages and hundreds of years of research and practice about the extremely complicated things humans needed to do to keep their bodies from falling apart, while knowing she would never need to worry about any of that herself. Nothing more complicated for her than *eat, sleep,* and *don't smash your bones into things because gods damn that is the worst feeling.*

She wondered that maybe if everything had gone down differently back when she was a young faeling, maybe she could have done something to make it this easy for all of them too.

A familiar voice interrupted her meandering thoughts.

Ravi.

"Oh hey, it's Nicole. What are you doing here?"

Danica was so distracted with her thoughts that she didn't even hear the beep of the electronic lock on the reference library door.

Ravi was carrying a large stack of papers, wearing an outfit that was just a little nicer than usual today that did a good job hiding their attractive warehouse-toned muscles and what little bust remained after their binder did its job. They had their shirt tucked in and buttons done all the way up to the top – which normally meant they had to teach a lab or meet with someone important about their research. That and the glasses and the tidy descruffled hair and the red pen in their pocket all added up to make what Danica could only describe as Ravi's Handsome Little Librarian Look – a rare treat.

"Ravi! Hi! Reading. I'm reading. Books."

Danica chewed on her lip a little after getting her answer out. This was going to be a tricky conversation to navigate.

Being bound by the universe to never lie is kind of a whole *thing* when you're trying to be sneaky.

"Oh, is *that* what those are for?" Ravi asked with a mocking smile. "I thought you were preparing for war, building a fort."

Now that Ravi mentioned it, her pile of literature had grown pretty unreasonably large – a bit of a wall. The poor *actual* librarian was going to have a lot of work to do putting all this away.

"Yeah, you know, reading and making a mighty castle wall. That return cart over there's been stockpiling its own books and making rude gestures. It's a bit of a cold war thing."

Ravi snorted at the bad joke.

"Why are you here?" Danica asked, to preempt any of Ravi's serious follow-up questions.

"Why am *I* here? In the library at the university I go to? *Asked the woman who is a proud college dropout.* How did you even get in the door? I have to tap my card to get back here."

Danica gave Ravi a knowing smile with no intent of answering the question.

"I'm not a *proud* college dropout, Ravi. I just didn't like all the stillness of it. You know how it is. Doesn't matter how many pretty words you write if you aren't out there doing something about it."

With much interest, Ravi noted the journals Danica was reading. "Medicine? I didn't know you were into that stuff. I thought you were in some kind of humanities program before?"

" *'Global Development'* they called it. Extremely 'write pretty words about doing something important and then never do anything about it' kind of program."

"See? Proud college dropout. I was right."

"Okay, fine, yes. Academia's not for me, but it never hurts to expand your mind. This medicine stuff is pretty neat."

Ravi let out another jovial little snort at that. "*Neat.* I'd say saving lives is neat, yeah," they joked. They shuffled their paperwork into one arm and flipped thoughtfully through a few glossy pages of one of the journals with their free hand. "I thought about being a doctor for a while, actually, but... uh... I never had a head for biology, I guess."

"Really? You wanted to be a doctor? You're so grumpy though."

Ravi shifted their weight a bit, uncomfortably. That stack of papers was starting to look awkward in their arms.

"I was going to be one of those grumpy genius doctors, I thought. I talked myself out of it, though. I just want to do something quiet now, I guess – something quiet that still moves things forward. I can do numbers, and chemicals are fun, so, you know, ended up living in the lab." Ravi eyed the seat across from Danica. "Nikki somehow you managed to pick the only table I like to sit at when I come here. Can I..."

"Oh! Of course! Sorry! I had no idea. I just like the lighting."

"It's warm, right?"

"Like candlelight."

"God I wish. In a big old library like this? How perfect would that be? Doing deep, dark, alchemical research in the middle of the night, steady little flame to keep you company and light your way through the stacks."

"Exactly!" *Yeah! Ravi got it.* "Exactly." Danica stood up in a hurry and started picking up her journals. "Yeah, the table's all yours, Rav. I'm just messing around in here. Let me get out of your way—"

"—Wait. You don't have to go. —Unless you want to be alone. I'm not going to push you out of your seat, Nicole, I'm not that much of an asshole. I'm sure there's another perfect paper-marking table in here somewhere."

Danica did actually kind of want to be alone. At the very least, she didn't want Ravi to find out she was researching the medical facts and figures of their illness. The whole *'find a cure for dear sweet Ravi'* thing was kind of a hush hush project – at least until she made some progress. But putting Ravi out in the cold wasn't right. She would just have to be coy about it. It'd be fine. She could do coy.

"—No! Have a seat! I'll just make some room."

Danica heaved a pillar from the wall of journals and textbooks over to the return trolley. When she got back, Ravi had already made themself comfortable with their stack of lab reports, red pen in hand, listening to a pair of earbuds that whispered tinny punk rock into the still air of the otherwise silent room.

With Ravi so focused on their work, it looked like Danica wouldn't need to worry about them figuring out what she was working on after all, so she carried on reading and looking up definitions with a furrowed brow and occasionally writing down a note or a name with a humble nod.

Ravi popped out an earbud after a few minutes of silently flipping through papers and nonchalantly circling mistakes. They told Danica she should have told them she was coming by the university. "There's a nice sushi place here. Cheap, but it's still good. I only get food poisoning there every fourth or fifth time. You want to go in a bit? I can probably get this stuff done in like... an hour?"

"You're really making a hell of a sales pitch on the food there, Rav."

"Hey, some places on campus make me sick *every* time. This place is a real gold medal eatery in my book."

Despite the questionable review from the questionable reviewer, Danica agreed to join Ravi for lunch when they were done marking.

In the meantime, she reviewed the densely packed pages in her notebook. It felt like she had gotten about all she was going to get out of a first pass here. She had a list of academics to visit, a few back catalogs to dig through, and a whole lot of unanswered questions with big swirly question marks next to them.

She wondered if maybe it would be a good idea to bring in some... big guns on this project. That oh-so-sagely and oh-so-sketchy old acquaintance of hers, it was his whole thing, digging up magical info, and tracking down regular info by magic. And considering the sorry state of human medicine on these *melanotic cysts*, magical intervention might end up being the only way. Angie was pretty convinced that the fae and the fae-touched couldn't do anything about this stuff, but there were always loopholes and workarounds. She'd find a way.

She made a mental note to give her guy a call tomorrow after Ravi left for work.

Ravi's pile of papers was about half done, and Danica had already returned all of her books to the trolley, when she started getting a little antsy. She picked up one of the marked reports and chided Ravi. "You don't put a smiley face or anything for a good grade?"

Ravi pulled out one of their earbuds again and smiled with an incredulous look. "Nicole these aren't children, they're like nineteen- and twenty-year-old kids."

"You don't like getting a smiley face on your work?"

"I think I'm a little too old—"

Danica ripped a page out of her notebook, wrote a little calculus problem on it, then handed it to Ravi. "Okay, tough guy, answer that."

Ravi dutifully put the answer down without much thought and handed it back. Then Danica put a big checkmark, 100%, and a smiling little bumble bee at the top of the page with a comment that read, *'Great job, Ravi Bee!'*

"Look, see? How's that feel?" she asked, proudly showing it off.

"Patronizing."

Ravi liked to put on a disinterested veneer, but Danica spotted a sliver of a smile when they saw the page.

She grinned and teased Ravi. "Oh, it's tough little Ravi, too cold-hearted for a little fun. I forgot I was living with a miserable unfeeling block of concrete. Come on, Rav, you don't feel warm and fuzzy getting a little praise like that?" Danica held up the page and pointed to the cheerful bee she drew. "It's not cute enough for you? What does it take? Flowers? Hearts? You want a butt? I can put a little bee butt here."

Ravi shook their head in disbelief for a moment, then clarified something that was clearly deeply troubling them: "Sorry, have you really been saying 'bee' this whole time? I thought it was just the initial. Like, Ravi 'B for Badass' Beausoleil."

" 'Cause you're so busy all the time."

"Okay. Fair."

"—And scary."

"I am *not* scary, come on."

"—And I bet you have a hell of a sting."

Ravi rolled their eyes in a poor attempt to hide the smile growing on their face, then they slid the stack of completed papers over to Danica. "I don't care enough to draw cute smiley bugs on all of these, but if you want to do it, go nuts. Anyone who got less than eighty percent gets a scary bug with a frown."

"That's so harsh."

"It's a harsh program." After a moment Ravi added, "Flowers are fine, but no butts, and <u>don't</u> draw any hearts."

"Aw, you don't heart the undergrads?"

"I don't 'heart' getting formal grievances or weird confessions. The last thing I need is a rumor spreading around that Amaira the TA likes the undergrad brats *a little too much.*"

"Amaira?"

"Oh. They use my… old name here."

"Why?"

Ravi looked a little put out by the question. But instead of explaining it, they just shrugged and told her it was easier that way. "Paperwork and stuff. You know."

She got a pretty strong feeling there was more to it than paperwork, but she wasn't going to push it. Ravi had their own reasons.

"Ah. Alright, no hearts, no scandal. Got it."

Danica felt pretty satisfied with herself by the time she'd finished processing Ravi's graded papers. It was a stupid little gesture, but it was nice adding a little light into someone's life whenever she could. And it put a smile on Ravi's face when they flipped through the stack. A smile on Ravi's face always felt like a little victory. They had a sweet smile when they let it out.

The sushi restaurant – simply called 'SUSH' – turned out to be a window in the wall of one of the university's large hallways. It had precisely three menu items – 'SALM', 'TUNA', and 'AVOC', written in angular letters in thick black sharpie on the wall next to the window – and the whole operation felt like it wasn't supposed to be there at all, like the window itself had been carved out of the brickwork with a chainsaw.

Danica puzzled over the simple selection. "SALM? Salmon?"

"Yeah."

"Salmon what?"

"Sushi," Ravi replied obviously.

"But like… rolls or… on rice…? Slices? Or that weird spicy pate stuff?"

"You're thinking about it too much. It's just sushi."

"Sushi."

"*Sushi.*"

"Right. There's not a pancake place or anything…? I thought I saw one on the way—"

"Nicole, I have exactly thirty-seven minutes before I have to catch a bus for work. That breakfast place takes longer than that to bring water to your table. It's the cheap mystery sushi or nothing. You'll love it, trust me."

After asking the gruff bot on the other side of the window for an order of AVOC – which seemed the least likely item to end up being weird or poisonous – Danica walked away with eight cubes of avocado on squares of rice. They looked like little tea cakes. Ravi's SALM order looked the same, but with orange cubes instead of green.

Danica sat down with Ravi at a scuffed up little table with mismatched chairs. It was right next to a wall made up of a single glass pane. The view would have been gorgeous – looking out onto a research greenhouse garden filled with shrubs and wildflowers – except the glass didn't look like it had been cleaned in a couple decades, so the view instead was the hazy suggestion of a greenish yard beyond.

"Your university has kind of a weird feeling to it, Rav."

"Yeah… It's not one of the 'nice' universities. But they have almost all the equipment I need for my master's research. And obviously, it's not 'nice' equipment, but it gets the job done, when it's online."

"Chemistry, right?" Danica put her elbows on the table and propped up her chin with her knuckles. Ravi didn't usually talk about their research. She wasn't going to pass up an opportunity to pry.

"Yeah, material science." They raised a curious eyebrow at her and asked in quiet disbelief, "You remembered?"

"I remember everything important," she teased them. Plus, it was at the top of every paper she just processed for them. Kind of hard to miss. "What's material science about?"

"Uh. I mean if you want the short version, in theory, I get to make *exciting revolutionary new substances* to make machines and prosthetics and spaceships out of. In practice, I've been making *existing* substances slightly lighter and stronger and more resistant to heat damage."

"What kind of substances?"

Ravi shoved a soy sauce drenched salmon cube in their mouth and waved their hand dismissively, words muffled by the mouthful. "It's not really that interesting, Nikki, you don't want to get into it."

"Is it for spaceships?"

Ravi raised an eyebrow, apparently surprised by Danica's interest. They swallowed the cube to answer before it was done being chewed properly. They had to swallow twice to get it down. "...Yeah—Yeah, actually, that's what I hope it gets used for."

"For the shell, right? Needs to be light and strong?"

They let a little grin slip. Ravi must not be used to this kind of attention.

"That's right. It's for the shuttles. There's a lot of fuss about reusing the rockets now, but the actual ships still get trashed when they come back into the atmosphere. My research should help protect the hull, if it works out."

Danica asked for more, and she listened with eyes full of wonder while Ravi cautiously went into detail about the science of their research. They were acting like a stranger trying to pet a nervous cat, like Danica was just going to dash away if they moved too quickly or said the wrong thing, but she didn't flinch. It was all pretty neat, despite their hesitation talking about it.

While they spoke, Ravi's food went entirely ignored, *such was their passion*. Danica smiled to herself when she noticed, but she didn't mention it.

They boiled their work down to 'shifting proportions of component materials by thousandths of a percent' – a little more of this stuff, a little less of that stuff. It truly was a super boring topic.

But Ravi, they knew it all so intimately, and so passionately, and explained it so patiently. By the end of it, Danica was genuinely invested in the exact ratio of carbon-to-boron-to-tungsten in Ravi's ceramic plating.

Danica hadn't spent a lot of time engaging with science people in the hundreds of years since she got stuck in this *Earthly form*. There was usually an air of arrogance and confidence in everything the *esteemed scientists* said and believed that didn't sit well with her, especially considering how easily their 'laws of nature' could be... *subverted*, and how frequently they changed.

Ravi was nice, though. Nice to talk to. Nice to listen to. They clearly held science in their hands with humility. It was a curiosity, a perfunctory tool that just happened to work the way it was supposed to when it was supposed to. For them, *understanding it* meant knowing how to use it, not knowing how it worked.

"Some guy said something like true wisdom is knowing what you don't know," Ravi said, when Danica asked how the science worked one layer too deep for them to explain. That question being, '*Where does all the heat go?*'

"Socrates," Danica noted.

"Yeah, some guy." Ravi paused again with a curious eyebrow to ask rhetorically in quiet bewilderment, "Why do you know that?" before they continued explaining with a quick shake of their head, "It's a good idea. That's the trick to science, I think. Good science. Seeing the holes. But there are some holes we can't even see yet, questions we don't know how to ask. So *absolute knowledge* is kind of a pointless pursuit when you think about it."

Danica grinned at Ravi's magic trick, their philosophical misdirection. "Rav if you don't know the answer you can just say that you don't know."

"Okay. I have no idea where the heat goes. The physics kids would say something about infinite vibrating strings or something. It's all magic past a certain point, you know? The math works. Let whatever god keeps the machine running sort out the details."

That wasn't a bad guess, though, Danica mused to herself. The truth wouldn't really change anything, but yeah, strings, basically. And magic. And gods. It was kind of funny, that the fabric of the universe was so pliable in the hands of the fae, so easy for them to bend and fold and poke holes in when it suited the terms of a tricky pact, and yet she still had no idea how any of the rules that were built on top of that fabric actually worked. Physics and chemistry were modern marvels, and it was a joy to hear the universe explained so humbly as Ravi did.

She wondered if the gods themselves even knew all these rules when they put it all together, or if it was just some intuitive expression of their will, as intuitive and thoughtless as whatever magic power she and her cousins managed to scam out of the universe. It felt like a big question for a human, and an absolute bore to any other faerie: Did the mechanisms of the universe come first, to be pieced together by human curiosity? Or was science just some fairytale humans told themselves? Just a palette of language to paint abstract portraits of reality with on the canvas of the mind?

Ravi interrupted her silent musing: "Why the sudden interest? Or have you always been this into chemistry? Have I been too stupid to notice...? God, could I have been ranting to you about my shitty lab equipment this whole time?"

Nicole gave them a satisfied grin. "You're just so fired up about it! And no one I've ever met talks about it like you do. I could listen to this stuff all day if it's you. Gods, I don't know why you're doing that warehouse job at all when you obviously love your chemistry stuff so much."

"The chemistry stuff doesn't pay the rent. Not yet. Not until I'm working in some lab, doing the same three litmus tests every day for the rest of my life. The warehouse gig lets me have a little more time here, doing my own research, playing around in a real science lab, *before the walls of my ivory tower transform into a passionless nine-to-five prison.*"

Danica had been working through her avocado cubes while Ravi was speaking, and just now managed to get the last one in her mouth. "Come on, Ravi," she said between chews, "Don't be so bleak."

"Hey at least I know it's coming. A lot of people I knew, they just jumped right into the nine-to-five prison thing, leapt right into the maw of the beast like it was a swimming pool on a hot summer's day."

"You scared of that?"

"You lose yourself. Who wouldn't be scared of that?"

"Sounds like all those people who hopped into the hungry maw weren't scared. Might be something to it if *everyone's* doing it." Danica didn't believe any of that, but it was fun to play devil's advocate with Ravi.

They didn't have a response to that. Their eyes lowered to their little plastic container of untouched orange geometry. They took a try at dipping a cube of salmon in soy sauce, but they couldn't muster the will to eat it, and just set it back down, dripping wet.

They asked Danica in a glum tone, "Isn't that why you're doing this?"

"Doing what?"

"The... job hopping. The never settling down. Traveling. Volunteering. Sleeping on couches. Aren't you scared of it too? Losing yourself?"

Danica had a lot of reasons for not committing to anything, to friends, lovers, to a home, to a career. Ravi was right, it felt suffocating, but there was a lot more to it.

She couldn't do anything to redeem herself to the world while she was working to fulfill someone else's ambitions.

And that's all it would ever be if she got into a real job – someone else's dreams, someone else's wealth, and she'd never have any control over what good or evil those dreams and that wealth would feed into.

She needed the freedom to fix things her own way, to make the world better on her own terms. And she hated the idea of being used for someone else's agenda – or using anyone else for hers. Not anymore. That was a life she wanted to leave behind, hard as it was to do that considering the many, many... *obligations* she had to fulfill – to Angie, to her 'generous' cousins, ...to Ravi.

And, on top of that, the fewer attachments she had in this world, the harder it would be for her family... to... ruin things again.

Ravi didn't need to hear any of that, though. They had a normal life to live, and Danica was going to do everything she could to keep it that way.

"I might be a little scared, yeah. But you're different, Rav! Just, *overflowing* with spite. You'd never let your job kill who you are. Look, you work in a miserable warehouse, but you're not '*a guy who moves boxes*', right? Why would you be '*a guy who does boring lab work*'?"

"Boxes isn't me by a long shot. That's easy. But the lab? That's too close to my heart. I don't want that getting twisted into something I hate."

Before the two of them could continue with that inappropriately heavy lunch conversation, Ravi noticed the time and swore loudly before leaping out of their seat, gathering their things in a hurry, and leaving Danica at the table with a hasty goodbye.

"Your lunch!" Danica called after them, pointing at their poor abandoned cubes.

"All yours!"

When they disappeared out the sliding glass doors at the end of the hall, Danica quietly pulled a set of keys out of thin air into her hand – marked with the city's transit logo. She admired the keychain for a minute – long enough for Ravi to sprint to the bus stop – then returned them to the driver's pocket.

A little favor for the free lunch and the good conversation and stealing their favorite table. Plus, you know, it would suck if Ravi was late and lost their job because of Danica. *That* would be a rough debt to pay off.

All that talk about losing yourself got Danica wondering if she might have managed to do the same, to lose something of herself at some point without knowing it. Leapt reckless into a soul-twisting prison all while convincing herself she was setting herself free.

She fondly reflected on Ravi's spiteful reverence for their true self. Living on the edge of poverty, twisting their bones and muscles for way too many hours at a thankless job, just so they could hold on to themself for one more day, just so they could keep what they loved sacred.

They were so strong.

And maybe if she were that strong, she could find the courage to keep herself too.

But she gave everything away, didn't she?

Who *was* she anymore?

She was proud once. Arrogant. Arrogant enough to save the world, no matter the consequences.

Now she begged and pleaded and sold off pieces of herself just to get one more chance at youth, one more chance to prove herself, one more chance to make everything right again. But every time around, she could only ever selfishly bring everything to ruin again.

Maybe this time would be different, though.

She ran her fingers over her notebook, full of hopeful research, and assured herself that she wasn't lost yet. Not yet.

I'm No Errant Knight, but I
Could Still Work for You

(Morning, Tuesday, 6th December)

Tuesday morning. Despite the freshly fallen snow and the fresh December chill, Ravi was leaning over the railing of the creaky old fire escape outside the kitchen, barely dressed after rolling out of bed twenty minutes prior, forearms soaked from the snow, formerly hot coffee in one hand, cheap tasteless cigarette in the other, staring woefully at the stop-and-go traffic below. A hard shiver shook them once in a while. Their punishment or something. Whatever. They didn't know. It just felt right to suffer right now.

They woke up an hour ago to an automated message on their phone indicating both their overtime shifts today had been sniped by a more senior worker at the warehouse. Eighteen double-time hours. Gone. They didn't want to be angry about it, but, on paper, if you took all the humanity out of the equation, it sure looked like Ravi just got robbed of a few days' wages for no reason at all.

And maybe they wouldn't mind so much if this came near the end of the month, when they were in a ridiculous amount of pain from their illness, but they were fine right now. Their shoulder was treated a week ago. It would just be a persistent dull ache for another week or so. And while that lasted, they needed to get in every hour they could, while they could manage the work pain-free, to offset the days they had to cut their hours because they couldn't.

It made them clench their teeth bitterly when they thought about it. They couldn't help feeling like they were being *punished* for something – that last lackluster performance review, for example – or maybe that fragile box they dropped the other day right in front of their supervisor when their shoulder was taken over by a sudden burst of sharp blinding pain, as it liked to do randomly in the last week of every month.

Patterns. There were patterns at play here. They'd already been written out of the schedule at four other warehouses since they started living on their own. It usually goes the same way, they figured: First a few of your overtime shifts get stolen. Then your hours get cut. Then suddenly you realize you haven't been to work for a couple weeks and you're desperately looking for a new job because your illness isn't 'bad enough' to qualify for disability support and you're out of amateurly refurbished electronics to sell.

They inhaled a rapid lungful of harsh, hot smoke from their cigarette to try to clear their head, grimacing bitterly while they exhaled.

It was just two shifts. It didn't mean anything. They were doing their best. This was just... just *one day.*

The door to the kitchen opened behind them, accompanied by a sweet voice asking if they were okay.

Nicole.

Ravi glanced over their shoulder at her with a smile to assure her they were fine. But she didn't seem to believe them.

"I thought you were working today? Are you sick?" she asked, settling in beside them to lean on the railing.

Ravi snuffed out their cigarette between their thumb and knuckle when Nicole got too close and stuffed it back in the pack for later. They didn't like exposing her to all that poison.

They noted that she was fully dressed today. Partly hidden under an open, thigh-length, black knit wool coat, she was wearing one of her rarer signature looks – seductively sheer, dark, wine-red stockings under a long, vibrantly floral dress that shimmered tastefully in the light when the breeze caught it, like a spring canopy of leaves and cherry blossoms piercing the grey weather. And today, as a special treat, she even had her wild amber hair tied and sorted into sharp hair clips. She looked powerful. Intimidating. Tall.

—*Beautiful.*

Ravi always felt so stupid and small next to her when she got dressed up like this – which, as far as they could tell, she only ever did when she was planning to leave the apartment to take care of some sort of important business.

They thought about their reply carefully. They didn't want her to worry. And they especially didn't want her to think they were hurting for cash.

After probably just a little too long side-eyed admiring how good she looked in her outfit and trying to think of an answer to such an easy question, Ravi replied that they just happened to have a day off today.

Nicole scrunched up her brow incredulously and teased them: "On a *Tuesday?* What happened? Warehouse burn down?"

Ravi stared at the street with dead eyes for a few seconds before they decided it would just be easier to tell the truth here.

"...I lost my shifts."

"Oh no."

—*And now she's worried. Great.*

"It's really not a big deal," they tried to assure her.

"Why did you—?"

"—I don't know. It just happens sometimes," they replied curtly, trying to dismiss her concerns. "System screws up. Clerical error or something. Really, it's fine, I can make it up another day."

Nicole smirked at them and joked, "How? Planning to clone yourself and work two shifts at the same time?"

"I wish."

"Me too! Imagine: If there were two of you, I might get to hang out with you more than three whole hours a week."

Ravi playfully parried her jab, "Since when do we hang out even three whole hours a week?"

"What, the time I spend watching you sleep doesn't count?"

"...Please tell me you don't..."

She shrugged with a playful grin, "I take whatever Ravi time I can get."

Nicole had a bad habit of skating on the edge of some emotionally devastating sentiment like this – something that, on a bad day, sounded a lot like, '*You're a bad friend for spending so much time working to keep the lights on,*' but, on a good day, sounded more like, '*I wish you could live an easier life so you could smile more.*'

Ravi knew that she meant it in the nice way, but they weren't sure she understood how bad it hurt that they *couldn't* spend more time with her, or anyone else. Like, they obviously would if they could, right? But as it was, they were lucky if they could even find an hour in a week for a loveless relief session with What's-Her-Name.

They shook those troubled thoughts out of their head and set the

"Thought I was supposed to be your muscle today."

"I'll let you know when I need your assistance, my dear minion. Just be cool until then? Low profile?"

Ravi stuck their tongue out at her, but agreed to follow her instructions.

While the two of them walked to whatever Nicole's first mystery errand was, Ravi took some time to admire the repairs she had made to their jacket.

"You really went all out on the embroidery, huh?"

"You like it?"

"I feel like I should be paying money for it. This jacket didn't even look this good when I stole it brand new."

"You stole it?"

"It was too expensive."

"Well, that's not a *great* reason to steal a coat."

"No no, I didn't actually *want* it. Just, on principle, it was too expensive, so I liberated it from the rack, then cut it up the moment I got home. I think I was going for some kind of anti-capitalist fuck you thing, I don't know. Who knows what's going on in a teenage poser punk's twisted little brain."

"...Wait wait, you stole it out of *spite* because you didn't like the price?"

"I do most things out of spite," Ravi replied with a coy grin. "I don't think I'd get out of bed in the morning if it wasn't to spite the sun."

"Not sure that's healthy, Ravi Bee."

They shrugged. "Better than lying in bed all day feeling sorry for myself."

"Did you steal a lot of stuff as a teenager or was this a one-off?"

"Oh man. Nicole. Don't get me started. You remember Fleece? Felicity? Vicente?"

"Little Filipina with the super short flax-dyed hair?"

"You are something else Nicole. Do you remember *everyone?*"

"I'm good with names," she replied with a proud grin.

"She was my best friend back then."

"I remember. You two were adorable together. I think everyone thought you were dating."

"We... were not." *Sadly.* She was very pretty. And fun. And her lip gloss on the cigarettes they shared was so... dangerous... "...I haven't seen her in years, actually. She moved away for university and never came back."

That wasn't quite the whole story, but Nicole didn't need to know every detail of how they fucked all that up.

They paused for a second when they suddenly realized it really had already been that long since they last saw her. If it weren't so embarrassing, they might reach out, but they hadn't really felt worthy of her attention in a very, very long time.

"...Anyways, me and her probably stole a hundred thousand dollars worth of criminally overpriced designer jackets over the years and donated them to good will. Out of spite."

Ravi opened the lapel of their jacket and pointed out a collection of a few dozen stapled-on designer labels that had all been vandalized with a razor. "Ripped off the stupid logo every time. These are my notches. This jacket's a testament to a hundred thousand bucks worth of lost profit."

"...Wow. That is... quite the spiteful jab at capitalism."

Ravi scoffed. "Yeah, I'm sure Big Denim is really hurting over it. God I was a stupid kid. Could've been doing something useful and I was out shoplifting for kicks."

"I had no idea I was working on something so valuable," Nicole mused. "That thing should be in a museum."

Ravi ran a finger over the new, beautiful, intricately embroidered quilted silk lining. "Honestly, I think it's worth twice as much after all this. And it's so warm and like... light? Seriously, I feel lighter just wearing it. And the silk is so smooth. I can barely feel it rubbing on my shoulder. Whatever you did, this is easily the nicest thing I've ever worn. Thank you, really. I mean it."

Nicole grinned wide and assured them it was no problem at all, and it was just a down payment on what she owed Ravi for their kindness in putting up with her.

"Nah, you don't owe me anything, Nikki. It's great having you around."

"...I'll still pay you back, though. I promise. I won't be able to live with myself if I can't."

"Sure sure, when you get your own place, put me up for a week and we'll call it even."

She grinned at Ravi, but didn't say anything more about it, because the two of them had arrived at the location of her first errand – an antique shop.

"What's going on here?" Ravi asked as the two of them walked through the door and kicked the snowy grey sidewalk slush off their boots.

"Picking up something for someone."

"Very specific," Ravi dryly teased her.

"Sorry Ravi Bee, some of this stuff is confidential."

Ravi touched the tip of their nose and nodded to let her know they understood.

Nicole looked around the building for a moment trying to size something up before she let Ravi know this would probably take a few minutes. "I gotta go haggle with the guy. So uh, I don't know, just wander around until I come get you."

"Really? Haggling without your big strong hired muscle at your side? You're wasting my talents here."

"I think I've got this," she replied with a warm smile. "I promise I'll come get you if I need your services."

Nicole discreetly disappeared behind a door to a back room of some sort, leaving Ravi alone to entertain themself.

It was a nice enough store. Cluttered, the way a good antique shop should be. Ancient furniture stacked on top of other ancient furniture. All of it a bit overpriced. All of it made to look old and genuine but, on closer inspection, a lot of the more expensive wooden tables and cupboards were laminated particle board instead of the purported solid oak.

Ravi assumed a lot of the appliances and lamps and toys were similar – replicas emulating a romanticized past. The false veneer of truth and beauty that, if Ravi could just get over their hangups about authenticity, they could probably entertain the idea of genuinely enjoying despite the falseness of it all.

They were drawn to a rack of clothes with a section of denim jackets. They ran their fingers over the fabric to find that much of it had been softened to the texture of flannel with time and use. One of the garments stood out: The logo on the chest matched one of the many not-so-surgically removed stolen patches hidden on their lapel.

They were depressed to find the jacket was also being sold for about the same price it would've gone for new on the shelf. And who knows if it was even authentic, especially considering the rest of the stuff in the building. There were always a ton of knockoffs for this brand floating around the market.

Looking at it got their mind back on poor neglected Felicity. God, what an untenable situation. Years of lies and hiding the truth of their feelings from her. They hadn't even told her their name. Hadn't even told her they weren't just a cute lovable tomboy anymore. Hadn't even told her they were sick with a crippling illness and unbelievably tired from overwork and utterly miserable except for what little time they got to spend in the science wing at the university.

They always just put on a face for her. Pretended to be someone else. Pretended to be the girl she used to love. Pretended to be good.

And it worked. Ravi's dear Felicity thought they were financially stable – living off grants and scholarships and their part-time TA work. She didn't know they lifted boxes to pay the bills. *Scholarships?* As if they could keep their grades up high enough for scholarships between exhausting shifts at the warehouse. They were a full year behind schedule, and had so, so many Fs on their transcript from missing assignments and exams – too many to mention to anyone – especially not to her. She still thought so highly of them from her memory of who they were in high school.

—Felicity.

She was just... so content to genuinely enjoy them, despite their shallow peeling veneer. It made them sick, doing that to her for so long. It was just easier, to just... disappear on her.

Like friends so often do.

She'd get over it.

For old time's sake, they checked around the store for cameras, and, finding none pointing in their direction, they discretely swapped the designer jacket's price tag with another one that was a couple orders of magnitude smaller, then stuffed the ridiculous overpriced tag in their pocket.

It gave them a giddy nostalgic exhibitionist rush to be hanging around the shop with the evidence of their crime hidden right there in their hand. They discretely fiddled with it while they browsed old books and records, trying very hard not to nervously glance over at the bored woman behind the counter.

God it was nice before, sharing this giddy excitement with Felicity. She always ran the distraction during their little heists. She was perfect for it – so animated and engaging. She made it so easy. She made it so *fun*. They were a good pair. Or a bad pair, depending on who you asked.

They missed her.

They missed so much of her.

They really did.

—Fuck.

God, get over it Ravi.

Nicole suddenly appeared behind them as if out of thin air and told them plainly that it was time to leave.

She was dutifully holding a little sealed wooden crate in front of her, with a label on it in a strange symbolic language Ravi had never seen before – and she looked *very* nonplussed, with a grim and distant look in her eyes.

Ravi noted that one of her hairclips had gotten messed up, leaving her hair in a bit of a state. Her coat wasn't sitting right on her shoulders. One of her boots was untied.

Ravi asked tentatively: "So... uh... How... did it go?"

"Bad. Thank you. Let's go."

She led Ravi out of the building with long impatient strides, leaving them practically jogging to keep up, and then continued on like that for a whole block without another word before she was finally stopped by a red light.

Once they got across the street, Ravi tugged at her coat. "Hey stop for a sec. Let me fix your hair."

"I'm fine," she replied coldly, without stopping.

"Okay." Ravi withdrew their hand from her uneasily. "You sure? It's kind of messing with your whole 'intimidating professional' 'take me seriously' vibe."

She took a few slowing steps before she finally stopped and hung her head in defeat. "Okay. Go ahead," she grumbly conceded.

Ravi put their hand on Nicole's shoulder to get her to lean down a bit so they could reach her hair properly.

"What happened in there?" they asked.

"Nothing good."

"Yeah, I'm getting that. You really don't mess around when you're haggling, huh? Did you get in a fight or something?" They struggled with the clip and the bit of hair that was out of place. They were never any good at this. They muttered quietly to themself, "How the hell did you have this before..."

Despite her grumpy demeanor, Nicole couldn't help letting out a stifled teasing snicker. "Why did you offer to help if you don't know how?"

"If I can't be your muscle, I can at least be your cut man." Ravi rotated Nicole's head slightly so they could study the other side to figure out what she did. "Over... under... twist... No, three twists? Oh, I see. Okay. Okay got it." They took a step back to admire their work. "There we go, looks great."

Nicole's grim scowl faded to a little grin at their optimistic assessment. "I'll take your word for it."

"No trust me, it's even better than before. I must have been a hairstyling savant this whole time. I'm wasting my life on this chemistry bullshit."

Ravi also offered to carry the box for her for a second so she could put herself back together a bit. Then they refused to let her take it back after she finished getting her boot tied back up.

"Mine now," they teased her with a smartass grin, playing keep-away with the box when she grabbed at it.

"Ravi come on. You said you'd behave."

"Let your hired goon carry your stuff."

Nicole rolled her eyes and gave up with a huff. "Fine. You're such a situation sometimes, gods."

"Hey, don't be like that. I owe you for getting me out of the house today. It's my pleasure to carry some of your stuff."

"You don't owe me. At all. But thank you."

Nicole shrugged off her displeasure and led the way to her next errand. While they walked, Ravi gently shook the box to try to figure out what was inside. Felt like a bottle suspended in crumpled packing paper. Wait, was something moving in there? Smallish... Mouse maybe? ...In a bottle?

Ravi turned the box over to look for an air hole.

Nicole noticed what they were doing and pleaded with them to stop fussing with it.

"Fragile?"

"*Confidential*. Ravi."

"Fine, fine. Lady of mystery and intrigue over here."

She shot them a coy grin and teased them, "If you don't like it, I can just hire a goon that doesn't ask so many questions."

The next stop was a little plant shop. She said she had to wait for someone here, so the two of them started looking around the store at the plants on display. Ravi picked up a cute looking succulent and called out to Nicole to come take a look, but there was no answer. Somehow they managed to lose her to some unseen back room again after only a few seconds of looking away.

How the hell was someone as big as Nicole so stealthy? Bewildering. She really was some kind of cat. Leopard maybe. Tiger? Something flamboyant.

Ravi was left waiting for a long time and getting kind of impatient about it after they'd made their rounds of the store and thoroughly exhausted their interest in the specimens on display. They started poking their head in whatever doors they could find around the shop when the cashier wasn't looking. No sign of Nicole, though.

Then out of nowhere, she startled them with a tap on their good shoulder. When they turned around, she placed a thick document-sized envelope on top of the mystery box Ravi was carrying and told them it was time to head out. The envelope seemed to have some notes on it in the same unknown language as the label on the box.

What was Nicole up to?

It was tickling Ravi's mind that they'd seen some of the symbols in this language somewhere before.

Once again, Nicole looked absolutely miserable about her success, and slightly flushed this time, like she'd been exercising, or wrestling. But it looked like she had taken the time to put herself together before she came back this time. Ravi noted that her hair was arranged slightly differently now.

They gave her an uneasy smirk once the two of them got back on the street to continue on with her odyssey, and asked: "You're at least *winning* these fights, right?"

"They're not fights."

"You're winning, though?"

She gestured lethargically at Ravi's burden and answered without answering, "The spoils."

They paused for a moment of thought before they asked: "You're really not into this, huh?"

"I'm really not into this."

"Why are you doing it?"

"Why do you work at your miserable back-breaking soul-sucking warehouse? Ravi."

They quirked an eyebrow at the odd comparison. "I mean I have rent and loans and research supplies to pay for. Manufactured nanoscale fibrous tungsten isn't cheap, you know. And it's *super* annoying to make in-house..."

Nicole took a while to reply to that. She was putting her words together very carefully, it seemed, from how slowly the heavy syllables came out of her mouth. "I have my own debts to pay."

"...Anything I can do to help?"

Nicole laughed at herself, like Ravi was a toddler asking to help cook breakfast. "You do. You already do. I don't know how I'll ever pay you back for it, Ravi Bee, but you're helping me more than I can ever tell you."

Ravi didn't really know what to say to that. If this work Nicole was doing was as emotionally devastating as it looked, they really wished they could do something to get her out of it. But it clearly wasn't something she could talk about, and it definitely wasn't something she'd ever accept their help with.

At least they got to carry her packages around. That was something. Maybe.

The rest of her grim errands that morning included getting a tidily wrapped book at a used bookstore, another envelope full of documents in a toy store – and a bag of toys for some reason. That didn't fit the theme at all. And then finally, yet another mysterious box, this time retrieved somehow from someone in a snowy wooded park. Each time Ravi found themself bewildered and abandoned while Nicole negotiated for her items. They couldn't even find her footprints in the snow when she disappeared in the park.

At last, she returned to them with the final box and a sigh of relief and said it was time for lunch, assuring Ravi that the rest of her errands for the day weren't going to be so weird.

"What else are you doing?"

"Mm. Let's see…" She held up a hand and counted off her list on her fingers. "Dropping off all that junk, picking up some food, delivering some toys, walking some kids home from school – you are going to behave <u>perfectly</u> during that one, Ravi Beausoleil, or you'll be in the river this time – and shooing some shitty protestors away from the women's health clinic."

"Oh, *please* tell me I can help with that one."

Nicole grinned. "Yes. Yes, totally, absolutely. That's *perfect* for your skillset. You will be deployed to maximum effect on that mission, I promise."

Ravi pumped their fist triumphantly. At last, they were going to be useful.

While they were eating, Ravi noted that, as usual, Nicole's lunch was actually breakfast. Pancakes. Lots of maple syrup. Clearly some kind of comfort food for her. Well-deserved after all the stuff she had to put up with that morning, including Ravi's bullshit.

Nicole left them standing in the cold with the bag of toys while she ran in to drop off all the packages she'd collected. The building was some ancient mansion-turned-apartments. They kind of wished they could get a look at the inside, which surely must have had radiators and hardwood floors and beautiful carved wooden molding on the ceiling of every room. That kind of stuff was a rare treat among the modern architecture of the city. Hell, it might not even be in there at all. Some of those old historic buildings were plagued by developers, hollowing them out to put modern condos in.

When Nicole returned to them, she looked so cheery that she must've been a solid four inches taller just from getting that weight off her shoulders.

The toys and walking the kids home were actually the same errand. She explained that the kids didn't really get a lot of fun stuff at home, and that she was picking up the kids to help out a few sweet moms she knew from a food bank she volunteered at – which was also where the food was being dropped off: A big box of free ugly vegetables and nearly expired bread from some charming bodega where an older Hispanic woman with a brilliant smile was working behind the register.

Nicole and the cheerful old woman shared a hug and a warm thanks before the exchange, and the two of them talked for a bit in Spanish and laughed sincerely at each other's stories. Ravi had never picked up more than a few twisted loanwords of the language from dear Felicity's family dinners, so they couldn't really follow along, but it was clear these two had a tight connection.

The kids loved Nicole, and from the glow in her cheeks she clearly had a lot of affection for them too. Turned out this was a little more than just a walk home. There was a lengthy stopover in a snowy park. Nicole got the children started on some game of territorial tag Ravi wasn't familiar with before letting them run wild. When she sat down with Ravi for a breather, she explained that the kids were let out early some Tuesdays, so she did this as a favor so their mothers wouldn't need to miss any work.

Ravi wasn't great with kids, so they tried to keep their distance when Nicole returned to the game, opting to stay safely on the bench, far from the action. But that didn't seem to deter a couple of them from breaking away from the group to come over to interrogate a bunch of uneasy single-word answers out of Ravi. Apparently Nicole didn't have anyone walking with her usually and that was a matter of grave concern.

"I like your jacket," one of the boys said, once he'd established that Ravi wasn't a threat. And the reason why he liked it was pretty obvious when he showed off a bit of pretty embroidery that was patching up a tear on his sleeve – very clearly in Nicole's style.

"Hey, samesies," Ravi coolly replied with a put-on grin for the kid, pointing at one of their own newly embroidered hole-patches.

"*Samesies...*" he echoed, kind of grim and confused, like he'd never heard the word before.

Ravi kind of smiled awkwardly in silence, praying the kids would get bored and leave before they said something stupid. Nicole would never forgive them if they messed this up.

Luckily Nicole noticed their predicament and came over to corral the kids back to the game so Ravi could recover from the intrusion into their safe little bubble.

"You good, Ravi Bee? You're looking pretty lonely over here."

They shook their head gravely. "I'm not a kid person. This is all you. I'll run security," they added, nodding at the precious bag of toys.

On the walk home, each of the kids gave Nicole a hug before crashing through the front door their little rundown apartments. Again, she chatted with each mom at the door for a minute or two, in whatever language they spoke, handing over a toy for the kid before leaving, smiling and laughing and ending the interaction with a cheerful wave goodbye.

That afternoon was such a shocking contrast to her grim errands all morning. This stuff gave her life. She was practically glowing with joy and satisfaction by the time she and Ravi made it to the wretched little group of anti-abortion protestors at the clinic. The two of them joined up with a few other counter-protestors and made quick work of them, being scary and loud and intimidating and annoying the hell out of them until they all gave up and dispersed for the day.

Ravi was probably never going to see any of the members of that noble crew again, but Nicole still introduced them to the others before the two of them headed out.

One of the women even gave Ravi the eyes and a flirty smile, tucking a cute lock of hair behind her ear. They flexed for her with a playful grin when they caught her, but more as a joke for themself than to flirt. They didn't have time to pursue anyone seriously. Even their casual thing with What's-Her-Name was too much.

And with that, Nicole's errands were finally done.

Ravi marveled at her on the walk home: "God, Nikki, for such a sweetheart, you're a hell of a punk."

"Am I?"

"Yeah. You are very, very punk."

"I thought that was your thing," she said, poking at their jacket.

Ravi rolled their eyes and waved their hand dismissively at the suggestion. "God. Self-righteous shoplifting was the stupidest shit I did as a teenager, thinking I was some counter-culture hero or something. But all the stuff you did today—"

"—Not all the stuff," Nicole reminded them with a grim tone.

"Oh whatever. Just because I work in a warehouse doesn't mean I support exploiting workers and shit. You do what you have to do to keep yourself alive. I get it. All this other stuff you did today? Being so sweet and good it makes my teeth hurt? That's you for real. Punk as hell. Making the world a better place. Helping little guys." Ravi smiled at her and clapped her on the back warmly. "Thanks for taking me out today. That was... really nice."

"You'll have to take me to the warehouse some day so I can carry some boxes for you."

"And then to the chem lab so you can mix some clay for me. I think you'd like that a little better."

Nicole smiled. "I would actually. Maybe I'll take you up on that."

"Hmm... No idea how I'd sneak you in, though."

"Oh, don't worry about that. I'm good at getting into places I'm not supposed to be."

"Like the reference section."

"Like the reference section," she replied with a wry grin. "Exactly."

That actually sounded like a fun activity, when Ravi thought about it. Mixing the two best parts of their life in one room. They couldn't help letting a flash of a grin shape their face at the thought.

God, Nicole was such a joy. And such a cool person? Her capacity for goodness was practically supernatural. Even just being near her made them feel like they were a better human being. Like they could *be* better. It was like she had a little sun in her, like they were some wretched withered plant soaking up her light.

And she even put up with Ravi's bullshit with a smile. What the hell was that about?

They felt so warm around her.

They felt—

What did they feel—

Something familiar—

—*God, she looks good in that dress, though.*

Their smile faded when their thoughts stung them with some bitter nostalgic sensation that they were sure hoping they'd never have to deal with again.

Nicole interrupted Ravi's mental grumbling with a cheerful invitation: "You're free tonight too, right? Want to head to the Serpent's Fang? There's a band playing I want to see."

Ravi hesitated for only a single moment of doubt and darkness before they buried all that to smile at her and nod yes, absolutely.

If You've Never Had a Fine Seafood Alfredo, Let Me Tell You, It's Hard to Stomach After Years of Ketchup and Wieners on Boxed Mac and Cheese

(Night, Tuesday, 6th December)

The brass bell on the door of the Serpent's Fang rang cheerfully when Ravi stepped in out of the cold and tapped the snow off their boots. They scruffed up their hair to get the snow out of it, checked they didn't look like a *complete* mess in a mirror near the entrance, then meandered around the lobby to try to find Nicole. When the two of them had gotten back to the apartment for dinner, she suddenly announced that she had some last-minute errand to take care of and just... dashed off. She said to meet up here at nine, but, alas, here they were, nine, and no Nicole.

They fired off a quick message, but it didn't get through for some reason. Dead battery?

They might be waiting a while.

This place was one of Nicole's favorite pubs. She was very fond of the old salt-and-pepper guy behind the bar, and Ravi had to admit he was easily one of the most playful bartenders they had ever met. Dressed extremely weird though. Like some kind of quirky reenactor, from some Victorian era ballroom or something. He definitely added something special to the ambience.

"Hey Henry," they said, sitting down at the bar, settling in for a long wait. "Hit me with a glass."

"Would you like something *in* the glass today, Mx. Beausoleil? Or are you just reminiscing?"

"I think I'll have my drink and reminisce about it too. I'm in a 'glass half-reminiscent' kind of mood today." Henry looked expectantly at Ravi for their selection. "Come on Henry, you know me by now. Just whatever's on tap there. Cheap. Tall. Cold."

Henry dutifully poured Ravi the cheapest, tallest, coldest beer from the old machine. The first sip was as refreshing as it ever was – not particularly. But it was a drink. You drink at a bar. That was the game. And Ravi played it right. They'd probably be leaving very drunk and very warm tonight.

"Meeting Miss Doyle?"

"I can't just come by to admire your moustache?"

"You can, but you never do, do you?"

"Fair enough. Yeah, I'm meeting her. She was actually supposed to be here already. Any ideas?"

"Miss Doyle is a mystery I think even to her own heart. I suspect that often keeps her lingering too long wherever she goes."

"Mhm. Cryptic. Love it. You're such a weirdo sometimes, Henry. You two go back, huh?"

"We go back," Henry replied with a knowing grin.

Ravi always got the feeling this guy was way, way older than he looked. And he always did this mysterious wizard act. The way he talked sometimes sounded like he'd seen more centuries than Ravi had seen years.

Ravi clapped their hands suddenly at a thought: "—Oh! Hey, speaking of Miss Doyle's mysterious heart, I think she thinks she still owes me a few drinks for making her dinner the other night. Which is ridiculous, since she bought the ingredients. —That *is* ridiculous, right?"

"She has a unique perspective on favors."

"Oh, I'm aware." Ravi checked over their shoulder to make sure Nicole wasn't there yet, then motioned for Henry to lean in for a secret. "Do *me* a favor? Don't let her pay?"

"Sir. Brief me on the details of the mission."

"When she comes up to pay at the end of the night, tell her someone was looking for her in the bathroom or something. Then wave me over and I'll get it?"

"Mm. You think she'll be happy about that?"

"Oh, no, she'll be pissed, but I love pissing her off about this stuff, so it's all good."

"You are truly one of the strangest customers she's brought to me. Mission accepted. I look forward to hearing her rant about your crimes the next time she's in."

"Nice. Thanks. You're a good man, Henry."

Half an hour later, there was still no sign of Nicole. It sure would've been nice if she gave them even a hint about how long whatever she was doing would take. But Ravi didn't mind waiting. It gave them a chance to get a couple drinks in before she started thinking she was paying for them.

They waved Henry over to get started on a second pint.

He had the glass poised under the spout when he suddenly paused for a long moment of quiet contemplation, hand frozen on the lever.

"Mm. Mx. Beausoleil, have you ever had a *nice* beer?"

"'Nice'? Come on, Henry, it's all the same. Rotten wheat juice – honed by the cold hand of industry into some extremely marketable, perfectly tolerable table topper. And it all gets you under the table pretty good just the same, doesn't it?"

Henry grabbed his chest in pain when he heard Ravi's words. "My good fellow, if she didn't smile so much when she says your name, I might have to share some bitter words with you over that. But she does smile, so how about we share a sweet drink instead? We can begin with something closer to that wheat-scented soda water you've got there." Without even looking, from below the counter, Henry produced a tall, ice-cold, fancy-curved brown bottle with a label in some foreign language and presented it to Ravi like it was his precious child. "This is a honeyed amber ale from a Belgium monastery."

"*Bijen knieën?*"

"Bees Knees."

"'*Bees Knees*'? Really? That's so corny."

"Look past the name." He retrieved the bottle from their hands, removed the cap and let it fall to the counter with a satisfying clink, then poured a tall glass for Ravi. It came out a beautiful sunset amber. Reminded them of Nicole's hair. "Give that a smell and try to tell me honestly that it doesn't take you away. I'll cry to hear it."

They had to admit, it was quite striking. But it did not smell like any beer they'd ever had.

"Honey in beer… Why ruin a good thing? Just make mead, no?"

Henry didn't reply. He simply silently poured himself a glass, to precisely the same height as Ravi's and without a drop left in the bottle. Then he offered it up in the air to Ravi for a toast.

"To Miss Doyle. She has excellent taste, even if her friends do not."

"To Nicole's terrible friends," Ravi said with a playful grin.

"Hi, excuse me." Nicole had snuck up behind Ravi and made them choke on their first mouthful of the bizarre tasting drink when she tapped them unexpectedly on the shoulder. "Which of my friends are terrible? And why are we cheering for them?"

Henry answered while Ravi was coughing that mouthful of intriguing and surprisingly strong beer out of their lungs. "Nice to see you, Danica. We are both terrible in our own way, it seems. They have no taste in beer, and to a fault I am endlessly kind and patient with their lack of culture."

Nicole gave the old man a coy smile. "I'm sorry, when did you become one of my friends, Henry? And are you really drinking on the job? I'll tell the boss on you," she added with a wink in her voice.

Ravi gave Nicole a playful shove and choked out a joking insistence that she should be nice. "He's just a lonely old man, Nikki, you're going to give him a heart attack if you're so mean to him."

"No, don't mind her," he said. "She's right. We are merely business associates. I'll remember that when I'm considering the 'friends of the bar' discount at the end of the night."

"Ah great," Ravi teased her. "Thanks Nikki, we could've saved like a whole dollar tonight."

Nicole sniffed the air curiously. "What are you drinking? Smells nice."

"Bee beer," Ravi curtly replied. They offered their glass, and she happily obliged to take a taste.

"Oh that's so sweet! I love it."

"*Of course you would,*" Ravi said with a smirk. They marveled at how the drink truly blended right into the color of her hair. "I bet you *bleed* honey, you're so ridiculously sweet all the time."

Henry offered Nicole a glass of the fine Belgian bee brew, but she cheerfully declined. "Something pink tonight. I'm feeling *floral.*"

The old man dutifully crafted a fragrant mixed drink that was so pink it was practically glowing, then Ravi and Nicole made their way over to their usual table by the window to get settled in for the night.

After a couple drinks and a lot of cheerful debriefing on the events of the day, Nicole's band started up: A three-piece grunge thing that worked some pretty, degenerating synth into the mix. It was fun. Bassline was great. If Ravi still danced, they could definitely entertain the idea of dancing to this. And Nicole definitely loved to dance, so it was pretty clear why this was on her list.

"Alright Nikki, where's this one on your extremely exclusive top ten thousand list of bands?"

Nicole grinned at Ravi's jab, letting it roll right past her, and answered earnestly, "Mm... Low 200s I think."

Ravi grinned right back and shook their head slightly in disbelief. "Fascinating. Just, right off the top of your head. I'm dying to know the criteria you use for this list of yours."

Nicole put a finger to her chin to consider it. "Cuteness is big," she said finally, nodding at the trio of musicians on the little raised platform in the far corner of the pub.

And fair enough, the members of the band were very stylish and nice to look at.

"Not sound?"

"Oh, obviously sound. I have to be able to dance to it. Nothing's on the list I don't love moving to."

"And humming to?"

"Of course!"

"Drums?"

Nicole shook her head, "Entirely optional. —Bass though, bass is essential. I need to feel it *everywhere*."

"And the singer?"

"Optional."

"But they've gotta be cute."

"Mhm. Essential. The bassist?" Again she nodded at the band. "She's cute enough for the whole band. And that *sound* she's making. Shivers."

Ravi took a few seconds to take a good look at the player on bass to try to get a sense of what exactly Nicole looked for in a woman. Short teal hair. Plaid flannel. Tattered black A-shirt showing off a salacious amount of her little fishnet-wrapped breasts. Tall black boots. Stripey stockings. Glasses. Staring directly at the bass the whole time with a dozy grin on, very into the music.

—*Noted. File that away.*

"You don't care about genre at all?"

"Nope. I'm not picky. Just gotta be cute and danceable."

"And you have ten thousand bands—"

"—I never said that. You said that."

"You're not denying it."

"...Closer to one thousand. I make a little extra room once in a while, though. If I kept at it for a few hundred years more, hanging out in musical cities like this? I could probably hit ten thousand."

"A noble ambition. May you live a hundred thousand years to bolster your exclusive catalogue to the millions," Ravi offered a cheers.

"May I live forever," Nicole replied with a wry grin.

After downing a healthy sip of their beer, Ravi challenged Nicole to put her body where her mouth was. "So does that mean you're going to go dance up there?"

She looked around the pub to take it in, get a feel for the vibe, and concluded with a smile that this was not a dancing establishment.

"Come on, anywhere's a dancing kind of bar if someone's dancing," they teased her.

"I don't think Henry would let me live it down if I scared his patrons off."

"Not possible. If anything, you'll bring more people in."

She was still wavering on it, but Ravi wasn't about to give up that easily. They leaned over and jokingly confessed, like it was some kind of secret, "I would love to see you dancing."

"Oh, would you? What's it worth?"

"Free drink? Fancy as you want."

"How about you come up with me and we'll call it even."

Ravi smirked sadly and shook their head, "Sorry Nikki, I don't dance anymore."

"How come?"

Ravi gestured at their infected shoulder.

"Mm. I see. Can't just be careful? I thought you just went to the clinic last week?"

Nicole was right. It wouldn't be the end of the world if they got tapped today. Hell, they barely felt it when they put on their binder right now.

But there was something else to it.

They didn't want to set unrealistic expectations with Nicole. The truth was, they'd never be able to dance like they used to. It'd probably be better if she just made peace with that. They had.

"...Okay, fair point, but you're still not getting me up there. Sorry Nikki."

Nicole tilted her head to the side slightly and failed to hide her disappointment with a grin.

"Alright," she conceded. "One free drink then."

Ravi cheerfully informed her it would be waiting for her when she got back.

They had already seen Nicole dancing a few times before. Sometimes at home, she just couldn't help herself when she put one of her records on. And sometimes the bars she dragged Ravi to had a little rectangle in front of the stage for dancing. It was nice to watch. She had a nice energy. There was something timeless about her movements. Something natural.

It looked like she was trying to make eyes with the bassist the whole time, but it wasn't going well, since the woman was absolutely entranced with her own instrument. A tragic love triangle, considering how much that bass guitar clearly loved moving Nicole's stunning body around the dance floor.

As the second song was starting up, one of the other bar patrons – a very pretty and provocatively dressed woman, Ravi noted – seemed to be taken with Nicole's performance and decided to join her in front of the band. When Ravi glanced around the pub, it looked like most of the patrons had lost interest in the band and turned their attention to the attractive duo.

While Ravi watched, they found their hand slipping to their pocket to sooth a burning heat there. It was the pocket they always carried one of those vials of tar in, in case they felt particularly inclined to crush it bitterly in their hand and demand answers out of it.

—Let me dance again. Please.

It remained silent as always. Useless to them as every sketchy, unreliable source of information they could scrape up on the internet.

It wasn't really fair. Erwin's bear was already dead. He was pleading with a corpse.

Ravi? Their bear still had its claws in them, slowly dragging out gashes in their back that bled and ached and how the hell were they supposed to ask it questions with its teeth sunk into their shoulder meat?

—Why? Please.

By the end of the set, Nicole and the stranger were dancing very close, close enough to lean in for a few coy whispers. They both looked hungry. When Nicole turned to return to the table, Ravi noted that the final look the stranger gave her traced her every curve from head to toe with a grin.

A new fan.

Ravi was vaguely aware that Nicole had a very *open* love life, though she rarely talked about it. Somehow since she started crashing at their place, Ravi had never caught her spending a single night in anyone else's bed. For someone looking as good as she did, it struck Ravi as a *little* suspicious. Surely she got lonely once in a while? Maybe she was just discreet about it, sneaking out for a romp whenever Ravi was out of the apartment, never talking about it? Hell, apparently she'd already hooked up with that attractive butcher at the meat shop. Lucky her. Lucky *both of them.* Yeah, that was probably it. Plenty of opportunities like that, since Ravi was barely home.

Hell, she might even be bringing people *over* while they were out.

Fucking, right there on the couch.

—Don't think about it.

But still, whatever she was doing to fill the hole in her heart, every morning, Ravi found her sleeping peacefully on the couch, curled up like a huge kitten.

After Nicole sat down and took a cheery sip of her reward, Ravi asked her who the stranger was.

"Mm... someone else who loves to see me dance, it seems." Nicole leaned over to tell Ravi a secret, "Apparently I have gorgeous eyes."

"You do," Ravi confirmed plainly.

"Yeah, I get that a lot. I don't think she was looking at my eyes when she said it though," she grinned.

"Yeah, that was a hell of a look she was giving you."

Nicole nodded. "I think she was hoping for an exclusive after-party."

Ravi hesitated for a moment. Something about the hard reality of that statement pinched something in their guts.

"...You gonna go?"

She shook her head, then smiled at Ravi warmly. "Not tonight. It's been a long day, honestly. I'm burnt out. It's nice just hanging out with you. —So? How'd I look?"

"Stunning as always."

She gave a little showy self-congratulating bow like she already knew the answer. "Thank you, thank you." Then she broke the act to titter at them. "You're so sweet, Ravi. Maybe next time I'll get you up there with me so I can get a look at your moves. I bet you're super cute and awkward on the dancefloor."

"Wow, thanks. Huge vote of confidence."

"I mean that in the nicest way possible and you know it," she said, playfully touching their wrist.

The warmth of her fingertips lingered on their skin and in their mind for a few seconds too many.

Every drink was making this... worse. They should really stop for the night.

Ravi shut that out and warned her off, "You can *try* to drag me out there, but I'll need *way* more alcohol in me to get me that stupid again."

"Mm. Well, I'll make a point of getting you absolutely sloshed before I ask next time," she said with a wink in her voice.

"Solid strategy," Ravi confirmed.

When they thought about it, they realized they actually might not mind that so much. Might be worth it – worth the crippling pain if things went horribly wrong and they got side-checked by someone with no sense of personal space. Might even be worth being *seen*.

Nicole's phone buzzed. She pulled it out of some mysterious hidden pocket in her bra. A brilliant place to store it for someone with such ample capacity, Ravi noted. Could probably empty a whole purse in there and still have room to swim.

—Hi hey Ravi? Can we maybe stop staring at our roommate's impressive curves please?

Nicole grinned to herself when she read the message, then put the phone face down on the table, showing off the pretty, minimalist, blue and pink and white floral pattern on the case, to ask Ravi a very prying question: "So how are things going with that TA of yours? Getting serious?"

—What?

Ravi's heart choked in their chest.

—What kind of question is that? Wait. Wait wait wait no. No. But. Maybe? Maybe, right? She's being really flirty, isn't she? Is she... asking...?

"...Why?" Ravi asked uneasily.

But they never had anything to worry about, apparently, because Nicole put their seemingly baseless concerns to rest in an instant when she named that flirty anarchist counter-protester she introduced them to earlier that day. Seemed like the woman was asking about them.

Ravi took a moment to think about how exactly they should respond to that. It was... a *whole lot* to get into, if they were going to get into it. Especially when they were feeling kind of loose on a bunch of beer. They'd lost count of how many they'd had. Too many probably, right? They were thinking stupid things already. Very, very stupid things.

They settled on lying to Nicole, that her very attractive friend wasn't their type.

"Oh? And what exactly is the type for Ravi Beausoleil?" she asked as a playful challenge, like she didn't believe them.

Ravi stumbled on the answer. They were caught in Nicole's gorgeous eyes, in her sweet smile, in her stunning outfit and her stare-worthy curves and her big heart and her sharp, playful tongue and... and they really, really didn't want to deal with the answer to that impossible question when they were ??? drinks in, thinking very, very stupid thoughts.

Trying and failing to sound convincing, they told her simply, "You just... You know when you know. You know?"

She sat back in her chair and poked at Ravi indignantly with her words: "How can you know already!" Then she leaned forward and put her hands out on the table in a pleading entreaty, "Just one date. She's so nice, Ravi! Everything you want, right? Wants to save the world? —Actually *does something* about it? I promise promise *promise* you she'll have plenty of interesting things to talk about. She's really smart."

Ravi looked away uneasily trying to find the words to explain this away.

Nicole took that as an invitation to up the stakes. She leaned forward and whispered, "She's great in bed. —You didn't hear that from me, though. But seriously: Magic hands. Tongue to match. Loves ropes and leather too, if you're into that."

Ravi put their palm on Nicole's forehead and gently shoved her away, "Nicole don't be… I don't care about that."

"What's it take! Come on, help me out here. Whatever you want, I bet she's got it. —She has a *motorcycle*, Ravi."

"…I'm just… I'm not interested, okay?"

Nicole's cheerful demeanor dissolved into glum disappointment. "Is it that TA?"

"It's not the fucking TA! Christ! I'm just not interested, okay? Please, just drop it. Please. Just… just tell her I'm not available. Okay?"

Nicole sighed in defeat, then informed them, "You're a real heartbreaker, Ravi."

Ravi scowled coldly at the table for a few seconds before they downed the rest of their beer and got up in a huff to get another pint from the bar.

When they returned to the table, Nicole seemed to have gotten the hint and finally let the conversation move on to some other topic, like what bands she was looking forward to seeing in the neighborhood that week and begging Ravi to find an hour in their schedule to come with her to any one of them.

A couple drinks later, halfway through Nicole's 200th favorite band's second set, her not-so-secret admirer stopped by the table to place her hand on Nicole's shoulder. She leaned over to whisper something in Nicole's ear, side-eyeing Ravi for a moment, and handed a slip of paper with her number on it to the cutely smiling target of her shameless lusty affection.

—Though, that cute smile of Nicole's broke for half a second, and in that half a second, Ravi could see a flash of dark ire in her bright eyes.

She made a show of stashing the note in her bra for later, but as soon as the woman left, she pulled it back out and folded it up to push it off to the empty side of the table.

Ravi quirked an eyebrow. "Not going to call her?"

Nicole shook her head. "You know, I'm not really feeling it anymore."

"She say something?"

"She did."

Ravi tilted their head to the side to implore Nicole to continue.

"Don't worry about it, Ravi Bee. She's just not for me."

Ravi grinned spitefully and jabbed at her, "What happened to 'just one date'?"

Nicole grimaced at Ravi for that. "I don't have any interest in someone who'd tell me to ditch my dear friend for a better time in her bed. I don't care how good she looks. You gotta have standards, you know?"

Ravi's eyes drifted to the bar for a few seconds of somber reflection before returning to the table to stare at their half empty glass. They swirled its contents around lethargically for a few moments. The vial in their pocket clawed at them with uncomfortable imaginary heat.

At last, with a bitter grimace, they had to make sure their precious soft-hearted friend knew something important:

"You don't have to hang out with me."

"I know."

"Don't let me keep you from having a good time—"

Nicole darted a hand out to grab Ravi's hand and shake them a bit to get their attention, to catch their dull eyes in the gravity of the brilliant, captivating galaxies dancing in her own irises. "I'm *having* a good time."

Ravi looked away and cursed at themself silently. They didn't want this pity.

"Ravi you're doing the thing again."

"What thing?"

"The pity party thing. Stop it. You're amazing."

"I'm not."

"You are!"

"I'm not. I'm not amazing. Fucking stop. God I'm nothing. All I can do is carry fucking boxes. And I can barely do that. Gonna lose my fucking job over it. Again. I'm not amazing, Nicole. *I'm broken.*" They choked on the words as they tumbled carelessly over their tongue, and they choked on them again as they repeated them, needing to hear the reality of them echo in the air, to feel the teeth of the knife they were driving into their own chest: "I'm broken."

Nicole got staggered on that one. Because they were right. They were right and she knew it and there were no words in the English language that could peel back some wretched false veneer to reveal some secret beautiful truth underneath. There was no veneer. Ravi was real. Real oak. Through and through. Stained. Splintered. Rotted. Overpriced.

—Ravi needs work. More work than anyone should ever have to put into such a futile restoration project.

At last, Nicole asked them in words dripping with concern and pity, "Is that why you don't want to give my friend a chance?"

Ravi scoffed at how reductive that was. "Sure. Sure, that's the reason, why not."

"Why not? Because you're... gods, Ravi, I know I can't get past your stubborn *whatever* right now, but you're really truly an amazing person and she sees that and she wants to get to see more of that if you just let her."

They lowered their head and glared bitterly at the table for a few long, aggravated breaths, until they found some calmness in themself.

"You're being... very sweet, Nicole. I know you can't help that. That's just who you are. But. I just. I can't. I can't make someone... *deal with me.* It never works, okay? It just makes everyone feel like shit by the time it blows up." They returned Nicole's sad gaze, "I'm sick of trying."

Nicole gave them a confused look and asked a bad question, "What about that TA—?"

"—We're just fucking. Nicole. Just. Just getting off and going home. She doesn't even know my fucking name. God, I even let her rip my fucking binder off and do whatever she wants to my tits. I hate that shit, but, like, she's not worth it. I don't give a shit. She's nothing. She lets me fuck her and she keeps me warm and she leaves me alone. All she has to put up with is not touching my fucking disgusting *pox* when it hurts too bad. She doesn't have to know anything else, and she never will, and I'm *happy* like this. I don't... You know? I just don't want to be..."

They tried to get the rest out, for her, so she could understand, because that was important for some reason, but they weren't strong enough to keep their dark thoughts from choking the breath out of their words.

They tapped their fist firmly on the table in frustration. They didn't want to talk about this. They didn't want to be *known* like this. They didn't want to be a fucking *burden* anymore. Not to that hot TA, not to this genuinely amazing woman Nicole was trying to hook them up with, and especially not to Nicole. Never again. Never again, please. Please.

Ravi exhaled a long hiss through clenched teeth and tightly pursed lips to try to cool down before they downed the rest of their beer again in one shot.

Nicole kept pushing them like this tonight. What was her agenda?

They tried to get her attention off of them: "What about you? Hm? Beautiful woman like you. Amazing... just... *amazing* woman like you. *Beyond compare.* Not a damn girlfriend in sight. What's up with that?"

Nicole sat up straight like Ravi was digging a finger into her sternum. "I'm just not into that. That's all. Being tied down with someone."

"Why not? Not even just to have a familiar warm body waiting for you at home?"

"Not even for that." Ravi looked to her for more, and she rolled her shoulders a little, uncomfortably, before she continued. "I guess it just feels... uncomfortable, needing someone like that, and... knowing it's going to end one day. Too soon. Always too soon. You know, I think I could have a hundred years with someone and it still wouldn't feel like enough time. But what do you get? Maybe twenty if everything goes well? Forty? But usually just a few months, right? Let's be honest about it. It's a blink of an eye. And I'm always leaving too, you know? I just can't stay anywhere too long. Feels weird. And it just... hurts saying goodbye all the time. But a hundred thousand warm hellos? I love that. I'll take that over the rapidly evaporating promise of a warm bed every time."

"...You don't get... lonely?"

Nicole scoffed at Ravi's apparently undue concern. "Don't worry about me, Rav." She nodded playfully at the discarded folded slip of paper that held the name and number of this evening's bold suitress. "I've got plenty of warm bodies to call on when I'm cold, I promise."

She paused for a few seconds of somber thought before she offered a gentle apology. "Hey, I didn't mean to push you like that, I'm sorry. I get it. I get it, I won't bring it up again."

"...Thank you."

Nicole nodded, then with a hopeful smile, she put out her hand for a handshake, "We still good?"

Ravi grinned right back and, with a firm grasp, they assured her the two of them were absolutely still good. "I know you're just trying to look out for me, Nikki. Sorry. I'm kind of a fucker about that stuff sometimes..."

"Oh, I know."

"You don't have to put up with it... Just tell me to fuck off if I'm getting shitty. You can do that. I won't hold it against you, I promise."

"I promise it's nothing to put up with. It's just talking, Rav. Figuring each other out, right? And like, yeah, you're a situation sometimes, but, you know what? I like that. You're fun. And passionate. And that comes out explosive sometimes. But I've got tough skin, and it's worth it, getting my knees scraped up once in a while. Promise. There's something really nice in you that's always peeking out even when you're hurting and spitting for it. You never hurt me. You never want to hurt me, no matter how bad you're hurting. I see it, you know. I see you. I just wish you wouldn't be so hard on yourself."

"Sorry."

"Oh stop."

"Okay. Sorry. Again."

"Ravi I swear, on every nameless god blighting the beauty of the eternal weave of their own creation—"

"...Are you gonna throw me in a snowbank again?"

"You're testing me," she replied with a cruel grin. "We've got a long walk home later, you know. And there's a *lot* of snow."

A Long Walk Home

Danica was following half a step behind on the walk home after running out the night at the Serpent's Fang, after that long day of errands and that fun night of drinking and *passionate* conversation with her dear Ravi Bee.

She was admiring Ravi's eloquent drunken footwork on the snowy pavement. Like a dancer without a song. They really had a style to them even when they were sloshed. She smiled to herself wondering how they'd move with a proper melody and a beat. She tried to do the math in her head: *Precisely* how drunk would they need to be, to get up for a dance without falling over immediately?

When Ravi stumbled a bit and caught themself on a wall, she cheerfully teased them: "You're kind of a lightweight, Rav."

They took a couple seconds to clear their head enough to realize Danica was speaking to them, and even then, they could only respond with a few half-slurred words at first before they heard themself and started trying to speak more clearly.

"Excuse... me? No. You. Excuse *you*. I had like a hundred beers I think I'm doing *great* considering." They were still clinging to the wall while they made this bold statement.

"Mm. I think it was eight, wasn't it?"

"Hehhehheh..." Ravi chuckled menacingly to themself, then looked at Danica with a devilish grin, "She doesn't know about the *secret* beers..."

They tried to stand up straight and take a few steps, but they stumbled again and cursed at themself.

"God, there's so much ice."

Danica silently noted that there was, like, *no* ice on the sidewalk – just a light covering of fluffy snow that was being eaten up by the salt and sand the city had put down earlier that evening.

But Danica wasn't going to get into a reality-checking debate with Ravi in their current state. She just wanted to get them home in one piece. And maybe smile a bit in the process. They were kind of fun to play with when they were like this.

"Need a hand?" she asked, already knowing the answer.

" 'm great. I'm great. *You.* You should be careful, Nikki. Can barely tell what you're saying, Slurry." They took a few more steps forward before they stumbled into her unexpectedly waiting arms. They clutched at Danica's coat and buried their face in her shoulder for a few seconds to curse at the world and get their bearings.

"Oh my god you're so fucking tall…" they marveled at her. Then they gasped a little in awe when they realized they had one of her breasts *firmly* grasped in a clumsily mislaid hand. They swore quietly and suddenly shoved themself away in a blushing panic and tried to stand on their own.

—Gods they were cute when they were flustered.

"Shit. Fuck. Sorry. Hold on. 'm fine." They managed to get themself stable for long enough to squint bitterly at the sidewalk. "God when did this street get so uneven? What are my taxes paying for?"

"I don't think you pay municipal taxes, Ravi Bee," Danica pointed out. "That's the privilege of the owning class."

"Fuck. I don't. Well what the fuck is our landlord paying for? He should be outraged about this. And he's not here. Should I call him?"

Danica reached out to still Ravi's hand before they could get their phone out of their pocket. "Do not call the property manager, Ravi. He's absolutely sleeping right now."

"Craig," they said, like they just remembered his name. "Fucker Craig. How long has our fucking hallway light been out?"

"Mm… Since before I moved in, right?"

Ravi stood stunned silent for a few moments. "Moved in." They shook their head like something wasn't right about that. "When did you move in?"

"Uh. Wasn't it October?"

"Wasn't it just crashing on my couch for a week? That's not moving in. Did you even have any boxes? *October.* How the fuck is there all this ice on the ground and you're still here?"

That cut Danica a bit. She knew better than to take anything Ravi said while they were this far gone too seriously, but… The two of them never really talked about it – about how long she was allowed to stay

– about this 'week' that, so far, didn't seem to have any end in sight. And that was by Danica's design. It was better this way, leaving it informal. Safer.

And this was probably a terrible time to talk about it. If she wasn't careful with her words, and if she wasn't able to keep Ravi careful with theirs, she might end up making things very bad for both of them.

Ravi continued, bringing their hand to their forehead in a gesture of confoundment. "I mean how long's a fucking week."

"Seven days…" Danica dutifully replied.

Ravi was stuck on this. The seed was planted. Even sober, they'd remember. Gods, there was no stopping this now…

"No. Must be like sixty now. Fucking… ISO standards guys are gonna be pissed when they find out what we're up to."

Danica didn't reply.

Ravi shot her a coy grin and prodded at her with a cutting dose of sarcasm: "I bet we can get it up to a hundred if we work at it," they said, like they were inviting her in as a co-conspirator on a mad science experiment.

"Mm…"

"—Ten thousand! Ten thousand even. One for every band on your fucking list."

"…Ravi. You're kind of losing the thread here. You're angry about the uneven sidewalk. Maybe we can get back on that?"

Ravi scoffed at themself. Then after a few silent moments of thought, they scoffed again in a sort of self-deprecating way before they resumed walking. …Well, stumbling. 'Moving forward'. Carefully.

After a dozen uneasy steps more, they looked over to Danica and playfully noted, "You're walking just fine, huh. God, what were you drinking? Fruit punch?"

Danica smiled at them. It was very kind of them not to ask her any hard questions tonight. Like, for example, *'How exactly can a human being drink eight cocktails and still be so sharp and sober?'* Because, obviously, the answer to that was, *'A human being can't.'*

She replied playfully, without really answering the question, "Takes a lot to knock me off my feet."

"I got you though," Ravi gloated.

Danica gave them a curious look when they glanced at her.

"Knocked you off your feet. Tricked you into the snow. God you were so pissed." They suddenly stopped short and held their breath. Danica could practically hear something pop in their brain from how their voice changed so suddenly into some pathetic mewling remorse, "Oh my god Nicole. Nicole I'm sorry. I'm so sorry. I was just playing. Don't hate me please don't hate me."

Danica smirked and snickered to herself at Ravi's earnestness, and shook her head in disbelief. Of course she didn't hate them. But there was no point trying to convince them of that when they were in this state.

"Ravi. Sidewalk. Focus here."

They brought their hands to their face to bury their eyes in their palms. "God you're gonna figure it out."

"Figure what out?"

"How long a week is."

"It's seven days, Ravi. I get it. You're right. I've probably been here a little too long, huh? That what you're getting at?"

They turned to her with a serious look on and clutched her by the wrist. "No."

She put her hand over theirs and pulled them off of her. "I can't keep sleeping on your couch forever."

"Yes you can. Ten thousand days. We'll stretch it out. I won't tell anyone it'll be our little secret."

"Oh my gods Ravi..."

"Yes to the eternal gods fucking the universe or whatever. You can stay. Stay. God it's fine I don't care. I don't care. Stay. Please. I'll call Craig and fix the light I'm sorry. I just hate calling him so much. Fucker never fixes anything right. I'll do it though just stay."

"...You're such a mess. Come on," she said, offering Ravi her shoulder – and wrapping her arm behind their waist to pull them into her when they refused.

She scanned the block for anywhere she could go to get something for them to sober them up a bit. Or at least to spare them a terrible hangover.

Ravi was grumpy about being carried around. They were halfheartedly cursing at her to let them go, but they clearly weren't putting much of an effort into getting away.

Danica finally managed to get them sitting on the frame of a snowy dead planter in front of a convenience store. She crouched down to catch their eyes. They were swimming. Almost falling asleep.

"Hey. Ravi. I'm going in this store here," she said, pointing and making sure they turned their head to see it. "I need you to sit here for me, okay? I'll be right back. Count to a hundred. Do not move. Okay?"

"Okay."

"One, two, three..." Danica got them started.

"Four."

"Mhm."

"Five... Six..."

"Thanks, Ravi Bee. Be right back."

She took one last longing look at Ravi from behind the glass of the door, then she hurried to the back to grab a bottle of water. Before heading to the register, she peeked out again and sighed relief that Ravi was still sitting where she left them. They were surprisingly fast when they wanted to be, and she really didn't want to have to pull out any magic tricks just to get them home tonight. It was normally a twenty-minute walk, and usually way faster than finding a ride, but this was turning into a bit of a hike.

But it didn't matter how long it took, as long as Ravi got home safe.

When Ravi noticed Danica had returned to them, they quickly sat up straight and pretended that they had been counting the whole time, "Nine thousand ninety-eight, Nine thousand ninety-nine..."

"Mhm. I said a hundred, Ravi Bee."

"I'm a good counter."

"You sure are."

"That's what they said. When I was a kid. Good at counting."

Danica couldn't hide a laugh at Ravi's bad joke. "Oh my gods, stop. Here." She offered Ravi the water bottle, already opened for them.

They dutifully took a sip, then coughed on it a bit. "Fuck. That's disgusting, what is that?"

"Finest bottled tap water money can buy." She sat down next to them and told them the rules, "Finish that off, then we'll keep going."

They nodded lethargically that they understood, then silently nursed the bottle while the two of them sat in the cold.

It wasn't frostbite weather, but it would still be great to get home before Ravi caught a cold or something. They had to work in the morning, after all. And they'd already lost two shifts today.

Danica stared at the faintly underlit clouds and the streetlamps overhead for a while to think while Ravi finished. She really had tried to be clever with her wording when she got Ravi's OK on her moving in. *I can be gone in a week.* No commitments at all there. And even if they did insist she had to be 'gone', there was nothing in there about how long she'd have to leave. She'd been 'gone' and come back every day since she 'moved in'. She'd been bracing for the inevitable 'get out of my apartment already' that she was owed for a whole month now, but Ravi just... never brought it up for some reason.

The unspoken stability of all that was all about to be messed up, though – though not exactly in the way Danica had imagined. It was nice that Ravi seemed to want to extend her 'week', but that wasn't the right way to game this arrangement, and she knew it.

She tried to conjure the perfect wording in her mind while she waited. Something that didn't bind either of them to a real commitment. Something that didn't exploit or cheat or deceive. Something *benevolent*.

—Gods, as if a faerie could be...

Ravi interrupted her planning with a marveling observation:

"Fuck. You're so tall. You know that?"

They were looking up at her from a very slouched position, the water bottle still in their hand, half-full, dangling lackadaisically near the ground.

She laughed at the earnestness of their statement. "Yeah Ravi, I know. It's so you don't lose me in a crowd."

"How'd you do that? How'd you get so tall like that?"

"Years of practice."

"God. I'm so small."

"You're a perfectly normal size."

"I stopped growing when I was six."

"Mhm."

"Three feet tall."

"Really."

"They won't let me drive."

"Ravi."

"This water really sucks."

"I know. Drink up. For me?"

"...And you'll stay?"

"...And I'll stay."

Ravi crushed the water bottle slightly with joy, then offered an unsteady hand out for a handshake on it. "Deal."

Danica shook their hand, noting to herself that she never said how long she'd stay, so this was safe.

Ravi made quick work of the bottle after that, and the two of them continued onward, Ravi leaning on Danica – now much less begrudgingly – while she helped them keep steady.

Unfortunately, this would-be little walk of theirs seemed destined to turn into an odyssey, because not even two blocks later, their paths crossed with the paths of some rowdy guys coming out of another bar.

Danica wasn't really paying much attention to what the guy said to her. It was some kind of catcalling. She'd learned to smile politely and roll with it to keep things peaceful. If Ravi weren't with her, she might push back a bit, call him out for being a pig, put him in his place – but she did have Ravi, and she really needed to get them home.

Unfortunately, Ravi was apparently still stuck in 'hired goon' mode, and they sprang to life right out of Danica's grasp when they heard the guy speak to her.

Danica tried her best to reel them in, to call them off, to hold their arms, to do anything to stop them, but they were too strong and wild with indignant rage for her to contain. There wasn't anything she could do other than watch helplessly as Ravi challenged the *much bigger* and *much taller* catcaller to a chest-bumping standoff, spitting words in his face and taunting him to throw the first punch.

He did.

And a moment later he was down, writhing on the ground with his face in his hands, surrounded by a fine spattering of his own blood staining the snow on the sidewalk.

Ravi was slouching over and staggered from the hit they took, but their posture and heavy breathing only served to give them the silhouette of a furious wolf in the dim red glow coming off the signage of a nearby storefront, and their sinisterly illuminated feral glare was enough to send the other two guys running.

Ravi was about to go wild kicking the downed guy's ribs when Danica took firm hold of their wrist and put a crushing force on them until they yelped in pain.

"Let's go," she told them sternly.

Ravi's hackles were still raised, even at her, but they calmed down after looking at her condemning glare for a few seconds.

Still, before turning to leave, they stomped the guy in the ribs hard with the heel of their boot, just once, and told him to keep his filthy tongue in his mouth – "Or I'll be back to rip it out when she's not looking."

They concluded their assault with a grin so cruel it gave Danica shivers.

She jerked them away and curtly commanded them to follow her – "Now."

They still resisted, but it was just a show this time, just to put a bit more fear in the guy, not that he was looking, curled up on the ground like that.

Just a show. They were following her now. She hurried them down the street until she could get around a corner and out of sight of the bloody scene.

"What the hell are you doing, Ravi?"

"...Protecting you?"

"That wasn't protecting me. Those guys were harmless until you picked a fight."

"You're just gonna let him talk to you like—"

"—I don't *care* how he's talking to me, Ravi! Don't do that ever again. *Ever.* You understand me?"

"What? Don't stand up for you? Don't punch assholes who deserve it?"

"Don't get yourself hurt in front of me for no reason."

She crouched down to get a better look at Ravi's scorned, stubborn, scowling face. Their skin was cut from the impact of the guy's knuckles on their brow. A thin trickle of blood was running into their eye. It looked like they just barely avoided getting knocked down with a shot on their temple. The guy knew where to aim. Ravi knew where to dodge. And they were lucky. That's probably the only reason they were still standing right now.

She hated to do it right in front of them, but it's not like they would notice right now, not in their state. She pretended to dig around in her bra for something while she subtly reached out through the Aether to draw some antiseptic wipes and gauze from the first aid kit back in the apartment. It'd look strange, sure, but Ravi could just marvel at how ridiculously over-prepared Danica seemed, while she doctored their wound and scolded them for being so stupid.

"Hold the gauze there," she told them after she was done cleaning them up. "And tell me if your vision gets weird."

She peered around the corner to see if it was safe to carry on walking home. The guy Ravi knocked down had disappeared somewhere. Hopefully he wandered off to sulk about getting messed up by someone a few inches shorter than him. As much as Danica didn't like seeing Ravi cut up, she had to admit to herself – and *only* to herself – that it was pretty satisfying seeing the prick crumpled up at Ravi's feet.

"Come on," she said, waving them over. "Let's go."

Bewilderingly, Ravi was *better* at walking straight after getting punched in the face. They grumpily followed behind Danica, moping about being scolded for their noble, self-righteous sacrifice.

Once the two of them made it back to the apartment building and stepped onto the scratched up, mirror-walled elevator, Danica spotted Ravi staring vacantly at the blood on their gauze. They murmured something at Danica that she couldn't hear the first time.

"I'm never gonna be tall as you," they repeated when she asked.

She let out a little huff of a sigh. "You're really stuck on this tonight, huh?"

The elevator door opened. Danica took a step forward, but Ravi didn't move from their place leaning against the far wall. She could see it in the mirror. They were looking intently at their reflection, far off in the distance, a short and dirty phantom slouching pathetically next to Danica's towering flesh and blood as she stood in the doorway waiting for them with a worried look on her face.

It was a perspective trick, but clearly it was still hitting them pretty hard.

"Ravi?"

They took a breath, crushed the bloody gauze in their fist, then lethargically followed Danica to their unit.

Once inside, Ravi kicked their boots at the wall, then stumbled their way to their room and flopped down in their bed.

They forgot to close their door, so Danica could hear their muffled sobs, though she tried to ignore it to give them some privacy.

When they seemed to have finished, she filled up a tall glass of water and knocked on the wall next to their door.

They forgot the light on too.

"What," they answered hoarsely.

"Water?"

"...Fine. Yes. Thanks." They didn't lift their head from its position buried in their pillows. They just kind of lethargically waved their arm at the nearest corner of the desk beside their bed.

Danica placed the glass down and took a moment to look around Ravi's room. She didn't usually get a chance to come in here. She noted immediately that their windowsill was even more crowded with dead and dying plants now – including every single plant she'd given them since she started living there. Heartbreaking. Though... even at a distance, it was obvious that the few that were still clinging to life were sick with yellowing leaves and rot.

—Overwatered...?

She picked Ravi's denim jacket off the floor where they had let it slip off their shoulders. It had some blood on it now. None of the seams were damaged, though, so that was nice – though, when she examined the lining, it looked like some of her delicate spellcraft had come undone over the course of the long day. She knew the seal wasn't properly set yet, but Ravi had wanted to wear it so badly, and she couldn't say no.

Oh well. She could fix it again. She didn't have much of this magic left to work with, but she could fix it.

Their desk was covered in scattered notes – among them, there were a couple vials of that black tar stuff, on top of a notebook that seemed to have notes about Ravi's own research into the substance.

Standing so close to the vials made her uneasy. Weird rumbling whispers spoke unintelligible words to her from the back of her mind when she looked too long. Something about oblivion. It didn't sit well with her.

She knew Ravi liked to carry one of these vials around in their pocket for some reason. She could feel it every time. A dull discomfort. Like standing just a *little* too close to a fire. But it was easy enough to shrug off as long as it was out of sight.

And what was she going to do about it? Ask them to stop? '*Hey Ravi I can feel some deep dark energy coming out of your pocket haha weird right? Please leave it at home? Or just stop hoarding this stuff at all?*'

Danica glanced over at Ravi, who was still woefully lamenting their circumstances facedown in bed. Seemed safe enough to snoop around – just a bit.

She carefully nudged the vials off the notebook with a pen so she could discreetly flip through the pages to see if they'd managed to make any more progress than she had.

Unfortunately, it was less of a detailed research journal and more of a record of Ravi's frustration at the substance for ruining so much of their life. She was surprised to see a number of pages with little more than a giant, all-caps, bold '**WHY?**' in the middle, surrounded by dozens of question marks.

Ravi, face still buried in their pillow, croaked out a few quiet words, startling Danica from her inspection:

"It's not fair. No one ever... No one ever showed me how... how to—" They choked a bit and ran out of words there.

"...How to what?" Danica asked softly.

Ravi shook their head, but they didn't respond.

But, considering their obsession with it tonight, Danica could guess they were still stuck on how to be as 'tall' as her. They really got weirdly poetic when they were drunk sometimes, hung up on metaphors.

Danica smiled sadly at them, then sat down on the edge of their bed and put a consoling hand on their back.

They took a deep stuttering breath before they turned their head to the side to face her. Their eyes were still closed, hiding the truth.

"I'm being weird. Right? God. I can tell. I can tell, it's okay. I'm being fucking weird I'm sorry. I just... I really like you, Nikki. I really like you I want you to know that okay. Okay? Don't. Don't listen to me. Just. I like you. That's all. I'm glad you're here."

"I know."

Ravi cracked open their wet, bloodshot eyes to look up at her pleadingly. Their swollen brow was clearly making it hard to open their left eye all the way.

"You'll stay?"

She placed a gentle hand on their bicep to squeeze them reassuringly. "I'll stay," she promised.

—*For now.*

"I don't care how long a week is," they continued, seemingly barely aware of her answer. "I was just kidding. I was kidding. Don't listen to me, okay?"

"I know. We'll figure it out tomorrow, okay? Get some sleep. It's been a long day. And you're working in the morning, right?"

Ravi scoffed. "Fuck. Fuck, I'm working in the morning. God this was a stupid idea…"

Danica gave them a warm smile and told them she had fun tonight. "And thank you. For protecting me. That was sweet of you."

"Yeah?"

The hope in their voice was enough to put a crack in Danica's heart. It meant that much to them?

"Yeah," she assured them. "Just, don't get hit next time. Okay? I don't like seeing you getting hurt."

Ravi cracked a stupid grin. "Promise."

In the morning, after Ravi had groaned and grumbled and apologized past Danica sleeping on the couch on their way out the door to get to work, she got herself set up seated at the little kitchen table, cheek held up by a half-curled fist. She was fussing with the wording of a contract for Ravi and herself, lazily waving her hand back and forth over a gods-cursed page of Archival Parchment, shifting the binding, promissory ink around to try to make everything fit, to make it so no one would get hurt.

But that wasn't how it worked, and she knew that. The best way to make a deal with the fae is to never, ever make a deal with the fae – herself included. No matter how well-intentioned she was, the gods would come for their tax, they would come to eat the misery that grew out of whatever twisted agony they could pry out of the loopholes in the contract.

No. The best way to make a deal was to just... not make a deal.

She took a deep breath, then waved her hand dismissively to clear all the ink off and release the blank parchment to return itself to the stacks of the gods' Archive of the Pacts Eternal.

She'd let Ravi make it.

And she'd just... not sign it. 'Nicole' wasn't her name. And Ravi would never question it if she just wrote that down instead of her true name. They'd never know. They'd never know she was betraying them. And then they'd never have to suffer for dealing with the fae.

Gods, a week should never have gotten this long.

It was probably time to move on, before Ravi got hurt.

But she still hadn't finished paying them back. And it was going to be a gritty rasp on the rest of her eternity if she couldn't make it fair.

Why couldn't they just have been like the others? If they would just *use* her. If they would just *exploit* her. If they would just *take* what they were owed out of her, then it could be even already. Easy. Over in no time. Everyone gets hurt and she could just move on already instead of spending all this time trying to pay them back for every kindness.

But instead, she was stuck, trying to swim against an endless torrent of their generosity. And no matter how hard she tried, she just... couldn't find anything to balance it out. She could feel it. She could feel it getting worse. She desperately wanted to spare them whatever pain was coming, but she was stuck until it was even. And she knew. She knew that it wasn't *even* yet.

Not yet.

But she'd figure it out. She just needed more time.

A hundred days maybe?

...Ten thousand?

Ravi didn't even want to do it. They thought it was a joke. And their contract was so... open. Never mind loopholes. It was like they *wanted* to be exploited.

The GUEST _Nicole Doyle_ can sleep on the couch of the HOST _Ravi Beausoleil_ until such a time as the GUEST gets sick of putting up with ~~Ravi's~~ the HOST's stupid bullshit. *(or vice versa)*

December 7

DATE

Nicole Doyle
GUEST

Ravi B (ee) 🐏
HOST

Danica felt like she had to at least balance out the terms a bit, make it so Ravi could actually kick her out if they wanted to.

They protested her late, humble, 'vice versa' addition, but she wouldn't let them scratch it out.

She later found that Ravi had snuck the signed agreement into one of her boxes under the couch for some reason. To remind her she was always welcome or something?

It was a very sweet gesture. An open invitation into someone's home was already worth more to any faerie than Ravi could imagine. And putting that on paper... Putting so much sincerity into it... It cracked her heart.

Honestly, though, nothing on the page mattered. It was all fake. A sham of a deal between a naïve, well-meaning human, and an impostor of a faerie who wasn't anywhere near as tall as Ravi wanted to believe.

That's Nothing to Be
Ashamed of, Is It?

"—Oh! Oh I have a hell of a story for you. You're going to be screaming by the end of this—"

Danica came home in the afternoon a couple Fridays later to find that Ravi had a boisterous high school friend visiting unexpectedly for the weekend from out of town: The nigh-legendary Felicity Aurelia Vicente - *the Golden Fleece.*

She had been a feisty, fighty little teenager. Aggressively defensive of Ravi whenever the preppy white kids made any comments about Ravi's grungy clothes or mixed heritage. *'Brown kids stick together,'* is how she used to justify it, but anyone could see there was more going on there.

It was cute to watch, honestly. She was Ravi's shadow, their protégé – apparently their partner in crime, too, from Ravi's stories. She followed after their every move, from the soft punk fashion and hair right down to their brand of energy drinks and pens. If Ravi's hair was blue – as it usually was back then – hers was a complementary golden hue. A subtle, subdued gold though, as if she was afraid to outshine them.

"Yeah, go ahead, hit me," Ravi encouraged their dear old friend with as much enthusiasm as they could muster after a long week of working overtime at both the university and the warehouse.

Danica noted that Felicity hadn't changed much since high school – still *very* attentive to Ravi. She sat a hair away from them, spoke with her hands, and grabbed at Ravi's arm or leg whenever she was excited—as she was now, to be relaying this thrilling tale. It looked like Ravi was forced to sit on the right of her just to avoid getting their sores crushed by Felicity's enthusiastic grasp.

Even her fashion seemed frozen in time – very short, platinum gold hair hiding the natural black, covered head to toe in some vague bubblegum facsimile of punk clothing that came off as manufactured and... *proper* somehow – despite that Ravi themself left their hair to return to the rich warmth of its natural chestnut brown these days, and only pulled out that final vestige of their old punk fashion, that freshly restored old jacket of theirs, when they were absolutely sure they weren't going to be seen by anyone they knew from work or the university.

"—You remember Nat, right Ames?"

Ah. *Right.* One *other* thing that she hadn't changed since high school was Ravi's name. Danica was having a hell of a time rewiring her brain to participate in the conversation.

Ravi shrugged in response to Felicity's question. "I'm gonna be honest with you, I don't remember most of high school. Hell, I probably only remember *you* because you keep coming back for some reason," they joked. —Which didn't quite line up with the story Ravi told her the other day, did it? That Felicity moved away and never came back?

"Well lucky for you. I'm worth remembering. Anyways, Nat, she's been travelling, yeah?—"

Danica watched and listened in silence the way only a third wheel can. She was waiting for some opportunity to jump in, but these two went all the way back to kindergarten, and Felicity was ready to fill Ravi in on every single detail of her life since she last set foot in the city, since she left, apparently, to pursue the dream and adventure of all the fieldwork involved in becoming an archaeologist. —Which was to say that she actually wanted to talk *specifically to Ravi*, about every single detail of her life *and also* the lives of every other person she could think of who might be remotely interesting to them, in what was starting to feel like a desperate series of mixed-success attempts to make them smile at her like they used to.

Sadly, Danica got the impression from Ravi's halfhearted enthusiasm – that they excused to Felicity as them being 'just tired' with no explanation for why – that Felicity had, in the eight years since high school and however many years since she last saw Ravi, seemingly lost her sense of what got Ravi's engine revved up.

"—So she falls off a mountain and breaks her leg. —Some country in Asia. —I can't remember. Hong Kong? Vietnam? Something like that. —She breaks her leg and didn't have any travel insurance. —And can you even believe that? She was out of the country for like... a whole year! With no insurance! It was bound to happen, don't you think?"

Ravi nodded thoughtfully and dutifully replied, "You gotta get insurance."

"You have to! You have to. So her leg is broken and it's costing her an arm and... and a leg. That wasn't supposed to be a joke. You know what I mean. But straight out of some stupid romcom, she ends up meeting this 'amazing' guy who's super rich or something, pays her bills, 'supports her' until she's walking on her own again, and just when she's ready to go—and I mean, airplane ticket in hand, luggage packed, taxi waiting—*last* freaking minute, this guy tells her she has to marry him! What the hell!"

Danica perked up at that. "He *told* her? Not asked?"

"Practically *demanded* it, Nat says."

"What, because he helped her?" Danica confirmed.

"Yes! Yes exactly! He thought he was paying for a beautiful Canadian princess with all that *philanthropy*."

Danica had to take some time to reflect on that. She knew it wasn't right for humans to do that kind of thing to each other, but if that were a 'relationship' between any of her own people, after all that he did for her, marriage would be a *generously* humble ask. Naïve, even.

Ravi spoke before Danica could put a response together: "That's pretty weird for a romantic gesture."

"Weird! Weird!? Amy, I don't know what crazy kinky romance stuff you've been reading or watching or whatever, but that is *beyond* weird. It's *extortion*. —Way, *way* deep in the territory of disgusting, after a pitstop in *fucked up* and *holy hell*."

"She should do *something* to repay him though," Danica insisted. "It sounds like he did a lot for her."

Felicity stared at Danica with a twisted, confused, and extremely judgmental look on her face. "Dani, no. What's wrong with you?"

"You pay back favors! It's perfectly normal! How could she *possibly* believe she could just live with this guy for *free* for *months* without even considering that she'd have to pay him back somehow?"

"Pay him back? *Pay him back*. Holy Jeezus Christopher, Dani, do you write bad pornos for a living or something?"

"I didn't mean with sex, you freak. Get your head out of the gutter. But, like, *some* kind of fair trade. A gift at least? He gave her so much!"

"Well if that's how you think about it, you're really going to get off on what she did." Felicity paused for dramatic effect before erupting with the punchline of her story, "She. Married. Him."

Ravi laughed in disbelief. "There's no way."

"There is a way and she found it and she is living a 'happy life' over there now and we will never see her again and the whole story makes me sick." Felicity ended her tale with a huff.

Danica had to ask, "What about the plane ticket?"

"Threw it away!"

"And she just stopped traveling?"

"Threw her backpack in the river!"

Ravi raised an eyebrow. "She did not."

"Okay that's an exaggeration but yeah, she's just done. Given up on life." Felicity rested her head on the back of the couch and brought a dramatically poised hand to her forehead. "You hate to see it. She had so much going for her."

"You don't think she's just found something else that makes her happy?" Ravi asked. "Just because *you* aren't ready to settle down—"

"—Nope. No this is *not* about me being forever painfully alone. It's about men being gross."

Ravi brought their finger and thumb to their face to rub their cheekbones in mild frustration before they chided their old friend. Danica noted, to her surprise, that despite Ravi's obvious exhaustion with Felicity, there was definitely a crack of a sincere smile under it all. "Fleece I don't know how but you always make these stories about something bigger than they need to be. There doesn't have to be a lesson here, does there?"

"There's a lesson in every story, Ames. That's what stories are for."

"Okay but maybe if there *is* a lesson, maybe it's not that men are trash? Maybe it could be more like 'sometimes people do nice things for other people, and they get along, and it's nice'? Please? No?"

They were really trying, but poor Ravi was seemingly approaching the end of their rope with their overbearing bestie – who had apparently only been over for a couple hours at this point, so, not a great start to the visit. Danica tried to get Felicity on another topic to spare her gracious host the struggle:

"So, Felicity, archaeology, huh? Are you digging up bones now?"

Her eyes lit up. She proudly jumped into a correction and an explanation of her *actual* work:

"Libraries. Actually. Books. Old, mystical, autographical books with faded words and pages practically *glued together* by time and weather. I get to use this cool machine. It like... shoots x-rays through the paper I think? —But <u>not</u> x-rays. The lab tech girl always yells at me when I say that, don't tell her I said that. But whatever it is – *fancy magic beam technology* – it can scan every speck of ink in a book all at once – stroke by stroke, word by word – even if it's so frail that opening it up would *instantly* turn the whole thing to dust. This tech is *revolutionizing* codicology. *Everything* is on the table. Old scrolls. Waterlogged stacks of paper. Crumbling journals." She clapped her hands together and brought them to her chin with a huge smile, like she was whispering a little prayer. "I have seen forbidden languages beyond human understanding describing worlds we were never meant to know."

While Felicity tried to explain the significance of the work she had been doing in collaboration with a very talented translator and a very sexy backhoe, Danica tapped Ravi on the knee and quietly asked them for some tea.

"Yeah," they nodded. "Green, right? Honey?"

Danica smiled at them. "Thanks."

Ravi gave Danica a subtle nod in response, which she took to mean, '*No no, thank <u>you</u>. I'm dying here.*'

"Oh can I get some coffee!" Felicity 'asked' when she saw Ravi going to the kitchen.

Ravi flinched slightly at the request – probably imagining the prospect of having an even more energized Felicity in their care – but they'd never say no. They were just like that. Accommodating to a fault.

Out of sight, on the other side of the kitchen wall, the kettle bubbled, and the coffee maker percolated. Danica imagined Ravi leaning silently against the counter watching the two contraptions racing to completion, recharging themself a bit, steeling their mind for the arduously long weekend ahead.

Felicity continued her stories and explanations at a volume loud enough for Ravi to follow along, clearly not content to talk with just Danica. Which was fair. She was nothing to this woman, after all. She and Felicity had barely spoken to each other in high school, even less than she'd spoken to Ravi.

By the time a hot cup of tea was placed in Danica's hands, Felicity had gone off in extreme detail naming all of the catastrophic events that had befallen the greatest of libraries since the dawn of time.

"Just last year! Just *last fucking year*, some bullshit missile blew up a whole historic library in Palestine. A thousand years of knowledge, turned to ash."

Felicity looked so genuinely hurt about it that Danica couldn't help feeling a bit of the dear, impassioned, mournful academic's pain in her own heart. She offered her condolences: "That's terrible, I'm sorry."

"Sucks you couldn't make a copy of those ones in time," Ravi mused.

Felicity nodded sadly, clearly still aching from the thought of that ashen archive. "That's why it's so important. Most of these books are just... handwritten, by some guy, some guy with a lot to say about his world. They've never been copied anywhere ever. We're doing it for the first time, making these words and these *worlds* permanent, for real. I'm building an indestructible library, you know? An eternal archive, for the future, for the rest of time. I have to. We can't keep losing this stuff."

Ravi tried to shift the conversation away from Felicity's mournful despair. "I bet you've seen some wild books, huh?"

Danica was amazed at how quickly Felicity shook off her depression.

"Oh, girl, you have no idea. *No idea.* I got into this thing thinking, *'Oh cool, diaries and letters and important philosophical manuscripts.'* No. We've got books that are just a guy counting and describing clouds for ten years. Some full of just... *incredibly* inaccurate medical advice. Math – but wrong. Also math – but in entirely the wrong place at the wrong time somehow? And just, tomes and tomes full of folklore and myths and superstitions, magical creatures and their mythical exploits, their revelations to their *chosen few* – secrets of the universe, guarded by the enigmatic creatures of our dreams and nightmares – and all of that all messily woven into *primary sources* of *historical accounts* of *actual real events*, twisted together so tightly that you can barely pull the facts out of the fiction."

Felicity leaned in to whisper, though there was no one else who could be listening, "Don't tell anyone this, okay? But I swear some of this magic stuff is written with such *unshakeable* conviction, and so consistently across time and space, that it makes me wonder if, you know, maybe... maybe it *was* real. Some of it. And maybe we did something to lose it all. Spat on the flowers of Eden."

Danica did her best not to react to any of that. She knew the reality that went along with that theory, of course, and it sure would be nice to have *something* to contribute to one of Felicity's one-sided conversations here. But she had to hold back. Just relax and calmly, quietly, nonchalantly sip at her tea, waiting in feigned disbelief for Felicity to continue.

Felicity sighed. "I don't know, it'd just be kind of sad if it was *all* lies, wouldn't it? Just stories we told each other in the dark to explain away our fears." Felicity's relentless enthusiasm... *relented*, and was replaced with an unexpectedly introspective melancholy. "Like, if all the spirits and gods and faeries in human history are just... *us*. Just reflections of us. The best and worst parts of us. The things we want humanity to be, the things we're afraid humanity will become, the knowledge we desperately wish humanity could have."

She looked at her coffee, swirling it around gently for a long, thoughtful moment before she continued:

"Like. The immortal gods. They just keep coming up again and again, and always immortal, eternal, always inexplicably concerned with us mortals for some reason. —No matter what you're reading, no matter where or when. Like, these stories, either there's some truth in there and someone *really is* watching and remembering and keeping our stories alive forever, or else every person since the dawn of time was just so afraid of meaning nothing to the universe that we had to shamelessly spew lies at each other, conjuring up some eternal unseeable caretakers, like maybe *they'll* keep us, maybe the deathless gods will remember us forever, even if the universe forgets and fades into nothing."

She laughed at herself. "Or maybe the best you've got is some dipshit girl who just loves stupid old books too much—enough to put a whole lifetime into immortalizing your dumb cloud journal forever. After painstakingly spending *months* x-ray scanning and translating hundreds and hundreds of pages full of chicken scratch notes. About. Fucking. Clouds." She gave Ravi a dire look. "I have never hated and loved a guy so hard at the same time, Amy."

Danica grinned at a thought. "So does that make you the cloud guy's god? His 'eternal keeper'?"

She gave Danica a coy smile. "I mean I wasn't going to say it, but I'm definitely the one who's going to keep his world alive forever. I'm sure he'd leave me an offering if he knew."

When Felicity excused herself to the washroom, Danica stole the seat next to Ravi and nudged them with her shoulder. "Hey buddy, how you holding up?"

"Tired," Ravi replied plainly.

"You're not much of a people person, huh?"

"No, come on, that's not true. I'm great with people."

Danica raised an eyebrow at that to show she wasn't convinced.

Ravi sighed. "Look, Felicity's different. I love her, she's always had my back, you know? And no one's known me longer. I would probably jump into traffic for her. Even now. But like, she's *special*, you know? She takes a lot out of me when I'm not ready for her, and she kind of dropped this on me out of nowhere. God, it's been years. Where did she even come from?" They put their head in their hands and grumbled, "I did *not* have enough time to prepare for her particular brand of friendship this weekend."

"Yeah, she's definitely got an intensity to her. Was she always like this? I don't remember her being so... 'passionate'."

"This isn't even close. You have no idea."

"You've got the patience of an eternal god, Rav. I'm proud of you."

"Aw thanks. And you've got the bullshit diplomacy of a seasoned politician."

Danica smiled and put her hand on Ravi's back to bullshit them. "You're doing great."

Ravi laughed. "Yeah. Great. Thanks coach."

Danica's smile faltered a bit at a nagging thought. She couldn't keep her mind off something that had been bugging her since she got home and got stuck listening to Felicity talk at Ravi, and she needed to get something straight before Felicity came back, so she jumped right to the point.

"Ravi. What am I supposed to call you?"

Ravi looked at Danica with a raised eyebrow.

"She doesn't use the right name," she explained.

"Oh! Oh." Ravi laughed. "I didn't even... Yeah, sorry, I didn't..." Ravi trailed off and got stuck thinking of an answer to Danica's question.

"Just... Amy is fine."

"You haven't told her?"

Ravi shook their head, "And I'm not going to. She knows me like that. I don't want to make things weird."

"You don't think she'll understand?"

"I don't want to find out."

Something about the way Ravi said that crushed Danica's heart, but this wasn't the time to talk about it. She just nodded and agreed – agreed to pretend she didn't know Ravi at all. It twisted her up.

"Nicole? Danica?" Ravi wanted to make sure they were getting it right too.

Danica realized she'd never really brought it up before, but Ravi was the only person in the universe that called her that. For some reason, she just didn't really feel like being 'Nicole' with anyone else. The best way she could describe it, if she were pushed to do so, was that it felt like a secret home, buried deep in the woods, a fire waiting warm in the hearth, a safe place to return and heal after a long time out in the cold. It was all pretend, but it just... felt right when they called her.

"Let's stick with Dani," she smiled. May as well keep it easy for everyone.

'Amy' nodded. There was an apology in their eyes. Danica wanted to tell them they did nothing wrong, but Felicity returned before the two of them could continue.

Felicity insisted on going out to check out some of her and Ravi's old hangs. First on the list was a hobby shop that no longer stocked the card game Felicity remembered playing every week with Ravi. Next was traversing a 'secret' path by a frozen creek, the end of which had a pile of fresh cigarette butts and empty beer cans. Then an old music store – "Oh right. It closed like two years ago," Ravi explained when the crew got to the locked door, which still had a sun-stained, handwritten note thanking the people of the city for their years of support.

It was a long day of disappointment after crushing disappointment for poor nostalgic Felicity, but she finally got a win when she found that one of her favorite greasy spoons was still open.

Unfortunately, it happened to be the only place in the history of mankind where Danica couldn't convince the chef to make her a plate of pancakes. She and that beautiful stubborn ox of a woman had been violently feuding about it ever since Danica returned to the city a few years back. And it was getting kind of intense lately. There was blood last time.

Ravi glanced at her when Felicity wasn't looking to silently plead with her to behave today. They'd already seen this turn ugly a couple times before.

Danica gave Ravi a subtle nod to assure them she'd keep a low profile today. For them.

Sadly, even Danica being on her best behavior wasn't enough to spare Felicity from getting her hopes dashed yet again: The restaurant's signature burger was, apparently, not as good as she remembered.

Danica silently reflected on it while she bitterly stirred the tasteless eggs and bacon around her plate – longing for pancakes, settling for this abomination – that you can't just go home after so long and expect everything to be there, sleeping, unchanged, waiting for you to shake it from its slumber. *What had changed in her home since she left?* she wondered. Would it even feel like home anymore?

Not that it did any good to wonder. She couldn't go back. And even if she could, she didn't *want* to go back. She didn't. Sure, staying here meant she would have to ache and long for the joyful memories of her youth to be real again, but it was probably better to ache in want here than to face the agony of disappointment that waited for her back there.

Yeah. She could just take a lesson from all of Felicity's disappointment today. Probably safe to assume that everything back home sucked now and be done with it.

The evening came and it was Ravi's turn to entertain. The three of them ended up passing around a huge, warm bottle of cheap red wine on a cold riverbank – apparently a regular hang for the two old friends. It was pretty. Ice floes bumbled up on each other in the dark, separated by the inky water that shifted and shimmered in the twinkling streetlight across the way.

The bottle was nearly empty in Felicity's hand before she broke down.

"Am I wasting my life, Amy? I'm wasting it all aren't I? Who the fuck cares about stupid old books. No one. *No one.*"

Ravi had their arm around their friend's shoulder, pulling her in close and letting her nuzzle her cheek into their shoulder. Danica could only sit off to the side and watch.

"Your stuff is so much cooler than mine," Felicity lamented. "Mixing mysterious chemicals together, shaping the *base materials of the universe* into new stuff. *Brand new stuff.*" She laughed at herself dismissively. "And I'm just dusting off old books. I feel like a shitty necromancer sometimes, a wretched old lich clinging to an empty life, resurrecting the dead, putting their words in my own little journal... Putting my name on it all like their brilliance was mine. They celebrate me, you know that? I got an award. For stealing from the dead. It's a fucking joke."

She was cackling at her own misery now. "God, how'd we end up like this, hey Ames? I got stuck digging up graves for a living, and you... you get to look *up*, at heaven, at creation itself." She laughed and spoke to Danica, "You think I'm a fucking god keeping dead words in a machine? *Amaira Fucking Beausoleil.* That's your god, Dani. *The creator.*"

Ravi seemed content to let Felicity pour her aching heart out without a word, but Danica couldn't stand to watch her flail and hurt like this without trying to do something to help. She tried to remind Felicity that her work was important, that it was impressive and valuable and that she *did* deserve to be celebrated for bringing those dead words back to life.

"Someone's going to read the books you save, Fleece. You're giving someone a chance to feel like they belong, like they were understood before they were even born. It'll be the first time for someone, that they get to feel the tug of the threads that connect every human together. That's the gift you're giving, you know?"

Felicity closed her eyes for a moment of thought before she exhaled a sharp and dismissive puff of fog into the cold night air. She didn't seem to have any response. She didn't seem to even care to try at putting one together. Another sharp breath came, then another.

Ah. She was crying.

Ravi brought a tender palm to Felicity's cheek and told her it was okay. She nodded solemnly like she believed it, like she barely believed it, like she could only have ever believed it if it came from Ravi.

❧

When they got back to the apartment, Danica and Ravi – after a fair amount of fumbling – managed the tricky maneuver of unlocking the apartment door and shuffling through with Felicity draped between their shoulders.

Honestly, Danica could've easily carried poor barely-conscious Felicity the whole way back like a sack of flour under her arm, but Ravi refused to let her do it alone.

The two of them pulled their old friend's boots and coat off, then carried her into Ravi's room to tuck her into bed.

That left Ravi and Danica to fight over the loveseat.

"You should take it," Danica insisted.

"No, it's yours. I'll sleep on the floor, it's fine, I have some extra blankets."

"Ravi. It is *literally* your couch."

Ravi shook their head. "I was planning to sleep on the floor anyways."

"That is not a plan."

Ravi sighed. "No, it's not. The *plan*, my dear Nicole – Plan A – was to sleep in my own fucking bed tonight and wake up early for work. Then someone showed up out of nowhere and said she was going to crash here for the weekend. *Plan B* was to make *her* sleep on the couch for just shoving her way into the apartment today without any warning. And I was still *supposed* to sleep in my room."

Danica let out a disappointed little, "Ah," before she teasingly confirmed: "Planning to stuff me in the closet I guess?"

"No! Of course not. You were supposed to get the bed. I was just gonna steal most of the blankets for a little floor nest in there."

"Me?"

"Yeah, you didn't do anything wrong here. I'll tell her she's on the couch tomorrow, okay? If she doesn't like it, she can find a hotel."

"What about you?"

Ravi shrugged. "How about you go find me a cheap air mattress tomorrow while I'm at work. It'll be good having one around anyways. Sounds like Felicity's finally sick of never seeing me, so I suspect this'll be the first of many weekends she ends up crashing here."

Danica laughed, then groaned in jest, "Oh good. Can't wait for

Drunken Existential Crisis 2: Return of the Golden Fleece."

"Don't laugh, okay. She's not doing great. Good or bad, she's still my friend. I love her."

Ravi really meant what they said about sleeping on the floor. They shoved the coffee table out of the way, then set up a spare comforter from the closet like a terrible bedroll. And Danica knew there was no hope in trying to get them to trade places.

Why were they like this?

In the dark, lit only by what little moonlight made it through the curtains, Danica watched Ravi for a long time while they tossed and turned trying to find some way to get comfortable down there.

When she was pretty sure Ravi had fallen asleep, she decided she couldn't stand the injustice – to sleep on the comparatively luxurious loveseat while Ravi slept on the floor? Unacceptable.

She whispered a gentle hello to Ravi to see if they would respond. And when they didn't, she cradled them in her arms and gently set them on the couch.

Something sparked painfully on the skin of her forearm when she pulled her arms away, like a live wire needled into her a dozen times all at once. She jerked back with a stifled swear.

What the hell was that? Were they hiding an electric fence under their shirt or something? Jesus.

After examining her forearm in the bathroom, she couldn't find any sign of a burn. So. Weird twitch or something? Human bodies spasm randomly sometimes. That's a thing, right?

Once she finished convincing herself that she wasn't crazy, she took Ravi's place on the floor, quietly struggling and failing to get comfortable in the dark, clutching at the painful spot on her arm.

She woke up to a pillow being thrown at her head, picked up, thrown again, and again, and again until she was awake enough to grab it and throw it back at her assailant.

"You ass," Ravi seethed. "Will you ever just let me do something nice for you? Just once? Is that so much?"

Danica gave Ravi a sleepy smile and pretended not to know what they were talking about, which earned her another pillow to the face. She graciously accepted the assault as fair punishment for her kindness.

❧

Ravi was at work by the time Felicity groaned her way into the living room.

"Headaaaaaaaaaa—" She paused in place, acting dazed, when she noticed the living room was missing her dear friend. "—*ache*. —Where's Amy?"

"Work," Danica replied plainly, with as much cheer as she could force out. She had entirely forgotten she was playing the 'forget Ravi's real name' game until Felicity spoke, and it kind of knocked the wind out of her sails. The whole thing was a mild annoyance.

Well.

No.

No, it felt more like something scraping the inside of her skull every time she had to say it wrong, so maybe 'annoyance' was underselling it.

"There's some pain meds in the bathroom," she helpfully informed her dear ailing friend.

—Friend?

Friend, sure.

The rattling of pills in bottles was occasionally paused for a few long moments whenever Felicity was presumably struggling to read the tiny words through the static of her hangover.

"This is for cramps!" she eventually shouted from the bathroom.

"Works for headaches too," Danica called back.

Felicity wandered back into the living room, intently reading the bottle. "It does not. Nothing about headaches on this."

"Fleece. It's a painkiller. It kills pain. It *does not care* where the pain is." For real though, they were very effective. Those pills were practically part of a balanced breakfast around here. They nearly went through a bottle a month between Ravi's hangovers, their overworked back and leg muscles, and the worst days of their illness. And also, obviously, as confoundingly indicated on the bottle, for either of their period cramps.

Gods, definitely one of the worst parts of this prison of hers. She had originally reveled in the authenticity of her carefully practiced form at first, so proud of capturing every little detail. But now, after six hundred years with no respite, she could only curse herself for it.

And for nothing at all! She couldn't even get anything out of it. Couldn't even carry a child – the only possible solace for all that suffering, but her body was just too damn good at healing itself to let her have even that bit of joy.

So stupid.

That weird pain in her arm after moving Ravi last night was almost as bad. Danica had tried to numb it a bit by popping a handful of the very painkillers in Felicity's hand. And it helped a bit, but not enough.

Gods, this really, *really* should have gotten better already. She was doing her best to ignore it in front of Felicity, but it still ached miserably.

Despite Danica's frank and honest presentation of the facts of how the medicine worked, Felicity still wasn't convinced. She continued humming at the bottle in disbelief, searching the label for the magic words.

Danica sighed, then put on a cheerful tone. "Oh, you know what! I bet there's a bottle of *regular* headache meds in the kitchen somewhere, one sec." Then she got up from the couch and went around the corner so she could discreetly wave a glimmering hand over the counter to pull a couple of the pills through the Aether out of the bottle in Felicity's hand.

Danica's stubborn, grumpy old acquaintance happily accepted the 'headache pills' and the glass of water Danica offered her.

"Thank you. Was that so hard?" she grumbled, after eagerly downing the medicine.

Danica tried to give a pleasant smile when Felicity returned the empty glass to her. It felt like it wasn't coming out right.

"Sleep well?" she asked.

Felicity wandered back into the bathroom to put the bottle of pills away and wash last night's stale makeup off.

"Yeah the sleeping part was fine," she replied after drying herself off. "Waking up suuuucks."

"You were really digging into that bottle last night," Danica said. She didn't want to judge, but... well, Felicity was here for a reason, wasn't she? Danica still hadn't quite figured out what that reason was, but it probably wasn't to get blackout drunk on wine.

Felicity didn't have an instant response to that subtle jab. "Yeah. I mean. Obviously. It's. My favorite brand."

"Which brand?"

"...Red."

Danica smiled, "Yeah. Boy, Red makes the best wine, don't they? That White company is just trash."

Felicity sighed and sat on the couch next to Danica, elbows on her knees, cheeks propped up in her palms, like she was bracing for a rolled-up newspaper over the head. "Okay. What did I do? Go ahead."

Danica warmly assured her that she had done almost nothing embarrassing. "You *did* throw up in a bush. I think some got on your boots."

"Noted." She hesitated for a moment before she asked, "I didn't... say anything?"

"Something about a general lack of job satisfaction," Danica said, to cradle the truth. No reason to embarrass her.

She chuckled to herself, "Yeah that's... definitely been scratching up the back of my brain. When's Amy back?"

"They—'Amy'. Amy takes long shifts at the warehouse on the weekend. Usually grabs some overtime too. The earliest is probably like... ten?"

"Warehouse?" Felicity's face twisted into a look of disbelief and concern, "She's doing TA work. What are you talking about?"

Oh.

Oh gods.

Ravi hadn't told Felicity about that yet?

Shit. What had Danica just done?

She gave Felicity an uneasy smile, but didn't say anything to confirm or deny what she just revealed.

But apparently that was enough for Felicity to take what she said as true for some reason.

She spoke bewildered, staring vacantly at Danica's chest. "Warehouse...? Until... ten? Seriously? Ten??" She started counting on her fingers, "That's like... what time is it?"

"Almost one."

"So... nine hours? That's crazy!"

"Yeah. I mean... the shift started at eight. ...'Amy' usually doesn't have a lot of energy when 'she' comes home."

"Yeah no kidding." Felicity flopped back on the couch and stared at the ceiling with her palms on her temples. "Jeezus. Whatever complaints I have about job satisfaction can get stuffed in a bag and dropped at the bottom of a lake, huh? How does she do all that *and* work on her thesis? That's crazy." Felicity suddenly sat up straight. It looked like a fistful of realization just hit her in the jaw. "She's not... I mean, I'm not judging, but is she... *on* something? Uppers?"

Danica raised an eyebrow and assured Felicity Ravi was not taking drugs.

"Okay but how do you know?"

"Felicity we are sharing like... 400 square feet here. If she was snorting coke or popping pills, I would be *extremely* aware of it."

She looked relieved – though not entirely convinced – by Danica's certainty.

Danica really wanted to get out of this before she accidentally revealed any more of Ravi's secrets. Hard to keep that stuff hidden when you can't lie.

"So!" she clapped her hands together and stood up from the couch. "There's tons of milk and the cereal's on top of the fridge. Eggs. Bread. Jam. Honey. Bacon. Go nuts. There's a little stool there for you short people. Coffee's in the cupboard beside the sink—"

Felicity scowled at her and put out a pleading hand for her to stop. "Wait wait, are you leaving?"

"Yeah! I have a bunch of stuff I want to do this weekend. Amy just asked me to stick around to make sure you didn't die of alcohol poisoning or whatever. And look! Here you are! So full of life! Mission accomplished. Really just a ten out of ten job on my part. Worthy of the highest honor in the land. I don't want a medal or anything though, Fleece, but you *could* leave us a five-star review—"

Felicity collapsed on the couch like a sack of potatoes.

"I can't figure you out, Dani."

She said that like she had been spending a lot of time on the topic in her head. She also said it like it was the first time she had given Danica a moment of thought in eight years. It was hard to tell which one was real.

Danica cocked her head to the side with a clueless, disarming smile.

Felicity mercifully went on to explain herself, kind of: "You know, the university I'm at now, they have a killer chemistry program. I ask the lab guys about it sometimes. Their equipment is expensive and new, they get flown all over for fancy conferences, get their papers pushed right to the front of academic journals by influential profs. Anyone would be happy to get in. Honored. And on a scholarship? That's an easy life, isn't it?"

Danica nodded along. She didn't really know where this was going. Felicity seemed to be falling into a funk again. Or maybe she never left.

"She didn't take it, you know. Amy. She got in – and got the free ride too. I didn't even know she had grades that good. I wanted her to come with me so bad. —Should've been easy, right? Easier than toast for breakfast. But she just stuck around here, in this decaying husk of a city."

"Hey, come on, it's not that bad. Give it a chance. I like it! Amy does too. You might—"

"—Does she? She *likes* this? This miserable, withering, *desiccated* hometown of ours? She likes the worthless equipment at that shitty bargain bin university of hers? She likes... what, she likes wearing herself out in a braindead warehouse? And after—ha—after all that— then after *all that*, she likes coming home to <u>*this*</u>?" Felicity gestured at the tiny, admittedly unattractive space in the living room. Chipped paint and distastefully stained carpets. The cushions on the couch were frayed and ugly. The TV was small. The coffee table was scratched.

It was all part of Danica's home now, and she loved every fault, but she got the feeling that everything she called 'home', and even her own presence here, all of it was probably included in the vilifying sweep of Felicity's arm.

She chuckled to herself in a fit of low despair while she continued her rant: "Ha... haha... God... She could have been changing the world out there. But no. No, she got stuck *here*. With *you*."

"...Wow. *Wow okay*. Amy told me to be nice because you're going through some stuff, but you need to chill out. I didn't do anything—"

"—Yeah. You didn't. And you won't, will you? You're not going to push her at all, are you? You're just going to let her stay stuck here, content in her misery. *Shit* apartment. *Shit* job. *Shit* university. And a fucking... fake, selfish, *shit* friend for a roommate."

Danica tightened a fist until her knuckles cracked. Felicity was really pushing it. But she didn't have even a second to jump in to defend herself before Felicity continued her bitter tirade.

"—Can't you see how broken she is? And you don't even care about her enough to try to help. You don't want her to chase after her *potential*, her *greatness*. You're just using her for a cheap place to sleep while you go out and fuck around all weekend doing *whatever*, hm? You think I'm stupid, Dani? I see how she looks at you. And I *see* what you're doing. Taking advantage of how nice she is. *You're <u>stealing her life</u>*. God, it makes me so... *fucking mad* seeing you leeching off of her like this! And she's just falling for it!"

Danica tried, but she couldn't stomach to just stand there and take this abuse. And she couldn't just stand there and let Felicity abuse Ravi's dignity like this.

She stomped away from Felicity to the other end of the room with a growl before she turned around with some bitter words:

"Fleece, it's not my job to fix her, okay? And it's not yours either. And they're not even fucking *broken*. You think you can just *pass judgement* on them? Why? What makes you the expert on how to live a good life, huh? The way you were talking last night, I wouldn't even pick you to coach me through the crisis of a *stubbed toe*. I don't know who you think you are to come here and tell me they're fucked up and tell me all about how I'm using them and holding them back—Like you know me? Like you know what's going on in my life? Like you know what I do here for them? —No. Shut up. You're done. —No! Back off, Felicity, I mean it. Just, back *right off*, okay? Just, step back, and look at what you're doing, and just... get it right the fuck out of your head that they need *you* to tell them how to be amazing. They're doing just fine without you."

Felicity shot up in a growling huff and aggressively stepped right up in Danica's face. ...Well. Right up in her chest anyways. Danica was at least a whole foot taller. But that didn't stop Felicity from *acting* like a towering, snarling beast in front of her.

She looked like she was ready to spit fire.

"You..." she sneered. The word rumbled viscously in the back of her throat.

"Yeah?" Danica shoved her chest into Felicity. She looked ridiculous down there. Felicity's ferocity might have made the little ingrate feel tall, but Danica still towered over her, and she wasn't afraid to show it off if Felicity was going to try to throw around what little weight she had. "What about me? Huh, Fleece? What *about* me? Please, *go ahead.* Don't hold back. How do you *really* feel?"

"Don't... *fucking* push me..."

Felicity sneered at Danica coldly, but, thankfully, she did have the sense to back off, and Danica was more than happy to let her retreat. She wasn't going to fight Felicity, but she sure wasn't going to let her talk poorly about Ravi either.

Danica didn't like the bitter taste of the air after all that aggressive posturing. She calmed her voice and tried her best to make peace:

"I don't get where all this is coming from, Felicity. None of it's true. Is that really what it looks like to you?" she softly asked, "You really don't think she's happy here?"

"Do *you?*" Felicity was still spitting her words at Danica. "Do you think this is where she's supposed the spend the rest of her life?"

Danica couldn't help letting out a dismissive little laugh. "She's 26. *You're* 26. You're talking like this is *it* for both of you."

"I'm 27."

"Oh, sorry. *27.*"

"Last week."

"Really? Well happy birthday."

"She didn't even send me a text about it. And I guess I see why now. Too busy working at the *warehouse*, apparently."

"That's what this is about??"

"No. ...Yes. But... No. It just... —You know what, I don't owe you a fucking... *explanation*..."

Danica took a slow breath and held it for a few seconds while she calmed herself down and took in Felicity's scowl with sympathetic eyes. She was clearly hurting about something deep that she wasn't ready to dig up yet. Danica wished Ravi had been a *little* more clear about what exactly was happening with her. And Felicity was right: Danica hadn't really earned anything from her. No trust or good faith. It didn't matter how friendly Danica tried to be, it clearly wasn't enough to offset the grave betrayal Felicity thought she was hitting Ravi with.

Gods, honestly, from how bitter she was, Danica couldn't even imagine a game plan for getting on her good side right now.

She exhaled deeply, hugged her ribs with a childish lack of

strength, and shifted her weight onto one foot to take all the power out of her stance. Maybe Felicity would get the point – that she wasn't a threat, and she wasn't going to fight her.

"…I'll listen if you want to talk about it," she softly assured Felicity.

"I don't," she replied sharply.

Danica rolled her eyes slightly before refocusing and trying to plead with Felicity: "…You know, I'm not your enemy here. I'm not. And I really don't like seeing you hurting like this. This doesn't do anything for me, Fleece. I swear I'm getting no pleasure out of this. I just want to help you, with whatever's bothering you, if you can let me."

Felicity clicked her tongue at Danica. Her teeth were grinding bitterly for a few seconds while she chewed off a biting response: "No. *No*. You don't like it? You want to help so bad? Then leave. That'll be a big help. Just that. Get out of her life. Go find some other sucker to take advantage of. Let someone who *actually* cares about her take over."

"I'm… not… Felicity, please, I'm not trying to hurt her, I swear. I swear on all the unspeakable names of every gluttonous gazing god, Fleece, I'm *not*."

"Tch," Felicity scoffed at her sharply. "Swear all you want, it doesn't matter. It doesn't matter what you're *trying to do*. You hurt her just by being here. How can you not see that? You're a burden. —You're a *poison*, and you're *killing* her."

Danica winced slightly to hear that and clenched her fists.

It wasn't true.

—It wasn't.

It wasn't.

Gods… But… how many…? Angie's words echoed in her mind. How many humans? How many… how many friends…?

~~Pets.~~

She grimaced and tried to shake it out of her head.

This entreaty with Felicity wasn't going anywhere.

Danica turned away from the stewing little white knight for a moment to consider what to do. She glanced at her boots by the door. Her old contact was waiting. She was wasting time here.

Though it didn't feel like a waste. She wanted to stay. She wanted to help. For Ravi at least. Even if there was no other reason, helping Felicity would make Ravi's life easier.

But there was another reason: Felicity wasn't a bad person. She wasn't a waste. No one worthless would ever get this pissed off about a friend's misery – imagined or not.

It was miserable to imagine leaving Felicity here alone, leaving her waiting, stuck stewing on her troubled feelings for Ravi, leaving her lying in wait here, hidden like a pocket of flammable gas, waiting to explode on Ravi when they got home and opened the door.

But there wasn't much to be done about it while Felicity had all her armor on like this.

"…I'm going out," Danica said at last, without turning around. Again she gestured at the kitchen in general, "Help yourself to anything you want."

"Gee thanks. So kind of you, to be so generous with Amy's stuff."

"Gods, stop. I'm going. Okay? I'm leaving. I'll be back for dinner. I hope you're cooled off by then."

Felicity watched in bitter silence.

Whenever Danica glanced up while she put on her coat and boots to leave, she found Felicity scowling at her.

She was about to leave, an inch from plucking her keys off the wall, when she caught herself and froze for a moment. That was the only spare set. Danica's set. There was no way to get back in the building without them. Not without cheating.

She slowly withdrew her fingers, and left the keys behind, calling back to Felicity on her way out the door, "Hey, there's a set of keys on the wall there, Fleece. Help yourself."

She didn't respond.

Danica didn't look back.

But her mind lingered there, with Felicity, while she hurried to the Serpent's Fang.

For all Felicity's vitriol, she was only trying to protect Ravi. It was hard to be angry at a loyal wolf for growling at a stranger getting too close to the most important person in her life.

Danica just wished she could prove to Felicity that she wasn't going to rip dear Ravi Bee to pieces. Hell, even convincing her that she wasn't planning to sit back and let them drown in a sea of misery would be huge a step forward. Sadly, the solution to that puzzle would end up being *remarkably* elusive – and extremely costly.

Is It an Art or a Trade?

When Danica opened the door to the Serpent's Fang and let a gust of cold air blow in from the street, she found Henry wiping stubborn water spots out of pint glasses in the empty pub.

"Well look who it is!" the old man crooned at her when he spotted her.

"Sorry! Sorry." Danica tapped her boots off on a mat by the door. Henry always chewed her out if she made a mess of his precious establishment. "There was this whole... *situation* at home."

"Oh? Is our dear Mx. Beausoleil okay?"

Danica laughed. "Yeah, they're fine. I think. They've got a disgruntled fan waiting for them when they get home tonight, though. —I'll tell you later," she said, dismissively waving it away. She looked around curiously and asked Henry if anyone was here.

"Not a soul. I've been keeping the place empty all day. Just for you." He gave her a grin that was pleasant and soft on the outside, but Danica knew that 'happy to help' smile of his concealed something sharp, as it always did. "I hope you're planning to pay me back for all the tips I lost out on."

Danica joked with her old collaborator, "You get tips? You're such a prick though."

"Only for you," he replied simply.

The door wasn't locked when Danica came in. But with Henry, it didn't need to be. Anyone wanting a drink today would get a mind full of the spell he put on the Serpent's Fang's front door, and they'd turn right back around to find somewhere with a more agreeable aura.

That little favor only cost Danica, as Henry so cheerfully reminded her, all the tips he would've gotten from the people he scared off for her. It amounted to two free drinks for the old guy. Danica wasn't sure how he was so confident in his math on that alternate timeline, but she couldn't really argue. He was the only dealer who'd still work with her. He set the price.

And it wasn't exactly breaking the bank, but his taste in liquor was refined with age, so it was a lot more than any pair of cocktails Danica had ever ordered. She reflected on her good fortune that Henry was one of the fairer and more reasonable creatures she knew. No tricks. Just business. That's why the two of them got on so well – as *professionals*.

With a *profoundly* aromatic drink in his hand, Henry led the way to a table in the back of the pub – solid wood that sat under a soft hanging incandescent lamp. Say whatever about the guy, he still had good taste.

"So?" Danica eagerly prodded him before she even had her butt in the chair.

"Weather's nice, isn't it?"

"Sure. Yup. Snow. Ice. Love it."

"How's the family?"

"You'd know better than me."

"Keeping busy?"

"Henry."

"What?"

"Can we get to business? Please. What did you find for me?"

Henry looked disappointed. "You love small talk."

"Not today. I'm burnt out on talk. Results! I want results!" Danica put on a mockery of a demanding mob boss. "Give me the goods or you'll never work in this town again!"

Henry closed his eyes, let out a quiet sigh, then shook his head sadly. "You owe me a nice little chat later."

"Yes. Later. Deal."

Henry fished a thick, plain-looking envelope from the breast pocket of his vest – an unnecessarily stylish and iridescent garment that went absolutely perfectly with the rest of his anachronistic attire. He never got his head out of the 1800s, and he was absolutely shameless about it.

From inside the envelope, he slowly drew and placed items on the table in a particular formation, like a medium laying out tarot for her fortune.

The deck he laid out consisted of a collection of neatly folded, frayed-edge notes, and weathered documents. After arranging every item in his own particular way – lining up edges and corners to be aesthetically pleasing for no one but himself – he presented the spread to Danica, offering to let her flip over whichever item she wished to see.

Danica didn't really care what order the information came in, she just wanted it as quickly as possible. She was sick of waiting. None of her leads on Ravi's melanotic cysts were leading anywhere. It was like all the people working on it had just disappeared into thin air. And, unfortunately, that meant Henry was her last hope of getting anything useful out of the universe before she had to resort to faerie trading. And she very much wanted to avoid faerie trades for as long as possible – in no small part because she was... *kind of* out of faeries to trade with.

She jabbed at some random piece of paper – a plain, mercifully unstained white document, folded up tidily to fit in Henry's envelope.

He delicately unfolded the letter and pressed the wings down before turning it to face Danica.

It wasn't the whole document, it seemed. The top of the page started halfway through a long paragraph. Every word had the tenor of a salesperson speaking to an acquisitions officer at a big corporation.

Danica tried to make sense of it. It was talking about some kind of 'campaign' project. There was a bit of a progress statement, and a few questions about how to proceed.

The only person named in the doc was a person the author referred to as Miss Ortiz.

"Who's this?" Danica asked, pointing to the name. It was the only thing she could pick out that might be even close to meaningful to her.

"A lead."

"Fae? Witch?"

"No. Just human."

Danica dropped her chin to her chest and brought her fingers to her forehead. "Okay so, I asked for magic. Right? I did ask for magic, right? Like, curative magic? And you brought me... a normal human in a business deal. *How* is this supposed to help me?"

Henry shrugged. "You know my investigative work is more of an art than a science."

"Is it? Is it an art Henry? Or do you just go around picking up random notes and documents and other pieces of trash off the ground and try to sell them off like they're *actual* information?"

"I'll admit, it's a bit of both."

Danica glared at him disapprovingly.

"You can't complain about the product, Danica. You know what I sell. Divination isn't precise. It's *never* precise. And it's rarely *generous.* These are just the materials, you get to do the work of putting it together yourself. Isn't that more fun?"

"Fun. Sure. So. Miss Ortiz. Business lady. *Shrouded in mystery.* Extremely helpful, thank you." She let out a defeated sigh. "Okay. Whatever. Let's keep going. Maybe there's something here that's not trash, hm?" Without a thought, she tapped the back of another folded piece of paper. "Go on. What's this one?"

This one had messily torn edges when Henry unfolded it for her. Another scrap of a document, but she knew without a hint of doubt what this one was.

"...And more scraps. Great. What am I supposed to do with a quarter of a page of a faerie trade, Henry?"

He didn't reply. He didn't even move. He just waited for Danica to finish making her assessment.

She looked it over nonchalantly. This was obviously a copy of the original. You don't rip an original to pieces unless you want to blow up a chunk of the Faelands. *Danica.*

She had to scoff at the language in the terms.

"Amateur work too, huh? Can't even bring me a scrap of something good?"

"What's so bad about it?" he asked with a curious eyebrow.

It occurred to Danica Henry probably didn't get a chance to see a lot of these, and he almost certainly never got a chance to see an expert's critical review.

"Look at this: 'The means to become immortal.'"

"...Sounds like a good deal."

"Are you kidding? No caveats? No definitions? Good luck!" She shook the paper in the air for emphasis: "This thing is just as dangerous to the faerie who wrote it as it is to the idiot human who signed it."

She stared at the phrasing again to let her imagination run wild for a few seconds. It was like it was *inviting* trouble. She could already imagine hundreds of ways it could go wrong.

"Gods. Like, just for an easy example, the universe could've just decided to let the guy be immortal in *stories* or something, or hey technically his atoms aren't going to die, or it could've killed off anything that might've threatened to kill him – including friends and family – entire countries at war – *anyone*. Hell, might even kill off the faerie who signed it if they were feeling particularly malicious when they wrote this."

"That's a stretch there, Danica. I've *never* heard of a faerie dying."

Danica snorted at that dismissively, then she jabbed herself in the chest over her heart to make a point: "Trust me on this, Henry. I didn't always have a heart like this, cursed with all this love and sympathy and regret. There isn't a faerie in the universe who can *ache* like me. Cost of my hubris. Make one bad contract and you'll see it: The cruelty and irony of the twisted whims of the universe can get very, very creative. If it makes the gods laugh, there's a way."

She returned her *hopefully* obviously disappointed glare to the page and shook her head in frustration, then she impatiently shoved it off to the side and jabbed at another one of the documents in Henry's spread: "Okay. This one. —And this one better be good. I'm at my limit here, Henry."

He took his time carefully unfolding the note and creasing it *just so* to keep it open in front of Danica.

A scrap of old parchment – just, nonstop, scraps scraps scraps today – ripped out of an ancient book it looked like. It was vandalized with some hand-written notes in the margin. —Not Henry's notes, obviously. His writing looked like what would happen if a typewriter grew a soul and got ahold of a fountain pen and a calligraphy book. No, these notes probably came from someone with far too many thoughts and far too little self control to keep them in their head.

Judging from the languages, the parchment itself was way, way older than it looked. She was impressed it was still in such good condition, considering what else Henry was presenting to her today.

She troubled over the symbols of the author's language and tried to remember any of it. It had been hundreds and hundreds of years since she'd had any reason to read this language. The last time was when she was dutifully helping her dad write vile faerie contracts. He was fond of using archaic barely remembered words from old forgotten dialects of Fae. And she might've known all of these archaic words once in context, but by now she'd even forgotten what the language called itself. 'Old Fae' was the best English could do, though this was probably better called *Old* Old Fae. Not even her older sibling spoke this language.

"Can you read it for me?" she asked her oh-so-worldly consort.

Henry's eyes widened, and a cocked eyebrow showed a hint of disappointment in her. "I'm surprised you can't. It's just ꝏꝛ ꝏꝛ ꝝꝛꝝ, it's not that old."

Ah. *That's* what it called itself. Well now she felt silly for forgetting it at all.

"*I'm* not that old, Henry, and my head's no good with this kind of stuff anyways, not like *yours* is." She smiled warmly at him to punctuate that compliment to show how 'sincere' she was in her admiration. "Please."

He let out a tiny sigh, then concisely summarized the note without even looking at it. "The author wrote about the art of trading with humans," he explained, pointing to the original text on the page. Then he pointed to the margin notes: "And this incorrigible margin vandal wrote about the art of trading with the fae, trying to tally up what exactly the fae considered the various parts of a human to be worth. In particular, the vandal wondered about the cost of 'mortality'."

"And?"

"It doesn't say exactly, though whoever it was *did* seem to understand that 'immortality' is more of a curse when dealing with the fae."

"Yeah, obviously Henry. I was literally *just* saying that."

"Not so obvious to everyone, little one."

"Well, shame the ones who signed that pact didn't read this book." She jabbed the page impatiently a few times. "Henry. Again, what's this have to do with Ravi's thing?"

Henry, again, could only shrug and shake his head.

"Okay. What was the *whole* book about? Did someone actually *know* about the fae? Or is this just some philosopher's fiction?"

"I don't know," he replied, entirely unfazed by Danica's growing frustration. "Whatever was left of the book was gone when I found this."

Danica frowned. The more she looked at this disembodied page, the more something was nagging at her. It looked... familiar? She had delivered a book to Angie not too long ago that was missing a page. Same size. Same language. Got a *huge* discount because of it, after a very heated negotiation. Angie wasn't happy though. Damn witch didn't even count that one against Danica's debt.

"...And where exactly did you find this, anyways?"

"It was on the ground in the parking lot at the mall."

Danica stared at him with the most expressionless, dumbfounded, condemning look she could put on. "Are you serious."

"Yes. Why would I lie about that?"

"I mean, gods, could you try though? Pretend it's from some mystic forgotten library in the Faelands? Some old witch's collection? A tomb? A dragon's hoard? —No. No, you're going with 'a parking lot'. Unbelievable. How do you stay in business like this?"

"I get results."

"Do you?" Danica glared at the remaining items on the table and shook her head, nearly shouting with exasperation: "Is it all like this? Did you get anything I actually asked for?"

Silence.

Not a yes, then, which also wasn't necessarily a no.

"Henry. Come on man. Did you at least find someone back home to *ask* about it?"

"No one wants to deal with you back home."

"That's why I sent you!"

"They know what you're doing, Danica. You don't keep it quiet. It would shake the Faelands if you could go even one of these cheating little lifetimes of yours without selfishly pursuing your Earthly pleasures. Just once, can't you just suffer quietly like you're supposed to?"

Danica crossed her arms and scowled at him, "You sound like Niede."

"Your high-handed sibling might mean you better than you're willing to believe. You could stand to give them a little more consideration."

Danica replied dryly, "Well, I'll take *that* under consideration, thank you Henry."

The old guy put his elbows on the table, brought his hands together, and rested his chin on his intertwined fingers.

After a breath to consider his words, he offered more dire, unsolicited advice: "I have to be honest with you, little one: You're sticking your neck out for the wrong people. I love Ravi. I do. They're good fun whenever you bring them around. You have to let them go. You can wait this out, let it fix itself. And you should. Just once. Just, do the right thing for once and leave these people alone. Be strong. Suffer through it. *Just once.*"

Danica scoffed at the suggestion. Like she would ever just sit back and let the world burn *or* let her family *win*.

Henry let out a little defeated sigh before he continued: "Why do you have to meddle? You'll never come out of this in one piece if you don't stop your bleeding heart, and the ones you love are always the ones that suffer for it. You know that."

Danica drummed the soft part of her fist firmly on the table in frustration. "Henry. I didn't ask you for advice. I asked you to get me information. Did you get me information? Because I'm not paying you for lectures and the trash you picked up while you were buying toilet paper." She gestured aggressively at the papers on the table and challenged him to be honest, "Is *any of this* even worth wiping my ass with?"

He didn't answer. Instead, he slowly brought his forearms to rest on the table. His gaze wandered just above Danica's head while he played his fingers in a pensive rhythm on the aged wood.

After a moment of deep thought, his chest swelled with a breath that came out through his nose in a long hiss, then he dropped his attention back to the table and drew a small, black, velvet bag from his vest's other chest pocket.

He handed it to Danica with a warning, "This is *not* free, and you are out of both friends and favors. Be careful."

Danica started to untie the gold thread that was cinching the bag shut, but Henry reached across the table and placed a calm hand on hers to stop her.

"Not here. When you need it, you'll know."

Danica pulled her hand away and standoffishly disregarded Henry's advice. She defiantly unsealed the bag and removed the contents.

Inside was a humble spool, wrapped with frayed and shredded scraps of thin, chromatic, pearlescent filament, tied together with ugly knots.

She unspooled a bit of it, and she knew what it was in an instant. It was obvious as soon as it grazed her fingertips. It was the same stuff that allowed Danica to slip anything she wanted anywhere she wanted around Earth's plane: Aethereal Tether. *Incredibly shitty* Aethereal Tether – exactly the kind of garbage Danica should have expected from Henry.

If this knotty mess of a line was sturdy enough to move an empty pint glass through the Aether, it would be a miracle.

But it was way *longer* than the scrap of perfect filament tied to Danica's finger. If this knotty mess of a line could move a pint glass at all, it could probably move it *all the way* through the Aether – *just barely* all the way to the Faelands – well beyond her current reach.

It might not arrive in *one piece*, but it'd get there. But being super unreliable like that made it practically worthless. Trash.

But... maybe if she folded it over a couple times? Triple plied it into rough knotted twine? It'd be a third the length, but *probably* strong enough to move stuff around on Earth at least. Could be handy if she ever lost her own pristine Tether somehow, though she sure as hell wouldn't want to bet her life on something so shoddy and fragile.

"And what exactly am I supposed to do with this?" she asked, while unspooling the shitty knotty mockery of a Tether and letting it unwind between her fingers into a cat's cradle.

While the two of them spoke, she busied herself with folding it back and forth to let it dangle playfully from her fingers. Then she tied one end of the tripled-over strands to her left index finger and started the long process of twisting them into a shorter, slightly stronger Aethereal... *Twine?*

At least she could make the useless thing *half*-useful.

"You'll know," Henry replied cryptically.

She rolled her eyes at him in a huff. "Great. Thanks. More useless garbage, then. How do you always—"

"Danica, you can call anything else garbage, but that is a handcrafted *gift*. It took a long time picking Niede's shredded fibers off the crags and spines in the Aether to put all that together."

She gave the shitty Tether a careful examination for a few seconds before she conceded and gave Henry a half-sarcastic thank you. If he put work into making it, she should be kind about it. And if he said she'd need it one day, then she would definitely need it one day.

But prophetic gift or garbage, it still wasn't very useful as it was. She'd have to put in a hell of a lot of work to fix it up. And since it wasn't 'free', whatever that meant, it probably wasn't going to be a very good 'gift' either. Probably more like Angie's debt-swindling trickery.

What exactly would she owe Henry for this?

She left it tied to her left hand, dangling idly and intangibly and imperceptible to anything born on Earth, so she could work on making 'Twine' out of it in her spare time. Something to keep her hands busy on the bus.

Then she collected Henry's trash off the table and slid it all back into the envelope before she stuffed it in her coat. Even if it was all garbage, she still paid for it, but since it almost certainly was all garbage, there was no point wasting her time here and racking up her tab with Henry.

She stood up from the table and started putting her coat back on to head off – utterly disappointed with the old man's results – when he had the audacity, even after all that, to remind her that she still owed him a chat.

"What? Now??"

"Are you in a rush?"

She was not. Unfortunately.

Henry graciously dispelled the ominous miasma that had been keeping customers at bay, then invited her to sit at the bar while he went about his day.

She slouched over the counter on her barstool and leaned on an elbow while she sipped away at whatever cocktail Henry made for her when she asked for something blue, and, in between orders, she chatted with the old man about whatever he wanted.

She could enjoy it any other day. He had a lot of good stories to tell. He'd been around a lot longer than she had, and it was kind of nice having someone older in her life to chat with who wasn't constantly trying to exploit her. Nice to let her guard down once in a while.

She never did get his story. Where he came from. What he *was*. She probably never would, so all she could do was guess.

Fae, right? But faeries always hate being human for long, and he'd been hanging around in this shape for centuries. But her imagination wasn't quite strong enough to imagine anything else in the universe that might have the kind of power either Henry or Danica had access to.

A punishment? Like her?

Or maybe, like her, he really was crazy enough to enjoy all the fun and misery that came bundled with these mortal forms.

"Is it different?—" she asked lazily, hoping desperately to derail Henry from this conversation of his: Marveling about the way humanity's troubles echoed endlessly though history, exemplified today by the inane specifics about the city's local politics. "—Back home?"

"No," he answered plainly without much thought.

Then he got struck still for a moment, staring at a point on the wall beyond Danica to reflect on his answer.

"...But maybe when you've lived this long, 'different' means something else." He gestured at the ancient, intricately pressed tin tiles on the ceiling of the lobby. "This bar was a laundromat last time, before that it was a bookstore, and before that it was a bar. A long time ago it was a place to store and buy furs. Before that it was parts of a forest and a few veins of rock and metal in the Earth. It's not different. It is what it has been."

"Okay *Sartre* chill out, I meant is it the same as when I was kicked out?"

"If you want to know that neglected walls have collapsed and ambitious trees have grown and precious people have moved from one place to another, then yes, it's different. Does any of that actually change it? The growing and the falling and the moving, that's the universe. Change isn't different."

"Yeah, great, existence is an undeterrable swirl of matter and energy made motionless in the vastness of the gods' eternal gaze. I get it. Can you go one week without reminding me? Write a book about it already. I just wanted to know about the first thing. Did they break my house?"

"Where do you live?"

"You know where I live! —Oh my *gods* are you doing more philosophy bullshit... THE PHYSICAL BUILDING WHERE I LIVED IN

THE FAELANDS. *HENRY*."

"Yeah, it's gone."

"...Ah. Well. That sucks... I liked the view there. The ocean's so calming. ...I should move to the coast. ...Should I move to the coast?"

Henry shrugged.

"Did they leave the garden at least?" she asked, hopeful.

"It's changed. Violently. But there are still plants there, tossed and upturned, undying, reaching for the light of the sunless sky. It's all the pieces of a garden, but I don't know if it's a garden anymore like that, without someone to take care of it."

"They tossed my garden??"

"They were scared."

"Gods, and none of my cousins cared enough to put it right again, huh? It was so beautiful. How could they *all* hate it?"

"Don't be too hard on them. It's all sealed off now – the whole swath of land. —Thank your dear sibling for that. Somehow, they convinced your father to give up some of his power to bind every faerie in the Faelands to an injunction. No one could get in even if they wanted to."

"Seriously?"

"You know how it is. They think you're sick. Some even think you're contagious. They didn't want to rule out 'environmental factors'."

Danica laughed, "Like what? They're worried a bunch of poached Earthen flowers are going to give them a case of 'The Empathies' or something?"

Henry shrugged, and in a way that suggested Danica wasn't exactly wrong.

Her family was so ridiculous.

"On the topic of maladies," Henry said, nodding at Danica's forearm.

She had been unconsciously massaging it since she sat down with him that afternoon. There was *still* a lingering tingling there from that strange, unmarked burn she got last night moving Ravi around. The sharpness was gone now, but it flared up with a dull ache every so often.

"What happened?" he asked.

He was right to sniff out that something was wrong. It definitely should've healed away overnight. Hell, it probably should've healed away even in the time she'd been sitting at the bar chatting with Henry.

"Punishment for being too nice," she smiled.

Henry laughed for the first time since she entered the building. "Even the universe is trying to get you back on the path."

"Screw the path," Danica said dismissively. She sighed and pushed her empty glass to Henry's side of the bar. "Henry it's been great. Really. But can I go home? Please? I'm hungry, and the sun's been down for too long."

He plucked Danica's tumbler from the bar and gave her his blessing: "May you find your way home unerringly, Danica."

She shook her head. "Takes a lot more than a few cocktails to make me forget the way home, Henry. But thanks for the concern."

"—Oh, and do give Ravi my regards," he added, after Danica had her coat on.

Danica shot him with a pair of finger guns to confirm she would do just that.

"And just for you, since you're usually such a sweetheart, I won't even tell them you'd rather let them suffer and die for no reason than give me anything useful to save them."

Henry smiled. "You'll figure it out, whether I want you to or not."

And Who Exactly Do You Think You're Playing With Here, Huh?

(Evening, Saturday, 17th December)

Felicity breathed some dwindling warmth into her cupped hands while she sat on the frozen front step of Amy's apartment building. If she knew she'd get stuck out in the cold for this long, she would've brought some gloves. But *why* would she *do that* when she wasn't *supposed to* be spending this long out in the cold? Hm? —Seriously, how the hell long was Dani supposed to be gone, huh? Felicity had been out here since the sun went down – which was at *least* a whole hour ago. Sundown is dinner time, Danica!

Ugh. This was all so... *stupid.*

Turned out in her *mild* flustration, not *only* did she somehow manage to forget her phone in Amy's bathroom, but she *also* kind of grabbed the wrong key off the wall, and then forgot to test it in the door before she left. —But it's not like they were labelled! Not her fault! Dani could've given her *any kind of hint* about what set to take, damn it. Why would they even *have* a second set of entirely useless keys, huh?

Sabotage. It was sabotage. Trying to freeze Felicity to death, get her out of the picture after that blowup.

She cringed to think about that Incident that afternoon. Had she really thought she could take Dani in a fight? That woman was a beast. A bear. She could probably throw Felicity across eight lanes of traffic.

And for a second there, from the look in her eyes? Felicity was pretty sure that vicious bear was going to shove her head right through the shitty drywall in Amy's miserable apartment and toss her over the railing of that rusty fire escape out back.

Amy.

How could she stand to live like this?

It made her so mad. Even just thinking about it made her stomp her boot in a huff. She'd give anything to bring Amy back with her, back with her to a better city, to a better university, to a better *life*.

She'd been playing out a dozen scenarios in her mind all day while she was wandering around trying to find anything redeeming left in this hollowed out husk of a city – scenarios where she managed to get Amy to leave this horrible place, where she burned the university down, where she... got her evicted? Maybe? No, that was too much. — Or maybe, against all odds, Felicity could just... look her in the eye and take her hand and tell her she deserved better, and she'd just... believe her.

—A warehouse??

It wasn't right. It wasn't *right*, damn it. Amy was too good for that. —Too good for all of this.

"...Fleece?"

Dani! Jeezus, finally!

Danica approached the building while looking Felicity over with an undue amount of caution. What was she afraid of? Felicity was obviously harmless to her.

She stood up indignantly and dusted off her lap. "Took you long enough. Let me in."

Danica came to a stop beside Felicity and stared at the door with a confounded look on her face. "You... lost the key..."

"I grabbed the wrong one, thank you for that," she said accusingly, tossing the fraudulent set of keys at Danica's chest. She fumbled to catch them.

"...You took the *laundry* keys..." Danica echoed in summary, staring bewildered at the set in her hand like she'd never seen them before.

"That's what I said. Are you going to rub it in my face all night or let me in?"

"...That was my only set of keys, Fleece. Unless one of us can break into the apartment, we're both stuck out here."

"No. Come on! Seriously?"

Danica nodded.

"Why would you leave me... your only... Jeezus, Dani, you're so... *confusing*."

Felicity joined Danica in her confounded staring at the building's front door.

"We could wait for someone to go in and sneak through?" she

suggested.

"There's a camera," Danica pointed out.

"Come on, is that even real? This building's so cheap, I bet it's a decoy."

"You want to risk it?"

"...I don't even live here, what are they going to do to me?"

"How about what are they going to do to Amy if they find out? You ever want to come back here?"

Felicity clicked her tongue at that. —Yes. Obviously, she wanted to come back.

Such a smartass, hey Dani?

Danica shook her head and explained why that still wasn't enough: "Doesn't matter anyways. You need the key to use the elevator. And even if you got up, the unit door locks automatically. We're stuck here. —Unless you know how to pick a lock and hack an elevator?"

"I could learn."

"What, right now?"

"How hard can it be?"

"Have you ever *tried*?"

"Whatever! Whatever. So what do *you* want to do, huh? Dani. Big Brains Danica Doyle."

Danica let out a tired sigh. —And how dare she. Felicity was a *guest* here. A guest who'd been sitting in the cold waiting for *hours*. —Almost. Almost hours.

"Amy's probably not done work until ten," Danica reminded her idly, while typing away on her phone. "I'll send them a message now, but they never have their phone on at work, so we're kind of on our own until they get back."

Felicity just remembered something that had annoyed her earlier that day. And it just happened again. She couldn't just let Danica keep getting away with it. "Why do you keep doing that?"

"Doing what?"

"They they they. You did it earlier too when you were freaking out on me."

"...Oh. —Did I?" Danica paused for a second to put together an excuse, which only made it seem *more* rude. "Sorry, I have a friend –

enby friend – with uh... an *extremely* similar name. I guess I get it mixed up in my head sometimes?"

"It's kind of *extremely* rude. Can you stop?"

"...That's... fair enough. Uh. Thanks. For pointing it out."

Danica put her phone away with a little sigh after sending off her message, then turned on a hopeful smile, "So. Where do you want to hang out until then?"

"Oh no. No no no no no, you're not roping me into... No. No thanks. I can entertain myself, thanks. I'll just come back at eleven, thank you."

Felicity turned to leave, but she was stopped by a set of strong fingers catching her by the arm. Her whole body started to tense up for a fight, but she knew better than to act on that instinct.

—Damn bear.

"Fleece. Listen. Please."

That soft voice. Seductive. —Almost, almost seductive. That was it, though. That was how Danica did it, how she manipulated Amy.

It was so obvious hearing it now, hearing it used against her, hearing Danica's tongue painting her pleading words with honey.

She continued: "Look, I can't pretend everything's okay in front of Amy if you're still upset like this. I just can't. If you're going to be staying here, it's going to be just... *super* awkward if you're pissed off at me the whole time. You want to make her deal with that?"

Felicity tensed up her body and mind for a few seconds to try to steel herself against the sweetness of Danica's words. But it was no good. She was just too powerful. A slow hissing sigh escaped Felicity's clenched teeth. As much as she hated to admit it, Dani was probably right.

Damn it.

She turned around to face her captor with a discerning glare before challenging her sharply:

"Fine. Whatever. And where exactly can someone 'hang out' in this *nothing* of a city for four whole hours? Hm? All the theaters around here shut down. The library closed at five. The park sucks in winter. And I'm <u>not</u> just going *drinking* or *shopping* with *you*. As far as I can tell, fun is just *banned* in this city."

Danica released Felicity's arm with a warm smile. She looked quite pleased with herself, didn't she? So cheerful. And... so... grateful? *Grateful.* Just for Felicity's *consideration?*

A little twinge of guilt pricked her synapses for being so harsh and short with this cheery, warm-hearted woman.

How the hell was Dani doing this to her?

Manipulation. It was manipulation. It had to be. Some tricky words and disarming smiles.

And it was like looking into the eyes of a pleading cat – a cat who'd just turn around and start scratching up the carpet the second she got what she wanted.

Felicity wasn't that stupid.

...Was Amy?

Something was weird about Amy now, sure. —Weird*er*. —But she wasn't... stupid. She was just... tired? Maybe? Probably, from what Danica said, right? Just tired.

Not that Felicity needed *Danica* to point out that something was off. By the end of last night, Felicity had a pretty solid collection of evidence that *something* was definitely wrong back home here. She knew there was something... off between Amy and herself. —But she'd been *certain* it was just... something wrong with *herself*, not with Amy. Right? Amy never changed. She was still the same old sharp-witted genius she always was. *Felicity* must've fallen. Become boring. Committed some cardinal sin. She thought she'd lost Amy's respect or something, lost whatever it was that made her worthy of the light in Amy's eyes and the warmth in her smile.

But after finding out from *Danica* of all people that Amy had been hiding things from her, like this miserable job of hers... Maybe there was more to it. Maybe it had nothing to do with Felicity falling from grace at all. Maybe something really was wrong here. Something devastating. Something bad enough to change her dear old friend beyond recognition.

It sure would've been nice if she could've spent the day with Amy—<u>alone</u>—to maybe give her a chance to open up about anything that had been troubling her. Instead, she had to find out some secret truth from resident parasite Danica Doyle.

How was it fair? This leech got to see Amy every day, bare and honest in her own apartment, while Felicity hadn't even *seen* Amy's apartment before this visit. Eight years of not-even-annual meetings in parks and restaurants, just naïvely sleeping at her own family's house, blindly accepting every excuse Amy had to not invite her over. All that time and she couldn't even put it together that Amy was hiding something like *this*. Absolute stupidity.

Danica knew Amy better in just two months than Felicity's two whole *decades* being her best friend?

How was it fair??

But suddenly, out of that fiery pit of despair, Felicity's mind sparked with a twisted thought: *Danica knew Amy better.*

And if Felicity couldn't get Amy to open up to her in person, maybe she could at least recoup her losses for the day by extracting some of that unjustly acquired 'intimate' knowledge out of Danica instead.

She grinned to herself and prepared for the hunt ahead.

In answer to Felicity's vitriolic challenge – about finding anywhere fun to spend the night – Danica suggested a venue for the evening: A bar that was easy walking distance from the apartment with music starting at eight.

Felicity kicked up a fuss about how terrible it would probably be, but still, she couldn't think of anything better. Might be good actually. After all, getting Dani drunk would surely loosen her tongue. Maybe Felicity could even lose a few stupid wagers or something to justify paying for all the drinks herself. Yeah. She'd drown Danica in hard liquor tonight.

"Gods, I'm so hungry," Danica lamented, while leading Felicity in some random direction away from the apartment. "I've had this old guy chewing on my ear non-stop for hours."

"Too much information."

"Talking. Fleece. He was talking. About *nothing* interesting, my gods. Today was just... not the day for it."

She gave Danica a mean grin and teased her: "Oh *my mistake*. So *sorry*. I just figured, the way you dress, with a body like that, you were probably the kind of girl who could keep a guy 'talking' all day."

Danica shook her head with a smirk. "Guys are better for... *chatting*. I think I'm a little better 'conversationalist' with the ladies. —After all," she added with a knowing wink in her smile, "they've always got such interesting things to 'talk' about, don't you think?"

Felicity's mind cringed at the revelation. That meant Amy wasn't just a mark for a cheap place to sleep, was she? She was a piece of meat. A ripe target for whatever cheap, manipulative tools of seduction this predator had in her arsenal.

Like that voice.

And those eyes.

And her sharp fashion sense.

And those damn... curves...

...Felicity filed that paranoid concern away for later. Amy wouldn't fall for some lay-about over such shallow stuff.

...Right?

"...Too. Much. Information," she repeated bitterly.

"You asked!"

"I didn't ask! I was making fun of you!"

"For being pretty?? Gods your heckling game is off the charts, huh?"

Felicity groaned at Danica. This woman was so frustrating. A whole night with her was going to be a damn marathon.

"Just. Shut up and tell me where we're eating."

Danica grinned at her like a smug child and silently mouthed the name of a restaurant.

Shutting up.

And telling her where to go.

Fucking... smartass... ten-year-old...

"...On God, Danica..."

But despite Felicity's sneering, Damica refused to drop the game or lose the stupid grin on her face. She just mimed turning a key in her pursed lips and flicking it away.

Felicity was at the end of her rope here. She was hungry, too, and this was not helping her mood even a little. She couldn't think strategy like this.

"—Atomic Slice," Felicity impatiently blurted out, taking the choice out of Danica's hands, desperate to go anywhere that wasn't in the bitter cold. "They still alive? —And you can stop shutting up now, brat."

"Oh! Yeah! I love that place. We order in from there all the—"

She interrupted Danica, putting up her finger sharply, grumbling,

"Too much information."

Felicity stoically led the way to the pizza place. The route was practically programmed into her feet once she got to the intersection in front of the arena. Back when they were teenagers, she'd bussed downtown with Amy a million times after school and walked the few blocks from the stop on the corner there.

The two of them would always split a decadent box of *Atomic Arrabbiata* deep dish, a pack of those long fancy flavored cigarettes, and a bottle of delicious, warm, fake ID Sauvignon in the park. It was always a recipe for a fun evening – usually capped with a little harmless vandalism before Felicity tried to convince Amy to crash at her place, because Amy's dad was apparently kind of shitty whenever Amy came home late and wine-toasted, and Felicity's mom loved cooking for Amy. —And... it was nice. Just... nice, listening to Amy's breathing at night, sleeping in Felicity's cozy bed, an extremely platonic twelve inches away.

It was nice.

Torturous too, though, obviously, having Amy so close and so far and all the rest of that 'crushing on your best friend' bullshit she never managed to get sorted out before she left the city and that she absolutely never would get sorted out now—especially with this *parasite* crashing at Amy's place. Fuck.

Wine. She needed wine damn it. Soon. And not soon enough.

"This music place have good Sauvignon, Dani?"

"Uh. I'm not much of a wine person."

"Okay. I didn't ask. Does this place have bottles of red alcohol that taste like warm spice and decadent old grapes?"

Danica assured her that if the place didn't have any good wine, she'd pay for whatever drinks Felicity ended up getting.

Which would sound like a great deal coming from anyone else but this swindler.

Also, Felicity was supposed to be the one with her hand on the tap, controlling the flow, getting Danica sloshed.

She scoffed at Danica's thin veneer of lovable radiance. "You're worse than the fae," she said simply.

Danica's smile cracked a bit when she said it. "What d'you mean?"

"This little 'best friend' act you're doing here? That tricky smile, those… eyes. —And how do you even get your eyes doing that, by the way?"

"Doing what?"

"The… like… sparkles or whatever."

"Mm… I've been told it's probably some weird genetic thing."

"Uh huh. Very believable. Contact lenses, obviously. And that… blue…? Or… is it… like… turquoise…? Whatever that is, it's totally the wrong color. Everyone knows it's better getting swallowed up in a pair of big beautiful brown eyes than getting charmed by some swindler's *chromatic gaze*. Mistake on your part."

"Just spitting venom today," Danica replied, her smile returned and unfaltering now. Cheshire cat. "You're kind of adorable when you're angry for no reason, you know. Like a bitey little puppy."

Felicity sternly chided her, "Don't flatter me."

Danica let a stupid sounding snort escape her nose at that. "Sorry. Sorry, I wasn't. I promise. You're just so little and fighty. It's kind of cute. I bet you pull even more guys than me with such a charming little act like that."

"First of all: Gross. If you see me pulling any guys, you have a sacred sisterly duty to tell them to back off, thank you very much. Second of all: I'm always charming. —And I'm always real; nothing's an act with me. Third of all: Don't try to get me talking about my stalled love life. I see your tricks."

"Mm. Should I add that to the list? Can't talk about *my* love life. Can't talk about *your* love life. What *do* you want to talk about, Fleece?"

"Nothing! Just, walk quietly, Jeezus. How hard is that?"

"You're just going to ignore me all night," Danica flatly tried to confirm, skeptical.

Felicity shook her head sharply and rolled her eyes with a huff of a sigh. "Just stop talking please. I'm hungry and cold and you're so fucking annoying right now I don't have words."

Danica scoffed again, "Wow you really *are* just *super* charming, my gods."

"You haven't earned any charm, Dani. How about you do something *good* with your life first? Make yourself even worth the effort of charming."

That finally put a real dent in her smile. —Finally put a stop to her endless 'playful' poking at Felicity, too. This was the first time all day that Felicity felt like she might have gotten a bit of an upper hand with Danica. Finally, Felicity managed to find a vulnerable little crack in her to abuse.

Against all odds, The Atomic Slice was, as Danica said, still open for business and still exactly the same inside as she remembered: Red vinyl seating everywhere, checkerboard floors, speckled white tabletops. Timeless. Maybe this place was sacred – a temple, an untouchable sanctuary against the decay of the city.

While Danica was distractedly humming over the menu board, Felicity approached the counter and ordered her old favorite – a spicy Hawaiian the owner called The Mauna Loa – then tossed her coat in a booth by the window before scooting down the seat to wait for the food.

Danica joined her a minute later on the other side.

"What'd you get?" Dani casually asked.

"Why do you care?" Felicity jabbed at her.

"Felicity. Please. Please just pretend. Just pretend you can put up with me for five whole minutes, holy hell."

She hesitated for a second before she answered, since it would be obvious anyways as soon as it was on the table: "...Hawaiian. And I don't want to hear one word about pineapples—"

"Oh, no way. That's hilarious—"

"—I just said I don't want to hear—!"

"—No no, I'm not making fun of you. I got the same thing." Danica put a discerning finger to her chin to look Felicity over. "I'd never have taken you for a Hawaiian kind of girl, Fleece. You've got more of a 'deluxe' flair. Or maybe something with artichokes."

"...It started out being ironic. You know, turning heads, like, '*Haha, who orders pineapples on pizza? So crazy.*' But it turns out if you pretend to like something for long enough, you run the risk of just liking it for real."

"Oh? So if I can just get you to pretend to like me for long enough – ironically, of course – then we might still have a chance here?"

Felicity scoffed. "Sure Dani. Terrible idea. Love it."

"So you'll do it?"

"Do what?"

"Pretend? Just for tonight! Ironically. You know, like, '*Haha, who could ever like Danica Doyle, the reprehensible scheming manipulative bitch with the tricky eyes? So crazy.*' "

Felicity sneered at the stupidity of it. Danica really was that naïve, wasn't she? Did she want to make things better with Felicity so badly? What, for Amy? What a joke.

But then it clicked for her – that this was the perfect wedge to drive into that little crack of hers.

It was a plan right out of the third-grade playground politics playbook. '*You want to be my friend? You want to get invited to my birthday party? Get on your knees. Beg. Lick the matte off my boots.*'

All she had to do was play along. Pretend, like Dani wanted. Get close. Give her hope. Then just pull away whenever dear desperate Danica refused to cooperate. Hold kindness for ransom.

After considering it for a while, Felicity eventually 'reluctantly' agreed to play along: "Sure. Why not. Like a B movie: You're such a bad friend that it's hilarious to watch you get away with it."

"There we go."

"I love spending time with my best friend's saboteur," Felicity continued, mocking the idea.

"Perfect."

"The fact that we like the same pizza is definitely cute and fun and not making me a little sick to my stomach."

"Wow you're so good at this!"

"Oh fuck off, Dani."

Danica crossed her arms and shot Felicity with another grin. This one was sly. Like a fox this time. Trickster behavior inbound.

"You really let me get under your skin that easy, huh? I bet you can't even go a whole hour without getting all huffy at me."

Felicity closed her eyes and took a deep breath before she shook her head and scolded Danica, "You really think I'm that stupid, don't you?"

"How's this: No swearing, no insults. Pull it off and dinner's on me. *And* cover for the show. *And* drinks. —<u>*And*</u> I'll sleep out on the fire escape tonight, if you win."

Felicity raised an eyebrow at that. The last bit of the wager there was actually an enticing proposal.

"Do I still have to pretend to like you?"

"Can't hurt."

But that was oh so very *au contraire*. The pain. Unbearable.

Danica put on a sad, pleading smile. It even looked sincere. Then she reminded Felicity why she was putting on this stupid show at all: "—For Amy?"

Felicity shot her with a subtle sneer. Unbelievable the nerve of this woman, seriously, holding Amy's happiness hostage like this. The monster sure wasn't planning to make this wager easy, was she?

Felicity looked over her shoulder at the kitchen to see what exactly was taking so long. She needed some food in her if she had any hope of getting control of this situation. She was starving.

She sighed and turned back to Danica and tried her very best to 'pretend' to be cordial. "Fine. Let's play out this little fairytale of yours, then. For Amy." Felicity shook her head, but figured this might be a good chance at a smoothish segue to start prying precious info out of Danica. "—And hey, speaking of Amy, what's she up to these days? Other than ruining her body at that warehouse."

"I mean, I think she looks pretty hot with all the muscle, no? You should see her abs. My gods."

"...And why have *you* seen Amy's abs?"

"Uh. You know. In a towel? After a shower?"

"In a towel. What, she's just, hanging out in that shitty little apartment with you, tits out, hot abs on display, and she's totally cool with you gawking at her the whole time?"

"I can't sneak a glance?"

"You can't just be normal?"

"It is *perfectly normal* to appreciate your roommate's dreamy midriff." She leaned over the table to offer a teasing jab at Felicity, "You wouldn't look?"

"...Of course I would look."

"See?"

"That's very, *very* different! I've already seen her in swimsuits and stuff! I'm her *best friend!*"

"Mhm. So *very* different. —Perv."

Felicity could feel some heat flushing her face. She planted her elbows on the table and buried her face in her hands. "Can you please be quiet."

"Aw, come on Felicity, I'm just teasing you." Danica ducked down a bit to try to catch Felicity's eyes. "Hey, I know you're worried about her, but she really does take care of herself. I promise. She does stretches and stuff, and sleeps as much as she possibly can."

"And how much is that?"

"Enough."

"No details, huh?"

"Sorry Fleece. —If you want to know what she's up to these days, why don't you just ask her yourself?"

"Lot of good that does," Felicity scoffed. "As if she'd answer me."

Danica's smile faded. She drummed her fingers pensively on the table while she scanned Felicity's bitter glare and mulled something over. At last, with words absolutely sopping wet with pity, she pointed out something that should have been obvious to Felicity:

"Would you even believe me if I told you?"

Oh. Huh. That was actually... a slightly critical flaw in her plan for the evening, wasn't it? What good would it do to carve information out of a stone that only ever chips out lies?

Danica put a pair of steepled fingers to her chin, pointing to her stupid smug grin, for a few long seconds while she waited for Felicity to respond.

But Felicity couldn't think of anything to say. There was no way to answer that challenge. Danica was... *right.* Bleh.

At last, when Danica was out of patience, she shot Felicity with a hopeful smile. "How about another game, then?" she offered, in a weird voice. Like... a *hungry* voice?

"A game?"

"A game. With rules. Right? I'm good at following rules. And if I'm following the rules, you can definitely trust me, no?"

"Rules...? What, like... Truth or Dare or something?"

Danica rolled her shoulders and swelled her posture, making herself even bigger than usual before she teased Felicity: "Oh, I'm sure I can do better than *that.*"

The grin on her face grew sharp and... frankly, kind of scary? A chill put goosebumps on the back of Felicity's neck when Danica smiled.

And she could swear those weird contact lenses of hers lit up in a greenish flash, like a pair of little fireworks, before Danica blinked that unnatural light away.

Seriously, how was she doing that?

Felicity hadn't seen this in her before. This... almost... *cruelty* in the way Danica was speaking to her and looking at her. Even when Dani was tearing into her back at the apartment, she hadn't been cruel or malicious. She was just defending herself, defending Amy. This, though... This was... *dark*.

Danica continued on with planning the game while Felicity wavered on the offer. She hummed to herself and spoke like she was walking through a fragrant garden for the first time in years: "Mmm... Give me a minute here... I haven't played a game like this with anyone in a long time," she said, her words dripping with nostalgia. "But for you, Fleece, I think I can make an exception. You've earned it."

"...And how did I earn it exactly?"

Danica only answered Felicity's question by sharpening her grin. Then she slowly splayed her fingers out on the table and presented the rules:

> *Three questions each, we'll play in turns*
> *about your dear Amy's concerns.*
>
> *Of the three, just precious two*
> *must be answered golden true.*
>
> *That vile other answer, though,*
> *true or twisted, you will never know.*

Felicity quirked an eyebrow at the childish rhyme and the stupidity of the game – though she had to admit, there was something strangely compelling about it. "So... Two Truths and a Lie? What is this? An icebreaker at some lame office party?"

Danica let that jab roll right off her, undaunted. "You game?"

"...Who goes first?"

Danica abruptly curled her definitely empty hands into fists and presented them to Felicity. "There's a coin. If you want to play, pick a hand. Winner chooses the order."

Felicity couldn't escape Danica's cunning gaze while she considered whether to play or not. This was definitely some kind of scam. Some scheme. Right? But she couldn't figure out the trick.

A seductive voice whispered in her ear, though, to challenge her better judgement. It was her own voice. A desperate voice. *What could it hurt?* Right? What did she have to lose? She'd get some information about Amy for free. And it was always easy to tell the truths from the lies in these games. She always guessed it right with other people. Danica was sharp, but there's no way she could outplay Felicity in a game like this.

Though she did say, '*You will never know.*' Sounded kind of ominous too when she said it, didn't it? Felicity assumed it meant she would never be able to confirm the truths and the lies. That's not normally how the game worked, though. The big reveal at the end was the funnest part.

"How do you even win a game like this if you can't guess the lie properly?"

"Oh, there's no winning. It's like tag. Just fun. Exercise. Enrichment. The terror. The *thrill.*"

"...You are being *real* creepy Danica."

"Oh, I'm just playing with you, Fleece," she said, relaxing her posture and letting all the malice out of her grin. Then she rattled her fists for Felicity to remind her that there was supposedly a concealed prize of a coin in one of them and a choice to make before the game could begin.

Felicity lowered her calculating gaze to Danica's hands. One fist was clenched slightly tighter, slightly less shaky. A decoy? How clever *was* Danica?

—No. Just keep it simple. Follow your gut.

She was amazed to find that she guessed correctly. She thought for sure Danica was going to pull some kind of shell game scam on her.

There definitely wasn't a coin in her hand when she closed that fist though.

Magic trick? Showing off?

"I'll go first," Felicity said, after considering it for a few moments.

"You got it. What's your question?"

Felicity shushed her and told her not to rush it.

"You don't even have a question ready?? I thought you were all pumped to find out about Amy already."

"I just said don't rush me! I'll tell you when I think of something.

Just, chill out."

Felicity crossed her arms and dropped her head to stare at her lap while she wracked her brain trying to think of the best way to ask these questions, to extract as much information as possible. She tapped her finger on her bicep while she worked away at it.

Yes-or-no questions would be easiest to tell if they were true or not.

Anecdotes would be the most revealing.

Some middle ground?

Not *what*...

"...*How*... did Amy... quit smoking?" Testing the waters there, to see how Danica was going to play the game. That one was way before Danica knew Amy. There's no way she could answer it. Felicity had a few big questions bubbling up in her mind, but those would have to wait until she was sure she knew how to play her hand.

Danica grinned at that, genuinely delighted. "Love that. Love that, Fleece, very clever. Sadly, I can't answer that one."

"What do you mean you can't answer it? That's not how this works. Just lie if you can't tell the truth."

Danica shrugged playfully. " 'How' requires the thing to have actually happened in some way or another. Can't lie about the details of a thing that doesn't even have a truth, you know? It's a good question. Practically a freebie, you devil."

Felicity stared dumbfounded at Danica. "You're taking this really seriously, aren't you?"

"I always take games seriously! Honesty and integrity are *extremely* important. What am I without my reputation, huh?"

Felicity thought about that non-answer and considered what exactly Danica had just revealed. "...So, she never quit, then? Is that it? It didn't happen? ...She's just been hiding it from me...?"

Danica shrugged. "I didn't say that. I just *graciously* explained the reason I can't answer. —Which means it's still your turn, Fleece. And how about you ask me one I *can* answer this time? Freebies aren't very *sporting*."

Felicity drummed her fingers on the table while she considered whether or not to play along with Danica's request to play fair. After all, Felicity *could* just be clever about it, mess with the rules like that all night. That was a hell of a loophole there. And there was probably *some way* to phrase any question to make it unanswerable in a way that still managed to answer it.

But she didn't really want to spend all night trying to figure that out. And if Danica was going to be so serious about it, it only felt right for Felicity to be 'sporting'.

She still wanted to get a question out of the way that she knew Danica would have to lie about. That way she'd know the other answers would have to be true.

So... something Danica would still be *able* to answer, but that she didn't have enough information to answer truthfully? About Amy. God, but Felicity didn't know anything more about Amy than Danica did anymore, did she?

...So maybe just something so *embarrassing* that she'd never tell the truth?

—Ohhh. Oh-ho-ho, yeah. That was good. The nasty swindler of a woman would never...

Felicity pointed her index finger dramatically at Danica when she challenged her:

"What was the biggest lie you ever told Amy? —That she still believes."

Danica's smile faded. Her eyes narrowed on Felicity. She was making a big show of putting a lot of consideration into her answer. Like she was trying to remember. Like it was heavy on her.

So, no way she was going to tell the truth here. Constructing a convincing fiction, right? What a shallow performance.

Danica asked to clarify before she answered, "Are we including 'misleading someone' in our definition of lying here?"

"Yes? Obviously?"

She paused for a long breath, and held it in for a few shaky, trepidatious seconds.

"I'll stay," she answered at last, morosely. "I told her I would stay. I even signed a little contract on it. She thought I meant for a long time. But I didn't. It wasn't even my signature," she laughed at herself pathetically about it. "She doesn't know. —And I'd very much appreciate you not telling her."

"You forged your name on a lease?"

"...Something like that."

"Sketchy! That's so sketchy! You are never allowed to pretend to be a good person again, Danica, that's awful!"

"Come on, Fleece, I did it to make her feel better. She was scared and lonely. —I think. I don't know. I don't know if it helped, but it was the only thing I could think to do."

"No excuse! Damn right I'm going to tell her!"

Danica crossed her arms and spoke sternly, "Okay. You could tell her. But do you know I'm telling the truth? For all you know, I've never lied to her at all, and I'm lying to *you* right now, just to make you look like a lunatic in front of her."

Felicity aggressively crinkled her nose at Danica. She was right. — Again. If Felicity did just start raving at Amy about some bullshit Danica made up, then she'd look like she was just... blatantly trying to make Danica look bad. *Felicity* would look like the asshole.

And... realistically, there's no way *Danica* would tell the truth about something like this, right? Forging a lease? She sure made it sound convincing with that little sob story there, but... come on. That was so fake. Outrageous. She was obviously just trying to play with Felicity's expectations, pretending to be extra sketchy, right? Just to trap her?

Felicity shook her head. *Unbelievable.* The rules sounded so easy, but Danica was still just going to play Felicity this whole game, wasn't she? Fill her with doubt.

What had she gotten herself into?

There must be some better way to ask these questions...

Danica didn't wait for Felicity to recover from that assault before she followed up with her own jabbing question:

"What's the biggest lie *you* ever told her?"

Felicity froze for a breath before she slowly, sheepishly raised her eyes to Danica's. She had very much forgotten, in her tunnel visioned machinations, that she was going to be subjected to a bunch of tricky questions herself.

And there's no way she could waste her lie on the very first question. Could she? Danica probably had some terrifying traps lined up for her. This obviously wasn't the first time she'd played this game.

...Though... nothing was really holding Felicity to the rules of the game. She could just cheat and lie for every answer. Danica would never know. It wasn't exactly sportsmanlike, but at least cheating wouldn't be obvious, not like the freebie thing.

Actually, for all she knew, even Danica was planning to lie every time.

Yeah. Yeah, sure, why not. She didn't owe this woman any dignity or honor. She sure hadn't earned it. Felicity just wanted answers about Amy. Rules be damned.

"Hold on," she said, holding up her hand to tell Danica to wait. "Unlike *you*, I've got like *two decades* of lies to sift through here, and none of them stand out as much as *yours*, you monster."

"Oh, that's fine, take your time," Danica said with a warm smile. "We've got a whole night to kill."

While Felicity was putting on a big show about humming over an answer, the guy behind the counter, finally, cheerfully, dropped off a little Mauna Loa pizza for each of them. He also placed a dry cider in front of Felicity and a bottle of some kind of pinkish vodka mixed drink in front of Danica.

She grinned at Felicity. "I see we're both on the same page here."

"Just get me through the night," Felicity said, offering her bottle up for a cheers.

Danica tapped Felicity's bottle with her own and added on, "May no blood be spilled."

"It'll be yours though, if there is any."

"Oh yeah?"

"I bite."

"You think I'm above biting, Fleece? I have pretty sharp teeth you know." Danica put on a huge wolfy grin, licking her canines hungrily to show them off, and sure enough, they were *way* pointier than they had any right to be at her age. It was like they'd never been used.

"You're way too big to need to resort to biting, Danica, Jeezus. — Hey, normal question for you: Were you actually going to smash my face in right after I woke up with a hangover today or were you just trying to make me piss myself?"

Dani didn't respond with anything but a playful grin, then she started in on her pizza, immediately yelping and whining from burning her tongue on the first bite.

How was this ridiculously soft and cuddly woman so intimidating? How was this towering *beast* so disarming? Seriously, just, flip of the switch, she could be however she wanted? There was no Earthly explanation and it made Felicity's head spin trying to keep up.

How was she supposed to know if this woman was a naïve puppy or a vicious wolf if she kept throwing Felicity off like this?

After a few minutes of eating silently, trying to think of a good lie, and being utterly distracted with troubling over how impossible and tricky Danica was, Felicity had to ask something, just to make sure:

"Do you believe in magic, Dani?"

Danica hurried through chewing a bite of pizza before she answered in a slightly more serious tone than Felicity was expecting: "I do. Why?"

"...Do you *know* magic?"

"I know some magic tricks, sure," she said, wiggling her fingers whimsically in the air before producing a quarter in her palm, just like she did earlier. "And some little blessings and curses and stuff."

"So, what, like Wiccan stuff?"

"Mm... not quite, but... something like that, I guess. Read enough books and you can pick up some pretty cool tricks, right? —Weird line of questioning here, Fleece. Tell me about your religious beliefs next, hm?"

"It's not... Sorry, I was just thinking you've got a kind of unreal... *vibe* sometimes. I can't figure you out."

Danica cocked her head to the side and gave Felicity an incredulous look, "So you think I'm... what, enchanted? —Hold on, did you actually *mean it* yesterday when you said you think magic might be real? I thought you were just being poetic."

"What's wrong with that?" Felicity asked in an indignant huff. "You believe it!"

"I just figured you were a woman of science and proof and all that. *I* bailed on a *humanities* program in second year."

"Like I said yesterday, *if you were paying attention*, it just seems *unlikely* that everyone everywhere forever believes in it if it's not real."

"So reality is a democracy now? Magic exists by popular vote?"

"It's unlikely! Okay! I just think it's unlikely that there's nothing magic in the universe. Just let me have my little fantasies about it, Jeezus."

"And your little fantasy is... that... what, I'm using magic on you? —

Oh! You think I put a spell on Amy! Is that it? Oh, that's <u>it</u>, isn't it? Oh my gods Felicity, you're so cute I swear."

Felicity bit her tongue. No swearing. No swearing, and then Danica would freeze out on the fire escape and all Amy's problems would disappear.

"Amy's not stupid enough to fall for some swindler's tricks like this," she insisted bitterly, to explain her theory.

"So—" Danica started, but she couldn't help stopping to titter like an idiot at herself for a few seconds before she continued, "Sorry. So let me get it right. Your equation here, is that I convinced Amy to let me stay with her, and Amy is too smart to fall for some huckster's con – and the *only way* to balance that equation for you is... *magic*."

Felicity felt some heat in her cheeks. She dropped her eyes from Danica's to hide what was clearly going to look like embarrassment, but it was *not* embarrassment, it was rage. Just pure, unbridled... rage.

Danica didn't wait long enough for Felicity to put a response together before she continued lecturing her: "You ever hear of Occam's Razor, Fleece?"

"Yes I've heard of Occam's Razor, *Danica*. I'm not ff... fr... freaking ten years old."

Danica grinned at her, "Good save."

"Shut up."

"And you don't think that maybe the simplest solution here is that I'm *not* actually taking advantage of her at all? Maybe she just wants to help me because she's nice like that? No? No. Magic. It's gotta be magic."

Felicity placed her hands flat on the table, trying to contain herself. "Okay can we drop it," she flatly insisted. "I was just asking. Ruling it out."

"Did you... Sorry, did you really think that if I *was* somehow using magic on her that I would just *admit it?*"

"I don't know! Maybe!"

"I'm sorry to mess up your fantasy, Fleece, but I've never used a single breath of a spell on her. I never would've needed to! She's just nice like that. Like, way, *way* too nice.

"Gods, it's frustrating, honestly. I'll probably be paying her back for all of this kindness for the rest of her life. —And I *will* pay her back,

Felicity. I pay my debts. Always. —And I will fight you to the first blood if you *ever* try to tell me I don't."

Felicity tapped her finger on the shiny surface of the table a dozen times before she gave up on finding a response to that.

Danica was very good at sounding earnest. At *looking* earnest. Very good. Too good. When Danica looked at her with those soft eyes, it made Felicity feel that even *trying* to dig into her was just as heinous a crime as trying to drown a helpless little kitten. It was infuriating.

Felicity continued turning over possible lies in her head while the two of them ate in silence under the serenade of a tinny speaker playing a local radio station – a station that felt the need to interrupt the music every other song to remind you that you were listening to an uninterrupted stream of the best rock music of all time.

Felicity scoffed to herself after hearing the announcement for the third time. "I totally forgot how much I used to hate this station. I swear they must've been playing the same ten songs on repeat for decades by now."

"Well, they *are* the best ten rock songs of all time. Can you blame them?"

Felicity let out a stifled snicker at Danica's bad joke, but she managed to catch the joy in her throat and swallow it down before it could do any harm. She was *not* going to be seduced by this villain.

She was *not* going to let herself see a glimpse of human warmth in this beast.

She was absolutely *not* going to let herself be poisoned with doubt.

Danica was a parasite, and Felicity needed to be strong here, to keep Danica out of her head and keep up her resolve. Because who else was there? Who else could possibly tell Amy how crazy all of this was? To let some random *stranger* into her apartment for *months*, just to leech off her kindness? It was insane. It was insane! Anyone could see it! But apparently there was just no one around to say it.

...But. But there was always a chance, wasn't there? Felicity could be wrong. It had happened a couple times before. And that might be... kind of a serious problem this time, because if Danica really *was*... as warm and as kind and generous as she pretended to be? If all that wasn't just an act? Then maybe Danica was actually... *good* for Amy. Maybe she was a source of peace. And stability. Hell, maybe she was the only thing keeping Amy going anymore, the only thing helping

Amy get through her miserable warehouse shifts.

The way Amy smiled at Danica? It made Felicity nauseous. But maybe that wasn't... Maybe it wasn't because Danica was a deceptive, manipulative monster at all. Maybe it was something else. Something Felicity *really* didn't want to deal with.

—Jealousy?

No. No she couldn't... —She missed her shot. She missed it and it wasn't...

—God, get over it, Felicity, fuck.

But... if it was... *that*. If *that* was blinding her? If there was even a possibility that she might be wrong about Danica, then maybe, somehow, she might also be wrong about—

She mumbled a few uneasy half-formed words, "...Hey. Dani. Is... is Amy—"

—happy?

She caught herself before she could finish giving breath to the question, though. She couldn't waste a turn in this truth telling game on something like that. *Obviously* Amy was miserable. Obviously. What a stupid idea...

It wasn't even her turn to ask anyways. She still had to feed Danica some stupid lie about a lie.

Felicity stared morosely at her nearly empty plate. She flicked an orphaned piece of pineapple around while she finished crafting her answer.

"I told her I liked her cooking."

"*That's* the worst lie??"

"I'll never forgive myself."

"What kind of food?"

"Blueberry muffin."

"What was wrong with it?"

"One question!"

"Come on. I gave you such a good answer. You can't add a bit more flavor?"

"...Fine. *Fine*. She put in way too much salt and somehow she managed to burn the outside while leaving the inside entirely uncooked. I ate it all anyways."

"That's very noble of you."

"I'm a good friend."

"I know. She's unbelievably lucky to have you." She paused for a moment before she replied with a cunning jab, "I've never seen Amy bake anything. She's not really into all that 'girly' stuff, is she?"

"...She... used to be?" Lie. Amy had never baked anything in the entire time Felicity knew her.

"Really?"

"Hey! Danica! You know what! It's my turn! Stop asking questions! Miss Freebies Are Unsporting."

Felicity silently swore at herself for coming up with such a terrible lie. How was she supposed to know Danica knew Amy well enough to know she hated baking? God, now it was all ruined. She'd have to tell the truth for the other two or Dani might catch her cheating, and there'd be no way to beat her if that happened.

And now she had to think of a clever question. —And she still wasn't even sure if Danica had lied for the first one.

This was not going to plan even a little bit.

She popped that last cold piece of pineapple in her mouth and went to the washroom to wash her hands and clear her head a bit.

By the time she returned, Danica had finished off her last slice and was just returning from clearing off the table. She gave Felicity a look like she wanted to head out.

The prospect of wandering around the city aimlessly with Danica wasn't exactly appealing to Felicity right now. But there was no use hanging out here now that their food was gone.

Once they got out the door, Danica looked up at the sky to think for a few seconds about where to go.

"Oh! You like books."

Felicity cracked a smile at the humble assessment of her interest in bibliography. "Yes, Danica, I like books."

"There's this cool book shop a couple blocks over."

"...Still open at 7?"

"It's a café-slash-bookshop thing. The books are kind of the attraction that keeps people in the building. They do readings sometimes. Open mic poetry and prose. Comfy chairs and coffee tables and stuff. It's nice! I bet you'll love it."

"I'm not really into *new* books so much."

"The new release section is like, half a shelf. 99% of the stock is decades old, and they have a huge collection of personal journals from patrons. It's kind of cool. They have a whole donation and exchange system set up. Like a library sort of."

Felicity was dumbfounded at the implications of that. "They're... they're storing... journals... and old books... in a *coffee shop*...? Oh my god, the humidity... Never mind that, the coffee smell is going to get caked right into the paper! This is a *crime*."

"Want to go?"

"Are you kidding? Yes obviously I want to go!"

Felicity had to confirm this atrocity for herself. She was outraged. Imagine if any *good* books were on the shelves. She couldn't forgive herself if she just stood back and let some limited-edition print get *violated* like that. —The journals alone would be priceless!

Danica explained on the way that the place also had a huge zine collection.

"Zines..." Felicity echoed distantly.

"Little... uh... like, pamphlet things."

"Yeah, I know what a zine is."

Danica gave her a quizzical look.

She mused on it uneasily, "I never even thought about... Wow, there must be... so many..." She shook her head, bewildered by the suddenly revealed gravity of this new branch of work she'd need to do to complete her 'aggregation of the humblest human literature' project in full. "Well, that's going to add like a whole... *decade* to my work... Maybe more. No, *definitely* more... Jeezus..."

"What will?"

"Tracking them all down, and scanning every little half-forgotten zine in the world, and translating them all into the database's universal language. Hell, just the ones in *this city* would probably take *forever* to catalog..."

Danica gave her a warm smile and suggested she might need a slightly bigger team if she wanted to immortalize *everyone's* forgotten stories.

Felicity's mind was swimming thinking about it, leaving her far too distracted to respond.

She'd have to...

—And then there was the...

—And the funding...

—And storing a print backup for every single...

—How would you even *translate* half the quirky ideas in a queer culture zine? Every one of them would need to be linked to some supplementary *textbook*.

By the time Danica stopped Felicity to let her know they had arrived at the criminally-run café-slash-bookshop, she had half a grant proposal written up in her head and a mental list of promising undergrads she could tap to help get the initiative started.

Danica mercifully left Felicity to explore the stacks for a while while she ordered a drink. She managed to find a couple rare books in the shelves, but they weren't for sale. As expected, the humidity and coffee oils in the air were wreaking havoc on the pages. She ached to see it. She'd have to have a chat with the owner about it when she had a chance.

She sat down to read, carefully opening the book only half-way to make sure she wasn't doing any extra harm to the poor thing's spine, while Danica sat nearby drinking a cup of tea and perusing some new romance novel.

After sitting and reading in silence for ten minutes, Felicity couldn't stand it anymore and had to poke fun at her: "You're surrounded by the literary pillars of humanity and you're just going to read some smut, huh?"

Danica looked up, shaken from her reading by Felicity's voice, and tried to explain that she'd already read most of the other books in the store. "The interesting ones, anyways."

"...What are you talking about? There are like—" Felicity took a quick glance around the shop and did a little visual calculus. "—three thousand books in here."

"Well. Okay, I might have skimmed a few."

Felicity noted that Danica was already halfway through the novel in her hand.

She caught Felicity's discerning gaze and told her that she was a fast reader.

"No kidding."

Danica shrugged. "You know, there are too many books. If I had forever, I don't think I could read them all. I mean, the world's going to burn to a crisp eventually, and your immortalization project there definitely won't capture all of them in time," she said. A playful jab, but it hurt a bit to hear it. The truth was a little cutting. Eternity is a long, and probably impossible time frame. But it was a guiding light.

But even in the short term – centuries scale – eventually Felicity's project would have to outlive her, and she'd have to trust whoever came after her to be as diligent in capturing even the most mundane of journals. And if her slow pace kept up, maybe Danica was right. Could she really hope to scan books, journals, and zines faster than they were being produced? How much of humanity's story would be lost by the end of the Earth?

Felicity looked down at the old book in her own hands. As far as she knew, it hadn't been scanned yet. And if she gave it priority, what other story would be pushed out of the queue and lost forever? What made a 'good' book?

Danica interrupted her deep thoughts to remind her, "By the way, your hour's almost up." She held up her phone, which was counting down a timer to the end of the restriction on Felicity's coarser language.

Twenty seconds left.

Felicity's brow creased in thought. She was supposed to feel like celebrating right now. The final stretch. Victory inches from her fingertips. What an easy win. Danica had barely been speaking to her for the last half-hour.

Ten seconds.

Did she really want so badly for Danica to suffer like that, though? Was she that vindictive? Making her sleep out in the cold?

Danica wouldn't *actually* follow through with it. Right?

Five seconds.

Four.

Three.

...Damn it...

"Ahh... Fuck you," Felicity said, bitterly, at the last possible moment.

Danica was shocked for a second, struck silent while the timer beeped. Then she silenced her phone and stuffed it in some pocket in her coat while blessing Felicity with a warm smile. Not smug. Just. Warm. Grateful. Disarming.

This woman.

"Just couldn't hold it in, huh?" she teased Felicity.

Felicity gave her a mean sneer, cut with a hint of a smile while she echoed: "Couldn't hold it in. You're just such a reprehensible, scheming, manipulative bitch, you know? What can I say?" She paused for a breath before she added, "And you were going to win either way, weren't you? Amy'd never forgive me for making you sleep out in the cold."

Danica gave her a coy smile, but she didn't respond, and instead just went back to racing through that trashy novel of hers.

The café kicked them out at 8, which meant they'd be late for the show, but Danica insisted it was no big deal. "Every one of their songs is amazing, don't worry."

On the walk over, Felicity's nostalgia was taking over her brain and feeding her a craving for one of those fancy cigarettes to chase the lingering taste of her old favorite pizza.

It had been years since she smoked, though. Probably not a good idea.

But just one?

She could have just one.

Right?

When Felicity told Danica she was going to pop into a convenience store to grab a pack, Danica was a little surprised.

"You still smoke? I haven't seen you with a cigarette since you got here."

"It's fine, I'm just feeling it tonight."

"...Is that a good idea?"

"What are you, the fun police?"

"...I mean, you gotta do you, just... I don't know, seems like a waste to throw away years of sobriety like that. You must've quit for a reason, right?

Felicity didn't respond to that.

So Danica continued, "I just want to go on record if Amy ever asks why you started up again: I'm not encouraging this *questionable* behavior."

"...Sure, Dani. I'll enter that into the record. You care about my lungs. Very sweet of you."

"Mm... that's not quite... I mean as much as I don't want you to junk up your lungs, it's not really about that. It's about your convictions, about who you want to be. I think people are at their best—" Danica said, starting in on some grand sanctimonious philosophy, "—when they're truly themselves, exposed to the world for who they really are, masks and chains thrown to the wind. And you're pretty amazing, Fleece, the way you live, mask off the whole time, shameless – real, right? So, like, why would you betray yourself and put your chains back on? You stopped smoking. That took a lot of work. You obviously want to be the kind of person who doesn't smoke, right? That's who you are. That's you at your best. At your most honest. It just sucks for me, seeing people compromise on stuff like that, especially just for some little moment of weakness, you know? I don't like just standing by and quietly *enabling* stuff like that."

"And yet, you're perfectly fine enabling Amy's shitty life."

"I'm not. I'm not fine with that. It hurts knowing she's not living her best life. But I have to respect her choices, you know? And help her make the best of that. I mean, *I don't know* what's best for her. This might just be who she wants to be. She might not want to pursue some grandiose higher purpose. That's *your* vision for her, Fleece. And it's a very sweet vision, it really is, but, honestly, have you even *asked her* what she wants to do? Who she wants to be? If she's happy?"

"...Dress it up however you want, Danica, but what you do? It sure looks a lot like enabling her misery to me."

"...It's different."

"And how do you know? How are you supposed to know, huh? What's the difference? What's the difference between supporting someone's dreams, and enabling their self-destructive behavior? How do I fucking *know*, Danica? *How do you know?* Because all *I* know is she could be so much happier doing *anything* else. So you fucking tell me. So fucking smart about it. Tell me right now: How am I supposed to know what to do for her?"

"Ask."

Felicity scoffed loudly and bitterly. "*Ask!* Fucking, *ask* she says. — She didn't even tell me she was ruining herself in that warehouse, Danica. Had to hear that from *you*. So what exactly am I supposed to ask? She's just going to sugarcoat it, hide everything from me, pretend she's happy. God, we used to be…—" She choked on the word before it could escape her throat. She shouldn't say it. It wasn't right. And even if it was right, it wasn't ready for the air. And even if it was ready, it wasn't for *Danica* of all people.

The look in Danica's eyes was full of an *embarrassing* amount of pity. Felicity looked away and left that bleeding heart bear outside to enter the shop to make her *conviction-betraying* purchase.

But apparently they were out of stock today – much to the surprise of the lady behind the counter.

After the cashier told her, Felicity chuckled low to herself before she snapped and crouched down and curled into herself to swear, far too loudly, at the floor: "*Fuck!* God *fucking* damn it!! Can't this *fucking* city get anything right??"

After a few furious guttural breaths, she noticed the cashier was standing back from the counter, terrified. Felicity gathered her composure and apologized profusely and told the poor woman she had done nothing wrong. "It has been. A *whole* day. I'm so sorry. You're good. I'm leaving. Thank you. Sorry."

Her face was hot with rage and shame when she returned to Danica, empty-handed. —Which *obviously* made the self-important bitch smile, like she'd won, like she'd convinced Felicity to be 'true to herself' or some bullshit.

"They didn't have any," Felicity grumbled, to wipe the smile off Dani's face.

"Lucky you."

"Yeah. *Lucky* me," Felicity echoed bitterly. "Let's just go. I'm sick of this…"

It sure felt like Danica was taking the long way getting to the bar. They definitely crossed the same street at least five times going back and forth. But it gave Felicity enough time to cool off and put things in perspective in her head. And once everything was in perspective, she had to bitterly admit to herself that it was, in fact, probably better that she didn't get any cigarettes. —But she would never, *ever* admit that to Dani. She'd never live it down.

They were about half an hour late getting to the show, as expected, but they hadn't missed too much. And Felicity had to admit, the music was pretty good. Maybe the city wasn't entirely irredeemable if it attracted bands like this here and there. Both her and Danica's toes and fingers were tapping the whole time. It was taking a *herculean* effort to keep from sprinting over to the little dance floor to get some of her aggression out, but she wasn't about to expose herself like that in front of Danica.

Felicity noted that her regrettable bar mate this evening seemed to be into fruity cocktails, which kind of felt like no surprise. And the wine was passable, so Felicity had to pay for the whole decanter herself, since she 'lost' that bet with Dani about the swearing.

Eventually, shortly after ten presumably – after the two of them were a good few drinks in – Danica's coat started buzzing. Amy calling.

She fumbled in her pockets trying to find the phone, and in her rush, ended up dropping the coat and spilling some documents out on the floor. She hurriedly picked them up and tossed them on the table in a rough pile next to their envelope before she rushed out of the noisy lobby to take the call.

—*Temptation.*

Felicity knew she probably shouldn't snoop, but obviously she was going to anyways. She might be warming up to Danica a little bit, but she still didn't trust her even as far as she could bodycheck her.

She looked over her shoulder to make sure Danica was well out of sight before she subtly thumbed through the stack of paper.

...Single pages of lengthy letters that didn't mean much to her... Notes in some... *vaguely* familiar language that *very much* hadn't been in use in at least the last century, from Felicity's fuzzy memory of her research... And one of the letters wouldn't unfold at all for some reason. Held shut. Not by glue, though.

She fiddled with it to try to pry the paper apart, and when she did, she saw something... remarkable. Something... Well, maybe there was some kind of experimental paper in some lab somewhere that had some kind of... tactile luminesce to it, but... she'd never seen anything like this before. The folded paper lit up in white ink in what looked like a stylish blend of a star chart and a circuit board when she pried a little too hard. Then the luminous lines and symbols faded away to nothing again.

So.

That.

Was.

Not a little Wiccan curse or blessing or whatever hokey magic Danica was hinting at earlier.

Her heart was pounding in her ears while she held the supernaturally sealed note in her shaky hands. And when she spotted Danica at the bar ordering another drink, she panicked and hastily stuffed the note down her shirt and into the modest space under her lingerie so Dani wouldn't spot her playing with it.

—Which was probably the stupidest thing she'd done all day – even more than grabbing the wrong set of keys off the wall *or* picking a fight with someone twice her size.

But it was far too late to put it back in the pile now. She'd only just barely managed to stash it away, just half a second before Danica turned around.

Dani apologized for leaving her papers all over the table and gathered them back up to return them to her coat.

She didn't notice.

Felicity's guts felt like they were twisting their way into her lungs from how sick and short of breath she was feeling. If Danica found out. If Danica. The. Fucking. Magic. Magic Danica. If Giantess Magic Danica found out.

She grinned uneasily at Dani and asked for an update on the Amy situation.

"She'll be home in half an hour. Maybe an hour if she misses the bus. So I figured one more drink and we can head out. Sound good?"

Felicity nodded and hummed affirmative. Nervously. Very obviously nervously. Oh Jeezus she was not hiding this well at all. She'd never been the cool-headed one in any of her old criminal escapades with Ames, and the unpleasant sensation of all those twisted, wracked up nerves of hers on every little heist was rushing back to her now, tensing her up, making her shake.

Not good. Very not good. Amy always handled handling the incriminating goods whenever they went out shoplifting and vandalizing stuff. Why couldn't *she* have been the one to find this?

Fuck.

Shit.

Shit shit *shit*.

The shaking wouldn't stop. Or the sweating. Or the *throbbing* with anxiety.

She had to calm down.

Wine. More wine.

"Actually uh. How about... how about a *couple* more drinks," she suggested uneasily. "Not like we're in a rush to get home."

"Oh? What a turnaround. You're enjoying my company that much now?"

Felicity put on as sincere a grin as she could muster and nodded. "Yup. Yeah. All this pretending is really paying off. You really won me over with your charms there, Dani. —And this wine is great! I'm getting another decanter. You want anything?"

Maybe if she could get Danica a little tipsy too, then she could get away with looking like a nervous wreck on the walk home.

Unfortunately, after Danica held up her freshly acquired cocktail and told Felicity she was good for now, it didn't seem like that plan was going to pan out. She was stuck heading up to the bar to get her wine, all on her own, mentally pulling her hair out the whole way there and back.

For the rest of the night, she pretended to be enthralled by the band, and did her white-knuckled best to nod along and give pleasant one-word responses to anything Dani said until she managed to finish off her wine.

Her head was nice and fuzzy, and her nerves were a lot calmer, but that didn't stop all the world-shattering questions from body-blocking all the other thoughts at the front of her mind.

Questions.

Oh she had a couple questions left in that stupid Two Truths game, didn't she?

What was the rule...? Questions about Amy, right?

So.

No asking about mysterious papers.

Not that that was a good idea anyways. Great way to get magicked out of existence, probably.

She poked Danica's arm to remind her about the game. Her words came out a little stupid though. Too fuzzy.

"I still have two questions left."

"Mm. Nope. You used one."

"What?"

" 'How am I supposed to know—?' "

"—what to do for her..."

"And I said..."

"Ask."

"Hey, you remember!" Danica said with a cute smile.

"...Great. So then, your turn, isn't it?"

"Mhm."

"Go ahead then if you *please*, Danica. I wanna get to mine already."

"Oh big rush now?"

Felicity rolled her eyes impatiently. *"Please."*

"Okay, well, in the spirit of good sportsmanship, since yours was so very easy, I'll give you an easy one too: What exactly would you do for her, hm? If she did need you. You don't live here anymore. You've got a whole new life out there. And I don't think she'd like being stuffed in some luggage and dragged halfway across the province."

"Anything."

"That is *not* an answer..."

"What, you can give a one-word answer and I can't?"

"Listen I love the conviction here but you're telling me murder and arson and *blasphemy* are on the table?"

"...*Anything.*"

"Hm. Alright. Noted."

"You don't believe me?"

"Hey, I know the first one was a lie," she replied with a coy grin. "This one's gotta be true."

It was. It was true.

Anything.

She'd fight God Himself for Amy if that's what it took.

If only she would ask.

Bringing her cup up for another sip, Danica pointed a finger at Felicity and reminded her, "Your turn, eager beaver."

Felicity stared at her empty wine glass, then glanced at her equally empty decanter, and decided she needed a little more before she could ask this one.

When she returned to the table and poured herself half a glass, it was gone in an instant.

"Fine. Fine, *Dani*. Danica Doyle. You know her so damn well. Smug prick..."

"That's not a question."

"...Is she happy?"

"Wow. Yes/no question, huh? Bit of a waste, isn't it?"

"Just answer me."

Danica's stupid grin and playful demeanor evaporated while she fumbled with the answer. At last she grumbled that it wasn't a very fair question. "You should really ask her..."

"You said you'd play by the rules Danica."

"Fine. *Fine*. Fine. Gods." She took a deep breath and finished off her drink to buy a few seconds more before she finally answered: "No."

—*Knew* it.

"I knew it. I knew it!"

"Fleece remember the rules please. You can't know—"

"—I sure as hell can know. What, you think I didn't clock your stupid lie at the start? Think you're so much smarter than me, huh? I'm not stupid." Maybe a little fuzzy from all the wine, sure, but not stupid.

"...Felicity. Please."

"God what was even the point of that whole fight today then, huh? If you knew. You know she's not happy. And you're not doing a damn thing to help her. How dare you try to tell me I'm stupid for trying to save her from this stupid life."

"I didn't say you were stupid."

"You meant it. You *meant* it you... you...—" A sudden fuzzy rush clouded her mind before she could finish that sentence. She couldn't find the right word for whatever Danica was. But it was bad. Oh it was so, so so bad.

It felt like only a moment later when she found she was walking down a cold street beside Danica, who was walking straight as a damn arrow and leading her with their elbows hooked together, like old friends or something.

She jerked herself away from Danica as soon as she found enough balance to do it.

"Oh good, you're back," Danica said with a hint of sarcasm.

No. No that was. A lot of sarcasm. Cutting. Cutting little bitch... No. Giant. Cutting... giant... ...*witch*...?

In a sudden moment of sharp sobriety, Felicity's hand darted to her breast to feel for the note that she'd tucked in her bra earlier.

Still there.

Felt kind of loose though.

Was it loose?

She couldn't help fidgeting and fussing while the two of them continued the march back to Amy's place, adjusting her undergarments through her coat every few seconds, so so subtly patting her tit whenever Danica wasn't looking to make sure that yes, the folded magical paper had not slipped away yet.

Unfortunately, to her absolute horror, Danica apparently noticed those so so subtle movements.

"Hey, you okay Fleece?"

"Mhm!"

"You're just, uh, real quiet all of a sudden. And fidgety."

"Mm! Yeah!" In her slightly toasty haze, she tried desperately to come up with a good excuse: "Sorry, just uh. This shirt rides up. And I'm quiet because... I'm thinking about... that... hypothetical zine project thing. Daunting. *Daunting* amount of work on the table."

Danica grinned at her warmly. That grin. That grin that hid a world of arcane knowledge from Felicity. That grin that hid the truth of the universe from her. What did she know? *What the hell did she know??*

—*Was Amy happy?*

"I'm not sure *how* I could help," Danica kindly offered, "but let me know if there's anything I can do. I've got a bunch of connections in some queer and anarchist circles around here. They're always pumping zines out like crazy." Danica paused for a moment of thought before she added, "Though you'll probably want to start with stuff in your own city, I guess?"

"Mm. Mhm. Yeah. Yeah probably." Felicity tried her best to dismiss the conversation so Danica would stop looking at her and she could go back to making sure that note wasn't going anywhere. And luckily it seemed to work, uncomfortably.

After at least a minute's worth of long silent seconds that left Felicity feeling like she was holding her breath past a graveyard, Danica suddenly stopped short in a panic and patted herself down for something.

—That's it. She knows. She's magic of course she knows. She knows it's missing. She can feel it.

You're dead, Felicity. Just, dead. Gone. Nice life while it lasted, ignoring all this stupid shit at the end.

But it seemed like Felicity was worrying for nothing:

"Shit," Danica urgently cursed at herself for her stupidity. "I forgot! I can't believe... —I had *all day!* Gods *damn it.* I'm an *idiot.* —Hey you think there's anywhere open this late around here that would sell camping gear?"

"...Sorry, what?" Felicity's mind was not in any state to think about camping gear at 11 at night. "No? Probably not? Who's going camping? We're not going camping. I'm not camping with you Danica you couldn't pay me—"

Danica ignored Felicity's protestations and put her head in her hands while she whined, "No... *No.* I promised..."

"Promised what?"

Danica sighed and explained through bitter frustration at herself, "I told Amy I'd get her an air mattress for tonight."

"...An air mattress?"

"Yeah, I don't know, she wants to sleep on the floor for some reason. I told her it's stupid and I don't care about sleeping on the floor myself but she's, you know, kind of stubborn."

Felicity raised a skeptical eyebrow at Danica's explanation. That was a very one-sided perspective there. It sure sounded like she might be exploiting Amy's kindness again, spinning it to make herself sound like some self-sacrificing hero.

This wasn't the time to pick a fight though.

Danica looked up and down the street, anxiously scanning the dozens of darkened storefronts until her eyes settled on one of the last illuminated holdouts – a late night dollar store.

"There!" she said with unshakably hopeful enthusiasm.

"...A dollar store? Would they even have that?"

"They've got *everything*, I'm sure—" She cut herself short to take in Felicity's skeptical gaze. "Look I don't have any other options here. You can head home if you want to, but I have to figure this out."

"...No, it's fine. I'll come along. Moral support."

That wasn't the real reason, obviously. It would've been great to get home first and warn Amy about Danica being some kind of witch or something. Not that she had... *any* idea how to broach that subject.

No, it was more that she didn't really trust herself to walk all the way back to the apartment in her current state. Plus, you know, being a svelte little Filipina princess didn't exactly lend itself to feeling safe wandering around on her own in an urban area like this. Cat calls. And worse. She did, after all, sadly, pull men. Far too often. And even if she had Danica's razor-sharp canines to protect herself, she'd heard that aggressive guys tend to just get meaner when you bite them. She wasn't eager to ever verify the rumors.

So instead of submitting to the cold uncertainty of a lonely drunken walk home, she morosely and dutifully followed Danica to the store, where only tragedy and disappointment awaited. Kind of nice that someone else could feel the sting of it for once after Felicity had been *stoically* enduring all the city's failings since she got there.

All it took was a quick hustle up and down every aisle to leave Danica's hopes in tatters. No camping equipment at all. Not really surprising, though, honestly.

The best she could find was a gross plastic neon-blue pool mattress.

"Amy likes blue," she insisted, though that bold insistence melted into an uneasy question to confirm: "Right?"

An uneasy question...

About dear Amy's concerns...

That must...

Be answered...

Golden... true...

Felicity's mind felt fuzzy and warm like wine had never done when she answered: "...Yes. But... not this blue..."

The strange feeling passed as soon as the words were out of her mouth.

What was that?

She was looking at a pool toy. It was an ugly blue. And worse, it looked extremely uncomfortable and gross. And... Danica wanted to get it for Amy? She was clearly grasping at straws here. "...But like. Danica. Doesn't matter what color: Would you sleep on that?"

Danica clicked her tongue at herself. "...Look, it's... *technically* what she asked for: A cheap air mattress. I'm fulfilling my end of the deal here."

Felicity raised an eyebrow at her and chided her, "I feel like you *probably* shouldn't be looking for loopholes for something like this, Dani. This definitely isn't an 'anything is better than nothing' situation." Felicity prodded the pool toy of a 'mattress'. The sound the plastic made when it rubbed against itself was *bad* stim. "Like... 'nothing' has to be better than *this*."

Danica crossed her arms and tapped her foot while she thought about it. At last, she offered a desperate consolation: "If it's bad enough, she won't use it. And then I can convince her not to sleep on the floor at all. My mistake, right? She'll have to let me sleep on it as retribution for my horrible crime."

Felicity shook her head. "That's... a hell of a scheme."

Throwing her arms up in the air in frustration, Danica insisted it was the best she could do right now.

Felicity helpfully pointed out that the wretched thing was not only: Not quite an *air mattress;* but it also wasn't quite *cheap*, at a dollar shy of fifty bucks.

But Danica bought it anyways and carried it home in merciful silence with a miserable distracted look on her face the whole way, which left Felicity all the opportunity she needed to finally adjust that note into a more secure position.

When they got to the apartment, Amy kindly buzzed them in and picked them up from the lobby, then, when they got through the door, she teasingly laughed and poked at the two of them for getting locked out at all.

"The key's right there," she said, pointing at the wall. "How did you *both* forget it?"

Normally Felicity would've felt like an idiot getting laughed at like that, but she would've done anything to hear Amy's laugh right now, to see her smile – especially after everything she'd gone through that day.

She stepped right up to Amy and gave her a huge hug. "I missed you. I had such a long day," she lamented, though she regretted saying it a moment later when she remembered that Amy had been out since before dawn working at that miserable warehouse of hers.

And it was all over her, that day of hard labor. Her eyes could barely stay open, her face looked exhausted, her hair was greasy, and she smelled thick with sweat, with just a hint of some boyish sporty deodorant that smelled nothing at all like what Felicity remembered of her from high school.

She almost broke down and cried in her arms when Amy wrapped them around her to comfort her. Amy didn't deserve this. God, she didn't fucking deserve this life. And Felicity sure as hell didn't deserve Amy's compassion here, useless as she was to her. But that idiot was too damn nice, wasn't she? Just like Danica said. Nice enough to put her up for a weekend unannounced. Nice enough to put up Danica for months. Nice enough to suffer forever in silence, hiding, hiding hiding hiding.

—*Ask.*

She clenched her teeth when Danica's answer echoed in her mind.

That one was true, wasn't it?

But she couldn't just... *ask.*

—And why should she have to?

Why hadn't Amy just told Felicity about her miserable back-breaking job?

What would it take? To earn enough of her trust? To be worthy? Worthy as that dear parasite Danica Doyle.

And... what else was she hiding?

Felicity was assigned to the couch tonight. She tried her best to ignore it, but she couldn't help feeling jilted, hearing the muffled chatter of Amy and Danica in Amy's bedroom while she tried to get comfortable on the little loveseat.

She sighed to herself while she tried to fold up the pillow there into the right shape. No matter how comfortable she got in this 'bed', it'd always be missing something, something she desperately ached for every time she returned to this miserable excuse of a city. But it was never coming back. Never. She was never going to get it back. She was never going to get to rest wrapped in the comfort of Amy's sleepy breath and steady heartbeat, would she?

Instead, Felicity was stuck suffering alone in the silence of the apartment, hours after the other two had already fallen asleep, silence broken up occasionally by distracting cars driving by below and the occasional muffled snore coming out of Amy's bedroom. And even those little bits of silence were ruined by the cacophony of her own anxious, racing thoughts.

Danica.

Who the hell *was* she?

What was she??

She pulled the note out of her pointlessly hopeful lingerie to fiddle with it, tugging at it over and over to trigger the little seal, to study the symbols, to try to find some hint in her useless brain about what it meant, but nothing was coming back to her.

What good was consuming all those books of hers if she couldn't even get something so simple as a couple arcane symbols to stick in her little encyclopedia of esoteric knowledge, huh?

She realized she'd have to return this to Danica's coat before she left. Even if Dani didn't notice at first, she might notice it later, and... God, Felicity didn't even want to imagine what might happen then.

But not yet. She still didn't have a plan.

Jeezus, this was so frustrating!

How was she supposed to figure this out?

And never mind just... *figuring it out*, how was she going to *prove it*?

She couldn't just take a photo of it.

No.

...She had to keep it, didn't she? She had to. It was super risky, but she had to. All she could do was hope Danica wouldn't notice. Or maybe she'd just assume she dropped it. Left it at the bar. It would be fine. Maybe. Probably. *Definitely.*

Yeah. That was the only way. She'd take it. And then she'd just have to find some way to connect it back to Danica. It couldn't just be Felicity's word against hers. That woman was way too tricky for Felicity to come at her with *nothing*.

She tugged at the note again, sending a ripple of light through the hidden lines and runes, which all seemed to encircle a larger, more complex symbol in the middle. If this thing was sealed *for Danica*, then surely Danica could open it. Right? If Felicity could just *catch* her...

But it's not like Felicity could just corner her and confront her about it. For all she knew, Danica could just erase her from existence if she started causing trouble.

And even if she did prove it, then what? Tell Amy? Expose the secrets of some dangerous magical creature and just hope she wouldn't make everyone who knew about her secret – including Amy – just *disappear?*

Ugh. She would never be able to get to sleep while she was sitting on this! Too many circular thoughts. Too much anger and anxiety and unanswered *unanswerable* questions and *nothing* like a plan coming together.

And on top of all that, some weird *sound* was annoying the hell out of her between the sound of passing cars. A buzzing or a humming or something. She threw the note on the couch and got up in a huff to frustratedly check all the appliances she could find in the apartment, but it wasn't the fridge or the TV or anything else she could unplug.

She tried to calm down and closed her eyes to listen carefully, to try to pinpoint the sound.

Was it... near the front door? Maybe the apartment hallway? A fluorescent light?

She took a few silent steps at a time, pointing her ears this way and that trying to track it down.

At last, she was pretty sure she had it. She carefully creaked open the foyer's closet and pulled Danica's coat off its hanger.

The letters?

Letters don't hum.

Letters don't light up in runes when you try to open them either.

She looked over her shoulder to check that Amy's door was closed tight. She could hear Amy snoring. If Danica could sleep through that, she'd definitely never hear Felicity quietly fussing with a bunch of papers out in the living room.

Hopefully none of the documents exploded.

But then she'd be vaporized anyways and she probably wouldn't have to worry about *noise* after that.

She turned on a lamp beside the couch and splayed out the stack of papers on the coffee table. It was pretty easy to find the humming note like that.

Unbelievable that she missed it earlier, honestly.

When she unfolded it, she found yet more impossible paper technology at work: Shimmering golden ink that was seemingly hovering half a hair off the page, faintly illuminating the paper underneath.

Ink does not float.

Ink does not *glow*.

Ink does not *shimmer* on its own.

Again the language of the words on the page felt vaguely familiar, but Felicity couldn't remember where she'd seen it before and it was driving her insane trying. Maybe her dear translator back at the university could help her figure it out? Virgil was pretty good at this stuff. Way better than she was, anyways. Worth every penny.

While she held the letter in her hand, she felt a subtle power in it. Hard to describe. Like gently fluctuating built up static maybe?

She needed to take this too. Right?

It was *real* magic. How could she not take it? Study it? Learn its secrets. —Learn *Danica's* secrets.

...Could she? Could she just... take this?

...Well. Why not? Right? She'd already taken one note, and Danica hadn't noticed. So. So, what's one more? There were more than a dozen random sheets of paper here. It looked like a pile of trash, honestly.

She steeled herself, took a deep breath, and balled up all the conviction she could find to do this probably extremely stupid thing.

After all, she did say, truthfully: *Anything.* She'd even fight a god if that's what it took to save her.

She ended up taking only three pages: The sealed paper with the white ink, the humming letter with the gold ink, and one other document – a page ripped from an old book, written in normal sepia ink on ancient parchment in a script that looked kind of similar to the golden letter. But this one had a second language on it, entirely different letters, written in the margin notes. There was no way she could leave this one behind. It might end up being a Rosetta Stone for her dear over-worked translator to figure out the other notes.

She wrapped the three pages in a thick sweater and carefully stuffed the bundle deep in her travel bag. The humming was muffled enough like that that no one would be able to hear it in the morning over the murmuring and shuffling sounds of even the earliest waking hour.

Lying down again, still miserably uncomfortable, her heart was racing, even harder than when she was standing right next to that *whatever-Danica-was*, hiding that stolen note in the nervously sweaty cotton of her lingerie.

This was the most dangerous thing she'd done in years. But she had to do it. She had to figure out who this... *thing* was, sleeping on Amy's couch, pretending at kindness, poisoning her with smiles. — <u>And</u> keeping Felicity away from her own best friend, damn it.

She had to save Amy.

From this life.

From this parasite.

From this... this...

—*What the hell <u>are you</u>, Danica Doyle?*

Sleep Apnea Can Cause Headaches, Depression, Fatigue, and Early Onset Heart Disease – and, of Course, Insomnia for Your Dear Unfortunate Bedmates

Ravi carefully closed the door to their bedroom, staring intently at the knob while they did. The click of the latch felt very... final... sealing Nicole and them inside for the night. They clenched their fists for a second while they tried to remember which side the door locked from.

Nicole was stripping out of her dress and stockings behind them.

Why was she so bold.

As if hanging out in her underwear around them every day wasn't frustrating enough.

Why did Ravi think this was a good idea? They should just sleep out on the floor in the living room with Felicity. This was too much.

God, not that sleeping in the same room as Felicity was any better, was it? Ravi should just sleep in the fucking bathtub for godsake, this was the most ridiculous...

—Just. Be cool Ravi. Be cool. It's not even the first time you've spent the night sleeping in the same room as this woman. This should be easy. Don't overthink it.

Though there was undeniably something very, very different, sleeping together in a living room, versus sleeping together locked away in Ravi's little bedroom.

Fuck... They hadn't even changed the sheets...

In a panic they glanced over at the fuck toy box stashed under their bed. Closed – check. Hidden – check. Thank god.

Hopefully Nicole wouldn't notice the sheets were a *little* overdue for a wash.

If she did notice, she sure wasn't saying a thing about it, lounging casually on their bed with bare thighs while she was changing.

They tried very hard to focus on getting the air mattress out of its difficult packaging, to avoid looking at her.

But she was so much, and they couldn't help sneaking a guilty glance when she dropped her bra and lifted up her arms to slip into one of those cute loose-fit t-shirts she liked to sleep in.

This was the first time they'd seen her chest so brazenly exposed, and Nicole did it so casually that she made it feel like nothing at all – not teasing, not flirty, definitely not seductive, just... like Ravi wasn't even worth considering.

Still, the sight of her, to see so much of her all at once, boldly in secret, it sent a voyeuristic wave of warmth rippling from Ravi's tightening throat down through every inch of their body on the way to their nervously clenching thighs. They hadn't felt this stupid and giddy looking at a woman's body since they were a teenager sneaking peeks at Felicity's cruelly forbidden breasts and tender skin in the changeroom. They flexed every muscle uneasily, trying very hard to crush their body into cold unfeeling compliance.

—But godsake Nicole could you do <u>anything</u> to hide how beautiful you are? Please?

Falling for Nicole like this was so ridiculous. So fast. So easy. All it took was a couple months of enjoying some beautiful woman's company, huh Ravi? Some beautiful, shameless, intelligent, amazing, playful woman who made their life fun and full and meaningful for the first time in...

They unfurled the unpleasantly highlighter blue, translucent, crunkled plastic rectangle that Nicole had brought them to sleep on and stared at it in disbelief for a few moments, prodding the stiff, rubbery material to test its tensity. They knew this wasn't *really* an air mattress, but seeing it unrolled like this kind of put it in perspective how much this was absolutely *not* made for sleeping on.

"...Nikki. I know you meant well, but what the hell is this? I said air mattress, not inflatable pool toy. ...It's so small. Isn't this kid size? I know I'm shorter than you, but this is just a *little* demeaning."

Nicole, after finally mercifully covering up most of her skin with that nightgown of a shirt of hers – though that shirt did absolutely nothing to conceal her breathtaking legs, or to ward off the irresistible temptation to peek at the forbidden delight of the shadow-guarded Schrodinger's underwear between her thighs whenever she carelessly exposed herself – had taken up a perch on the corner of Ravi's bed and was watching them as they examined the unpleasant pool toy with apprehensive consideration.

Her face went from 'uneasy' to 'scolded puppy' in an instant when Ravi complained.

"I know... It was all they had, though."

"Who's 'they'? Where did you even get this?"

"The dollar store."

Ravi hummed and nodded in a mockery of thoughtful consideration for the mattress. "Yeah. That checks out. This thing is absolutely worth one dollar. They didn't have anything at the sports shop or something?"

Nicole shamefully admitted that she didn't have a chance to try anywhere else. "It was super last minute. ...I almost forgot entirely, to be honest. Really, you're lucky the dollar store was even open."

"Yeah," Ravi replied, looking grimly at their bed for the evening, "'Lucky'." They heaved their shoulders slightly with a little sigh. It was too late at night after far too long and achy a day for them to deal with this. "Hey, listen, I appreciate the thought here, and I'll give it a shot, but boy, if you had just forgotten altogether, I could be shamelessly sleeping in a pile of laundry or something."

"...Points for trying?" she asked cutely.

"...Nicole, puppy, I think you literally did the worst possible job you could've done short of building something out of garbage bags and packing tape," they said, trying to sound playful, but from the look on Nicole's face, it was clearly coming out tired and grumpy and mean. "Hey, come on don't look like that, you're breaking my heart. A hundred points for trying, okay?"

"I can sleep on it," Nicole offered, a miserable, hopeful compromise.

"Nope."

"Come on Ravi, it's not fair."

"My room, my rules. And my rule is you're sleeping on the bed. — Do *not* move me this time, I mean it."

Nicole crossed her arms and gave Ravi a grumpy little huff, "You're such a prick sometimes, Ravi. You don't deserve this."

"Yeah, I'm with you. I definitely deserve something a little nicer than this," they held up the miserable pile of blue plastic for emphasis. "Think of it as your punishment, knowing that I'm down here suffering for you," they added playfully.

Nicole gave them a pleading look for a few seconds before she finally accepted that she didn't have any hope of convincing Ravi to swap beds any time soon and gave up. She miserably flopped back in Ravi's bed and sorrowfully called them a stubborn idiot before she threw the blanket over herself.

Which was fair enough. She wasn't wrong. But Ravi couldn't bear to let their guests sleep on the floor. It just wasn't right – no matter how heinous Nicole's shopping errand crimes might be.

They sat cross-legged on the floor to get started inflating their terrible bed. There was some weird stiff rubbery plastic nipple that they needed to bite down on while they blew into it, and the thing was so damn stiff that it let half a breath escape for every whole breath they put into it. The exercise left them winded and light-headed and with a very sore jaw. God, they were too tired for this after working all day.

They ended up flopping on their back after a couple minutes to take a break to catch their breath – and the damn thing wasn't even half-full.

Nicole crawled over to the edge of the bed to peek over with a cute smile to offer to take over.

Ravi considered putting up a fight, but they were so damn tired, they just didn't have it in them anymore. They lethargically tossed the wretched pool toy up on the bed and told Nicole to go nuts on it.

It gave them a *little* satisfaction to hear Nicole struggle with it just as much as they did. She occasionally took a few seconds to gasp desperately and swear a little, "Holy fuck... This thing is awful..."

"Yeah."

"I'm so sorry."

"You're not done yet. Keep going, you monster."

"Yes sir, sorry sir."

Ravi grinned at that. They would never boss Nicole around for real, but it was fun playing, and the way she said it, she was clearly having fun pretending to be in trouble.

At least, they hoped she was pretending.

While they listened to the steady rhythm of Nicole's dutiful efforts to inflate their bed, they closed their eyes and let their mind wander tiredly.

It wasn't actually so bad just on the floor.

Maybe they could just tell Nicole to stop.

They could just sleep like this. Listening to her.

They woke up with a start a few minutes later when Nicole prodded them with her finger. She was leaning over the edge of the bed.

"Hey. Ravi." When they didn't reply right away, she teased them: "Oh, my most loud and honorable Lord Chainsaw Woodchipperington—" Apparently they had started snoring already. "—your bed is ready, my liege."

Ravi looked over to where Nicole was pointing, and sure enough, there it was, their tiny regal bulbously overinflated bed. They lethargically crawled over to it and told Nicole to throw them a pillow and a blanket.

She teased them about their ability to fall asleep so easily on the floor like that: "Just nothing in your head at night, huh? Anxieties, fears, regrets: Not for Ravi."

They groggily corrected her, "I have so, so many regrets Nikki. The trick is you just count them. Like sheep. Knocks you right out."

She grinned at them warmly. "Good trick. I'll remember that. You good down there?"

"Mhm."

"Can't convince you to trade?"

"'Night Nix," Ravi replied, to cut that inquiry short.

"...'Night Rav," she replied, with a warm, honey-sweet pleasantness in her voice.

Ravi started counting their regrets and before they even got to number three, they were out.

...Only to be brought back again almost immediately when they rolled right off of their miserable fucking pool toy and startled themself awake with a little swear.

Something annoying was rattling around their brain in the dark tonight, making them toss and turn a bit. It was something that had been interrupting their thoughts since yesterday. Something Nicole said about their name.

—*Not important now. Time to sleep. Please.*

They tried to get settled again, and again they were out in a minute, and again they were brought back when they rolled over in their sleep in a troubled state of mind and tumbled onto the floor.

They mumbled quietly to themself, "Fuck... This fucking..."

"Ravi." Nicole was still wide awake in the dark.

"Sorry. Sorry, I keep falling off the stupid—"

"You know there's like... tons of room up here."

They considered it for a few tense seconds. That was a generous description of the situation in that little double bed of theirs. But still, they cautiously responded, "...Is that weird? It feels weird."

"You're the only one making it weird, Ravi Bee. It's just a bed. I promise I won't bite you *or* grope you."

Ravi tried their very best not to imagine either of those pleasant scenarios – though they would much, *much* rather be doing the groping and the biting there.

—*Making it weird, Ravi.*

"...Okay. Okay fine. *Fine*. Move over."

They crawled up into bed next to Nicole, got settled in with their pillow and their blanket, as far away from her as they could – though that still left them inches from rolling into her – then said their sweet goodnights again.

Sadly though, even in the comfort of their own bed, it seemed like Ravi still couldn't get to sleep. They must've spent a solid ten minutes switching between lying on their good side and their back, kicking their blanket off their feet, shifting their pillow around.

Nothing helped. They couldn't reduce their anxieties to integers tonight. —And they were failing *miserably* at trying their best to not remember the last time they had someone they loved in their own bed, or the last time they opened up to someone they trusted, or the last time they spoke to anyone in their family, or the many dozens of other fears and regrets and painful memories they had, most of which tonight seemed to involve getting a little too close to someone a little too important.

...But even when they managed to quiet those troubled thoughts, they still couldn't find any peace, because they couldn't get Nicole out of their head. But it wasn't for anything good. Not for their stupid crush. Not for her captivating eyes, or for the way her laughter shaped her face just right to make Ravi smile every time, or even for the way that oversized t-shirt of hers was hanging on her curves so dangerously tonight as it did every day but never so close to them.

No, tonight, they were stuck on the same thing they'd been stuck on in every rare idle moment at work all day. They were stuck on the way she looked at them yesterday when they told her to use the wrong name: Aching, pierced, betrayed.

—She didn't understand.

And it was... *important.* She *needed* to understand.

After a final failed attempt at contorting their limbs into some magic shape that would grant them the peace of oblivion, they splayed themself out flat on their back and let their arms flop pathetically at their sides in a show of frustration. One of their fingers brushed against Nicole's thigh—and they quickly retracted it in and grabbed their offending wrist in embarrassment, hoping she was too unconscious to feel it.

After a few seconds to gather themself, they whispered Nicole's name into the dark.

She responded instantly, to their surprise, sharp and sober like she had been awake the whole time: "What's up Ravi Bee?"

Ravi was probably keeping her up with their constant inconsiderate huffing and shuffling around.

They were hoping to have a few more seconds to put their words together here, but there was probably no sweet way to say any of this.

They took a deep breath before they let out their heavy thoughts, "So. The first time I told someone to use my chosen name, and to stop calling me a girl, she stopped... talking to me."

"Oh," Nicole responded plainly, miserably, but she didn't add anything else, so Ravi had to continue.

"—Not right away," they clarified. "Just, every time I reminded her, she apologized and made an *embarrassingly* big deal about it, but she *still* kept using the wrong name with everyone we knew. It hurt. I pushed her about it, over and over again, and I guess she eventually just got sick of me and never talked to me again."

"That's... really shitty of her."

"I know. I know that, but... I didn't, back then. I didn't know. I thought I fucked up. Like maybe I pushed too hard. Maybe I was making things weird for her, making her *suffer* through explaining who I was to everyone she knew. —And I got over that, got over making excuses for her shittiness. She was the one who screwed up. Not me.

"But it doesn't *matter* who screwed up. I still lost her. Forever. And every time—*every time* I got enough confidence to try to correct one of my friends or anyone in my family, it just kept happening the same way. I just wanted to disappear and never have to deal with it again. So... you know, I did. And here we are: Lonely Ravi Beausoleil, with all of like... four people who know my real name – all people who never knew 'Amaira'."

Ravi turned their head to rest their cheek on their pillow, to look at Nicole. She was already watching them intently. There was a deep sadness and sympathy in her eyes. It hurt to see it, but they had to push through here.

"You get it, right?" they pleaded with her. "Felicity doesn't know. She's the last one. The last good thing I have from back then. —Except for... Sorry, except for you, obviously. But it's just... different with her. I didn't know you at all back then."

"I get it."

"I love her so much, Nikki. I would die for her if she asked. I would. She's so important to me. I can't stand it."

Nicole scrunched up her brow in confusion. She challenged them: "If she's so important, why don't you just tell her?"

"Because. You know?"

Though Nicole obviously did not know. And it was really hard for Ravi to put it in words. They'd never done this before, never talked about this, never even written it down, and barely thought about it.

But still they tried. They had to.

"I could get over anyone else. Anyone else. But... she... I don't know, Nicole, she looks at me like I'm a good person. Still. Even after all this. She doesn't know I'm a piece of shit. Somehow, I've managed to trick her this whole time. —This is the first time she's even seen this apartment, you know that? God, eight years I kept it from her, and she just barges in here like it's nothing and finally sees the truth – and the way she looked at me... it felt... I didn't feel *human* anymore..."

Nicole was barely listening it seemed, because all she managed to find to respond with was a quiet, mumbled, "You're not a piece of shit..."

Ravi let out a little huff of a sigh. Nicole didn't get it. Why did they think she would?

"...You know... it's... Fuck, just..." They closed their eyes and turned to face the ceiling again. "Forget it... It doesn't matter..."

"It does. It does matter. I'm sorry, I'm not just going to lie here and let you talk bad about yourself like this. You're <u>not</u> a piece of shit."

"...Look whether I'm a piece of shit or not isn't what *matters* here. *She* thinks I'm made of gold. But it's just... paint. It's gold paint on cracked oak. —And I get it Nicole, you see something cool about cracked oak or whatever, and that's very sweet of you, but I'm supposed to be gold. To her, I'm supposed to be real fucking gold. And I try so hard... But I haven't been good like she believes I am since I was a girl, since I was her little crush, her tomboy princess, big and tough and cute.

"But I can't *be* Amy. I don't know how anymore. The only thing I have left of her is the name. But I need to pretend. I have to. You see that, right? I can't lose Felicity. I can't lose her the way I lost everyone else. I just can't." Ravi shook their head and tried to calm their breathing, but it wasn't working very well. They brought their palms to their eyes to hold it in, but still they choked on their words a bit while they spoke. "She's too big, Nikki. She's in me too deep. I need her to look at me like I'm *worth something*. I need her. —And I fucking know how pathetic that sounds. I know it's not healthy. But I don't know what I'll do if I lose this."

Ravi turned to face Nicole again, hoping the darkness in the room was enough to hide their watery eyes. "Tell me you get it. Please."

After a long pause, after Nicole's eyes took in Ravi's miserable face for a few tense breaths while she thought about her answer to Ravi's pleading request, she hit them right in the chest with a steak knife of a question:

"Do you really... think it's better? That she loves this... *shadow* of you? Like, it's safe. I get that. But is that really better than taking a chance on being loved for who you really are? Is being loved that much more important to you than being known?"

Ravi was staggered for a few seconds while they tried to put together some defense to that attack.

"...You know, I've just... I've taken that chance so many times already, and I know what it's like when it goes wrong, I know what it's like to be hated for who I really am. God, honestly, it's happened enough by now that I've even figured out how to not give a shit about it—with *anyone* but her."

Again, Nicole's eyes silently scanned Ravi's face in the dark, looking for something to say, but she clearly couldn't find it. She rolled her head to face the ceiling and closed her eyes in silent contemplation.

Why was this so difficult? It wasn't a lot to ask, was it?

...Was it?

Were they... being a burden on her...? Even on Nicole...?

She interrupted their anxious thoughts: "I love who you are, Ravi."

So shameless. Always so shameless.

"...I know."

"You're worth knowing."

Ravi looked away from her. What was she trying to do?

When they didn't respond, Nicole half sat up and let her blanket slip off of her to lean over to try to catch Ravi's eye.

"Anyone could see how amazing you are, Ravi. She'd be stupid not to. And trust me, after being forced to spend a whole night with her, I can promise you she is a lot of *very* frustrating things, but she is *not* stupid."

Ravi couldn't help scoffing and smirking at Nicole's frank-but-polite assessment.

"You're being very generous."

"She doesn't make it easy."

"I know. You're very brave."

"Not by choice! She was in such a mood tonight. I practically had to drag her kicking and screaming around the city to show her a good time. Gods. She's such a handful."

"Thanks for not throwing her in the river."

"There were moments, Ravi."

"She's not a good swimmer," they solemnly warned her, in case she really *was* considering it.

"Well, obviously I'd save her if she was drowning."

"Oh, obviously."

"I would!"

They paused for a moment to smirk at themself. "...I know it's hard to see it, Nikki, but she's really good to me. I really appreciate you being nice to her for me. I want her to like you too."

"That's very optimistic of you."

Ravi grinned at her smugly. "You'd have to be stupid not to like you."

"Well maybe there's hope then. She's a lot of things—"

"—But she's absolutely *not* stupid."

Nicole, still leaning over to keep Ravi's eyes on her, glanced away from them for a few moments to put some words together before returning to their gaze.

"...It's just not fair, you know. To either of you. To not give her a chance to know you. I cannot emphasize enough, Ravi, you are worth knowing. I promise. Firsthand experience. I'm practically an expert on the matter."

Ravi couldn't help a crack of a smile from escaping at Nicole's earnestness. She really did a good job of sounding sincere about that kind of stuff. It was almost enough to break them sometimes. Almost.

After a little breath, they morosely informed her, "I'm just not ready."

"Will you ever be?"

Another signature Nicole-brand lung-piercing needle of a question. Ravi wished she would let up on them even a little tonight.

Again they didn't have a response. They just looked her in the eye, taking in the profound sadness there. But there was something else. Hope maybe?

Nicole's eyes fell, after a few expectant breaths, when she realized Ravi wasn't planning to answer her question. She sat herself up properly, on crossed legs, and drew

on one of her knees

tense

pensive

shapes.

Uneasy.

Sulking.

Over and over... and over...

"...Just say it," Ravi implored her.

Nicole curled a soft fist and tapped on her knee a few times before one final drop, pressing her fist into herself firmly in frustration.

She said, at last, reluctant, but still stern and selfish: "I hate calling you the wrong name. I hate... *pretending* I don't know who you are."

Well, that was painfully obvious. She'd been saying that all night, hadn't she? With every word.

They rolled over on their elbow and reached out a bold consoling hand to rest on her knee. They spoke the words *they'd* been trying to say all night, imploring her to understand: "It's just for one weekend," they assured her. "Please."

Nicole silently chewed on that sentiment for a few seconds before she morosely nodded her understanding, though she couldn't seem to look Ravi in the eye when she did.

"You're a good friend," Ravi reminded her of the obvious.

"Oh, I know," she said with a sad attempt at a proud grin – a grin with a profound and poorly-concealed misery in it.

Still, Ravi responded like it was sincere, because it ought to be: "Good."

It felt like a bittersweet conclusion, but after all that, they were pretty confident Nicole understood. —Better, at least. She understood better. And hopefully she understood well enough that she could feel at least a little less shitty about helping them with their façade. That was all they could ask.

After getting all that off their chest, Ravi's mind was finally warm and silent for just long enough that they could find the peace they needed to fall asleep – no counting required.

Breathe True Thy Words, Oh Golden One, Though They Flutter Only on the Shadows of the Dead. ...Please?

(Early Morning, Sunday, 18th December)

Ravi woke before Nicole, and hours before the miserly December sun. They wished they could say she looked like a sleeping angel, but she was making a hell of a face there, half pressed into the pillow, a steady drip of spit spilling out of her mouth, absolutely soaking the cover.

But there was still something sweet and disarming about her, even like that. —Especially like that.

Lit only by what faint streetlight and moonlight bled through their blinds, they silently made their way around their room to get themself ready for another borderline-criminally long day of work, feeling guilty the whole time they were getting into their clothes – guilty that they couldn't spend more time with poor troubled Felicity during her visit.

But it was easier that way – easier to hide the truth from her when they weren't in her affectionate, discerning gaze. She was many things, but she wasn't stupid, and she'd figure it all out eventually, they knew that. But just... just a little longer. They wanted to stay good in her eyes just a little longer.

If only she would stay away, then the two of them would never have to change, frozen in time in each other's memory, and just... remembered, perfect, forever. That was enough, wasn't it? To pretend to be loved?

Wasn't that better than being known?

—You're worth knowing.

...They took great care to silently close their bedroom door behind them. Nicole deserved a bit of rest. It had been a long time since the poor woman got to sleep in a real bed. Honestly, Ravi would give it up for her – once in a while at least – if she'd ever accept it.

They peered around the corner of the living room wall to spy on Felicity sleeping on the couch. She, too, was not exactly an angel in her sleep. And she looked woefully uncomfortable, arms tangled up with her pillow, all curled up on herself miserably – even though she practically fit perfectly between the armrests of the loveseat.

...She was breathing so peacefully.

Ravi remembered this.

They'd fallen asleep to this dozens of times in their youth.

They stood there for a long time, listening again. Maybe it was creepy to do it now – hell, maybe it was even creepy back then – but they couldn't help themself.

Their own breathing was impeded slightly today, unnatural, different, as it usually was, by their binder constricting their chest, reshaping them so they could be themself, so they could be at least a little closer to being known right by the rest of the world.

And it had never felt tighter than it did right now.

While they listened to her, shamefully, filled with voyeuristic guilt, they couldn't help lamenting all of this. They would never be able to enjoy this again. This wasn't their life anymore.

Felicity loved Amy.

And they could never be her Amy again.

I Know It Looks Cool, but
Alchemy Still Isn't Magic

"What does this one do?"

Nicole.

Running wild in the chem lab.

She was a living disaster, a time bomb just waiting to blow the whole building away.

Ravi was trying very hard to focus on weighing out the materials for this evening's ceramic composition trials. Nicole was making that very difficult, since she was entertaining herself wandering around the lab and trying to touch every dangerous thing she could get her hands on.

"That one will explode the lab if you touch it."

She crossed her arms and gave Ravi a playfully grumpy huff. "That's what you said the last three things would do."

Ravi grinned at her and shrugged. "What can I say? There's a lot of ways to blow up a chemistry lab."

"It literally says 'IN CASE OF CHEMICAL FIRE' Ravi."

"Oh, you *can* read."

"I'm going to press it."

"Don't press it."

Nicole hovered a teasingly shaky finger dangerously near the pin-locked button.

Ravi never knew how serious Nicole was about this kind of thing, so they figured it was better not to risk it. They sternly told her what it actually did before she caused a disaster, which was cut off all the gas to the burners in the lab and then bathe the entire room in inert fire suppressant foam.

"Takes a week to clean up, I hear. I'll be in a lot of trouble if you press it for no reason, so please don't."

Nicole pulled her finger away with a hint of trepidation and took a step back before she returned to Ravi's bench.

"Ravi, you told me I could play with clay."

"I have to measure it first, Nix. This takes a while."

"How long is a while?"

"It's kind of precise. Twenty more minutes?"

Nicole kind of showed up unexpectedly tonight. It was still a very welcome intrusion, even though she refused to tell them how she got past the security doors.

Unfortunately, this truly was not an especially exciting part of the process, and Ravi couldn't help feeling a little guilty about that for some reason.

They let out a little sigh, then stood up and beckoned Nicole to follow them to the stock room.

They opened up a little locker in there that was specifically set aside for them and presented her with a spool of nanoscale fibrous tungsten.

"This is worth more than your entire wardrobe," they assured her. "So don't waste it."

She unspooled a bit of the coarse fiber to examine it. "Feels like wool?"

"Yeah. It's fibrous. Furry little filaments growing off a solid central core. It's meant to increase the surface area. And I have a very special task for you!"

"What's that?"

"You're going to increase the surface area even more!"

Ravi grabbed a few special tools out of the locker as well, then locked it back up and led Nicole back to the bench to sit beside them.

They got her set up with the gear she needed to get to work: A simple face mask; A clamp to put tension on the coarse tungsten filament; A little magic tool with a hook-shaped diamond blade; And finally, a glass orb with an electrostatic generator inside.

Ravi gave a quick demo: "Just shave the strand back and forth until it's smooth. You should get fibers sticking to the orb there, about half a centimeter long. If not, you're doing something wrong."

"And this is helping... how...?"

"We'll be mixing the fibers into the clay. Makes it stronger. Better at handling heat. Tungsten's kind of magic – but only if you get the right amount in there. Which is—" Ravi gestured at their precise measuring equipment. "—kind of the whole point of my research."

Nicole examined the razor-edged diamond of the stripping tool curiously, then took a preliminary stroke with the blade and watched, with her head tilted slightly to the side, as a plume of the freshly harvested nanoscopic fibers tumbled through the air until they got caught in the static field and stuck conveniently to the glass orb of the generator, ready to be collected later and mixed with a bit of water to give them the consistency of a thick paste.

"You figured all this out on your own?" she asked, while she found her rhythm with the stripper and the spool.

"Some of it. Tungsten's already used in a bunch of ceramics. Usually powdered though, in compounds. Using pure metal fibers changes the behavior a bit – in just the way I want, conveniently."

"Who makes the weird wool?"

"It's a custom process. I could do it myself, but it takes forever with the stuff we've got in this shitty lab. I get a specialist in Germany to do it for me. —It is. Very expensive. So, like I said, please don't waste any of that."

Nicole gave Ravi a dutiful salute with the stripper tool, then carried on with her work with a renewed dedication to the process.

About twenty minutes later, Ravi's measurements were complete. Ten batches, each with tiny deviations in the ratio of materials in the mixtures. They smiled at Nicole and announced that they could start on the next process, which was actually fun.

"Aw, I was just getting into this," Nicole lamented. "It's kind of relaxing."

"Isn't it? It's a bit tedious, but I like just sitting down and working on it sometimes when I'm having a rough day. *Not so fun* when I've run out of the stuff and have to spend an hour restocking. So, thanks for that."

"What's next?"

"Mixing the clay. You do it by hand to get it started, like kneading dough, then throw it in the machine to finish it off. Takes a couple hours to get it smooth and homogenous and work all the water out. So I'll take you to my very exciting data entry console while we wait."

Nicole raised an eyebrow at Ravi. "You get excited about the weirdest things, Rav."

"Hey I wouldn't have invited you for this part, Miss Shows Up Out Of Nowhere All The Time Somehow. The actual fun starts after it's done mixing – forming it into plates and throwing it in the fire."

"How long do you spend here?"

"Mm... usually until three or four AM I guess? Yeah, I guess you're always asleep when I get back, aren't you?"

"Gods. That's like... what, eight hours?"

"Nine. Ten if I'm lucky. Gotta put in a full day's work. I don't get to come down here as often as I'd like, you know? And sometimes the lab's busy, so I can't get much done. Not enough equipment to go around. As I have said before, this is a very, very shitty university."

Nicole very much enjoyed playing with the clay dough. She kept making little abstract animal sculptures out of her batches and showing them off proudly, each time acting more and more disappointed when Ravi reminded her that she would not be able to bake them like that unless she wanted to mix a new batch and pay them for the materials.

Despite the distractions, it was kind of nice having a second pair of hands for this part. Saved a ton of time. And Nicole was... fun. She made this fun. They caught themself wishing she'd come by more often.

Ravi sincerely thanked her once everything was thrown in the mixers for the night.

When they got to the door of the engineering lab, they handed Nicole some cash and their access card.

"Go get us dinner? Use the card to get back in, please. Whatever you're doing to get in here, it can't be safe or legal. I'll be over there behind that blue machine," they said, pointing.

"I can get it," Nicole insisted, trying to put the cash back in Ravi's hands.

"Nope. Not letting my lab assistant work for free, Nikki. That's criminal. Chinese please. Something with chicken. Make-me-cry spicy. I don't care where from. You're the best," they reminded her before they turned abruptly and closed the door behind them before she could protest.

While Ravi monitored the measurements coming out of the

machines that were trying very hard to destroy their ceramic plates with pile drivers and plasma torches, they realized this might actually be one of the fun parts. Nicole would be sad to miss it.

Last week's batch turned out pretty well, it seemed. One of the combinations worked a whole 2.1% ± 0.3% better than the others. Not quite the best they'd ever seen, but it was easily the best they'd seen in a while.

When Nicole returned, they were making graphs and writing up a report about the results this week, trying to predict which one of their mixtures next week would do best. Hopefully the kiln wouldn't destroy too many of them during the baking process this time. As much as the stuff was super strong once it was done, while it was half-baked, it was pretty sensitive to bursts of heat, and that kiln was so, so shitty.

The two of them enjoyed the food over cheerful conversation, mostly about what Nicole had been up to that day – more charity work today, bless her heart. Ravi told a little story about one of their students in the lab today who got the concentration of a reagent wrong and cracked a beaker from the heat – which they realized too late sounded a whole lot less exciting out loud than in their head. Nicole still smiled, though. Sweetheart.

When they were done eating, Ravi had to get back to writing their report, so they told her she could go find something else to entertain herself while they finished off their analysis, warning her to stay away from about 90% of the science wing first.

"Oh, uh, there's a greenhouse over that way," they gestured vaguely in the direction of the biology wing. "You *shouldn't*, but I bet you could figure out how to get in."

Nicole gave Ravi a coy grin and said it would be a fun challenge, but before she could escape the tedium of the engineering lab, her attention got caught on one of the whirring machines. She was mesmerized by the towering contraption's bright, colorful display.

She asked what it was, and Ravi explained that it was a spectroscope. "It's trying to figure out what molecules that sample is made of."

"Is this one yours?"

"No. I already know what goes into my stuff. Someone probably left it running overnight on some mystery substance."

Nicole hummed on it. "So… someone could just put your ceramic in here and figure out how to make it?"

Ravi hadn't considered that, but yeah, she was right. "The compounds are pretty common. The only weird thing is the fibrous form of the tungsten there. That might throw someone off."

Nicole watched in awe for a while as the thing clunked and whirred while the rainbow bars of the histogram gently shifted around.

After a while, her eyes lit up. She asked excitedly, "Could you use it on something biological?"

Ravi quirked an eyebrow at that. Biology wasn't their thing, but… they didn't really see why not. "I guess? Why? Want to see what you're made of?" They grinned at her and offered a preliminary hypothesis: "I'll guess… 75% pancakes, 10% pure honey, 10% green tea, and 5% whatever a regular human's made of."

"Are you trying to say you think I eat people?"

"…No. That came out wrong."

"Because I don't."

"Hm. Kind of defensive there, Nix."

"I don't!"

"Mhm. I won't tell, you know. Just don't eat anyone I know."

"Ravi."

They grinned at her, then turned back to their report.

While they were working, Nicole continued staring at the machine pensively. After a minute or so, she confessed something:

"I saw your notebook the other day, Ravi."

"Which notebook?" they asked absently, distracted by their work.

"About your uh… 'samples'. Those vials you keep stealing."

Ravi froze with their fingers on the keyboard. They wouldn't mind if she was reading through any of their academic notes, but that one was… a very personal journal for her to stumble across.

"Sorry. It was just right out on your desk. I couldn't resist."

"Mm… Anything juicy in there?" they asked uneasily without turning around. There was a whole lot of embarrassing stuff in there. They were trying to enumerate it all in their mind to imagine the absolute worst-case scenario here. It would be great if Nicole hadn't seen any of it.

Though... honestly, it would be... nice, if they could talk to her about any of it, wouldn't it? Maybe she'd understand.

"You want to know how the tar works, right?"

"That would be nice. There's nothing legitimate online about it. Kind of frustrating."

"So. This machine..."

Ravi turned to look at the steadily humming spectroscope in front of Nicole.

Their mind was glowing with a realization.

"You're... thinking..."

Nicole finished their thought, "You could throw it in here, right?"

"Right..."

"And figure out—"

"—figure out what it's made of," Ravi mumbled, to finish her suggestion.

"Might help, right?"

"Yeah. That. Might help..." Ravi trailed off in thought.

—Wait. No. No, come on, you can't do that. That's like... mad science stuff, experimenting on your own body. <u>Dark</u> path.

They shook their head about it and tried to come up with an easy excuse. "It wouldn't help that much, though. Everything organic is just made of carbon and some other random stuff, if I remember *anything* from that one biochem course I had to take in second year. And the output from that machine has to be matched against known patterns. I don't know any patterns for organic molecules."

"So? You could look it up."

"Nicole people spend years studying to figure that stuff out. I'd be playing catchup with postgrads in the field."

"Okay. So, you know any postgrads in biochem?"

Ravi rolled their fingers lightly on the keys of the keyboard while they considered what Nicole was suggesting.

"I can't just... That's not ethical, bringing a biohazard like that into the lab, without even running it by any of the administrators...?"

"So don't tell anyone?"

"That doesn't make it more ethical! In fact, I'm pretty sure that makes it much much less ethical, Nicole."

"Okay fine, but who's it hurting?"

"I don't know! I don't know anything about this stuff, Nikki, it's all shrouded in mystery and coverups and bullshit reports sponsored by *InThetics*. It might be *contagious*. It might be *airborne*. I don't know." Though every report they read suggested it was entirely benign once it was out of the body.

"So? Just be careful. Just assume it's all of that and be careful with it. They study viruses all the time, right? That's way more risky, isn't it?"

"...I guess?"

"So."

"...Just be careful..."

"Easy!"

"...I don't know anyone in the bio department." Half-true. There were a couple TAs they'd seen in the break room who seemed very passionate about very obscure bits and pieces of microorganisms. But Ravi had never spoken to any of them.

"You're just making excuses now. Do you want to get answers about this stuff or not?"

"...Why do you care so much?"

"*You* care! Don't get in your own way! This is important to you!"

Ravi grimaced about it and looked away to consider Nicole's unsavory premise without having to look at her pleading eyes.

They did often have time to kill in the lab waiting for various semi-automated processes to finish, like the mixers. It wouldn't be... *impossible* to work on a little research on the tar in parallel.

But it was so sketchy. They'd never be able to get someone in the bio department to help.

They sighed and told Nicole, "We'd have to do it in secret."

Nicole was absolutely glowing when Ravi agreed to her proposal.

"And the chem lab doesn't have what I need to be safe about it. Nothing for handling biological substances safely. We'd need to get into a bio lab somehow. —Without anyone knowing."

Nicole brought a gracious hand to her chest and bowed to Ravi, "At your service, my liege."

"What?"

"You need to get in somewhere, I'm your girl."

"You're serious."

She grinned at Ravi proudly, "I'm very serious! Let's do it right now! I bet you've even got some on you right now, don't you? You do, don't you? I know how much you've been obsessing over this stuff." She didn't wait for an answer before she grabbed them by the wrist and tugged them out of their seat. "Come on! Show me where the bio labs are."

Ravi tried to protest, but there was no saying no to this woman. They were going to the bio labs tonight.

God, they hoped she never wanted them to pull a heist or bury a body. They'd roll over in a second.

Unsurprisingly, the door that led to the hallway with all the bio labs was locked behind keycard access, and Ravi obviously wasn't cleared to get in there. The lock blinked red when they tapped their card. —Which was just a *stellar* experiment to pull here. Now there would be a record of them being here. *Why* did they think that was a good idea?

While Ravi was struck stupid and lamenting that absolute *idiot* move there, Nicole shot them a wry grin and told them to wait there.

They were suddenly having second thoughts. And third thoughts. Fourth. Fifth. If they got caught, it could be catastrophic for their academic career. This was a very, very bad idea.

"No. Nicole come on, how are you even getting in these places?? Nicole!" They called after her while she hustled down the hall and around a corner out of sight. "Nicole!! Do not break into the biology labs!!" They jogged up to the hall she just disappeared down, but there was no sign of her, and no response to their calls.

They cursed at themself. They'd be in so, so much trouble if anyone found out about this.

And seriously! How was she even planning to—

"Ravi!" she called from behind them with a singsong voice.

She'd done it. And in less than a minute. How was she so familiar with the university she could just slip in there? This was a *huge* security concern. There were dangerous machines in these labs, godsake. Nicole could get hurt if she was messing around in here on her own.

"Come on!" she called them over.

Ravi looked over their shoulder apprehensively. Surely there was some kind of security camera monitoring the door. But they couldn't spot one.

This shitty university didn't even care enough to properly secure their science labs. Unbelievable.

"Nicole, seriously, how did you get in here?"

"Did you know you can trick open an emergency exit if you get it just right?"

"...Aren't the emergency exits alarmed?"

"Do you hear an alarm?"

Ravi shook their head. "Were you a jewel thief in a past life or something?"

She grinned at them. "Something like that."

While the two of them wandered the forbidden hall – Ravi: very cautiously; and Nicole: brazenly peering in every window she could find – Ravi reflected on how insane this was. Really, what were they hoping to do here? They were so, so unfamiliar with organic chemistry. They'd been focusing on material science and their own research for so long, they'd practically lost everything they knew about even basic compositional analysis techniques.

They trawled their mind for some strategy to deploy. They could run the tar through a centrifuge, split it into layers, put each layer through a battery of decomposition reactions, try to pull out every imaginable compound one by one...

But there was a proper way to do that. Some ideal sequence of particular chemical baths to run a substance through to be efficient with the sample – and they didn't exactly have an unlimited supply of the sample to work with here. Since September's treatment, they'd managed to grab a vial every month – at the end of October, November, and one more just last week. Four vials. Not a lot of room for fucking around.

Ravi stopped beside Nicole, who was staring in awe at a big lab – bright white with a bunch of fridges along one wall, a few big glass incubation chambers with subtle red lights warming plants and petri dishes, and a bunch of large machines that Ravi couldn't hope to guess the purpose of.

Then they spotted their salvation: There was a humble lab desk, off in the corner, with a scale, a centrifuge, and a few sterilized vials next to a handful of bottles of various solvents. Presumably, solvents that were well-suited to breaking down biological substances.

—And, most importantly, a bunch of single-use HEPA masks, and a very powerful looking fume hood.

They could work with that.

Nicole looked at them eagerly, practically begging them to go inside.

They sighed at her relentless enthusiasm. There was no hope. They couldn't say no to her.

"Come on," they conceded to her silent insistence. "Let's get this over with before security finds us and expels me."

"Oh stop, no one even knows you're here, this place is dead."

Ravi noted to her that the lights for the lab were on. "They're automatic. Someone's in here. So, act natural." Ravi looked Nicole over head to toe discerningly. "Actually... god, I hate to ask, but could you use your incredible breaking and entering skills to track down a lab coat? You look *incredibly* out of place in a dress and stockings. There's probably a locker room around here somewhere. Good place to start."

Nicole dutifully gave Ravi a salute and started to scope out every door in the hallway in search of some promising place to borrow a coat from.

In the meantime, Ravi tried, as casually as possible, to enter the lab and get settled at that workstation of their dreams. ...Their nightmares? God what were they doing...

They glanced over their shoulder and spotted the person who was keeping the lights on – a postgrad student – or... probably a professor, actually. She looked in her thirties. She was wearing headphones and staring lethargically at the output from a machine that looked *surprisingly* familiar.

—*They actually did use spectroscopes in biology? Nicole was right?*

And <u>*why*</u> *is that one nicer than the one in the engineering lab? God damn it.*

Ravi noted something interesting about the mystery woman. It looked like she was equipped with an InThetics prosthetic on her left arm. A couple models behind. The obnoxious green logo on the back of the hand gave it away. The ink popped brilliantly against the synthetic perfectly tone-matched dark brown skin – even from thirty feet away.

It was *interesting* because she was also using a wheelchair. Ravi wondered why, if she was cool with getting prosthetics at all, she would only get one for her arm. Too much money maybe?

Ravi considered it for themself. If they had to pick just one limb, which one would they save?

Something felt wrong about that grim thought experiment, considering the inspiration for it.

—*Disability tourism, no?*

They returned their attention to their work and hoped that they were innocuous enough off in the corner that the mystery woman wouldn't call security on them. But it would probably be fine. Ravi was doing science, after all. This was a science lab. And even if they were floundering, these labs were open even to second year students. They could just lie.

They drew the vial of tar from their pocket and set it down on the stainless-steel surface of the desk, then sat down on the stool there to vacantly stare at the thing while they considered the implications of what they were about to do.

—*Just be careful. Right?*

Ravi looked around the large room and spotted a dozen signs about various countermeasures to avoid contamination in the lab. They didn't even know what half the terminology on the signs meant. But they knew it would be bad if they fucked this up.

It *wasn't* contagious, they reminded themself. It wasn't. For sure. Every report they'd ever read about it made that clear. Never, ever, had it spread from one person to another, as far as any research could prove.

Statistically speaking, this was perfectly safe. Bayes' Theorem never let them down before: Previous results informed the probability of future events. Thousands of nil outcomes would *obviously* lead to nil probabilities.

...Right?

This was the first time they'd broken the seal on one of these things.

Growing in their shoulder was very, very different from sitting under their nose.

The smell wasn't terrible, though. Kind of metallic? Or like molten glass maybe? It was hard to place it.

They suddenly realized they had opened the thing with neither a mask on nor the fume hood active. They remedied that in a hurried panic.

A quick glance over their shoulder confirmed they hadn't done anything suspicious enough yet to earn the attention of the woman at the whirring machine.

They were safe.

For now.

Nicole returned with a very ill-fitting lab coat on – way too small. She couldn't button it up if she wanted to – though it did a *phenomenal* job accentuating her ample bust.

—*Ravi. Stop.*

She shrugged when she got close and assured Ravi it was the best she could find. Ravi handed her a HEPA mask and told her how to put it on so she could actually sit near them while they worked.

However, she opted instead to stand three whole paces back.

"What's with you?" Ravi asked her teasingly. "You're the one who wanted me to do this."

"Yup! Definitely want *you* to do this. That stuff kind of weirds me out, not gonna lie."

Ravi rolled their eyes. That *was* perfectly reasonable, but it felt very silly that she was so invested in this while being so squeamish about it.

Ravi laid out a few petri dishes under the fume hood and plucked a pipette from a jar on the desk to put a drop of the tar in each.

While they were getting set up for their first round of observations, Ravi realized they hadn't actually... told Nicole that they were carrying a vial of this stuff in their pocket.

"Hey, how did you know I had this?"

Nicole was idly spinning in a chair she found somewhere else in the lab while she waited for Ravi to do their work.

"Mm... How did I know... Uh. Good guess? You're kind of obsessed with it. You take it out sometimes and fiddle with it while we're hanging out. You don't notice?"

"...I do?"

"You do."

Ravi froze in place for a few seconds trying remember any time they'd ever done that. They did carry a vial with them everywhere. They did fiddle with it in their pocket sometimes. They really took it right out in the open sometimes? Just, unconsciously?

What the hell was wrong with them? They were as bad as Erwin, waving his tumor around in their face.

"God, sorry I did that to you."

"Oh, don't worry about it. Hopefully getting some answers about it here will get it off your mind, hey?"

"...Yeah. Hopefully."

God, they almost forgot why they had been collecting these vials at all. It wasn't to just feel bitter at the stuff, or to keep it close to them, contained in a way that felt like they had some semblance of power over it. They wanted to know it. To know *why*. And maybe Nicole was right that the first step there was figuring out *what* it was.

After a couple of hours working at it – though they'd completely lost track of time and had no idea it had already been a couple hours – they took a break to look over their notes and their rough sketches.

The tar came out thick and gritty when they spread it across the surface of the petri dish. Under a microscope, long chains of little black crystalline strands separated from the fluid medium. They looked a little like fiberglass or asbestos – which certainly might explain why it hurt so bad, getting their flesh cut up every month by millions of glassy microscopic needles.

But aside from that, there wasn't much else they could make sense of. According to some basic manuals lying around the workstation, the results of the various litmus tests showed, unsurprisingly, that the thick tarry medium was rich with various hydrocarbons they couldn't hope to see the significance of – no struggling with a spectroscope required to prove that. There also seemed to be some iron compounds in there, and some other common organic molecules they couldn't put any meaning to.

Looking at it all together, they almost felt more lost than they did when they started. It really just left them with more questions.

But that was the right way. That was science at its best. Now they knew just a little more of what they didn't know. There was a gap in the universe that only they could see now. And there was still a lot of work to do to patch it shut – work that would probably only open up more gaps – but it was a start.

They dropped the empty vial of tar in a nearby biohazard bin, then got to work sterilizing and tidying up their station.

After they had everything cleaned to their satisfaction, Ravi looked around to try to figure out where Nicole had got to. She was nowhere to be found in the lab, though.

That mystery scientist was still staring lethargically at her monitor. She was drawing something idly in a notebook now. Two hours of staring. That's a hell of a lot of patience.

Ravi picked up their own little notebook and flipped through it one last time. They knew they were on the right path, but they couldn't help feeling a little frustrated that even though they knew what they didn't know, they couldn't even imagine the questions they needed to ask to get any answers.

They had been right about one thing: They were years behind any postgrads on this stuff.

But... there was some kind of a postgrad right here in front of them.

A postgrad who had apparently not cared at all about Ravi's obvious floundering use of the lab all night.

This was probably the best chance they had, to introduce themself to someone who might be able to help.

They took a deep breath and steeled themself for a very awkward interaction, then put on their very best lost puppy act and took the dive.

They waved in the woman's peripheral vision and started in when she got her headphones off: "Hey uh... Sorry, this is a weird question. I'm trying to figure out what's in this... uh... weird black slime sample I've got. But I kind of have no idea what I'm doing."

All the woman's lethargy shed away in an instant as she perked up at the sound of Ravi's voice. She gripped the hand rims of her wheelchair, then whipped around enthusiastically to give Ravi a big grin. She was clearly eager to have an excuse to do anything else but what she was doing.

"That's what you were up to over there? You were *really* into it. I was wondering."

"Yeah. Well. Sadly, I didn't make much progress. I'm very bad at this stuff."

"What're ya looking for?"

"Oh. I mean. Anything? I guess?"

"Mystery slime?"

"Yeah. From my fridge," they lied, probably very convincingly.

"Neat. Love it. For a lab assignment or something?"

"Uh... kind of a personal project. Groundwork for a thesis."

"Oh cool. Brave of you to do a thesis on something you suck at."

"It's uh. Very *ground-level* groundwork."

"Sounds pretty subterranean, yeah. You want a species then, right? So, DNA? Maybe a protein profile? Could probably find a name for it in the database if you can get some kind of a fingerprint on it."

"Yes. Yes all of that sounds cool. I don't know how to fingerprint a slime."

She leaned back and looked Ravi over head to toe, then gave their eyes a good, uncomfortable peering into. Now that she wasn't sluggishly leaning over the counter looking at her monitor, Ravi was surprised to find that she had a confidence and control and comfort in this space that simultaneously scared Ravi and put them at ease. They picked the right person. This was *her* lab.

She spoke frankly: "You are *not* in the biochem program. Where are you from?"

"I uh... I'm working in materials."

"Ah ha. Yeah, this is... *completely* unrelated."

"Yeah, I can tell."

"How'd you even get in here?"

"...Special access?"

"Uh huh. You're gonna want to work on your story there a bit."

"It's not—"

"—Hun, I was watching you clean up that station with *rapt awe.* You have no idea what you're doing. Go take the training before you come back, okay?"

"...Yes ma'am."

"Anyways, I'm not going to stand in the way of anyone's bold scientific endeavors, so long as you don't contaminate everything. So: Getting down to it: You probably want to start with something easy," she said, asking Ravi to stay where they were. She dramatically shoved herself away from her station at that fancy whirring spectroscope and wheeled herself over to the back of the lab.

The powerful lab master of a woman hummed and murmured to herself while she examined the spines of a pile of crisp textbooks on some half-hidden shelf in the corner of the lab. Reminded Ravi of some wizened wizard in an arcane library. At last, she seemed to find the one she wanted. She cheerfully wheeled her way back and tossed it to Ravi. "Start here. And welcome to the dark side," she said with a coy grin.

It was an old first-year biochemistry book with some sticky notes poking out on a few pages – pages covered in radiant pink, blue, and yellow highlighter ink, and all related to elementary DNA analysis. This book had seen some things.

"I'm Carrie," the biochem wizard introduced herself.

Ravi extended their arm for a handshake and offered their name in exchange. "Ama—"

—Wait. No. This woman's cool, right? She seems cool, at least.

And… you're… <u>worth knowing</u>, right?

"…Ravi."

"Ama-Ravi—"

"—No. Sorry. It's just 'Ravi'." They paused for a moment before hurriedly adding: "And I'm non-binary."

"Ravi. Pleasure. I'm *told* I'm some kind of lady-type, but as you can probably tell from the hair and the eyebrows and such, I cannot even pretend to give a shit about acting like one. Boyfriend hates me for it, but I don't keep a guy like him around for his unsolicited opinions, if you know what I mean. Anyway, there's a manual for sterilizing a station in the cupboard over there. Do it properly before you leave."

"Yes ma'am."

She laughed, "Okay you have to stop with that. We're all the same here. Just humble students under the enigmatic tutelage of the eternal cosmos. I'm very happy to help, I mean it. I'm usually pretty busy down here, but if you see me sitting on my ass staring at this piece of shit machine, you feel free to come ask me whatever you want."

After cleaning up properly, Ravi found Nicole hanging out in the hallway, shed of her poor disguise of a lab coat, reading a copy of the very same first-year biochemistry textbook they were holding in their hands.

Ravi shoved her playfully in the shoulder when they approached. "Just abandon me in there, huh?"

"Oh sorry. I figured you didn't want any distractions. You were extremely in the zone." She snapped the book shut and asked to confirm, "Ready to go?"

Ravi led the way back to the chemistry labs. They had a long night ahead of them still. And they were now a fair bit behind on their reports and on firing their clay in the kiln.

But it was worth it.

They had a powerful ally now.

They told Nicole about Carrie. She was overjoyed that Ravi had managed to make a new friend – as if Ravi was normally incapable of succeeding at even the most basic attempt at human warmth. Which... to be fair, might be kind of accurate lately.

They felt good about this, about going forward with all this. Answers. They'd finally have answers.

...Though, they still had no way to get into the bio lab on their own. There was no way they'd actually be able to get special access added to their card.

While Ravi and Nicole worked away at fitting the newly mixed clay into Ravi's molds, Ravi turned their little puzzle over and over in their head.

At last, seeing no better option than the one right in front of them, they took the plunge and made a big, big ask:

"Hey Nicole, can you... get me in the lab again next week?"

Nicole looked absolutely shocked at the request, bringing a teasing set of fingertips to her lips to hide a mock gasp. "Ravi Beausoleil. Are you *asking for help?*"

"Oh, shut up. I ask for help all the time. Can you do it or not?"

"Yes! Absolutely! I'd love to. Gods, you're finally putting me to good use. You know how long I've been waiting for this?"

Ravi shook their head in a little show of frustration. "You're such a weirdo Nicole, I swear to god." The way she phrased that sounded extremely wrong. They spoke to her very sternly to assure her: "You <u>do not</u> have to do this for me just because I'm putting you up. Tell me you understand that or we're not doing this at all."

Nicole grimaced a little before she repeated, "I don't have to do this."

"For any reason."

"For any reason."

"Okay. Thank you. It's very sweet of you to help me out. I appreciate it. You're a good friend."

"Correct," she replied, breaking her grimace for a proud little smirk.

After getting everything in the kiln, Ravi headed back to the engineering lab to finish off their report. They told Nicole all the fun stuff was over, but she insisted on sticking around, even though she was clearly bored stupid.

She was reading that textbook and spinning around on a chair waiting for Ravi to finish up their reports when she sighed and woefully chided Ravi with something that had clearly been weighing on her for the last half-hour:

"You really won't ever let me pay you back properly, will you? You're such a monster, Ravi Bee. You have no idea what you're doing to me."

Without looking away from the screen or even halting their typing, Ravi automatically responded, "There's nothing to pay back, Nix." It was practically a reflex at this point.

Another sigh from their dear misguided friend.

They knew they'd never convince her, but at the very least they had to keep reminding her. She paid them back with every smile. They wished she could understand that.

And the push she gave them tonight? Ravi would never be able to pay *her* back for *that* – not that she'd ever believe them if they told her that.

Ah well. That's just the way she was, wasn't it? It was mostly endearing when it wasn't gravely concerning, and they made a point of correcting her whenever it *was* gravely concerning. They didn't mind being careful with her about all that. It was kind of fun, really. Like a game. A playful perpetual little battle of wits.

And maybe if they kept at it, they'd finally make the winning move and convince her she'd paid them back a hundred times over already.

You Know You Probably Shouldn't Need to Get Security Involved in Academic Engagements

(*Afternoon, Monday, 9th January*)

Virgil – Felicity's dear translator – normally wasn't late coming back from lunch like this. And normally Felicity wouldn't care either way. She was barely in the office the two of them shared, and when she was, she usually had her own work to do. Cataloging scans. Reading through the latest news for any hints at some newly uncovered ancient forgotten manuscripts or journals. And now, thanks to that insightful conversation with *dearest* Danica, reaching out to universities around the world soliciting for collections of nearly forgotten zines.

Once in a while, she even sat down to write out a few pages to summarize the status of her growing bibliography for her thesis paper – because apparently, helping set the groundwork for the greatest stride humanity has ever taken towards immortalizing even the most mundane of its people just wasn't enough of a testament to the significance of her research. Nope. Needs a *report*.

Normally Felicity wouldn't mind keeping herself busy while she waited, but Virgil set her expectations pretty high today with an all-too-brief message that morning: "Found something for you. Office after lunch."

Felicity could only assume he'd finally found some time in his oh-so-busy schedule to look at those notes she liberated from Danica's coat last month. —Last month! The guy was busy with his own research, sure, but come on! This was mission critical. Lives on the line.

Though, to be fair, the details Felicity could provide about the secretive project were... sparse. Hard to convey the urgency of the request with a bunch of 'Just because!' justifications.

And she couldn't really entice him with the arcane nature of the pages either. She wasn't about to hand over magic paper with glowing ink to *anyone*, so she just gave Virgil a couple photographs and told him to track something down for her. Told him it was a lead on some important manuscript or another.

Luckily the month of waiting was enough time for her to do some research of her own – into Danica herself. With the help of a pricy private investigator, she managed to find out that there was a mysterious string of misfortune that seemed to follow Danica around wherever she went in the last few years. Evictions. Accidents. Scandals. Almost everyone she associated with for longer than a couple months seemed to come to some kind of ruin.

It wasn't much to go on, but it sure was suspicious. Bad luck could only explain so many coincidences. Once you got up past a dozen? Probably something else going on.

Felicity was getting impatient waiting for Virgil, so she opted to wheel her chair over to his desk to start fussing with the papers there. It was a whole lot of interesting stuff, sure, but nothing related to what she came here for.

She was halfway through making a little flip-animation on a pad of sticky notes she found on Virgil's desk when he finally made his appearance.

He entered the room mournfully apologizing.

He entered the room mournfully apologizing with a hell of a lump on his face and a black eye.

Felicity shoved herself away from the desk and looked at him wide-eyed. "What the hell happened to you?"

"Don't really want to talk about it, Miss V, if it's all the same."

"Well it's definitely not all the same, but I can't force you. —Unless giving you a matching black eye there would squeeze it out of you," she added with a grin.

"...Dr. Fern hit me."

"Ha!" Felicity couldn't catch herself in time from letting out a big laugh. "Aw Virgil. She's smaller than me, Jeezus. How'd she do that much damage to you?"

"I'll tell you, Miss V, you can't go challenging her etymology thesis assertions without both a hefty body of evidence and a large bodyguard."

"I'm guessing you had neither."

"Didn't occur to me to come prepared to the staff lounge, no." Virgil sighed and flopped down in his chair. "She left in a huff and returned promptly to my surprise to educate me in melee with a briefcase full of her research notes."

"Come on. Seriously?"

"I would never lie to you, Miss V. We have a professional bond of trust."

Felicity tried to get Virgil at least a *little* more incensed about being assaulted like that, but he seemed determined to roll over and take it. Shame. Just because Fern was a prof didn't make it okay for her to assault a poor graduate student like that. God.

After a few failed attempts at trying to convince him to get some petty revenge, Felicity asked, "Well, were you right at least?"

Virgil waved his hand lackadaisically in the air while he glumly answered: "The violent weight of a briefcase full of research suggests that being right was never an option, but I still don't think her conclusion fits, even after she tried to forcibly insert it into my skull."

Felicity mused: "You know some academics make entire careers out of feuding with each other. This could be really good for you," she said with a grin. "Go on TV, nerd out about the origins of words and how to pronounce them, get into fist fights. I hear there's big money in the lecture-boxing circuit."

"I doubt I have the reflexes to stand up to Dr. Fern in a fair fight, Miss V, but I appreciate the confidence. Real sweet of you."

Virgil sat in silence for a few breaths while Felicity waited eagerly for the conversation to drift naturally to the thing she was waiting for.

Sadly, there was rarely anything natural about conversation with dear Virgil.

At last, as if waking from a stupor, he waved his hand in the air in front of him again, miming the motion of a waterwheel, while he tried to gather his thoughts.

"I couldn't write it down," he started, slowly pulling it together. "You told me not to."

Felicity remembered no such instruction about these artifacts of hers, but she assumed Virgil would explain it all in a moment.

He heaved himself out of his chair, then made his way to his full-to-bursting, double-layered bookshelf, shoved some books aside, and pulled one out from the hidden second layer of books, then handed it to Felicity.

"Page 210."

Felicity opened it to find a copy of a page she'd given to Virgil to translate – that annotated page that was torn from some book.

It was entirely untranslated.

"What's this?" she asked disappointedly, holding it up and showing off the lack of progress.

"Mm... so the text from the book's no good. I can only guess at a few words. The margin notes, though," he gestured at the page in Felicity's hand. "Some person writing very earnestly about negotiating with mystical brokers. Apparently, whoever they were, they were very interested in bits of human." He gave Felicity a slightly condemning look, "You bring me some weird stuff sometimes, Miss V, but this is the weirdest yet."

"Why didn't you write any of that down?"

"You remember GH1703X?"

Felicity raised an eyebrow at that and rolled her shoulders uncomfortably. "Hey we uh. We agreed we weren't talking about that anymore..."

"I'm not talking about it. Are you talking about it?"

"Okay good."

Again, Virgil gestured at the page, "Same language. Same words here and there. Still no idea what any of it means. But at least this one didn't have any drawings of *flayed children*. So, thank you very kindly for *that* mercy."

Felicity looked at the page again in disbelief.

"...You're thinking..."

Virgil shrugged. "Miss V, I promised you I wouldn't ask, but I'll let you know, I've never seen anything like 03X until you brought me this. Wherever you got *that* book, that's probably your best bet if you want more info about that *page*, I'd say."

"...Okay. Thanks, Virgil. Good work."

"No problem, Miss V. Still working on the other two."

"You're too good. I don't pay you enough."

"You pay me just right, don't worry."

This was the only used bookstore Felicity had ever been in that didn't have a bell on the door.

"The real Faust," she said, when the lethargic 'owner' asked what she wanted.

He nodded, knocked on a wall behind him, then informed Felicity she could find the book in aisle thirteen.

The bookstore had twelve aisles.

She met her contact in the back alley.

"Aurelia!" the round, well-bearded old man greeted her with open arms, coming in for a warm hug.

He smelled so thick of ink and mildew that even Felicity, seasoned spelunker of ruins and tombs filled with rotting *everything*, had to hold her breath.

She tolerated this guy with a grin because there was simply no one better in the world to get what she wanted than this man.

Unbelievable she had to travel all the way back home to this husk of a city just to see him, but he refused to communicate any way other than face-to-face, and this was his home base this year.

"How's my beautiful golden girl?"

"Great! Doing great," she answered, as sincerely as she could. Then she jumped right into it, pulling the copy of the disembodied page out of her pocket and handing it to the eccentric man. "You gave me a book a while ago…"

Felicity never did learn her black-market bookseller's name. To be fair, she never gave him hers either. Her middle name was enough. To her, he was simply the Dealer.

The Dealer unfolded the printout and all the joy drained right out of his face. He asked very sternly, "Where did you find this?"

Felicity quirked an eyebrow at that. "Why? Familiar?"

"Familiar?? This *single* page dropped a whole zero off the price of that book! Torn right out. I can't believe the buyer even noticed. I was this close—" He pinched his finger and thumb together a micron apart. "—to retirement."

Felicity jabbed at him skeptically, "You'd never retire."

"I could have though!" Again, he stared at the page dumbfounded for a few seconds. "Aurelia, I must insist, where did you find this?"

Felicity hadn't prepared a lie for this situation. She was actually hoping to ask the Dealer some similar question.

She laughed nervously when she replied, "Internet?"

"Aurelia."

"...Okay. Okay, it was on the ground."

"Where?"

"In a bar."

"Where??"

Felicity gestured in the general direction of the bar she and Danica had been drinking at the night she found this. It was true at least. It had been on the floor. Then she found it. Honest enough. Better than trying to keep up a lie. She wasn't very good at that.

The Dealer gave her a discerning look for a few tense seconds. She, again, smiled at him nervously. At last, he accepted her answer, but not happily.

He ran his fingers through his beard while he contemplated what to do with this. "You have the original?"

"I do."

"You can give it to me, yes? We're close like that."

"No. I need it. It's for my research. I was actually hoping to get the book it came from." Felicity let out a little huff of a sigh. "I don't suppose you can just tell me who you sold it to."

The Dealer let out a hard laugh at that. "What's it worth to you, my dear golden girl?"

Felicity closed her eyes and braced herself to let go of her apprehensions. This, she was prepared for. At least, she told herself she was. She told herself that every time. But every time, still, she hated to do it, hated herself a little for it. It felt so... seedy.

But maybe it wasn't so bad? The books she scanned for her research, the originals, they weren't exactly useful once they'd been scanned. Frankly, storing them was a huge hassle, especially considering how fragile they were.

But the Dealer, he was always looking for rare originals – even ones that could never be opened again. And... you know, some of them probably ended up in museums, right? Or extremely professionally protected private collections?

Yeah, they were probably going to good homes, it was fine.

Felicity handed him a tablet, open to an album of photographs of some of the books she had recently recovered and immortalized, each accompanied by a synopsis of the work.

He browsed the list with hungry eyes.

Felicity could never quite nail down what this guy wanted out of the books. He had such varied tastes. Some days he would lean towards something mundane like some ancient farmer's almanac. Other days, he wanted formal religious texts. Other times, recipes, songs, medicine, folklore, architectural sketchbooks, 'spell books'. There was no way to know, so Felicity always had to bring everything she had and wait, leaning against the wall lethargically staring at her neatly painted pomegranate nails, searching out imperfections and trying to file them off with the edge of her thumbnail, until at last he returned to her with a list of asks.

She scrolled through his requests today. Larger than usual. She normally tried to negotiate. But there was no negotiating on this. Amy's safety was at stake here. If Felicity couldn't figure out what all this nonsense with Danica meant, she could never rest, never knowing what kind of creature was preying on her dear best friend.

She sighed to herself about it. Normally she'd at least get an actual book out of the deal too.

Half-heartedly, she asked, not really expecting a 'yes': "Don't suppose you can throw in some old manuscript for my trouble? You know, a tip for the courier?"

He grinned at her, "No hassle today, Aurelia? You're desperate."

"It's personal, this one."

"Well, for my most loyal customer—"

"—Oh, please. Don't call me a customer, that's so callous. We're research partners. This is a material exchange. Sharing academic knowledge and historical resources."

"Call it what you will—"

"—I'm calling it research partners."

"Yes yes, well, for my most loyal 'research partner', I'll throw in a box of disintegrated journals, how's that?"

Felicity closed her eyes and reminded herself again and again, like a mantra, what she was doing this for: For Amy. Amy was counting on Felicity to figure all this out, whether she knew it or not. No matter how much it hurt to accept such a terrible deal, she had to accept that there was no way around it.

With much trepidation, she uneasily offered her hand out to seal the deal, and the Dealer happily, eagerly shook on it.

"So who bought the book?" Felicity asked, ready to write the info down.

"There's an old eccentric collector in town. I only hear her called the Witch."

"Yeah, that fits," Felicity nodded. Magic book, right? Obviously? Considering where she found the page? "How do I contact her?"

"You don't. There's a go-between. I only ever deal with her."

"Okay. Who's the go-between?"

"Big woman. Tidy braided amber hair. Very blue contact lenses. Grin sharp enough to cut glass. I don't have a name for her at all. But I'll tell you something, Aurelia, you don't want to mess with her."

"Mm. Why's that?"

"You know I don't part with my zeroes that easily," he lamented. "I barely came out of that scuffle in one piece."

"She fought you??"

"Worse. Worse, my dear, worse worse worse. I can't even describe it properly, but she got in my head about it. Made a game of it. I lost. *Soundly.* I'm lucky she didn't get the whole thing for free. And I have no idea why I even agreed to play for it at all. You know me," he said sternly, crossing his arms. "I don't play games when it comes to books."

Felicity stared at the man in stunned disbelief.

"...Her... 'contact lenses': *Pure* blue? Or do they kind of... change in the light? Sparkle in other colors?"

"...They do indeed sparkle in other colors – especially when she's got that *grin* on. You already sound very familiar, my dear Aurelia."

—Danica?? That was Danica for sure, no? Her hair wasn't braided, but everything else...?

Hold on, did that mean... Did Danica secretly rip a page out of this book and then negotiate a whole zero off the price because it was missing?? Is that why it was in her pocket??

What a scam!! This woman was a devil! A devil for sure!

Felicity realized she was doing a very bad job hiding her bewilderment. She tried to shake it off before she asked as calmly as she could, but still a little eagerly: "When are you meeting her next?"

"Why?"

"Because I need to track down this Witch if I want this book, and the only way I'm going to do that is if I can follow her go-between. If this vague little description is all you're planning to give me, then you're *dramatically* overestimating my detective skills. I can't just look up 'big women with sparkly blue eyes' in some database and track her down like that, you know."

"You already seem to have an idea, though, Aurelia. That's really not enough for you? You're very clever."

"Yeah I know I'm clever, but an idea doesn't do me any good. I need to know for sure."

The Dealer hummed on whether to give up that precious info for a few seconds, but at last he had to acquiesce to Felicity's request. He was, after all, getting a stupid number of books about it, and Felicity's continued loyalty as a 'research partner'.

"The last Tuesday this month," he informed her. "In the morning. In this very alleyway." Then he gestured to a fire escape on an adjacent building. "I normally have my 'security' hiding up there. I'll let them know you'll be joining them that day."

Felicity looked up, and sure enough a cheerful hand waved over the edge of one of the platforms a few storeys up.

"Keeps us both safe," he assured her when he saw the troubled look on her face.

"I bet."

He grinned at her. "You will be discreet, yes my dear? Because if she finds out my appointment book fell out of my pocket like this, I doubt I'll live out the hour."

That checked out. Anyone with even one half-functioning braincell would be afraid to mess with that grinning bear. 'Dead in an hour' was probably a merciful end.

Felicity nodded and assured him she'd be extremely professional about it. "She won't even know I'm following her, I promise."

"For both our sakes, I hope you're right, Miss Vicente."

She cringed when she heard her name. He knew, then. He'd always known. She really had hoped she'd managed to maintain any amount of power or control in this little professional relationship. But apparently, she had always been at his mercy.

Luckily, she was valuable.

But she really didn't want to imagine what exactly he'd do to her once she *stopped* being valuable. He'd almost certainly find some way to *keep her* valuable, whether she wanted to be or not.

Once she got back out on the street, she composed a casual message to dear Amy: "Hey Ames, I'll be in town in a couple weeks. Low key book conference thing. Time to hang? Pizza? Wine?"

As much as Felicity wasn't much of a computer smarts detective, she'd read enough books to know how to do this kind of thing properly. She'd scam a tracker off that PI of hers, drop it in Danica's coat, and then, come the big day, all she'd have to do is follow the glowing dot after Dani met up with the Dealer to find where she was delivering her ill-gotten books. Easy.

And once she tracked the Witch down, she'd have two very important questions for the mysterious woman:

What was that book really about?

And who the hell is Danica Doyle?

∾ *Part II* ∾

There's a Chance It Is Not, in Fact, Enough for Now

With a quirked eyebrow and a weird smirk, waving their fork around, Ravi was telling Danica what they thought was a pretty wild account of a weird ceramic knife hocker they encountered on the metro the previous night. —And Danica figured it would've been weird enough to find a guy hocking knives on a subway car, and absolutely weird enough that the guy picked Ravi in particular out of the dozen people in the car, but then they kept going and going, and every extra detail they revealed was prickling the hair on the back of Danica's neck with concern.

They were getting really focused on the knives – because, ceramic, so, obviously - but Danica was aching to circle back to the *guy* because he sure sounded weird in just a particular enough way to make her stomach turn.

"—It wasn't even that zirconium dioxide stuff regular ceramic knives are made of," they explained in disbelief bordering on disgust. "It was all chipped and toothy like it was just regular old porcelain. Like the guy just made it himself in his garage or something."

"Mm... yeah... —So you said his fingers were weird? And teeth? Too many?"

"That's what you're worried about?"

"How many though, exactly, would you say...?"

"Six on the one hand. Seven on the other."

"Teeth?"

"I didn't pry his jaw open to count Nikki. He had three front teeth though," they said, pointing to their own. "And a second canine over here," they added, hooking a finger in the corner of their mouth and prying it open to the right to show off their own canine for example. "I've never seen that before."

"Nice suit though?"

"Right? Listen, not to judge, but guy like that? Sketchy as hell? With a perfectly pressed three-piece?"

"Yup. Definitely… definitely pretty weird."

"—Oh! And two watches! One on each wrist. No hands though! Just a fashion accessory I guess?"

Danica gritted her teeth and tried not to let her concern show through a pleasant put-on smile.

She managed to work up the courage to ask, to set up Ravi to put a cap on the story with a joke, "So did you buy one?"

Ravi put up a finger without a word and finished off a mouthful of food before standing up and digging around in the foyer closet for something that Danica was really hoping wasn't there. They peeked around the corner with a menacing grin and, like a killer ready to strike, brandished a perfectly white mockery of a knife.

That was absolutely not the right punchline.

Ravi actually bought a cursed knife.

Danica could feel her eye twitching in frustration.

"Ravi Bee…"

They approached the table and sat down, observing the knife carefully, turning it over in their hands. "It's probably useless, but it looks kind of cool? And it was only a buck."

"You didn't give the guy your name or anything did you…?"

"He kept asking but that felt sketchy so I lied." They offered the knife over to Danica to take a look.

She could feel the magic in it the second it touched her skin. No way to know what the curse was without tracking down the faerie trade that made the thing but it was definitely cursed.

"Don't suppose I can keep this," Danica asked hopefully.

"Oh sure. All yours. Don't cut anything with it though, it'll chip right away."

"Thanks for the tip."

Ravi shot her with a playful finger gun and returned to their meal with a satisfied grin. They probably thought they just got Danica a fun little trinket of a gift.

Before they left to get to the university for a TA shift, Danica asked them a small favor: "If you see that… guy… again, can you call me right away and let me know where he is?"

"What, don't believe me? Gotta see him for yourself?"

"I'd like to see his wares."

There were only four faerie doors in the whole city, made of trickily intertwined branches in parks and backyards. A couple of them were being repaired by the slow and steady pace of nature reclaiming its natural form from the damage caused by ambitious landscapers that cut the branches away. And may they rest in peace all of them because a human doesn't tend to live long after breaking one of those doors.

There were also transient circles that came and went all over the city. Usually mushrooms. Sometimes moss. Rocks. Even a ring of ants once formed a little door home right in front of her. Scared her shitless when one of her cousins jumped out.

None of her cousins were particularly brave on Earth. Humans are prey, but they're ominous prey. Everything in the 21st century is made of steel, which from a distance sure *feels* just as dangerous as pure cold iron, but it's made much safer by the ashes mixed in. But since raw cold iron is enough to leave a lesser faerie burned and broken for centuries, and most of her cousins weren't quite savvy enough about the human world to tell the difference between safe steel and devastating iron, they all tended to stay within screaming distance of the nearest escape.

So Danica did a little map work, based on the train Ravi was riding the previous night and the location of the last two intact faerie doors – and the fact that transient mushrooms and moss don't grow super well in January and rocks are all hidden buried under the snow – to pick out a little search radius to track down her dear little brother so she could strangle the reason why he was trying to curse Ravi out of him.

Dashing with her Tether roof-to-roof when no one was looking, and peering over the edge to the streets below, she managed to track him down – exactly as Ravi described, in a beautiful purple three-piece suit with trendy hair with an utterly inhuman grin and hands – peering through the window of a high-end electronics store with a hungry look in his eyes.

During a lull in pedestrian traffic, Danica slipped herself down to the street and crept up behind her poorly-disguised brother as best she could, crouching down to avoid being spotted in the reflection of the glass, until she was close enough to grab him by the ankle.

A moment later, the two of them were atop the tarred gravel roof of one of the tallest buildings downtown, and Danica had flipped her dear little brother onto his back, eliciting a childish little yelp out of him.

"Krell," Danica greeted him coldly, standing over him with one leg on either side of his waist, the skirt of her dress pressing hard into her shins on the windy rooftop. She summoned the cursed porcelain knife to her hand from its safe spot in one of her boxes under the couch and gave him a playful grin before falling to her knees and plunging the fragile blade into his chest. "Found something of yours, buddy."

He didn't scream in pain like a real human ought to do, because it wasn't a real human body at all. Not even close. Not like hers. As much as Krell had picked up a bit of Danica's love and fascination for humanity when he was young and looking up to her, he ended up being more into their *toys* than their *bodies*. He didn't have the patience to create such a perfect emulation as she *insisted* on having, didn't understand the beauty in every little detail of the human form. *He* didn't want to sweat and ache and freeze. *He* didn't want to shiver and tickle and writhe with joy. And *he* didn't want a knife buried in his chest to hurt.

And fair enough. It hurt like a bastard that time *she* got stabbed in the chest. But gods what a rush – the fear, the adrenaline, the red red *red* drowning every sense and synapse. She screamed in pain then, like a human, like she'd never done before. She might have painstakingly perfected every nerve and vessel in this body but it *still* surprised her sometimes.

But Krell, instead of reacting like a human, reacted like the indignant monomillennial child that he was, whining at her, "Would you get off!" while slapping her legs.

"Make me."

"Danica you're such a bully."

"Oh I'm the bully?" She drew the knife out of his chest and coldly repeatedly plunged it back into his body like a trowel into sand, to put a few ugly holes in that suit of his while she berated him. "You little shit. Why the fuck are you here? It's not time to fuck with me yet and you know it."

"Hey! Would you stop? That suit wasn't cheap."

"Yeah? What'd you trade for it Krell? Get ripped off? Drive someone off a bridge for it before you could even collect your whole prize again? Huh? You stupid little troll. *Why are you here*, Krell??"

Danica's pathetic darling little brother scowled at her and writhed and struggled trying to get out of her grasp. He couldn't shed his physical form while she had him pinned, and especially not with an equally physical knife lodged in his chest. And she knew that the second she let him loose, he'd just discorporate his mockery of a human body back into that uncertain little primordial cloud of sparks and light and wispy tendrilous smoke that was the same beautiful natural form he had when she found him and handed him over to her dad for naming. And if he wasn't *material*, she'd have a hell of a time keeping him in one place for this little interrogation.

After a few more seconds of whining and complaining, he finally relented and laid his head back on the roof with a bitter sigh.

"You're such a bitch."

"Hey. Watch your mouth young man."

"Niede's right. You suck now."

"Yeah? Well, you tell Niede I said I love them too when you see them, hey? Really. They never write. Real terrible older sibling behavior, ignoring their poor lonely little sister doing her best in the big hard world."

Without moving his head, Krell's eyes darted to Danica's to take in the look on her face intently. There was a question in that glare he wasn't asking.

"What?" she said.

"Are you lying?" he asked.

"I didn't *suddenly* gain the ability to lie, Krell."

"Well how am I supposed to know?? I figure if anyone could figure out how to lie it would be you, Danica. And Niede says you're barely fae these days at all, you've been pretending at being a human so long. Who knows what you can do anymore?"

"That's real nice of you buddy, but I'm not *that* good at pretending to be human."

"...Then you really didn't get Niede's letter?"

"...What... letter?"

Krell's too-many-toothed smile curled up far too far when he heard that. "You don't know. Oh that's *delicious*. Serves you right though. Serves you right, Danica, you deserve every bit of it, you monster."

"Every bit of what?"

"They're sick of you screwing around over here Danica. Your time's up."

"Niede is? Niede. *Niede* is sick of me screwing around. They're way older than me, Krell. They're older than *bread*. How exactly did *they* run out of patience after just six hundred years of me 'screwing around'?"

Krell gave the closest approximation of a shrug he could manage from his position pinned under Danica. The knife shifted oddly in his body when he did, like he was full of shrugging gravel instead of meat and bones. "I just hear rumors. And get fun little missions. I'm not about to turn down a big bag full of good favor and a chance to mess around in the city and play some fun little games with my favorite big sister's latest human. You always pick such *fun* ones. Shame this'll be the last one though. I'll miss all this."

"Alright kiddo I feel like we're not going to be making much progress like this. You ever taken a dip in molten iron before?"

"<u>Wait</u>. Stop. Don't you dare—"

Before Krell could even finish trying to convince Danica to stay her hand, she had instantaneously slipped the two of them through the Aether to the floor of a dark and dreary metal refinery, the walls and ceiling and loud machinery and conveyors and tumbling slag lit up only by the orange of the flame of the smelters and the glow of molten iron metal.

Danica flicked him in the forehead to tease him and remind him he was powerless under her before cheering, "Field trip!"

"I hate you..."

"Oh Krell, don't be so bitter. Just tell me what I want to know and you can run on back home and warn everyone to never bother my lovely and painfully generous roommate ever again. Or—" she gestured with a finger in the air to summon a solidified wayward splash of iron on the floor into her hand with a flamboyant sparkle. Danica gritted her teeth bitterly at the pain of holding it, but she turned that pain into a cruel grin, even as the flesh touching the scrap of metal sizzled and burned and smoked. Then she slowly brought the devastating hunk of fae-poison iron closer and closer to Krell's writhing fearful face. "—<u>or</u> you can *crawl* back home and *be* the warning."

"Stop. Stop! Danica stop please. You can't do it like this! Make a damn deal Danica for godsake stop! You're better than this! You fucking *changeling!* There are <u>rules</u>!"

"I stopped following the rules a long time ago Krell. —Now tell me exactly why you're here picking on my roommate."

Krell writhed as far away as he could from Danica's hand until he realized there was no hope of forcing her into a deal or pleading with her for mercy.

"You didn't RSVP!" Krell shouted at last to answer her question, glaring bitterly at the iron in Danica's hand, continuing to glare at it even when she withdrew it and tossed it on the ground a few feet away – a safe distance, but still a constant reminder that it'd be back to torture Krell again if he misbehaved. "Niede thought you needed some extra pressure to commit."

"Commit to what?"

"Your court date."

"My court date," she echoed flatly. "What, dad's little make-believe court? *...In the Faelands??*"

Krell sneered at the iron on the floor and bitterly added, "I can't believe they're thinking about bringing you back. You're just as horrible as ever. Monster. I bet half the Faelands is ash and dust before you exhale your first breath of the sweet summerly air of our home again."

Danica scoffed at the obvious misunderstanding. "They're *not* bringing me back."

"You won't come?" He seemed excited at the possibility that she was going to refuse her summons.

"I can't come. The terms are pretty clear, buddy."

Krell quirked an eyebrow a bit comically too far at Danica for that and told her that's what he was told. " 'Make Danica's human suffer until she agrees to come back for her court date.' That's our job."

" 'Our'?"

With a coy toothy grin, Krell informed Danica he wasn't the only one on the job. Then with a little nod at Danica, sitting on his torso and pinning him down as she was, he justified it by saying, "Niede doesn't trust any of us to stand up to you alone after last time. It's a bounty this time. The first one to make you crack wins."

"...And you picked *Ravi* to try to manipulate me? We're not even... I mean they're just my roommate, Krell. I've had tons of roommates this lifetime. Why them?"

He shrugged. "Got you this upset, didn't it?" he teased her, pointing at her hand all curled up in pain.

Danica glanced at the bitter iron burns on her palm. They were painfully healing away, like she learned to do even before her exile – and thanks for that handy trick there, dad – but the scars would still last a whole day or two, longer than even a would-be deadly chest wound with a ceramic knife. It sucked for her, but it was way better than the centuries it would've laid up Krell to touch it.

But it *did* hurt her. A lot. It was taking all the grit she had to keep a straight face.

Why <u>was</u> she doing this?

Because she hadn't paid Ravi back yet, right? And knowingly letting one of her cousins harm them, that'd just make the debt worse, obviously. She couldn't let that happen. It was already bad enough.

Yeah.

Right.

That's all.

Ravi was just an unwitting debtor.

They weren't worthy of being killed just to hurt her.

She just had to convince her family of that somehow. But sending Krell back home scarred with iron lashes wouldn't exactly be sending the message that this targeted campaign wasn't bothering her.

She scowled at him and informed him that Niede's math was wrong. "You're just complicating my arrangement. This isn't affection, it's debt and duty. I can't let them get hurt if I can protect them. Especially not by you psychopaths thinking it's actually enough to twist me around on some decision you haven't even given me to make yet. What kind of discount courier did Niede use to deliver that letter that it didn't even make it to me, anyways? —And they couldn't just put it in my hands themself? Gods I hope they got their money back. Go back and let them know I haven't read it yet, and *stop* wasting your time picking on my roommate."

Krell grinned at her. "You don't want to hurt me, do you?"

"I already owe you enough, Krell."

"Not enough. Make another deal, Danica. Promise me more favor than you can possibly deliver. If I'm going to be getting on Niede's bad side, I want my own unstoppable protector. Then I'll go."

"I can't protect you from Niede. They're stronger than me in a fight. By a lot."

"But you're smarter. You're smarter about them, anyways, even if you've turned utterly *stupid* about yourself. No one in the Faelands could figure out why you'd roll over for them like you did, until you showed everyone how stupidly *happy* you were rolling around for them over here."

"I didn't roll over. That had nothing to do with Niede. They just happened to be the one with the pen and the paper and the courage to make the terms. I was just accepting responsibility for what I did. — Even if I *was* right doing it."

"How so very *human* of you, punishing yourself for nothing important. You really *have* been poisoned by them, haven't you?"

"Don't *you* start with that. I get more than enough of that from Niede."

"Offer me all the protection you can give me Danica and I'll promise never to 'complicate your arrangement' with that human of yours again."

Danica gritted her teeth about it. You *don't* make trades with the fae if you can help it. There's always more to lose than what's written on the page. But there weren't a lot of options here. The only way to send Krell back with the right message for her cousins was to craft the words herself in a binding contract.

With a little huff of a sigh, she summoned a stack of magic paper in her hands to make a new contract with her brother. She waved her fingers back and forth over the pages to stage the ink of the terms, then handed it to him to do the same. They passed the shifty-inked document back and forth for at least an hour there on the floor of that noisy refinery, in near silence except for the occasional little incredulous snicker at the other's ridiculously overreaching terms or silly insulting margin doodles.

Even if he pretended at hating her now, Krell still obviously had some affection for Danica – though in the fae, affection normally meant something more like... appreciation for the potential for exploitation. He was clearly trying to act tough and independent now, but he hadn't changed much since the last deal she had to make with him a couple hundred years ago. Honestly, he'd barely changed at all since she was letting him dote on her all those centuries before her exile. Just a little smarter. A little more confident. A little more playful. It would be nice, if it weren't dangerous.

At last, when the two of them were satisfied enough with all the tricky language and bitter concessions, they locked eyes and nodded grimly while they let the ink settle into the paper forever. If Danica had a shred of pride left, she'd probably find it pretty demeaning to be made a loyal guard dog for her own little brother. At least she couldn't really be called on to help too much while she was stuck on Earth, unless he came seeking sanctuary. But she figured by the time he knew he needed sanctuary, he'd probably already be beyond any help she could offer. It was kind of an empty arrangement, but it made him happy enough to work with her and that was all that mattered.

They each glided a finger over their respective signature lines, leaving behind an unspeakable glimmery blue sigil that represented the will of their true names, and then the enchanted document triplicated itself, leaving behind a copy for each of them before disappearing itself to the gods' Eternal Archive.

Krell was delighted to abuse his power immediately, insisting that Danica 'protect' him from the trouble of walking back to the faerie door home by giving him a ride back on the Aethereal Tether.

Not exactly a fun first assignment. Danica wasn't super fond of being anywhere near those doors. She had to keep herself well away from them to avoid getting yanked into the gap between the door and the Aether by the fae-hungry creatures in there. You only need to experience that once to learn your lesson, that's for sure.

After bidding him farewell and reminding him to spread the word about how much of a waste of time harassing Ravi would be for her cousins, and tossing that cursed knife after him through the portal before it closed behind him, Danica returned herself to Ravi's apartment.

She sat on the little couch and read over the terms of the contract. Her own personal archive of these things would be big as the public library downtown if she stacked them all on shelves instead of hiding them in random little spots all over the planet to keep them safe. Some of them were even complicated enough to require *binding* and *multiple volumes.* Like, for example, the terms of her exile – bound and rebound and rebound again from how many times she'd read them over making notes in the margins.

She was more clever than Niede. Krell was right. Even before the ink dried, she'd already figured out how to turn this punishment of an exile into something fun – too fun for Niede to tolerate when Danica was supposed to be here suffering and withering away forever. And in the centuries since, she'd found dozens and dozens of loopholes. Her dad drafted it, after all. Alone. Niede was just a signatory. A witness. And even though her dad used to be *very* talented at writing these things, he'd kind of fallen out of practice after so long leaning on Danica's talents to help him in his compositions.

Unfortunately – or maybe fortunately, depending what parts of herself she loved more – her heart was far, far too tainted with a mockery of humanity to weasel out of the stricter contractual obligations of that exile. Something in her felt like she deserved this, deserved *something* to pay back everything she'd done. But her head, her base instincts, they were far, far too fae to let a contract full of loopholes go unexploited. The thrill of it, of a good contract, of winning a game of wits, it was intoxicating, and she did her honest best to avoid it.

This, though, this punishment, on her terms, this was enough. It was as much as she could bear, to be a love-cursed immortal among mortals, to suffer the pain of the loss of everyone she loved over and over again. It was enough. If only Niede could understand that, they might even leave her alone for it.

An hour later, by the way, Danica discovered what the curse on that porcelain knife was, when she found herself screaming bloody murder as a dozen phantom knives pierced her chest and completely ruined the blouse of her dress with blood and holes – one for every hole she'd put in her brother earlier.

Luckily, Ravi was still out at work, or that would've been a hell of a thing to explain.

A concerned neighbor did knock on the door, though.

"Messed up cutting something!" she shouted through the door, desperately holding a bloody towel to her chest to soak up the mess before it stained the carpet. "I'll be fine! Sorry!"

Gods. Good thing she got rid of the cursed little thing before Ravi decided to chop up a carrot with it or something. She stared abhorred at the rapidly healing wounds in the mirror, imagining exactly how the curse might have manifested on them to echo a bunch of casually eviscerating food prep.

She wondered if saving their life like that might have done anything to ease her debt, but it sure felt like a break-even incident, considering it was her fault they were in danger in the first place.

Ah well.

She'd find a way.

There was still the sliver of hope of helping them figure out a cure. Maybe that would be enough? It had to be enough.

But she was starting to worry it might not be if this went on much longer. Ravi's generosity really was piling an increasingly insurmountable mountain of debt on her with every passing day. At the rate it was growing, she'd end up serving in the shadows as their loyal dog for the rest of their life, even if she cured them, and even after all that she'd still never pay it back well enough to avoid spending the rest of her eternity enduring the agony of having never made it square.

She really needed to get this under control already...

In Case of Chemical Fire

(Morning, Friday, 13th January)

MAN-021-C: Instructions for Handling Emergency Situations in Lab C.

–   In case of emergency, follow the yellow lines on the floor to the nearest exit. Consult the map on the door for the nearest assembly point.

Miss Beausoleil!
I think I messed up!
—Achttch!
—Shit!!
...Oh. That's not good—

–   In case of fire, use provided hand-held fire safety equipment. Refer to Appendix B for operating instructions.

The extinguisher's not working!
Where's the fucking blanket—!?

–   In case of volatile chemical fire, pull the safety pin from the emergency switch on the wall and hold the button for five seconds.

Miss B!
Help me!
He's not breathing!
Miss B where are you—!?

–   In case of leaving one of your first-year students behind, unconscious on the ground, getting drowned in fire suppressant foam, cnwo m, we'd os, sharow who n em ma coov w o va [text corrupted and illegible]

—Oh my god...
Please breathe...
Kid you better fucking breathe...
Please...

Lost, Found, Forgotten: Some Things Should Never Be

Since dear Ravi Bee was going to be stuck on a warehouse shift tonight as usual, Danica was stuck drinking by herself, enjoying Henry's company and mixological prowess while she waited for the band to start.

"Danica my dear I don't understand you, wasting money on these," Henry nodded at her latest drink in a string that the playfully incredulous man definitely knew was going to keep growing every hour for the rest of the night.

"I've explained this before, Henry."

"Humanity."

"It's all the humanity in there! It's human. To drink. To make drinks. To turn death into life. I don't know, why do I have to get drunk to drink? It's just nice! Sitting. Relaxing. Enjoying *their* magic. Tasting the fruit of tens of thousands of years—"

"I'm more wondering why you're wasting money at all, little one. I thought you were eager to pay Mx. Beausoleil off for their kindness."

Danica laughed at the suggestion: "Ha! Henry, if money could pay them off, I'd rob a casino tonight and be done with it. They don't care about money. It's *extremely* frustrating. —Another one, please~ Green. Something green."

"...You couldn't take even an hour out of your eternal life to learn the names of some of these?"

"It's all the same to me, Henry, I just like the colors. And the magic, as previously discussed."

"I know. But for me? This is my *profession*, Danica."

Danica scoffed and teased him playfully. "This is your *hobby*, Henry, don't kid me."

Henry's skillful hands captivated Danica while he mixed some arcane concoction of liquors and bitters and juices together with a splash of indigo to swirl among the green. There were some things on Earth Danica wanted to stay ignorant about, so she could still experience a little whimsy and fun watching the masters of those strange magics at work. Humanity's gastronomical defiance of death was one of those. Henry's art was another.

She marveled at the glass for a few seconds when he placed it delicately in front of her and gave it a little twirl. Somehow Henry had even managed to get little flecks of light to dance around in there for her.

"Gods, I love the way you do these. Like little galaxies."

"Just for you, little one, to match your careless eyes."

"Oh shush, my eyes are beautiful."

"Too beautiful, no?"

"I worked so *so* hard on these, Henry. I'm not hiding them for anyone. —And no one cares that much. Part of the *design*."

"Mm. I don't know, little one. I see the way your consorts look at you. I think you may be a little more transparent than you mean sometimes. Honestly, it's a bit of a wonder that you can still act surprised when you get caught."

"...Well maybe I *like* getting caught once in a while. Ever think of that?"

"I do. That's the only reasonable conclusion, isn't it?"

"How's that?"

"You'd have to be a real fool to make such careless mistakes over and over again."

"...And I'm too smart? Are you calling me smart, Henry? That's so sweet of you."

"No, that would stretch the definition of the word a little too thin I think, but you're definitely too clever to think you could keep getting away with it forever."

Danica shrugged. "It's not the end of the world if someone finds out, you know that. Just means I have to shuffle things around a bit. —And I'm usually gone before anyone cares."

"Mm. How long does that normally take? For someone to care. A couple of months?"

"...Why?"

"Just seems to me you've been bringing a certain someone by the bar for a lot longer than 'a couple of months'."

She gave Henry a mean grin through clenched teeth. "Yeah, yeah, I get it. Thank you for your concern. But you know what, honestly, I can't think of another human being I'd rather get caught by."

"Oh?"

"Honest. I can't even imagine them trying to exploit me for a *back rub*. They're *incorruptible*."

"Mm. I see why you're struggling with them, then."

"Right?? Gods. I'm this close—" She measured out a centimeter between her finger and thumb. "—to just giving up on paying them back at all. Just, roll over and curl up in their lap and give over to the sweet misery of living under their oblivious benevolent thumb. Why not!"

"...How's the investigation?"

"Terrible! None of the junk you gave me led anywhere and you know it. You monster. The best lead I have now is *Ravi*. They're using some science stuff to try to figure out how the infection works."

"Science stuff."

"You know, like, chemistry magic and cool machines and computers. I don't know all the details. Just—" Danica wiggled her fingers in the air like a magician pretending at a spell. "—science stuff."

"So you're going to get them to do all the work to make the gift you're giving them? That's quite the scam. I was worried you had truly given up your beautiful craft forever, Princess. Your father would be proud."

Danica shot him a cold glare. "Stop. I'm not playing any tricks here. They already want to do this, I'm just making it easier for them."

"And getting out of your little debt to them in the process?"

"It's the only lead I've got for now!"

"Is it?"

"Isn't it?? If you have something, Henry, you better spill it *immediately* because I am *suffering* here."

"I distinctly remember putting a few very promising leads in your hand some chilly afternoon in December."

Danica scoffed and teased him, "Come on Henry, that pile of trash? I just told you there wasn't anything useful in there."

"Wasn't there?"

"Was there??"

Henry cocked his head to the side and gave her a suggestive shrug, but he didn't answer.

"Well just tell me!"

"Not how this works," he replied morosely, like he was sick of repeating it. And Danica was equally sick of hearing it.

"Gods. You're such an ass, Henry."

"I don't know what any of it means either, Danica. It means what it's supposed to mean to you. It will mean what it was meant to mean when you need it."

"Well maybe I'm just stupid or something, but I don't know what I'm supposed to do with random bits and pieces of books and reports and contracts. It sure just looks like trash to me."

"...Is that everything I gave you?"

"Oh sorry, and an old user manual for a fake arm, *my apologies*. I'm keeping that one *real safe*, honest. Could *definitely* come in handy if I ever get mine ripped off and my body suddenly decides to stop 'fixing' itself."

"Fascinating..." The old man drummed his fingers on the bar for a few pensive seconds before he decided to broach some subject that had clearly been troubling him: "I wonder if maybe you've lost something recently, Danica."

She quirked an eyebrow at the strange suggestion. "Uh. What, like a receipt? A game?"

"A letter."

"...I don't really get a lot of mail, Henry."

"Mm... Well, I thought I saw something with your name on it in the lost-and-found this morning. Maybe I'm mistaken."

"...What are you talking about?"

Henry nodded over to a big wooden box in the corner – the home of orphaned and forgotten unmatched mittens and trodden-on tuques and scarves.

She crossed the room and crouched down to rifle through the box to find a single sheet of paper in the cluttered tangle of clothing.

She unfolded it where she was standing, which was apparently a bad idea, because it staggered her enough to send her backing into a table, knocking over a menu there.

Without looking away from the gold-inked page, she hurried back to the bar.

"Henry what is this? *What is this?* What the *hell* is this Henry *why is this here*??"

She slammed it flat on the bar and turned it to face him. "Why do you have this??"

"I don't have it. I haven't had it since I gave it to you, little one. Like I said, it just seems to have made its way to the lost-and-found over there."

"Since you gave it to me…? Are you saying… this is one of those pieces of trash you gave me??"

"I really wish you wouldn't call my work trash, Danica. I do have feelings, you know."

Danica turned the page back around in a rush to read it over again.

"You really didn't read it?" Henry asked, disappointed.

"No, I didn't read it! It was with all that other garbage you gave me! And I was busy that night!"

"Ah. I was wondering why you never mentioned it. I wonder how long it's been lost."

She stared at the page, bewildered. "…You think I dropped it?"

It would be extremely bad if a human with any kind of curiosity found this. It was written in the enchanted ink and in the language of her dear family – of her heartless cousins and her bitter siblings and her vile father back in the Faelands – the family who condemned her to this Earthly prison.

"…And how did you even get this? It's addressed *to me*."

"Well Danica, some of the things I find in my searches are placed directly in my hand by interested parties."

"…*You*. You were the shitty courier?"

"Danica please you're going to make me cry if you keep this up…"

"Who gave you this?"

"Your most attentive sibling."

"Niede. It really was them."

"The very same."

"Did you read it?"

"Oh, no, it was addressed to you. I wouldn't betray anyone's trust like that, you know that."

"Why wasn't it sealed?"

Henry shrugged. "Not my business."

Danica groaned. Gods, it was probably on purpose, wasn't it? Just more trouble. Just leave it open for *whoever* to find it. Make everyone around here suspicious. Force her to move again, leave behind every shred of happiness she was stitching together.

"Anything interesting in there?" Henry asked.

—*Nosy.*

Danica read it over again. It was written in modern Fae at least. Easy enough to read. So very kind of Niede to accommodate her like that.

The details were more-or-less as Krell described them. Go home. Or else.

"It looks like they want to talk to me. In the Faelands. About my... appeal? I'm not appealing anything." She shook her head and creased her brow in consternation. "I can't even get across the Aether. What do they want me to do?"

"Your sibling's quite *mobile*, aren't they? You don't think they can handle the simple matter of transportation?"

"Okay but I'm not even *allowed* to be there! My sentence is *extremely* clear about this."

"Danica. You've never found a single loophole? In all this time? *You?*"

"...I mean. *I* have. But why would *they?*"

"I assume because they want to talk to you *in the Faelands.*"

"Just come here!" she exclaimed, whacking the page with the back of her hand indignantly. "This is the stupidest... And what the hell is this? About... my... '*my* human'..."

That 'or else' in there wasn't just some nebulous 'or else'. Roughly translated – and there was always a bit of ambiguity between Fae and any human language – it was heavily implying that the 'or else' would involve 'Danica's human' suffering horribly if she refused to accept this generous 'invitation'.

It couldn't be anyone else, could it? Krell was so set on them.

"They mean Ravi..." she said, bewildered by the obvious truth of it.

Henry didn't respond.

The deadline on her response was unclear, but apparently it had passed long enough ago that Niede was already issuing bounties on Ravi's misery.

"They can't *do this!* They can't do this already! I'm not even... I didn't *do* anything this time! I'm not even happy! I'm miserable! I'm working for that fucking witch and I can't pay off my debt and nothing is working out for me this time—*what the hell are they doing this for!?* "

Henry gave her a sad grimace. "I did say you should sit this one out, didn't I?"

"You knew??"

"I have eyes. Danica, there are patterns to your pain. A tide. A revolution. The water is rushing out. The sky grows darker every day. I don't know how you can't see it after all these years. How many of these agonizing false lives have you suffered through and still you can't see all this?"

Danica gritted her teeth. Of course she could see all *that.* And she was going to be prepared for it this time, when it came. But...

"It's too soon," she replied bitterly. "It's too soon, damn it. I'm not ready."

Henry ducked down a bit to catch her sinking gaze. "Perhaps it's time to cut ties with your human, Danica. For their own sake?"

Danica clicked her tongue harshly at the suggestion. As if she could. As if she could just walk away from her debt like that. —And forget the debt! As if she could walk away from *Ravi.* They were too important. Without them, how would she have any hope of finding a cure to this tar stuff? Of saving humanity from this vile illness? Of paying off her debt to Angie? —To *them?* —And what would it help anyways?? Ravi wouldn't even be safe if she walked away! Not now! Not now that they were in her vindictive family's sights!

She crushed the letter in her palm and hammered a furious fist on the bar, growling in frustration.

Henry watched stoically as ever while she blew up.

"They think they can do this to me? *Me?* They know who I am! Did they forget?? I'm the damn scourge of the fae! I brought my father to his knees and pissed off every nameless god just to do it! I can destroy his precious little kingdom on a *whim!* And I will! They want to play with me? Threaten me into coming back with their pretty golden words while holding my friend hostage?" She clenched her teeth and sneered, spitting her seething words: "I'll *ruin* them... They can't do this to me again... I don't care how long it takes, I won't let them get away with this... It's too far, Henry. For nothing! It's too far!"

After that little outburst – and no help, no response from Henry – she found a dark table in the far corner to fume in solitary silence for a long while. The band started but it was just noise tonight. She cursed at her cocktail. Henry refused to stock the good stuff, not even for her. She longed to get her hands on the nectar of those ambrosial Lethean lilies back home. To be lost in madness for a night. Oh, to be gone, to be obliviated, to taste the end of all things for even a moment again.

...Obviously she wasn't going to destroy the Faelands or raze her dad's ill-gotten kingdom lands or any other ridiculous fantasy she could conjure up in her fury.

But she also wasn't going to let them hurt Ravi. She wouldn't. She could keep them safe. She had to. It wasn't *even* yet.

The letter indicated this dire meeting with her family was scheduled for the following month, though the date was written strangely. Her family never could quite get the hang of knowing the significance of this or that number, couldn't even count the right number of fingers or teeth in a human body, so the code tumbled out in a long, disorganized string with repeating patterns that were hard to make sense of: *1442'144:14'21-4144'1'42.*

Danica knew what it meant though. February 14th, 2:14 in the afternoon. The anniversary of her banishment.

Revolutions. Tides. Her pain had patterns. And somehow she'd become blind to them – blind enough to think she was still miserable enough right now to keep her family at bay, miserable enough to keep them satisfied that she was indeed suffering from her punishment for now.

But apparently, the vast ocean of her misery had receded far further than she imagined while she was playing in the sand, and those devils were eagerly waiting to charge down the surf to make her suffer for it.

❧

When she got home, miserably sober, she was surprised to find Ravi awake and not at the warehouse at all, tired, hazily watching an old episode of one of the shows the two of them were slowly working through whenever they had a spare hour here and there.

They greeted her with a warm, tired smile, wakened from their stupor by her dour hello, and invited her to sit beside them to watch. "I was waiting for you," they said, morose and teasing at the same time, so that Danica wasn't sure if it was a joke or not. "Couple new episodes came out this week. You up for it?"

Danica couldn't say no.

But it was extremely difficult to pay any attention – not while she was troubling over what to do with Ravi and with her cruel family. She found herself looking at Ravi more than she was looking at the screen.

Their hair had an odd smell to it tonight. Some special chemical in the lab they didn't usually work with maybe? And there was a strange look in their eyes – something beyond the exhaustion from working too much that normally dulled the light in there. Whenever their show went too long without showing anything exciting, their eyes fell and started to search for something in the darkness that wasn't there.

Danica found herself wondering in one of those heavy silences if she would've done anything different if she had gotten that warning letter of an invitation when she was supposed to – if she *could* have done anything different.

When she asked Ravi if they were okay, they gave her an uneasy grin and shrugged it off. "Sorry, am I thinking too loud?"

Danica grinned back. "Like a blender full of glass."

"...Yeah. Sorry, just... rough day at work today."

Danica offered Ravi sympathetic eyes, but they didn't seem to want to elaborate. Instead, they returned their attention to the show and started very obviously making an effort to look like they weren't troubled – which, of course, only made them look more troubled.

Poor Ravi Bee. It wasn't fair. It wasn't fair what she had done to them. She should've left. She should've gotten that warning in time and left right then and there to save them from whatever was coming. They already had to suffer so much just living day-to-day. It was hard to imagine what her family could even do to make it worse for them. But her cousins were very, very creative at this sort of thing, and the lot of them always managed to surprise her with the viciousness of their punishments for the people she loved.

But this wasn't... She didn't... It wasn't *like that* this time! She was just paying them back. Just... just suffering endlessly with them, while she desperately tried to pay them back... to pay them back for that... that *bottomless* fountain of joy that spilled out into her hands with every motion of their heart, with every kindness, with every breath and joke and smile... and...

...and...

...

...

—Oh.

...Well fuck...

Okay I Get It but Do You Have to Be so Rough About It?

(Morning, Friday, 20th January)

So, admittedly, it was probably not a great idea for Ravi to accept that enticing overtime at the warehouse last week – overtime that started the night before they were supposed to be running a big chemistry lab test with the first-year kids – overtime that went all the way up to the very hour before they needed to be back on campus to set everything up.

Maybe if they had instead just *gone home* at the end of the night, then they would have been rested up enough to notice that they had mistakenly picked up the jug of *concentrated* acid solution instead of the *ten times diluted* one when they were hurriedly setting up the couple dozen open-air stations.

And, sure, there was a pretty good chance that if they hadn't had a migraine from all the coffee they had been chugging all morning to keep their eyes open for the entire duration of the lab, then they probably would have had the sense to attribute the unusually high number of explosive reactions – and the resulting fires and the excessive smoke and noxious fumes – to something *other than* almost every single student somehow getting their calculations wrong.

They might even have pulled the alarm and triggered the chemical fire suppression system on the lab in a timely manner. But at the very damn least they might have remembered to check the lab for stragglers on the way out – you know, just in case one of their students passed out and got buried in suppressant foam and almost died in their hands while they struggled to remember the rhythm to that stupid old disco song to keep his chest compressions going, fearfully refusing to stop even after he screamed out in pain when his ribs *cracked*.

But unfortunately, they *had* accepted the overtime, and as a more-or-less direct consequence of that, the chem lab needed to be shut down for a week to clean it up and reset the suppression system, and a kid got a set of broken ribs and almost died – and, of course, this morning, once the investigation was complete, Ravi was called into their supervisor's office to be informed that they would no longer be performing their TA duties for the university.

On the plus side, the students were all very grateful to them for the extra time to study – the ones who didn't fearfully drop out of the program immediately afterwards, at least.

Ravi stewed on it all afternoon before returning to their supervisor's office to plead for another chance. They couldn't lose this.

But it was too late. It was already gone.

"Miss Beausoleil. You have a lot of nerve to be back in here."

"I'm sorry. I just... I want to apologize. Really. I know I screwed up and I want to make up for it."

"You can make up for it by accepting your suspension of duties with grace and being grateful you aren't being expelled from the university outright."

Ravi wanted to protest, to explain that they had learned their lesson, that this would never happen again, that they would do anything to make it up to the school, but there were no words in their head that sounded convincing enough now to earn back the respect of their professors.

That stern condemnation was echoing in their head that evening while they sat alone in the dark at the little kitchen table in their apartment. In one hand, they held the letter of reprisal from the university. In the other hand, they had pulled up on their phone the payroll records from the day of the incident. They were solemnly staring at one line item in particular to see what exactly it was worth:

OT @2.0 | 7.98 hrs | $ [illegible]

They didn't feel time pass in the apartment while they considered the value of their reputation. And the closest their mind could get to some kind of productive self-reflection was, "*You're a fucking idiot, Ravi.*"

Their head was planted firmly on the table in the dark, in a small pool of tears, when Nicole finally came home.

"Huh," Nicole said plainly after hearing Ravi's story. "Yeah that's... Look I'm not gonna lie, Ravi, that's probably the stupidest thing you've ever done."

Ravi was so sad that they couldn't help laughing at Nicole's candor. "As far as *you* know," they said, playfully challenging Nicole to imagine something worse.

Anything.

—Please.

"Come on, there's no way you can top almost killing a room full of undergrads and nearly disintegrating the university's whole science wing."

"It wouldn't have disintegrated, it would've just... had a lot more holes in it... More ventilation in a chem lab is never a bad thing."

Nicole gave Ravi's shoulder an encouraging pat. "There we go, positive thinking. I love it."

Ravi tried to smile, but it wouldn't stick.

"Nicole they're never going to trust me again."

She peered into Ravi's eyes for a long moment of deep consideration.

They weren't sure if they should even be putting all this on her right now, but there was just... no one else. But Ravi was already half-convinced they did something to fuck things up with Nicole somehow. She'd been avoiding them a lot this week. Skipping dinner. Staying out late without even inviting them – not that they felt much like going out in this state. She didn't even protest when Ravi cancelled their regular Thursday night biology lab break-in, and she loved that stuff.

But maybe all that was just in their head, because after that terrifyingly long moment of heavy consideration, that dear impossibly sweet angel of a woman summoned them to stand up so she could put her big soft arms around them to squeeze them tight against her chest.

She didn't have any words for them. She didn't need any words. Ravi wasn't wrong. It was gone and it wasn't coming back.

But the longer Nicole held on, the more Ravi could hear something else in her silent embrace, something else that wasn't wrong: *It doesn't matter.*

They weakly returned Nicole's embrace and buried their face in her shoulder.

—God, if she weren't here...

It was hard for Ravi to believe that that warm and comforting and impossibly sweet angel of a woman was the very same creature as the demon who stubbornly refused to let them sulk in their room forever, in their precious peaceful solitude, in the embrace of the all-consuming blinds-drawn darkness.

After too *mercilessly* few days of letting them wallow – stuck in bed, barely getting up to use the washroom, calling in to waste every last one of their sick days – Nicole rudely barged into their sanctum, their nest, their shelter from the cruel world, and clawed them from their bed by the ankle.

Before they could even protest, they were being shoved in the shower and locked in the bathroom. Nicole informed them that she would not be opening the door until Ravi had at least done the bare minimum to take care of themself.

They stewed on their anger at Nicole while they washed their scruffy hair and put it right for the first time in days. They didn't deserve tidy hair. They didn't deserve clean skin or sandalwood scents or warmth or comfort. They had a whole lecture ready for their *impetuous* and *unwelcome* houseguest when they yelled through the door to bitterly assure Nicole that they were good and clean now and that she could open the fucking door.

But when they saw the woeful look on Nicole's face and heard the sincerity in her voice asking if they were okay, they couldn't get out anything more biting than a grumbled begrudging 'yes' and a quiet 'thank you'.

Nicole wasn't trying to force Ravi to go to the lab or the warehouse, but she did throw their boots and coat at them to insist they go out and do *something*.

"You're not usually like this," she lamented on the walk over to their favorite diner.

"I'm not usually such a huge fuckup."

"Wow! Okay you need to stop talking about yourself like that! You made a mistake. Everyone makes mistakes."

Ravi sneered at that. "I've never seen *you* make a mistake. So... fucking *good* all the time. You've actually got your whole life put together. It's disgusting." They meant it as a joke, but they realized too late that all that came out sounding a little bitter and jealous – you know, maybe because it was, just a little, bitter and jealous.

Nicole retorted defiantly: "Rav, I've been sleeping on your couch for months. I don't have a job. I have no idea where I'm going or what I'm doing. My whole world is kind of coming crashing down around me, you don't even know. So if you think you can beat me in a fuckup pissing contest, sorry to say you're just dribbling on your feet over there—"

"—Okay that's *extremely* gross please never say that again—"

"—But we are *not* having a fuckup pissing contest. Because everyone sucks sometimes. And most of the time you're amazing. Think big picture! You're definitely net positive on the 'not a fuckup' scale!"

Nicole managed to charm the familiar waitress at the diner into giving the two of them a lunch menu discount, even though it was way too late in the afternoon for it.

Definitely one of the best things about having Nicole around: She was somehow sharp and soft all at once. Like... like a banana? Sure. And today she was sharp enough to understand that 'Ravi losing one job for being a fuckup and missing a bunch of days at the other job because they're bedridden with sadness' meant 'money is tight'.

"You're going to the stich-and-bitch tonight," she informed Ravi – between mouthfuls of the pancakes and bacon that the kitchen was definitely *not* serving this time of day. She informed Ravi of this as though she were their executive assistant and had already booked them in for the appointment.

"I'm not."

"Your seat's already paid for."

Ravi smirked. "Nicole I know it's free."

Nicole rolled her eyes and huffed. "Can't you just play along? Fine, yes, it's free, but you still have to go. I already told them you're coming. They went and got a whole extra chair out of storage just for you. Just for you! It's practically a throne! Do you have any idea how hard it is for those old ladies to carry those chairs? And they had to lift it up three whole flights of stairs, too. You're going to tell them it was for nothing? Don't you have a heart?"

Ravi gave Nicole a vicious, toothy smile and told her through gritted teeth that they hated her.

"You do not."

"I'm taking your pillow away."

"No! You wouldn't dare. I love that pillow."

"One week pillow suspension. *Zero* comfy things on the couch. Violators will be forced to sleep on the floor."

Nicole gave Ravi a stern look, but she refused to back down. They *would* be joining her tonight, she stubbornly insisted. "If that's the price I must pay, then so be it."

It turned out Nicole had lied about the chair. In fact, the group was actually *missing* a few chairs up there, which meant that after the two of them arrived at the cheerful, welcoming clubroom on the third floor, Ravi and Nicole were the ones who had to go back down all those stairs to the main floor, dig the chairs out of storage, and then carry them all the way back up the stairs. Ravi felt like they were back at work heaving boxes around – without pay.

After they got up to the studio and distributed the collection of 'thrones' around the pair of large grey folding tables in the center of the room, Ravi gave Nicole a firm punch in the arm for the betrayal.

"Ow! Hey! What did I do??"

"*Oh Ravi they got a chair just for you,*" they mockingly echoed Nicole, then added under their breath, "You're an ass."

"I didn't know!"

The room itself was on the top floor of an old brick-walled warehouse that had been converted into a collection of studio spaces. There was a massive, dusty, paneled window that looked out onto the abandoned, snow-covered, amber-lit streets of the ancient shipping district. One panel in the window was missing, and though it seemed to normally be covered with some tape and paper, tonight it was left open to invite the cold air of the evening in – cold air that did battle with an over-worked space heater on the floor underneath it. A tall bookshelf was stuffed with magazines and thick books filled with sewing and knitting patterns. The floors and shelves on the perimeter of the room were absolutely overflowing with bundles of colorful yarn and stacks of fabric. One corner was just... just *full* of cotton stuffing, piled taller than Ravi's head. It looked like the perfect place to get swallowed up and hide from the world – and also a huge fire hazard. Ravi eyed the ancient, ungrounded wall sockets nearby with suspicion, then started scanning the room for anything that could be used to put out a massive blazing tower of cotton.

It was a small list. Just a large industrial sink on the opposite end of the room, and a kettle on a hotplate on a small table next to it. And right beside that, a pile of torn up teabag wrappers. So, joy, another fire hazard.

To say they were *on edge* about the possibility of a catastrophic exothermic chemical reaction – like, say, for example, one that turns a few beakers of reactive over-concentrated hydrochloric acid into a series of explosions that almost burn a chem lab down and kill a kid, or, say, for another example, one that transmutes a spark and a harmless bundle of cotton into a burning building – was a little bit of an understatement.

Deep breaths. It seemed a little dark to imagine it, but, you know, maybe a bunch of old ladies happily knitting and chatting would be thrilled to go out in a literal blaze of glory. *'Died doing what they loved – being on fire.'* But Ravi, they were so young. They had so much to live for. A reputation to rebuild.

—*Please don't burn to the ground. Not tonight.*

The teapot, the only vessel Ravi could see other than the kettle that might be used to ferry water across the room in case of emergency, was making its rounds in the hands of a... *familiar* woman, though Ravi wasn't sure from where.

The group consisted of six grannies and one cheerful young man, who were all happily accepting a cup of tea... from... Oh, who *was* that...? It was going to drive Ravi nuts...

Oh! That was Nicole's friend! The one who had helped Ravi cut in line at the clinic that one time. How long ago was that? A few months by now, wasn't it? Same day Nicole started staying on their couch.

—*For 'a week'. A delightfully, miraculously everlasting week...*

"What's her name again?" Ravi whispered to Nicole.

"You can call her Angie."

Ravi raised an eyebrow and smirked. "Is that not her name?"

Nicole replied with a sincere smile: "It's the best we've got."

"Mysterious."

"You don't even know."

While 'Angie' was doling out cups of tea – which Nicole vehemently refused for some reason—

"I'm a green tea girl forever, Ravi. She's only got that nasty cheap black stuff."

—the sweet old woman greeted Ravi with a warm smile.

"Oh, what a joyous day!" Angie said, in a dramatic show of

motherly affection. "My dear, sweet, long-lost child has returned to me again. My heart can rest at ease."

Ravi stopped an unsolicited hug with a halting hand gesture, but returned the smile and gave the woman a sincere thank you for her help before.

One of the other ladies – who Ravi later learned was named Sammy – asked Angie with surprise, "I didn't know you had children, Angela! Why didn't you tell us? What's her name?"

Nicole interjected with an insistent correction, "*Their*. Their name."

Sammy quickly apologized and asked the question again properly. Which was... refreshing.

Angie replied, "This is Ravi, and you know full well that I'm far too old to have a child so young and charming."

Ravi was surprised the old woman remembered their name with such confidence. They'd only introduced themself once, and for a five-minute conversation. That's practically a superpower.

Maybe it was just because she'd been so *bitter* about learning they'd given up their birth name for it, though.

Sammy beamed with recognition. "Ravi! Danica always says such nice things about you—"

—Another 'Danica' crowd.

Both Ravi and her were living double lives, it seemed.

They had yet to meet a 'Nicole' acquaintance, actually. So much for experimenting with a new name. It must not have meant nearly as much to her as she pretended at home. Which was fine. It was still her name, to them. 'Danica' was... someone else.

"—You're so sweet to take her in, dear. She's such a troublemaker, I hope she's been good to you."

Ravi nodded and assured her, " 'Danica' has been... just... great to have around. Would be nice if she'd cook dinner once in a while, though," they awkwardly tried to joke. They nudged Nicole playfully with their elbow.

But apparently she didn't find that funny, judging by the cold shoulder she gave Ravi in return.

A flop of a joke. Ravi felt their face flush with embarrassment. They weren't super into being the center of attention, and they were already floundering here. All hope of this being a quiet, keep-to-yourself kind of thing was disappearing. At this rate, there'd be no escaping a real conversation – especially with everyone seated so close at the same table like this – and with Ravi being in such a disastrous mood lately, well, that couldn't go well.

Luckily, the others had a lot to chat about, and soon everyone was caught up in exchanges that didn't involve Ravi at all. And what a relief, since none of what they were talking about was anything Ravi could be bothered to care about. They'd have found absolutely zero joy in comparing notes on technology that was moving too fast – *oh but what wonders, to have a prohibitively expensive mechanical man cleaning and cooking at home;* complaints that the kids never called – *such a joy when they do though;* or cooing over that handsome so-and-so at the grocery store – *way too young for you, Sammy!*

Even the only guy in the group joined in once in a while when the grannies started talking about some new show that was out – *how long do we have to wait for the next season? The writers are on strike though. Well we're suffering for it!*

While the group was distracted, Ravi took a little walk around the room to figure out something to do for however many hours they were going to be stuck here until Nicole was ready to leave.

They ran their fingers over dozens of bundles of yarn of diverse thicknesses and textures and colors. There were so many to choose from. It felt important to grab the right one, to look at least a tiny bit like maybe they knew enough about this stuff to belong here, but there wasn't a single scrap of knowledge they could dig up in the recesses of their mind about the forbidden textile arts.

In fact, they had kind of gone out of their way to avoid it. Too girly, they had thought in their misguided youth, though now they knew that was a pretty childish way to think about it. And it made them a little sad now, as an adult looking back, knowing how powerful it was to be able to turn these primordial strands from nothing into something. They drew a line of soft wool between their fingers, feeling the life and potential in it, potential they could never hope to realize, all because silly little Amaira couldn't help sulking in the corner of the arts and crafts room at school, determined to learn nothing at all.

They settled on something garishly bright pink with strands of silver twisted in the yarn – offensively girly, to spite their younger self – and returned to the table to... well... they didn't really have any idea what to do, so they just unraveled the bundle a bit and started tying the strand into increasingly larger and uglier knots.

Nicole spotted Ravi struggling and cheerfully told them where the spare knitting needles were – in a box buried under a mountain of loose yarn. So now, big step forward, Ravi could tie increasingly larger and uglier knots to a pair of metal sticks.

Maybe they could build some kind of molecular model out of the stuff. Something simple. Iron oxide maybe. Rust. To match their dingey mood.

"You don't know how to knit?" Nicole asked, clearly more disappointed in herself for never thinking to ask than in Ravi for not knowing.

They shook their head no. "But it's fine, I'll just... do my thing here."

"No!" Nicole exclaimed, dropping the beautiful, intricately multitextured piece she was working on. "Let me show you! It's super easy once you get the hang of it."

Nicole then proceeded to show Ravi that knitting was actually incredibly hard and complicated and impossible for someone of their skill level.

"No, it's... That one goes... under. No wait stop, not that way, the other... the other way! Ravi!" Nicole sighed impatiently. "And it's unraveled again... Are you doing this on purpose?"

"I put it under! How many different kinds of 'under' are there? Huh?"

"Apparently exactly enough for you to pick the wrong one every single time! What are the odds!"

Ravi dropped the yarn and the needles on the table and scowled at Nicole. They whispered harshly at her, "I told you I didn't want to come here. Just leave me alone. I don't care about any of this."

They grabbed their coat off the chair and stormed out of the room to stomp down every stair on the three flights down to stand outside in the snowy cold to blaze through a bitter cigarette on their own.

So fucking stupid. They should just walk home right now. What a waste of time. How dare she be so fucking presumptuous to make all these stupid plans for them. She thought she knew them so fucking well? She didn't even fucking know they had fingers that were just absolutely useless for *anything* beautiful. Those hands were made to lift boxes and mix clay into cold emotionless shapes. Those hands were made to make armor hard enough to withstand any attack, even the cruel embrace of the Earth after a catastrophic reentry. *Nicole's hands were made for beauty.*

They crushed their spent cigarette under the heel of their boot in a bitter huff.

The walk back up the stairs sobered them of their rage a bit.

And what they saw when they got to the top instantly turned whatever rage was left into vapor on the subtle breeze coming through that broken window.

The whole crew looked at them with concern, but all they could see was Nicole. She looked so crushed and heartbroken and apologetic.

Ravi had been... *way* too harsh with her.

After they settled in beside her again, they had to immediately and quietly apologize to her for being so cold.

How could they take their frustrations out on her like that? She didn't deserve that. She deserved their kindness and gratitude for everything she was trying to do for them, even if it wasn't exactly making things better. She was trying.

And besides, she was... she was clearly just joking with them about screwing up, right? Teasing them. Like she always did. To make them smile.

But the apology wasn't really enough to make up for their shitty behavior. Obviously. She couldn't hide it. Even though she said she forgave them for the outburst, she was clearly still hurt.

Before they could do anything to properly reconcile with their dear heartbroken friend, Sammy, that kindly granny, snuck up behind the two of them and interrupted with a big toothy grin. She had apparently been keeping an eye on Ravi's struggles all night, and Nicole's futile efforts to help their clumsy hands learn to shape anything beautiful in the world.

"You've never knitted before have you, 'ey kiddo?" she asked.

Ravi scoffed at themself and replied in a poor attempt at playful sarcasm: "Cat's out of the bag, huh? Ravi's just a crafty fraud over here."

She took a look at the mostly-unraveled... *whatever it was supposed to be* on the table in front of Ravi and chastised Nicole for it: "Danica! You monster. What are you doing to them? This pattern would be a *nightmare* for a sweet naïve virgin to our refined, holy craft. Don't you remember being a baby knitter? I always thought you had a big heart, but this is just cruel."

"It's not hard! It's a super easy one, come on. It's just a little teapot coaster thing."

The old woman cackled. "Just because it's a little project doesn't make actually *doing it* any easier. You're going to scare them off on their first night."

"Well sorry for being so naïve. Guess I'll let the expert pick a project," she said, passing the metaphorical baton over to Sammy.

The teasing old woman grinned and looked at Ravi for permission. "You up for it?" she asked. "No trouble for me, kiddo. I'm not making anything important today."

Ravi wondered how anything about knitting could possibly be 'important'. They didn't have the guts to say no to her offer, even though their mind was screaming '*I refuse!*' and trying to send them running out the door. They absolutely did not want to keep embarrassing themself in front of a group of strangers like this.

But the woman was actually... remarkably helpful. She set aside the needles and focused on teaching Ravi 'finger knitting' instead – just to get them comfortable working with the yarn, she said.

"You'll love it," she cheerfully insisted. "My grandkids all got started like this, and the look in their eyes?" She gave Ravi a smile tall enough to crinkle her eyes closed. What a cheerful old lady Sammy was.

They had to start over a couple times when the knots got all tangled up and too tight on their fingers, but once they figured out the right tension and fell into a rhythm, it felt... very relaxing. There was something extremely satisfying about watching the orderly tangle of woven fibers grow out of the back of their hand into a long, twisted vine. It reminded them of a fun chemical reaction they liked to show off to first-year students, where an endless wiggling tube of black ash erupted from a pile of *mysterious chemicals*. Of course, that had very little to do with anything those dewy-eyed freshmen would be doing for the next four years, but it still looked cool.

Nicole had been watching Ravi and their new mentor intently. Apparently, even though she was clearly experienced with the needles, she had never learned to finger knit, and decided to follow along with the lesson.

When the two of them were all set up, Sammy left them to carry on and returned to her own project with an encouraging, "Keep at it, you're doing great."

Nicole quickly got the hang of the new technique and got bored, so she went back to the thing she had been working on before the interruption, which left Ravi some time to work on their own without distraction. By the time Sammy came back to check on them, Ravi had absentmindedly produced a length of finger-knit rope that was easily long enough to extend from the ceiling to the floor.

"You planning to make an escape rope there, Ravi?"

"Huh?" Ravi looked up and noticed for the first time how large the coil of highlighter-pink rope they had been making had become.

She laughed and asked 'Danica' why she didn't stop them.

"Are you kidding? They were in the zone. You don't touch someone when they're in the zone, Sammy, you know that."

Ravi was bewildered at what they'd done. "No uh… I think she's right, Nic—Da—Danica." Ravi silently cursed at themself for the slip. "You definitely should've stopped me, this is… a lot of useless rope."

"Wrong!" Nicole defiantly asserted. "We don't make anything useless around here. Even if you can't do anything with it, you made it. The making's what matters."

Sammy pointed out that it's still nice to finish a sweater once in a while. She nodded at a pile of half-finished projects in the corner, which Nicole seemed to take as a little jab at her.

"Hey! I said I'm working on it!" she protested. "I'm just trying out a new pattern today. I'll work on one of those next week."

One of the other women jumped in to poke fun at Nicole. "*Another new pattern, 'ey? How many weeks in a row is that? You're going to tie up every skein of yarn we have at this rate.*"

Nicole grumbled that if it was such a big problem, then she'd unravel some of her unfinished projects to free up some of the yarn, but the others just laughed and assured her that they didn't care.

"It's fine, Danica," Sammy reassured her. "Truth is half of those are mine anyways. If they make you ball all of yours up again, they'll make me frog all mine too. And I won't, I just won't. It's too sad to throw away all that work. And so *tedious*."

Nicole smiled and raised her fist in the air. "Solidarity, sister."

"Procrastinators unite!"

"*You can't steal our right to never finish anything!*"

Angie put her hands up to stop the two revolutionaries. "Girls please, no one is going to make you do anything with your orphans. But—" She turned to Nicole with a peculiar look in her eye. "—As a favor to me, *Danica*, maybe you could take some time next week to undo your work. There's some lovely wool in there going to waste."

When Angie made her request, it felt to Ravi like the air in room froze for a moment. Just a fraction of a second. Less than a blink. But in that moment, Ravi could see Nicole's jaw go tight with frustration, and her whole body shifted down slightly, like her chair had just been kicked out from under her.

But the moment passed, and the air moved again when Nicole brought the tense silence to an end with a nod and a quiet, defeated utterance: "Deal."

The night wrapped up before Ravi knew it. Sammy showed them how to tie off the end of the finger-knit weave tidily, and now that they knew the whole process start-to-finish, they took the opportunity to quickly make a smaller cord – a bright little bracelet – a gift – a thank you – an apology.

On the way out the door, the old ladies cheerfully waved at Ravi and said it was a pleasure to meet them. And Sammy specifically approached Ravi to give them a huge smile and handshake that lasted a bit too long. "See you next week," she said, hope in her eyes.

Loneliness too.

Ravi wondered how long it had been since the old woman had a doting student in her care.

"We'll see," they replied, with a put-on grin.

Look, I Never Read 'The Art of War' but I'm Pretty Sure It Didn't Cover This Shit

The air was biting on the walk home. Ravi jokingly wrapped their obscenely long pink rope loosely around their neck to make an entirely useless scarf. Nicole assured them it was absolutely charming and anything but useless.

"So?" Nicole asked nothing playfully.

"So what?"

"Felt good to make something, didn't it?"

Ravi held up one end of their evening's labors for Nicole's consideration. "I turned a cord of twisted animal fiber into a slightly thicker and more complicated cord of twisted animal fiber. I don't exactly feel like I've transmuted the fabric of the universe here."

Nicole only replied with a knowing smile.

After a few minutes of idly listening to nothing but the cheerful crunch of fresh snow and ice underfoot, Ravi had to get something off their chest.

"Hey, sorry I've been so... shitty about everything lately. You were right. It was good to get out and do something."

Nicole let out a quick, dismissive breath through her nose, sending out a plume of fog. "Come on, it's fine. You've been having a rough time. I get it."

Ravi took Nicole by the arm and brought her to a stop. "Nicole I mean it. I'm sorry. This doesn't make up for it, but I wanted to give you this," they said, offering that hastily and slightly unevenly knit little bracelet. "Thank you. I had a good time. Really."

Nicole looked at the gift in Ravi's hand for a moment with a blank expression on her face. Was it that surprising to get a gift from them? That didn't speak well for Ravi's reputation.

She cautiously plucked the bracelet from their hand and thanked them for it.

"I'll pay you back," she insisted.

"What are you talking about? You don't owe me anything for this, Nikki. If anything, it's just a down payment for putting up with me these last few days."

"You sure?"

"Of course! Christ, what kind of home did you come from that you think you have to repay a friendly little gift like this?"

Nicole smiled. "Clearly the *wrong* home if I could have just been accepting gifts no strings attached this whole time."

"Yeah, no kidding. You've got a problem, Nix."

"You don't even know."

Nikki tied the bracelet to her wrist. It didn't fit well, so she had to wrap it around a few times to keep it from just slipping off. But she loved it and proudly held out her arm to show it off.

"Hey," she suggested, pointing at a little pub of a bar with a few patrons smoking outside, "You want to grab a drink? Keep the fun flowing?"

Normally it would sound like a terrible idea to drink in the middle of a deep dark depression – which had *not* been magically cured through the power of knitting and friendship, unfortunately. But, while it *normally* wouldn't be safe, it didn't feel so dangerous with Nicole. She always kept them good.

Ravi always had to laugh at Nicole's choice in drinks. No consistency with her, always a new color of the rainbow.

Tonight, it was something that captured the waning twilight hours before a warm summer's night.

"What is that?"

"Margarita. You'd don't know what a margarita is?"

"I don't know any margarita with a dead flower in it."

"It's a hibiscus!"

Ravi looked over at the bar, which was lined with expensive bottles of scotch, rum, and gin, and primarily patronized by gently wrinkled, leather-jacketed, salt-and-pepper men well into the second half of their lives.

"You come here a lot, don't you?" Ravi asked, hoping to confirm a suspicion – that Nicole's influence spread far and wide in this city. Why else would a no-nonsense place like this even keep the ingredients for such a pretty floral drink in stock? if not specifically to fulfill Nicole's singular desires.

"Yeah! I know the owner. She's super sweet. I walk her dogs sometimes. They. Are. *Even sweeter.* —Don't tell her I said that."

Confirmed. Nicole owned this town. She probably used the same subtle strongarm tactics against the bar's owner that she did against Ravi when she insisted on moving in, and the same tactics she used to get them out of the apartment all the time – and even today. This woman was far too powerful. Ravi was very glad to have her on their side, even if it meant that they occasionally had to put up with being thrown into the deep end of a cold metaphorical lake.

Ravi's drink was much less flamboyant, as usual. Just whatever pale ale the place had on tap. And, as usual, it wasn't bad, because despite Henry's attempts to sway them to the dark side, they were still pretty sure that beer was beer at the end of the night.

They spent the first hour of the night chatting with Nicole through smiles and subdued laughter about the other patrons in the building, and the décor, and the dirty words scratched into the surface of the wooden table, and the ladies at the stitch-and-bitch. They also chatted about the most interesting stuff Ravi could ever hope to get stuck on, the stuff they always loved talking to Nicole about – the good in the world, the injustice, the wonder and the disappointment, the reasons to be alive in the face of all the misery, reasons to laugh. Just, the usual stuff that always came up whenever they were hanging out. The usual stuff that made Ravi glow, to know anyone at all wanted to talk about it, and to know they had one of them so close by.

While they were hanging out, Ravi noted that Nicole was eyeing up the band now and then – a duo that was playing intriguingly melodic grunge – music that absolutely didn't feel like it fit the vibe in the building, but no one was complaining.

During a set break, she left Ravi alone at the table to get the attention of the lead singer, tapping the young woman's shoulder. Nicole was met with a beaming smile, a long hug, and a sweet bump of their foreheads.

After a quick chat, it looked like Nicole asked for a favor, and the woman cheerfully agreed. Nicole gently touched the woman's arm when she left, then returned to Ravi with a huge smile.

"Friend of yours?" Ravi asked. They had been tapping the rim of their pint glass idly while they supervised Nicole's interaction.

"Sort of! This used to be one of my favorite bands, actually – and we hooked up a couple times," she added, like it was nothing. "She's really good! Don't you think?"

Ravi gave Nicole a playful grin, trying to hide their miserably inappropriate bitterness, and teased her: "On stage or in bed?"

"I meant music! Gods you're awful."

"Bad in bed then?"

Nicole dodged the question with a bit of red in her freckled cheeks, as she tended to do whenever Ravi was getting a little too close to uncovering her secrets. "Her old stuff is really good, I was just asking her if she's playing my favorite song tonight."

"Danceable?"

"*Very*. I wasn't expecting such a good band – and definitely not *her*. It's usually just boring rock cover bands in here. I guess the owner's developed some taste."

"Mm. *Taste*." Ravi was skeptical. "You sure you didn't put the idea in her head the last time you walked her dogs? —And maybe some ideas about floral cocktails?" they added, pointing to Nicole's drink.

Nicole smiled at Ravi but didn't answer the question.

As usual whenever they went out and Nicole felt like gracing the dancefloor with her beauty, Ravi guarded the table – sneaking in a couple extra drinks for themself when she wasn't looking.

Though this wasn't much of a dancefloor. It was like a whole ten square feet in front of the stage. She was the only one up there, which made sense considering the crowd, but she looked right at home there, drink in hand, never spilling a drop, filling every beat of the music with life.

She was nice to watch.

Ravi noted, as they quickly made their way through their first secret pint, that the lead singer was very much singing *to* Nicole tonight. The two of them had their eyes locked every song – including during one that sounded very much like it might have been *about* Nicole, from all the poetry about a beautiful woman with an intoxicating smile, starry eyes, and a body delicious enough to make you feel hungry all night.

To Ravi's surprise, Nicole hurried back to the table to drop her glass off, then put her hands on Ravi's wrist to plead with them to join her for the next song. It was her favorite, she insisted – probably the one she requested.

Ravi was hesitant. They had sworn off dancing, and for months now they'd told Nicole that every time the two of them were out, but she had just kept right on asking with so much hope in her eyes and it really was wearing away at them.

But their shoulder was absolutely not in good shape tonight. It would be devastating if they got knocked around.

They clenched their teeth, looked down at their half empty glass, then over at the bright-eyed singer who was still grinning cutely at Nicole even all the way across the room.

—Annoying... That's... so... <u>annoying</u>...

Fuck it. They'd done stupider things for smarter reasons.

They quickly finished their drink and let Nicole drag them up to the foot of the stage to make a fool of themself in front of a room full of strangers – for the second time that night.

Ravi noted with childish bitter jealousy that the singer was still very much trying to make eyes with Nikki, but Nicole wasn't looking at her, or even at Ravi. She was just lost in it, eyes closed, warm look on her face, moving her intimidating form along smooth Bezier curves that made her look like what Ravi could only imagine was the shape of the wind in summer.

Yes.

That was it, wasn't it? That was her. The wind. She was sweet summerly living wind, riding alongside the sweet breath of its favorite voice, right next to Ravi's awkward, pained, polygonal, side-stepping, not-quite-dancing. They were more like a dilapidated old windmill in the breeze, wagging back and forth but never making a full rotation.

They put on a smile for her whenever she did open her eyes to glance their way, though, or when she took their wrist to pull them into her intoxicating flow for a few bars of the song.

This was the first time they'd been this close to her while she was dancing, and the show was much, much more intense at this distance. They couldn't keep their eyes off her forbidden ample curves – which were torturously right up in Ravi's face – whenever she bounced and swayed and *gyrated* to the rhythm. —And for some reason, she grinned at them warmly whenever she caught them appreciating the shape of her.

—God damn, seriously, does she <u>know</u> how much she's torturing you?

When the two of them finally returned to the table after what *felt* like hours but was certainly only a few minutes, she was beaming.

"I never thought I'd get you up there dancing with me," she said with a hint of a thank you in her voice. "You told me you didn't do that anymore!"

Ravi looked away from her, casting their eyes down, and sheepishly tried to explain it away like it was nothing. "Yeah. Well, if some beautiful woman keeps asking, I'm gonna crack eventually. I'm not *that* fortified, and you've clearly figured out my one true weakness: A healthy dose of alcohol at your favorite band while I'm feeling shitty and grateful for everything you do for me. It's a rare synchronicity, this – a hundred-year comet hanging in the night sky next to a meteor shower during an earthquake."

"You get so poetic when you're drunk."

They snickered at that dismissively. "Drunk and depressed. *The stars must align to unlock the gate.*"

Nicole touched Ravi's wrist and somberly assured them everything would be okay.

And you know, looking in her bright eyes, at her hopeful smile, they had to believe her. They really did.

During another set break and a lull in conversation, Ravi glanced over at the singer, who seemed to be looking over at Nicole hopefully, and Ravi didn't want to lose her again, so they tried to distract Nicole with a question. Unfortunately, the only question they had at the front of their mind was something that had been bothering them all night, and one that they finally felt bold enough, on their fifth beer, to ask about:

"Nikki, I have to ask: Are you *really* friends with that woman? She seems to have a weird... uh... connection... with you."

"What? Who, the singer? I don't know, not really. I mean she's nice. Cute smile, great music, and I do *so* miss how she just *gets me* in bed. Those lips have quite a few talents beyond shaping her pretty voice," she added with a sly grin. "But I wouldn't say we're 'friends'."

"Too much info. And I meant that old woman... Um... What's her name...? Why do I keep forgetting..."

"Oh. Angie," Nicole confirmed lethargically.

"Yes! Angie."

She didn't answer right away. And Ravi wondered if there could be any real friend in the world that needed to take so long to say *'yes'* to such a simple question.

But she did, at last, say, "Yes," like she had only just accepted the truth of it. "Yes, we're friends."

"Really?"

"Yes."

Ravi looked off beyond Nicole's shoulder, letting their focus wander about the dwindling crowd of rowdy patrons at the bar who were stumbling into each other with smiles and drunken comradery.

They rubbed their cheek aggressively with their palm. They didn't know what it was that bothered them so much about this, but it felt wrong, something felt very wrong.

"I just... When she told you to undo your sweaters back there. That was weird. Wasn't that weird? It just felt kind of... I don't know, pushy? Mean? *Controlling?*"

Nicole lowered her eyes and gave all her attention to the crude words carved into the surface of the table, while her glass moved under the edge of the table to find itself hidden in her lap. The faint hum it made while her finger lazily drew circles around its rim was the only response she seemed to be willing to give at the moment.

Ravi didn't know if they should push this. But it wasn't going to go away just because Nicole didn't want to talk about it. They both knew that.

After a long silence, Nicole set her cup down and placed both her hands on the table. She narrowed her gaze and looked directly at Ravi – not at their eyes, but at their lips, very intently avoiding eye contact.

"She takes care of me," she assured Ravi. "I owe her a lot, and I have to pay her back for that."

They didn't know how to respond to that obvious lie. The way Nicole said it, it sounded like Angie was some kind of mob boss, hounding her for protection money, with a horde of bat-wielding goons at her disposal to crush Nikki's kneecaps if she didn't pay up.

Ravi could hear an echo of Nicole's words in their head, a common phrase in the apartment: *I'll pay you back.* She even said it earlier that night, just for the shitty apology bracelet that she still had wrapped playfully around her wrist. They had always thought that it was just the way she showed her gratitude, just an over-the-top *'thanks'*. But after seeing how she reacted to Angie's 'request' earlier...

"Hey," they spoke as sternly and soberly as they could, "You don't owe me anything. You get that, right?"

Nicole's intense gaze didn't shift a millimeter from the tip of Ravi's lips.

They reached out to take her hand and dipped down to try to catch her eyes.

"Nikki. Nicole. You're a gift. You don't owe me. Okay? You have never owed me anything. Ever."

She clenched her teeth, then pulled away from Ravi. After a few bitter silent moments of consideration and parted lips seeking out some words to dismiss Ravi's pleading entreaty, she gave up, finished her drink in one go, and stood up to leave the table.

She grabbed her coat off the back of her chair and informed Ravi she needed some air. She lingered for a moment, though, looking at Ravi for something with pleading eyes, but only for a moment before she stormed off.

—What did she want to hear?

No, more importantly, what was her damage? How does someone so sweet end up so weird about favors and debts to friends and old ladies?

—What did Angie <u>do</u> to her?

Ravi waited impatiently, trying very hard to avoid drinking their beer, because they were already too deep in it to hold their tongue properly, but every time they thought about that look on her face when she stormed off, they had to take a swig of it.

At last, when their glass was empty, and Nicole was still nowhere to be found, they grimaced at themself for a few seconds before they stood up, almost knocking over their chair, and followed after her, fumbling to get their coat on over the bitter cutting pain in their shoulder while shoving their way out the door.

They found Nicole outside smiling warmly, talking to that singer, who was just crushing one cigarette butt under her boot while she coolly knocked another one out of her pack. Premium brand. Ravi could smell the pleasantly warm and fragrant, almost *floral* smoke even from a dozen meters away, even through the half-dozen other smokers out there. She offered one to Nicole, but she declined with a playful grin and teased the singer like she should know better.

These two really had some history.

Ravi froze in place when they saw the two of them talking like old friends, when they saw Nicole looking so happy, after they had just made her so agitated at them that it was worth abandoning them inside.

Someone bumped into them to shove them out of the way of the door and hit their shoulder the wrong way, which made them tense up and wince and yelp out in pain, and forced them to take a few steps out into the cold in a clumsy stagger that drew Nicole's attention right away.

She told her dear singer to wait for a second before she hustled over to check on Ravi, who was avoiding eye contact and trying not to show their face all flushed with embarrassment.

"Hey Rav, you okay?"

"Mhm. Sorry, just uh. Got bumped a bit there," they grinned uneasily. "I uh..." They glanced over at the singer who was looking at them with a snide grin. "...figured I'd come out for a smoke."

Nicole looked over her shoulder at the smiling woman, then invited Ravi to join the two of them.

They tried to refuse, but there was no good reason to say no, so they reluctantly followed after Nicole to make a little triangle with the two attractive women.

They almost forgot to take out a cigarette in their flustration.

There was what felt like a very awkward silence, so Ravi interrupted it to compliment the singer on her performance. "It's good music. Uh. What do you call it?"

"We try to avoid labels," she replied stoically. Her speaking voice was just as enjoyable as her singing voice.

"Yeah. Yeah, that makes sense. Well, it was nice. Thanks for playing."

"Still have another set, *comrade—*" She pointed teasingly with her fragrant cigarette at one of the faded anarchy patches on Ravi's denim jacket when she said that, guiding their dumbfounded eyes to it when she did. "—Or are you leaving?"

There was something cutting about the way she asked that. Like she was telling them the bar would be better without them.

They looked at the ground while they took a long drag of their cheap cigarette, and by the time they were done, they had entirely forgotten the question, but they did manage to remember that the answer absolutely out of spite had to be, "No."

Nicole perked up in the silence with a cheerful apology when she realized she hadn't properly introduced either of them. Ravi didn't remember the name of the woman, just as much as they were certain she immediately erased theirs from her mind. Nicole introduced Ravi as a good friend, and as a talented chemist, and not as a colossal fuckup, which all felt quite generous.

"A chemist? Lucky you, Danibelle. Unlimited transcendental contraband at your beck and call. Bet you two have a lot of fun on the farthest liminal edge of reality. Should we invite your talented good friend here to the afterparty?"

She was very much speaking about Ravi and not to them. They were nothing to this woman. And that seemed fair. Ravi would never be able to put so much beauty into the world as she did. They would never be able to captivate Nicole the way she did. They would never be able to make Nicole move so beautifully as she did. And that ached in a way that wouldn't go away for a long time.

Ravi dryly explained that it wasn't that kind of chemistry, though they weren't about to elaborate. A suave singer like her definitely wouldn't find anything interesting about the kind of work they did and they knew it.

But still, Nicole tried to defend Ravi against the truth of the humble nature of their work, trying to sell them as a genius on the cutting edge of making the exotic shells of future spaceships that would go to the stars and back on a whim. She really thought that about their work, didn't she? God, if they could get her writing their grant applications with all that enthusiasm, they might actually bring in enough funding to cut back their shifts at the warehouse.

Unfortunately, unsurprisingly, that still killed the conversation immediately, with a little bored affirmative hum from Nicole's enamoring old hookup.

Ravi was... very obviously making things weird here.

They watched the ash on the end of their cigarette lose its orange glow and fall for nothing to get lost in the snow.

"...Nicole can I talk to you?"

The singer looked at her and smirked. " 'Nicole'?"

'Danibelle' smiled back. "Long story. Tell you later."

Then Nicole graciously followed Ravi around a corner into a quiet alleyway, away from the small crowd of people in front of the bar.

"What's up Ravi Bee? You okay?"

Ravi still couldn't make eye contact. They scuffed their boot on the ground and kicked a few clumps of hardened snow against the wall before they dropped their half-finished cigarette on the ground and crushed it out. They hated... exposing her to that poison.

The smell of that charming singer of Nicole's fancy cigarillos was still lingering in the air, even over here.

This was so stupid. They were so fucking stupid, to keep pushing this, what was obviously a very sensitive topic for Nicole, while she was obviously just trying to have fun with that beautiful talented woman over there, but it was too important to just let it go.

At last, they found the courage to look her in the eye and implore her, "I need to hear you say it. Please. Just say it. You don't owe me."

No response, except for all the joy in her face to drain away in an instant, and for her to turn away from Ravi. For a second it looked like she was about to storm off again, to return to that lovely singer's pleasant company, but she graciously stopped herself.

"...Nicole. Please."

She let out a huge huff of a sigh that sent a massive cloud of fog into the night, followed by an impatient admission: "I know."

"No. That's not... That's not enough. I can't keep... *doing this*. This stupid game. You're so fucking stubborn I'm never going to win and it's... I can't live like this. I can't be your *friend* like this. Just say it. Please. You don't owe me—"

"—I know! Gods, I know, okay? I know."

Ravi clenched their teeth bitterly. They didn't know how to handle this at all. How many times did they have to make it clear their kindness wasn't part of some scheme? Some loan? Some *transaction?* How many fucking times would it take?

There was something in all this that they couldn't see, that they couldn't understand, that Nicole refused to talk to them about. And maybe they should respect that. If they had any sense, or any decency, they'd respect that and let it go.

"Is that all?" she asked impatiently while Ravi was stuck in their head. "Can I go?"

The tone of her voice was both like the eardrum popping roar of an antagonistic revving engine, and the violent squeal of burning rubber. She didn't need to ask; she was already gone.

Where was that warm loving Nicole that dragged them out of bed in the depths of their darkness and thrust them into the light?

Why did they have to fuck this up tonight? Everything was going so well.

—Just let it go!

Why was this so hard for her?

—She'd tell you if she could! Drop it, you fucking idiot, what's wrong with you?

They couldn't stand it.

—Why though? Why doesn't she trust me? After everything…

They had to know.

—Fuck, aren't we friends? Or what the hell is all this?

Ravi couldn't catch their tongue. It was too loose, and it was too late in the night, and they were far too deep in their own head now to even realize they were speaking aloud.

"What did she do to you?"

Nicole let out a couple of restrained hissing huffs through her nose before at last she turned to face Ravi and took two stern steps to get right up on them. Her face was red with either cold or anger – *probably* anger, since she was making herself tall and menacing, standing over Ravi in a way she had never done before except to tease them, in a way that made Ravi small.

But Ravi didn't move, though they were shaking – either with cold or fear. Probably fear, since Nicole would *destroy* them in a fight. Lucky for them, Nicole was holding herself back, still as a statue, frozen in place, frozen solid holding herself a mere moment from speaking words that would probably cut Ravi in half, holding herself a mere moment from reaching out to grab Ravi by the coat to throw them into a dumpster, holding herself a mere moment from following through on what already felt like a silent threat on Ravi's life for their asinine meddling.

She stood like that, holding herself from destroying them, towering over them, for a few enraged breaths—furious clouds of fog that erupted through bared teeth over Ravi's head before they faded into nothing.

—She's so tall.

Ravi lost count of the breaths between them, but at last, Nicole backed off and let off on that 'fuck off and die' stance to relax into something softer and more forgiving.

As the vapors of her rage drifted away into the quiet winter night, only her body was left behind, stuck in the discreet darkened laneway there with her stubborn, prying, ungrateful, insufferable little shit of a roommate – stuck there with her terrible roommate, and all the angry words she was too nice and too good and too *indebted* to Ravi to give a voice to.

It must have felt like a mountain of seething cold kindling without a spark of ire to light it up.

That missing spark seemed to leave her struggling to speak. Ravi could see the words hesitating on her lips, tripping on the tip of her tongue, caught in her throat. But she swallowed and choked them all back, and instead she only managed to get out an apology that must have tasted like the bottom of a boot from the look on her face.

"I can't talk about this, Ravi. I can't. I'm sorry. Just... It's fine. Trust me. We've just got... *history*, I guess, okay? And even if we're not whatever you define as 'friends', I still need her, just as much as she needs me."

"Well she doesn't have to be so shitty about it."

Nicole's scowl broke for a second. A hint of surprise. A subtle shift in her brow. A spark in her eye. A silent concession that Ravi was right.

"Just... drop it. Please."

There it was. Clear as day. Nicole wanted Ravi to back off, and they hated to do it, to watch Nicole get jerked around by that shitty old mob boss of hers, but if that's what Nicole wanted, they'd do it. They'd pretend it was okay. Bitterly. Silently.

"...Okay. I'll drop it. I'm sorry."

"Thank you." She paused for a breath before she asked, less impatient this time, "Can I go?" like it was up to Ravi, like they were keeping her.

Ravi dropped their gaze and shook their head at themself. "You don't have to ask, Nikki. You can go whenever you want..."

She didn't move for a few tense seconds. And when she did move, it wasn't to leave. Once again, she took two steps up to Ravi – and all their courage was gone now. They flinched and took half a step back, but it was too late. She had them in her hands.

But she wasn't throwing them in a dumpster.

"Thank you," she said to them softly while she hugged them and pulled them into her soft chest with an arm firmly wrapped around their good shoulder. "I promise I'm not going anywhere, you baby. Stop being so dramatic about every little thing, gods."

Ravi grinned to themself stupidly. They felt like an idiot for doing it, but still, they weakly brought their hands up to hug her back. They didn't deserve this.

Despite her assurances, though, Ravi couldn't follow her when she turned to walk away. They could only helplessly and disappointedly watch, while hiding around the corner to stay out of the way, as Nicole and the singer regrouped, shared a few pleasant words without them, and then went back inside together.

Nicole looked back, but she didn't spend more than a few seconds before giving up on finding Ravi.

It felt like a bit of a betrayal.

Maybe the singer was right. Maybe the bar would be better without them.

They gritted their teeth and cursed at themself bitterly before they followed after Nicole.

When they got back to their table, they found it had been taken over by another group. They looked around and spotted Nicole closer to the stage, exuberantly waving Ravi over to a new table – a round four-seater. Ravi noted a couple extra drinks waiting, including a fresh beer for them at the seat counter-clockwise from Nicole's.

"There you are!" she said, loud over the music. "Thought I lost you. Sorry for abandoning you back there." Her hands were pressed together like a humble prayer to plead for Ravi's forgiveness, implying the beer was repayment for the crime.

They scoffed, then lifted their beer in the air for a cheers to show Nicole there was no bad blood about it.

After they set their drink down, they asked about the other seats.

Nicole explained that the two musicians on stage would be joining the two of them after their final set to close out the bar. "Sounds like there's a fun party after this," Nicole said with a grin. "They've got a couple hotel rooms booked for the night."

"What's the vibe?" Ravi asked, pretending to be interested.

"Mm. She mentioned some other musicians, probably some jamming, drinking until dawn. And if I remember correctly, there are usually some pills in the mix with her," she added, bringing a fingertip to her lip like it was some big secret. "The kind that make you feel *warm*."

"Ecstasy?"

Nicole shrugged. "I don't *usually* partake. Though I might make an exception tonight…" she added, looking over at the singer with hungry eyes and a playful grin. "Gods not that I need anything to warm me up right now."

"You're really hurting for this one, huh?"

Nicole grinned at Ravi while she absently tapped the rim of her cocktail glass. "I've been a little *occupied* lately. And it's been a long time since I got a chance to enjoy one of the five-star entrées in my little black book."

— *'Occupied'.*

Dealing with Ravi's bullshit, probably.

"She's that good, huh?"

"She's an *experience.*"

"You're making me jealous."

"Oh, come on, I bet you'll find *someone* to have some fun with. — You're coming, right?"

Ravi put on their best poker face and told Nicole they'd absolutely follow her to the ends of the Earth tonight, "—As long as I don't have to carry any more chairs."

"I do solemnly swear," Nicole said, raising her hand in the air to swear an oath on it. Ravi swatted at her hand and told her to stop being so serious about it.

In the middle of the next song, they told Nikki they were going out for another quick smoke.

But, instead of lighting up outside and hanging around with the other drunken patrons in the cold, despite their assurances about travelling the Earth for Nikki's delight tonight, they decided to send Nicole a message: A humble apology, explaining that they'd caught a ride home in a rush, to get some sleep before an entirely fictional early morning shift that they 'only just remembered'.

"Have fun tonight," they capped it off, before turning off their phone.

Then they dutifully stumbled home on their own, to spare poor Nicole the trouble of looking after them all night. They were sick of getting in the way of her fun.

When they got back to the apartment, they reluctantly turned their phone back on to read a flurry of messages from Nicole that arrived all at once. At the end of a few messages thanking them for spending the evening with her, they found one final message informing them that she definitely wasn't coming home tonight, with a few salaciously suggestive symbols to prophesize exactly what kind of fun was in store for her that evening.

Ravi replied with an impotent, "Have fun," and an *incredibly* forced winking face, and then spent the rest of the night trying very hard not to imagine how happy that singer must be making Nicole tonight.

Ravi tossed their phone, then sat down on Nicole's cramped little couch of a bed and closed their eyes to take deep breaths and clear their mind. But all they could see in their mind's eye was that singer's pretty, sly lips mocking them, and that quickly led into a frustrating vision of the woman nipping at Nicole's ears and teasing off the ribbons on the bodice of her dress to unwrap her – and it would only get worse from there if they let it, so they opened their eyes and abandoned that exercise entirely.

With a huff of a sigh, they let themself collapse dramatically on their side, to flop their head right into the pillow Nicole always slept on. It was Ravi's pillow, really. The good one. Not that it was very good. Glorified polyester stuffing on terribly deformed foam. Nicole had been borrowing it since she moved in. But after so long of soaking her up, it did not smell like Ravi at all anymore.

It smelled like heaven.

They took the pillow out from under their head to lay themself flat on the couch, and hugged it to their chest to drink in Nicole's intoxicating scent. They let their eyes fall closed again and immediately their mind returned to that torturous scene. Now the singer was delighting Nicole's bountiful breasts with her oh-so-musical lips and tongue, playing her moans in a sweet melody like a beautiful instrument.

Ravi found one of their hands had managed to wander down to their midriff. It was digging into their abs with clawed fingers, trying to hold itself back from claiming what they so desperately wanted tonight.

—*This is sick, Ravi. Don't do this.*

But their control of their hand slipped away as that vision in their mind warped to sate their perverse hunger, doing away with the pretty singer entirely and putting Nicole in *their* bed, her intimidating thighs parting happily for *their* enjoyment.

They bit down on the pillow while that devil's hand of theirs clumsily unclasped their belt and undid the fly of their jeans so their desperate fingers could easily slip under their boxers to feel the wildly inappropriate wetness between their thighs.

—*You're so disgusting.*

Yeah. And? Who gives a <u>fuck</u>.

The loose buckle rattled obnoxiously in a rapid rhythm while Ravi fucked themself and assaulted their clit and coaxed quiet, shameful gasps and whiney moans out of themself, right there on Nicole's bed, suffocating themself in her pillow, breathing her in, dreaming of *her* moans. They built themself up to a sharp hip-bucking climax, on the image of Nicole's body writhing and convulsing uncontrollably in their hands.

When they finished, they brought their perverse lust-drenched fingers to their lips and licked themself clean, pretending it was her.

But there was no way Nicole tasted as mundane as they did. She was a goddess. It was a poor substitute for her ambrosia that only made their longing more painful.

God, that singer was right with that song of hers: Nicole was so delicious it was enough to keep them hungry all night. But all they could do to sate themself now was shamefully hug her pillow in the dark, curl up in her bed, and long for the impossible, for the unreasonable, for her to find them there and understand what it meant and, with a piteous smile, kiss them until they melted in her hands.

❧

Nicole wasn't back by the time Ravi woke.

In the regrettable sobriety of the morning, the hangover made it hard to tell whether they were feeling nauseated because of their disgusting behavior or because of the alcohol.

—*You're vile. Really truly just a disgusting carnal <u>animal</u>.*

They found they had passed out in Nicole's miserable bed with their belt and jeans lewdly undone. They paused on fastening the clasp, and considered just... doing it again, fucking themself in her bed like some horny witless degenerate, just to wallow in how disgusting they were for it. They still wanted it. Even now. The heat and temptation of the *forbidden* was eating away at them. They *wanted* to get caught now. Better than living with some miserable secret shame every day forever.

And it wouldn't even be new behavior for them, would it? Jerking off in their best friend's bed. Back in middle school, and even in high school, whenever they would stay over at Felicity's place, forced to sleep in her bed at her giddy insistence, they couldn't stop themself from getting overwhelmed by the thought of her, the smell of her, the subtle building warmth under the sheets from her body mere inches from theirs, remembering all of the salacious secret side glances the two of them tried to sneak past each other in the locker room, overheating with newly discovered hormonal lust – until Ravi found their hands acting of their own accord whenever Felicity left the room to use the bathroom or get some water, trying desperately to start and finish themself off in the time it took her to return, *aching* to be discovered.

They were never quite fast enough back then, though, which just made the rest of the night even more torturous, filled with subtle thigh clenches every time their mind stumbled into the wild image of just rolling over right there to take her for themself – to take her stunning little breasts in their hands, to slip their curious fingers between her thighs, to slide their eager tongue along the back of her neck and put dark love bites there to claim her.

—Yeah. This isn't new. You've always been like this. Just do it. Filth. This is your couch too. Your apartment. You can jerk off wherever you want.

And why would it matter to stop now? You can't undo this, even if she never finds out. Just like Felicity. You'll always know. You defiled her bed.

...But that wasn't right, was it? At least they'd have an easier time excusing themself for it, last night – excusing it as just... a stupid drunken jealous one-time mistake. They'd done a lot worse. It'd just be added to their list of countable regrets that sent them off to sleep on troubled nights.

They thought better of it, and instead returned to their own bed – to work this... *frustration* out of their system – to fuck themself stupid with the most reliable vibrator they owned, thinking instead about something that always got them off properly: That time, in the depths of the darkness of their third year at the university, when, after proffering half a hand job under the table, they let some nameless cock shove them face-first up against the wall of some filthy bathroom stall in a half-drunk haze, their bottle of piss-weak beer still in hand, to drop their jeans to their thighs and fuck them raw and reckless with the stall door wide open for anyone to see.

God, they really were disgusting, weren't they? Who does that? No decent human being, at least. The depravity of it always got them very, *very* hot though.

They couldn't even remember now whether or not they pleaded with him to pull out and finish himself off fucking their throat raw – you know, to be safe. That was their go-to, and the best preventative birth control they would let themself have back then, they were so brutally self-destructive.

But in their fantasy, it didn't matter how much they begged or what they offered up, because no matter what they said or did to protest, he just treated them exactly like they deserved, like a filthy used-up piece of garbage, a disposable cum rag. Then he left, leaving them shuddering and incomplete, alone in abhorrent solitude, to clean up the sloppy mess he made of their cunt and the back of their shirt and jeans. And he didn't ever pull out in time, no matter how many times they remembered it.

In the memory, that was where the dangerous disappointing encounter ended. Ravi remembered closing the stall door after he left so they could feverishly massage the selfish fucker's cold sticky mess into their clit until they got some release.

But in the fantasy, they never got to finish cleaning themself up before some other rough nameless cock stepped up to try and fail to finish the job, and then another, and another...

And this fine shameful morning, laying in bed, fucking themself and bucking their hips slightly to guide their vibrator to the right spot to make them swear, that lengthy ordeal in Ravi's fantasy had to culminate in something big – in the image of some long, thick, drool-slickened cock, buried deep and twitching in their throat, making them gag, leaving them red-faced short of oxygen, eyes welled up with pathetic silent tears, until violent spurts of liquid heat coated their throat and filled them up while the guy's fingers dug into the back of their skull desperately to keep them from escaping before he was done with them.

Felt good.

Felt *right*.

To be wanted so violently.

To be taken.

To be needed.

—*Need me. God, just need me. Please. For even one night...*

After they recovered from a long, writhing orgasm and got their breath back – their cunt still twitching on the patterned pulses and vibrations of their nameless silicone stand-in – they had to have a little laugh about that old memory's pathetic, disappointing anonymous bar patron. What a stupid fucker. If he was gonna cum inside anyways, he could do it properly at least, fucksake. Grab their hips and force his filthy cock up to the hilt inside them so they could actually enjoy every throbbing defilement of their cunt, so they could pretend they were worth fucking at all.

And seriously, it was an expensive fucking pill the morning after. Make it worth the money, asshole.

They switched off the vibrator and let it slip out of their cunt to drop pathetically onto the little mess of lust staining the bed between their thighs. After a few long, peaceful, euphoric breaths, to drink in the endorphins and the catharsis, they brought the heels of their palms to their eyes and chuckled at themself for how stupid they felt.

This was just... so idiotic, letting this crush get so *in* them, letting it drive them crazy like this. They weren't even fucking *lonely*. What's-Her-Name was always down to fuck – just a horny booty call away. Wasn't that enough? *Why* wasn't that enough? Why wouldn't that *ever* be enough?

They didn't even bother cleaning up the mess they made of their lust-stained bed or their tossed hair or their beer-scented and stale sweat-caked skin before they pulled on last night's jeans and let themself out for a walk to gather their thoughts. Hopefully getting all that frustration out of their system had been enough to clear the stupidity out of their head.

By the time they got back to the apartment, hours later, well into the afternoon, Nicole was finally back from her own adventure, and Ravi had managed to wrestle with their mind for long enough that they had come to two important conclusions:

One:

They were done with this idiotic half-pulled-out crush. This wasn't healthy. And if they weren't going to grab this situation by the hips to commit to making a huge mistake for real – and at least get a little fun out of it in the process of fucking everything up – then there wasn't any point.

They were sick of the disappointment they kept thrusting on themself, sick of cleaning up the mess it made of their emotions, sick of getting hurt by Nicole just because she didn't want them, just because she never would want them. None of that was her fault. She didn't even know. And she *couldn't* <u>ever</u> know, obviously. They saw that.

After all, how could they possibly tell her? Nikki was easily the best friend they had now – even better than Felicity, wasn't she? Not for any fault of Felicity's though. Ravi was the one who spoiled all that. Let it turn to bitter ruin, just because they couldn't get over her, because they couldn't be honest with her, because they couldn't stand to be near her anymore. They couldn't let the same thing happen with Nicole. It would be so, *so* stupid to let some childish obsessive bullshit ruin all that again.

And the only way they could keep her in their life, *and* be honest with her, was to clean up their mind until the honest truth wasn't '*I want you to look at me like you looked at that singer last night*' anymore.

Two:

They were done letting Nicole get away with thinking she owed them anything. It made them sick to think that she might look at them one day the same way she looked at that miserable old mob boss of a woman, that smiling pretender. They couldn't stop being kind to Nicole. She deserved every kindness in the world. But they had to figure out some way to turn each and every kindness around, to turn every gift they gave her into a favor *for them*. They'd wracked their mind over it for hours on the walk home.

It wouldn't be easy, but they were pretty smart. After years of jumping through hoops and twisting words around to fit the criteria for every impossible grant application, they'd gotten pretty good at this kind of stuff. Thinking in rhetorical loopholes like that, it was just part of their wiring now. They'd figure something out.

They'd have to, because they weren't kidding last night, and they weren't being dramatic: Getting rid of this fictional debt between the two of them was the only way they could stand to be her friend anymore.

Nicole was in the kitchen when Ravi returned, preparing some tea for herself. Ravi joined her with a pleasant hello and put on some coffee.

"Good time last night?" they casually asked her while they loaded up the filter.

—Immersion therapy. Wreck me with details. I'll get over it. I'll have to.

Nicole leaned back on the counter and dragged rough fingers through her wild hair to draw her eyes to the ceiling and, with a giddy beaming grin, told Ravi emphatically *yes*. She played coy, kept the details fuzzy as she always liked to do about her sexual encounters, but she let out a few hints about the wild, orgiastic afterparty in the singer's hotel suite – and about the subsequent private session with her after everyone left or passed out – that pretty well confirmed what Ravi had suspected about the talents of that stunning woman's musical lips and tongue.

And they did a *very good job* not thinking about it.

—Click-click. Good dog. Have a treat.

Nicole had a nostalgic smile on when she admitted how happy it made her to spend a night with the woman again.

"Gods, I missed her. She's always on the road."

"Why don't you go with her? Nothing keeping you here, right? I bet she'd love a goddess of a groupie like you hanging off her arm."

Nicole gave Ravi a sad smile before she explained to remind them, "I told you before, Ravi Bee. I'm not good at that long term stuff."

"Doesn't have to be long term. Just go for a couple months. You deserve to have fun, you know." They paused for a second before they added, "And I'll still be here. Just come back when you're bored."

Nicole sighed and looked at the ceiling for a few seconds to try to put together a good answer.

"I don't know how to put it right, but... I don't like... being happy for too long. Always feels like things are going to fall apart. Makes me anxious. And the longer I stay with someone so... delicious like that, the harder it is to say goodbye. It's just a recipe for disaster. A little fling once in a while like this is better."

Ravi rolled their fingers on the kitchen counter pensively while they considered that. What did that mean, then, that she'd been staying with them for so long?

"You're not happy here?"

Nicole's eyes opened a bit in shock at the question. And she didn't have an easy answer on hand. Looked about as tricky to find this answer as it had been to figure out if Angie was her friend last night.

—And what happy person in the world would have such a hard time answering such a simple question?

"...You... make me... less anxious," she said at last. "I don't know how to explain that... But I'm happy here, I promise. And... I don't want to leave. Not until you're sick of me."

Ravi fiddled with their fingers for a few seconds while they rolled that around in their head. Nicole was counting on them, then, for something, for some kind of stability and comfort. She needed them to be a good friend. She... needed them, didn't she?

Or... *did* she?

"...You're sure you're not just sticking around to pay off this imaginary debt of yours?"

"Well, maybe that's part of it, but... you're..." She stopped to laugh at herself before she admitted some apparently well-kept truth: "You're the best friend I've had in a long time. ...I don't want to lose that."

They were about to respond with a little joke about how unlikely it was that their name could possibly be that high up on the list, but they stopped themself when they noticed something unexpected about Nicole's ensemble today: That pink bracelet Ravi gave her last night, she was still wearing it, even after changing into a new outfit today. The knot looked different now, though. She'd taken it off and then taken all the time and care to put it back on?

...They wondered if she had been wearing it all night, or if she managed to spare it from witnessing every minute – every *hour* that singer was sliding that deft tongue of hers all over Nicole's body.

—Bad dog. No treat.

Instead of a joke about being unworthy of such a lofty title, Ravi simply replied with a hesitant, "You too," that felt a little too painfully earnest on their tongue.

The coffee maker gurgled to a halt, and they poured themself a cup before they invited Nicole to sit with them on the couch.

They tried their best to ignore the pang of guilt about defiling it last night.

—You were drunk and stupid. Forgive it. Move on. Be a good friend.

...Wait. Where's the pillow?

Oh <u>christ</u> did she notice??

While Ravi had an expertly contained little panic attack about maybe being found out for carelessly leaving some sick stain on Nicole's pillow, she cheerfully sat beside them, with a hot cup of her special honeyed green tea, apparently completely oblivious.

—Be cool. Ravi. Be cool.

The pillow probably just fell under the couch. Right? It was fine. Not like they could ask about it anyways.

It was fine.

Forgive it.

Move on.

Nicole idly rotated the cup in her hands with a dumb smile on for a few seconds before she spoke up with a playful little challenge for them:

"You didn't actually have a shift today, did you?"

Ravi was bracing for a much more cutting accusation there, but it seemed like their worrying was for nothing.

They tried to be normal, like a normal person wouldn't, and let out a playfully defeated chuckle at her sharp detective work. "Wow. Found me out! How'd you know?"

She shrugged. "You're not... *tired.*" She paused for a few seconds before she continued to show her gratitude: "Thank you. For that. Though you didn't have to lie."

"I definitely did have to lie. Are you kidding? You're too good a friend sometimes, Nix. That was the only way I could get you out of babysitting me all night. —And *please* don't thank me for that. Don't even mention it. It was the least I could do after everything you've done for me these past few days." Ravi gave her a very dire look, "Nicole Doyle, you look at me. I'm serious. Do not mention it again."

"As you wish," she said, with a playful little bow, "my most generous liege."

"Thank you."

"...Hey, I'm sorry I was so... *short* with you last night about... You know."

"I sure do know."

"I really... *I know*. I know how you feel about all this. I do. I promise."

"And you're still..."

Nicole let out a little sigh. "I grew up in a weird home. It's not easy to shake all that. Like. *Painful*. It's painful. Everything has a cost. That's just how I was raised." She looked at them pleadingly and tried to assure them, "I'll try to shake it though. I know it's important to you."

"God, that would be *so* nice for me."

"Oh? Well, if I do manage to get over it, you think that'd be enough to pay you back for everything?"

"With *interest*."

She grinned at them, then assured them, in that case, that she'd put in an honest effort.

ॐ

A week later, while Nicole was out doing errands, Ravi made discreet arrangements to put her convictions to the test – her convictions, and the proficiency of Ravi's rhetorical gymnastics.

"Erwin, you sure you can do this?"

The old man was making a herculean effort – without a word of complaint – to help Ravi maneuver a gently used three-ton pullout-bed couch into the apartment's cramped little elevator. It wasn't going well.

"Don't underestimate the old guard, Ravi. My creaky old bones carry the same freight all over that floor yours do."

"Yeah, on a forklift."

"That thing's reserved all the time and you know it. I'm stuck on the floor half the time just like the rest of you *uncertifiable* peasants. — You know that, you goat! You knocked me over a couple weeks ago with your head down!"

"Oh right. *Right*. God sorry about that, Erwin. I was so far behind. Fuck, I didn't even... apologize, did I?"

"I think you managed to bleat out half a 'sorry' at me before you *shamelessly* scampered off. Don't worry about it, though. I'm not some frail seeding dandelion. It'll take a little more than a running tackle to send my head flying."

"Running tackle... Did I really trip that hard? My god. I'm so sorry. I think some kind of gremlin undid my bootlaces or something."

Ravi glared at their boots discerningly. Double knot. Every time. For decades. They never came undone. But it had been happening a *lot* lately for some reason, even after they switched to a triple knot.

—Sabotage?

Sadly, despite Erwin's improbable confidence in his ability to lift this humanly impossible weight, this wasn't actually a *lifting* puzzle.

He took a break from supporting the couch at its weird angle to let it settle on its side, then took a few steps back to give the geometry of the situation a careful assessment. The hand he brought to his chin was that old InThetics model with the wonky pinky. Still hadn't been fixed. Poor guy must be having a rough time getting the money scraped together for a repair. Might explain why he was selling the couch for *way* too cheap. Ravi set him straight on the price, though. Even if they could barely afford it, they weren't going to exploit the poor guy.

Ravi suggested that there was a chance the couch could fit without either of them inside the elevator, and sure enough, with a lot of grunting and groaning and shoving, it worked—*barely*. Ravi leaned in and desperately stretched to press the buttons to send the elevator up on its own, to hit every floor on the way up to slow it down, and then sprinted up the stairs to catch it before it went back down.

Huge success, though they barely made it – and they were wheezing by the time they did. They weren't a cardio person, and the half a pack of smokes a week didn't help.

When Erwin finally joined them and spotted them out of breath, he applauded their athletics and asked why they didn't just get him to send the elevator up *after* they got to their floor.

They did not reply.

With a bit more enthusiastic struggling at the door to their unit, the two of them miraculously dragged that little old loveseat out in the hall and shoved the new full-sized couch into the living room – though it was a little too long for the wall and ended up sticking out a bit around the corner, destined to forever slightly obstruct the hallway to the bathroom and Ravi's bedroom. But that was fine. It'd be worth the drunkenly stubbed toes.

Turned out that sullied pillow *had* fallen off the couch – directly into one of Nicole's boxes. Very weird place for it. Very... *intentional* place for it.

...Wait... Did she... take it seriously when they said she was banned from having a pillow for a week?

Fuck. Somehow that felt even *worse* than jerking off in her bed... Jesus...

No. Forget it! Move on! New couch! New life!

And this new one was so modern – and *clean*. It didn't fit the ratty aesthetic of the rest of the apartment at all. But it was a *bed*. An honest-to-goodness queen size bed when it was pulled out – even bigger than Ravi's. More comfortable too, honestly. Finally – and well-deserved – a real bed that Nicole would be able to stretch out on, that she could put real sheets on, that she could laze about in and drown herself in luxury with all the lush downy pillows she deserved, instead of trying to make the best out of the beat-up two-seater and the limp old sack of foam and stuffing that Ravi had lewdly *sullied* on her – and then forced her to hide away with their careless words, apparently.

They stuffed a week's wages in Erwin's good hand and christened the new couch with him with a cold beer and some delivered pizza before helping him load the old couch on his truck to find a new home at the good will.

He was a good man. Too good. While Ravi finished securing the straps to the truck bed, they reflected on how heartbroken they'd be when Erwin eventually kicked the bucket. They didn't really want to have to deal with that, ever – someone dying.

Hopefully he'd have a long life ahead of him.

—Though, honestly, Ravi was probably going to die first, considering everything, so it probably wouldn't come up. Lucky them.

After Ravi shook his hand and said one final thanks, Erwin turned to get in his truck, but he got stuck frozen still with his hand on the door handle. He stood there for a few silent seconds, pensively clenching and releasing the handle, until at last he cleared his throat and spoke in an uncharacteristically slow and morose tone: "Hey Ravi, you ever... think about changing careers?"

—*What a strangely serious question.*

"Are you kidding?" they replied sarcastically. "You know lifting boxes is my lifelong passion."

"Mm. I've just heard rumblings that you've been... having *trouble* lately."

Ravi was startled by Erwin's frank assessment. He was right. They'd been tripping and dropping boxes and losing track of shipments and equipment for weeks now, despite their best efforts to get it together. It was getting bad even on the good days, even when they weren't suffering through the blinding pain in their shoulder, even when they should've been at the very top of their game.

But... they thought no one had noticed. No one had spoken to them about it, at least. But Erwin was hearing... '*rumblings*'?

He continued, trying to sound at least a little encouraging: "And you know, you're too smart for a place like this. You'd be better doing something where you get to work out your brain matter a little more, don't you think?"

Erwin was still looking at the door while he spoke. He was hiding his face. Why was he saying all this?

They tried to make an uneasy joke with him, "Come on Erwin, are you really so mad about that little goat tackle that you'd try to get rid of me?"

"...Lost a lot of overtime last month, huh?"

"...Yeah...?"

"Have you checked your schedule next month?"

Ravi's guts twisted slightly at the line of questioning.

Patterns. There were patterns. Losing overtime is first. Then... shifts get cut back...

"...Not yet?"

"Just, you know, like I said, I wonder if you ever think about changing careers. That's all. I hear things on the floor sometimes, you know, and some people were talking about it, about career changes. Just... got me thinking."

All the joy fell out of Ravi's heart.

They were going to be fired.

This was a warning.

Unless they could get it together, they'd be on the street.

After a few long, still seconds of grim silence between them, Ravi finally spoke up: "Thanks Erwin. I'll think about it."

He nodded silently, then got in his truck and drove away without another word.

Ravi returned to their apartment to sit on the new couch and work through another beer in quiet contemplation, occasionally crushing the bottle in a tight fist when they were overcome with a little spark of rage – mostly at themself.

There was no use sulking about it, though.

They'd start looking for a new job in the morning. Start over again at a new warehouse, keep the illusion of their competence up for as long as possible, then move on, again, and again, and again...

A career change wasn't happening. Nothing else would give them the hours a warehouse did, or so livable a wage. And they needed that money. They had a mountain of loans, and an education to finish, and a whole lot of expensive research to do, and they weren't ready to sacrifice their convictions just yet by taking a military or a corporate grant. They could hold out. They had to. Would they even be *Ravi* anymore if they couldn't? Would they even deserve Nicole's respect if they gave those convictions up? Or would they just... *die* in her eyes right then and there?

They couldn't stand to find out.

When Nicole got home, she was devastated by Ravi's all-too-generous gift – which was exactly what they were expecting. They came prepared for this.

"What was wrong with the old couch?" she asked in frustrated disbelief while she stood with her arms crossed glaring at the pristine offending usurper. "It was fine! I was *fine* with that. *You* were fine with that!"

"Come on, Nikki, that thing was awful. And way too small. I don't care if you were fine with it, *I* wanted to replace it for ages."

"Yeah? Really? First I've heard about it!" She huffed at them and glared.

"What's your problem?"

"I see what you're doing! You think I don't see?"

"What am I doing?" Ravi asked with a coy grin.

She grumbled at them. "You can't pretend this isn't a favor to me. I'm not stupid."

"It's not, though. It's for me."

"Uh huh."

"Nicole, puppy, I am sick of listening to your spine pop when you straighten yourself out every morning. That's not normal and it freaks me out and you are *doing me a favor* by sleeping on this thing and fixing your back for me."

Nicole clenched her teeth and growled quietly at Ravi, curling her fingers into a tight fist until her knuckles cracked—which caused her to splay her hand out immediately and glare at it like she'd just accidentally crushed a butterfly. Apparently, she took Ravi's lie to heart immediately there. They didn't actually care about popping joints, but if that's what it took, they'd lie as shamelessly as they needed to.

Ravi got behind Nicole and assertively shoved her with both hands towards the couch while firmly encouraging her, "Come on try it! It's so good. I love it. *You'll* love it. You'd *better* love it. Not loving it isn't an option so don't tell me if you don't love it."

Nicole halted herself a few inches short of the couch before she asked, "How much was this? You can't afford—"

"—Fifty bucks! Delivered!—"

It was much, much more than fifty bucks. They'd be cutting back on smokes and beer for a few months – maybe a whole year, honestly – but that was... definitely for the best, considering their miserable cardio performance and their impending financial crisis.

Ravi had already resolved to never, ever tell Nicole about their troubles at work. The last thing they wanted was to make her worry about them. They'd sort it out on their own, even if it meant some... *creative* financing strategies.

—There's always... dear old dad...

"—Can't believe I got it so cheap."

Nicole turned around and gave them a skeptical glare. "Ravi I can't... pay you back for this. You get that, right? This is too much. Why did you do this?"

"I swear to god Nicole if you say those fucking words to me ever again, I'm going to dump a whole bucket of ice water on you. Now sit your ass down on these luxurious cushions and tell me how comfortable this thing is."

She grumbled about it, but she did at last accept Ravi's firm invitation and plant herself down on the couch. She tentatively placed her hands on the cushions and gave it a little bounce like she was afraid it was thin ice about to shatter under her weight.

Ravi was looking at her with an expectant grin, and when she spotted that, she let out a little sigh of defeat. "It's very nice. I promise to use it to fix my back for you."

"Thank you! Was that so hard?"

"You're an ass."

"Oh shush. Here, let me show you how to pull out the bed—"

"There's a *bed!?*"

"Didn't I say that?"

"Oh my gods Ravi…"

Nicole stood up and buried her head in her hands, absolutely red with frustration while Ravi moved the coffee table out of the way and pulled the bed out for her.

"I can't believe you did this," she said to herself, quietly repeating it in despair: "I can't believe you *did* this… I can't *believe—*"

And she refused to sit down on her own, so Ravi had to put their hands on her shoulders to <u>sit</u> her down.

Still she wouldn't take her hands from her face.

"Nikki that is not how to test a bed."

"You're a monster."

"Lie down, fucksake. Stop being like this! You promised you were going to work on this stupid debt shit *– for me.*"

After a long, deep breath to gather herself, she did at last admit defeat and flop back on the bed. She stared vacantly at the ceiling for a few seconds before she closed her eyes, took another deep breath, and admitted it was very comfortable.

"Right? What a steal."

"What a steal," Nicole echoed incredulously.

Ravi dug a hidden shopping bag out of the closet and threw a couple brand new pillows and a set of nice sheets at Nicole. Pastel pink with subtle floral patterns. They were pretty sure she'd love it – which she would absolutely hate, of course.

She pulled one of the sheets out and crushed it between her fingers and thumb to test its quality while she lethargically challenged them, "Alright. Go ahead. Let's hear it."

"Well, I just thought it'd be nice – *for me* – if the bedding was really pretty, you know? Make the whole room look nice and clean whenever the bed's out."

"Mhm. And the pillows?"

"You've been borrowing my extra pillow since you got here! I want it back already!"

"You really thought of everything, huh?"

Ravi played stupid, "I have no idea what you're talking about."

"*Okay* Ravi. Good game. You win. I'll make your new bed pretty and get my spine all straightened out *just for you.*"

"That's all I'm asking."

Nicole put the sheet set down and picked up one of the pillows to inspect it. She hugged it to her chest as part of her assessment and rested her chin on it with her eyes closed.

"*For you...*" she mumbled to herself. "So stupid..." She shook her head solemnly to herself with a bitter grimace, but after a few seconds she shook it off with a sigh and goofy little grin. "...Well. Thank you for all this."

"Don't mention it. Ever again. I mean it."

"No, I mean..." She paused to scoff at herself, then looked at Ravi with an earnestly grateful gaze. "Thanks for letting me pay you back for once."

Ravi smiled at her warmly, but they didn't acknowledge her gratitude with any words.

Finally, they won this stupid game.

Now they just had to keep this up for as long as Nicole stayed here.

Easy.

That night, when Ravi was setting out a freshly cooked fish curry dinner for the two of them, they nonchalantly informed Nicole that they had decided to start experimenting with their cooking – for every meal, for the rest of time – and that she would be doing them a *huge favor* by being a test subject for their culinary experiments.

She tapped her fork on the plate pensively while she grumpily glared at Ravi in stunned disbelief.

"That is the *stupidest...*"

"Means a lot to me!" they cheerfully interrupted her. "Just let me know how it tastes and I'll add your data points to my research notes."

Nicole rolled her eyes, took a forkful of the curry, then dryly informed them that it was delicious, "—As usual. *Ravi.* What exactly did you do differently here? Tastes just as amazing as it did last time."

"Put a few extra grains of salt in the rice."

Nicole couldn't stop a little snort of a laugh from escaping at that. The grumpy scowl and the misery in her eyes disappeared when she teased them: "You're really pushing the envelope of culinary science here, huh?"

"Hey, you know my philosophy, Nikki: Science is about incremental change. And meticulous documentation. Thanks for the feedback. Looking forward to the results of the next experiment."

She had a soft grin on when she admitted that she was happy to help.

The Thorns of the Garden Are Dripping With Blood, but Jeezus, Those Raspberries? To Die For

It should absolutely not be this hard to follow someone with a tracking device in her pocket.

But somehow, after every building Danica went in, she suddenly blipped away to some random location halfway across the city.

The tracker must've been faulty or something.

Except the location wasn't random. It was the same place. Every time. Half a dozen times. And every time, she returned empty-handed.

When Felicity looked up the address, it was some old mansion. One of those ones that got gutted of all its beauty to cut it up into little overpriced units. She looked up a couple adverts for rentals in the building, and holy Jeezus it was ridiculous how much these cost.

By the afternoon, despite her best efforts, Felicity's day seemed wasted, all because of that broken tracker. Though strangely, broken as it was, the final blip seemed to take Danica halfway back across town, right to Amy's apartment.

—She's <u>definitely</u> some kind of magic, right? So. It was impossible, but... was she... teleporting?

Felicity made her way to that refurbished mansion to scope it out, finding a seat at a café across the street—with an absolute darling of a barista, wow, immediately worth the visit—to keep an eye on everyone coming in and out of the apartment building.

"Ristretto," she answered when the barista asked for her order.

"Uh. We don't... What is that?"

"You don't make ristretto??"

"Sorry I've never even heard of..."

—This city...

Felicity sighed to herself and waved her hand dismissively. "Just a double shot then, it's fine."

Felicity got set up at a window bar seat while she waited for her compromise of a drink.

Witch. She was looking for a Witch. And she didn't want to be prejudiced or anything, but you know, it was probably safe to assume the Witch probably looked a lot like a witch, right?

So, what, old, miserable, weird clothes?

When the barista brought her drink over, Felicity challenged her to describe a witch.

She was caught completely off-guard by the question.

"Oh. Um. Like, green skin, right? And weird hair? Purple eyes? Isn't that how it goes?"

"What about a witch hiding in plain sight, though?"

She gave it some serious thought, ignoring a customer that was at the counter waiting to order just to answer Felicity's question.

"Well, if I had a ton of magic, I wouldn't care about getting caught. I'd probably make myself look like a faerie queen and destroy anyone who challenged me about it."

Felicity smiled at her. "How would you dress if you were a faerie queen, then?"

She started to describe her vision, for a powerful member of the Summer Court, tall and regal with glorious wings folded into an elegant gown, but she had to cut herself short before she could finish describing the floral patterns of the gilding on the royal's hypothetical bodice when she glanced over her shoulder and turned sharply with a little swear and an apology as she hurried back to the counter to deal with the impatiently toe-tapping customer there.

What a cutie.

Felicity noted her drink was a lot smaller than she expected for a double. When she tasted it, she was surprised to find it was, in fact, a strikingly concentrated shot of ristretto.

That barista was a gemstone shining through the splintered grains of a forest of rotting wood.

Felicity tried to adjust her criteria for 'witch' while she watched the people coming and going across the street, but, unfortunately, within the hour, she noted at least half a dozen old ladies with a very eccentric fashion sense, so it wasn't exactly enough to narrow anything down – and none of them were quite worthy of the title 'faerie queen'.

This wasn't the way.

She pulled the scanned replica of that orphaned page from her pocket and stared at it, hoping to find some kind of guidance in it.

She had no idea what it meant.

Though whoever wrote those margin notes definitely did.

And Virgil could figure out what those margin notes meant.

There was some chain of knowledge here. If the rest of the book was vandalized like that? It'd practically be a Rosetta Stone.

And the Witch had to understand it too. Why else would she have any interest in a book like this unless she could understand it?

"Excuse me?" Someone approached Felicity from behind her seat at the window. That darling dewy-eyed barista. "Did you drop this?"

She was holding some random receipt in her hand. It didn't mean anything to Felicity, so she just waved it off and thanked her for asking.

Honestly, even if it was hers, she didn't want it. From a bookstore or something it looked like. Unless she wanted to return a book, it was useless.

While Felicity watched the barista show off the receipt to every other patron, she wondered who could possibly care about a receipt for a book. No one returns books. What kind of insane person would try to return a book?

Unless it was damaged. Missing a page or something.

So... who could care about a receipt?

...Only a person who bought a damaged book, right?

Felicity noted, once the barista's search was at an end, that the guy the receipt belonged to reacted completely differently from everyone else – though he still didn't want it.

It meant something to him.

...The person...

...Who bought it...

Felicity slammed her hands on the table in a rush of excitement, then shoved the copy of that mysterious page back in her pocket, grabbed her coat, and rushed up to the barista to thank her and promise her a huge tip when she got back. Then she dashed out the door without even waiting for a reply.

It was a shame to do it, but she had to abandon her comfy warm seat to relocate across the street to a bench in the cold in the mansion's little front yard. She settled in, pretending to read a novel, while keeping her little duplicate of that defaced orphaned scrap of a book tucked away in the depths of the novel's pages – an orphaned scrap of a book that would mean nothing to anyone at all, except for the person who spent however many thousands of dollars on the tome it was torn out of.

"Excuse me?" she said, disarmingly, approaching every person who made it a few paces past her. "Did you drop this?" She held out the scrap, and watched the reaction intently.

A dozen earnest 'no's left her a little disheartened. There were only like twenty units in this building. She was more than halfway through the tenants. Maybe this plan of hers wasn't quite as brilliant as she thought.

And she was getting super cold. The sun set hours ago. She called up the café across the street and managed to charm that cute barista into abandoning her post to run across the street to deliver a rejuvenating cup of coffee. Felicity handed over that massive tip she promised earlier, and it seemed like the barista snuck a phone number in the insulating sleeve of the cup. Fun. Cute. Clever. Shame Felicity didn't live here anymore.

Sadly, the coffee was nearly gone and ice cold by the time Felicity was on the verge of giving up.

This was getting nowhere at all.

She had entirely dropped the innocent puppy act, and lost all of her enthusiasm, by the time she approached the next one – an old woman with a beautiful scarf and a bit of a limp – and asked her, "Hey, miss, did you—" But she didn't even need to finish speaking before she saw the dire spark in the woman's eyes at the sight of the page. *That* was new. "…drop this?"

The woman immediately tried to hide that intense glare from Felicity behind a warm smile, but it was too late. Felicity found her mark.

"Oh, thank you dear, yes," the old woman pretended. She reached out her hand, expecting to collect the page from Felicity. "I've been looking for that for weeks. Wherever did you find it? Just on the ground here?"

Felicity quickly withdrew the page, well out of the old woman's reach. "...No."

The woman's grin faded slightly. She retracted her hand with an uneasy look in her eyes. "...I see."

"I want the book," Felicity said bluntly.

What little was left of the Witch's cheerful demeanor disappeared in an instant, replaced with a dire scowl.

"That's not how this works," she replied.

"That's how I'm saying it works," Felicity insisted. She took a few full steps back and drew a lighter out of her pocket to hold it threateningly underneath the page. "What's it worth?"

The old woman scowled at her, but she didn't seem to be falling for the bluff. Or rather, she seemed to genuinely believe it was just a bluff, but Felicity sure didn't care if the copy got burned up. The original was safe and sound back in a sturdy little safe back home.

"More than your life, dear," the woman coldly replied. "And I don't think you want to test the *precision* of my scale."

"What's that supposed to mean?"

"It means you shouldn't try to intimidate your *superiors*." The woman stood tall, and Felicity noted an icy radiance in her eyes. There was something in there that shook her – something that she had only ever seen before in her own dear sweet *lola*'s eyes when Felicity had stepped over some boundary with her stupidity. It was the unbearable weight of impatience and ire of someone who had seen entirely too much shit in her long life.

Felicity couldn't help feeling small, on instinct. You don't stand up to your *lola* when she looks at you like that. But this wasn't her dear sweet *lola*. This was an old Witch who had the information Felicity needed to save her best friend.

She was about to straighten up her own posture to put on an aggressive counterattack, but she was suddenly very aware that this little escalating negotiation was taking place in plain sight, in front of dozens of passersby, a few of who were already turning their heads to see what exactly the source of all the tension in the air was.

"You want to take this inside?" Felicity asked, provocative and patronizing, like the old woman was the childish one who should know better. "I hate talking business in the cold."

Her adversary grimaced at the suggestion, but after a few moments of tooth-grinding consideration, she agreed and led the way.

While her back was turned, Felicity finished off her bluff and set fire to that worthless copy, leaving it behind to burn to ashes on the stone bench. It would be far too dangerous just holding onto something like that in the woman's home. Who knows what tricks she might have at her disposal to pry it out of Felicity's pocket.

And lucky for Felicity, her arson went unnoticed.

The woman's apartment was more or less exactly as Felicity would've expected an old Witch's apartment to look. Strange artifacts on every wall and counter. Cupboards filled with random jars with who knows what inside. Beautiful clutter that came together to feel like a preserve-dried botanical garden. And a wall full to bursting with books – probably more books than even Virgil had on his bookshelf.

"I know who you are," Felicity bluffed, getting herself comfortable on the couch while the Witch got settled uneasily in an armchair across from her. Felicity plucked a little sealed, filigreed, wooden box off the coffee table and started fiddling with it, to be rude, to take up space.

"Please don't touch that."

Felicity grinned smugly, and silently refused to put the box down, now that she knew it was definitely going to bother the old woman. She rotated it idly in her hands while she tried to bully the Witch. "What's it worth?" she repeated, referring to the book. "—And don't threaten me again, or this precious little page of yours is going to be a pile of ash before I leave this room," she bluffed.

"…I won't be parting with my book, dear. I promise, you don't have anything I could want. But perhaps I have something *you* want. I do have—" She gestured to the multitude of wonders in her living room. "—a wide selection of baubles and treasures you might find… interesting."

Felicity felt her gaze lock onto the old woman's library. Stupid of her, being so careless with her eyes.

"Oh, a fellow bibliophile I see," the Witch said with a mean grin.

"I've been known to read a few books," Felicity replied nonchalantly, tossing the woman's little filigreed box in the air and catching it on the back of her palm over and over again, much to her visible frustration.

"What's your favorite subject? I'm sure I have something for you."

"Ancient magic. Witches. Forgotten languages." Felicity paused for a moment, then leaned forward with a cool grin, "But you know what? Recently, I'm really interested in books about tall, amber-haired, flashy-eyed, sharp-toothed women. You know, the kind who can make you do things you regret. The kind who can get in your head. The kind who can move halfway across the city in an instant."

The Witch straightened herself in her chair and rested her folded hands on her lap. "Well well well, that is a very specific subject, isn't it?"

"Isn't it?"

The old woman smiled, then slowly returned to her feet and made her way over to the bookshelf to glance a finger over the multitude of cracked and tired spines there. She thoughtfully drew three books from the shelf and returned to Felicity, putting the small stack in her hands, forcing Felicity to finally put that little wooden box back where she found it on the coffee table.

"You might be surprised, dear, to find I have just what you're looking for."

Felicity gave the woman a queer look, then took the time to open the first book and flip through the first dozen pages.

It was messily handwritten in what she *thought* looked like Old Gaelic. Illegible to her, but Virgil would have an easy time with it.

As she flipped further, she found sketches of mystical creatures. Faeries and spirits and great fearsome beasts.

One in particular caught her eye. A towering black bear of a wolf, with fire in its eyes and a grin sharp as a dagger.

"...How old is this?"

"Oh, older than me." She smiled at Felicity. The old woman clearly had no intention of being more specific than that, but from the way she said it, Felicity could probably assume that the Witch had been around for many, many more lifetimes than any human being deserves, and that the book was probably only *barely* older than she was. "She wasn't so kind back then, I hear. And I don't think she had her beautiful amber hair yet."

—Danica. She really was some kind of devil, wasn't she?

Wait. Why was Felicity just trusting this old woman?

She snapped the book shut with a grimace. "Why should I trust you? This could just be random bullshit. Myths. Folklore. How would I know it's her?"

The Witch considered it for a moment before she provided Felicity with an important question: "Do you know her name, dear?"

"Danica Doyle."

"Oh, my dear, you're missing so much of it, aren't you?"

"What? Does she have a middle name?"

The woman grinned at Felicity warmly but didn't quite answer: "It's not *true* you know, if it's only *pieces*."

" 'True'? What do you..." Felicity's mind was running on nitro. There were dozens of mythical creatures whose power was in their 'true' name. That didn't narrow it down as much as it should've, but it was a hell of a hint. "...What is she? Really. And why is she working for you?"

"She's working for me because I *do* know her name. We're close like that. As for what she is, you'll have to ask the puppy yourself. Though she won't tell you unless you guess it right. And if you guess it wrong, I don't suppose you'll have long to regret it."

Felicity looked down at the little pile of books the Witch was offering. "And the answer's in here."

She grinned, but she didn't reply.

"You won't just tell me?"

"Would you believe me if I did?"

Felicity considered it for a moment before she conceded that the woman was right. Unless Felicity could figure this out on her own, she'd never know if anything about it was true. This woman just wanted that page. She had no reason to be honest to get it. She could easily just be telling Felicity whatever she wanted to hear.

Felicity tapped the top cover in the pile with a pensive finger. Getting into a deal with a Witch seemed like probably a bad idea. Not that Felicity had any evidence this woman was magic. She might just be... weird.

But there was something unnatural in the way she moved. Something arcane in the way she spoke. It almost felt like the air in the room moved out of her way, like the electricity fluttered when she blinked, like the mysterious bottles locked in her cupboard rattled when she grinned – all in *fear*. This room *feared* her.

After a few heavy contemplative breaths, she finalized the offer in her mind and told the Witch: "If this leads anywhere—" She rested her palm on the stack of books. "—I'll give you the page. Until then, I'm keeping it."

The fire in the woman's eyes didn't fade, but she did clench her fists gently until her knuckles went white. After a few tense seconds, she offered Felicity another empty grin. "You're quite shrewd, aren't you?"

"That's a new one. Shrewd. I like that."

"Very well, dear. If you come up empty, though, I expect you'll return to negotiate again, yes? That wouldn't be my fault if you don't know how to find the truth in there."

Felicity grinned. "Sure thing, my dear Witch. How about if this doesn't pan out, you cut me a library card for your impressive collection there? It'll make a fine consolation prize."

The Witch didn't respond. She just offered Felicity a false smile and invited her to leave the apartment.

This felt like a pretty huge success, honestly. Yeah, she had a solid lead. Maybe. Time to celebrate, maybe do something to make the hellish hours-long commute out here worth it.

Felicity returned to that café and gave that darling barista a warm smile to ask when she was off and if she had the energy for a little date tonight, explaining first that she very much was only in town for one night, and that she never knew how to have a good time when she was here, and that the stunning young woman looked like she would be a good time no matter where she took her.

—*Felicity Aurelia Vicente is <u>always</u> charming, <u>Dani</u>.*

You know, if this miserable city had nothing else, at least it still had a few attractive women to play with. And, sure enough, this darling barista was very fun to play with – especially when the two of them got caught up in a wine-fueled haze that sent all of their clothes flying to every dark crevice of the woman's apartment for a challenging game of hide-and-seek in the morning.

God it was nice to get laid again. Especially with someone she'd never have to see again. Especially with someone so eager to be coached into all the right places. No strings, just fun. It really had been a while. She'd almost forgotten how deliciously devastating it felt to have someone else doing all the work.

The euphoric refresher made it frustratingly apparent that she'd been way too focused on her research lately – *probably* distracting herself from that growing unease rumbling in the back of her mind. — And now this whole thing with Danica. Fuck.

It was very nice to get her mind off it all and just enjoy herself in the afterglow for a while before she had to leave in the morning – after losing that game of hide-and-seek with half her nice lingerie, damn it – to fight the highway through a hangover and throw herself right back into the misery of wracking her brain over all her troubles.

The barista's number found a home in Felicity's wallet – for next time. If everything went right for her, she'd have a reason to celebrate again—and soon.

Felicity dropped the Witch's trio of books on Virgil's desk and told him this was priority one. "I'm tripling your rate," she insisted. "I want this translated by the end of the month."

Virgil stared at the books dumbfounded for a few seconds before he plucked one from the pile and opened it to the title page. *"The Thorns of the Garden?"*

Felicity shrugged. "I don't know, Virgil, I can't read any of it. But I know you've got me covered, yeah?"

"...Sure thing Miss V."

"Thanks Virgil. You're the best."

He absently flipped through the first few pages, silently mouthing the syllables of the words there, creasing his brow in consideration of the meaning. He was already gone, lost in the work. Felicity would almost feel bad doing this to him, but she knew this was what he lived for. And the chance to get his hands on some never-before-seen manuscript – with pictures! She could see it in his eyes: He was practically salivating.

"Oh and throw it in the scanner while you're at it, please."

"...Mm."

"You're a sweetheart. I mean it. I don't deserve you."

"...Okay Miss V."

" 'Night Virgil."

"...Okay Miss V. You got it."

Sometimes the Journey Is so Bad That It's Easy to Forget the Destination – Which Is Also Bad, but for Different and Much Worse Reasons

(Afternoon, Tuesday, 14th February)

So, that whole 'stay away from Ravi as much as possible' plan was not going great – especially since Nicole had to spend so much of her time now following them around in secret, trying her best to foil whatever her mischievous cousins were up to, in their attempts to spite Nicole by making Ravi's life miserable.

Unfortunately, even her best efforts weren't enough to keep Ravi from having the occasional little disaster. Splashed by swerving cars. Nearly knocked over by falling branches. Dropping boxes at work even when they weren't in pain.

Apparently even Krell's best efforts to throw her cousins off weren't enough.

What a waste of a trade.

Ravi told her all about every improbable demoralizing scare in harrowing detail, and with every incident, Nicole was growing more and more furious at this sabotage disguised as mere misfortune. They blamed themself for every bit of it, while she was stuck knowing every bit of it was on her. And these weren't just her cousins' apparently-not-so-misguided attempts at making her suffer. She'd already done her best to RSVP to Niede. Nicole was going home, whether she wanted to or not. Apparently that wasn't enough though. Apparently, she still needed a cruel demonstration of what was coming if she didn't play along with whatever her sibling wanted out of her.

If she could stand to look at it, her phone would say 12:48 PM, but she couldn't. She desperately wanted to forget what was coming.

She'd been expecting it for a month now, with quiet fear and seething fury. Even Ravi noticed sometimes, when she got too quiet in front of them.

And poor Nicole—

...'Nicole'?

Why was she doing that...

And poor <u>Danica</u> still had no hints about what exactly her dear meddling matronly sibling had in mind for her. She'd spent hours reading the ambiguous letter over and over, seeking out hidden words, hidden meanings, loopholes, but nothing was coming through. Maybe she was just too stupid at it now. After all, she hadn't interacted with Niede since her exile – a little more than six centuries ago, also on the 14th of February.

This was supposed to be her birthday.

But she was absolutely certain there wouldn't be any cake or fun songs waiting for her back home when she arrived.

You will appear before the court.

Direct. Ambiguous. It was amazing how much Niede had grown in their wordsmithing since Danica was young. The stern and stoic antisocial socialite of a faerie hated writing contracts and dealing with humans – just terrible at it – preferring to make use of Danica's prodigal talents for all their work, just like her dad. And Danica was happy to oblige, once upon a time. For the fae, there was no familial bond of debt greater than the truth and power in a name, and Niede gave her that gift when they stumbled on Danica's primordial spark in some distant corner of the Faelands some countless years ago.

They raised her. They watched her grow and surpass them. And then they grew bitter about the attention and adoration their dad gave her ahead of them.

It was so crushing, that everything fell apart so badly between them.

She missed them dearly.

She missed dancing with them. Singing with them. Delighting them with stories of her exploits on Earth and her daring ventures into the Aether. They hated the Earth and everything on it. Or maybe it was fear. They never explained it, but it was obvious from their reluctance to ever join her, even just for a little sight-seeing. But for some reason, despite all that, Niede loved to hear Danica's stories, once upon a time.

Now, all she had left of them was that little scrap of Aethereal Tether. It used to be much *much* longer before – when Niede first gave it to her to help her complete their errands a little more efficiently – but it had been cut pathetically short as a bitter final trade with them, to end any lingering obligations of their tainted kinship – and, of course, to ensure there was no hope of Danica finding a way back home.

To even call them her sibling now was a stretch, especially considering all the bitterness between the two of them, but Danica could never forget what Niede meant to her once. She didn't have the right kind of heart to forget.

You will appear before the court.

She was dreading the commute, whatever it would look like. And it would *probably* look like being yanked through the Aether by Niede's own Tether, long enough for her to weave it into every inch of reality if she wanted. It was a wasted gift in her hands from how little she used it to do anything but *watch*.

Danica would love to make the trek herself, of course. To be in control of her own body instead of being dragged around like a disobedient dog. But she had no safe way to cross the Aether after her exile. Her wings had been torn off and sealed away as a cruel unnegotiated retaliation even before the terms of her exile were put on paper. All the gates and tunnels and faerie circles in the world were too dangerous for her to use now. There was a hairline gap between the Earth and the Faelands in every one of them. —Big enough for her to be grabbed and pulled in by the tendrils of the terrifying creatures in there – and, wingless, alone, she'd never have the strength to escape their grasp. Only the impossible strength of that perfect scrap of Aethereal Tether was strong enough to pull her out now – and the only thing that scrap was long enough to do to keep her safe was desperately bind herself to the underlying fabric of the universe on this side of the Aether.

She could get lost in the Aether forever if she even got too close to an entrance unprepared.

If today's journey to the Faelands was going to happen the way Danica suspected, it wasn't going to be a fun trip. She'd have to trust Niede not to drop her halfway through, trust them not to leave her at the mercy of those merciless glass-bodied tendrilous fae-corrupting Aether-born monsters. And Niede wasn't known for being gentle.

"You okay?" Ravi asked.

Nicole shook herself from her distressed meandering thoughts, letting her mind return to the present – the living room, the couch that was *explicitly* not a gift, the stale tea on the table, the show she had not been watching for at least an hour. She returned to that precious mundane reality of hers to answer Ravi that she was fine. Just fine.

Stretching the truth just a bit. She was in good health, at least.

"Okay. Just you've been choking out that pillow for a pretty long time," they pointed out. "I think it learned its lesson."

Nicole released her grasp and looked down at her poor victim. She'd managed to squeeze it into an hourglass shape. An innocent bystander. It had done nothing wrong. She shook it out a bit in a failed attempt to fluff it up again, then tossed its unsightly corpse at the end of the couch.

And now she had nothing to crush. She picked up her tea – cold from negligence – and started fiddling with the cup.

"Sure you're okay?"

"No." There wasn't any point in pretending. Ravi always knew.

"What's up?"

"Have to visit my family today."

"Ohh. Yeah that would do it. Lot of drama?"

"Drama is kind of underselling it. They basically disowned me. I don't even know why they called me up, but now I gotta go deal with whatever they're about to throw at me." Nicole looked down at her knees. "I don't know what's going to happen this time. And I'm like, scared, I guess. And angry, that they can just... make me feel like this, out of nowhere, and have the fucking nerve to talk to me after everything—" Nicole cut herself short when she realized she was just about to offload way too much baggage on Ravi all at once here. "Ah... sorry." She laughed and put on a smile. "I need to get a real therapist."

—No, you <u>need</u> to stop talking to Ravi about your personal problems, <u>Nicole</u>. This is <u>not</u> the way to keep your distance...

"It's all good, I don't mind. You can talk about whatever if it helps. I didn't know you had all that going on. It's kind of nice hearing other people have fucked up families too. *Extremely* relatable. My shit's so bad that I got made into a little exile over at the *maison Beausoleil*. Only went back for one Turkey Day since I moved out. Big mistake. Never again."

Nicole couldn't help laughing, and she couldn't help opening up, stupid as it was to do it, when Ravi was being so bare in front of her. "You know, I think having family bullshit is about as easy as having a family at all."

"Yeah, no kidding."

Ravi was absently nursing a cup of coffee, with something clearly on their mind. After a few moments of deep thought, they got up and offered to make Nicole some fresh tea. She happily handed over her cup.

They returned with a clean cup that had a drip of honey already waiting for her, and set the teapot down on the table on an extremely poorly knit coaster – one of their own creation, one that Nicole refused to let them throw away. This new little hobby was so good for them, and she couldn't stand to see them being so hard on themself about it.

After Nicole said a quiet thank-you and Ravi got settled, they said something idly to Nicole while staring pointedly at the TV, though obviously not watching what was happening on it:

"You don't have to talk about it, but I'd like to hear what happened if you ever feel like you're, I don't know, ready? No pressure. It's just… I think it's good to share that stuff sometimes. Share the weight, you know?" Ravi glanced over at her while they flexed and patted their bicep with a grin. "I'm pretty strong, you know."

Nicole gave Ravi a warm smile and thanked them again. "Same offer's on the table for you, Rav."

"Oh nice. Yeah, settle in. I've got baggage for *days*. You want me to go first?"

Nicole didn't want to go first or second or *at all*, but she did want to hear about Ravi's life. And she lived for trades, whether she wanted to or not. How could she say no?

"Alright, you tell me something, I'll tell you something."

Ravi smirked. "Nothing's ever free with you, huh?" They took a big breath before they told Nicole about what it was like at home. They didn't call it home, though. They corrected themself the first time they made that mistake.

"It's just a house. It's his house." They meant their dad. "I guess sometimes even a home is just… a place. A place you used to be. A place you can't go back to. I thought it was more, but it's not. Just a three-bedroom house and a little yard that I can only remember fondly if I look at old photos and squint real hard to see the beauty there.

"I felt like a tourist last time, or maybe like... an unwelcome emigrant.

"You know, I've lived here my whole life but it still doesn't feel like my hometown. I lost so many connections, ruined so many memories... I had to make a whole new life here, a whole new home."

They shared far more than Nicole expected them to. Vague, most of it. Dad sucks – relatable. Mom tried her best. But even she didn't seem to know what to do with Ravi – even before they tried to come out to her a few years ago. To her, there was always something wrong with them.

"*Maman* never said it, but I knew she wanted something out of me I couldn't give her. My clothes were a big sticking point for her. One time she threw out *everything*. Gave it away to a shelter or something. Right down to my boxers. I came home from camp and found all my torn-up jeans had transformed into skirts and slacks, all my ratty t-shirts were blouses and tanks. My jacket, my favorite jacket, covered in a hundred super cool patches that I painstakingly stapled on myself – gone. Everything in my closet and drawers was suddenly hand-me-downs from cousins and aunts. Nothing even fit properly. But I guess it fit her, like, *whatever she wanted out of me.* It's sad to think about it. I feel bad for her. She just wanted me back, how she remembered me, some cheerful caricature of a kid she could still talk to, still understand, her little cabbage. I think I was a jar of *achaar* or something by the time she realized we didn't connect anymore."

"Achaar?"

"Spicy pickled stuff. It's really good, actually, but it sure doesn't taste like cabbage anymore."

Ravi shook their head and continued. "After that, the only real clothes I had left were in my luggage from the camp. I wore the same three shirts and jeans and underwear every week, and I kept them hidden when I wasn't wearing them, for months, until I could get my friends to steal some cool clothes from their older siblings for me. And when I could finally afford to buy my own stuff, I kept it locked up." Ravi laughed. "God I must've been the only kid with a padlock on their closet.

"The funny thing is I was totally okay back then, being a tomboy. It felt like I could own that, a girl acting like a boy, messing with expectations – if anyone would just leave it alone. But I just got so sick of being told I was doing it wrong. Like no matter how boyish I acted, no matter how obviously I did not give a shit about being pretty, that's all everyone saw – not me being awesome at being me, just me being terrible at being what they thought I should be. —But being non-binary, no one can expect me to be something else. I can't be 'wrong' like this, you know?

"God, I just wish she could've figured that out. It would've been cool if I could've made her see that after I switched over – that I wasn't a failure of a daughter, that I wasn't broken, that she didn't *fail* me."

Ravi went quiet for a few long seconds after that, watching their fingers as they crushed their palm uneasily, until suddenly they shook it all off and cheerfully asked, "Hey I have some achaar in the fridge, actually. You want to try some?"

Nicole smiled at them warmly and nodded that she did very much want to try some.

Ravi returned a few minutes later with a little spread of fruit and pitas and cheese and a little bowl of extremely colorful, intoxicatingly fragrant pickled somethings.

The first bite blew Nicole away.

"Wow. This. Is. Amazing? Oh gods my eyes are watering up, it's so spicy…"

"Good, right?"

"So good. —You were right: Doesn't taste like cabbage at all."

"Oh," Ravi laughed. "Sorry, full disclosure, this is *mango* achaar. The storebought cabbage stuff around here kind of sucks."

Nicole had tears streaming down her cheeks from the building heat of the spice on her tongue, but she couldn't stop herself from eating more.

She hoarsely asked, "Why don't you put this on everything?"

Ravi couldn't help themself from grinning wide at her, mercifully holding back their laughter. They put a concerned hand on her arm and chided her, "Jesus Nikki slow down you look like you're going to die."

She shook her head and defiantly shoved another helping in her mouth with a proud grin.

"You like it that much, huh?" Ravi clicked their tongue at themself. "I woke up a demon… Listen, don't eat it all, okay? It's kind of hard to find. The only store that sells it is like... halfway across the city, and they're sold out half the time."

Nicole nodded and gave a dutiful salute. "I'll find some way to contain myself."

"Alright I gave you a sob story and a little snack, your turn."

Nicole was kind of hoping Ravi had forgotten their little deal, but nonetheless, she agreed to this, and she had to accept her grim responsibility.

If she was stuck sharing anything at all, she wanted to share something that was as... *personal* as Ravi's – and she had no shortage of stories about her family – but she was struggling to think of how to recontextualize her charged relationships back home in 'human' terms.

She'd never really opened up about that stuff to anyone. In hundreds of years – and thousands of friends and lovers – and even through every single one of a handful of loving, intimate, and ultimately doomed 'marriages', both before and after her exile – even in all of that, no one had bothered to ask as sincerely as Ravi was asking now. There was only one she could remember, long, long before her exile, who had ever known her well enough to even know *how* to ask about her real family <u>and</u> loved her enough to care about the answer.

And that knowing, imploring look in Ravi's eyes was... *uncomfortably* nostalgic, for a time before her heart even knew how to love.

A brief, '*I moved away*,' was usually more than enough for her casual acquaintances. Even for her lovers. And if it wasn't, she would just talk about her adopted families – though she never really had anything to complain about there. She couldn't find it in her to complain about that kind of generosity, no matter how she was treated.

But that shallow empty stuff wasn't what she wanted to share with Ravi. The spirit of the deal was sincerity and truth and trust, and Nicole would honor that as best as she could.

"My dad," she started. "His job was bad. Like, morally bad. A lot of people got hurt because of him. He was basically... like... your stereotypical skeezy insurance guy, finding loopholes and ways to screw people over when they came to him with... claims. He'd set up their contracts *maliciously*, full of mazes only he knew how to get around – and he *loved it*. He loved all of it.

"I was young, and I looked up to him. I didn't get how bad it was, so I loved it too. He was my hero. I cheered for him whenever he won. We celebrated. He even got me to help him make contracts sometimes, and whenever one of my tricks worked, I was in heaven for weeks. I loved the praise. He showed me off to his friends with pride. *'My daughter is a prodigy,'* he'd say."

Ravi gave her a puzzled look and asked when exactly Nicole had been doing all this. "You sure didn't seem like an evil mastermind when you were in high school."

Nicole laughed. *Right.* That part of the story didn't really fit with the timeline of this lifetime, did it? She tried to explain it away. "Smiling and being friendly is all part of the scheme, Rav. I had the whole school under my spell." She gave Ravi a coy smile. "You're lucky you kept your distance back then."

"Yeah, I bet. Looks like you still have the whole city wrapped around your finger, from how many restaurants are willing to put a plate of pancakes in front of you in the middle of the night."

"Hey no, come on, I'm not like that anymore. I've just earned a lot of goodwill around here. People like me."

"You've changed your ways. Really? You still seem very good at getting people into *arrangements*."

"No. I mean, yeah, but I'm better now, I promise. Grew a heart and a spine years ago, finally figured out it was all really, really wrong, doing all that horrible stuff for his 'love'."

"Is that why you started all that philanthropy volunteering stuff overseas?"

Nicole laughed. "Yeah, actually. Yeah that's... right. I wasn't just trying to be better myself, though. I tried to help him too. I wanted him to be my hero again, you know? I tried to get him to stop being so shitty. But he wouldn't listen to me, so I did what any good daughter would and tore up his paperwork and razed his 'office'."

"You did *not* commit arson on your dad's office."

"Mm... arson is such a strong word... But I did definitely destroy a pretty huge chunk of his place of business. —Felt good, not gonna lie."

"Christ, Nikki. I didn't know you were a felon. —Oh god I've been harboring a felon..."

"You're not gonna kick me out, are you?"

"Oh, hell no. Sounds like the fucker deserved it. Wish I had the balls to burn down my dad's office."

"There's still time," Nicole said with a coy smile. She let out a little sigh and continued her story, "He kicked me out after that. His little *prodigy*. Turned everyone in our family against me. I'm not worth anything back home now."

"Hey no, that's not true."

"It's true."

"You're not worthless anywhere, Nicole. Not there, especially not here – not anywhere. If anything, it sounds like they need you back there to burn down an office once in a while, scare them straight."

"Yeah. Well, unfortunately, I made a promise not to ruin any more of his precious paperwork, and he made a promise not to be so shitty that everyone *dies*. So, my legacy lives on in some small way I guess."

"You think he'll keep it?"

Nicole gave Ravi a confident grin and assured them that he was far too much of a coward to break a promise like that.

"So why do they want to see you?"

"I don't know… Gods, I really don't want to see them, Ravi. I don't want to hear *anything* they have to say. I'm really… Fuck, I just… I don't want to go…"

Nicole found her hands had gotten too shaky with frustration to hold her tea steady anymore, so she left the cup on the table. She squeezed her palm with her fingers to try to calm down.

"I'm scared, Rav."

"…Do you have to go?"

She nodded yes. "They won't leave me alone if I don't. They'll come *here* if I don't go. They're crazy, and dangerous, and I really don't want to have them messing things up here. I like this whole thing we've got going on."

Ravi scoffed cheerfully. "What, with the tiny apartment and the sofa bed and the borderline poverty?"

"With my friends. This life. You. And yeah, even the sofa bed and the *humble* budget. It's really good here. And I couldn't…" Nicole paused for a moment to collect herself. She wasn't supposed to be this close to anyone. Never again. She promised herself so many times and she always let herself down. Every gods damn time. Why couldn't she ever learn? "...I couldn't deal with it if they did something to you, Ravi. And they would. So, I have to cooperate."

After listening to Nicole, Ravi simply said, "Okay."

They looked like they wanted to say something else. A lot else. Their lips parted and closed silently a few times before they finally gave up, took a deep breath, and sat in quiet thought for a long while.

Which was fair. What else was there to say? There wasn't really anything they could do—

"You want me to come with you?" they bluntly offered, out of nowhere.

"What?" Nicole's mind took a moment to process what Ravi just said, and when it clicked, she scrunched up her brow a bit in confusion at the offer. "No. No, that's... Aren't you working today?"

Ravi shrugged. "If you don't feel safe with your own family, that's not okay. I hate that, actually. I really hate that. So, if you want backup, I'm there. Dropping a shift to help my friend out, zero regret." They smiled and added, "Plus it'll make our budget *even more* humble. You love that, apparently."

"Wow. Ravi that is... incredibly sweet of you—"

Nicole genuinely considered saying yes, letting herself forget for a moment that bringing Ravi to the Faelands would be an extremely bad idea all on its own, even without having to deal with her family.

"—but this is my thing. I don't want you getting dragged into it. I'm not kidding about them being crazy. Like, *super* crazy. And the last thing I want is to get them chasing after you with pitchforks and torches just for being in my corner." She tried to give Ravi a convincing smile. "I'll be okay. I promise."

Ravi looked her in the eye, like they were checking an old beaker for cracks before dumping a jug of acid in it – and they didn't look happy with the state of the glass by the time they spoke.

"Okay. Well. Call me if you need me, okay? If shit goes down or you're just... I don't know, freaked out or hurt or something. I'll have my phone on 'scream' the whole time, and I will bail on work no questions asked if you need me."

Nicole smiled stupidly. "Noted. Thank you."

The two of them chilled out and relaxed a bit over tea and shows and charcuterie while Nicole's final precious minutes of peace ticked away.

Despite her earlier assurances to Ravi that she'd contain herself, she still somehow nearly managed to get through that whole jar of Ravi's spicy mango achaar, turning her cheeks red with warmth, embarrassing her eyes with childish cayenne chili tears, and filling her lungs and ears with sweet teasing laughter.

Time could stop now.

Or… now.

Now?

—*Please?*

But she knew there was no power in the universe that could stretch this moment out to infinity the way she needed.

When she noticed her miserable appointment rapidly drawing near, she sighed and informed Ravi that she needed to go:

"Time to go face the fam. Wish me luck."

"*Good luck.* Stay strong. You can do this. Call me if you need me, okay? I mean it."

Nicole was just about out the door when she remembered something important. She went back to the couch and dug around underneath for one of her boxes. There was a good luck charm in there she'd need today. Something pink and ugly and important.

"You kept that thing?" Ravi asked, sounding embarrassed but looking *just a little* proud.

Nicole tied Ravi's gift – that badly knit 'thanks/sorry' bracelet – around her wrist a few times. It fit like a massive elastic band – poorly – perfectly.

"It's probably the best gift I've ever gotten," she said with a smile. Then she waved Ravi off on her way out the door.

And then. What?

She was standing in the hallway and only just now realizing she had no idea where to go. All she knew is that wherever she was supposed to wait, it should probably be out of sight, so she made her way to the end of the hall and into the privacy of the spiral concrete stairwell of the fire escape. She got settled in, sitting on a stair between floors while she anxiously watched her phone tick towards 2:14.

Words Mean Something, Damn It

"Our father is [illegible]ized," Danica was told – in mercifully modern Fae words – entirely without ceremony – before she even had a chance to get her bearings after being pulled violently out of the stairwell through the Aether by her dear sibling's will.

She was still recovering from the rush of the rapid journey while she processed Niede's words. She hadn't had a chance to touch those deepest most dangerous depths of the Aether like that in so long. It was a thrill she assumed had been put to rest forever, but that slumbering exhilaration was very awake right now. Every nerve and synapse sparked on and on with extremely inappropriate delight, making it kind of hard to focus.

What did Niede just say?

Something-ized?

Necro...tical...ized?

...Dead?

...That's not an adjective that touches a faerie. It sounded very wrong when Niede gave it a voice. Some new euphemism? The dialect here must've changed while Danica was away – or else Niede was being very, *very* dramatic.

Once she had her wits back, Danica replied, bitter with sarcasm, and pointedly in English: "Good joke—" Her family always hated when she spoke in human words at home. "—and here I was worrying you were going to be all humorless and miserable when you dragged me back here."

Danica had been forcibly seated – but not bound – at a massive circular table made of braided and woven living wood that sang slow subtle melodies to itself at her touch. The table was surrounded on all sides by a massive circular clearing made of deep clover that extended right out into the shadows of the tall woods beyond – except for one arc of black withering rot that extended out from the center of the table and continued on in that direction to the end of the infinite expanse of the Faelands. The parting gift she left behind for her family. She didn't want to look at it.

When she nudged the undying carpet of leafy green and blossoming white with the coarse leather toe of her boot, she was hit with a heady scent, of dew and nectar and eternal *summer* that was fragrant in a way that nothing on Earth could be – in a way that saturated and *punctured* her physical senses, all the way through to the ethereal abstraction of her being, to stir and delight and *torment* the underlying tangle of her essence – essence that she had spent countless years training into the shape of her human body even before it became her prison – a human body that was very much never meant to be *here*, in the land of the fae.

The brilliant, sunless sky above was eternally blue as ever – though... maybe a *shade* darker than she remembered, but that was probably just her eyes adjusting.

Niede was the only one at the table with her. They were rudely opting to forego a corporeal form today, instead shimmering and swirling and fluttering before Danica to show off the full spectacle of the breathtaking storm of their primordial pyre.

It felt like they were taunting Danica. All of this, it was all part of some grand performance that said something like, *'This is what you left behind. You'll never be this beautiful again. Suffer. Suffer suffer suffer. —Are you suffering yet?'*

She was not.

But she had to acknowledge that it was a solid effort.

They might've been the only one at the table with Danica, but Niede wasn't the only one witnessing this... *whatever* this meeting was supposed to be. Hundreds of fae of all shapes and sizes were gathered in the branches and shadows of the periphery woods to watch Danica uneasily adjust herself in her seat. Cousins, all of them, whose names and faces still warmed her thoughts. They were all tittering and chattering in anticipation.

The Exile returns at last.

They were probably charging for tickets.

Everything was the same today as it had been six centuries ago— except for one very notable difference: No scowling disappointed bitterly betrayed dad.

...Well, *that*, and the fact that she was stuck in her human form this time. No entertaining the crowd with cruel cackling abyssal theatrics today.

"It's no joke, Danica," Niede replied in stern earnestness.

Danica smirked and chided her sibling to drop the act. "Come on, Dedes. Did I hear you wrong or something? You expect me to believe he's dead?"

"That's a crude way to put it," they replied, their swirling form taking on a demeanor that matched the tone of disgust in the complicated melody of their words.

Danica looked on into the beautiful shifting mass of their sibling's form and tried her very best to sus out whether they were messing with her or not. Because there were rules. And some rules can't be broken. And one of those rules is:

"Faeries can't die."

"And yet..."

"And yet *what?*" Danica slammed her hands flat on the table and leaned forward with a cold incredulous grin. "What do you mean? 'And yet'? He's dead? He's *actually* dead??"

She laughed sharply at the idea. This joke was so stupid. He was obviously hiding somewhere, just waiting to jump in and catch Danica making some mistake.

He deserved a proper 'eulogy'.

"Well good! Good he's dead! Gods, the miserable crazy piece of shit. Like he'd be missed! Does anyone even like him? Honestly? Come on."

She stood up from her seat and shouted to address the diverse audience of chittering fae creatures observing the 'appeal' from the boundary of the clearing – using fae words just to make sure everyone understood how stupid this was: "Hey! Raise something in the air if you like my dad!"

No one moved. The quiet chatter didn't stop though.

"See?"

"Danica. Sit down. Please be serious. We're not here to play games. There's too much at stake. With him gone, we need a new guard to care for the fae."

"Sure. Bet this place barely functions without him, gods. He's got his nasty hooks in everything around here, doesn't he? Right down to the very last mote of pollen." Danica rolled her eyes and let out a little impatient huff of a sigh. "Dedes, can you please drop the act already. Where is he hiding? Get that coward to come out and talk to me face-to-face."

"You're being very difficult. I would think someone living among mortals for so long would have a bit more reverence for the dead."

"You just won't quit, huh?" She leaned forward and dropped her palms and forearms on the table with a huge smile. "And here I thought this was going to be serious. 'Dead'. What a tasteless joke. I mean you *know* I'd just love to believe it, but stuffing me in a human body didn't make me stupid. If you couldn't even kill *me*, there's no way the guy holding everything together over here is dead. What's your game? I don't have anything left to take, Dee. What could you possibly get out of me now?"

"Your cooperation."

Danica let out a sharp scoff of a laugh. She waited for more – the deal – the trick – whatever game they were playing to make her suffer just a little more before they destroyed everything she loved on Earth again.

This was so stupid.

But Niede didn't continue. They just let Danica's bitter doubts linger in the air. And Danica was starting to feel a little uneasy about that.

A lot uneasy.

An awful lot uneasy.

Niede had never been the kind of faerie that told jokes.

They'd also never been the kind of faerie that used tricks or stretched the truth to swindle the naïve. That had always been Danica's area of expertise.

Niede's silence grew heavy. It grew *sincere*, and *pleading*, and *old*, until at last, it was too much for Danica to ignore.

"...You really mean it, don't you? He's really... dead."

Niede's nebulous form swelled with disappointment while they spoke: "That's honestly the best this ugly language of yours has, that you're souring the air of our sweet home with, isn't it?"

"Hey, don't knock English 'til you try it, Dee. It's *delightfully* ambiguous. Especially the last few decades, wow. You're really missing out hiding over here. You should come visit once in a while."

Niede completely ignored Danica's joking invitation, instead continuing their derision of her choice of words: *"Ambiguous.* I can imagine that being a delight to you. It's quite annoying to me."

They then went on to do their condescending best to explain the difference between the mortal concept of being 'dead' and whatever the hell they were trying to convince Danica had happened to their dad.

And it sure sounded a whole lot like he was gone, and he wasn't coming back, and he didn't even leave a spec of his essence lying around the Faelands to spit on.

Danica collapsed in her seat, her arms hanging loose at her sides. She stared for a long time at the table, finding nothing there for her eyes to catch on.

He was dead.

Faeries can't lie.

Faeries don't die.

There were *rules.*

Danica had kind of zoned out to crunch through all this, but she realized after a while that Niede was still speaking:

"—you can see why I've summoned you, can't you? Please tell me being in a human body for so long hasn't actually made you stupid."

"...What? What are you talking about? You summoned me for an *appeal* or something. This sounds like it's turning into a will reading."

"We'll get to your appeal. I just want to make sure you understand the gravity of the situation. Many of his contracts are... *broken* now – contracts no one ever expected to expire. The most important of those, I think you'll agree, was with you."

Danica's eyes went wide at Niede's words.

"...The extinction pact?"

"Yes. He held the power that enforced it."

"...And now that he's gone..."

"Nothing is left to protect humanity. We're all free to make that mistake again, unlikely as it may be."

"...Well fuck."

The fae didn't have any good reason to *want* to erase the entirety of the human race, but gods damn some of them were *absolutely* stupid and greedy enough to almost do it by mistake once in a while – and it had already happened once before. *Dad.*

Niede continued by reminding Danica: "And since he can't fulfill his side of that pact, that means you have some new freedoms as well."

Danica stared at her hands pensively. That little deal there was made to keep everyone safe – Humans. Faeries. The Faelands itself. *Everyone.*

The terms she set out had been simple – but powerful and dangerous in their own way, as these contracts always had to be.

From her dad, he could never allow anyone to make a contract again that threatened the entire human race – and the universe, much to every other faerie's frustration, opted to give him vet and veto over all faerie contracts after that, just so he could fulfill his side of things.

From Danica, she would never be allowed to touch the archived, genuine copy of a faerie's contract again, to keep her from furiously tearing another shitty deal in half – which, apparently, was a blasphemy *annoying* enough that the gods figured it was appropriate to turn a massive chunk of the Faelands into a broken, mortal wasteland forever, as a *warning*.

But now, according to Niede, her dad was gone.

Which meant no one was keeping any faeries in check.

And nothing was stopping Danica from carelessly pissing off the gods enough to destroy more of the Faelands.

It sure *sounded* like a stretch – but there was an easy way to check.

She flicked her finger and sent the deft tip of her Aethereal Tether darting down to the distant depths of the forbidden Archive of the Pacts Eternal, until it glanced upon the edge of the original copy of a very special agreement.

The air glimmered for a moment before the hefty document appeared in her hand – the terms of her exile, signed by Niede, dear old dad, and herself.

The *original.*

Not a 'wait eight-to-sixteen weeks for delivery' duplicate.

The real thing.

This was never supposed to be in a faerie's hands at all. The Archive was for the gods' enjoyment. But Danica had some dangerous freedoms that other faeries didn't enjoy.

She could feel the power in the stack of paper as she flipped through it.

She could *also* feel the danger in it. In her hands, thanks to Niede's gift, it was as frail and vulnerable as any normal stack of paper on Earth. All she would have to do is drag it through the Aether the wrong way and it would be torn to shreds, just like last time, when she 'scorched her dad's office', as she explained it to Ravi.

She could be free. Right now. The key was in her hands.

"Please put that back," Niede scolded her with tired impatience. "I'm not telling you all of this so you can cause another disaster."

"It would be *beautifully* ironic, though. I think the gods would get a kick out of it," she teased with a cruel grin.

"More than you know," Niede replied with a heavy, darkly melodic sigh. "Please. Show us you've learned anything at all from your exile. Put it back."

Danica grimaced and gave Niede a little sneer. She didn't need to be scolded about it. She would never tear it up. She just wanted to see if she *could* tear it up – and maybe make her ever-stoic not-quite-loving caretaker sweat a little.

With another subtle gesture, she returned the document to its place.

—*So long, freedom.*

She took a short breath to collect herself, then conceded to the reality of it:

"So he's really... dead."

"He's really 'dead'," Niede confirmed, even debasing themself enough to use the English word for it so there was no ambiguity left between the two of them.

"How?"

"That's not why you're here, Danica. You're here to appeal the terms of your exile."

"I am?"

"You are."

"...Why?"

"You've suffered enough."

"Oh, I don't know about *that*," she scoffed, rolling her bicep around her shoulder to show off her muscles while she teased Niede, "Pretty sure I've got at least a *few* more eons of suffering left in me."

"Danica."

"—No, hold on. You really think I'm stupid, don't you? I see your game here. Dad's dead and you need me to fill in? Take over the family business of being a monstrous despot? That it? You think you can guilt his scared, heartsick, broken little prodigy to come back and save the day or something? And I'll just be so *grateful* for the *opportunity* that I'll roll over and do whatever you want?"

"That would be ideal."

"Uh huh. Right. Okay. Uh. No? How about 'no'? How does that sound?"

"Selfish."

"Selfish!? I'm sorry, you're calling *me* selfish? Our debts are *cleared*, Niede. You made that *very explicit*. I owe you *nothing*."

"You do, however, owe a rather large debt to every one of your dear cousins after all the desperate trades you've made to try to get out of suffering properly on Earth. You owe an uncountable debt to the Faelands for the damage you caused. You owe an unspeakable apology to the nameless gods. And you're still going to selfishly say 'no' to taking responsibility for your crimes?"

"...I... That's... that's not what we're talking about here. —And I *am* taking responsibility for my crimes! Why the hell am I living in exile!? Sure as hell better be for my 'crimes', Niede! I'm not doing this for fun!"

"Do you really think your little exile is enough to pay for all the damage you've done here?"

"I... yes? Wasn't that the point? Hell, I'm still *pretty sure* I'm getting ripped off here. According to my math, an eternity of suffering is a *little* heavier than a plot of land, no matter how big it is, no?"

A ripple of sparking yellow light erupted from Niede's core, giving the impression of a dismissive snort. "*Pretend* you're suffering at least, then," they chided Danica. "Not that it would matter. Math wasn't the point. *Balance* wasn't the point. The point, Danica, was for you to *suffer* until you understood that you were *wrong*."

"Okay. Well. Mission failed!"

"Clearly."

"Hey I *wasn't* wrong. Pretty sure I saved like... the *entirety of existence* with that little stunt. Losing a chunk of the Faelands is worth it, don't you think?"

"I haven't forgotten your side of the argument."

"You know I never did hear your thoughts on it, though. You were so *quiet* at the hearing. Remind me what you said?"

Niede didn't reply.

A stunning reprise.

"Right. Right, yeah, nothing. That's right."

"It's not my place."

"Right! Sorry, that's right, that's what you said. Then you witnessed and signed my exile, standing right next to dad, just like you always wanted, right? *That* was your place, wasn't it? At his side?"

Again Niede didn't reply. Cowardly.

"—And what, now that he's gone, you're getting cooked under the heat? Don't have anyone's shadow to cower under? Still haven't figured out how to be your own person, huh? Unbelievable. Hundreds of years to figure yourself out with me *totally* out of your way, and you're still *nothing* on your own. —And <u>*I'm*</u> the one who hasn't learned anything." Danica scoffed at Niede and crossed her arms in a huff.

"That's enough."

"Tell me how he died."

"It doesn't matter."

"Why not? Because it's embarrassing? Did you do it yourself? Was *he* in your way too?"

"It doesn't *matter*, Danica. Let it go."

"How does a faerie *die*, Niede? There are *rules*."

"I'm sure no one would dream to doubt your expertise in the art of breaking unbreakable rules, Danica. I hope you can trust that the faerie who taught you everything he knows is just as capable of foolishly defying the laws of the universe as you are."

"...He did it on purpose?"

"I don't know."

"Well, tell me what you *do* know!"

"...I know he wanted you back. Desperately."

"Oh go _on_ about that. I am *so* interested." She found herself practically spitting the sarcastic, venomous words.

"He wanted you to give up. Find a loophole. Escape your prison. He always expected you to find a way."

"Yeah, I bet he did. That would've been a big win for him, huh? Prove I was always *exactly* what he wanted me to be. Gods, he's so ridiculous."

Niede's intimidating form shifted uncomfortably while they spoke in discordant tones: "I think we can both agree on that now. He started making plans to free you, kept secret even from me. He was recording them in a journal before he died. If you don't believe me, you can read them for yourself. —You *can* still read, yes?" they asked, with a hint of derision.

With a subtle glimmer, Niede pulled a messily scrawled notebook through the Aether and let it land in front of Danica, open to a page halfway through.

She leaned over it and tentatively flipped through the pages one at a time. It was written half in Old Fae, which she was extremely unpracticed in now, and half in a *super* archaic dialect of Fae that she had never quite been *fluent* in – the same one that was in that weird page among the trash Henry gave her months ago – but she had read and edited enough of her dad's contracts that she could get a general sense of the meaning from context when he used it. He had a very *particular* way of abusing old words when he wrote, finding ways to make even the clearest indisputable language *ambiguous* with beautiful, intricate, spiraling webs of circular conditional definitions.

No one else could write like this. He composed all of the most beautiful contracts ever signed – when Danica was at his side, at least, guiding his pen to make shapes more clever than he ever would've considered without her.

But honestly, even before he got his hands on her, he was the best there was. She only elevated his cruel craftsmanship from mere *eloquence* to refined, exquisite *art*.

And Niede was right about the journal. It was full of dozens of schemes to break Danica out of her exile.

Gods. What was his problem? Sentence her to an eternity of misery then spend however long trying to undo it?

And then *die*?

And no regret! No apology to be found anywhere in there. Just plans.

She gritted her teeth and clicked her tongue at herself when she realized a bunch of those schemes were supposed to exploit the exact same loopholes she had already found in the agreement herself, in the hundreds of years that she'd spent musing over the terms.

She truly was that bastard's precious little prodigy, huh? So *clever.*

—Monster.

She noted, too, that some of those brilliant ideas had been crossed out. On closer inspection, it looked like he'd tried and failed a bunch of times already. She remembered every disaster written there, every disease and war and famine, every torment she had to endure at humanity's expense. He truly had been trying to make it harder for her on Earth, exploiting the weakness in her heart, hoping to push her to her limits until she gave up and cheated her way back.

She snapped the book shut and slid it across the table in disgust.

"So, what, you think he died trying at one of these schemes? Trying to 'set me free'? —You think it's my fault? Is that what you're getting at? Because that's a *hell* of a stretch, Niede."

"It doesn't matter. You're here to appeal your exile, and to accept a new set of less *restrictive* terms, in exchange for a little cooperation."

Danica threw her hands in the air in frustration. Not like she had a lot of choice here. She was stuck here until the very moment Niede had the inclination to send her back home.

"Guess I am! Okay then! Oh, great and wise and *meddling* Niede, please consider my request for an appeal so we can get this show over with and I can go back to my prison cell!"

Without comment or celebration, Niede's swirling form collected into something more formal, to conduct her business 'professionally'. They cast out a pale-yellow plume of sparking dust and light over the journal on the table to open it to a particular page. Another firm gesture pushed the book back to Danica for her consideration.

"I'm fond of this one," they said. There was a hint of a smile in their voice.

Danica looked over the raving words of her dad's prisonbreak plan. It was sharp, she had to admit, exploiting some trick of the language he had written into the agreement – a convoluted cascading cluster of interdependent definitions. You couldn't do *that* in English, gods. She'd forgotten how extreme the trading game was back home.

If she wanted to play along, it looked like she'd have to put in some grim work herself back on Earth to set things up – and the only way it could ever have worked at all was if her dad *was* somehow removed from the signatories on her exile's paperwork – which shouldn't have been possible, since, you know, faeries don't die.

—And yet.

... ...Did he... <u>know</u>?

The most troubling part of the plan was Niede's contribution:

"You'd have to be my warden," Danica confirmed.

"Like old times."

"You were never my warden," Danica scoffed. "You just gave me all the fun chores you didn't want to do and took all the credit."

Niede's form shifted sharply at Danica's words, but they didn't acknowledge what she said at all, they just continued explaining their proposal.

"The humans are poison to you—"

"—So you and dad keep saying."

"Living as one is only making you sicker and sicker. It's obvious now that you can't change while you're drowning in the very thing that taints your judgement. No amount of suffering will be enough while their numbing poison seeps into you. So, you'll be confined here in the Faelands, where you'll be safe under my care—" Danica's dear spectral-bodied sibling gestured with a wispy golden tendril that drifted away in the breeze. They were pointing in the direction of the broken part of the Faelands. "—in the barren valley of the Traitor's Waste—"

"—<u>Wow</u>. *Fun* name."

"An *appropriate* name, for the dread magnum opus of The Heartsick Fallen, The Daughter of Ruin, The Great Betrayer – *Danica*."

"<u>Fun</u> names! Wow! What else are you guys calling me behind my back over here? You know I had a pretty killer garden before you ruined it, maybe you could spend even a single breath in six hundred years remembering that? You can call me the *Queen of Green* or something!"

Niede didn't answer, they just continued with their abysmal sales pitch: "You'll be safe there, cut off from any human contact. And while you're taking on the work our father left behind, you'll have a chance there to be cleansed of the poison of your own… *humanity*, free and forbidden from this rotting mortal cage of yours."

"My *cage?*"

Niede again gestured with an ethereal arm, this time at Danica. The sharp cloud of sparkles and sweet dust hit her gently, right in the chest, before it faded away.

"What, my *body?*" Danica snidely laughed at the idea. "You're really still trying to convince yourselves, huh? After all this time, you still think this thing is a punishment, don't you? I don't *miss* this," she said, waving her hand dismissively at the beautiful, bountiful Faelands around her, at her home, at the world she could never forget and never return to. "And I like it in here—" She defiantly pressed her fist into her chest. "—and I love it over there. You're gods damn right I'm not suffering. You got played. I beat you. And my life is amazing when you're not trying to *sabotage* it like some spoiled child throwing a tantrum. You think I don't see through you? I know why you've been doing this to me, and it's nothing to do with making me come crawling back. You just can't stand that you got screwed on this agreement, can you? That I *won*."

The stormy countenance of Niede's form shifted uneasily, but they didn't respond to that.

When Danica took a breath to center herself again, she could hear it: A dead silence fell over the clearing. She smiled to herself.

—That's right. You won. You always win. Even now, broken and pathetic and terrified, you're still winning.

And she would never show them a moment of hesitation or a hint of regret. Niede, her dad, every one of her cousins – they all thought they were taking her life away when they cast her out, but all they did was give her a new one, and she'd never let them think they won. No matter how much it hurt out there, no matter how agonizing and itchy and exhausting and hungry and cold and sweaty it was, she would treasure every moment, to spite them.

And just as much out of spite, she would convince herself that she didn't ache for home, until it was true enough that it wasn't a lie when she said it. She would deny herself any joy in the beauty of the Faelands. And she would deny herself even a moment to consider Niede's terms.

She wasn't going to let them win.

But as she looked around the clearing, she didn't see any reverence for her in her victory, or any fear of what she stood for, or any sympathy for her situation. No kindness. No joy. Not even a look of hopeful greed that they might be able to con something out of her. Just hundreds of cold eyes, staring, watching, waiting.

So much had changed in the six centuries she had been gone.

So much had been lost.

And now, all of her cousins, they had all moved so far beyond her influence. She'd used up every favor – favors she had spent *eons* earning with each and every one of the fae. Now, she was surrounded by nothing more than a muttering ocean of impatient debtors.

Henry was right: Danica had run out of friends.

Here. She had run out of friends *here.*

Her eyes lingered on the pink, misshapen, poorly woven bracelet binding her wrist.

Niede wanted her to come home. Home to nothing. Home to no one. Home to a thankless job taking over for her dad. There was no love for her here. No hope. No fun. No future.

Niede wanted her to come home. But this place wasn't home anymore. It never would be again, would it? It was just... a house. A house with all its walls torn down. A house that would only ever be beautiful in her memory if she squinted real hard to ignore all the misery of it.

She still had a home, though. A real home. A real home she desperately wanted to get back to.

Nicole shook herself out of her thoughtful musings and turned her attention back to Niede. Her dear floundering sibling's nebulous form was still shifting in a steady, patient rhythm waiting on her to respond properly.

She crossed her arms defiantly and broke the silence in the clearing:

"Sorry, maybe it wasn't clear. I'm not coming back here. Not for anything, and definitely not for whatever 'freedom' you think you're offering me. —And if you're hurting so bad for someone to guard the fae from your own self-destruction, why don't you step up and do it yourself? I'm not spending the rest of eternity on your leash doing your paperwork for you."

"You haven't even read the terms—"

"—Anything else you want to chat about, Dedes? Or can I go home now?"

Niede's nebulous form swelled for a few seconds of bitter raging frustration at Nicole's stubbornness, but that gave way to something softer, something that left Nicole with the impression of a piteous smile.

"Home," they murmured, seemingly just to themself. "You really are gone, aren't you Danica? Is it really too late?"

They sharpened their presence once more to be formal and rigid and heartless, then said with a tone of miserable finality, "Here—"

A gilded leather-bound book appeared before Nicole with a glimmer. Its pages quickly flipped before her eyes – about a hundred of them, all dense with fae legalese. Niede's writing, surprisingly.

"—The terms of your new arrangement," they explained. "Sign it, and we'll get you out of that prison. Or don't, and you can spend eternity rotting away in *joyous* agony."

"I'm not signing it," Nicole said, pushing it away from herself.

"Read it, before you decide. Please."

Nicole waved playfully at her stuffy sibling's amorphous form and told them she'd look forward to seeing them at the next underwhelming will reading.

Once Niede sent her back, Nicole sat motionless in the fire escape's stairwell for a long time, staring at her knees.

The soft leather cover of the proposed agreement remained closed while it sat in her lap.

A fluorescent bulb clicked and flickered on another floor.

It must've wavered ten thousand times or more, before she bitterly peeled back the cover to peer at the first page.

In the dark of the apartment, Nicole stared at her phone intently while she slowly, methodically rotated Ravi's bracelet around her wrist, over and over again, like a monk praying on a rosary. She was looking at the message Ravi had sent her at 2:15 that afternoon:

"Call me if you need me, okay?"

Need you.

Need you.

If I *need* you, I will *call* you.

It felt like a little contract on its own, bound in glass, written in liquid crystal ink, archived forever in the modern magical embrace of some distant electro-magneto-mechanical disk.

If Nicole *didn't* call Ravi, did that mean something?

There had been a note from Niede, tucked secret between the pages of the contract, revealing Nicole had already failed Ravi worse than she could possibly have imagined:

Your world will burn. Your human will suffer for you, and their precious lab alight will be the least of it. Come home.

Rosée de fleurs maléfiques

❧ ✽ ☙

(Late Night, Tuesday, 14th February)

When dear Ravi got home, they saw right through Nicole's attempts at pretending nothing was wrong. How was she so bad at faking things like this? Centuries. *Centuries* in this body and she still couldn't pull this off.

—*Need you…*

The words wouldn't stop echoing in her head.

Did she *need* Ravi to grab every blanket they could find to wrap her up cozier than she'd ever been in her life? Did she need them to make the sweetest most perfect stack of pancakes for her in the middle of the night? Did she need them to, without even asking, like they'd committed it to memory, put on the only show she ever watched on the rarest occasion when she was having a bad enough day to get caught looking miserable?

Did she need them to sit with her in silence, in a silence that said she was *home* and she was *safe*, in a silence that saved a space for her to say anything she needed – even nothing at all – a silence that said, *I'm listening.*

—*Need you?*

How dangerous could it be? To need someone again?

"Nicole," they said so softly when she cried, when they held her and told her things would be alright, when they tricked her into believing things would be alright. Their words were a warm embrace, wrapping around her heart with gentle fingers. It felt like they knew every vessel, every muscle, every beat. She felt so broken. And Ravi was holding her together. Ravi was the only thing holding her together.

Did she need them to call her like that? To call her by a name that she could pretend was really hers? A name that Ravi made her *believe* was really hers. A name that had never been stolen from her or tricked away. A name that *wasn't* a constant reminder of every vile contract she'd ever proudly signed. A name that wasn't attached to the memory of every vile celebratory word of praise she ever received for her vileness – from a vile creature that expected his same vileness to pour joyously and endlessly out of his precious *Danica* – and how *right* he was.

Oh, to be Ravi's *Nicole*, to be free of everything that was her vile father's *Danica Llewellyn Doyle*.

Ravi let Nicole lean on them and rest her head on their shoulder while the two of them wasted the night on episodes of a show they had both already seen so many times before that it was all just pictures and noise now. Nicole could only hear Ravi's calming rhythms now. Beats and breaths and predictable laughs in between the lines of the familiar dialogue.

She smiled to herself, to be home.

Someone's nail brushed against the back of a hand. Accidentally. The fingers entwining? The reassuring *I'm here* squeezes? Accidents. Just accidents. Stupid, stupid accidents. Just as stupid as looking them in the eye in the tender silence and falling falling *falling* into them.

Ravi's tireless embrace felt so safe, their two sturdy arms a fortress that Nicole couldn't bear to leave – but all fortresses crumble in time, and all embraces have to end. That's just how it is with mortals.

But even when Nicole reluctantly pulled away, Ravi's arms held fast, keeping her close. And when Nicole raised her tired gaze to meet her steadfast guardian's, she was startled by the vastness of the dark sepia ocean of Ravi's eyes as they took her in, that so much love and light and warmth and care could fit in there – and that even with all that, there was still enough room for her to get lost in them.

She caught herself staring, but she couldn't stop, and she couldn't stop being drawn in by their gravity, pushed speechless and unwilling, millimeter by millimeter by heartbeat after heavy heartbeat, until she was close enough, dangerously close enough, to lean her forehead on theirs – close enough to feel Ravi's breath on her lips when they spoke to her.

They whispered her name softly. They hesitated for a long, heavy moment. Then, at last, they wrapped her aching heart in an impossible cashmere vow:

"I've got you. I promise."

She didn't have any words to express how true Ravi's words were in her heart. She had no words. But she desperately needed them to know. And in her haze, all she could think to do to tell them was to tenderly caress their cheek with her fingers, pawing at them, beckoning them to her to meet her for a tender kiss, a kiss so light it could have been mistaken for a passing breeze.

When she pulled away, she hoped to see it in Ravi's eyes that they understood. That they understood the words she couldn't say. That they understood that she needed them more than anything else in the world right now. That she would do anything to keep them. That she was theirs. That they had her. That they could take her.

—*Take me. Please. I need you.*

Nicole was shaken when Ravi's lips took hers over, but, unlike her kiss: Theirs? Their kiss couldn't possibly be mistaken for *anything* else.

—*Gods, how could something so poisonous be allowed to taste so sweet?*

Nicole was suddenly tossed and lost in a stupor of emotional turmoil, only anchored to reality by Ravi's gentle fingers woven through her hair, cradling her head. She reached up her own hands to theirs, to check they were real, to hold them there once she was certain they were real, squeezing them, fearful. This was dangerous. This was the edge of a cliff in a stiff wind. But Ravi clearly wasn't afraid of any of this. They were boldly walking the edge without a thought, reaching a hand out for Nicole to join.

Their kisses were so soft, so gentle on her. Not hungry. Not desperate. They were cherishing her. They were soothing her. They were pressing love into her uncertain lips, into her trembling skin, calming her fears and drawing hope out of her despair.

After too many exhilarated heartbeats to count, Ravi finally pulled away from Nicole's lips for a moment to take in the adoring light of her eyes, and to give her the gift of getting lost in theirs again.

They asked softly, pleadingly, "Is this okay?"

Nicole hesitated for only a second, because she knew there was *something* that wasn't okay about this, but she wasn't in any state to remember what.

With a stupid grin, she touched her forehead to Ravi's again and nodded emphatically to assure them without words this was everything she needed.

With Ravi's next kiss, while Nicole's mind was distracted by slow dancing tongues, she felt a welcome intrusion as Ravi's weight shifted into her. They were pressing their chest into hers, forcing her down while they wrapped an arm around her to guide her gently onto her back on the couch.

The blankets fell away.

Forceful. But careful. Tender. Nicole hadn't imagined Ravi loved like this.

But Nicole hadn't really let herself imagine Ravi's love at all until tonight.

Ravi paused only for a moment to warn her, "Careful about my shoulder."

She nodded her understanding and made special note to keep track of wherever her arms and legs and desperately grasping fingers might land on their body tonight.

Oh gods, Ravi was really planning on pushing this until she *was* grasping at them, weren't they?

Her unspeakable question was answered immediately: As they continued on top of her, they pressed a bold knee between her legs, easily parting her heavy thighs and pinning her in place while they continued blessing her with their lips. Nicole instinctively rolled her hips into them when they did, feeling the first hint of the warmth of their body against her, even if it was through a few frustrating layers of clothing. A wave of heat coursed through her when she felt them against her there, swelling her mind with a hazy desire for more. She was wet for their touch in an instant.

Nicole lost track of both time and misery while she was showing Ravi how to play with her. She patiently moved them around her, guiding their fingers to touch her here and there, guiding their hands to free her cumbersome breasts from the blouse buttons of her dress and take her in handfuls, guiding their head and tongue to just the right spot on her neck to make her shudder and coo. She gently grinded herself into their thigh while they played with her.

She was ready.

She was ready to give every part of herself to them.

Nothing else mattered now.

Nicole couldn't help herself in the throes of her gentle ecstasy, from calling their name into the night.

"Ravi…"

—I need you.

She wouldn't say it. She wouldn't say that. Even just in her mind, it sounded like an exhilarating *catastrophe*. She didn't need to say it, though. Ravi made the contract. She only had to call them now and they would know.

Her insides fluttered with glee and uncertainty whenever she looked Ravi in the eye, when she caught their warm smile between rough and tender kisses on her neck and her bawdily exposed chest.

She fluttered with euphoria and terror when they held her wrists over her head, to her unspeakable delight, while they breathed warm flattering whispers into her ear, illuminating their deep adoration of her beautiful bountiful body with sultry words that warmed the back of her mind. She never imagined those intimidating, solid, muscular arms would be holding her like this. When she playfully resisted their grasp, she realized with a rush of warmth that their vice grip was impossible to escape, even for her. Nicole could normally carry even Ravi's dense mass around in one arm if she tried, but, unless she wanted to magically slip away, she was entirely at their sweet benevolence like this.

That fluttering in her grew more intense and uneasy when Ravi's curious fingers released her wrists and started exploring every curve of her body unguided – and that uneasiness exploded into the chaos of a crowded aviary when she realized those fingers were descending below her hips in pursuit of Ravi's darker desires.

They were trying to test when she would stop them.

She wouldn't.

They crawled down her body towards her toes, dragging their fingers over her along the way, until their hands boldly slid under and all the way up the skirt of her dress, intent on peeling off her leggings and panties, with a look so devilish that she was afraid for a moment: Maybe she'd made a terrible mistake, and wound up desperately longing for the taste of a demon.

But no demon would ever ask so sweetly, with eager fingers curled around the waist of her undergarments, poised to peel them off: "Can I?"

She wanted to say no. And yes. And no and yes and yes yes yes.

She nodded silently. *Yes. Please. Yes.*

Of course *yes*. Of course. Of course they could do something so stupid. Of course she would let them, and she'd do it with a giddy grin on. She was pretty sure by now that she'd even beg them if they refused.

Once Ravi's venerating affection was locked onto her legs, she couldn't do anything to catch their eyes, couldn't do anything to pull them away from their game, of teasing her with suckling kisses and a slow, seductive slithering tongue all up and down her bare, vulnerable thighs, drawing coos and stifled moans from her, to their obvious delight. Whenever she made a sound for them, they seized firm, assuring handfuls of her legs or her ass in their wandering hands.

Ravi teasingly hiked up the front of Nicole's dress inch by inch with every movement, and slowly spread her legs as they did, like they were carefully prying open a beloved book without cracking the spine.

But Nicole wouldn't mind a little spine cracking right now. This prolonged affectionate *torture* left her feeling like her whole world was turning inside out with fear and anticipation.

Despite the butterflies messing up her stomach and a pink fog taking over the part of her mind where her reason should have been, Nicole managed to find enough composure to hazily respond to Ravi's obsessive focus on her legs. She put a crush on them with her thighs to catch their undivided attention and teased them, "You know, for someone who's always bugging me about wearing pants..."

Ravi grinned in response and simply told her, "You've been torturing me, Nix," before gently asking again, "Is this okay?"

Without hesitation, Nicole eagerly nodded again, and Ravi went right back to tantalizing her thighs when she released them from her grasp.

With the front of her dress hiked up above her waist now, she was fully exposed to them. She could feel their teasing breath on her, and their eyes were trapped by the sight of her, dewy and flush and blossoming for them. It was such a rush. To be seen by them. To be so vulnerable and raw and brazenly beautiful for them when for so long she had kept so much of herself hidden and unknown. It was such a gods damn dangerous rush. Her thighs clenched them gently to slow them down. They were getting dangerously close to taking the two of them beyond some unspoken point of no return. But she could stop this right now. She still had a chance. Close her legs on them. Push them away with a smile. Laugh it off.

Yeah.

Yeah this… this wasn't a good idea…

Time to stop before it went too far.

She gingerly placed her hand on Ravi's head, putting the slightest pressure there to bring their eyes to hers, to hold them back.

But somehow, when she got caught in those big pleading eyes of theirs, her hand slipped. And instead of pushing them away, she found her fingers tangled in Ravi's rugged unwashed hair, found her fingers drawing their head in, to invite their sultry tongue between her subtly drawing thighs for a taste of her – and instead of laughing awkwardly and saying stop, she let out a mewling whine and begged them to keep going when they accepted her foolish invitation.

They brushed their fingers affectionately through her lush, downy, golden-amber bush, then reassuringly grasped the thick tuft of her mound to gently coach her beautiful blossoming flower to their lips while they took their first eager taste of her.

Nicole was a rippling puddle of bliss from even just their very first lingual caress.

They paused after a few deliriously pleasurable strokes of their tongue and marveled at her with a curious look on their face.

"You taste… a little like… honey…? How…? What do you *eat?*"

Nicole's stomach twisted painfully when she realized: Ravi could tell. Gods, of *course* Ravi could tell – they weren't new to this. They knew how a woman tastes.

Stupid of her. So stupid of her.

In the heady fog of her passion, apparently Nicole had forgotten one or two details about that fae-crafted body of hers that might give away too much of her secret – details like, for example, that she'd made this form of hers so long ago to taste of ambrosial nectar to captivate her lovers, which was normally a great feature, when she wasn't delighting the tongue of a deeply curious mind. If Ravi wanted to dig deeper, Nicole couldn't lie to them – and any of her usual half-true excuses would definitely just make them want to dig deeper, scientist that they were.

Which meant that if she couldn't get their mind off of it, they might discover what she was, here, now, at the worst possible time.

She grinned uneasily at Ravi's bewilderment and playfully answered without answering, "Pancakes night and day. You know that. Why? Too sweet for you?" she added as a little poke of a challenge.

"Should taste like maple, then, no?"

Nicole took their hair in her hand again and pleaded with them, "Ravi. Don't make me beg."

Ravi grinned at her coyly for a moment before they dove right back in to draw out more of her sweet enchanted nectar and her gentle moans with their sly tongue.

Crisis averted. For now. She could go back to enjoying being in Ravi's tender care. Hopefully while they were exploring, they wouldn't pick up on any other *revealing* traits Nicole had forgotten.

Ravi managed to shudder all the anxious tension out of her body with their relentless lusty affections, building up a heady swell of warmth and crackling electricity that pulsed from her tender clit up through every inch of her body until it flooded out her fuzzy mind.

Nicole tried to hide her joy-twisted face behind the crook of her arm while she involuntarily pressed her clit into Ravi's face to match their rhythm. They really knew what they were doing with her. How did they figure her out so quickly? The scientific method at work? Or maybe they just really *really* knew what a woman tasted like.

She almost felt bashful about it, about being so exposed, so known – but that was how the two of them got here at all, wasn't it? Nicole was so obvious to them. She was open to them even at her most guarded. They knew just how to pry her armor off and get at the tender wounds underneath. And that made Ravi dangerous, just as much as it made them safe and soothing.

Nicole marveled at this unbelievable change in their manners. Ravi was so cool and brash normally. It was extremely endearing, especially when she managed to poke holes in *their* armor. But this was so unexpected. To think that their brusque tongue and rough hands might have such a talent with something so delicate.

And they refused to let up on her. Even when she placed her hand on their head to get them to ease off, they simply took her hand in theirs and let her squeeze them through every twist and tremble they pulled out of her.

"Ravi," she pleaded breathlessly, "Ravi... you don't... have to... Oh gods... Please... It's so much..."

They slowly pulled themself away with one final loving lick of her tender swollen clit – their lips and chin soaked, a salacious strand of Nicole's juices dripping from the tip of their tongue before they swallowed it down with a grin – to ask what she wanted: "Stop? Or keep going?"

Nicole shook her head. She didn't want to answer. She wanted both. It was too much too fast and she desperately wanted *more*. More more *more*. But she also desperately wanted more *time* with them, lost in them, wrapped in them, safe in their tender care.

Gods, no wonder this felt so fast, though. Her dress wasn't even off yet. Just lewdly undone and shifted all out of place. She hadn't even made it to the *bed* yet and Ravi was already burying their tongue in her. They were skipping entirely too many steps here.

"A break..." she pleaded. "A little break."

Ravi smiled at her softly and agreed to a brief ceasefire. They sat up and invited her to get nestled into their chest, to be wrapped in their arms while she recovered. She happily accepted.

Safe again in their embrace.

Nicole didn't know how long any of this would last, but she knew she needed to spend as long as she could, sheltered in these doomed fortress walls.

Their fingers felt so calming, running through her beautiful, wild hair, barely glancing over the tips of her ears. Their gentle almost *meditative* handling of her tender breasts was so easy to get lost in. But even those subtle sensations were enough to send an occasional swelling wave of pleasure through her. She wasn't going to last much longer like this.

"You're being so good to me," she spoke softly to them, turning her head to look them in the eye. "Can I do something for you?" It needed to be fair. She needed to give them what *they* needed too, or she would go crazy thinking about it later.

They returned her adoring gaze for a few seconds of silent consideration before they shook their head and softly replied, "Just let me take care of you, that's all I need. I just want to make you feel good, and safe, and special, like you deserve."

Nicole grinned to herself. Once again Ravi was playing her, somehow managing to twist this *devotion* of themself to her pleasure into a gift *from her*.

How were they so good at this?

"Well, you're doing a great job," she assured them.

They beamed at her with a playful smirk. "That's what I want to hear." But that smirk only lasted for a few seconds before it melted into something soft, melted into some warm adoration that inspired them to draw closer to Nicole for a kiss – a kiss that grew from soft nips to tangled tongues and grasping hands – and lasted for just too long enough that Nicole had to dramatically pull away, stand up, and drag Ravi by the hand to their bed in a huff.

In a second, she had her dress and bra off, tossed who knows where for the morning to worry about. Then she dove onto Ravi's bed, shamelessly showing off the secret faded seals tattooed onto her back, kicking giddy heels in the air, and beckoning them over with a playful smirk.

As they crawled up next to her, she pulled her hair aside to expose the joyously vulnerable nape of her neck for them.

Ravi – because of course they would – got the hint immediately. They leaned over her, letting the weight of their muscular chest rest on her back, then curled gentle fingers around her throat to hold her still while they whispered in her ear and delighted her neck with their lips and tongue.

She could feel her own heavy heartbeat pulsing aggressively against the precious arteries in their grasp.

The sensation was like drifting away in an ocean of warm red wine – intoxicating, all-encompassing. She barely noticed Ravi's other hand as it traced over the lines of the arcane ink in the tattooed seals that bound her to the Earth, giving fresh new meaning to this joyous prison of hers. She barely noticed as they teased their fingers up and down the length of her spine. She barely noticed, until Ravi apparently couldn't resist their desire to crawl a little further down.

Nicole involuntarily curled her back and raised her hips up to meet them, and a moment later, the drunk sensation of Ravi's tongue on her neck was joined with a comforting pressure on the tender rolling hills of her labia.

She pitched her hips and pressed herself into their hand while they massaged her, and clenched her thighs whenever they had the audacity to tease her with a wayward finger, to stroke her shudder-inducingly sensitive clit, or to dip into the hot and *very* willing entrance to the depths of her lust.

It wasn't long until her whole body was twitching and contracting to match the pace of Ravi's touch. She lost track of time in their hands, measuring out the night only by the tidal swell of heat in her mind that was quickly approaching some delicious delirious crashing crescendo.

She moaned Ravi's name, summoning their ear to her lips to whisper to them, "Stop teasing me…"

Nicole couldn't see it from her position, pinned on the bed by Ravi's weight, throat in their gentle grasp, face pressed into the sheets that smelled so deliciously of *them*, but she could hear the grin in their voice when they told her to say what she wanted properly.

"Take me…" she desperately replied, "Please… More… I want more of you…"

Ravi still wasn't satisfied with her performance.

"You know what I want…" she pleaded.

Still they teased her, circling the trembling entrance to the eager target of their mutual desire, showing they knew *exactly* what she wanted, cruelly holding her prisoner in their grasp. Even when she desperately pushed back into them, they refused, pulling the tips of their fingers back.

She bit her lip hard for a few seconds before she could find the resolve to sully the air with her desperation:

"I need you… *in me*… Please…"

At last, she stumbled on the magic words.

Ravi, without a word, and without loosing their grip on her throat, eased a pair of firm fingers past ethe ager, slick folds of her hot, rosy, dew-dripping petals to come to rest deep inside her, drawing a long cooing sigh of relief out of her.

As they churned her insides – making shameless, debaucherously slick sounds with her sweet, fragrant, thigh-soaking juices – every inch of her body, from her hot, blushing cheeks down to her desperately writhing toes, was overtaken by rhythmic waves of pleasure at their touch, waves that were growing more and more intense with every heavy breath, drawn desperately through her dear guardian's reassuring grasp on her throat.

She felt so safe in them like this, so excited to be treated with such care and reverence and passion, that she could almost let go – she could almost forget that the two of them were running now, sprinting along the edge of a cliff on the ocean, with crashing waves lapping at her feet, slickening the stone. This felt more dangerous than anything she'd done in ages – but she had no intention of stopping anymore. 'No' was gone.

They'd fly off the cliff together if that's what it meant to keep going.

Fuck the heartbreak.

Fuck the debt.

Fuck the fae—Fuck the whole fucking world.

It was all going to end anyways. Everything she loved was going to be taken from her, so why the fuck should she care about any of it? She didn't need it. She didn't need any of it. All she needed now was Ravi. There was nothing else.

Nicole felt Ravi's hand withdraw from her throat slightly. It seemed like they wanted to change their focus to some other part of her. But she wasn't ready to be let go. She needed them. Desperately. She quickly darted a hand out to catch them, to try to keep them there, to keep them holding her life in their hands.

They responded exactly as she needed, by tightening their grip on her throat again. She felt them draw close to her, reassuringly resting the warmth of their chest against her back, feverishly rolling firm fingers over her clit and decorating her back and neck with their tongue and lips in thick, warm graffiti.

It felt so good. <u>This</u>. *This* is what her body was for. This and nothing else. To be shaken to blissful oblivion by greedy human hands. To be a commodity to trade. To be *used*. But *fuck*, Ravi was doing it wrong in such an exhilarating way. They were drowning her beautiful body in pleasure without any of the *expectation* that's supposed to go with this. She was *nothing* to them, and nothing she could give them would *ever* be worth anything, but somehow they still cherished her, like being nothing at all was enough to be treasured. It felt sickening. Twisted.

Perverse. It filled her mind with an exhibitionist rush, and every time she thought about it, it shuddered her body with immoral pleasure.

She was sparking and quivering and melting all at once, moaning Ravi's name between swears she barely remembered from her youth, clenching her thighs together and curling her toes until they cracked. She grasped at Ravi's musky bedsheets desperately, and tightened her grip on their wrist, silently begging them to do the same to her – and they obliged.

Their fingers constricted around her throat, held her perfectly still, muted her moans to hoarse whispers. They held her heartbeat hostage while they built her up for a few seconds of intense exhilarating oblivion. Nicole felt delirious at the height of it, before Ravi pushed her over the edge and released her throat to unleash an overwhelming swell of convulsive orgasmic euphoria into her blood-starved mind.

When her senses came back, her body was buzzing and she was overtaken by shudders at the slightest touch. She found herself once again held in the fortress of Ravi's embrace, their fingers entwined with hers, their soft breath on her neck while they waited for her to come back.

As Nicole's uncontrollable little convulsions slowed and her breath returned to calm, Ravi released her just enough that they could lean over her. Her face was still smushed into the bedsheets in a little wet spot of her own drool. They had to wedge their fingers between her cheek and the bed to turn her jaw to face them for a tender kiss on her unsteady lips before they asked her softly, "More?"

After letting out a heavy sigh of relief to gather herself, Nicole said in a bit of a haze, "That was so much…"

Ravi didn't repeat themself. They just patiently waited for an answer while they continued kissing her neck, sending shivers and little bursts of warmth down her back whenever they slid their tongue over her sensitive skin.

—There's <u>more</u>?

Nicole's love-slickened thighs clenched at the thought.

She squeezed their hands in hers for a few long breaths before she finally released them and got out from under them to roll over onto her side, to look into her bold guardian's adoring eyes.

This was all she needed. It was all she could ever need.

Nicole shook her head softly. Right now there was only one thing in her mind. "Just hold me," she said, one note flat of begging.

Ravi wove their fingers with hers and pulled themself into her until their foreheads were touching and their thighs and calves were knotted tight together, feet seeking the caress of their newfound lover's tender soles. They spent a long while like that, gently tangling into each other while they shared warm breath and nuzzled into each other's cheeks.

Nicole closed her eyes to bask in it.

Home.

This was home.

She didn't remember falling asleep, but when she woke, tucked warm and safe in Ravi's bed, she found them breathing peacefully, snoring adorably, curled into her back, holding her hand, and keeping her safe in the unbreakable fortress of their arms.

She felt drunk on them, drunk on whatever this feeling was – until she remembered where she was and what she'd done, and then it suddenly put her in a sharp, sober panic to realize it: This was probably the single gods damn stupidest place she'd woken up in over a century.

A Few Good Ones

There are a lot of reasons to avoid sleeping with your roommate. Unfortunately, Nicole couldn't think of a single one the night before. But now that the night before had turned into the morning after, and the sun was making soft orange projections on the wall, on the sheets, on Ravi's beautiful sleepy smile – now she was writing a book in her head, an essay for every reason why it had been incredibly stupid to do what she had done, to let herself fall in a moment of weakness.

—*Again.*

This mental exercise was making it a bit hard to enjoy Ravi's sleepy lips on her neck and their fingers tracing potent love spells on her skin.

—*Chapter 1*

This is the best friend you have in your life right now. Why did you think complicating that was a good idea? Can you even just hang out now? Who are you going to talk to when you can't talk to them? Henry? And get lectured for every little thing? No thanks. Felicity? Come on, there's no way. That woman is borderline insane. And also she hates you. That's probably worth noting—

Ravi lifted themself out of bed a bit, letting sheets fall away, revealing the strong shoulders and arms that had protected Nicole from the dark all night.

"What language was that?" they asked idly, between cute adoring kisses on her tummy and chest and that sensitive spot under her ear that was definitely one of the highlights of having a human body and *why did they have to do this right now while she was trying so very hard to focus on finding some graceful way to stop them from ever doing this again.*

"What?" Nicole lost track of Ravi's question.

"Last night," they continued, mercifully laying off their assault and settling in to cuddle in Nicole's unfortunate embrace. "I've never heard words like that before. It sounded pretty. What were you saying?"

Nicole must have gotten lost in her pleasure and started

desperately singing out in some old fae tongue.

—Chapter 2

They are going to find out. You can't get this close to someone without them finding out who you really are. What if you're in bed together and you just start drawing sigils in your sleep? Or the seals on your back start to glow or something? What if they ask for your name? What if you <u>give them</u> your name because you're so fucking stupid that you would absolutely do something like that.

Again.

"Good things," she assured Ravi with a smile. "—I think. I picked it up a long time ago, but uh, I haven't really spoken it in a long time." True, that. It was probably just a bunch of untranslatable exasperated swears, honestly, but she truly couldn't remember what she said.

—Good things, probably.

Ravi grinned playfully at that and gave her a little jab that elicited a stupid, giddy little squawk out of her while they teased her:

"It better have been good things! Would be a *little* rude of you to start talking trash about me when I had you so blissed out that you forgot the English language."

She shouldn't have been using fae words in front of Ravi. This always happened. She always gave too much of herself away. Why did she *always* let this happen? She closed her eyes and tried to push her regret down, tried to find some way to enjoy this. After all, it might be the last thing she got to enjoy for the rest of her life, if Niede had their way.

—Chapter 3

You can't do this again. Every time you get close to someone, the world gets set on fire. Your family is already hunting them to hurt you again.

No, there was no way she could enjoy this. It had to stop. She couldn't do this again. She loved them. She loved them way too much – *way* too much now. Gods, so much for keeping her distance.

She shouldn't have let them get so close to her heart. She should have recognized it a long time ago and just walked away, debt or no debt. But it was too late to turn it off now. Ravi had their loving claws in her skin, and their ambrosial poison had seeped into her *blood*.

But gods, just Nicole's affection and devotion weren't going to be enough to keep Ravi safe.

Something bad was coming.

Something bad would be coming for *everything* she loved, like it always did.

And she couldn't stand to bring that down on Ravi.

And not just them, right? All of humanity would suffer again. No one deserved whatever disaster was coming if Nicole refused to play nice with Niede.

And... if she just cooperated with their request now, she could break the cycle. If she just signed that shitty agreement, Niede would never have a reason to torment another human being again.

Right. She *had to* stop it, didn't she? If she did... If she just walked away from everything she loved, if she just walked away from her home – again – she could fix this, for real, forever.

Yeah. She had to. She *had* to *go*. This had been going on too long.

Plus, it was time to be real about it: It's not like she was ever going to finish paying them all back. Not if she kept bringing calamity to the world whenever her family wanted to deliver a little retribution for her crimes – retribution for crimes like, for example, living there with a smile on her face, like living with a friend in her life and a lover in her arms.

Gods, never mind paying the *world* back, she couldn't even figure out how to pay *Ravi* back.

It was time to give up. Give up and just... live with the aching burden of her debt forever, on Niede's leash. Maybe she'd be lucky, eventually manage to fix enough terrible contracts while she was slaving away over there that she could balance things out with humanity.

She had to go.

There was no easy way to do it, but she had to go.

She gave Ravi a soft kiss on the forehead, then got up from the bed to start collecting her clothes off the ground. She had no idea how to tell them this could never happen again – that she had to leave, forever, for no reason – that the two of them would never meet again.

Maybe she shouldn't say anything at all. Just... disappear. Ravi would get over it. Humans are like that. They forget. And then they die.

She made the mistake of turning around when Ravi beckoned her, when they sweetly called her precious name with a hint of concern discoloring their voice. She made the mistake of getting lost in the immeasurable depths of the ocean of their eyes again, of getting charmed by that smile, of getting trapped in the unwavering fortress walls of their arms and ensorcelled by the somatic spell of those loving fingertips on her skin. A spell of stay. A spell of just one more. A spell of what could it hurt. A spell that turned one uncertain kiss into a *night* of kisses. A spell that turned one ill-advised night into a whole *week* of nights. A spell that made it so very hard for a forgetful number-numb faerie to remember just how many nights were even *in* a week.

How many *was it* now, Ravi?

Seven?

A hundred?

...Ten thousand?

❦ *Part III* ❧

Honeymoon Crush

(Afternoon, Thursday, 16th February)

Ravi couldn't help snorting and pulling away from Nicole's ambrosial pussy, trying and failing to hide a huge, incredulous grin.

"Sorry, your *what?* Your 'flower'?"

"*Yes*. What about it?" Nicole asked, playful and indignant, crushing their head between her thighs until, with a lot of effort and a little grunt, they managed to pry her open again.

"So, I guess these—" They put tender suction on one of Nicole's sweet, rosy pussy lips and tugged on her until she slipped between their lips with a sexy little snap. "—are your delicate little 'petals'?"

Again, Nicole put a squeeze on them, and this time even Ravi wasn't strong enough to get out, or breathe.

"Ravi Beausoleil I'm going to crush you until you pop if you keep teasing me."

They tapped her thigh three times, pleading for a truce.

But despite the truce, Nicole wouldn't let them back in. She jabbed them in the forehead when they tried.

"Nuh uh. Nope. *You* are being *rude*."

"I'm not!"

"You are *teasing* me and you are *banned* until you apologize."

"I'm sorry! Forgive me. It's just so stupidly cute. 'Flower'. —And *perfect* for you. Seriously, it's perfect. I mean, god, you *taste* like overflowing nectar. You make such a pretty pink blossom for me whenever you're excited. I could get lost *forever* in this sweet perfume of yours. And I love love *love* burying my tongue in you – I'm such a stupid bee for you Nikki. —*Please* don't ban me."

Nicole huffed playfully, absolutely failing to hide her grin. "Say it properly then, like I said."

"I love your beautiful flower, Nicole."

She was practically radiant with joy hearing them say it. She graciously let Ravi spread her out properly so they could marvel at how appropriate the word was for her, before they happily returned to licking and sucking the sweet dew off her 'petals', pulling even sweeter coos and moans out of her lips.

—How could this woman be so fucking adorable?

[REDACTED]

(Late Night, Thursday, 9th March)

Ravi was cheerfully humming to themself while spending a long night alone in the engineering lab – very much in the zone formatting a graph *just right* for their report – when they noticed the time. 11:03. They were late.

They hurriedly saved everything they were working on, then jogged through the halls of the dark, eerily silent university, triggering the motion-activated lights in every hall they entered.

As usual, Ravi found Nicole waiting patiently for them on the not-so-legal side of the security door for the bio labs.

This was becoming a regular Thursday night date for the two of them – though it wasn't quite as romantic as the starry walks in the riverside park they loved to take her on, so they always tried to set aside an extra night every week for her to make up for it. It usually meant dropping a shift at the warehouse, but it was worth every lost penny to hold her in their hands all night without feeling absolutely exhausted.

Back before the two of them hooked up, they always tried to pay her back for her generosity here by paying for dinner. But now, so many exciting possibilities were available. Tonight, Ravi was planning to spice it up for her a bit by dragging her to some dark corner of the campus for some harmless not-so-legal exhibitionist fun. She liked that, they quickly discovered – being fucked and eaten out on the edge of being discovered for her stifled moans – usually in supply closets and stalled elevators and busy bar bathrooms – but Ravi was having a *great* time teasing her and pushing the envelope to see just how far she'd let them go.

No end in sight yet.

They would probably never figure out exactly how she did this thing with the doors. Every time they tried to catch her at work prying one open, she managed to disappear on them somehow. Apparently, this woman just had some secrets she really, really wanted kept secret. And sadly, her proprietary breaking-and-entering technique was on that list. Maybe she was worried Ravi would use the power for evil or something. Which was fair. They would.

Nicole opened the door for them with a little scowl, then held up her phone to point at the time.

"See all these weird numbers after the 11 there? Mm. See? Those are supposed to be *zeroes*. Ravi." She was acting upset, but it wasn't a very good act. It clearly didn't bother her that much, she was just putting on a show.

"Sorry! Sorry, thank you for waiting, you're very sweet."

"You'll be paying me back for my time I assume," she teased them while they made their way through the halls to Carrie's bio lab.

"Absolutely. Once I'm done with this stuff tonight, I'll be at your command. Ten minutes enough to satisfy your needs?" they asked with a playful wink in their voice.

Nicole grinned. "Oh I see. You want me to put your mouth to work, Rav?"

"My lips are yours to command."

"Great! There's this cool karaoke bar, open super late—"

"...I have *reconsidered* my offer and I will not be paying you back for your time."

"Wow rude."

"Not rude. My life is at stake. I'll have to throw myself in the river from shame by the time you're done with me."

As usual, Carrie was poking around the lab doing her own work when Ravi came in. She never offered them any direct assistance, but she was always very happy to point Ravi at resources that contained the answers to their questions.

Today was a very special day for them, because the process they started their tar samples on last week was finally done.

Actually, it was done days ago, but there was no way for them to come check without Nicole. They'd been eagerly waiting for this.

They cracked open the sealed container and tentatively drew out one of the dozen redundant thin strips of a very special translucent membrane.

It had a beautifully clear barcode made of blue ink. Each bar represented the density of a different member of the substance's protein families. And only this specific substance should have this specific pattern.

This was it.

The fingerprint.

They carefully checked and compared every one of the dozen strips. They'd used multiple samples and confirmed that every single strip had the same pattern.

At last, they had something.

Good timing, too, because they were down to the last vial of tar.

Ravi was absolutely beaming when they showed it off to Nicole. "I did it! I got it. Finally, we have something to move on."

"What's next?"

"Carrie said there's a national database of biological samples. If this thing has been processed before anywhere in the country, it should be in there – and if nothing else, that'll give us a name, someone to talk to, whoever first reported it."

Ravi called Carrie over and showed off their results with a proud grin.

"Holy, Ravi, I had no idea you were this close already. You missed your calling, hun."

Ravi couldn't help feeling a little giddy getting praise from their unorthodox mentor, but they managed to keep their cool in front of her.

At the database terminal, Ravi took the chair while Carrie guided them through the process of scanning the barcode of the tar's fingerprint and then fussing with the painstakingly slow, extremely ugly, grey-scale interface for the connection.

In fact, it was taking long enough that Ravi was starting to think they'd done something wrong, but Carrie assured them it was always slow.

"Pretty sure the servers are connected to the network with a tin can and a ratty mile of string. Just give it a minute."

But a minute turned into a few minutes, and Carrie got sick of waiting. She told Ravi to just call her over when it loaded.

Nicole only came over to sit next to Ravi and watch what they were doing once Carrie was away from the station. It didn't come up much, since Nicole was generally free to wander around wherever while they worked in here, but for some reason Ravi hadn't figured out yet, Nicole seemed to be uncomfortable around Carrie in the lab – and she never joined in when Ravi went for a couple drinks with Carrie – which was very strange, since Nikki was normally the most pleasant and sociable person they knew.

They wanted to ask about it, but this definitely wasn't the right time for it.

Sadly, Ravi's patience with the computer was not rewarded with promising results. In fact, they were pretty certain now that they had messed something up, because every one of the handful of digital records and photo-scanned documents in the database was either blanked out or covered in thick black lines obscuring most of the text. And every page of the scanned documents was marked with a big red stamp – PROTECTED C.

When they called Carrie over to help, she was stunned dead silent when she saw what Ravi had pulled up on the screen.

In a panicked rush, she shoved Ravi to the side to pull the power on the computer.

Then she returned to that grim silence.

"...Carrie?"

"I'm dead..." she muttered.

Ravi raised a concerned eyebrow. "Did I screw something up? I swear I didn't press any weird buttons."

"Those records were redacted. Government secrets. We're not supposed to... Oh my god, I'm so *so* so dead. I'm dead! That was my user account! The logs are going to point right at me!" She brought her hands to her temples and growled in frustration, then she spoke to Ravi in cold deadpan disbelief: "Fridge slime."

Ravi didn't respond with anything but an uneasy smile.

"Hell of a fridge slime, to get the *government* this freaked about it."

"Um. Maybe it's... *really* poison?"

"No. No way. I'll eat my good hand if that's *fridge slime*. Tell me what it really is."

Ravi looked away uneasily.

"Ravi do you know what 'Protected C' means? *National threat.* International spy stuff. Biological warfare. Economy destroying tech. This is the kind of thing people *disappear* over."

"...Come... come on, Carrie that's a little..."

"You ever hear of Terrance Paul?"

"...No?"

"*And you never will.* He was in too deep on *something.* No idea what. Never found out. —And thank god for that or I'd be gone too, I'm sure. He started getting these weird letters warning him off. Anonymous. Blackmail stuff. He didn't take it seriously until it was too late and then one day, just: Poof. Gone. Disappeared. Never worked here. Never lived in the city. Never *born.*"

"...And you know about this because...?"

"Did some marking for him, and apparently I've just got a face you can trust. When I gave him back the first batch of papers, he asked me if I was getting any weird spam in my inbox lately. By the next batch, he was sweating, on the verge of a breakdown, told me everything except what he was actually *working on* that got him in trouble. And by the third batch, there was no one left to give the marked papers to. *Terrance Paul* was no more. I ended up handing back the assignments myself and covering his lectures the rest of the year. *Sabbatical,* they told me. And let me tell you, every prof I know who goes on sabbatical spends the whole year leading up to it bragging – and he didn't say one word. By the next semester, his name was erased from every record at the university."

Ravi and Nicole shared an uneasy glance to silently confirm that this sounded insane. But Carrie didn't really seem like the kind of person who would get sucked into conspiracy theories. If she was genuinely worried about this, it might *actually* be dangerous.

"...You think I should stop," Ravi said, morosely, knowing the answer.

"You want to keep going??"

"I'm not done figuring it out yet, Carrie. Look this is your lab, your rules, okay? You tell me to stop, I'm done. But if you let me keep going, I promise I'll keep you out of it."

Carrie rolled her eyes and let out a little huff, "Well I'm already *in it* now. I feel like my condom just broke, holy lord..."

"...Well, since you're already fucked, might as well keep going...?"

"That's how you roll, huh?"

"Hey if I'm taking a big expensive 'fuck you' pill anyways, might as well have fun with it."

"...Ravi you're literally going to get me killed thinking like this..."

She closed her eyes tight and pinched her cheek bones between her finger and thumb for a few long seconds of tense thought before at last she returned her tired gaze to Ravi's face. "Let me think about it."

Ravi nodded gratefully.

Then they turned their grim attention to the dark monitor and the silent computer.

Ravi knew Carrie was only doing what was best for herself there, and they couldn't hold it against her, but it sure would've been nice if they could've kept looking at those documents for a few minutes more before she killed it all. Even if they were redacted, there might've been something useful in there.

They let out a depressed little sigh. Months of work for nothing.

Carrie put a gentle hand on Ravi's shoulder and apologized for freaking out.

"It's all good," they said as kindly as possible. "Just wish we could've at least gotten something out of that if you're going to get in trouble anyways."

"...Yeah, I didn't think of that. ...I bet you're good at chess, hey?"

"I've made a few boastful boys cry, yeah."

"I'm terrible. I lose one horse and I'm ready to throw in the towel."

Nicole – who had gone back to casually leaning against some equipment a few paces back once Carrie returned – cheerfully corrected the two of them: They *had* gotten something. "I spotted a few names before you killed it."

Ravi looked at her dumbfounded. "How? It was only on the screen for a few seconds."

Nicole grinned at them. "I'm good with names."

To Carrie's relief, Ravi agreed to hold off on following up on any of the leads Nicole miraculously committed to memory, until she had a chance to think about it and get back to them on whether or not to proceed. Give it a week, she said. And then, pleasantly as possible considering that Ravi had maybe just ruined the poor woman's life, she invited Ravi and Nicole to have a wonderful rest of the evening anywhere else but the biology wing.

"Keeping your word, Ravi Bee?" Nicole asked lackadaisically on the grim walk back to the engineering lab.

"What?"

"About the names. I have a guy who's good at looking into stuff like this. I can get him on it tonight if you want."

Ravi scoffed at her. "Nicole Doyle, I didn't know you were such a coward."

"What!?"

"I keep my word," Ravi assured her.

"Mm. Okay but *I* didn't promise anything, and I'm the one with the names."

"Oh, that's a *gross* loophole Nikki, don't. Whatever Carrie decides, I'll respect that."

"...You'd just give up because some random woman tells you to?"

Ravi stopped short and gave Nicole a discerning glare. "Do you have a problem with Carrie?"

"She's great! Why would you think—?"

"You're always avoiding her in the lab."

"Oh, that? Her shampoo isn't my favorite smell, you know?"

Ravi quirked an eyebrow at the lame excuse. "Nicole be honest with me please. If you don't trust her, I need to know why."

Nicole tilted her head back to look at the ceiling for a few seconds. Why was this such a big deal for her?

"Okay," she started in on a meandering explanation, "So you know how some people get skeeved about like... the feeling of dry styrofoam or chewing sounds or whatever?"

Ravi scoffed and shook their head. "What, you don't like the way her voice sounds or something?"

"Um. Okay listen I know this sounds bad, but I promise it's not..."

"Not a great start, Nikki."

"Sorry. It's um. Her hand."

"Her hand. The InThetics one?"

She nodded grimly.

"Nicole. That's..."

"I don't know why! I'm sorry. I don't know why, it just... I don't know, it weirds me out."

"You have some body horror hangups or something?"

"Not usually!"

"What's so special about her hand then?"

"I don't know! I don't know. I'm sorry. Honestly, they always weird me out, those InThetics things. I was trying to be cool about it. She seems really nice, and I have absolutely nothing against her, honest. I totally trust her. I do. —But that has nothing to do with my question! You barely know this woman. I know you respect her a lot, but you're really just going to let her tell you to give up on this? I thought you really cared about figuring this out."

"Not if it's going to get someone killed or whatever!"

"You don't think she's overreacting a bit?"

Ravi crossed their arms and gave Nicole a stern stare down. "It's not up to me to decide that for her." They looked Nicole in the eye for a few tense seconds, trying to get a read on her, and they were a little worried at what they saw there. "Promise me," they insisted, "that you won't do anything about those names until Carrie says it's okay."

"Aw come on Ravi."

"Promise me."

Nicole let out a disappointed little huff, then raised her hand in the air to solemnly swear: "I'll keep it to myself until you say so. Okay?"

"Thank you." Ravi let out a little sigh of relief. "God for a second there I was worried you were jealous or something..."

Nicole laughed. "Sorry Ravi Bee, I've never been a very jealous creature. Just want you to be happy."

Nicole's earnest answer evaporated Ravi's uneasiness, letting their head and heart returned to their plans for the evening – and to the sudden vacuum in their schedule for the next couple of hours.

They took a few assertive steps forward to back Nicole up against the windowed wall of a darkened bio lab, then wrapped their fingers around the back of her neck to pull her down to their level. They spoke in a low, seductive voice:

"—If you want to make me *really* happy tonight, you should follow me to this oh-so-dark-and-quiet hallway by the cafeteria I found – let me entertain myself finding ways to tease out all those cute little happy noises you make for me."

"Mm..." Nicole stole a soft kiss from Ravi, sucking on their bottom lip a little too long and tugging it playfully with her teeth until she let it snap back with a coy grin. "What's your gameplan there Rav?"

"Oh, I was just thinking maybe I'd get lost in a horny little daze, pop a few buttons off your dress…" they said, brushing their fingers through her hair and teasing the tips of her ears with their fingertips the way she liked.

"I sure hope you're planning to sew them back on," she replied with a dreamy coo. "I like this dress."

"Staples good enough?" they teased.

"How about you just stick to licking the sweet dew of my pretty little flower off your fingers for now? We'll see where that goes."

"Deal," they replied with a big grin, then tugged her by the wrist to rush off in the direction of the cafeteria.

I'm Not What You Always Wanted, but Maybe I Can Still Be What You Always Want

Ravi twinged to note that Nicole had a hungry look in her eyes when she unbuttoned and stripped their shirt off, as the two of them faced each other on their knees in bed, preparing for another long night of making love.

She was insatiable now – not that they were any less hungry for her – but it was a lot, to be in such high demand all the time. They'd never lived with a lover before, and it was... tiring, between serving Nicole and the warehouse and the lab. But they powered through it with a smile, just to hear those heart-melting sounds of hers when they had her losing her mind under them.

But she didn't want to be *under* them tonight.

Ravi twinged to note that hungry look of hers because they had seen it before, in dozens of lesser lovers' eyes.

It was a hungry look that lingered on their chest a little too long.

Ravi put out both their hands to gently push Nicole away.

"Wait," they said firmly. "Stop. I don't think I can do this."

"What? Did I do something wrong?" Nicole looked utterly dejected.

Ravi pulled their shirt back on and started doing the buttons up to seal their chest and binder away for the night.

It wasn't skin that bothered them. Cunt? No problem. Hers for the taking. Back? Legs? Hell, they'd happily spread ass for her. God, with absolute *pleasure*. But their chest? They just... couldn't... With her...? *Her*? What if she hated them for it...?

—*What if she loves you for it?*

It was becoming a point of pride by now, that they'd managed to go a whole month without letting Nicole take charge in bed – and managed to keep most of their clothes on the whole time, too. It was wonderful, to just get lost in her, to feel her pleasure, her shudders and shivers and pathetic whining. The way she moaned their name was like a song. But they knew that winning streak couldn't go on forever. As much as Nicole obviously loved being treated like a princess, worshipped like a hedonistic goddess by Ravi's reverent prayers – lips and tongue and fingers all incanting for her ecstasy – they knew she'd eventually want to have her way with them on her terms.

But it sure would've been nice if they could've stayed in control of all this forever.

While they slowly did up their shirt, they spoke to Nicole, but they couldn't bring their eyes to meet hers.

"Nicole… you're…" They hesitated for a moment before they smirked and scoffed at themself stupidly. Why did they think this was a good idea? "You're really into women," Ravi said plainly, to confirm the obvious truth.

"Yeah? Why do you sound so unsure, Ravi Bee? I thought we had a mutual affection for the female form." She gave them a seductive grin. "You sure love mine."

Ravi's fingers froze on the third button up, leaving a little showing, as a test, as a trap, while they watched Nicole's wandering eyes. "…You… You get that I'm… not…"

Nicole's eyes went wide with shock, but for a fraction of a second, she betrayed herself, she fell for their trap, stealing a glance at what little of their chest was left exposed.

—Obviously…

They continued buttoning up the rest of their shirt with a sad grin while dear sweet Nicole tried to explain herself:

"Ravi. Rav. I have been living with you for a long time. I think I know that you're not a woman."

"What am I then? When I take all this off, what am I?"

"You're Ravi!"

They rolled their eyes. "That's such a cheating answer."

"Listen, whatever you are, you're not a woman, that is abundantly clear. I have *zero* issues with that I promise."

"Okay but I'm not like… 'woman lite' either—"

"—*What* is 'woman lite'? All the taste half the sugar?"

"It's… I don't know, it's how it feels with basically *everyone* who gets me on my back, soon as the tits and cunt come out. I'm sick of being treated like a precious little *girl* when I take all my clothes off. Like it's some kind of… *game*. Like they want to catch me *pretending*. —I know you're used to being with women, Nix. Women with sweet, beautiful breasts just begging to be sucked on tenderly and treated with deifying reverence like yours so very are—*my god I love your breasts*—"

"They are pretty amazing, aren't they?" she asked playfully, framing her chest with her biceps and rolling her shoulders around to show off the heft of her bosom for Ravi. "Made 'em myself you know," she added with a wink.

Ravi let a little laugh escape and congratulated her: "Artisanal work, Nix. Really. —But my… tits… —I just… —It's *not* a…" Ravi couldn't find the right words. And Nicole was offering them what sure felt like a damn piteous smile for it. They couldn't help clenching their teeth and curling their nails into their palms. After a sharp inhale, they finally gave her what little they had to give: "I just don't like it. Okay? That's… that's it. —And I don't want to disappoint you, or fuck with your expectations or whatever, so just… pretend they're not there or something, I don't know. Just leave my shirt on. Okay? You can do anything else to me, I don't care, just… not that."

"Okay. —But I want to make sure you know: You literally cannot disappointment me. I have no expectations here. I just want to drink in a little more of my lovely Ravi Bee. I'm having fun no matter where that goes, I promise."

"I… get it. I get it. Just. Not yet," they said, one note shy of pleading with her. "Okay?"

She nodded in understanding, without a hint of disappointment in her eyes.

She generously let Ravi take over from there, let them push her back on the bed, crawl on top of her to taste the otherworldly sweetness of her lips and tongue, to let them knead her oh-so-stunning breasts to coax gentle coos out of her.

They were sliding teasing fingers up her stockings when she asked them idly, apropos of nothing at all, "…What kind of game, anyways?"

"Huh?"

"You said people treat your tits like a game. Like, what, skeeball?"

"Nicole..."

"Horseshoes?"

"Oh my god..."

"...Darts?"

"...More like *chess*, I guess. —Nikki can I focus here?" they asked, firmly gliding their fingers all the way up her thighs to show off what they were chasing after.

She didn't seem to be interested in focusing on any of that anymore though. Instead, she continued her silly line of questioning, in playful confusion: "...How does a nipple piece move...?"

Ravi sat up in a defeated little huff, then spoke as plainly and to-the-point as they could to try to cut this exercise short: "I can make you melt. —If I figure out the right moves, I can melt you. I can turn you to sweet bubbly butter in my hands, Nicole. There's something divinely *feminine* about the way you move for me and the sounds you make when I've got you undone. —I don't *do that*. There's no special sequence of moves that unlocks my secret girly moan. It's not a *battle of wits*. I'm not *pretending*. I don't fucking *like it*."

"...Hm... so... no tender tit sucking. Noted."

She wouldn't give up on this, would she? And she was being so curious and understanding. Ravi couldn't help grinning at how stupid it felt being so guarded before, asking Nicole to put up with their bullshit. As if she had ever failed to do it before. But this felt bigger in a lot of ways than anything they'd asked her for before. If only she'd let it go.

But she wasn't going to let it go. They could see that now. She wanted to *know* them.

But there was more about it than just... tit sucking. Something way bigger that just avoiding their tits didn't quite capture.

Ah... damn it... Alright, fuck it, they'd gone this far.

They took her hand and caught her eyes to speak right into her with a stern entreaty: "There's more to it than just not sucking on my tits Nikki, if you're so set on this."

Nicole didn't respond with anything more than a sincere dutiful nod while she waited for Ravi's guidance.

They took a deep breath. This was something they'd never put into words. Maybe an example would help? "You know that TA?" they started.

"Dear What's-Her-Name. The *consumer*."

Ravi laughed at Nicole's memory of their complaints. "Valerie."

"Oh you *do* know her name!" she teased them.

"We were fucking for like four months Nix. I had to moan *something* in bed."

"First *I've* heard it."

"There's just something about how she does me. Tenderly, like she was trying to undo me. But like a conquest too...? I don't know how to put it, it was somehow... demeaning? I want to be in control. I want to be on equal footing with whoever's fucking me. I want to be respected. Being coddled feels so stupid, so *fake* when all the attention's on me like that. It's like this with everyone. Like, it doesn't even matter how obvious I am about what I am, seems like just seeing my body flips a switch and suddenly I'm a cute puzzle of tomboy who needs to be treated ever-so-special until my *façade* breaks.

"—But it's not a façade," they added with a firm sense of finality.

"No kidding," Nicole said with a teasing squeeze of their hands.

"I know you get it... I just... I know how fun it is to do that, to win that game with someone. Making big butch women and oh-so-stoic tough guys writhe and coo like that, breaking them with tenderness until they're begging pathetically in my hands... I get it. I get why it's fun. I'm sure you get it too."

Nicole nodded to confirm.

Ravi continued: "—But I don't give a shit about tenderness and foreplay and sweet words and stuff, you know?"

"Treat you rough. Got it—"

Ravi shook their head sharply. "No. No it's not that either. I don't know... how do I put this... I don't want to be fucked like some brainless sex doll. Just, like, jerk me off like a normal person and don't act like a smug prick because you can get me off, I guess. —I mean it's not hard. I can do it myself in a minute flat, you know? I don't need you."

"A *minute??* Holy hell Ravi."

"...Okay, maybe not quite that fast, but you know what I mean."

"I mean it kinda sounds like you just want to be treated like some fleeting encounter with a guy in bed. No? Crass and casual?"

"Kind of. Not quite but kind of. But whatever, can't even get something like that: Doesn't matter the vibe I give off. Doesn't even matter what I *ask for*. My *fabulous tits* just throw everyone off for some reason and everything *I* want gets thrown out the window."

"That sucks. It doesn't sound that hard to figure out."

"Right?" Ravi paused for a second before they realized they weren't sure this metaphor was actually going to land, but it sure sounded like Nicole was catching on strangely easily considering... "—Wait. You've fucked a guy?"

"Oh, yeah, lots."

"Huh. I thought for sure you were exclusively into women. You're always..."

"Oh. No." Nicole laughed and glanced away for a second with a dozy reminiscent grin. "No, dear sweet Ravi Bee, I am a multiplatinum-star bisexual." She brought a playful fingertip to her lower lip and explained coyly, "I want to experience the full gamut of bodily delights. —I get why the confusion, though. I'm way, way more into women usually."

"Huh. Well that probably makes it easier to explain this. You know that feeling? When you're climbing on top of a guy, pushing him down, knowing in the back of your mind he's kind of just *cooperating* with you, knowing that he could take control any moment, knowing that even when you're in control, *he's* fucking you."

"Mhm. Though it takes a pretty big guy to get that out of me, Rav. I'm pretty *voluptuous*. Not a lot of guys could follow through on a promise of throwing me around the bed."

"God, I wish I could throw you around Nikki..."

"Mm... but I *love* the way you hold me down. The way you... *push me*. You make me feel like I'm going to come apart at the seams in your hands – and I love *breaking* for you. —You put me back together so nice," she added with a playful grin, like she was already imagining it.

Ravi couldn't help grinning stupidly back at Nicole's shamelessness. But they shook the grin off their face to get back to their point:

"But you know what I mean, about being on top of a guy? About the unspoken agreement? The *truce* of it? I know the look in my eyes when I'm doing it – the look that says 'I'm hungry let me take you' and

'I'm yours do what you want' all at once. —Just once, I want that look in my partner's eyes. I want to see that *reverence*, like they <u>know</u> I'm *letting them* have me, that even when your fingers are buried in my cunt, *I'm* fucking *you*."

After Ravi finished explaining it, Nicole's eyes slowly wandered away and traced meandering arcs over their head while she thought about their words.

This was... a lot, wasn't it? —God, it sure *felt* like they were asking a lot.

Why did they have to do this? Why even bother bringing this up? Make things so complicated and *particular?* How many people had they lost just trying to get this kind of thing right? They could've just let her do whatever. It would be fine, right? Just to keep her. They didn't care that much, did they? No one had ever got it right before, maybe it was a stupid thing to fantasize about.

But Nicole told them over and over and over, with everything she did, that she wanted to know Ravi for real. She wasn't going to let this go, they knew that. And, you know what, fuck it: With her, they'd rather take a risk on being known properly. This was the best thing they'd ever had in their life, and what made it the best thing was how open and honest they could always be with her, how she'd never once betrayed their trust no matter what they let show, and they weren't about to betray her by hiding this if she was going to be so goddamn devoted to figuring it out.

...Still, they were clenching their jaw and fiddling with their fingers waiting for her.

"...Nicole?"

She closed her eyes for a second and nodded to herself, satisfied with the conclusion of whatever thought exercise she was running through.

"Okay. Okay, I think I got it: Fuck you hard, with a giddy sense of fear in my heart that you're going to hold me down and fuck me right back if you feel like it."

"...That... sounds... *perfect—*"

—*Yeah. That was it exactly, wasn't it? Reverence. Respect. Trust. Desire.* <u>*Mutuality.*</u>

"—It doesn't even sound hard when you say it," they added in a kind of relieved disappointment at how easy she was making this.

Nicole snorted and teased them, "Yeah, it doesn't sound hard to *do*. But it really isn't quite as simple as 'fuck me like a guy', huh?"

"...I just... I don't want to be *wrong*, Nikki. Not with you. I don't want you to see a woman when you look at me, but I definitely don't want you to see a man when you look at me either. Especially not in bed. Every man I've ever fucked, I felt... I don't know, used? I'm sure that's not every guy in the world, but you know, I think my sample size is big enough by now to draw a pretty sound conclusion. Ready for peer review."

Nicole nodded. "Yeah I get that – though I promise there are *plenty* of outliers."

"And sometimes I want to feel like that – used – you know, just, get something out of my system? —But I never want *you* to feel like that."

"Aw," Nicole cooed. "That's sweet of you."

"Oh shut up. You deserve to feel like you matter. Because you do."

She grinned coyly at them. "You know I want to be used sometimes too. I'm not *just* an innocent little princess in bed."

"Princess? You're more like a queen. —And I know you love when I'm on my knees for your *worship*."

"You want me to show you how serious I am?"

She leaned forward to meet Ravi for a deceptively sweet kiss that was hiding a cruel bite of their lip that sent an electric rush through them. When they tried to pull away, she took their hair in a tight fist to keep them still while she pulled their skull back to expose their neck for her to bite them again and tend the sharp pain with a long seductive lick.

Ravi couldn't help letting out a stifled little moan, which immediately shook them out of it and caused them to reflexively push Nicole away a little.

"Hey," they said in a slightly confused daze. Nicole had never taken the lead like that. It was terrifying, the thought of letting her... keep going...

"Too much?" she teased them.

"No."

"More?"

Ravi grabbed the bodice of her dress in both hands to pull her closer and whisper in her ear: "Don't ask."

They'd explained all the rules, and she sounded like she understood them. She didn't need permission for every little thing. They'd stop her if it went too far.

—Let her know you, Ravi. You have to let her try.

You deserve to be known.

Ravi spent the next few minutes stunned to silent gasps by how lewd and aggressive Nicole could be, even with all their clothes on. And the further she went roughly handling them while they resisted and fought with her, the more giddy they were feeling about the thought that she might actually be able to follow through on that whole 'reverently fuck you hard' thing.

She was also graciously avoiding their chest with the assertive rasping of her fingers about their body, instead focusing her attention on grabbing and biting at their thighs and ass, and fiercely holding them down to force an eager hand down their jeans to roughly handle their cunt just so, *so* nicely – with such a crazy look in her eyes that it made them shudder slightly just imagining what else she might be capable of doing to them.

However, when she gave them a brief reprieve and retreated from them, Ravi caught her eyeing their hidden chest again. When she saw Ravi's discerning gaze, she sharply caught herself too and gave Ravi a serious look.

"I'm not admiring your tits," she said. "I promise. Your chest just looks very handsome in that binder."

"...Thank you."

"If you ever feel up for it, I'd love to get my claws in your pecs. I love a little muscle, you know. And I can see you have so very much muscle under there."

"...I'll think about it."

"Promise I won't fondle your tits."

"Noted."

Nicole smiled at them, reached out twinkling fingers to take Ravi's hands in hers, then pleaded with them playfully: "Ravi Bee. Can I *please* take your shirt off? I *really* want to ride you. And your abs are so hot. It *is* a crime to hide them from me and I may be forced to call a lawyer if you keep this up."

"Uh huh. And what kind of lawyer would take that case on?"

"Abdominal law. For abs-related crimes. You've never seen the billboards? 'You may be entitled to a huge abs settlement.'"

Ravi snerked at Nicole's stupid joke. "Right. Obviously."

"*Obviously.*" Nicole echoed them. Then she started eyeing up the buttons on Ravi's shirt again and hit them with the cutest puppy dog eyes. "Please?"

She was clearly being sincere. She wanted so badly to fuck them exactly the way they'd always wanted. She deserved a chance, didn't she?

How could they say no now?

Ravi took her hands in theirs and guided Nicole's fingers to the buttoned seam of their shirt and smiled at her while she undressed them – all the way down – shirt, jeans, boxers. —And of course she had to make a teasing big deal out of marveling at their cunt to embarrass them.

"Are you proud of that hot throbbing clit of yours Rav?"

"I have days."

"Today?"

"Well the way you're looking at me..."

She teasingly massaged the sheath of their clit to elicit a subtle roll of their hips for her. "Should be every day, honestly. It looks absolutely delicious."

"Thanks..." they said uneasily. "Made it myself...?" They felt so exposed. Would she play by the rules?

"Artisanal," she said with a wry grin. "Let me taste?"

—This is it then. Moment of truth. Be brave Ravi. You can trust her. You <u>*can*</u>.

"Yeah Nix go for it."

She didn't take her eyes off theirs while she dipped down, slick tongue dangling in anticipation.

Ravi braced for the teasing flicks that always started the stupid game of trying to undo them.

But Nicole put on a stunning demonstration of her familiarity with sucking off a throbbing cock, sliding the whole length of her tongue firmly from the base of their clit to the tip, finishing the hungry gesture with a slow suckling kiss that filled their guts with a shuddering wave of warmth.

They darted their hand out to grasp her hair and push her away slightly before she could go for another.

"Okay that's... that's good..."

"Mm... More later?" she hazily pleaded with them.

"If you're good," they assured her with a dozy grin.

Nicole shed her own clothes until she was naked with them in all her beautiful glory, showing off those artisanal breasts and that delicious kissable tummy and those enticing thighs of hers, all for them. Then she started crawling up on their waist, firmly tracing the lines of their abs and on to their biceps and wrists while she did, bringing their arms helplessly over their head for a few moments to let them get lost in her shimmering green-flecked sapphire eyes and the sweet scent of honey on her breath.

"...Hey. Binder's staying on this time, okay?" Ravi reminded her before she got too ambitious in her groping.

A rolling rush of heat coursed through their body when she agreed without a single note of complaint.

—*Still. Still? She wasn't just trying to wear them down? <u>No one</u> did this with them...*

When Nicole straddled their waist, she sat up tall and raised her arms above her head to show off how her breasts hung so perfectly off her frame. She was so close, but oh-so-far. All they could do was wrap their hands around her bountiful thighs and enjoy the warmth and weight of her on their body. If only she'd move up a bit, they could get a taste of heaven. Torturous.

"Just going to sit on me, Nikki?" they teased her. "This good for you?"

"Just want to make you squirm a bit."

"Oh, it's a power play thing?"

"Something like that," she said with a coy smirk.

"Can't convince you to come a little closer?"

"Oh? You hungry?"

Ravi grinned at her. She knew the answer to that.

She mercifully crawled up their torso a bit and leaned over them to let her heavy breasts hang teasingly close to their lips, but she cruelly pulled away whenever she happened to grace their tongue with her nipples.

When they tried to wrap their hands around her back to pull her down, she took firm hold of their wrists and held them down instead.

"That's not how we're playing," she informed them. "Now! Where's that fat cock of yours hiding?" she playfully asked them, abandoning her position over them for a moment to lean over the side of bed to dig around in Ravi's little box of toys.

The position gave them a tantalizing view of her ass, but they restrained themself from taking her. That wasn't how they were playing tonight apparently.

"And how do you know about my fat cock, Nicole Doyle?" they poked at her. "You really can't stop yourself from snooping around, can you?"

"I was looking for the strap earlier," she explained without looking up from her investigation. "Thought you might like that tonight. But imagine my delight when I found out you've been hiding *this* from me:" She dramatically produced what was truly the fattest silicone cock Ravi owned, a little bigger than the biggest guy they'd ever taken, but with some *sensationally* alien morphology and none of the stamina considerations. For *particularly* special occasions and *particularly* bratty conquests. "You think your delicate princess can't handle this? Hm?" She jabbed them in the sternum with the head of the toy teasingly.

"Well you just have to ask, Nix."

"Mm. You said no asking tonight, though, so—" She shoved the hefty mass of stiff silicone into Ravi's hands. "—I'm not asking."

Then she guided Ravi to wrap their fingers around the base of their cock, and positioned their hand *just so* on the mound of their pelvic bone. After a few moments of slickening the shaft with the wetness between her thighs that had apparently been building in her since she started teasing them, she leaned forward and raised her hips to let the head settle into a firm resting position between the petals of the so very proud, so very rosy, so very beautiful blossoming flower of hers.

And finally, in that position, Ravi could steal a taste of her breasts while she warmed herself up on their cock and inched that fiery hot pussy of hers down the shaft. She let out stifled little moans with every stroke as she let all her weight settle into Ravi's hips to force the head of their cock deeper and deeper inside her. They could feel it bottoming out in her over and over again, but she pushed herself to take more and more of it with every plunge.

When she finally had it buried in herself deep enough to disappear, leaving her rosy pussy lips pressed firmly into Ravi's fingers where they were clutching the base of the toy to hold it steady for her, she leaned in and sighed hot contentment in their ear before she generously let them have a taste of her lips.

When she pulled away, she gave Ravi a stupid grin. "Still think I'm a delicate little princess?"

Ravi gave her a mean grin, but they didn't reply. She knew the answer. That was very much an expectation-defying performance, and quite a feat all in one go like that. They were clenching their thighs remembering how amazing that thing felt in them, imagining how good it must feel in her. They desperately wanted to throw her on the bed and fuck her properly with it now, to drive her mad with pleasure, sliding every tantalizing ridge and swell in the shaft over the deepest sweetest spots in her, but before they could even try to move to do that, she shook their mind with a pleading request:

"Let me ride you. Please."

Without waiting for an answer, she started slowly gyrating her hips on Ravi's makeshift cock and looking them in the eye, hungry and pathetic, begging them to let her stay like that, begging them to let her fuck them. That was it. That was the look they'd imagined, the look they'd fantasized about for years. It was the look Ravi had given every guy they'd ever fucked when they were straddling him and hungry for it – and it was... *delicious* to see it on her face.

She really nailed it. In one shot. How did she get so good at this? So good at *them*?

God, it didn't even feel like a performance when she did it.

Nicole got into her own rhythm on them, using their thick sturdy cock to build herself up, shifting her weight slightly now and then to mess up her hungry pussy exactly where she needed. They could see it in her face and feel it in the shudders of her thighs when she teased her own cervix with the head or firmly pressed the bulge of it into her g-spot. They intimately knew the map of these secret delights in her already, knew exactly how to coax these shudders out of her now, but watching her draw it out of their cock herself was so... different. All Ravi could do—all they were supposed to do—all she would *let them* do—was lie there, hold their cock steady for her to grind herself into, and enjoy the show.

She was looking quite warm and pleased with herself when she sat up straight – eyes closed – lip pierced between her sharp teeth – thick amber hair bunched up with grasping fingers into a messy ponytail – dropping all her weight on her favorite new sex toy while Ravi desperately tensed up their abs under her so she wouldn't knock the wind out of them in her fervor. They had to keep a death grip on the base of that cock every time Nicole pulled away, she was clenching it so tightly inside her.

Her pace and ferocity let up a bit so she could lean in to give Ravi a teasing kiss before telling them, dreamy and sultry in their ear: "I'm going to jerk you off so fucking good, Ravi…"

Ravi raised a startled eyebrow at her. "What?"

"I said—" She leaned back, without missing a beat in the gentle rhythm of her hips, and slid her hand up the slick contours of Ravi's cunt until she had their clit trapped firmly between two fingers, simulating the same kind of grasp they'd learned to use around the base of a twitchy throbbing cock. "—I'm going to jerk off that <u>artisanal</u> clit for you until you come *hard*, like the big tough guy you are. —Just how you like, right?"

She started working Ravi's clit, matching the rhythm of her hips with deep, rough strokes up and down their little shaft, drawing back the sheath and exposing the stiff, sensitive little nub to the cool air with every stroke.

It was a lot to get hit with all at once, and they couldn't stop their own hips from bucking and thrusting into the air for her, raising her into the air slightly with every motion.

"How's that?" she asked with a dozy grin. "Think I can finish you off in a minute?"

"You can try," they replied, trying and failing to keep their cool. They kept interrupting themself with little swears and whining gasps whenever Nicole took a few seconds to double the pace of her assault on them. "I'm not—nnffuck—I'm not that easy—"

"Mm, you sure? You're getting kind of *shaky* there Rav. Sure feels like you're getting close *already*. —How many seconds was that?"

"I don't know…"

She paused her attack to lean forward and whisper in their ear, "Count for me."

They hesitated for a second and apparently that was the wrong answer. She took their scruffy hair in a tight fist, drawing a little yelp out of them, and said in a low commanding voice, "I said: Count for me. Did you forget how? Or are you just being... *difficult*." She punctuated her teasing words by painfully tightening her grip on their hair for a second.

Ravi grinned at her. They could see it in her eyes. She was playing. She was playing right, by the rules. She knew they were just letting her get away with this. And it was a fun game. They'd play along.

"One... Two..."

She released them with a satisfied grin. "Don't miss any this time, you cheater," she said playfully, then leaned back again to continue mercilessly jerking their clit off.

Her leaning back like that gave them a perfect view of that beautiful blossoming flower of hers, eating up their cock in that slow and steady rhythm that left her dripping dew down the silicone shaft to drench their desperately clutching fingers in her sweetness. She was really into this, and it was a hell of a distracting show.

"I don't hear counting," she teased.

"Ten... Eleven..."

Ravi's abs were flexing uncontrollably, but they couldn't move at all under Nicole's weight. All they could do was clench their thighs desperately to try to slow her down, but it was no use.

They really were quivering pathetically for her.

"Tw... twenty-five..."

Their toes were curling hard enough to crack.

"Twenty...six..."

Their breath was stuttered and shaky and decorated with little swears.

"Fff... seven..."

Fuck. *Fuck* this wasn't fair, it was too fast.

God, it was their own fault for taunting her, and it sure didn't help that they hadn't had a good chance to get themself off in at least a week.

There was only one way they could think to stop her:

A counterattack.

With their free hand, Ravi used their thumb to press rapid, rough circles into the mound of *her* clit, which got her twitching uncontrollably to match *their* rhythm.

Nicole wasn't going to set the pace anymore.

They kept up their count for her, though: "Thirty-seven... Thirty-eight..."

She offered no resistance and no complaint to Ravi's attack. In fact, she seemed pretty pleased about it, playing along and pressing herself into their assault. Then once she was giving herself over to them, entirely at their mercy, they started rolling their pelvis into her, driving their makeshift cock into her at their own pace, churning her insides up however they wanted to to draw gentle coos out of her.

The steady pace of her fingers on their clit faltered for a moment.

They were winning.

"Ravi that's cheating..."

They continued counting – defiantly now: "Forty-nine..."

—*Almost there.*

Unfortunately, they had unwittingly undone themself with their attack, because apparently in their fervor they didn't realize that out of habit, the rhythm they were using on Nicole happened to be the same rhythm they used to finished themself off, and Nicole took advantage of that, copying them perfectly to shred their resolve, to drag unwilling stuttered gasps out of their lungs, and to utterly paralyze them with involuntary convulsions.

They forgot to get her off.

They forgot to hold themself back.

They forgot *numbers.*

And they had no idea exactly how long it took, but they definitely never got to sixty before they were shuddering at her touch, squeezing desperate handfuls of her thighs, searching for anything at all to grab hold of while they held their breath through that sharp and shallow climax.

They found Nicole grinning smugly when Ravi opened their eyes and took a breath. She'd left that love-drenched cock of theirs lying callously on their sternum, her slick sweet juices rudely staining their binder. The scent of her sex was maddening. They wanted so badly to lick the sheen off it, but they got the feeling that wasn't part of Nicole's game. If it was, she'd probably have already shoved the thing in their mouth for her own entertainment.

They casually tossed the delectable toy aside and bullied her about that smirk of hers: "What are you looking so happy about, huh? I told you, you're not special 'cause you can get me off."

That smug grin turned cruel when she dropped one heavy hand right beside their head and used the other to grab their jaw and squeeze their cheeks like they were a bratty child. "You're so mouthy, huh? I beat your record. You don't get to talk trash like that unless you win, Ravi Bee."

She roughly turned their head to the side when she let them go, to show she was in charge.

Which was absolutely ridiculous of course.

Ravi showed her that in a second by digging their fingers into the most sensitive part of her thighs to get a yelp out of her and force her off of them.

They rolled over and shakily got on their hands and knees to crawl up to her, getting right up in her face until she was forced to put her hands out behind her to keep herself from tumbling backwards. The look of barely-pretended fear in her eyes was sending waves of heat through Ravi's body and putting mischief in their mind.

"So you think you're better than me, huh?" they teased.

She grinned at them. "Prove me wrong."

"*Prove you wrong*. First of all, that was the worst orgasm I've ever had."

"*Sure* it was."

Ravi gave her a toothy grin, wrapped their fingers around the back of her neck to pull her upright again, and snatched her wrist in their hand.

"You really need me to hold your hand, huh? I'll show you how to fuck me properly."

They made themself tall on their knees in front of her and parted their thighs for her, staring her down with a mean smile, so they could guide her hand to their cunt. "You know, I've been eyeing up those big powerful fingers of yours for a *long time* Nix." They shaped her hand until only her index and middle finger were extended to show her exactly what they wanted. "Go <u>hard</u>. Make me feel it. If you're not fucking up my cervix, you're not doing it right. Got it?"

She nodded with a barely hidden smirk.

They didn't manage to stifle the embarrassing little sigh when she first buried her fingers in them. And they were even worse at holding themself back while she was *withdrawing* her fingers, tracing every twitchy spot their innards had to offer along the way, drawing a hard gasp out of them when she passed over their cervix, and stealing a pathetic mewling coo out of them when she pressed the pads of her fingers, firm and unforgiving, into their g-spot.

Then she began her audition, dutifully following their instructions, to Ravi's absolute delight.

While Nicole was roughly thrusting her fingers into them, they clenched their teeth and firmly grasped her hair at the base of her skull in a tight fist to keep her eyes on theirs the whole time, showing her that she was doing it right with a snide grin.

They rewarded her efforts by leaning back on one hand to give her a better angle, forcing her to follow them with that firm grip on her hair.

It felt good, but she wasn't *quite* getting it, so they took over her rhythm for her, grasping her wrist and driving their cunt into her fingers to bottom out with every hard thrust. She figured it out quick and got down to fucking them hard enough to ache, knocking her knuckles into them with every pump of the heavy piston driving her hand, backed up by the hefty weight of her arm, truly shaking their bones with every impact.

They grunted with each hit, darkly imagining the salacious achy bruises they'd be recovering from for the next few days. Their breath started coming harder and heavier, and, as Nicole brought them closer to their end, they squeezed her hair tighter, forcing her forehead into theirs while they closed their eyes and exhaled hot breath dripping with swears and blasphemy and Nicole's exquisitely breathtaking name.

"This you fucking me, Ravi Bee?" she teased them.

"Shut up…"

"Seems unfair you're the only one getting off tonight."

"I'll do you later… Don't you dare stop…"

Ravi didn't see it with their eyes closed, so it came as a rush of shock when Nicole grabbed their scruffy hair in her own tight fist and once again twisted their skull to face the ceiling. "Selfish," she snarled in their ear before sending them to the very edge with a cruel bite and a hickey on their neck.

But that wasn't enough to satisfy her it seemed, because she kept on, relentlessly, slipping her tongue between their lips, fucking *their* tongue with slithering thrusts to match the rhythm of her fingertips drawing firm circles around the devastating hotspots around their cervix, sending crackling shockwaves of pleasure through their body over and over and over with every other beat, until she ripped the air right out of their lungs in a huge cluster of desperate gasps.

They clawed at her and tore free from her grasp to madly hold her still to catch their breath before they pulled her back in for a rough kiss, to bite her right on back as cruelly as she's done them, tugging at her lip with their teeth until they could taste a hint of her blood.

But even as they shuddered in her hands, she refused to let up on them at all, and as much as they desperately wanted to stay in control here, keep her hair in their hands and their breath on her lips, they couldn't help losing it all as they tensed every muscle in their body, fully lost their grasp on her, and slammed themself back on the bed, sending a wicked shock of overwhelming hyperventilating pain-made-pleasure when their fucked-up shoulder hit the mattress. They frantically grasped the sheets over their head in knuckle-cracking fists just to hold on to anything at all as their sense of reality slipped away, writhing pathetically for her as she relentlessly hammered away at their g-spot until their vision started to flutter.

It was too much. They were too pathetic there. But they couldn't say stop. They couldn't let her win.

—*Fuck. Fuck fuck fuck <u>fuck</u>.*

...When they got their senses back, they once again found her leaning over them, this time with utterly disappointed eyes.

She teased them: "You're so pathetic when you come, hey tough guy?"

"Shut up..."

"I thought you were supposed to be fucking me 'even with my fingers buried in your cunt'. That's what you said, right?"

They scoffed with a grin. "What is this?"

For a second they thought it was an act, but the longer she looked at them with those mean eyes, the more it became obvious she meant every word.

She brought her lips close to theirs, letting her hot honeyed breath tease them, then looked in their eyes hungrily while she ran fingers through their sweaty hair, until she grabbed a fistful of it in a fierce grasp.

"You said you were going to fuck me," she reminded them, whispering the warm bullying words in their ear. "I'm waiting, tough guy."

The way she said it put a giddy fluttering in their guts, leaving them hot and wild to take her up on her taunting.

This was so different than anything their past fuckers had done before. This wasn't trying to undo them. This wasn't trying to *trick* them. —This was a *challenge.* A fun one, on reverently hallowed even ground.

And they sure as hell weren't about to let her win.

They were still shaky from how well she worked them over, but they hid it pretty well they thought, sitting up proudly and returning her mean glare.

"You want the usual treatment, *princess?*"

"Mm. How about you treat me like I deserve after embarrassing you like that? You really were *so* pathetic."

Ravi slid tender fingers up Nicole's sternum to bring them to rest around her throat, holding her captive there while they confirmed: "So, a *bad* princess, then."

She leaned in sharply, forcing their hand into her windpipe, to whisper sultry in their ear: "Just take me. *Use* me. Make me suck the taste of me off of your fingers. Force that cock of yours down my throat and make me *choke.* I promise I won't look at you like a man for it. Just fuck me like you promised. Make it even."

Ravi was a little startled by her frankness. They'd never seen this side of her. But they couldn't help grinning at her darkly delicious, salacious requests.

And they couldn't *stop* grinning as they strapped their cock into its harness for her. This was going to be a fun night.

Even the Strongest Heart Is Made of Strands Most Tenuous

(Afternoon, Friday, 17th March)

When Nicole collected the mail from the dark and dingey mailroom in the apartment building's lobby, she couldn't help peeking at the return address on each envelope. She was surprised to see one from InThetics. —She was surprised to see one from InThetics with a startlingly familiar name in the corner: Miriam Ortiz.

Miss Ortiz? From that piece of a progress report Henry gave her months and months ago?

She dug the forgotten document out of her boxes and read over it again. Status report. Lobbying effort. Projected harvest. Nothing clear enough to glean anything useful, of course, but Henry's little puzzle pieces were always like this.

It pricked her curiosity all day waiting for Ravi to return, and when they did, she was practically hanging on their arm when they opened the letter.

They smirked at her and assured her it wasn't important:

"I get these once in a while. They always want to give me a 'grant' – to privately commission some of my ceramics research, pay me to lock some of it away behind patents and copyrights. It's a scam, but I still wouldn't work for them even if it was legit."

"Why not? I thought you were super into their tech?"

"I love their tech. I hate their side gigs. They make war machines and sell weapons to both sides of these bullshit international proxy wars. They keep it quiet, take all the heat whenever it comes up and bury it with silky smooth PR, but they work with the Canadian Government on it too, take contracts from them specifically to arm these conflicts."

"Ah. Right. I had to write a paper on this before I dropped out. Destabilize the region to justify stepping in to support and puppeteer the more Canada-friendly regimes?"

"Yeah, stuff like that."

"Depressing."

"Sure is! Not something I want to contribute to even a little bit. Bad enough my taxes pay for that shit."

Still, Ravi scanned the letter to see what it was about.

When they did, the smug indignation on their face melted into cold shock.

Nicole asked them with a bit of concern: "What's up?"

"They... want to hire me..."

"...Right? As usual? You just said—"

"No. This is... They want to hire me for real. Permanently." They read over the details again and again to confirm before they summarized: "They want me working on a research team. —On some modern ceramic tech. —And... this isn't even an entry level job. Looks junior level."

Nicole raised an eyebrow. "Junior sounds pretty entry level."

"No this is a 'seven years professional experience' kind of gig. This would put me... *so* far ahead in my career..."

Ravi let the hand holding the letter drop to their side to vacantly stare at the wall.

"Can I read it?" Nicole asked.

Ravi handed her the letter without moving their head at all. This was really getting to them.

Nicole looked over the offer. She noted a few concerning items there – nondisclosure noncompetition was bold and flaming in her eyes. Ravi wouldn't be able to continue their own research. Their thesis would be dead – or else InThetics would own it.

And their research into the tar...

"You'd have to give up... everything," she summarized.

Ravi didn't reply.

"No, right?"

Again no reply. Nicole was talking to a corpse here.

She put a concerned hand on their shoulder and shook them a little to bring them back to life.

"*Ravi.* No. Right?"

They closed their eyes and took a deep breath, swelling their chest and holding it in for a long time.

At last, they let it out and confirmed, "Right. Right, obviously. Sorry, it's just a big… thing. It's big."

Nicole handed back the letter, and Ravi folded it back up to stuff it in the envelope. They hesitated in an uneasy pose, poised to rip the thing in half, before they finally pushed themself to follow through. They tossed the two halves lackadaisically onto the table.

"This is better," Nicole assured them.

"It's better for my soul, whatever that's worth."

"It's worth a lot."

Ravi nodded in agreement, though they weren't very enthusiastic about it. Nicole opened her arms for them and invited them to snuggle into her chest. They lethargically accepted the offer. She spent a long time running loving fingers through their hair, hoping to assure them they made the right choice with soft affection alone.

…But even Nicole had to accept that maybe it would be better for Ravi to spend whatever short lifetime they had ahead of them in a career that satisfied them. A career that didn't break their back and drain their bank account. A career that paid off their debt and gave them a real chance at a comfortable life.

Souls weren't real anyways, though she couldn't really tell them that.

But that's not what they meant anyways.

They meant that *this* path, ignoring the offer, would keep the Ravi boat floating. Making an ethical compromise like that might end up being the final swapped piece of the hull that changed the ship of Ravi Beausoleil into some vessel beyond recognition, a vessel that may never float again.

And that? That was worth a lot.

In the morning, Nicole noted that the torn letter was neither on the table where Ravi left it, nor in the recycling bin where they had supposedly convinced themself it belonged.

She didn't ask about it.

There Are No Life-giving Stars in a Sky of Endless Blue

(Late Morning, Sunday, 19th March)

The kitchen had always felt like a forbidden zone for Nicole. —Not that she wasn't able to cook. Cooking was easy. Put a bunch of things on some heat and presto: Food. Even easier once you have a few recipes in your head.

But it felt like the world shrunk for her whenever she learned a new recipe. She couldn't forget it. Every word. Even the meandering stories that cluttered up most of them in the 21st century. That remarkable curse of a memory of hers was one of the oh-so-special perks of having been bound to thousands of picky contracts in her life. You forget one *comma* and you're in trouble.

And then, once she knew how something was made, the magic was gone.

She still cooked for Ravi once in a while, but it always felt a little depressing, and of course they noticed her misery and kindly offered to cook most nights instead, to Nicole's absolute guilt-ridden delight. Their food was too good to say no to, though.

There was something else about cooking that troubled her, though: It was a *human* activity. The fae just *conjured* their food – the handful of specialists who could, anyways – and never for hunger, just to *taste*. Thousands-year banquets, a million courses of heavenly tastes and textures and just... just... *emptiness*. Filling, sure, but just... completely *empty*. You can only remix a dish that tastes like perfection so many ways before it all starts to taste the same, before the mind-tingling sweetness of it all starts to rot in your mouth and tire your mind.

Though that sensory exhaustion didn't seem to be a universal fae experience. As far as she knew, she was the only one who ever had any complaints about the food back in the Faelands. She had always been a bit of a weirdo among her cousins, even before she screwed up her heart. But she was pretty sure if a human could figure out how to live forever, they'd get just as bored of it as she did.

Humans, though, they could *cook*. They could transform filthy dirt and manure and *rot* into vegetables and spice and meat and cheese and bread and so many impossible creations, creations that created an experience that *shook you*. They turned *death itself* into raw ingredients and combinations of flavors that were so unbelievably shocking and so diverse, so full of life on the tongue, filling the air with giddy *anticipation* of their *imperfection*, that it was unbelievable to Nicole that any creature in the universe could look on any of it with scorn. This was art, painted in a palette no immortal faerie in the Faelands could even *imagine*.

But they did. They scorned it all.

It was funny, though, how empty that scorn was. Her dear stubborn cousins always scoffed at it at first, but Nicole had never met a faerie that didn't hum with delight at the taste of a fresh loaf of bread. And that was just the start. It was a guilty, secret pleasure for any of her cousins once she got them hooked.

But, fae as she was, it seemed that whenever Nicole tried her hand at it – at imagining new flavors, at creating something full of love out of the cold abhorrent death of the mortal realm – her food always came out more like the product of a cold dead machine, like storebought factory-sealed goods. Seemed that even her aching, death-fearing, love-cursed heart always fell short of the inarticulable criteria required to make something that tasted like a *transformation*.

And that made sense, really. Why should it taste like life coming out of her? She could never die. Not really. So how could she dare to hope to tap into the power of humanity's magic, that turned death into life-giving love?

What made humans *human* was mortality. An immortal pretending couldn't hope to understand.

So she had always figured.

But today, she decided to forget all that and bite the bullet and rip all the magic out of a food that made her cry with joy the last time she had some, a food that was apparently very hard to find in this city, a food that meant a lot to dear Ravi Bee: Achaar. Spicy pickled cabbage, to be precise.

Maybe she could pull it off, turn a little rot into love. She'd done crazier things before, right?

Unfortunately, despite that she was *certain* she had the mix of spices perfect according to the precise, particular numbers in the few dozen recipes she stole the best parts of, the taste still wasn't coming out right at all. As usual, as expected, despite the spice, it tasted dead on her tongue. Manufactured. A cold recitation. —And nothing about it tasted like *Ravi*. And that was the whole point. It was *for them*.

She sat on the kitchen counter next to that bowl filled with a colorful mixture of spice and disappointment and lethargically jabbed the spoon into the mess over and over while she tried to figure out what was missing.

What did Ravi like? Spicy food. But they had such diverse food taste that it was hard to pick out any one thing in particular.

Coffee? Beer? *Honey*, obviously, she grinned to herself salaciously.

Oh, that was it then, wasn't it?

She popped over to the Serpent's Fang to flag Henry down.

"Hey bestest buddy."

"Oh ho, I'm your 'buddy' today?" he asked, incredulous, arms crossed, with a playful grin.

"You sure are. Give me a bottle of that beer you gave Ravi before."

"...'Before'. When is 'before'?"

"Like... Uh... Oh gods I don't know, it's been a while. It was something to do with bees and honey. They liked it, right?"

"Ah that, yes. They did indeed like it, though they haven't ordered a bottle since."

"Well, it's expensive, yeah?"

"It is."

"So?"

"Right. I see your point."

Nicole put her hand out and curled grabby fingers expectantly.

"Sorry my dear, I'm completely out. They stopped selling it for the season. You'll have to track down the monastery it came from and hope they've got an extra cask lying around."

Nicole groaned. It was always such a *thing* finding anything in Europe. Even being able to fling herself anywhere she could imagine on Earth wasn't enough to make it easy.

"Don't suppose you have an address?"

"Best I can give you is the bottling facility."

"Well, that's fine! They've gotta have an extra bottle."

"If they had bottles, they'd probably still be selling them, no?"

"Oh whatever, just give me the address. Time sensitive here. Gotta get this stuff before Ravi gets home."

"Oh?"

"It's a surprise for them."

"I fear your dear beloved beer connoisseur might not be as surprised by a bottle as you're expecting."

"No no, it's what the beer's *going in*. Trust me, they'll love it."

Nicole gave Henry a cheerful wave once she had the address in hand, then disappeared to begin her investigation.

It took hours of discreetly flitting around and desperately pleading for plainly spoken directions, but at last, she finally managed to find the monastery and convince them to trade her a corked bottle of the sweet, honeyed beer, fresh from the cask, in exchange for a few chores around the facility. She really preferred using cash for this kind of thing. Cash had some built-in curses that made it a lot safer than exchanging favors as a faerie had a tendency to be. She hoped the monks wouldn't mind too much when the floors she swept spotless inevitably ended up being so dangerously slick later that someone slipped and sprained an ankle or something.

They'd be fine.

It was fine.

Once she returned home, to her absolute delight, it turned out that she was right: The beer was exactly what she needed. The flavor profile of the new mix was perfect, she could feel it. There was no way Ravi wouldn't love it.

The next part of the recipe was letting the concoction spend a few days in the heat of the sun, so she whisked the freshly sealed jars of perfectly spiced pickled cabbage to some discrete sunny cliffside in some warm, sun-kissed equatorial country she'd grown fond of visiting, and then she tried her very best to put it out of her mind so she wouldn't look like a giddy child waiting for it.

But she couldn't help herself from absolutely beaming with joy every time it crossed her mind while she was eagerly waiting for her surprise to make itself ready. Ravi noticed and kept asking her about it, but she managed to keep it secret:

"It's a special surprise, Ravi Bee. You'll see when it's ready."

"I hate surprises, though. Just tell me?"

"Nope. And don't worry, it's not a surprise now, since I warned you. Now it's just a *mystery*."

"Oh. Good. Yes. That's completely different. I love mysteries."

"Everyone loves mysteries."

"Normally mysteries have clues."

"There are clues, you just have to look carefully."

"No hints?"

"Hint one and only: Wait three days."

Ravi tried guessing a few dozens times while they were waiting, but they didn't get even close before Nicole's gift was finally ready. When she presented them with a cheerfully wrapped little bundle of vibrant jars, the glass was still warm from the tall equatorial sun.

"What's this?" they asked with a suspicious raised eyebrow, plucking a jar from the package to examine its contents through the glass.

"Hm-hm-hm. I wonder. Why don't you try it?"

Ravi tentatively opened a jar and gave it a sniff, which immediately opened their eyes with shock and wonder. "What *is* this?"

"Try it! Gods!"

Nicole was giddy with pride when she saw Ravi's reaction. They were lost in the taste. She really nailed it. Gods, maybe her whole 'humanity' act was actually getting better. Next she'd be writing poetry that actually meant something to anyone, or painting paintings that captured some otherwise inexpressible mortal ennui.

"Where did you get this?" they asked, rotating the jar in their hand, seeking out some kind of label, finding only clear glass. "Did you make it?"

Nicole grinned at them.

"Shit. Really? It's so... *good*. Is this your first try at it?"

"I know, right! I'm surprised too, honestly."

"Yeah, no kidding. I thought you hated cooking."

"I do! It's awful! Thanks for noticing!"

"Well, fuck, you should do it more anyways if you're making stuff like this. You're wasting your talent."

"Noooo thank you. I like your cooking way better. It's always so full of love."

"Sappy."

"Oh shush. You cook, I do the dishes, you know the arrangement."

"Well now I feel cheated on the deal, honestly."

"*Too late~*" Nicole replied in a singsong voice. "You shook on it."

"Idiot move on my part."

Ravi couldn't resist snacking on that first jar for the rest of the night. It was mostly empty by the time they put it away. Good thing Nicole made a whole batch.

It turned out Ravi had a special surprise for Nicole as well:

"Carrie said we can go ahead."

"Really?"

"Yeah. Actually, she seemed strangely committed to it. She even asked me to explain what I'm *actually* doing, even though she was pretty confident it was going to get her in trouble to know anything about it."

"She likes you."

"She likes the scientific pursuit of *truth*. —And apparently, despite all the danger, she really likes the excitement of it – dark science, forbidden secrets, government coverups. I kind of love her."

"She really bought your 'in for a penny' argument, huh?"

Ravi shrugged. "Might as well have fun if you're fucked anyways. I stand by that."

"You ever actually put that theory to the test?"

They scoffed at themself bitterly. "Oh yeah. Yeah. And let's just say it wasn't always the condom that broke down."

"Really? I didn't realize you were so *adventurous*."

"Oh god, Nicole, you have no idea. I've done some very, *very* stupid things when I was drunk, or just... *depressed* – and once you've broken the skin, it sure doesn't feel like anything to keep going for blood. I'm such a self-destructive idiot sometimes, god. I'm glad you never had to see any of that. Not exactly the proudest years of my life..."

Nicole gave Ravi a concerned look. "You're not doing that right now, are you? With this *'fuck you, shadowy government spooks, come get me'* stuff?"

That question seemed to catch Ravi by surprise. Their eyes fell and they started fussing with their fingers while they considered the answer.

At last, they assured her: "It's different. This is different. All those other times, it was because I didn't care. I wanted to die. I wanted anything to kill me. Finish me off. Put me out of my misery. I wanted some proof my life could even *be* worse. I was in shadows chasing darkness and oblivion. But this is more like... I don't know, I'm doing something important, something I want to live for. There's some kind of light I'm chasing now. And it's a light worth teasing oblivion for. I'm not going to let it scare me, and I'm not letting it take me without a fight."

Nicole grinned wide at them. This was peak Ravi. It was so good seeing them in such high spirits about all this.

"Well, I'm with you all the way, Rav. You just let me know whatever you need."

"Thanks Nix. You're up next. See what you can find out about those names?"

Nicole gave Ravi a dutiful salute. "As you command, my righteous and most noble liege. I'll have a report for you as soon as I hear back from my guy."

Some Tattoos Are Drawn Inkless by the Tender Tips of Fingers in the Dark

(Late Evening, Saturday, 25th March)

"You really don't have to do this," Nicole assured poor Ravi.

They had their fingers paused apprehensively on the zipper of their binder. Their bottom lip was pinched between their teeth. Their eyes were closed. And Nicole could swear they were shaking.

"Ravi?"

"Shh. I'm visualizing."

Nicole couldn't keep a playful little snort from escaping. "Sorry, what are you visualizing?"

"Mm... Nudist beach. Public showers. The privacy of my own lonely apartment."

"Ravi."

"Almost got it."

"Please don't do this if you're not ready."

They let out a long hiss of air before they finally committed to it and undid that charming restrictive chest piece that gave a boyish shape to their unwelcome bust, letting the thing slip lethargically off their shoulders and arms, eyes still closed, seemingly afraid to look at Nicole's reaction.

She noted the dark impression left behind by the elastic, framing their chest with deep red grooves. According to her research, Ravi wore this thing far too often for far too long at a time. And they had to know that. They weren't stupid. Self-destructive, yeah, but not stupid. But that wasn't something she was ever going to be qualified to correct them on. Their body, their rules.

This wasn't actually the first time Nicole had seen Ravi naked. They were always bare-chested for the last few days of every month when they couldn't bear the pain of wearing their binder, leaving them stuck trying to hide their body with baggy clothes instead. Even now, in the final week, it was pretty obvious that it hurt to wear it, but... it was important to them.

This, though, this was different. This was the first time that they were making themself bare *for her*.

A sharp prick of guilt accompanied the unspoken thought in her mind when she saw their chest:

—*Such cute breasts, gods.*

<u>No</u>. *No, fuck, don't. Don't. This is important.*

Ugh, but she couldn't just *turn off* her thoughts or her lusting affection for the shape of *Ravi Beausoleil*. But she could do them right with her actions – and just hope they would never ask her a question she couldn't sneak out of answering about how beautiful they looked with everything finally out for her to enjoy.

—*So, so beautiful.*

She really did want to push them down and slide her tongue over every inch of their body, even their forbidden breasts, their tempting, perky little nipples – she wanted to cherish them like they deserved, joyously celebrate every feature with reckless abandon like she always did with her lovers, but that wasn't right. That wasn't how to celebrate *Ravi*, and it was time for Nicole to learn how to do it properly.

—*This is <u>important</u>.*

"Nicole the stunned silence isn't very reassuring," they chided her, eyes still closed.

Nicole grinned at them, though they couldn't see, then she reached out a hand and placed it, fingers splayed, on their sternum.

They flinched slightly when she did, but relaxed when they realized what she was doing and leaned their weight into her.

The muscles there were so dense. They really had quite an impressive physique under that binder.

She traced the sinews of their pecs up to their collarbone with rough fingers, taking care to avoid their breasts as best as she could, then slid her fingers along the lingering impression of their binder to the sensitive crease of their armpit so she could drag a firm finger-padded claw down the side of their ribs and on to their clenching abs, pausing only for a moment before returning her hand to rest on the flat space between their forbidden breasts.

She was tracing a loving frame around their chest. Would they understand?

She watched Ravi's face the whole time, looking for any sign of discomfort, but they looked fine. They… really *trusted* her, didn't they? Unquestioningly. Absolutely.

When she withdrew her fingers from them, they opened their eyes and looked right at her. There was an intense fear there for a few seconds, but when they saw the softness and adoration in her eyes, their fear transmuted into confusion, and then into relief.

"…That feels nice," they told her.

Nicole held out her hands, palms-up, for Ravi to take. "Please show me what to do."

Ravi looked at her hands contemplatively for a few long seconds before they reached out and took her wrists to guide her.

Nicole was surprised just how much of their chest was available for her enjoyment. They seemed to be more concerned with *how* she touched them than where. As long as she avoided lingering anywhere too sensitive, and as long as she was fairly rough with the pressure of her massage – enough to get right down to the muscle and bone underneath – then Ravi seemed to actually enjoy having her attention on their chest.

They even wrapped a hand around the back of her skull to guide her to where it was okay to lick them, to kiss them, to sharpen her teeth and leave dark love bites.

It was a map of Ravi's secret pleasures, and she made sure to perfectly commit every line and landmark to memory forever.

By the time Ravi was done with their tour, they were grasping Nicole's hair in their hands like a cat kneading a blanket and letting out soft coos and wincing hisses of pain at her touch as she oscillated between firm caresses and rough handling with tooth and nail. They were lost in the joy of it, until, after a satisfied sigh, they drew her up to meet them for a kiss of bit lips and dancing tongues that sang a few long silent minutes of *'thank you'*s and *'I love you'*s and *'I want you'*s and *'I need you'*s and *'you're impossible'*s all at once.

It was a rare treat to find Ravi so soft in bed. Some hidden switch in their head flipped like this once in a while. They were practically a puppy in her hands tonight, pawing at her clothes and pleading with her to take them off and share her beautiful body with them. This was one of those nights where they were willing to sacrifice all their control to her – and she intended to treasure every moment of it.

The giddy fun of the night culminated in a beautiful view of Ravi's sweaty, exhausted body, splayed out on their stomach with their face pressed firmly into a growing little spot of saliva that was staining the bedsheets. They were still clutching the sheets pathetically and twitching with orgasmic aftershocks while Nicole, slow and teasing, withdrew her big colorful strap-on from their desperately clenching little asshole.

When she finally slipped the last of it out of them, Ravi let out a huge satisfied sigh and moaned quietly, "Oh my *god.*" They lethargically wiped a bit of drool from their cheek and marveled in a hazy stupor: "I've never gone that <u>deep</u> before... Fuck. *Fuck*, I swear I was almost choking on it... That was... Wow..." They rolled over a bit to catch her eyes with a dozy look of love and admiration, "You're way too good at that."

With a mean grin, Nicole playfully jabbed their ribs and teased, "Shame *someone* never wants to put my *extraordinary* talents to good use, huh?"

"Sorry, puppy," they replied with a tired grin. "The stars must align..."

"Okay well can you tell me which ones? Maybe I can pull some strings and make a new constellation for you."

"Aw. You'd move the cosmos around just for me?"

"If it means I get to do this to you every night? Yes. Very yes."

After the two of them got cleaned up properly, Nicole was overjoyed to find herself settled into bed for the night to cuddle with her dear, newly fully revealed lover.

At long last, Nicole could wrap her arm around Ravi's bare chest in bed. She could wrap her arm around them and they could grasp her hand and bless it with gentle kisses that, each and every one, said a silent, "I love you more. And more. And more."

When Ravi finally drifted off, Nicole smiled to herself in the dark, listening to them breathe, feeling their heart beating under her palm, mentally retracing the precious map of their body in her mind.

Finally, she knew how to celebrate every inch of Ravi Beausoleil – inside and out – and she could think of nothing more that she could possibly need now.

It's Just a Thought
Experiment, Don't Take It Too
Literally

(Late Evening, Saturday, 1st April)

Virgil finally got back to Felicity with the translation of that book. *The Thorns of the Garden*. Ended up being a pretty useful resource to cross reference a bunch of other texts on the supernatural throughout time and space. *Lot* of patterns in the entirety of human knowledge about some *particular* creatures.

Felicity was sitting in her car a block away from Amy's apartment that evening, notebook open under the vehicle's ceiling light, drawing and drawing a very special sigil over and over again – a sigil inspired by dozens of similar sigils, sigils that were drawn by dozens of authors over hundreds and hundreds of years, out of dreams and feverish visions and deathbed hallucinations – a sigil inspired by the nightmarish half-rememberings of dozens of victims of a powerful figure that came up again and again in stories old and older – the great Black Dog, the Grinning Dagger, the seducer of even the most steeled minds, the one who hungers for the misery of mankind, who feeds on the greed and desperation of men, women, and children without discrimination.

It was the only common factor between the three books the Witch gave her, so it sure felt like an important lead – especially because the sigil bore a *striking* resemblance to one of the glowing white-inked symbols on that sealed note of Danica's.

—*It's not true if it's only pieces.*

The Witch's words stuck with Felicity while she was doing her research. That every sigil was similar but slightly off was frustrating. It confounded her until she was bored in her frustration and playing with a new little flipbook animation she was vandalizing Virgil's sticky notes with. Frame by frame. Pieces of something bigger. Then it hit her: Inspired by the very tech that she used to scan her ancient books – page by page, slice after slice, all bits and pieces of a greater whole, dismantled into two-dimensional frames of something more, nothing on their own, everything together.

And that insight was a hell of a lead. The sigils – when stacked up and ordered by the subtle shifts in the lines according to the scanner's algorithm – turned the scattered scraps into a three-dimensional model and took on a new meaning: It wasn't a dozen shifting flat symbols drawn in the area of a circle. It was a bunch of flat slices of a dozen twisted twirling ribbons in the volume of a cylinder, woven in tangles folding back and forth over themselves, disappearing and appearing as the ribbons' loops ended and began – *seemingly* at random, by nonsense, until the variations were put in order and the underlying structure was made clear.

But the only thing any human could see of it, the only thing they could put on a single sheet of paper, was just a slice – for example, a slice that might be represented by the ink of a signature on the page of a contract – the signature of some magical creature – *true* but never *complete.*

Obviously, Felicity couldn't draw it all on a page. And she couldn't quite extrapolate the model out to whatever full depth it might extend to – infinity? Who knows. But she could know it well enough to write a piece of it, to write a dozen pieces of it, to bluff that she knew it all, to construct some countless interpolated versions of it that had never been put on paper before.

It was Danica's true name. Felicity was sure of it: She did *science* on it.

She also cross referenced the runes in that white-ink-sealed note she stole from Danica with everything in the database. What she found seemed to indicate it was a locking spell. And in some of the books she had, she read that locking spells can be unlocked with key spells written in iron ink. Unfortunately, none of her books had concise guides on this kind of stuff, so she set her computer to work, eating all the info she had, spitting out runes in likely unlocking patterns, building counter seals with different slices of the multidimensional ribbons of Danica's true name, and printing those permutations out in bulk in iron doped ink.

And that week, it finally clicked. She returned to the lab to find that the iron sigil on one of the hundreds of printouts was burnt to ash, and the sealed note was finally unfolded on the table beside it.

It was blank. —Or rather, it *looked* blank, unless you looked at it with the right equipment – in this case, an old illusion-piercing scope made of flint. Peering through the hole in the stone revealed the indecipherable words of a letter of some sort. Tables of figures. Dramatically circled symbols.

When Felicity wrote the letters out and fed them to the machine, it looked like they matched bits and pieces of a bunch of folkloric wards and banishing spells, which lit her eyes up bright as the sun to realize how much power she had just unlocked.

She had the machine generate a bunch of promising patterns from the symbols on Danica's sealed note and memorized them. No guarantee any of it would work, but it was *something*.

Felicity's plan was to make a big show of it. Draw Danica's name and the spell by hand like she knew it and a thousand more. And if she could bluff that she knew all of Danica's name – that she knew all of Danica's name *and* the spells to banish her – then she might have at least a little chance of intimidating the beast, maybe even enough to scare her off for good.

But even if the name and the amateur spellcraft weren't enough, Felicity was ready to defend herself. She brought a whole duffel bag full of surprises for Danica, wards and protective charms and devastating anti-magic weapons inspired by the words of warning in that Thorns book.

She had narrowed it down to a few candidates, for exactly what Danica was, but she needed to make sure – absolutely sure – so that there would be no way for the creature to wriggle her way out of this.

She clutched the chain on her neck to double check and triple check it was there. A circle of knotted iron links. Polished to a shine by the industry of human hands and oiled to protect it from rust – nature's only defense again the cold, indisputable-by-historical-consensus magic-warding metal.

It wasn't the only thing on her neck to protect her, though. She hated to do it, to use a cross for something so tawdry, but she also had a silver crucifix hanging from the chain, just in case Danica was something a little more unholy than some mere murderous trickster spirit.

Her *lola* would kill her if she ever found out she was using something so holy for something so blasphemous, for *pagan magic*, but there was no other way. She'd pray for forgiveness once she was sure Amy was safe.

She looked over her sketches, compared them to the model she had on her phone, and tried to assure herself it was good enough to deceive the creature.

Then she took a deep breath, flicked off the ceiling light, and got out of her car, slinging the heavy duffel bag over her shoulder.

Show time.

Danica wasn't expecting her to show up so early. Amy was working late, as usual, the poor thing. Felicity had just confirmed with Danica that Amy wasn't going to be back for hours.

And that coy trickster, she was far too invested in keeping up that friendly act of hers to refuse Felicity at the gate.

Danica was clearly startled to hear her on the lobby intercom, but on the elevator up, she was sure acting like it was a pleasant surprise.

"And here I thought you didn't want to spend any more time with me, Fleece."

"Well, special case here. I'm trying to pick out a gift for Amy, and I figured, who knows Amy better than you these days?"

"What's the occasion?"

"Well! I got to thinking: If I can't be here to protect her myself, I should at least leave a little good luck charm for her. Keep any dangerous spirits out of her home."

Danica raised a curious eyebrow at that while she opened the door to invite Felicity in.

"You're really on this magic stuff these days, huh? —Coffee?"

"Sure," Felicity said, dismissively. She wasn't here for coffee or chitchat or these stupid mind games. She was here for an *exorcism*.

She kneeled in front of the coffee table across from the couch and let her duffel bag slip off her shoulder onto the ground beside her, then casually undid the zipper with a grin.

She wanted to jump right into trying to bind the creature with her true name, but that was far too dangerous until she knew she could defend herself against whatever this beast might be able to throw at her.

Time to find out exactly what this thing was.

When Danica sat down on the couch across from her, Felicity pulled out the first warding artifact in her list and placed it just so in the center of the table.

Rabbit's foot.

She watched Danica's reaction attentively.

The creature eyed it incredulously while running a finger over the soft fur. "Is that real?"

"You bet it is."

"I don't think Amy would be... *super* into an amputated foot."

No reaction. Okay. That was low on the list anyways.

She put that one away, then brought out a wreath of various herbs that the Thorns book – and a few others – had assured the reader would ward off any malicious pixies.

Danica put a considerate finger to her chin, then informed Felicity that it should go in the maybe pile. "Is that really good luck, though? I think she'd probably just end up cooking it all off in a couple weeks."

Right. That made sense. Amy cooked for Danica all the time, and she was pretty damn good at it. If herbs were really Dani's weakness, she'd already have been driven out of the apartment by now by all the delicious food.

Which also ruled out *garlic* and *bread* and every other food-related ward.

She let out a little sigh. Snacks for later.

Next up, a little wall-hanger crucifix. Pure silver. Not cheap.

Danica picked it up to admire it, but casually informed Felicity that Amy wasn't very religious. Kind of extremely nihilist, actually. "Don't think they're into all that Jesus stuff. —Uh. Sorry. No offense if that's your thing."

"Nah it's fine, I get it. It's mostly a family thing for me," Felicity assured Danica – though she had no idea why she felt the need to justify that. Maybe because of the *guilt*. Dabbling in all this pagan magic stuff sure felt pretty sinful. Truly, if her dear sweet *lola* ever found out, she'd be excommunicated.

She tried a few more items – special plants, bones, symbology – with little effect, and much skepticism from the *expert*. That spread was supposed to help narrow it down, too – what Danica was – but with no reaction at all, it didn't do anything to get Felicity closer to a diagnosis.

At least the useless crucifix ruled out the undead and the demonic.

This wasn't looking good. Felicity was *really* hoping some of this less powerful stuff would have any kind of effect. Either Danica was too strong for any lesser wards, or the tips and tricks in that Thorns book were less reliable than Felicity was hoping, or else Danica really was truly some kind of horrifying *thing* that, even in dozens of books over hundreds of years, no one had ever figured out a countermeasure for – other than sharing terrifying tales of warning. Tales of warning that... Felicity had... entirely ignored...

She grimaced at herself. This might not be going as planned. But she wasn't giving up yet!

Time for the big guns.

Four leaf clover. Name like 'Doyle'? Amber hair? Blue-green eyes? She was definitely from some kind of Gaelic mythos, right?

And, to Felicity's delight, for a change, Danica made no effort to pick that trinket up.

Very interesting.

"Take a look," Felicity insisted.

Danica just grinned at her, "I know what a four-leaf clover looks like, Fleece, I promise. It's cute. Classic. Where would you uh... put it?"

"Oh, I don't know, I'm thinking whatever we pick out should probably get nailed right to the front door."

"Hm. Right. That would... definitely annoy any spirits trying to get in that way."

"Right?"

"Wouldn't cover the windows or the back door though."

"I'm sure I can get a few more of these. They're all over the internet."

"Mm... But, you know, evil spirits and stuff, they aren't supposed to be able to get in anyways, right? Without an invitation? Seems a little silly to try to ward off the doors anyways."

"Ah but that's the trick, isn't it? Amy's so nice, I bet she'd be naïve enough to invite *anything* in, if whatever it was gave her some big old puppy dog eyes."

Danica snickered at that and admitted that there was definitely some truth in it.

"So?" Felicity asked, " 'Maybe' pile?"

"...Yeah. That's a pretty good one."

Felicity quirked an eyebrow at that. Why would Danica play along with this? Would she really go so far in her efforts to exploit Amy and deceive Felicity that she'd even accept some anti-magic wards all over the apartment?

Or was she really so powerful that even being subjected to oppressive wards like that wouldn't be enough to make her flinch?

Felicity was a little deflated by that idea. Maybe this plan wouldn't work out... But she boldly carried on with her show-and-tell.

Next up was that flint scope she used to read that sealed note – a plain flint stone that had managed to get a hole bored in it through centuries of dripping water wear.

Again, Danica refused to pick it up.

Felicity peered at her through the hole playfully. It was *supposed to* reveal magical illusions, but she was disappointed to see it didn't have any effect on Danica's visage when she looked through. Somehow, she just looked like *Danica* underneath whatever magic she was using.

"What's that one?" the monster asked, like she didn't know.

"Flint scope! Reveals glamours, supposedly. Faerie magic. Illusions. *Hidden text*. Figured it'd be good for Amy, so she knows what she's inviting in." Felicity gestured at the front door. "Could mount it on the eyehole there."

"You sure could."

" 'Maybe' pile again?"

"...Yeah."

Danica was starting to lose the cheer in her cheeks.

She folded her hands in her lap uneasily and asked Felicity in a grim tone, "Are we... really doing this, Fleece?"

"Doing what, my dearest *Danica Llewellyn Doyle*?" A gift from her private investigator, that one.

She cringed a bit to hear her full name out loud, then bitterly chided her: "Fleece this is... not a good idea..."

"Hold on, I think you'll really like this one," Felicity said with a cruel grin.

A special acquisition from an old pioneer village's blacksmith.

She tossed it to Danica as a surprise: "Catch!"

The fear in Danica's eyes at the prospect of being touched by that old-school iron horseshoe was everything Felicity needed to see to confirm it.

Fae.

Only the fae could be that afraid of cold iron.

That afraid of cold iron and flint scopes and clover and *nothing else* in her bag of tricks.

Instead of catching it herself, Danica, moving faster than Felicity had ever seen her move—and in fact faster than she could even see at all, truly, like the instantaneous strobe of a flash photograph—brought one of the pillows on the couch in front of her like a baseball mitt to catch the dangerous charm.

She folded the pillow over it and calmly set it aside.

"What's wrong, Dani?"

"Uh. I've got like... an allergy."

"To iron?"

"Yeah."

"The... stuff in your blood. You've got an allergy to *human blood*."

"...It's different when it's pure like that. Messes up my skin."

"Okay." Felicity put a finger to her chin and gave Danica a discerning stare: "How did you know it was pure iron?"

Danica gave her an uneasy grin before she sheepishly answered, "...Good guess? What else would a good-luck horseshoe be made of, right?"

Felicity just silently glared at her to say that she was absolutely not buying it.

The grin on the beast's face dissolved in an instant. "Gods, Fleece, you're really... just... *really* set on this, aren't you?"

"Set on what, Danica?"

"You know what you're doing..."

Felicity scoffed. "I sure do. And I'm not done yet."

A hint of a scowl was growing on Danica's face. "It would be *so nice* if you were, though. Could I convince you to lay off here? Maybe we can work something out? A little... *deal?*" Her eyes flashed with a hint of excitement when she said the word – though, oddly, despite the spark of joy, she tensed up and rolled her shoulders like she was trying to shake off an uncomfortable shiver.

Felicity finally had her in a corner, pleading for cooperation. Iron was the key. She could push Danica as hard as she wanted as long as she knew she had a sturdy ward against the beast's magic.

With a cold, confident grin, she drew out the most devastating anti-fae weapon in her arsenal – a replica of an ancient ceremonial iron dagger, made deadly sharp and shiny with protective oil just like her necklace. Without a word, she held the blade out between the two of them to take in the unease in Danica's eyes before she placed it on the table with the blade facing the beast. Then she went on to continue with her attack:

"Why do we need a deal, Dani? I'm just showing you my cool charms and trinkets here. —Here, you're going to *love* this last one. Guaranteed to get any miserable mythical creatures out of Amy's life," Felicity said, pulling a blank sheet of old parchment from the bag, a calligraphy brush, and a bottle of iron-doped ink. "It's real special, this one. *Just* for you. *Absolutely* to die for."

Danica rolled her shoulders uncomfortably. "Fleece please."

The monstrous unmasked faerie in disguise watched with a growing display of horror as Felicity drew, with practiced strokes, a fragment of the creature's name. This was it. The result of weeks of labor and practice and memorization of impossibly complicated tangles of ribbons. With this interpolated slice of that complex shape, she'd be able to scare Danica into cooperating, into running off with her tail between her legs.

She asked Danica while she carefully, painstakingly prepared the detailed sigil: "You ever hear of the Barghest, Danica?"

"...I know of the Barghest, yes."

"Mhm. Intimately, I bet."

"Felicity."

"Terrible creature, that one. Mythical, of course. Fiction. Right? But boy, lots of stories, lots of the same stories, all over the place, all over time. A big terrifying black beast who offers irresistible treasures to the selfish and the desperate, only to grin and cackle in a voice that shakes your *bones* while you sign away your *everything* for *nothing*."

Silence.

"How many did you kill, Dani?"

She looked away at last, in shame.

"How many?" Felicity clutched her brush in her hand in a fit of indignant rage and demanded an answer from the beast: "Can't answer me? Can't lie? What's the number, huh?"

"The... *Barghest*... That monster killed... too many," she confirmed, cold and distant. "Way too many... I wish I could prove it to you, Fleece, but there isn't a heart in the universe that aches more than mine does for the innocent people she hurt... But... I can't tell you the number."

"How come? You forget? Lose count? So much blood dripping off your claws that it all just blends together in a sea of red?"

Danica didn't reply. She probably couldn't do it without lying or outright admitting to being a monster. And she wasn't allowed to lie, if everything Felicity read was true.

And it was true, wasn't it? The great and horrible not-so-fabled Black Dog of a thousand tales and a hundred thousand feverish nightmares was sitting and sweating right there in front of her, wasn't she? Felicity was proud she figured it out, but terrified that every stroke of her brush brought her closer to the truth that she was sitting in front of a creature that had brought perilous ruin to countless ill-prepared fools.

But she was prepared. She glanced at the deadly iron knife on the table keeping the beast at bay, and rolled her shoulders to feel the safety in the subtle weight of that iron chain on her neck. She was *safe*. She made sure. Iron was the beast's true weakness.

She returned her attention to the page and continued writing out the sigil that she could use to cast this demon out of Amy's life for good.

While she carried on, Danica huffed a little sigh and flopped back on the couch in a miserable funk.

Felicity didn't look up, but she did prod at her, "You're looking pretty calm for someone who's about to get banished."

"You're not about to banish me, Fleece, that's not how this works."

"Oh, no, no no no, you're not tricking your way out of this. You're done, Dani. It's over."

"Where'd you find that, anyways?" she asked, trying very hard to seem disinterested.

"Books."

"Yeah, I bet 'books'. You're all books." She paused for a few seconds before she offered a teasing piece of bait, "You know I really thought I got them all."

Felicity's grip on the brush tightened, almost enough to make her mess up a stroke, but she managed to stay calm. "What do you mean 'got them'?"

"Oh sorry, you're right, I should be more specific: I thought I *destroyed* all those books. Hundreds and hundreds of ancient, one-of-a-kind manuscripts, and diaries, and bundles of tragic deathbed love letters. So full of beautiful diagrams and artful initials, and so lovingly cared for for *centuries.*"

"You're trying to make me mad..."

"I guess my guy isn't always as reliable as he says he is if you managed to track down that much of it. I should call him up and try to get a refund."

"...That much of *what?*"

"You know what it is."

"Your name."

"And what would you do if it was my name, Fleece? Write me a love letter in iron ink? What's that supposed to do?"

Felicity paused between strokes to consider it. "I know how to banish you, Danica. I know the spell. The books said..."

"The books said 'rabbit's feet' and 'salt' and 'dill' and 'bread' and all sorts of stupid things. —Like, come on, *bread?* Seriously? Who thought that one up? What *insane* creature would hate *bread?*"

"...Maybe faeries have a universal gluten intolerance?"

Danica scoffed. "You're so adorable Felicity, I swear. If you weren't trying to ruin me, I would love to keep you, as a little pet, feed you old books, tell you how pretty you are and how good you are and let you pretend you're saving your best friend from a horrible monster."

"You *are* a monster."

Danica laughed at herself and brought her fingers to her forehead for a few seconds before she revealed something that no length of iron chain would have prepared Felicity for: "We're sharing a bed now, you know. Did she tell you?"

"...What... does that mean?"

"She didn't tell you," Danica echoed herself, disappointed. "Gods... I mean she didn't *have to*, but that's still a little cold... It's been a couple months already... How long do *you* usually wait to tell your best friend you're sleeping with someone?"

"...No. No she... wouldn't..." Felicity lowered her head bitterly, grinding her teeth together and snarling at Danica: "You... you fucking *monster*..."

"You think I tricked her."

"I *think* the moon's a big rock and the ocean's full of salt. I *know* you tricked—"

Felicity was startled to feel a gentle set of fingers caress her cheek and come to rest behind her ear.

Danica... the *faerie*... crossed the *iron knife*...?

A warm palm pressed into Felicity's cheek and lifted her up to draw her bitter gaze away from the page. Danica's eyes were so soft then, so powerful, so *ancient*. They glistened in the light like a thousand stars were dancing in the air between she and her. There was powerful magic in that gaze. These were the eyes that swayed a thousand witless fools into signing away their souls.

Felicity sure wasn't planning to become some witless fool tonight, but she couldn't bring herself to look away while Danica spoke into her, in words that *tasted* like the gospel truth, that thickened the air with the power and the honesty of a thousand parishioners singing in unison for the collectively unquestionable glory of their God. This was a voice that had always spoken the truth, for thousands and thousands of years. This was a voice that didn't know how to lie.

"I have never stolen from your beloved friend. I am giving her everything I have left to give. I am *sacrificing* everything for her, to protect her, to keep her close to me. I love her dearly, I love the life we share, and I will not let you take this away from me just because you're *afraid* of me, *Felicity Aurelia Vicente*."

Felicity shuddered uncomfortably when Danica gave sound to her name. Her mind flushed with heat. No one had ever... made it... *sound* like that... Sound so... *so*...

—True...?

Felicity suddenly felt weak and feverish and pathetic before this playful, earnest, towering monster.

"What are you... doing...?"

"Human names are so *shallow*, you know," she calmly explained without removing her palm from Felicity's cheek. "Your ego's so caught up in just the *sound* of it. It's cute, really. Naïve. You just... hand it out! Proudly! Give all your power to anyone who asks!"

Felicity tried to resist, to pull away from the gentle, seductive touch that was warming her cheek, but her lethargic body wasn't listening to her panicked mind.

The beast continued, with a dark look in her eyes, "I don't like doing this, Fleece."

"I bet…"

"It's not humane."

"Sure isn't…"

"I'd rather just be civil."

"What do you want…?"

"Let's make a deal."

Felicity scoffed at the idea. "Yeah. A deal. With the Black Dog. The Grinning Dagger."

She grinned at Felicity, showing off those impossibly sharp canines. "So many *books* you found!"

"I'm not making a deal with you…"

"You'll like this one," Danica cheerfully assured her.

"Bet."

"I'm going to give you my leash, Fleece. How's that sound? Hm? Want a pet? A faithful dog? If you back off – if you forget *all about this* – it's yours."

Felicity sneered at her. "I already own you, Danica…" Then she clutched the collar of her top and clawed it far enough down to show off the iron chain there. "You can't hurt me."

"Aww. Iron chain. That's cute." Danica's eyes lit up playfully when she spotted the crucifix. "Oh! Is that a cross, too? Oh my gods, I can't get over how sweet you are, Fleece. You really had no idea, did you? I thought you were just having fun with me before. You really thought I was a vampire or something? A devil?"

"Can't be too careful…"

To Felicity's horror, though, Danica proved that she had apparently failed to be careful enough, by bringing the fingers of her other hand to Felicity's neck, dragging a reticent fingertip along the oiled loops of her chain with a proud, wincing grimace. Felicity could hear the sound of Danica's skin burning – she could *smell* it, acrid and metallic and *detestably* sweet and floral. But she didn't stop caressing the chain until she had undone the clasp and freed the chain from Felicity's neck, to hold it up and marvel at it as it burned the skin of her palm.

"This is really pretty. I like the knots. Celtic, no? Thrift store? Antique shop? ...No? Oh my gods, don't tell me you commissioned this just for me. You sweetheart."

"...What the hell are you?"

Danica finally freed Felicity's cheek from the uncomfortable warmth of her palm so she could teasingly uncurl Felicity's uneasy fingers one by one and return the chain to her shaky palm in a tidy spiral.

The links had turned wretched and bright bloody red with arcane rust wherever Danica's fingers had caressed them. And when she showed off the skin of her own hand, Felicity noted with fear that the burns there were already healing away.

"It's in my blood," Danica assured her, repeating Felicity's teasing words from earlier. "So, you know, I guess it really is more like... an *allergy* now." As another arrogant show of her power, she casually plucked the not-so-deadly iron dagger from the table by the handle and held it to the light to examine the edge and the intricate inscriptions. Again, the metal caused her flesh to burn with a horrible sweet smell, but she was barely flinching from the pain.

With a cruel grimace, she explained: "It's annoying. Painful. But I'm not going to wither away from *this*—" She said with a little jab in her tongue and a quick lunge forward to press the cold razor's edge of the dagger to Felicity's vulnerable throat. When she flinched away, the beast tittered at her, then she turned the knife around in her hand to offer the hilt to Felicity with a friendly smile.

When Felicity uneasily grasped the handle and drew the blade away, Danica pinched the edge between her thumb and finger, leaving every inch of its surface red and flaked and marred with the same bloody rust that had ruined Felicity's chain.

Felicity examined the damage in horror. <u>Nothing</u>. Nothing in <u>any of her books</u> said anything about <u>this</u>.

By the time Felicity looked up, Danica was flexing her fist and opening her palm for Felicity to show off the fading burns with a teasing grin. She gave Felicity a playful warning: "Careful with that edge there. Don't want you getting tetanus or something."

Iron was useless. Truly pathetically useless.

Felicity might as well have brought a damn cardboard tube for all the good it did.

Danica shook out her gently singed hand a bit, then spoke calm and cold to Felicity:

"Let's get this over with, hm? I don't like this any more than you do – making deals. I hate this stuff with everything in me. The Barghest, the Black Dog, that legendary beast in all your books, that monster thrived on it. She hungered for it, desperately, shamelessly. And I never want to be like that thing, hurting people for nothing good.

"But this means a lot to you, doesn't it? For Amy. You'd do anything for her, wouldn't you? You'd even face off against something you're convinced is just as powerful as a god. There aren't a lot of people in the world brave as you, Fleece. Big talk. There's a lot of big talk. But that's not you, is it? I can see it in your eyes. You'd die for her. But I won't ask you to.

"So, how about we tempt the gods, together, and make a little deal to keep your best friend safe? And then you can stop trying to mess around with immeasurable powers beyond your comprehension?"

Danica finally released Felicity's body and mind from her spell and let her return to a comfortable position, kneeling across from her on the floor. She suddenly felt very, very small. She had always been small in this woman's eyes – in this *beast's* hungry gaze – hadn't she? But now she knew how little she was. An annoyance at worst.

But... an annoyance big enough to threaten the peace of the beast's life.

Yeah. Felicity might be small, but she sure wasn't nothing, even if Danica could destroy her with nothing more than the fae-poisoned syllables of her very own name.

Though... she got the feeling the only reason Danica hadn't destroyed her already is because it would make Amy cry.

"...Why do you care about her so much?" Felicity asked, pathetic, defeated. It sure felt like she was stuck here. She'd have to agree to whatever Danica's terms were, but still, it would sure be nice if she knew why all this had to happen at all.

"Why do you?" she answered with a jab of a question.

"She's everything to me. What is she to you? Some... toy? A diversion? Food? I don't get it. Why would a god need a human?"

"I'm not a god, Fleece. And whatever you think I am, you have to get it through your head that I'm not immune to pain, and loneliness, and fear. I'm scared of what's waiting for me out there, and she makes me feel like that doesn't matter. It's a gift I figured out a long time ago I can never pay back. So I'm wallowing in the bittersweet misery of it, trying to make it fair, to make her as happy as she makes me. And I think I'm doing a pretty good job, honestly. Gold medal performance, really."

Felicity clicked her tongue at that. "That doesn't sound like love to me. Sounds like *obligation*."

The beast lowered her glimmery eyes from Felicity's for a few somber seconds before she returned to her with a sad smile. "Maybe you're right. It's... hard to explain, but my family's a little messed up, and back home, debt's about as close to love as I ever had. Maybe it's not how you'd love her, but it's the best I've got to give. Maybe it's enough?"

Felicity lowered her own eyes and shook her head bitterly. That couldn't be enough, could it? Love had to be something more than debts and obligations. It had to be.

But she was struggling to figure out exactly what the difference was, between Danica's description of her devotion to Amy, and the way she felt herself when she looked in Amy's eyes and knew she'd give that woman anything in the world to make her happy again – to pay her back for all the years of happiness they shared.

Maybe Dani was right.

Maybe *obligation* was enough.

She scoffed at herself. Owned again by Danica's silver tongue. How was she so pathetic?

"You really are a twisted monster, Danica. Fine. Fine, give me your fucking leash. Tell me your stupid deal. Let's get this over with."

"Sorry Fleece. I know this sucks. But you'd never let this go, would you?"

"No."

"You'd do anything for her. To keep her safe."

"Are you really asking me that?"

"And what about to keep her happy?"

Felicity looked away bitterly.

She hated to admit it, but... if Amy really was happy, really was in love with Danica... It would be cruel to cast her out, wouldn't it? That might be even worse for Amy than just... letting things stay like this – than just letting her stay with a... 'reformed' monster.

Danica moved the parchment with the half-finished sigil on it off to the side, then waved her hand over the coffee table to summon a different sheet of paper.

With another wave of her hand, she drew ink to the surface of the page, as if it were bubbling up from deep within the pulp of the paper itself, and in only a few seconds, the ink formed into words in Danica's own handwriting.

A pact.

She lifted the paper up to read it over, then nodded to herself and turned it to face Felicity with a grim look on her face.

"For your consideration. We can change any terms you like," she said, demonstrating the fact with another wave of her hand, shifting the order of some words around without changing the meaning. The ink was alive, crawling on the page, shaped by her will.

This was her real power.

It felt somewhat underwhelming, though, after being subjugated by her mere *words* earlier.

Felicity read over the document herself to get a sense of exactly what Danica thought a good deal looked like.

The gist of it was that if Danica ever harmed Amy, then Felicity would be free to tell Amy everything, that Danica herself would answer anything about herself to Felicity's satisfaction, and that Felicity would be free to banish Danica from Amy's life forever.

"What's the catch?"

"You forget everything you think you know about what I really am," Danica said, pointing out the clause in the document, as if Felicity had missed it. "You forget that you think I'm 'dangerous'. You might even *like me* after you sign it."

"...Well let's not get carried away."

"Yeah, I won't get my hopes up, I promise. But it means you'll never be able to warn her about me, until after I've done something to hurt her. And for all you know, that first hurt might be the very last hurt she'll ever suffer."

"You could kill her before I can save her."

"Correct."

"...You're just... telling me the catch."

"I told you Fleece, I don't like doing this. I don't like hurting people. I never want to be like that monster."

"But you're cool holding someone hostage until they sign their life away for you."

"I'm not holding you hostage. But you're pushing me up against a wall here. Did you think I wouldn't push back?"

Felicity sneered at her bitterly, but she didn't have the heart to admit that she did in fact kind of hope Danica wouldn't have been able to push back, because that did sound a *little* cowardly in her head.

Danica let her shoulders fall with a little sigh before she recentered herself and tried to explain calmly: "Look, I'm not forcing you, okay?"

"Not forcing me? You're *threatening* me!"

"This isn't a threat. It's just a friendly warning. I bite. My teeth are sharp. You will bleed. If you hurt me out of some senseless jealous malice, I'm going to hurt you back. That's fair. It doesn't matter what you think I am – that's *fair*. Don't pretend you're above that. But you absolutely still have a choice about how this goes. I'm not taking that away. And I'm making it easy for you to walk away from this safely – in a way that's good for all three of us."

Felicity grimaced at the beast, and she wanted so very much to resist Danica's influence over her mind, but there wasn't any dark influence to resist. This... this was just... *words*. She wasn't using that dark name magic of hers anymore, whatever it was. She wasn't *forcing* Felicity. She was just trying to talk. And Felicity was apparently just arrogant enough to listen.

It occurred to her that Danica probably only used that power with her name *earlier* to show off that she wasn't using it *now*.

"You understand, don't you?" Danica continued in a hopeful entreaty. "If we leave things like this, none of us can be happy. You'll be miserable holding your secrets, I'll be living in fear of losing her, and when you finally crack and tell her, she'll be heartbroken – either because her best friend has turned into a jealous lunatic, or because she actually *believes* you when you tell her that her lover is some horrible irredeemable monster. No one wins like that. This is the best way. I know you're smart enough to understand that."

Felicity scoffed at the flattery.

But... she was *right*, wasn't she? If Danica really was making Amy happy, then it would be really shitty of Felicity to ruin all that. But... she couldn't just... *sit on this*. It was *way* too big to keep quiet about.

But if... she could just... *magically forget...*?

...Danica would never risk losing Amy, from the sound of it. And that meant she'd never risk hurting Amy and getting exposed by Felicity and losing this easy life of hers.

...Which meant she'd never offer a deal that would *actually* put herself at risk like that.

Something was up with this. Obviously. *Faerie.*

"...You said we're *both* tempting the gods with this deal. What do you mean?"

"It's like... monkey's paw stuff. Always some kind of horrible catch with these. You know how it is, right? After all your *diligent* research. But no book written on Earth could've told you *why*. The gods, they want to suck the misery out of these deals, find loopholes and tricks and stuff. I try to spot all the catches first, when I draw it up, before any surprises come up. I'm good at it – best there is, really – you lucked out with me – but even I can't see everything. This could just as easily screw *me* over." She paused for a second before she scoffed bitterly at herself. "Wouldn't be the first time."

"Okay. Well, what's the catch for you, then? if you're so smart about this."

"Oh, yeah, mine's easy. I'm leaving you a *naïvely* generous definition there. What's it mean to 'hurt' someone? Who knows what counts there? I might just slip up and say something insensitive that hits her a little too hard. Might turn on the light too fast and make her squint in *mild discomfort*. And then that's it. I'm done. Completely at your mercy."

"...Why would you leave that in there, then?"

"Because. Just... because. You need to know she's safe, right? I get it."

"...Okay. Well, if you're going to be so *accommodating*, then I want to change something."

Danica took the contract back and dutifully twinkled her fingers over the ink in preparation to make Felicity's changes. "Brand new car? Kitchen set? Library of Babel? Whatever you want, Fleece. We'll make it work. Go for it."

"I want to know *before* you hurt her."

Danica's hand didn't move. The ink didn't change.

Apparently this wasn't going to be as easy as she was pretending it would be.

"You want to foresee the future," she echoed in grim summary. "That's... a *dangerous* one, Fleece. Doesn't usually end well." She closed her eyes and hummed to herself for a second before she shook her head and confirmed to herself, "...*Never*, actually, when I think about it..."

"Don't care. The whole *point* of this is to keep her safe. I don't want to come around crying after you've already bitten her head off. I want a week's notice; I want to know what's going to happen; and I want to get my memory back as soon as I know, so I can get rid of you properly before you become a real problem."

"Okay but... Ugh... Fleece... That's not how it... *works*. Humans can't *move* worldlines. You can't change the shape of the universe like that. You're on rails. Even if you find out ahead of time, that won't do anything to save her. It might even make it worse. It might make *you* the cause. —In fact, it will *almost certainly* do that."

"The hell is a worldline?"

"Uh. Hm... How much do you know about physics?"

"Not much. Amy's the science wizard."

"Atoms? You know atoms?"

"Sure. Matter of the universe."

"Great. Electrons?"

"Little bits of atoms."

"Right. Negative charge? Yes? Okay you get it. So there's this guy named John Wheeler like a century ago. Knew about electrons and these other things called positrons. Same size as an electron, same number of them in the universe, but they're positive."

"...Why... does a horrible magical monster... know about physics..."

"Science is fascinating! Listen for a second, gods. So Wheeler's got this idea: What if there's <u>only one</u> eternal electron in the whole universe? One electron that goes back and forth through all time, that pierces *this moment* in time, and every moment in time, over and over again like a needle and thread through a quilt with an infinite number of sheets. Going one way, it's negative. Going the other, it's positive."

"...And that's a worldline. The electron thread thing?"

"Basically. Threads of possibility, stitched unmovable into the eternal immutable weave of space and time. He was wrong about the *electrons*, but the idea's right. And <u>you</u> can't change the path of that thread, Fleece. It's already going where it's been and coming from where it's going to be."

"...Hold on, why are you emphasizing the 'you' there?"

Danica waved her hand dismissively. "Don't worry about it."

"I'm worrying about it."

"Well, you'll just have to wait. Ask me again if you beat me at this deal, I'll tell you whatever you want to know about all my secrets before you get rid of me."

—So... <u>something</u> could change fate...

But never a human...? Or... never <u>Felicity</u>?

Felicity looked over the contract and considered the weight of it for a few long seconds.

What good would it do, to know about a tragedy that couldn't be avoided? Not much good for the universe, or for Amy, but at least Felicity would be able to convince herself she really did everything she could to prevent it.

And fighting fate always worked out great in the stories. She'd figure something out if it came to it. —Especially if she had unlimited access to all of Danica's carefully guarded faerie secrets, right?

"...Alright. Well, whatever, I don't care if I can't change it. I still want to know before it happens. Put it in or I'm not signing it."

Danica sighed and slumped her shoulders. "Okay. I warned you, though. I did. You can't be mad at me later."

She grumbled to herself miserably about it while she waved her hand over the contract and shifted the ink to change the rules to Felicity's satisfaction. Then she handed it back for a final review.

Felicity read it over a few times before she cautiously confirmed: "So... So I just... sign this, and I forget."

"You sign it and you forget and I'm at your mercy – to keep Amy safe. And with this, we can *all* be happy."

Felicity closed her eyes and took a deep breath before she slowly exhaled and, at last, gave her affirmative on it: "...Okay—" She put the pact down on the coffee table face-down, then gave Danica a discerning glare. "—After I ask her."

"Ask her what?"

"You said you make her happy. You think I'm stupid enough to just... *believe* that?"

Danica smiled and shook her head, laughing to herself. "Gods my life would be so, *so* much easier if you were, though."

"I'll ask her tonight. You go out, grab a drink, have a night on the town, leave us alone so I can talk to her. And... if she says yes, I'll sign your deal in the morning." Felicity put her palm flat on the contract and glared at Danica. "But if she says no, I'm nailing every clover and flint scope and horseshoe I have to every surface in this shitty apartment – with iron nails – and that won't be the end of it. I won't rest—"

"—I know."

"Good."

"...You won't tell her?" Danica cautiously confirmed, eyeing the tabled contract uneasily.

"Yeah, no. Really don't want to get hit with that... *name* thing again."

"Yeah. Sorry about that."

"Not forgiven."

"That's fair. I will absolutely do it again if you cross me."

"Great. Glad we're all on the same page here with the betrayals and revenge stuff."

Danica smiled at Felicity warmly, then stood up from the couch to dust herself off and headed to the front door to get dressed.

"Wait. You're leaving already?"

"Aw, Fleece, you gonna miss me? Need someone to glare balefully at? I know I'm pretty, but you're making me shy with all this attention."

For a moment, Felicity felt sick to admit that she did, in fact, want Dani to stay. She had so many questions and theories and... she was... *scared*... of all this, honestly. It was so far beyond the kind of trouble she'd ever dreamed she'd be getting into. And for some reason, it felt like Danica, that demonic fae beast, was the only one in the world who could possibly put that fear to rest.

The Grinning Dagger was really twisting her way into Felicity's head.

She shook her head no and waved Danica off dismissively.

When the beast was gone, Felicity put all her trinkets back in the duffel bag, then sat on the couch and picked up the contract to read it over and consider exactly how bad the worst-case scenarios were.

Who was more likely to get screwed here?

...Or were they both going to be screwed 'when the gods came for their misery'?

—You can't change fate...

Felicity wondered, after finding out tonight that so much of the lore in her books had been wrong, if it was even true that dread fae beast Danica Llewellyn Doyle couldn't lie.

She rolled her fingers on the back of the page while she held it, then, at last, she hid it away in her duffel bag, and returned to her half-finished sigil to fill in the rest of the lines.

Danica had definitely been scared of this thing. Felicity wasn't stupid enough to get fooled by her coy deflection. And she wasn't about to throw away a trump card in a situation like this.

⁂

When Amy got home and found Felicity alone on the couch watching some TV, she casually looked around the corner towards her bedroom and asked, "Where's Nic... a?"

"Nica?"

"Da-nica. Sorry. Choked on my spit there."

"...She said she was meeting some friends for drinks. 'Don't wait up.'"

Amy quirked an eyebrow at that, then pulled her phone out of her pocket to check for a message. Finding none, she let out a little sigh, then returned her attention to Felicity with a tired accusation:

"Did you kick her out? Are you two *still* fighting?"

"No! No. She just wanted to give us some time to catch up."

"...Okay. Because you *told me* you were going to be nice to her."

"I'm being nice!"

—Lies lies lies. Shame on you Felicity.

"...Alright. Well. Thank you. —Coffee?"

"It's like 10PM Ames."

"...Right, right. You're one of those people who likes to *sleep* at night. Hm... so... wine?"

"Oh my God *yes* please."

—*Ca~ber~net Sau~vi~gnon. Bless your heart Amy.*

The two of them snacked on charcuterie and got lost in a few glasses of wine, listening to a carefully curated sample of the couple dozen records Amy dropped in front of Felicity to choose from.

Amy was finally talking openly to Felicity about her miserable warehouse work, though she refused to complain about it as much as it was obviously owed. She *did* gravely mention tonight that she wasn't sure she was going to last much longer at that particular job, but when Felicity asked, with hope in her heart, if that meant Amy was planning to find better work, she just assured Felicity with a dismissive wave of her hand that she was fine working at another warehouse after everything went to shit.

She distracted Felicity from that misery by chatting at length about Danica. She bragged about the spicy pickles on the platter when Felicity complimented them – better than storebought – homemade by the beast herself just last week – and, admittedly, delicious. — Though Felicity nearly choked when she realized she was technically eating fae food, and decided to avoid the tempting treat for the rest of the evening.

Somehow, that topic led into a little show-and-tell with Amy's freshly mended jean jacket, the one the two of them had gleefully stolen together in their high school days, the one that was previously covered in charming, awkwardly stapled and half-dangling patches that were so very *Amy*. She was proudly showing off the new lining, which was covered in arcane symbols and runework that Felicity recognized from some of the dangerous books she'd been reading lately chasing the Dog down, but that Amy clearly just thought were very pretty. And now, every seemingly unwelcome hole in the denim that showed the age and experience of the jacket was darned with beautiful weaves and embroidery – Danica's – and every patch was untidily sewn down – Amy's proud handiwork, done under the *occasionally* frustrated tutelage of that dear and talented beast.

"I'm terrible at this," she said, drawing a tender fingertip along the edge of a skull patch, adorned with uneven stitches and half a dozen stray threads. "But she *refuses* to give up on me."

And *that* led into Amy's gushing adoration of all of the impressive charity work Danica was up to lately in her spare time – news to Felicity. Shocking news. What was she up to? More trickery, no?

Apparently her latest project involved cajoling her knitting club into putting together warm, water-resistant blankets for people stuck living outdoors in tents and doorways.

It was too much for Felicity to endure. That light in Amy's eyes grew brighter and brighter with every word. This ridiculous, endless praise of that vile murderous creature was making Felicity sick to her stomach – that Amy had been so... so... *sold* on Danica's trickery.

Felicity changed the subject to get back on Amy's work, on her research this time. And she looked much happier chatting about her research than about her doomed warehouse gig—obviously. She told Felicity that her results were really promising lately. Everything about the work had been smooth as silk since Felicity last had a chance to talk about it with her. Even the kiln was behaving, she said with a grin.

And, apparently, she was also working on some top-secret project that she absolutely glowed to hint at, even though she refused to provide any details.

"Tell you once it's done," she said with a drunken grin. "Promise. — God and Nicole's been such a sweetheart about it."

"Nicole?"

"Sorry! Sorry. Danica. Sorry."

"...Nicole?"

"It's uh. A nickname, I guess. Sorry. *Danica's* such a sweetheart. She's been helping me out in the lab just for fun. Works for food. And for other fun... *favors*," she added with a coy, dozy smirk.

Felicity grimaced at the poorly enigmatized act. Amy absolutely wasn't being as coy as she was trying to be after a few glasses of wine got settled in her. Why wasn't she just being honest and *telling* Felicity about the fact that she and Danica were sleeping together? Why keep it a secret if she was so *happy* about it?

—Did you just... forget about me, Ames?

At last, though, Felicity had a proper chance to confirm Danica's doubtful claim: "You two are... kind of close these days, huh?"

Amy cringed a bit and held her tongue. She stared at her wine glass for a few seconds, rotating it awkwardly back and forth while she put her words together.

At last she asked, sheepishly: "...I'm being stupid aren't I?"

"Yeah. You're being a little stupid Ames."

Amy put her glass down and clasped her hands together like she was pleading with Felicity. "Okay listen. I know you've got reservations about Dani, I know our situation's kind of weird, but I promise I put a lot of thought into this. I promise. I need you to promise me you won't freak out about this."

Felicity nodded grimly. "Go ahead."

"...We're together now."

"Yeah."

"You knew??"

"I mean. Amy, the way you've been talking about her... Yeah, it's pretty obvious, really." Felicity sighed. It really was obvious. Even the last time she was here, months ago, planting that tracker in Danica's coat, there was something different about how Amy looked at Dani. So stupid of Felicity to miss it... "How long?" she asked, trying her very best to be pleasant and encouraging about this miserable confirmation.

"A couple months, I think? I don't remember... —Actually... I think it might've been Valentine's Day? That's so corny, god, I didn't even think about that..."

So Danica wasn't lying, then.

Only a couple months... God, if Felicity had just... done something sooner...

"You didn't tell me?" she asked, doing a pretty bad job hiding the hurt in her voice.

"I wasn't sure it was real! —I mean... Okay, I knew it was *real*, but, I don't know, you know how it is. I wanted to make sure. I didn't want to freak you out."

"...She really loves you?"

Amy nodded with a grin. "She's so good to me, Fleece. So supportive. She pushes me in all the right ways, makes me feel so... alive. Worth something. Worth so... *much*. I owe her so much. And she makes me smile. Every day. —God, it's so embarrassing: I was crushing on her for *months* before we hooked up. And she's so *beautiful*, my god. She was *torturing* me. It's not fair. I should get a fucking *medal* for holding back that whole time, don't you think?"

She placed her fingers on Felicity's wrist and caught her eyes, showing off those big beautiful brown irises of hers that always melted Felicity whenever she got this close. Those eyes were so full of warmth and joy tonight in a way Felicity hadn't seen since high school, with so much light in them that Felicity could swear for a moment they had the same impossible twinkling in them as Danica's unholy eyes.

She spoke to Felicity like she was pleading for something.

—Forgiveness? ...A blessing?

"I just... I can't even believe this happened. I sure didn't do anything to deserve this. I keep expecting to wake up and find out it was all a dream, or she's just *gone* or something. I mean she just showed up one day out of nowhere, right? And she was always talking about it before, how she hates staying in one place too long. —God, she's gonna just disappear one day, I know it... But for now? This is so good. I can't believe how lucky I am. She's such a *gift*."

Amy was grinning like a giddy child confessing a crush. *Months* in love already, getting all that honeymoon stuff out of her system, and *still* she looked so *stupid* about it...

Felicity let out a little sigh, then gave Amy a genuine smile and assured her, "You absolutely deserve this, Ames. You deserve to be happy. —And, you know, I've seen how she looks when she talks about you. That's not the look of someone who's just going to disappear on you. You're... *obviously* a gift to her too." She reached out and rested the tips of her fingers on the back of Amy's hand. "I'm really... happy for you, Ames. —But if she ever does *anything* to hurt you, I'm going to gut her."

Amy let out a hard snort of a laugh. "Okay, Miss *'I'm Being So Nice'*. I'll let her know she's on thin ice."

"Make sure you do. I'm not joking – and it's only fair that she's ready for her grisly fate if she screws this up."

Amy nodded solemnly. "I will absolutely sic you on her if she turns out to be some horrible monster. I promise. But I can't even imagine how. She's so sweet to me—to *everyone*. I've never seen her hurt a soul. You don't have to worry."

Felicity clenched her teeth until her molars creaked and subtly shifted around on her jaw, but she swallowed what she wanted to say.

It was time to let it go.

All of it.

Months of work.

She had been so sure Danica was going to hurt Amy – so sure all of this was part of some grand scheme of hers to steal Amy's soul or something.

But that didn't matter anymore, did it? Scheme or not, there was no way Felicity could take this joy away from Amy now, no way she could snuff the light in her eyes – not when she was so happy.

—*Danica. Maybe she really <u>couldn't</u> lie.*

...But... What did she say that time? At Atomic Slice? Her biggest lie...? The lie Amy <u>still</u> believed...?

...I'll stay?

After Amy helped Felicity get the bed pulled out of the couch and said goodnight with a cheerful hug that ached Felicity's heart with nostalgia and bitter jealousy, Felicity found herself once again sitting and suffering in silence in Amy's miserable living room – which, tonight, suddenly felt... a lot *less* miserable, for Amy.

Danica tried to be quiet coming in, but Felicity was still wide awake with her thoughts when she got back.

"I'm ready," Felicity said, grim and quiet into the dark.

It took Danica a few seconds to reply, then she told Felicity to close her eyes before she turned on a light and invited her to sit at the kitchen table to sign the contract with her.

There was one more change Felicity needed, though.

" 'Hurt <u>or</u> leave'," she insisted. "—And I want two weeks. One's not enough."

Danica hesitated for a moment before she confirmed: "You sure about that Fleece? I thought you *wanted* me to leave."

"What I want is for Amy to be happy. And she clearly needs you for that now. So you get <u>one</u> <u>warning</u>, Dani: If you try to leave her, I'm going to hunt you down and wrap you in the thickest, coldest iron chains I can find while I figure out how to make you pay."

Danica sure didn't look happy about it, but she dutifully waved her hand over the document to command the ink to accommodate Felicity's demands.

Then the two of them started to sign the pact.

But Felicity wasn't content with the names on the document.

Something felt off.

"Amy doesn't... call you Danica, does she?"

"No, why?"

"...Nicole. *Nicole Doyle*, right?"

Danica subtly twinged half her face in discomfort when she heard Felicity say it. "...That's right. But... no one else—"

"—Put that name too. AKA. I don't want you squirming out of this one based on some weird... faerie... nickname bullshit."

This contract is a binding agreement between the Promisee _Felicity Aurelia Vicente_ and the Promisor _Danica Llewellyn Doyle (a.k.a. Nicole Doyle)_ concerning the person known to the Promisee as _Amaira Geneviève Beausoleil_ (Amy).

The Promisor hereby swears to never hurt or leave Amy. In exchange, all of the Promisee's knowledge and suspicion about the Promisor's secrets will be sealed away.

If the Promisor breaches this promise by hurting or leaving Amy:

1. The Promisee will be informed, two weeks prior, by way of the ringing of the Silver Bell (to be provided to the Promisee upon signing this pact), that the Promisor has failed in this obligation.

2. The Promisee's sealed knowledge will be unsealed.

3. The Promisor will be compelled to answer, honestly and without obfuscation, to the Promisee's satisfaction, any questions about the Promisor's nature.

4. The Promisee may command the Promisor to exit, without exception or delay, Amy's life, forever.

This contract will remain in effect, without exception or recourse, until the end of either signatory's life.

Danica Llewellyn Doyle (a.k.a Nicole Doyle)
Promisor

Felicity Aurelia Vicente
Promisee

The very instant the ink dried solid, the document triplicated itself – one copy for Felicity, one for Danica, and a third – the original – that disappeared into shimmering thin air.

Felicity wanted to ask about it, but the moment it disappeared, she forgot why that was even strange at all.

Reading over the contract, it seemed almost… silly. Whimsical. Childish. What did it even mean? She'd remember something about Danica? What could she possibly have forgotten? She barely knew the woman. Just that Amy was head over heels for her, and as much as it hurt to see that, it was what made Amy happy, and Felicity wasn't about to do anything to ruin that.

That night, on that remarkably comfortable couch-bed in Amy's living room, in Felicity's dreams, she saw a strange… symbol? Or… a rune circle? A sigil maybe? When she woke, she tried to draw it out. It reminded her of something she had been researching for a few months – some mythical creature that kept showing up in a bunch of fascinating books of folklore, a creature that she was certain she'd tracked down some complicated unspeakable multidimensional *name* for – though the idea of a name having *dimensions* at all seemed extremely strange.

Like, what, would you just… stack the letters on top of each other or something? How could you even read it like that?

When she went to borrow Amy's shower, she found the beautiful iron necklace she'd gotten for herself had sadly lost its crucifix, replaced with a charming florally formed and ornately etched Silver Bell that refused to ring no matter how she shook it or struck it. A gift from Danica, she vaguely remembered from the night before.

She must've had more to drink than she remembered.

According to the childish agreement she and Danica signed, this Bell would warn her if something bad was going to happen to Amy, though she couldn't imagine how. It felt superstitious, but, somehow, she knew it was true – like staying away from faerie circles in the woods – so she made sure to keep that Bell on her neck at all times, and to keep that contract carefully guarded in her document safe at home.

She was startled to find, when she cracked open that safe in her closet, that it contained a couple of strange notes – one of which was *sealed shut* with a frustratingly familiar sigil.

—What was that? And why did it feel so... important?

᪥

A week later, Virgil informed Felicity that he was about halfway done one of the documents she had asked him to translate. —Urgently, she had insisted, apparently, from the most recent installment's invoice – though she couldn't imagine why she cared so much about it.

He sent her a copy of the partial translation to read over to assess the quality of the work. The fragments weren't especially enlightening.

...come home...

...renegotiate...

[Some string of numbers.]

Your human will suffer.

She didn't really know what to make of it, entirely out of context – though the clarity and confidence of that final sentence was kind of ominous.

When she asked Virgil about where it came from, he thought she was joking.

"Miss V, you've been on me for months about this. Don't tell me you forgot."

"...Sorry, uh... Having a senior moment. Remind me?"

"Not much to remind you about. You were very hush hush about the project. You just told me to put everything at the highest priority for triple pay – this letter and the torn page from December, and the three manuscripts you gave me in February. —Which by the way has been an absolutely confounding exercise, to split five ways my undivided attention."

The document in her hands – the letter – was obviously a copy of a copy from the smudgy artifacts fuzzing up the original text.

"Where's the original?"

Virgil shrugged and shook his head at her. "I've only ever had the copy. ...Are you really okay, Miss V?"

She brought her hand to her sternum to clutch the precious Silver Bell hanging from her iron necklace and thought back to the silly terms of the contract she'd signed with Danica when she got the uselessly unringable little thing.

What exactly did she get 'sealed away'?

"…Just… keep working at it, Verge. I think I'll need it later…"

Yet another week later, Felicity got a call from some old woman asking about a page missing from a book. It was that old woman in that mansion-turned-apartments back home. She'd completely forgotten.

It was a hassle making the trek for nothing else, but she *had* agreed to give the page over if those books the old woman gave her helped out with her research – and from the look of her notes, it sure seemed like the books had been helpful, so she had no reason to hold the page hostage anymore.

"Did you find everything you were looking for, dear?" the old woman asked her gently, with a warm serpentine smile, as she plucked the page from Felicity's fingers.

The woman's strange eyes captivated Felicity. She was. *Old*. Older than her dear *lola*. By a lot. And it felt like something was *slithering* in the depths of those unwavering pupils.

Felicity uneasily nodded yes, but she didn't elaborate. That woman gave her the creeps, and she was happy to be done with her.

She stayed overnight with that fun slightly-more-than-one-night-stand barista from the café across from the old woman's apartment.

Strangely, the delicious young woman *also* asked if Felicity had found what she was looking for. Apparently, she'd been on a whole braggadocious quest the last time the two of them hooked up.

"What was I looking for?" she asked curiously, between warm kisses on the sweet, deliciously soft skin of the barista's breasts.

"Mmm… keep doing that…" the woman cooed, digging her fingers into Felicity's skull. It took her a few long writhing seconds before she realized Felicity was waiting for an answer. She dozily answered, "Something about your friend's roommate I think…? Did you forget? Silly. Are you *really* a genius resear… cher…? Hey…? Hey, don't stop… Aury? What did I say?"

Felicity withdrew an inch from the barista's stiff nipple, a thick trail of saliva leading to her dangling tongue, stunned still and silent while she tried to make sense of those words.

Amy. Danica. The books. The old woman. The… the Witch…? …A… dog?? Was that… Was that *something*?

"Aury?"

Felicity's mind blanked. Like waking from a dream. She had apparently zoned out while enjoying the taste of this rare snack of a woman. She muttered a dazed apology, then returned to her meal while the barista guided her head with clutching fingers and seductive moans.

In the morning, Felicity joyously reclaimed her long-lost lingerie and left the woman with a slightly too intimate kiss, then returned to the highway and on to her apartment.

When she tried to play the trip over in her head, she felt some inarticulable sense of regret – a feeling that normally accompanied a night of heavy drinking, and *not* a mostly-sober evening trading sweat, sex, and saliva with a beautiful woman.

But no matter how hard she tried, she couldn't find anything amiss about the evening, so she just resolved to put it out of her head. If it was important, she'd remember later.

&

A few days later, on her computer, Felicity stumbled across a program that was built around a three-dimensional model of a tangle of ribbons. There were a lot of useless artifacts in her notebooks and on her computer from the last few months that she couldn't make good sense of, but she knew what *this* was, at least. After all, it took a *lot* of work putting it together.

But like Virgil's translations, she couldn't remember *why* it was so important – just that she was compiling a bunch of information from *dozens* of books about some… creature? A demon? A mythological dog? Something like that.

This tangle of ribbons wasn't just pretty art. She knew that. It was a *name*. A name with *dimensions*.

She pulled a little scrap of paper out of her pocket. Something she'd been keeping close to her since that last visit with Danica and Amy – the strange sigil from her dream that night.

She scanned it into the computer and told the system to shove it into the ribbony model wherever it was supposed to go.

```
Line 387: Error: Array index out of bounds:
keyframe = keyframes[-1];
```

—Useful message. Lazy dev.

When she got the programmer to explain the error properly,

apparently it meant the sigil couldn't fit into the model. Didn't line up with anything.

So.

Different name?

Or... not a name at all, more likely, right?

Which made sense. It was just a random fragment of a weird dream. It probably wasn't even related.

She spent a lot of time after that, turning the frozen tangle of ribbons in the simulation over and over and over again. It felt so familiar that it was driving her nuts, but she couldn't find the clarity of mind to put together why.

But, useless as it was for *anything* related to her thesis, she couldn't bring herself to delete it.

She could feel it, like dire, *incontrovertible* superstition:

She'd need it later.

Pros and Cons Don't Really Matter When Your Life Is on the Line, but It's Nice to Have a List of Reasons for Your Suffering, Isn't It?

Nicole was slouched forward on the couch, waving her hand back and forth over the coffee table. The air shimmered under her palm. With every stroke to the right, she pulled the last vial of tar in Ravi's possession out of its hiding place to hear its vile influence on her mind and feel the uncomfortable heat radiating through the glass, then disappeared it back where it came from with every stroke to the left.

She had snuck out of bed an hour ago, wiggled out of Ravi's sweet grasp. Her guts were all twisted up and she couldn't stand to stay in bed like this.

Henry had finally gotten back to her on those names – the scientists on the redacted documents in that database of Carrie's. Henry got back to her with... nothing.

They were gone.

All of them.

Academia forgot their names.

No papers in archives.

No books on shelves.

No records of professorship at their respective universities.

Carrie's words echoed in her mind: *'Ever hear of Terrance Paul?'*

Swipe to the right, to feel the heat again, to feel how dangerous this stuff was just to be near. And not just for her, apparently, but for Ravi and Carrie too. Whoever was making these scientists disappear like this would be coming for them next if she let them continue down this reckless path.

As if Nicole didn't have enough to worry about with keeping Ravi safe from her malicious cousins – practically a fulltime job now, and still one she was barely able to keep up with.

She sighed and swiped her hand to the left, to feel the relief of sending the vial out of sight.

She could disappear it. This vial, and every vial Ravi ever had the stupidity to bring home again. But that would only make Ravi more curious.

And... what hope did she have of finding a cure for this stuff without Ravi working on this? Nicole couldn't do any of this work on her own. Angie was right. This disease, the darkness, it was untouchable – by her at least. *Iron and malice and greed* – whatever that meant, it seemed to be an accurate assessment. Outside the glass, the tar sizzled the skin on her fingertips like raw iron when she brought it near. Behind the glass, it was uncomfortable. And in Ravi's shoulder, it was... challenging. The blacker Ravi's cysts became, the more unbearable it became to brush against them. She learned that the hard way a few times already while the two of them were having fun in bed. The slightest graze left Nicole's skin feeling shredded up for days with invisible wounds. —Though, judging by the way Ravi twisted and yelped at the touch, it was definitely worse for them. At least Nicole could avoid the pain by being careful. Ravi? It was in them. Every day.

She couldn't do anything about this illness on her own. But it was too dangerous for Ravi to get any closer to this. It was just too dangerous! She couldn't stand it, if Ravi just disappeared one day, knowing she could have done something to save them.

But there was no way Ravi would just quit. Not now. Not after Nicole had encouraged them for so long. Not after their obsession had grown so deep.

And even before Nicole got them set on this unorthodox research, Ravi already had a... strange obsession with their extractions. They explained it once, why they had been so keen on collecting this stuff even though they weren't doing anything with it for so long. They explained, though Nicole didn't quite understand it, that this disease was their 'bear' and that they 'weren't done wrestling with it'.

Whatever it meant, it was important enough that it kept Ravi going. They had started to get *excited* for their impending agony – as long as it meant they would get another round in the ring with that bear.

How could Nicole stand in the way of that fight?

Swipe to the right. The vial appeared again and spun around on its base until it stopped, standing perfectly upright with a satisfying clap of the glass against the wood.

Holding the little mislabeled vessel between her thumb and finger, it didn't nettle up her hand like the stuff inside Ravi did, but it was hot and heavy as lead in her hand. It felt wrong in the world like nothing else she'd ever seen. She hated to be near it.

She had resolved to endure it, though it felt like the contents of the vial were inviting her to dive into some darkness she couldn't understand.

But what was the point of enduring it if Ravi was just going to get disappeared for it?

"Nicole?" Ravi sleepily called out to her from the hallway.

She panicked and fumbled the vial, sending it flying in the air. In a desperate attempt to save it, she waved her hand over it midair and tried to slip the glass back through the Aether, back into Ravi's desk, but she was in such a rush she couldn't be 100% sure it landed right back where she got it.

Hopefully they wouldn't notice.

"Hey, you're really *not* dead," Ravi said, rounding the corner into the room, with a hint of relief in their voice. "Cool. My brain is an idiot." They let out a quiet yawn. "You're up so late. It's like 3 in the morning. You okay?"

"Yeah! Yes. Just great." Nicole didn't know where to put her hands. She was rapidly shifting them back and forth between adjusting her baggy t-shirt and flattening out her bare thighs like there was a wrinkled pair of pants on them. "I was. Uh. Just... hanging out. Watching something."

Ravi looked at the TV, which was dark and silent.

"—And now I'm reflecting! Just thinking. Big thoughts. Complicated themes. A whole lot to digest."

—Great. Doing great, Nicole. How the hell are you going to get out of this without lying?

"What show?"

"Um. Might have been... T...twilight?"

"Twilight. The vampire movie."

"No! No, uh, what's that one you like? Twilight... Space?"

"The Twilight... *Zone?*"

"Yes! With the guy. 'We control the horizontal.' Spooky. Deep."

"That's *The Outer Limits* I think."

Half-truths, partly deflected questions, and willful ignorance. She was really balancing on the very edge of the truth here, and it was making her skin crawl.

She clenched her teeth and gave Ravi an awkward smile. Maybe if she just looked cute enough.

They raised an eyebrow and smirked at her. "Nikki, babe, if you were jacking it in here or something, I do not care."

"I was *not!* I was..." *Wait, that was actually a pretty good excuse, wasn't it? And the 'or something', what a perfect out. Bless you, Ravi.* "Okay, fine, you got me. I'm a real deviant. Can't keep my hands off myself tonight. Color me red."

Ravi yawned again and waved their hand dismissively before leaning into a big stretch. "It's fine, I'm not judging. I'll just knock next time," they added with a playful grin.

Nicole *really* wanted to switch focus here. "Did I wake you up? I was trying to be quiet."

Ravi laughed quietly. "Yeah, kind of. My dreams got all freaked out about you falling out of a plane or something." They looked at the ceiling while they put the details back together. "I was diving after you. I kept missing and missing right up until we hit the ground. I think I grabbed for you for real in the bed and you weren't there and I got all panicky or something."

Ravi shook their head and scoffed at themself. "You know, I never thought I'd get so messed up by an empty bed. What have you done to me?"

"You never loved someone enough to miss them?"

Ravi thought about that playful question for a lot longer than Nicole expected them to, and then they didn't even answer it.

"Anyways, thanks for not being a pancake on the ground. Huge relief."

"Yeah for sure, Ravi Bee. I'm here for all your not-being-a-pancake needs." Nicole gave Ravi a little salute. "Service with a smile. Happy to help."

They returned the playful gesture, then groggily staggered into the kitchen and offered to make Nicole a sandwich.

"Uh, yeah, sure, if you're making one anyways. You're not going back to bed?"

"Uh big 'no' there. When I close my eyes, I'm back in the dream, smashing into the ground, so, need some time to chill out."

They put an unevenly assembled, entirely unseasoned tuna sandwich in Nicole's hands – no plate – and sat down on the couch next to her.

Ravi ate in silence, clearly deep in thought about something, and Nicole joined them in that quiet. Not so much out of solidarity as it was because she kind of didn't know how to talk about *anything* right now, since her mind was stuck on trying to find the perfect words to explain to Ravi how dangerous what they were doing might be.

And while she was stuck juggling those words in her thoughts, they were getting all jumbled up at the front of her mind, trying to force their way out and blocking any other thoughts from forming there. She was really hoping Ravi would bring up literally anything else to talk about.

And unfortunately, it seemed that, tonight, Nicole might be destined to get everything she wished for.

With a little huff of a sigh, Ravi tossed their half-eaten sandwich on the coffee table, then leaned back on the couch, pressing their palms into their eyes. After a moment of that distressed pose, they cleared their throat.

"So. Uh. I didn't want to talk about this but it's not going to go away so let's just get it out there. I lost my job."

Oh.

Well, that was bad. That was extremely bad.

Nicole's mind immediately started calculating how much stuff she could sell, how many people she knew who might have a gig to offer, how many loans she might be able to persuade a bank to give her, how to run a casino scam...

Nicole ran those calculations while she waited in silence for Ravi to continue.

They took a few deep breaths before they explained it. No eye contact.

"I don't know what's been going on with me lately, but for like… god, months now… I've been dropping stuff a lot, tripping into people, crushing boxes under forklifts, tipping pallets. Somehow I even jammed up a conveyer so bad that everything had to stop for a few hours – *multiple times.*"

Nicole gritted her teeth bitterly. Her cousins at work, surely. Gods, she couldn't just hang out in the warehouse, though – and her cousins clearly knew that.

Nicole wanted to assure them it was nothing to be ashamed of, to lose their job. It happens. But that wasn't really something Ravi would be able to wrap their head around right now, and Nicole knew it. To them, this was something to be ashamed of, and that wasn't going to be up for debate.

So instead, she just sidled over and took their hand in hers. They leaned their head on her shoulder before they continued with a sigh:

"So, the last straw, I was on a forklift, just to get something out of the way real quick, and I toppled a whole fucking shelf. Hundreds of boxes full of thousands of dollars of stuff, *destroyed.* Which would be *bad* if I had a forklift license, with insurance. But I *do not* have a forklift license. And I *do not* have insurance. So, it was pretty far beyond bad. I'm fired and they're suing me for everything I broke."

"No."

"Yeah."

"How much?"

"They're saying 130k."

"*No!*"

"Yeah."

"…And you don't have that, obviously."

"I do not."

"What are you… going to… Gods, can I help?"

"I don't know, do you have 130k I can borrow?"

"No…"

"Can you *get* 130k?"

—You sure could.

Nicole wasn't quite done with her calculations, but… There was one way to do it without lifting a finger. With the right kind of deal, she could get anything. If she could entice the company's lawyer maybe. Bribe the judge? Yeah, she could get it, or she could make it go away, but it would be... *expensive*, in different ways. Faerie trades were always... dangerous. And the more valuable the trade, the greater the danger.

"...Not... *simply*," she replied.

Silence filled the room.

Nicole's thoughts filled the silence.

—*Your human will suffer.*

Niede's grim warning.

Maybe she should've taken that warning more seriously – you know, instead of selfishly giving in to every one of her stupid childish little whims, instead of indulging herself in the joy of Ravi's love, instead of doing literally <u>nothing</u> at <u>all</u> to prevent whatever catastrophe was coming.

She had convinced herself it would be better for them if she was *here*. She could protect them here. She <u>could</u>.

But apparently, she was pretty good at deceiving herself, and pretty terrible at being a bodyguard, and even worse at being a good lover, for putting Ravi in danger like this in the first place.

It was too late to change her mind now, though, wasn't it! If she left now, she'd be leaving Ravi to deal with that debt alone, to deal with the fallout of *her* bad decisions. And she couldn't bring herself to do that.

She broke this. She could fix this. She <u>could</u>.

"—I can try though," she offered, squeezing Ravi's hand to assure them she'd do everything she could to keep them afloat.

And she would try. The human way. Working, gambling, stealing, selling what little she had. Each had its own price, but none of those ways would cost so much as the interest the universe would demand from a faerie's trade. Using that kind of magic to help Ravi would be a terrible idea, and would almost certainly make things worse.

Ravi took a few breaths to sincerely consider Nicole's offer, but in the end, they quietly turned her down. The faintest hint of a grateful smile flashed on Ravi's face before returning to a grim look that matched the gravity of the situation.

"I was kidding, Nikki. You can't bail me out. This isn't your problem," they told her, patting her hand, completely unaware that this was *very much* her problem and *almost certainly* her fault. "I'll figure something out. Even if it means swallowing my pride and asking my shit parents for help."

Ravi sat with Nicole in silence, fallen over in misery and leaning on her chest while Nicole wrapped an arm around them like a protective wing. They weren't crying or anything, but they were clearly feeling pretty broken. Nicole wondered how long they'd been sitting on this news. Ravi wasn't usually shy about talking about their fuckups.

Though it didn't take much consideration to come up with a good reason why they'd be acting different now.

Love was supposed to open you up to your lover. And Nicole had never felt closer to Ravi. But now she had to *be* loved. To be good for them. To be good to them. That meant keeping some of the bad things hidden – the things that would make her seem *less* in their eyes.

Ravi was probably afraid of the same thing now, as if Nicole could somehow love them less just because they made a little mess at work. ...Okay a big mess. At least no one got hurt?

See Chapter 1, she thought. *Sleeping with your friend makes things complicated and shitty.*

Ravi pressed their forehead firmly into Nicole's chest before they admitted they had something else bothering them – something they wanted Nicole's mediation on.

"You remember that letter I got a while back? Job offer of a lifetime?"

"InThetics?"

"Yeah."

—So Ravi did keep it.

They took a breath to collect themself before they continued: "I'd have to bail on my thesis. But... it's full time, you know? And it's still... science – and still in my field. Hell, still *ceramics* even."

"But... if you stop working on your thesis... what happens to all your work?"

"Yeah... All for nothing. And... there's no way I could be on campus after I leave, which means... no more breaking into the biotech lab, so... all my *secret* research would have to stop too."

Nicole's eyes opened wide at that for a moment.

That was… perfect. That was perfect! Talk about spinning the shredded flax of misfortune into gold! There was so much… good about this. Ravi would be kept away from this dangerous research of theirs. They'd have a normal day job – no more awful back-breaking overtime. And they'd still get to do some kind of science that was close to their heart.

Nicole tried to forget why it was such a problem for Ravi to take this job at all. But she couldn't. She remembered. InThetics was evil, so they said. And working for them was some moral failing in their heart. And she saw the danger in it – the risk of losing themself with that immoral sacrifice.

And all their research would be gone.

Everything they'd been working towards for… so many years… So many late nights… So much miserable labor at warehouse gigs just to fund it all… Throwing all that away was… a lot.

To Nicole, there was a lot of good in it, but for Ravi, it didn't seem like it should be much of a dilemma. They had so much to lose, so '*no*' was kind of a no-brainer answer.

For them, there was only one thing that could make this a hard decision:

"It pays well, I guess," she said, completing an unspoken thought that was hanging in the air.

"*Yes*. Yes, it pays… extremely well. I could take care of this 130k *and* all of my student loans in like… four years…? Maybe even three if I live *humbly*."

Nicole studied Ravi's face for what to say here, for what Ravi needed to hear, but there was no answer in their troubled gaze. Only a question. A question *Nicole* was supposed to have the answer to. A question that had a *right* answer, and a devastatingly *wrong* answer, and she had no idea which was which.

"You want me to tell you it's a good idea?" she asked.

Ravi leaned forward on the couch and buried their face in their palms.

"I don't know, Nicole. I want to make the right choice and you aren't supposed to go shopping when you're hungry. I can't weigh all the money and the morality of feeding the war machine and the loss of everything I've worked for for the past eight years – not when I'm about to lose my apartment and my freedom and everything I own because I fucked up at work too much. What if I fuck this up too? I'm *losing it*. I fucked up the warehouse, I already destroyed the lab at the university, and if I keep going like this, I could *very easily* fuck up the most expensive science lab at the most influential tech company in the country, and then I'd never work in my field again."

Ravi sat up and pressed tight fists into their thighs, punctuating their exasperated words with percussive bone-shaking thumps. "But if I don't have any money, I can't afford school anyways! So what's the point if it's the same outcome either way, right? Either way my research is dead. And what's the fucking choice anyways if I lose everything? Be homeless or, what, go back home? Live with my shit dad? Admit I never had any clue what I was doing on my own? I can't fucking go home, Nikki, I can't. —But if I take this job, I never have to make that choice. I get to live somewhere nice, have a car, have a family, have a real life."

Nicole had spent a lot of lives on this Earth, struggling, watching humanity, even living through a little taste of their miseries. And one thing she'd seen over and over again was that living, for the most part, was spent fighting to live. The in-between parts? They were only ever good out of spite.

And maybe, for Ravi, this peaceful little in-between part was over for now. It might just be their turn in the ring. And they'd make it. They were so, *so* strong. Nicole could count on one hand the humans she'd met in thousands of years torturing humanity who had more strength in them than her dear beloved Ravi Beausoleil – and Ravi would still give each and every one of those champions a hell of a fight if any of them ever stood in their way.

But there was something… cold, cruel, and utterly unforgivable about telling someone they were 'strong enough to suffer'. She absolutely didn't want to say something so crushing and horrible to her troubled lover while they were laboring over a choice like this.

Nicole was caught on Ravi's words there – '*A real life.*' She remembered something Felicity had said to her, that Ravi had a choice once to go with her to her prestigious university on a free ride, on a handsome all-you-can-eat scholarship. Why had they turned that down? If it meant they'd be stuck in this miserable concession of a life? What was so appealing about staying? What was so terrifying about leaving? *What was the 'real life' they wanted?*

Ravi was waiting on Nicole for an answer.

As if a woman they had only really known for half a year could be trusted with their whole future.

As if those pleading eyes of theirs could pull some profound truth of the universe out of Nicole's heart through her clenched throat – a profound truth that also happened to be the *right* answer to their question, and not the devastatingly *wrong* one.

Unfortunately, the only answer Nicole could ever give was the *honest* one, the one that she had been feeding and growing for centuries, while desperately carrying on, living life again and again, and doing her best to stave off the pain that came along with that.

She crushed her palm with her fingers while she spoke, barely able to glance up at Ravi's eyes between uneasy assertions.

"I don't know what you should do, Rav. I'm sorry. But if you want to know what I would do, I would do whatever it takes to stay safe, to stay alive. I won't get into the details, like, *ever*, but I have done some pretty shameful things to get my hands on some kind of a tomorrow. One more day to live. Begging, stealing, helping shitty people. You know, if I'm around tomorrow, maybe there's still a chance I can make it right, all the horrible things I've done, staying alive." She rested her hands flat on her lap and looked Ravi in the eye before she continued: "You want my take on it? Being alive one more day is worth more than a lifetime of pride. Which, you know, wouldn't be a very long lifetime anyways if you traded all your tomorrows away for it."

Ravi's eyes sunk deeper into darkness with every word Nicole said. They gently pulled away from her after she was done speaking.

—*Wrong answer, then.*

They didn't tell her what they were planning to do before they returned to their room. And they said they wanted to spend the rest of the night alone. So, for the first night in a long time, Nicole slept on the couch, arms empty but for one of those precious not-a-gift pillows Ravi gave her so long ago, her heart full and heavy, thinking about what shameful things she would do herself just to get Ravi a tomorrow they could still be proud of.

The next evening, Ravi grimly informed Nicole they had an interview Friday morning.

They returned Friday afternoon, dressed in the most sterile, professional outfit Nicole had ever seen them wear – tidy hair styled flat and tame, thick-rimmed glasses, solid forest green neck tie, tightly buttoned cuffs and a charming blazer that accentuated the tie perfectly. They returned in that costume bearing a brand new InThetics badge and a dossier of orientation material that they studied for a long time in the solitude of their room before they finally returned to Nicole to prepare dinner for the two of them, and to explain their new schedule and duties at the company that shattered their soul.

How to Win Friends and Influence People and Break Into Carefully Guarded Facilities

"And this is you!"

Miriam Ortiz. The intense CEO and *de facto* mascot of InThetics.

Ravi never imagined *she'd* be the one giving them their onboarding. They found out later that apparently this is standard procedure for *every* new hire in the research department. The woman liked having her claws in every member of her 'tiger teams', and ended up being the unofficial project leader on nearly every 'mission' the department undertook.

The chain of command here was made of exotic matter.

"Desk. Chair. Computer. —You're going to love that chair, by the way. Color good?"

—Red? Like a gamer? Sure.

Ravi noted with a subtle quirked eyebrow that the whole open concept research area had a red-and-black gamer vibe.

The letter of offer had promised an 'extreme' workplace. They didn't realize it would extend all the way down to the décor.

"It's very energizing," Ravi confirmed with a put-on smile.

They weren't used to being falsely pleasant. None of their jobs for years had required playing nice with management. Their professors and administrators at the university were no-bullshit types. And the warehouse? If you spoke to your supervisor at all there, it wasn't for anything that could be smoothed over by deepthroating a pair of pristine managerial boots, not when devastating single-digit disruptions to the bottom line were on the table.

Miriam, however, contrary to Ravi's initial assessment, might actually have been a no-bullshit sort of manager too, since she saw right through their false pleasantries.

"You're not into it," she confirmed with a hint of disappointment. "Here," she said, flipping open a fancy touchscreen device on her wrist and typing out a rapid email to Ravi's inbox, "give the procurement team a call, they'll get you whatever you need. My tiger teams need fertile soil, Amaira. Don't be shy, okay? You're precious here, I'm not letting you wither away."

"Thanks, Miss Ortiz. I think I'll be fine though."

"Miriam. Miri if you want." She gestured for Ravi to have a seat so she could continue her tour. "Your eyes and your access card there—" She said, pointing at the card dangling from a spring-loaded tether on their hip. "—get you in your terminal, the cabinets, the storage facility, the elevators, the bathrooms – basically every door in the section."

"...There's an *eye scanner* on the bathroom doors?"

"Can't be too careful," Miriam said with a stern finger in the air.

Ravi gave their intense guide a nervous half-smile and nod that she was absolutely right about that and it was silly to even question it.

"—And please don't go wandering too far," she added suddenly. "Don't want to lose *another* new girl in a vat of nanite prototypes." That grim sentiment was punctuated with a playful grin.

Ravi gave her an uneasy smirk and asked her to explain: "Nanites?"

"Joking! We're not there yet. —Soon, though! The Singularity, Amaira, it's coming. Bionic *perfection*. Before I die, I'll see it. You too, I hope."

"Not sure I'm ready for immortality, Miriam. But it's a nice dream. Happy to contribute."

"You're sure I can't convince you to move on campus? We have *amazing* facilities in the research dorms. Cutting edge. —*Fertile soil*," she added to remind them.

Ravi smiled warmly. "I'm very happy where I am right now, I promise. I'll let you know, though."

It was InThetics' policy that only married couples – couples bound by hefty contracts of law – could be trusted to sign the non-disclosure agreements required to live in the company apartments. Flighty boyfriends and girlfriends were not to be trusted, apparently.

The thought of leaving Nicole behind to move here was too much to even consider. Ravi felt like they'd be entirely lost without her loving words and comforting touch, supporting them through all this. They were abandoning everything they'd been working for just to pursue this *conflicted* opportunity. Everything except her.

"We'll get you yet," she grinned at them confidently. "So, do you have any questions about the project?"

Ravi had spent the last three days poring over the extremely confidential document – as evidenced by the big red stamps all over every page – that detailed the work they'd be contributing to.

Armor. Right off the bat, just, military-grade armor.

—See ya, ethical integrity. The untested illusion of your existence was nice while it lasted.

Specifically, it was a new composition of lightweight, impact-tolerant plating for exosuits – *and* medical prosthetics, so, at least it would also help *some* normal, 'not murdering people for money' people...? Yay...?

As much as Miriam was hyping up Ravi as some extremely valuable talent, and trying to convince them they were contributing to some elite tiger team, InThetics was already at the point in development of this solution where they were just tweaking the mass-scale production processes for the molded parts.

Ravi's role on the project was pretty mundane. Really, just fiddling with knobs, adjusting temperatures and timings by hundredths of a percent, then running stress tests on the resulting product, tallying up failures, guessing lifetimes, writing reports, that kind of thing.

There was no real chemistry here, just... tedious lab work and data entry. A high school grad could probably handle this with a few weeks of training, but they got the impression that Miriam liked to say she had 'field experts' doing the science stuff, so, here they were. Field expert. Science stuff in hand.

And looking around at the monochromatic demographic palette of the office, they couldn't help feeling a bit like a living, breathing, 'brown person wearing a lab coat holding a flask' stock photo.

But hey, for a modelling gig, it paid pretty well. And all it cost was their soul. And ambitions. And work satisfaction. And self-respect. And—

Ravi realized that they would probably be seeing a lot of Miriam, so it was probably a good idea to make a good impression here, ask a question that was also a show of their talent – you know, a product demo. *Here's what that shiny new Amaira Beausoleil can do. You're getting your money's worth, Miriam. Please never ever fire me.*

"I noticed—" Ravi started, to answer Miriam's question about reading the project primer with a question of their own, "—you've only been adjusting the thermal coefficients in stage 3. Are we stuck isolating that stage for now? or is it possible to make adjustments on other stages at the same time? Do more testing in parallel?"

"Ooh. Hm. I don't think we've tried. Wouldn't that muddy up the results?"

"Oh definitely, but it's faster, if you care about that. I prefer to test a few variables at a time in my work. If there's a significant change, it's not that hard afterwards to isolate the major factor with another round of tests. Doing it one at a time is extremely tedious and expensive. Us time- and money-strapped grad students don't have endless funding or months to wait around for results, you know?"

Miriam laughed, "Amaira we certainly love improving efficiency here, but we also don't want anyone shying away from the tedium of pursuing perfection. I'll run it by the tech lead though." She leaned in to tell Ravi a fairly obvious secret, "Anything that gets this thing in under budget and ahead of schedule makes me look like a hero to the board. Listen, the senior staff on the project might try to shut you down, but don't be shy about bringing up *challenging* ideas. That's the whole reason I tap young blood."

—Tap. Like… a maple tree? That was an unpleasant image. No, she probably meant it like a tap on the shoulder. She must have.

After Miriam disappeared, Ravi got settled – but not comfortable – in the stiff, jagged, modern-looking gamer chair, then waved their access card ambiguously at the computer to log on and started reading through the dozens of soon-to-be-hourly emails that were already plaguing their inbox.

This was their life now.

❧

Ravi managed to assemble a little crew of allies in the trenches of the InThetics research labs in the first few weeks. Mostly guys. Mostly extremely awkward flirty guys. It was a huge change of pace from the warehouse. There, they had been one of the guys, and they didn't stand out at all on the floor. Here, among the scrawny lifelong desk jockeys, Ravi was like... *the* guy, despite that they were hiding behind the wrong name with everyone in the building. And apparently, buff brown androgynous science 'women' were in high demand in a special little chunk of the population in the office. And Ravi quickly found that having a crew of awkward flirty guys from every area of the organization was pretty handy for getting into all sorts of places they weren't supposed to be in.

It felt a little unsavory, a little... *unfaithful*... to be flirting around like that, but they were so bored waiting for their test results every day, and the doors their access card and dull irises would open didn't lead anywhere nearly exciting enough to keep them entertained. Luckily, Nicole gave them her blessing to have a little harmless fun when they lamented their situation, the sweetheart. Ravi had never been with someone so trusting and free from the bondage of jealousy before. It was extremely refreshing. Though... a little unfamiliar, a little... uncomfortable.

—*She does... <u>want you</u>, right? Right. Right, yes, obviously. Obviously...*

Tedious as it was to wait for the thing, they had to admire the autokiln they were in charge of fiddling with the knobs of. It was a technological marvel, of pristine white walls and platinum controls, with an impossibly heat-resistant filtered glass window that let them peer into the brilliant thermal light radiating out of the oven while it was baking.

The terminal had hundreds of parameters, organized into the most user-friendly interface Ravi had ever touched, all on one of those monitors that was just a disembodied sheet of black glass, mounted stylishly to the machine's wall on a free-moving swivel.

If Ravi had had access to something like this back at the university, their research probably would've been complete after a few months instead of still in progress after a couple years.

Through the window, they could watch as the device fed various composite clays through tubes and nozzles to lay purpose-built sculptures out in layers.

The design they were working on now was some kind of shin guard, with a smooth, modern shape. Each of the thin layers of clay was interspersed with a dusting of scattered shreds of some proprietary fibrous material that Ravi had never seen before.

Actually, the process was remarkably similar to the one they were developing themself with their fibrous tungsten composite clay, though much more precise and structured. They wondered if one of their papers might have inspired this technique. That would probably explain why InThetics had been so persistent in recruiting them in the first place.

The exact composition of the clay itself was carefully guarded. Which was fine. It wasn't what they were there to tweak, after all. No chemistry for them. Not here. Just manufacturing parameters. But more than the clay, which Ravi could probably guess at, those fibers were a fun mystery that they couldn't help puzzling over. What could possibly work better than their most beloved darling, the impossible miracle metal, tungsten?

Ravi speculated about the nature of the fibers while they drummed their fingers idly watching the machine get itself set up. Probably some kind of proprietary alloy, right? The only info Ravi could glean about it came from the label on the hopper: *InThetics™ 54f-White™*.

This company sure loved naming its tech after colors. Like for example, every new generation of their prosthetic tech was some new hue of the rainbow. They were looking forward to the company being forced to dig into the pool of crayon colors.

At least 'White™' was accurate. The little shreds were as brilliant as pure titanium oxide, even in the dull light of the autokiln, with a beautiful shimmering hint of deep crimson at certain angles.

It always took a pretty long while for the autokiln to finish its bake cycle, so Ravi was left with a lot of time to wander around the facility. They'd been getting a little bolder in their boredom, lackadaisically waving their card at every door they passed by while they walked up and down the halls of the facility. It didn't open every door, they found, but it did open some doors they didn't expect.

InThetics had a wide variety of R&D sections with a large number of teams at work, and, for the first couple of weeks after they got hired, every scrum room Ravi stumbled on in their meandering exploration of the sprawling research campus was inexplicably giving their card a green light to use the iris scanner to get inside. Someone on the security team was clearly not doing their job if Ravi had this much leeway, but they weren't about to shy away from taking the opportunity to poke around at some of the other work InThetics was engaged in. —It was the least the company could do, after all, to compensate them for the tedious work they were stuck on. —You know, in addition to the healthy salary.

While they explored, they reminded themself of Miriam's warning and made sure to be extra careful near any suspicious vats.

Unsurprisingly, the computers that Ravi wasn't assigned to refused to unlock for them, but other staff regularly carelessly left their machines on and open while they were busy working away on the other side of their teams' laboratory glass. Whenever no one was looking, Ravi took a moment to subtly peruse whatever files were open on screens or strewn across desks.

It turned out that military armor was, surprisingly, *not* InThetics' bread and butter. They had built their empire on pharmaceuticals, prosthetics, and augmentations. —And lately, autonomous robotics, which were more-or-less just amalgamations of prosthetic parts hooked up to a compliant intelligence core, as far as they could tell from the schematics.

Ravi wasn't much of a robotics nerd, but it seemed neat. It occurred to them that this tech could be a huge leap forward for Miriam's vision for the Singularity. If she could somehow find a way to swap the compliant intelligence for a real human intelligence, well, that'd be it, wouldn't it? As long as that still counted as a 'human', then immortality was on the horizon.

Though robots still break down, Ravi figured. So, not perfect, not yet, unless you were careful about how you wanted to define 'immortality'.

It was their habit of idly wandering and poking around places they weren't supposed to be that led them to meet most of the guys they ate lunch with now. Whenever they inevitably got caught, they would pretend to be lost on the way to the cafeteria, and make innocent puppy eyes at their kind escort the whole walk there, asking deeply probing questions about the guy's work to keep him interested.

It was funny how easy this was. They had always assured Nicole that they were a people person, and now that they had the energy and patience for it, they finally got to show that off.

It was a good thing they made all these connections early, too, because their lax access was tightened up soon after.

Though oddly, it wasn't the exploring that seemed to trigger it. It was only after Ravi started poking around the backend systems from their computer terminal, searching for more information about proprietary mystery substances and confidential project plans, that they found their access to the facility started getting restricted, quietly.

Whoever messed up on the security team must've figured out what they did wrong and fixed up Ravi's access permissions, hoping not to get caught on the mistake.

That little corrective action would've put an end to their trespassing fun, but luckily, they had the good fortune of acquiring that little squad of inside guys.

Today, Ravi was feeling especially bored, running this particular sample through the longest bake cycle yet, so they wandered over to visit one of those guys: Dear sweet Alexander Mack in the cybernetic implant section.

Ravi tapped on the glass beyond the security door to get the naïve young guy's attention, which was always enough to get him to let them in with a smile that said he just won something.

They stood next to his terminal and bowed low to peer at the documents he had open on his monitor.

"Whatcha workin' on, Lexy?"

The low dip and the fake interest were all part of the show, to keep him doting on them for nothing at all, to keep his carefully guarded doors open.

It did feel like a bit of a silly performance, though. Ravi didn't really have any cleavage to show off with their binder on, and they wouldn't know the secret to showing it off tastefully even if they did have any, but they knew it always put a little flush in anyone they were courting to lean over and show off a *little* extra skin peeking through a half-buttoned button-up.

It sure made Nicole happy, at least. And What's-Her-Name back when that was still a thing.

Alexander was always delighted to spill a little more info than he ought to when they played with him like that.

"Don't tell," he warned them, as he always did.

Ravi raised their hand in the air in a solemn oath.

Alexander pulled up a couple schematics and reports he was tidying up so that he could gesture at something while he over-explained everything, as he liked to do, like he had forgotten already that Ravi was a published post-grad dropout with an extensive science background.

He showed off some of the implants his team was working on – implants scheduled for release to the public in about five years, according to the roadmap in the tech lead's report.

Ravi pointed out one very interesting piece that was coming out of alpha soon.

"Yeah, this one's neat. Doesn't even need to be installed subdermal with that new White™ tech in there – though, obviously, you would still *want it* to be implanted subdermal, to keep it out of sight. It targets nearby pain receptors—nerves that send signals to the brain," he explained, like Ravi was a child who had never heard about pain before. "It's for chronic pain. You know, when someone has pain that won't go away, because they have an illness or something. It would also work well—" he said, pointing to a section on the report that Ravi had already read while he was talking titled '*Mitigating Implant Rejection Pain*', "—for implants that don't take well. Could be used to make the pain a little easier to deal with if you put it near the site of the rejection."

"Mm. Works better than painkillers?" Ravi asked, silently noting to themself that there was no comparative analysis in the report against existing pain control methods, which seemed like a kind of important thing to include.

"That's what the tests show."

Now *that*, Ravi was genuinely interested in, and they couldn't hide it at all. They could feel the grin creeping across their face and the sparks of intrigue firing in their eyes.

"How much better?"

Alexander leaned close to Ravi to whisper: "In animal trials, it's enough to stifle the pain response for *broken bones*."

Ravi raised an eyebrow at that. "You're breaking bones in animal trials? That's a little…"

"Whoa whoa," he put up his hands defensively, clearly aware of the monstrosity of it, but wanting to make it clear he was entirely innocent of any wrongdoing. "*I'm* not doing anything. I'm just making the schematics and the reports look nice."

They gave him as sincere a proud grin as they could put on. "Well, that's a relief. I was worried you were a real monster for a second there." Ravi gave the docs another once-over for show and complimented Alexander's work with a proud smile. Then they casually asked, "They do the testing in the building?"

He nodded and confirmed, "In the basement over there," while gesturing at some distant unseen corner of the campus.

"Can I see?"

"You want to watch them break some bones? That's dark," he added, like it was a compliment.

"No, I just want to see the tech. I love this kind of stuff."

"Mm... Sorry, Amaira, wish I could. I don't have access."

"Aw. Come on, Lexy, you don't have anyone who could sneak us in? Just for a little bit? I'd love a little hands-on demo with you. I used to work in a warehouse, you know. My back is always acting up on me," they said with a pathetic whine. They twisted around to point to a spot on the small of their back, which did genuinely cause them a twinge of pain sometimes, even now. Then to put a little flourish on the show, they slid a hand down their backside to grab the back of their thigh to show it off: "Down here too. Hard to reach all by myself, though, don't you think? I bet it's tricky to set the thing up right. You could... *help me* put it on, right? You know how it all works?"

He was turning a little red thinking about it.

"...Of course," he confirmed timidly.

Mission accomplished. Poor guy.

"You're such a nice guy, Alex, I can't believe you don't have any friends down here who owe you even a *little* favor."

He anxiously drummed his fingers on the desk for a few seconds of consideration before he suggested he'd ask around about it, then followed up with a hopeful question about maybe grabbing dinner later.

"Oh, that would be fun, wouldn't it? A little one-on-one tech demo and a fancy meal after?" Ravi didn't commit to anything, but they led him on a bit, asking what music he was into, what bars he liked around here, if he had anything fun to do at home.

He lived in the company dorms, and didn't get out much, so sadly he didn't have any fun suggestions.

But it was enough to spark his imagination and get him feeling a little extra motivated, which was encouraging, but Ravi still didn't have a lot of faith in his ability to deliver on this one.

⁊

"You really love playing with these guys, hey Ravi Bee?"

Nicole was giving Ravi a little head massage on the couch while they rested in her lap after work. They were debriefing her about their adventures for the day. And this constructed office intrigue was the only fun topic they could find worth talking about, since everything else about their day was always so tedious. Honestly, they were starting to feel like it was imperative they keep going with it now, like they were only toying with these guys at all so they could have stories for Nikki.

"I must've stumbled back into my slut era or something," they replied, joking. "I was *sure* I got all that out of my system back in third year."

"Well well, don't let me hold you back if you want to let loose," Nicole replied with a warm grin.

—*God. She's actually serious, isn't she? Who* is *this woman?*

"Nah, I'm good. The attention's nice, but it's all just pretend, Nix." Ravi took her hand in theirs and brought it to their lips to bless her with chivalric kiss. "My heart's yours, I promise."

"Just your heart?"

Ravi gave her a sly grin, "Don't act like you don't already know you've got every part of me at your pleasure."

Nicole traced teasing lines down their midriff and confirmed, "*Every* part?"

Ravi didn't reply, but they didn't have to, Nicole was already cheerfully undoing the buttons on their shirt and unclasping their belt.

God it was nice to unwind with her after work. It was especially nice having the *energy* to unwind with her. Tedious as it was, there was something to be celebrated about the relaxed pace of a steady nine-to-five.

After the two of them had their fill of each other, Ravi got started on dinner while Nicole doted on them, sitting on the counter in her underwear, perfumed in the intoxicating blend of their sex, taking up far too much space in the little kitchen in the best possible way.

While they were stirring up a heavenly base of onions and garlic in a sauté pan, they were hit with a fun idea.

"Hey, you love breaking in places."

"Well, 'love' is maybe the wrong word for it," she replied, playfully kicking her feet in the air while she waited for dinner to materialize.

"Oh sorry, you *live for the thrill* of breaking in places."

She grinned at them. "That's better."

"Want to help me break into the deepest darkest depths of the InThetics research facilities?"

"You don't trust little Lexy to come through for you?"

"Let's say my expectations are low, but I really do want to get my hands on one of those prototypes. It sounds really neat. —And it would be nice if I could nick one without having to endure little Lexy awkwardly staring at my ass and feeling up my leg."

"You're going to steal one?"

"Borrow! Just borrow. For a few years. If it works."

Nicole's grin didn't falter, but she did raise a skeptical eyebrow. "Don't let me talk you out of crime and adventure or anything, Rav, but you've only been at this place a month, you sure you want to get into trouble this early?"

"That's the trick. The earlier I get in trouble, the easier it is to pretend I didn't know better."

"Ah I see. You're running out of time."

"Not getting any younger."

"You can't just wait five years for the thing to come out for real? Probably safer than messing with some untested tech."

"Come on Nikki, I'll be lucky if this shit doesn't kill me in five years," they said, gesturing at their infected shoulder. "Wouldn't it be nice if I didn't have to be in agonizing pain the whole time?"

Nicole's face soured at their grim justification. "Don't say that…"

"What? It's true."

Her scowl didn't fade. Apparently this was a serious topic for her.

Ravi rested the spatula in the pan and shuffled over to Nicole to lean their waist against the counter between her legs and wrap their hands around her hips while they spoke to her with all the warmth and sugar they could pull together:

"Nix, puppy, I know it's tough, but you gotta accept that you're going to live a whole lot longer than me, unless you get hit by a bus or something. And please don't get hit by a bus, it would be so stupid if you died first, my god."

Nicole hugged Ravi with her calves, cradled their skull tenderly in her fingers, and drew them close to kiss their forehead. "Ravi Bee, I know it's easy for you to talk about this stuff, but I wish you'd be a little kinder about it."

"You want me to sugarcoat it?"

"I want you to imagine a world where you're around for a long time to take care of the people you love."

"...That's not real, Nikki."

"It's not real *yet*. And it won't be real at all if you give up."

Ravi's eyes turned away from Nicole's, but they couldn't escape her. She ducked her head down to keep her bright eyes in theirs.

"Nicole. Stop." Ravi tried to squirm free from Nicole's grasp, and she was kind enough to let them out.

They went quiet for a while, pretending to be fully entranced by cutting up some bok choi, peppers, and carrots for the meal.

Nicole graciously returned to sitting quietly and kicking her feet, though she clearly wasn't doing it in that same childish carefree way she was before.

—As if it mattered. What difference could it possibly make, giving up or not?

Hoping and fighting and flailing wildly wasn't going to do anything. It wasn't going to do anything but make every day of the rest of their little life just feel like they were making pointless moves in a losing game. A chess match with nothing left but a king and a knight and an opponent who just won't let you die.

Nicole didn't speak up until Ravi had the rest of the vegetables sizzling in the pan:

"Why does it scare you so much? To think about some kind of future where you get to live a long life."

"Scare me... Is that what it looks like?"

"What is it then?"

Ravi stared at the steaming contents of the pan for a few long seconds before they started putting their answer together: "...You know, some people think they've got a whole century on Earth to fuck around. So you see them just wasting time, working in an office, absolutely miserable, absolutely convinced they're going to retire one day to some easy life where all their suffering was *for something*." Ravi rapped the end of the spatula on the center of the pan a few times before they continued: "My suffering is never going to be *for anything*. You know? There's no reward at the end. It's pointless. The suffering is pointless, and pretending it *isn't* is just as pointless."

"Oh, *I see*. We can't do pointless stuff anymore. Boy that sure takes a whole lot of fun activities off our rotation."

"You can do all the pointless stuff in the world Nikki. I have to make everything count. And every pointless little thing I do *with you* gives my short little life a bit more meaning. I want to have fun fucking around with you as long as possible, knowing it's all going to end soon, enjoying every moment, you know? And it's easier to have fun for me if I can just... accept that I can't do this for very long. I don't want to spend every day of my life feeling like I'm failing myself and everyone around me because I can't magically get better by sheer *force of will*."

Nicole looked down at her feet while she continued flicking them up in the air nonchalantly. She creased her brow while she considered something for a few seconds. Then, at last, she agreed to Ravi's proposal. She even sounded kind of confident about it. "Okay. I'll help you break in."

"Don't let me pressure you with sob stories here, Nikki. You really don't have to," Ravi assured her emphatically.

"I want to."

Ravi shot her a big grin. "It'll be a fun date."

Nicole returned their grin with a nostalgic smile and nodded. "I haven't had to outrun the authorities for ages."

"Okay well we're not supposed to get *caught*."

"No promises," she said with a wink. "Almost getting caught is half the fun."

"What's the other half?"

"You know, making out in closets and such."

"I feel like there should be at least a little fraction in there about exploration and discovering untold secrets."

"That's the backup second half if there aren't any closets."

"You're kind of a perv sometimes, Nikki."

"Maybe," she said with a playful shrug. "—Or maybe I'm just having fun *corrupting* you," she added, grinning so salaciously sly that Ravi had to turn off the stove to drag her back to bed.

A Forbidden Autonomous Factory Might Actually Be a Bad Location for a Date

Sadly, there were no easily accessible closets in the InThetics basement.

And after wandering around for half an hour, Ravi was pretty sure the two of them had ended up in entirely the wrong part of the facility. This looked more like a manufacturing wing. The main corridor loop featured a massive glass wall along one side, and as Ravi meandered down the hall with wide eyes, staring at the full-auto manufacturing processes happening on the massive factory floor a solid thirty feet below, they were surprised to find Nicole was the one shying away from the windows this time.

"What's with you? I thought you 'lived for the thrill' of this stuff."

She was walking around hugging herself, looking very much like she was on the verge of throwing up from anxiety.

"Nicole?"

"Um. Sorry. Sorry, there's... I don't know, something in the air maybe..."

Ravi sniffed the air with intent. Years of working in a chem lab had definitely desensitized them to a wide variety of acrid smells, but she was right, there was something a little off-putting about the scent, at least to a *normal* human being.

"Want to leave?"

"No. No, this is important to you, I'm fine, just do your thing."

"You feeling okay is more important to me. You look sick."

She made a show of shaking it off and put on a look of determination. "I promise I'm fine."

"...Okay. Well since you're down here making yourself suffer anyways, you sure you don't want to look at this stuff? It's crazy, I've never seen anything like it. Look," Ravi waved her over to the window.

Below them was a massive pool – big enough to hold Olympic competitions in – filled to the brim with some dark chemical soup. Dozens of spider-like arms suspended from the ceiling were moving in pairs in perfect sync – one tip sparking the surface of the pool with electricity while the other drew an uninterrupted filament out of the sparks into a massive spool. When it was full, each spool was deposited on a conveyor at the back of the room to send it off to its destination.

The thread was a striking bright white color, even from this distance, and pearlescent in a deep crimson when the light caught it just right.

—*And isn't <u>that</u> intriguingly familiar.*

Nicole uneasily approached the window and watched alongside Ravi in dead silence. When Ravi looked over, her eyes were shifting about uneasily, and she was slowly, silently whispering something.

"Nikki?"

"…Ravi… I don't… think we should be here…"

They nudged her shoulder, "I told you we can leave."

She couldn't take her eyes off the black pool below, and she was so transfixed that she was apparently having trouble hearing Ravi. They had to poke her a few times just to get her attention.

"Nicole. What's going on with you?"

She turned her head slowly towards Ravi, barely able to pry her eyes away from the spectacle down on the factory floor.

"Can we leave?" she pleaded with them.

"I already told you we could go!"

"Yeah. Yeah, let's go. Sorry. This isn't… I don't know… Let's just leave. Please."

She led the way with long, hurried steps towards the nearest stairwell that would get them out of the basement. She didn't even wait for Ravi before rushing through the doors. They found her curled into herself, leaning against the wall on the next floor up with her head in her hands.

"Nicole, seriously, what's going on?"

"…I can't… I can't… Gods, Ravi, this isn't…" She turned to them with a shattered look in her eyes. "What are they making here?"

"All sorts of stuff. Implants and prosthetics and robots and, apparently, that super secret white thread. I'm pretty sure that's the stuff they put in the ceramic at my station."

"…You don't know anything else about it? About that thread?"

Ravi shrugged. "If that is what it is, it's kind of hard to get any info about it. No one I ask seems to know or care about it. I found a couple documents, but security cut off my access before I could save anything, so, big proprietary mystery."

"Ravi that black stuff down there. What is it?"

"No clue."

"Can you… —Can we find out?"

Ravi raised a curious eyebrow. "Why?"

"It's just… I can't explain it. I'm sorry. I just think it might be kind of… uh… *urgently* important."

Ravi wracked their brain trying to think of some way to figure it out without having access to any of InThetics' secretive documentation.

The best they could come up with on the spot was the same method they'd been using before to figure out what their own mysterious black stuff was made of – compositional analysis and painstakingly searching databases for fingerprints and spectroscopic patterns.

"If I can get down there, I can collect a sample, do some tests on it. But seriously, you look awful, we should get out of here before you throw up or something. I'll come back another day."

Nicole grimaced, then shook her head with determination. "No. No, you don't know anyone who'll let you down there."

"I can find someone."

"That someone is right here."

"Nicole."

"…Wait here, I'll figure out the way."

"Come on Nicole, this isn't that important. Let's get you home."

"Ravi. I am never coming back to this building. It's tonight or never."

"…Alright. Okay. You don't want me to come with?"

She shook her head. "Faster by myself."

Ravi let out a little huff of a sigh. They had to trust her, no matter how uneasy it made them feel.

"Be careful," they said, before giving her a tender kiss for good luck.

Nicole disappeared down the stairs to sneak back through the security door using whatever that trick of hers was.

While Ravi waited, they scuffed their foot on the tile floor uneasily. What was going on with her? She was never… nervous like this.

And she was never sick. Ever.

Was she allergic to something in the air here?

God, this was just supposed to be a fun little date. Play with some fancy painkilling implants, sneakily make out in a dark corner, maybe get some dinner after, go to a bar, *drunkenly* make out in a dark corner…

It was a good few minutes of worrying and waiting for Nicole to get back before she made her appearance again at the stairwell door.

She looked awful. Staggered, nauseated, exhausted, leaning most of her weight on the wall to stand.

Ravi rushed to her side to hold her up and get a good look in her eyes. She was not well.

"Jesus Nicole what the fuck…"

"Shh. I'm fine. Here," she took Ravi's upturned wrist in one hand and placed a shaky fingernail on their palm, then traced a path there while explaining every turn through the halls to get down to the factory floor. "I propped open all the doors. You can just slip in and out."

Ravi looked at the skin of their palm with a quirked eyebrow. The white impressions there lingered a lot longer than they expected. A map. Nicole sure had a lot of cool tricks at her disposal.

"You sure you're good?"

Nicole nodded and tried to smile through a grimace.

"…I owe you a real date, Nix. I'm sorry this sucked so bad for you."

She shook her head to dismiss Ravi's concerns. "It's all good. I'm glad we did this, honest. Please just go. Don't worry about me." She slid her back down the wall until she was sitting on her butt, "I'm just gonna wait here. Take your time."

"…Okay."

Ravi, of course, did not take their time. They had to get Nicole out of here already, but she clearly wasn't going to let them go until they got that sample.

Why was she suddenly so obsessed with it?

They jogged through half a dozen doors, following the lingering white impression on their skin the whole way, until they found themself hustling down a long staircase that let out onto the factory floor with the giant pool.

The machinery was remarkably quiet. Well-oiled. The only sounds were the muted electromagnetic hum that accompanied every motion of the spider arms' servos, and the near-constant crackle of the arcs of electricity that were materializing those uninterrupted white strands out of the surface of the strange black fluid.

As they approached the edge of the pool, they remembered Miriam's words of caution, and crossed their fingers that this wasn't secretly a dark mass of some super experimental flesh-altering nanites or something.

The surface of the matte liquid was perfectly still.

And the smell was... familiar...

And unique...

Kind of... metallic...?

Or... like... like molten glass...

...They stared at the pool bewildered for a while before they shook it off to hurriedly search through every nook and cranny of the massive room for some kind of container they could gather the sample in.

At last, they managed to find some sealable plastic bags. Probably good enough, unless it ate the plastic.

They put one bag over their hand like a glove, then dipped it into the mysterious black fluid to scoop some of it into another bag.

It was... thick.

Like...

Tar...

...They uneasily sealed the bag and then sealed it inside another bag before stuffing it in their pocket and hurrying back to Nicole.

She still looked awful. Pale. She swayed in place and her eyes were swimming. They hurried her out of the building and called a ride for the two of them. The bus was not an option in her state.

She was barely speaking the whole way home. Just a nod and an, "I'm fine," whenever Ravi asked.

They helped her to their bed and got her comfortable.

By the time they got back with a glass of water, she was unconscious, breathing weak stuttered breaths.

What the hell happened?

Ravi called in sick the rest of the week to sit at Nicole's side. She didn't have a fever, but she was sure acting like she did. Ravi had to help her to the bathroom and help her bathe and eat while she was in that fugue state. It took two whole days before she was even able to keep up any kind of conversation. But by the third day, despite clearly still needing help, she was very earnestly trying to get Ravi to stop doting on her.

"You don't need to take care of me—"

"—Stop. I'm staying until you're better and that's that. They don't need me at work, it's fine."

When she was finally sitting up in bed, Ravi caught her glancing uneasily at the far end of their desk. They had hidden the last vial of their shoulder's tar in one of the lower drawers, right next to that stolen sealed sample.

Ravi gave her an apprehensive look when they noticed her troubled gaze. There was no way she saw them put that stuff down there. She was way too out of it when they had.

But she knew. Somehow. She was looking right at it.

And she couldn't look away from it when she asked: "...Did you figure out what that stuff is?"

Ravi reached out and placed gentle fingers on her cheek to turn her eyes to theirs. "Hey. Let's not talk about that right now, okay?"

"...I was right, wasn't I? It's the same."

Ravi took a long look at Nicole's pleading impossibly green-flecked sapphire eyes. They couldn't keep this from her after everything she did for them to get that answer.

"I think so," they reluctantly confirmed.

They still hadn't properly put together what that meant, though. How was something that looked and smelled exactly like the tar in Ravi's shoulder ending up in a giant pool in the basement of an InThetics factory floor?

They paused for a long while before they asked to follow up, "How did you know?"

"Secret."

"Really. 'Secret'. After all that, you're not even going to tell me why you got yourself all sick like this just to send me down there?"

"Sorry, Ravi Bee. I've got some secrets I can't share."

Ravi clenched their fists uneasily. Nicole was hiding something from them? She was hiding something from them that was so important she would put herself in bodily harm and not even tell them why?

Nicole placed tender fingertips on their wrist and pleaded with them. "Please. Let me keep this."

"You can *feel it*, can't you?"

She didn't reply.

"Nicole. Please. Is it bothering you? I can get rid of it." They got off the bed and crouched down in front of their desk to open the offending drawer.

"Ravi stop. I'm fine. Okay? It's fine there."

They froze their fingertips on the handle of the drawer. "This is what made you sick. Isn't it?"

"I don't know. I don't know, Ravi, maybe. It doesn't matter."

Ravi had been right all along, hadn't they? When they started experimenting on this stuff. They were right. It was some kind of... some horrible biohazard. Not to them, but to Nicole. They were... They were so *obsessed* with it, they didn't even notice. But she had always hated this stuff, hadn't she? They thought it was just because it was gross, that she was just keeping her distance, poking at it with pens, afraid to get too close to it because it was some disgusting byproduct of their illness, but... this whole time, it was actually... *hurting* her, wasn't it?

They curled their nails into their palms furiously. "Are you kidding me?? It doesn't *matter?*" Ravi fell back on their ass and laughed pathetically. " '*It doesn't matter.*' —You're insane. I *make* this stuff. My body *makes* this stuff. I'm *poison* to you, aren't I? This whole time, I've been... I'm just hurting you... Oh my god..." They buried their face in their hands and tried to keep it together. "Nicole what the fuck is wrong with you? Why would you... You can't let me do this to you."

"...Do we have to do this right now? I'm still not feeling great..."

Ravi heaved a heavy sigh. Their breath was stuttering slightly. This was so stupid.

This wasn't Nicole's problem. Ravi had to fix this. She just needed to rest and get better.

They ripped the drawer right out of their desk and left Nicole in the bedroom, safe from their poison.

They placed the vial and the double-bagged sample on the little kitchen table and glared at the both of them, trying to think of what to do.

Incinerate them. That was the answer, right? This was biological *poison*. If it hurt Nicole, there's no telling who else it was going to make sick if they just left it lying around. Just being *near it* was enough to do this much damage to her? How could they be so stupid? So careless? So fucking *selfish?*

What did the nurses do with it when it was extracted? Incinerate it? Incinerate it. They incinerated it. Like any biohazard. They incinerated it for fucksake they incinerated it what else could they possibly do with it? Just... just toss it in a giant pool??

They cackled at themself madly. That was insane. Insane. There's no way that... that it was all... God damn how many people would they need to tap to fill that pool? *Millions.* Easily millions.

How many people were sick with this? How many...

Every month...

Millions of people...

Millions of little vials...

—*Incinerated.*

They grabbed their coat and rushed out of the apartment with the vile stuff in their pocket, then called a ride to rush them to InThetics.

They hurried through every security door, not even sparing a smile for the security guards at every checkpoint, right to their station, the autokiln.

They opened the manual door and threw both samples in before sealing it and sitting at the controls to turn the kiln up to the highest temperature it would allow.

They watched with vitriol in their eyes as the disgusting samples cooked to ash.

Though in the middle of that ash, they noted a chaotic tangle of fibrous black material, like asbestos or fiberglass, left over after the fluid cooked away. The kiln wasn't hot enough. They growled at it and dug through the user manual to find the safety override, then turned it up to a temperature hot enough to turn the controls red with dire warnings.

The inner pane of the viewing window of the million-dollar kiln cracked from the heat. It got hot enough that Ravi had to step back. As the crack spread, some emergency thermal breaker tripped and shut the whole thing down.

When it cooled down enough that they could get a good look, it seemed to have been enough to at least powderize the fibers. So they were right. They were right. It could be incinerated. And that must be what the nurses were doing. That pool downstairs, it must be something else. Something just... similar. Synthetic. Obviously. It wasn't full of... of biohazardous *extractions*.

Satisfied with their observations, Ravi left before anyone could ask why they were there on a sick day.

The ride home was grim. Like, sure, the sample was gone, never to bother Nicole or anyone else again, but they still had an unlimited supply of something growing right inside them that *smelled* the same and *burned* the same and *fucked up Nicole* exactly the same as whatever the stuff in that pool was.

How were they supposed to deal with this...

When they got home, they didn't return to Nicole's side. Instead, they sat down on the couch, slouched forward, wringing their hands uneasily. They tenderly prodded one of their cysts to feel how bad it was today. They winced slightly at the touch. This was the fourth week. It was mostly black with tar already.

They had to stay away from her.

God, could they ever be near her again?

"Ravi?"

Nicole was peering timidly around the edge of the living room wall.

"Don't," Ravi said sharply to keep her from coming any closer.

"What did you do?"

"I got rid of it."

Nicole stood silently, a distant look in her eyes.

"Go back to bed," Ravi implored her. "Please. I don't want to hurt you like this."

"It doesn't hurt when it's… I mean as long as I don't touch it… When it's in your shoulder, it doesn't bother me, I promise. It's only when it's… out."

"…When you *touch it?*"

Nicole blatantly ignored Ravi's pleading request that she stay away and decided to come sit right next to them on the couch. Ravi tried to shift over away from her, but she refused to let them escape.

"Stop!" Ravi tried to shove her away, but she only grabbed their wrists to hold them still and try to calm them down. "Stop already, Jesus Nicole, why are you being like this?"

"You're not poison."

Ravi laughed dismissively. "You really don't believe in the standard scientific method, huh? God, you'd make a terrible scientist like this. Hypothesis: The bullshit in my body can make you sick. Methodology: Expose the subject to just a crazy amount of that bullshit. Observation: She's fucking sick. What's the conclusion there, huh Nix?"

"Pretty sure you're supposed to have a bigger sample size. Some statistical analysis? Peer review? No?"

"Oh, shut up, don't turn this around on me."

"Well, I can't let you call me a bad scientist when you're missing half the process. Sounds like you're the one throwing some wishful biases in the mix there, Ravi Bee."

Ravi scowled and wriggled their wrists free of Nicole's grasp, then slouched forward again and pointedly avoided eye contact.

Nicole sat with them for a long time in silence, watching, waiting. Ravi could feel her eyes on them, trying to pull their attention away from their dark thoughts, but they weren't ready to leave that dark place yet. They had to do *something*.

She placed a soft hand on Ravi's thigh to try to shake them from their misery.

"You know it's convenient, actually," she said. "Whenever your shoulder's bad for you, I can't touch your sores."

Ravi laughed pathetically. "Yeah. Wow. Super convenient. Until your hand slips or something."

Ravi shook their head and looked Nicole in the eye. "Nikki why... When you *touch* me...? That doesn't... even make sense... If it was something in the air... Or like... I don't know, *radiation* or something? That only affects you? Somehow? But when you *touch me?*"

Nicole grimaced and looked away. "It would be really cool if you stopped asking about this..."

"Why? Because of your secret?"

Nicole nodded sadly.

"You can't just tell me?"

She shook her head. "...I want to. I want to so badly. I'm sorry. There are just... rules. Some rules can't be broken."

Ravi creased their brow and squinted at her, trying to read whatever it was she was hiding.

She caught them staring and pleaded with them again, "Please stop."

"...How do you get past all those doors, Nikki?"

She looked away with a miserable grimace. And she didn't answer.

"You're never sick."

"Stop."

"You can drink me under the table every time."

"Ravi."

"...You're not normal, are you? No one... no one has eyes that shimmer like that – and I've *never* seen you put contacts in. And your hair? How does fragrance-free shampoo smell like that, huh? How does *anything* smell like... like *summer*. —All the time! *All the time*, no matter how hot and sweaty I get you. —God, you *taste* like magic, Nicole..."

She stood up in a huff and shouted at them, "Shut up! Just. Shut up Ravi. Please. Just stop. —This is good! Isn't this good?? I love you and you love me and you still... you look at me like I'm a human being. Like I'm good. I don't want to lose that. Please."

"...You're not though, are you? —Human, I mean. You're still... You're still good..."

Nicole growled in frustration and turned away. "Can't you just leave this alone?"

"Leave this alone...? Nicole I'm sleeping with... with... what? What are you?"

"I told you I can't *fucking* tell you! Would you just stop!"

"...You said there's a rule. What's the rule?"

"I'm not allowed to... I can't make it obvious. You have to figure it out."

"And all this... this... whatever you've got going on, that's not making it obvious?"

"Well, no one else is putting it together like this! Normally takes a *lot* more work than this to figure it out! Gods... I'm so stupid..."

"Jesus Nicole... Are you serious? What the hell is this game? Fine, what, aliens? You a body snatcher? A renegade android? Magic? Is it real? Real magic? Like Felicity was going on about? Faeries and wizards and gods and stuff?"

Nicole didn't answer.

Which was becoming a very interesting pattern.

"Why can't you answer that?"

"Because I can't lie to you."

"And, what, I can't handle the truth?"

"Can you?"

"I mean *not answering* is kind of giving away the answer here."

Again, no response.

"...So. For real, for real for real, you aren't human..."

Nicole brought her palms to her eyes and walked away, to return to the bedroom.

Ravi didn't chase. They had a lot to put together.

Maybe the tar wasn't a biological poison at all, then.

Maybe it was just... poison to... to *whatever* Nicole was...

—What the fuck is sleeping in your bed, Ravi?

Android...? Didn't make sense. No reason for an android to get sick from a little biological discharge – or even from a *lot* of biological discharge. —Also, Ravi was intimately familiar with Nicole's body, inside and out, and she was definitely flesh and blood through and through.

So. Alien? Maybe. Better fit than android. Maybe the tar was... some kind of kryptonite to her? Maybe the aliens were infecting people? Working with InThetics? Big conspiracy? And she'd still be made of meat and bones. Might explain the weird eyes and the heavenly taste of her.

But come on, how impossible would it be? for some alien species to look *exactly* like a human? Humans weren't special, just evolutionarily *lucky*.

Body snatcher, then? Still have human anatomy. But then there'd be no reason to be vulnerable to some kryptonitic tar. Not like that, right? If it was hurting whatever parasite was in there, you'd think it'd make the host healthier, not sicker.

God, so, what was left?

Something that wasn't human, that could look and feel extremely human, with special rules that didn't fit regular humans.

It couldn't be. It just *couldn't*... but... it sure sounded like something out of a myth. Ancient Greek gods and tricky spirits and stuff. Dragons? Dragons can look human, right? That was a story they vaguely remembered hearing once. Witches can do magic, illusions, transformations. Trickster foxes could pretend to be people. What else was there?

Felicity would know. She knew all of this stuff. But how the hell was Ravi supposed to ask her about something like this? It was insane. This was insane. And Felicity already didn't trust Nicole. This would only make it much, *much* worse.

—*But _you_ still trust Nicole? Even now? Are you stupid or something?*

God, whatever the answer was, Ravi was going to have to crack their own skull open to rewire stuff in there to accept the truth of it all...

But what kind of scientist would they be if they were afraid of pursuing some new truth of the universe?

They rapped their fist on their knee a few times before they stood up and finally followed after Nicole.

She was rolled over on her side, pointedly facing away from the door.

They sat cross-legged on the bed facing her, trying to put their words together, trying to find the perfect question, but all they could think to ask was what they already asked:

"Are you magic?"

She still wasn't answering.

"Look I'm not asking 'what you are', just tell me if you're using magic to do stuff. Like getting past doors, is that magic?"

Nicole let out a long sigh before she subtly nodded yes.

She was sulking about it.

"It's magic. Okay. So. Magic is real."

Again Nicole nodded.

"Great. Cool. So. What the fuck am I wasting my life doing all this science bullshit for then? Holy fuck. Magic is real. —What can you do? Can you tell me that? It's not like I can guess what you are just from a little magic show, right? That's not 'making it obvious' any more than I already know."

"What can I do...?" Nicole echoed lethargically. After a few seconds of thought, she scoffed at herself. "Not much. Not anymore. I can show you the whole catalog of tricks in less than a minute."

"Okay. Can you?"

Nicole rolled over to face them. She was bleary eyed with wet cheeks. This was really devastating for her. But Ravi couldn't just let this go. She had to understand that.

After she took in the pleading look on their face for a few long breaths, she let out a little huff of a sigh and sat up cross-legged to face them.

She held up her hands to show off they were empty, like a magician, then with a subtle gesture of her fingers and a glimmer in the air, an empty teacup appeared in her hand – a teacup Ravi recognized from their own cupboards.

"Ta da," she lethargically cheered, handing them the cup to examine.

Ravi held it in their hands, stunned silent for a few breaths while they rotated it to confirm it was in fact real.

"You can teleport things," Ravi summarized in disbelief. "No. No I'm sorry, there are rules. The amount of energy required to... to... The planet should've just... vaporized."

"It's not teleportation. It's *moving it*, through... I don't know, like, a wormhole I guess is how you'd explain it, pulling it through a different kind of space. I usually just call it the Aether."

"The Aether. Why?"

"Sounds cool?"

"'Sounds cool.' Okay. I mean, I think that word already means something else, is the thing. Like, isn't it supposed to be some kind of trans-material medium for radiation or something?"

"It's also supposed to be some guy who represents the sky beyond the sky, if you ask the old Greeks, and a bunch of other things. It's all the same kind of idea, though – a layer of space next to this one that lets things move weirdly."

"That's... okay. Alright. So, you can move things through magical wormholes that go through some kind of alterspace. Got it. Suspending just, all my disbelief here, then. Okay. What else have you got to shatter all my long-held beliefs about the way the universe works?"

Nicole shook her head sadly. "Not much else, honestly. I had a lot more cool tricks before, but I uh... lost most of them. I can do this?—" She lifted her finger into the air and waved it around like she was drawing on a chalkboard. The tip of her finger left a brilliant white line in its wake that shimmered in the shape of a little heart for Ravi for a few seconds before it disintegrated in a shower of dim sparks. "— Which is remarkably useless, but still kind of fun. Is that belief-shattering?"

"Mm... not really, I guess."

"Darn."

"That's it?"

"I also have just a tiny bit of magic left in an old bone needle. I was using that to fix up your coat," Nicole explained, nodding in the direction of the closet by the front door where Ravi's jacket was hanging.

"You enchanted my jacket."

She nodded. "Though it keeps coming undone for some reason." She tapped her own right shoulder to mirror Ravi's. "Right there. Like your sores are... I don't know, ripping apart the spell or something. Which... you know, kind of makes a lot more sense now, considering what it was doing to me..."

Ravi was still struggling to put their words together. They handed the cup back to Nicole, who promptly returned it to where she pulled it from.

That was how she did it, wasn't it? How she got past locked doors. She just... moved herself through this... *Aether.*

Crazy.

God, this was crazy.

She was fiddling with her fingers like she had something left to add, something that she very much did not want to add.

She pierced her lip painfully between her teeth before she swore at herself and admitted there was one more thing.

She reached out her fingers to caress Ravi's cheek and bring their eyes to hers.

"I know the power of your true name, *Ravi Beausoleil*."

An intense wave of warmth coursed through Ravi's mind and body at the unreal sound of their name on Nicole's tongue. Their strength wavered and they felt all their weight collapse into her lovingly outstretched palm.

"I'll never use it to hurt you," she promised, with a voice painted in a misery deeper than Ravi had ever heard. Then she withdrew her hand from Ravi and whatever spell she had just put them under disappeared. They couldn't even tell if it was real after. Was it just… a daydream? A fantasy?

Could there really be that much power in just the sound of their name? They'd always loved hearing it in Nicole's voice, but… was that only because of some… spell…?

—No. It's never felt like that before. That was something _else_.

When they recovered from their disorientation, they scrunched up their brow in confusion and asked, "Why are you here?"

"Mm… Define 'here'."

"I don't know, in my apartment, in my life at all. What did I do to deserve someone so amazing?"

Nicole let out a little laugh at the question. "You are so much more amazing than me, Ravi Beausoleil, and I wish I could do anything to make you understand that. I'm here because of your kindness and your love, and I just… I don't know how to leave anymore. I don't know how to leave you. I owe you so much, and I can never pay you back."

"…Are you just sleeping with me because you think you owe me…?"

"No! No. No, it's not like that. It's not. I promise. Gods, if anything, I feel like I'm more in debt to you every day we're together."

"So why?"

"I just… like you. I like you. A lot. You take care of me. You make me smile. And, you know, I love people, in general, but no one else makes me smile like you. No one else looks at me the way you do. You make me feel like maybe I can be good for real."

"I'm sorry, *I* make *you* feel like *you* can be good? You're practically due for some kind of sainthood as far as I can tell, Nikki, what are you talking about?"

She smiled warmly at them, then pointed at their eyes playfully. "Yeah. That's what I mean. No one else looks at me like that. Gods, if you were telling my story, I really could be a saint instead of a demon." She lowered her head with a grim look. "I wish I could've hid it from you forever, Rav. But I'm not the person you think. I'm not good. I never will be. All I can do is try to pay it back but I can never undo the things I've done. And I can never stop being what I am."

"...And you still can't tell me what that is."

She shook her head sadly.

Ravi stared at the space on the bed between the two of them. Nicole really was ashamed of who she was, wasn't she? And after all that stuff she was always saying about being true with the people you love.

Was she really planning to just... keep pretending the whole time they were together?

Ravi clenched a fist tight until their knuckles cracked when it occurred to them that they had no right to judge her for that. As bare as they were to her, they were still hiding the worst mistakes of their past from her too.

They reached out their hand to entwine their fingers with hers and tugged at her gently to catch her gaze.

"Hey. I've done some pretty shitty things too, you know."

She scoffed at that. "Oh my gods Ravi you cannot *possibly* compare what you've done to what I've done. There isn't a single person in the entire history of the human race who's done worse than me."

"Does it matter?"

"Yes it matters! We're talking stealing a chocolate bar versus murdering every child in an orphanage here! You have no idea what you're talking about! I can't be forgiven. I can't just... forget and move on. I'm a monster. And you know, if I can't pretend to be human anymore, I've at least gotta save you from getting it in your head that I'm some kind of innocent angel. I'm not."

"...I don't think that's true."

She scoffed at them, "Well I can't lie, so it better be true."

"Is that a rule too?"

"Yeah."

"...That's... Wait. How would I... Hold on, this is one of those logic puzzles, right? One guy tells only lies, the other tells only truths... Fuck, we're missing the lying guy, though."

She grinned at them playfully. "Don't lose any sleep over it, Ravi Bee. There's no trick to figuring it out. You just have to trust me."

Ravi stared pensively into Nicole's eyes for a few tense breaths. They couldn't hope to guess what she was. And they didn't have any interest in asking about her horrible crimes, whatever they might be. All they wanted to do was keep going with her, keep loving her, keep making her smile.

"I trust you," they said at last. "And I trust that you're good. For real. Whether you want to accept it or not. —And do not try to prove me wrong. Everything you say, everything you do, every moment I have ever shared with you, it's all screaming how good you are. And I don't... care what you are. I love you. You're still the same Nicole, whatever you are. You make me happy, every breath we share."

Nicole smirked at that and teased them, "Sappy."

"What?" Ravi asked indignantly. "I can't tell the woman I love how much I love her?"

"You can't do it a little more stoically?"

"Oh sorry. *Dearest Nicole Doyle, I have a deep affection for you. I hope it's reciprocal. Sincerely, Ravi Beausoleil.*"

"Perfect."

Ravi got caught in Nicole's warm, adoring gaze – got lost in her eyes, as it had always been so easy to do – and no wonder, now. Those gemstone irises were surely enchanted just as much as every other part of this beautiful woman's body.

But it didn't feel like a trick, or a trap, or some kind of manipulation. Her eyes could be any color, could be dull as stone, and still there would be that loving warmth, shaping every curve of her face into that heartfelt smile.

...She really loved them, didn't she? God, what the hell.

They broke from her gaze for a few seconds to put together an important desperately hopeful question.

"...You really can't lie?"

"I really can't lie," she answered, confident as always. And in all the time Ravi had known Nicole, they had never seen her lie. She definitely played coy sometimes, dodged questions – and they could see why now – but she had never, ever lied.

"So... you were telling the truth then: You really aren't bothered by the stuff in my sores? Unless you touch them?"

"I really, truly, honestly – on the cruel indifference of every nameless god – am not bothered by your sores unless I touch them. And even then, only when they're turning black. I promise. And I've already learned, the hard way, to be very very careful with your shoulder so we don't hurt each other, I solemnly swear."

"...Then... can I... I can really still be close to you? I can still kiss you and everything else? It's not going to make you throw up or pass out or something?"

"Oh my gods... Come here," Nicole said with a roll of her eyes before she pulled Ravi in for a long kiss. When she finally released them, she teased, "See? I'm fine. Honestly, we've done that like... hundreds of times already, why are you freaking out about it now?"

Ravi touched their lips tentatively, bewildered at the sensation, finally knowing what it really was.

"...You really taste... Even just your lips... God, how did I never put this together before now? I'm so stupid."

"Most people never put any of it together. Don't beat yourself up about it, Ravi Bee."

"It just really sucks that it took making you violently ill with some magic-fucking tar to catch you on it..."

"...Yeah."

The two of them went quiet for a long while.

Nicole broke the tense silence with a difficult question – one that needed to be asked, unfortunately: "What should we do? About that... factory?"

"...I don't know," Ravi replied.

Nicole fiddled with her fingers a bit before she offered a suggestion: "Your research..."

Ravi let the half-spoken sentiment linger in the air for a few long seconds, until Nicole seemed to think it was necessary to try to finish it for them:

"If they're… collecting all that stuff from people… like you…—"

"—*Stop*. Stop. Please. —We don't know, okay? We don't. It might not be… —It couldn't… —It… it's just something… synthetic. Okay? It has to be. …It has to."

Nicole pinched her palm between her finger and thumb painfully enough to make herself wince before she looked up and challenged them: "Ravi. Look me in the eye: Do you really believe that? Because if you don't, if there's even a chance—"

Ravi refused to meet her gaze, but she wasn't content to let them get out of this so easily. She cradled their jaw in her palm and drew their eyes to hers to silently pry the truth out of them.

They tried to look away, pleading with her: "Even if I wanted to, what am I supposed to do, Nicole? It's too big."

"Lead paint was big, too," she said, as a cold reminder of something Ravi *really* didn't want to remember right now.

"What?"

"If this is killing people," she continued, to lead them on. "If *InThetics* is killing people, and you *know* that…"

They looked her in the eye for a long time – and what a look was complicating the impossibly shimmery green-flecked turquoise of her eyes. She sure as hell didn't want to remind them, that was painfully clear, but she obviously felt some duty to do so – to remind them what they said so long ago, chastising What's-Her-Name the TA for so callously ignoring the plight of the world – to remind them what they promised they'd do: Anything at all but sit on the truth.

"You really want me to do something so… dangerous… —It's *suicide* Nikki."

"We can find a way to be safe about it. —*I* can keep you safe."

Ravi scoffed. "What, with your magic?"

"With everything I have, Rav, I'll keep you good. I promise. I'm not letting the Ravi boat forget how to float."

Ravi laughed at the idea. They were sure they'd swapped out every last bit of what made them seaworthy – what made them human – what made them *Ravi* in Nicole's eyes – the very moment they signed on with InThetics. But Nicole was still looking at them like they could cross the damn Atlantic in a week.

Still, that question remained unanswered: What should they do?

The weight of the answer to that puzzle sat heavy in Ravi's mind. Whatever they were going to have to do, it was going to be... a lot. It was going to be dangerous. It might even be impossible.

But Nicole was right: They couldn't just sit on something like this and pretend it didn't matter.

Luckily, whatever they decided to do, at least they'd have this amazing woman at their side to help out. And, magic or not, that was an incredible advantage.

The two of them agreed to come back to it later. Nicole was still exhausted from her exposure to that vile poison, and Ravi pushing her so hard sure hadn't helped. Now that they were done harassing her about the nature of her being, she desperately needed to continue resting.

While she was lying down, Ravi curled up with her, resting their head on her chest, arm wrapped around her.

In the silence, Ravi found themself listening attentively to Nicole's heartbeat for anything strange about it, but it sounded so goddamn human that they figured it almost excused how long it had taken them to figure out it wasn't.

They noticed for the first time how carefully Nicole's arm was cradling them, perfectly avoiding the dangerous spots on their shoulder. She really had learned how to hold them. She really loved them enough to figure that out without a word of complaint.

They lingered on it a little too long, the realization of just how much they had been a burden on her, this whole time. They had no idea. And the whole time she had been silently making room for them in her life in spite of it all. They lingered on it just too long enough that they couldn't help a few silent tears running down their cheeks.

Ravi figured they must've been a goddamn saint in a past life or something, because they couldn't imagine a single thing they'd done in this one that warranted a gift like Nicole.

They squeezed her tight and whispered a gentle thank you, but she was already asleep. She probably knew though. She had to know.

The Razor Edge of Reason
Might Actually
Be a Very, Very Good
Location for a Date

"Dragon," Ravi guessed, pointing at Nicole with their fork over breakfast, the very morning she was back to her usual energetic cheerful self.

"Can't say."

"Witch."

"Okay no. Definitely not. Thanks."

"Elf. —No: *High* elf."

"Ravi Bee, love, all my love, I swear to all the unspeakable gods, I'm going to leap over this table and shake you senseless if you don't stop."

Ravi huffed. "No hints? Seriously?"

"No hints."

Ravi groaned teasingly, then grinned at her: "If I guess it right, do you have to tell me?"

"Yes."

"Okay so I just gotta find an encyclopedia of magical creatures or something, right? List them off one by one."

Nicole smiled and shook her head. "Doesn't work like that. You need some *conviction* behind your guess. You have to *believe* it. Have some evidence, you know?"

"Wow. Seriously? Do I need to do a whole thesis? Peer reviewed? Come on, that's so stupid."

She shrugged. "Sorry, my dearest love. I don't make the rules."

Ravi spent the next few weeks prying as much information out of Nicole as they could about her life. Her *real* life.

Little things at first. Just testing the waters. Seeing exactly how far Nicole would let them push it. But it wasn't long before they were feeling a little too bold, asking questions that shoved her stumbling over the very final boundary of her comfort zone.

Still, they got a lot out of her before she put a stop to it all.

Like, she was old. Really old. Though she wouldn't be any more specific about that than that she was far older than Ravi. From the way she said it, though, they were guessing a few centuries.

She used to be some kind of *royalty* or something. Famous, at least, and influential, wherever she was from – which was... *absolutely* crazy, that they had somehow earned the affection of, not just some mysterious magical creature, but the affection of a *celebrity* of a mysterious magical creature. They felt stupidly starstruck when they found out, even though Nicole refused to give them any details about her notoriety.

And she was banished from wherever her real home was – stuck in a miserable human body – thank god, though, right?

"Lucky me. If you got stuck in a snail, I don't think I'd have fallen for you quite so hard."

"So shallow," she teased them.

"How'd you end up in such a beautiful body anyways, if it's supposed to be a punishment? You sure don't *look* miserable."

"I made it myself."

"You made your own prison? That's dark."

"Isn't it?" she replied with a bitter, sarcastically exaggerated smile.

"Who's punishing you?"

Nicole shook her head. No dice on that one.

"What for?"

"I broke a rule. A big one."

"Right. I mean, obviously. Some super powerful magical creature wouldn't get sentenced to some prison of a mortal body for just frolicking in endless fields of flowers or whatever."

"Correct."

"So, you're, what, a criminal? Or some kind of rebel? A martyr? Fighting the system?"

"Something like that."

"God, you're so fucking punk. Seriously."

"You're really overselling it, Ravi Bee, but thank you."

"Is this… common? Are there a lot of magical creatures stuck in human bodies? Because Felicity has a real otherworldly vibe sometimes…"

Nicole laughed hard at that idea. So at least Felicity wasn't magic. Probably.

"No, just me," she assured them, "as far as I know. You might see something pretending to be human sometimes, but I'm the only one *stuck* like this."

"…You must've really fucked up then."

"It was worth it. I promise."

"…Forever?"

"Forever." Nicole hesitated for a moment after she said it, then she added, as if someone were twisting her arm to do it: "Nn…*shit*… Fuck. Okay, *sort of*. Sort of forever. With… *unpleasant* exit conditions." She grimaced at herself miserably. "Uh hey how about no more questions about this stuff? Wouldn't that be fun?"

Ravi shot her with a playful little finger gun. "You got it. Question box: Sealed. You just let me know when you're up for more, okay?"

"Is 'never' an option?"

"Yeah, of course. I will be writhing with curiosity forever but if you never want to talk about this again, I won't. Promise."

Nicole slid her hands across the table for Ravi to entwine their fingers in and pleaded with them with a warm smile, "It would be so very cool if you never asked me about any of this ever again."

Ravi replied with a weak attempt at a cheerful smirk. "Okay—" They paused for a moment before they felt compelled to add, "—I just… Sorry, I didn't mean to push you. I just want to know who you are, you know? You don't have to hide anything from me."

"I know, Ravi Bee. I'll let you know if I change my mind, I promise."

She looked genuinely relieved when Ravi moved on to other subjects, and they were true to their word: They never asked again. But it never left their mind, that curiosity. They wondered about it all the time, with every reminder that she wasn't quite normal. When they tasted the impossible sweetness of her lips. When they saw that supernatural sparkle in her eyes. When they traced the mysterious unexplained runes on her back. When they admired her arcane stitchwork on their jacket.

It took a long time, but they found a way to make peace with the mystery of it. She was just... amazing, in a way they could never hope to fully understand, and that was okay. They could be okay with that. Really. Honestly. They could.

They had to be.

And it didn't matter anyways. They didn't fall in love with whatever she was before. They fell in love with *Nicole*.

The two of them somehow managed to maintain some semblance of a mundane way of living together and loving each other after that, though Nicole did occasionally delight them with a little magic, disappearing and reappearing with some gift or another, teasing them with a lewd display from some unreachable bough in tall trees in the park, drawing pretty white lines on their skin in shapes and words they couldn't hope to understand. And the sounds she moaned in bed sometimes – words from some forgotten language, they figured – they were *musical*, warming the back of Ravi's mind, flooding them with ripples of pleasure whenever they heard the ancient melodies on her tongue.

She wasn't afraid to use her magic in front of Ravi now, but she never used her magic to *move* Ravi. Too dangerous, she insisted, and they had to trust her on that. But the two of them did go on a whole lot of trespassing dates after that, with her brazenly slipping past any locked doors that stood in the way, exploring the forbidden corners of any building in the city they wanted. Ravi discovered it was one of her favorite activities – trespassing, exploring, tasting the forbidden – right up there with dancing and making love and savoring her most beloved foods.

They marveled at her, at the way she lived. Her body was supposed to be a miserable torturous prison of some sort, but as if out of spite, she went out of her way to do everything she could to relish every pleasure she could milk out of it – and Ravi was very, very happy to assist.

She was right, of course: Half of the fun of trespassing was making out in secret closets, and Ravi was quickly getting addicted to the rush of it. Opportunistic exhibitionism was one thing. Breaking and entering *just to fuck*? That was... something... <u>*else*</u>.

This half-revelation of Nicole's magical nature truly seemed to unlock something reckless in her—in *both of them*. After only a few weeks, it was getting to the point that Ravi could barely remember the last time Nicole wore anything at all under her dress when they went out together – she was so eager to let them take her, anywhere – eager to let their bold fingers crawl up her skirt to part her thighs and slip inside her, or to hear them command her to bend over against a wall so they could get on their knees for worship to bury their tongue in her – sometimes only separated from a business meeting or a busy conference hall by nothing more than a curtain or a closet door or a corner wall – other times, only *barely* more discreet, in some towering commercial building with her bare chest and grinning face pressed violently right up against the floor-to-ceiling glass of a dark unoccupied office's window, dress hiked up to show off her beautiful dripping wet pussy and slick thighs to the whole city, careless gasps and guttural moans escaping her lips at Ravi's salacious command for anyone nearby to hear.

It was getting so, so dangerous, but god they were loving riding on the edge of oblivion with her. They were ready to do anything for her to make this newly revealed torturous existence of hers more exhilarating – *anything*. It was the least they could do, for how wonderful she made them feel while they faced their own torturous existence. They felt a deep kinship with her when they held her – especially after devastatingly enjoyable evenings in bed. —And before hurried, desperately passionate weekday mornings before work. — And during every tender moment of the long, *long* afternoons on the weekends that tended to bleed right into evenings again. The two of them were just spitefully making the best out of the bitter promise of an endless parade of misery, together, against the uncontestable will of an unfeeling universe – and Ravi had never felt more understood, never felt closer to anyone in their life than they did with her now.

They even found the courage to follow her, hand in hand, to the dance floor any night she asked, no matter how dangerous it was to do it. It didn't matter any more. The delight in her eyes was worth more to them than anything they could imagine, worth any pain.

If they could only spend every single one of their far-too-few days left alive like this, with her, it would be worth more than a whole long lifetime without her. If they could only have even one year – hell, even just the few months they already had – it was more than they could possibly deserve. But here she was, cherishing them like gold, like real gold, with no end to her adoration in sight.

Unfortunately, in between the joy of *her*, they were still living under a cloud of dire malaise, working at InThetics, desperately trying and failing to dig up information about where that tar in the basement came from, in between hours of lethargically peering through the still-cracked glass of the autokiln, feeling again and again, every day, the same desperation they felt when they were trying to destroy that vile poison to keep it away from Nicole forever. Every time they fiddled with the controls, the feeling came back just as powerful, fresh in their mind, just as intoxicating with rage and self-loathing as it was the first time.

They were done stealing the vials of their own monthly extractions now. They couldn't possibly subject Nicole to that anymore. That was a closed chapter of their life. Finding some sense of closure about their own illness wasn't on the table. —Though, after every treatment, they still found themself staring longingly at the tray of loaded vials, aching to grab one and run.

But even if they were done experimenting on the mess of their own sickness, they still had to confirm exactly what InThetics was up to with this stuff. If there really was a chance that what the company was doing was actually as vile as their worst imagining, then millions of lives might be on the line here.

After all, they already knew that there was no profit for InThetics in finding a cure for an illness that they sold the only treatment for. Conspiracy theory or not, that was a cold hard capitalist fact. But combine that with their ability to extract the byproduct of that illness to turn it into some rare, proprietary, extremely profitable super material? Well, that might be enough for the company to do a lot more than just *suppress a cure*.

❧ *Part IV* ❦

I Hope This Message Finds You Well

(Morning, Tuesday, 20th June)

Ravi was in the biotech department at dear sweet Lexy's desk after sending him off to grab the two of them some coffee. They thought they were alone in the team's office; no one else had been in the room when they turned their focus on fussing with Lexy's terminal in search of any interesting leads on their secret investigations.

They were startled wrong by a not-quite-forgotten voice behind them:

"Uh excuse me?"

They quickly smashed some keys on the machine to close the files they were poking around in and turned around in an adrenalized rush to see who it was.

"...Carrie!?"

The guardian of the biochemistry lab back at the university? What the hell was she doing here?

"It *is* you. I thought I recognized that gremlin posture of yours. You're going to need a back brace if you don't fix that, ya know. What are you doing in here?"

"...What... am... I...?" Ravi was stunned stupid and stammering. "I was... waiting for... Alexander...? —Hold on, never mind that, what are *you* doing here?"

"...My job?" She let out a skeptical little huff. "How is it I always seem to find you getting into trouble in the wrong lab, Ravi Beausoleil? What are you messing with there?" she asked teasingly, with a nod at Lexy's terminal.

Ravi didn't answer. They were too focused on the sudden appearance of their old abandoned mentor. "Wait. But. What about your... research...? Did you quit the university or something?"

Carrie's lips briefly cracked into a sad smile before she confirmed it was the latter: "Or something. Sorry, Ravi, but I can't let you mess around in here. Let's go," she coldly insisted, gesturing for Ravi to step away from the desk and follow her to the exit.

Ravi squinted their eyes at her discerningly, trying to figure out what was going on with her. She was being so curt. This wasn't like her. But if she wasn't acting normal, there was no point trying to have a real conversation here. They'd just have to play along.

"Right. Sorry. Lead the way."

Ravi gravely followed after their old colleague – their... *new* colleague? – trying to think of what to ask to get to the root of this. But from how she was talking, it sure sounded like she wasn't about to answer anything honestly right now.

When they arrived at the exit, Carrie held out her arm to direct Ravi through the security door out of the biotech wing. They noted the old green InThetics logo on the back of her prosthetic hand had been replaced with a modern version of the company's insignia, in brilliant white ink.

Ravi lingered for a moment before they informed Carrie there was a cool band playing at the Serpent's Fang in a couple days. "Wish I could go. Would be a nice place to catch up with an old friend," they added coyly, hoping she got the message. "Anyways, nice seeing you."

"Nice seeing you, Ravi. I'll tell Alexander you were looking for him."

No hint at all that she was even listening. Hell of a poker face.

"...Thanks."

When Ravi got back to their own terminal, they pored over the archive of emails they had been filtering out of their inbox – among them, the frequent and ever-so-cloying *'Welcome to the team!'* announcements for newly hired employees.

And sure enough, there she was, announced a few weeks prior: Carolyn Carter, subject matter expert, biotechnics department.

They flopped back in their company-reissued deviant blue extreme gamer chair of theirs and spun around lethargically while they rolled that around in their head. It had been months since they'd spoken to Carrie, since Ravi's cold and shameful and perfunctory goodbye. They hadn't told Carrie where they were going, or why. It all felt far too embarrassing to admit to. She gave them her best, of course, and they said they'd keep in touch as much as they could.

Which was... *not at all*, sadly. Ravi wasn't great at that kind of social upkeep stuff.

Thinking back to their time together in the lab, and the occasional nights out of it at the bar, they were 99% certain that Carrie was *not* interested in leaving academia. She was always very enthusiastic about continuing her research. She even seemed to enjoy teaching, and she *loved* encouraging her students in their own research. It lit her up every time she talked about some new challenge her little junior research teams were hurdling.

She wouldn't just *leave*, would she?

Ravi pulled up the university's website to poke around in the department directory.

Carolyn Carter wasn't a registered account anymore.

The biotech faculty roster didn't list her name.

The book store and library pulled all her books and copy packs.

Even the recordings of courses that Ravi *knew* she taught over the winter semester had been removed from the archive.

There was just... *nothing left.*

— 'Ever heard of Terrance Paul?'

Carrie's warning grumbled in their head for a minute before they had the morbid curiosity to look up the missing man's name.

Like Carrie had warned Ravi before – when she was freaking out about the possibility of being disappeared by government spooks for prying into classified documents – there was no record of Terrance Paul at the university.

But, to their grim surprise, they *did* manage to track down a record of him – at *InThetics*. According to the staff directory, he was hired a couple years ago. As a subject matter expert. In biotechnics.

—*What the fuck...*

Ravi rolled their fingers on the keyboard while they stared at the blinking cursor on their terminal and considered how exactly to compose an internal email to a dead man to ask why he's alive actually.

Like...?

Hi Terry, so great to hear you're not dead! You don't know me but I heard you got erased from the face of the Earth for climbing the tower of academia in pursuit of the devil's most unholy forbidden fruit. I see you have an opening in your schedule at 2PM today. Can I block a quick meeting with you?

Thanks!

Two exclamation points to be friendly. Call to action to get a quick response. Maybe 'Dr. Paul' would be more professional—?

No! What the fuck!? Obviously no! God damn it, how the fuck were they supposed to do this!?

They erased the draft and logged out of their terminal before storming off to sit in front of the cracked autokiln and brood over their situation while admiring the glow of the heater.

Oh, if only all problems could be solved by the purifying heat of the kiln... Turn us all to glass, O great and tireless wyrm...

As much as they wished the machine had any answers for them, they really didn't have anything to extract from it but the day's manufacturing trial.

They spent the rest of the day distracting themself by actually doing their job and running mundane tests on the freshly baked and cooled ceramic until they could clock out.

They lingered by the parking lot exit for a long while, hoping to catch Carrie leaving for home, but even after hanging out in the shade there for a few long cigarettes, there was no sign of her. She'd probably accepted Miriam's enticing offer to live in the company's fancy apartments on campus.

They'd have to wait until the night of their fabled 'great band' at the Serpent's Fang if they wanted a chance to talk to her now.

While they rode the elevator up to their apartment, they tried on a few explanatory phrases to get a feel for how crazy this was about to sound coming out of their mouth. They were hoping to stumble on some magic words that could explain it all without freaking Nicole out, but, you know, it was freaky, so they left the elevator empty-handed.

After explaining it as plainly as they could and pleading with Nicole not to freak out, she was, in fact, disappointingly calm.

"So InThetics poaches troublesome scientists?" she asked curiously.

"Seems like it."

"...Do you think they poached *you?*"

Ravi opened their mouth to protest, because that definitely wasn't what happened, right? They just had... *extenuating circumstances.*

But they stumbled on the uncertainty of it.

—*Oh god. Oh god damn it...*

"...They... they poached me..."

But <u>why</u>? Their ceramics research? Nothing about that stuff was worth *suppressing*, even if it did have some similarities to the processes they saw at InThetics after they started working there. It wasn't like Ravi was in a position to stir up trouble about that kind of intellectual property theft stuff.

But... their secret research into the tar... *had* been moving forward around the time that InThetics sent them that enticing letter. Might be a coincidence. Might be. But even if they had no idea what exactly they were stumbling into, they had nonetheless been getting closer to *something*. If they had kept going, would they have gotten close enough to connect the dots somehow? Could they really have been close enough back then that it scared the company into action like this? Scared them into trying to secure Ravi's cooperation and complicity?

Had InThetics been *watching*? Carrie had made it sound like the government was the big problem.

God, which would be worse?

If the government really cared, they probably would've made Ravi disappear for real. InThetics, though, what a strategy. Forcibly transform risks into assets under your control. Why not? If this was how they got people out of the way, it was certainly *economical*. It wouldn't even look weird from the outside, would it? Ravi had just changed careers. They made themself disappear all on their own, to start a new life, chasing brighter opportunities. No need for black suit spooks in vans, no murder, no coverup. All InThetics had to do was set up a little bait and quietly drag Ravi away from their secret scientifically incendiary research, take away the gasoline and molotovs and give them a pathetic little fire stick to poke some pointless embers in a cold corporate industrial fireplace to keep them under control.

Terrance probably never even *knew* he got erased. Maybe he and Carrie both just accepted a tempting job offer in desperate circumstances, just like they had.

How many others were there?

They tapped their fingers on their knee for a long time before they worked up the courage to ask:

"Nicole. Those names."

"Mm? Which names?"

"From the redacted docs in Carrie's database. Can you write them down for me?"

"Ohhh... Oh no. You think?"

"I don't know. I don't know, but it would be a hell of a thing, wouldn't it? To find a bunch of academically erased scientists working at the same place?"

"That would... be a hell of a thing..."

And it was, in fact, a hell of a thing, because, in the company directory, under the prestigious and ambiguously defined title of subject matter expert, Ravi managed to find almost every single one of the names Nicole remembered from those forbidden classified documents.

Poached.

Like them.

It's Just One Little Step, How Hard Could It Be?

From a dark table at the back of the Serpent's Fang, Ravi watched with guilt and trepidation as Carrie expertly hurdled the single harrowing half-step up into the lobby with her wheelchair before she paused to scout out the tables. They sheepishly waved her over when they caught her attention.

"Had to pick the place with the one pointless bastard stair, huh," she chided them playfully.

"Sorry! Sorry. I totally forgot."

She smiled at Ravi and assured them she was just kidding, then shoved the chair opposite Ravi out of the way and got settled in across from them.

"So, what's the band?" she teased them.

"Uh. Yeah. No band tonight, sorry."

"Oh no," she replied, dry and sarcastic, "I have been deceived. You scoundrel. Guess you're buying the drinks then, huh? To make up for my crushing disappointment?"

Ravi was dumbfounded at how cheerful Carrie was about all this.

"Carrie. Is that really you?"

"You bet. —Well, 98% of Carrie anyways," she replied playfully, showing off the fancy new replacement for her synthetic hand. "Boy you sure looked terrified to see me the other day. Thought I was a ghost for a second, I swear. You were more afraid of my face than the fact you got caught poking around where you don't belong. —Again."

"You're not supposed to *be there*, Carrie. It's not a good place to work."

She laughed. "Ohhh, I see. *You* can run off for this amazing mysterious job at the big scary tech company, but I'm stuck at the university forever."

"You weren't 'stuck' when I left. What happened?"

Carrie looked over her shoulder at the bar. "One sec, need something to sip on dramatically if I'm telling you all this." Then she excused herself to get a drink from Henry.

She returned with a fancy looking and very fragrant dark beer and a very pleased look on her face. "Holy shit I can't believe they had this on the menu. Where'd you find this place?"

"...It's Nicole's favorite."

"I can tell why! I can't believe you never took me here before. Hiding the good stuff, huh? —That guy behind the bar has such an *energy* to him. You think he's single—?"

"Carrie. Can we focus? I've kind of been freaking out for a few days here."

The playful sparkle in Carrie's eyes faded a bit when Ravi asked for details. She took a long savoring sip of her drink before slouching over the table and getting settled in to mercifully explain as plainly as she could.

Turned out that some of the university's funding comes from a weird work exchange program. The federal government coordinates the program, and creates 'opportunities' for corporations to 'borrow' researchers for specific projects, without hiring them outright.

"Which sounds great for everyone," Carrie added, bitter and sarcastic. "I don't even get paid any more than I did as a prof, *and* I don't have a permanent contract, *and* I can't do my own research anymore, *and* I didn't actually get a choice. Just, one day, letter on my desk from the dean. Something like, '*Hey Carolyn, you like InThetics, right? You've got one of their hands and everything! Cool, well, you'll be working there starting Monday. Cheers.*' —Prick."

"That sounds a little less sinister than I was imagining."

"Does it? Because it sounded pretty shitty to me when it happened!"

"...Did you know they erased you from the directory? Pulled your books?"

"Did they now?"

Ravi nodded grimly.

"Great. Great! That's great."

"Carrie, that guy who disappeared from the university – Dr. Paul – he's been working at InThetics for two years."

Carrie's eyes glazed over while she rolled her fingers on the table for a few silent breaths, until at last she hoisted her glass to her lips, tipped it all back, then dramatically whirled her chair around to meander back to the bar in silence to get another one. She returned with a refill and a couple of clear shots.

"You like tequila, right?" she asked without asking, putting one of the fragrant little cups in front of Ravi.

"Not... usually..." they lied. Though it would've been true a year ago.

"Well tonight you do! Let's get fucked, since you're paying, and since we're already fucked."

She lifted her shot in the air for Ravi to follow, and slammed it down with a hiss. No salt. No lime. Ravi did the same, and it sent a miserable shiver down their spine, but they stuck it out to look tough for Carrie.

"So," Carrie said with a renewed sense of chaos, "I *am* fucked, right? Is that I'm hearing?"

"Well. I don't know..."

"Okay let me be more clear, then: I'm *as fucked* as our dear Dr. Paul?"

"...Seems like it."

"And how is the previously *stalked* and *terrified* gentleman doing?"

Ravi shook their head and shrugged. "I can't just message him about this, obviously. They're watching our inboxes. And I can't find him anywhere in the building. He doesn't have an office listed, or a phone number. I don't even know what he *does*. He's got the same title as you – subject matter expert. I was hoping maybe you could... explain what that means?"

"Ha. Me too! I was even more confused than you are about my lack of job description or permanent address. I'm mostly just wasting my time pointlessly puttering around and attending meetings that I don't really have anything to contribute to but a pretty smile and the occasional nod along." She clicked her tongue and muttered, "Certainly doesn't make me feel like an expert on *any subject* aside from the esteemed science of Shoving A Thumb Up My Ass, frankly. And there are plenty of profs back at the university who are far more qualified. —Looking at you, dean."

Ravi rotated their pint glass in their fingers pensively while they tried to put all that together.

There were patterns. At the warehouse, first you lose your

overtime, then your hours get cut back, then…

"You lost your access to a research facility," Ravi muttered to themself, "then you got put on a *nothing* job, and then you got erased from academia." They paused for a few long silent seconds before they absently addressed a question to the bodiless council of signatures carved into the surface of the table, as though they could answer, "And then what?"

Carrie lifted her pint glass in the air in a cheers to the miserable mystery: "The question of the hour: Exactly *how* fucked are we?"

"I guess we need to track down Dr. Paul for an answer."

"Great. Well, that'll be easy and not suspicious at all, arranging a meeting between each of the three scientists InThetics pilfered from the very same university in the last two years. —I'll book a conference room! You like 1-13A? Comfy chairs, I hear. —Oh, I *loved* the view in 10-20C though. You can see the whole river."

Ravi leaned forward to rest their elbows on the table and buried their face in their palms. There was an answer to this. They knew it.

"The trick is… not being suspicious," they muttered. "So, get someone else to organize the meeting? Make it look like a coincidence?"

"And do *you* know anyone high up enough to organize a meeting between three extremely specific subject matter experts from all over the building?"

Ravi let out a little sigh and admitted their pool of contacts on the corporate campus was limited to pretty low-level employees.

"—There's Miriam, though."

Carrie laughed at that.

But Ravi's eyes sparked with a plan that formed chaotically on their tongue as it tumbled out of them: "No. No wait, take it seriously. She's everywhere, right? Micromanager supreme. You've met her, right?"

Carrie gave Ravi a knowing smirk that was more than enough to confirm that Carrie had definitely had the Miriam Ortiz Experience when she was brought in.

"She onboarded *me* Carrie and I'm *nobody* there. I just fuss with knobs on a big machine all day. So she *definitely* knows her precious subject matter experts. We could use her. We just need her at the table for a big enough project. Then we could convince her to bring anyone we wanted into any room of our choosing, in the name of the project's grand success. We just have to make sure she knows which people are the right people for the job. —<u>Our</u> people."

Carrie's grin slowly faded while she drank in the determination in Ravi's eyes, until that nearly-dead grin sparked into a huge laughing smile. She raised her glass and took a drink in celebration of Ravi's insanity. "Can't ever complain about being bored with you around, hey Ravi? You're the only one in the world nuts enough to hand your exclusive poached scientist guestlist directly to the head of the company poaching your scientists."

"Just have to be clever about it, Carrie. If we get it right, she'll write the guestlist herself."

"And you're that clever, huh? Ego."

"Hey, I went to university."

"Everyone at the company went to university."

"Miriam didn't."

"Really?"

"She's a self-made prodigal visionary, Carrie. The bold entrepreneurial heiress to the InThetics throne. You didn't know that? It's in the employee handbook."

Carrie laughed at that and admitted she'd been a little too bitter about the circumstances of her employment to read any of the literature the company handed her.

She swirled her drink around for a few somber seconds to take that in. "So you're telling me this internationally renowned, scientific paradigm shifting megacorp of ours is being run by someone who *doesn't actually know science?*"

"That's what I'm saying. She's a fanatic, not a scholar. You haven't seen her talking up the Singularity?"

Carrie laughed at the idea, then flexed the digits on her prosthetic to show off her derision, "The immortal merging of man and machine."

"Brought to you by InThetics AugMe™ with Saffron Aquamarine™ Technology," Ravi continued, echoing the tawdry commercials.

Carrie rolled her synthetic fingers on the surface of the table for a few bars before she clenched them into a tight fist and knocked on the table twice with a resounding sense of finality. "Alright. Alright you nutjob alright if you think you can do this without getting us disappeared into the deepest darkest depths of the InThetics basement laboratories—"

"I can."

Carrie scoffed, approvingly. "You could've been a con man, Ravi."

"Always time for a second career," Ravi said – though they knew that was absolutely not true for themself. They had a very limited time to do anything with the very important information they had – a few years maybe, before their sickness spread and ruined them. —Hell, maybe a decade if something miraculous happened, or if Nicole's optimism had any base in reality. But even with a decade, there was no time to drag their heels. No time to hesitate. No time to play it safe. No time for half-pulled-out fucking around. There was only time to bury every reckless inch of themself into this, until they could figure out how to stop whatever evil InThetics was doing to the people of the world.

And considering how desperately InThetics was trying to bury their secrets, how surgically and thoroughly they were neutering all these scientists, it sure seemed like whatever those secrets were would definitely be worth dragging up out of the ground.

All they needed to do was figure out some kind of project that would require a handful of 'subject matter experts' from all over the company to get together in a room – some kind of project that would make Miriam salivate at the thought of its completion:

The Singularity.

It's Not Exactly a Scientific Method

(*Afternoon, Friday, 21st July*)

"Immortal brains," Ravi said excitedly, once they had Miriam captive in an elevator on the way to the last meeting on her calendar before the weekend. They had exactly ten seconds to catch her attention.

But those two words were enough, apparently.

"Go on."

"I've been reading about some breakthroughs in composite ceramics. And this one stuck out like crazy: Suspended cascading capacitive optical semi-organic webs."

"Never heard of that."

"Very new. Very *stable*. But they haven't worked out all the kinks yet, haven't even started looking at manufacturing. It's basically a complicated matrix of fibrous optical filaments in a self-healing composite. Looks a *lot* like a brain when you send a pulse of light through it, and any cracks in it have the ability to *heal* and form new connections."

Miriam's eyes lit up at the possibilities.

The paper Ravi handed Miriam to read over was... a *little* fake. A little... *not quite* peer reviewed. A little... —Okay, fine, so maybe Ravi committed a *little* academic fraud to get a paper published that was full of lies and then was almost immediately retracted.

But who even reads those retractions? Definitely not science-fanatic heiress to the InThetics empire Miriam Ortiz, that's for sure.

And, as they hoped, Miriam ate it up when Ravi handed her the fraudulent preprint.

They had her.

All they had to do was convince her to put them on the project – a project that would necessitate collaboration from every part of the organization – a project that would need *no excuse* to summon *anyone* in the company's directory for a casual meeting of the minds.

They humbly offered to be a fly on the wall, taking all the notes at meetings and organizing a growing library of confusing documentation about a fictional technology that would never exist.

Miriam, in her fervor to encourage the rambunctious paradigm shifting new generation, opted to make Ravi a project coordinator instead – a position they were absolutely not qualified for. But that didn't matter. They only needed to hold out until they had their chance to meet with the disappeared scientists wandering the floors of the InThetics campus like useless listless zombies.

Easy.

A couple weeks later, Ravi was entirely swamped with paperwork and diagrams and budgets and presentations and preliminary pre-pre-meetings, and they were absolutely hating every minute of it. Their inbox was overflowing with emails from every corner of the corporate campus that literally *demanded* urgent responses, *or else.* — And the *or else* there turned out to be for random strangers in the company to spontaneously sublimate out of the air near their desk to ask about the cause of the entirely unreasonable delay and make it entirely impossible to answer their *other* emails.

They hadn't even had a chance to touch their lovely autokiln in *days*. They never imagined they'd miss the thing.

This... may have been a mistake.

But they had to push through. If they held on, just a little while longer, just until the project started, they'd get to a point where they could finally start tapping people for talent and arranging discreet meetings with the missing scientists.

Soon.

Another couple weeks later, on what should have been a lovely Friday evening, hours after everyone else on the floor had already left for the weekend, Ravi was frustratedly trying to make sense of the instructions for some workorder form they forgot was due *yesterday* – stuck on a little menu on the form that was demanding they decide whether to request funding from 'Research' or 'Development' and turning half the document red with errors no matter which option they chose – when they realized that this plan kind of sucked. A lot.

And not only did it suck—a lot—but it was also absolutely going to take way the hell too long.

The entire bus ride home their mind was swimming with stupid corporate lingo and mind-numbing forms and a triple-booked meeting schedule and they couldn't help groaning to themself in misery, enough to attract the scornful glare of a few passengers, but they didn't give a shit. This whole situation was a slurry of bullshit of their own stupid creation and they were sick of nothing <u>happening</u>. —And if the back of the damn bus had to hear them groaning so they didn't fucking explode about it then those poor innocent passengers were going to god damn well hear them groan.

When they got home, they flopped on the couch and buried their face in Nicole's heavenly lap to continue their lamentatious vocalizing while their beautiful lover did her honest best to cure them of their ails with nothing more than gentle caresses and soft words. And it helped, but it sure didn't move the project's slovenly timeline up.

"I just feel so powerless!" they complained when they finally got all the groaning out of their system, rolling over to rest the back of their head on Nicole's thigh. "I'm basically in charge of half this damn project and I can't even move it the three fucking inches forward I need to get what I want already. —Fuck!"

"Poor Ravi Bee..."

"Ughhhh... I thought I was being so fucking clever..."

"It's a smart idea. You just have to be patient. It'll come together."

"I don't have <u>time</u> to be patient!"

"You do."

"I don't!"

"You <u>do</u>, Ravi. Stop letting yourself get caught up on how much time you have left and just, go. Don't look forward, don't look back, just go. You'll get there. Or you won't. But you're doing everything you can right now, right?"

"I don't know! Am I?"

Nicole tried to assure them that she couldn't think of anything else they could possibly be doing right now.

"Me either! But it's not like I have any brainpower left at all to think about it like this. I haven't felt this abused and exhausted since I worked at the warehouse, god..."

Nicole pressed her palm into Ravi's abs in soft soothing circles while they complained, until they finally got it all out and fell silent, clutching her other hand in theirs and holding it against their cheek.

"I wish I could carry you in my pocket all day, Nikki..."

"That would be very cute."

"Take you out for a little recharge..."

"Well," she said, as she teased them with a ticklish finger down their thigh and a dozy grin, "I can't fit in your pocket, but maybe I could charge you up enough all at once to get you through a whole week?"

Ravi grinned at her, and drew the hand they were holding against their cheek to their teeth to bite her fingertips playfully before telling her she was welcome to try.

Unfortunately, Nicole's best efforts and Ravi's willing body didn't seem to be enough tonight. Their work-warped mind kept pulling them right out of the moment. Not even the sharp giddiness of Nicole's cutting canines in their thighs or the normally irresistible temptation of burying their tongue in the delicious rosy folds of her pussy seemed to be enough to keep Ravi's attention from drifting to idiotic corporate-flavored thoughts – like, hey, maybe they should go in tomorrow for a fun Saturday morning full of feverish catching up on overdue paperwork, just to move the project ahead a whole quarter of a day or something.

They couldn't even take the time and care they needed to get Nicole off before they found themself impatiently losing focus. They ended up kind of forcing themself to hurry to the goal, taking rushed aggressive shortcuts that normally finished any one of their lovers off in a grand display – but apparently you can't get away with using heartless prepackaged finishing moves on Nicole Doyle.

She took them by the hair to pull them away from her and chide them for pushing themself like that: "It doesn't feel good if you're not into it Rav."

They apologized profusely for their disappointing performance. This never happened. Ever. What the hell was this job doing to them?

Nicole was lost in quiet thought for a few minutes, running loving fingers through the sweat-licked waves of their hair, while Ravi's mind crunched through static and half-formed plans that all amounted to nothing at all.

She startled them from their grim meditative quiet by patting their head repeatedly like she was stimming on a gameshow buzzer while she eagerly exclaimed: "Oh! Oh oh oh I know. I know what you need."

"A lobotomy."

"No."

"A vacation. To the sun maybe."

"No no no tonight I mean tonight."

"...Mm... Can we circle back to the lobotomy thing? I've got a drill—"

Nicole scowled at them and covered their mouth with her hand to playfully squish their cheeks and shut them up. "Would you stop." Then she poked them in the chest teasingly and told them to go get cleaned up and dressed in something *business*. "Wear a tie," she said with a coy grin.

"Not sure how doing more paperwork is supposed to rev up my engine, Nix—"

Again Nicole shushed them with a pincer grip on their cheeks and told them to follow her instructions please and thank you and she would be right back.

Then she disappeared and left Ravi to change.

They knew she was fond of their semi-formal outfits but she'd never specifically requested it. Cosplay? Business cosplay? Was that really enough to get her going?

They put on their sharpest slacks and their pressedest sand-colored shirt and adjusted the businessyest deep forest-green tie in their repertoire with the tidiest half-Windsor knot they could manage. Blazer too? Yeah. Blazer too. Do the whole suit, why not. She'd like that.

They were just putting the final touches on their hair and fussing with their glasses when they felt Nicole appear behind them in their room. When they turned around, they found her sitting straight and proper in their desk chair looking like the most well-done-up secretary they'd ever seen. Wild hair tamed in tidy braids. Subtle, professional makeup and eyeliner that perfectly accentuated a couple bold strokes of *striking* black-cherry lipstick. Floppy black satin bowtie secured *tight* around her throat, holding up the collar of a white half-sheer half-frilled blouse that did very little to hide her curves or obscure the promising raspberry colored lingerie underneath. And that revealing blouse was tucked into a plain, far-too-short-to-be-professional black skirt that led to shiny wine-red stockings that perfectly matched her temptuous lips – stockings that were *begging* for Ravi to peel them off at the very first opportunity that arose, as soon as they could slip the straps of those pretty black heels past her toes.

Her hands were folded. She was putting on an act of being nervous, fussing with her thumbs, biting her deliciously-painted lip, and looking at Ravi with the mousiest eyes they'd ever seen her put on for them.

"Nicole. Looking good."

" 'Miss Doyle' is fine!" she replied, in a put-on, eager-to-please voice. "I'm so sorry I'm late, Mx. Beausoleil. —And on my first day. Oh my gods I'm so so sorry. —Please don't fire me," she added, pressing her palms together in a humble prayer. "I'll never do it again."

Ravi grinned stupidly for a second before they let out a little laugh. It *was* cosplay, then.

They were a terrible actor for this kind of thing. Butterflies gathered in a fluttery crowd in their guts in an instant.

"This is your big idea?" they asked teasingly, trying their best to hide their uh... *unfamiliarity* with the situation. They'd done a lot of reckless things in bed with a lot of people but they'd never done this kind of thing – acting. Felt silly. Ravi didn't pretend in bed. Period.

Nicole broke character for a moment to explain: "Exposure therapy," she said, closing her eyes, putting a finger in the air, and nodding sagely, words dripping with old wisdom, like this was the de facto prescription for workplace misery. "It's been so long since we messed around in your place of business, Rav. You need to have a little fun at the office before it drives you insane. And it *sucks* that I can't visit you after hours for the real thing anymore, but I promise this'll be the perfect substitute."

"And here I thought you just wanted to drag me around in a tie."

"No Mx. Beausoleil, never. You're the boss. If anyone's dragging anyone around by the collar, it's you," she informed them with a wink in her voice.

Again they couldn't help scoffing through a stupid grin at the silliness of the game, but they'd play along for her. "Alright, I guess I can try. So how does this work? I tell you to call me 'sir' or something? That fun for you?"

'Miss Doyle' jumped right back into the act: "Of course sir, I'm sorry."

"And I guess I'm supposed to tell you the only way to make it up to me is... what, suck me off under the desk—?"

"Sir!" Nicole immediately went flush and flustered with pretend embarrassment at Ravi's bold request. "—I mean! I mean that's... That's so... —I've never...! —I mean I'm not that kind of girl, sir. —And... and I'm... I mean there's someone at home. —I'm sorry. Please understand. —But! Anything else. I'll do anything else to make it up to you. —To this company! I... I can't lose this job. We're... having a rough time, you see. My partner, they're counting on me to bring in this money. Please."

Ravi smirked out of character and complimented her, "You're good at this, huh? Lots of practice?"

Nicole replied with a cute smile and broke character to reply that she was a very good actress sometimes.

"*Very* good," Ravi replied, as smooth as they could pretend. "It'd be a shame to lose talent like yours, Miss Doyle. But I'm afraid it'll be hard to find any use for you like this. You can't show up on time, and worse than that, you're telling me your pretty lips are entirely useless to the company."

"They're not! They're not, sir, please, I'm very useful I promise. Just not... not for that."

"Mm. That's very disappointing. I'm just not sure what to use you for now." Ravi took falsely confident steps up to Nicole and put a heavy hand on the armrest of the chair. Their other hand gripped the knot of her tie, choker-tight against her throat, in a firm fist to hold her still against the back of the chair, then they assertively shoved their face right in her space to tease her: "I'm afraid, Miss Doyle, that I'm going to have to throw you away, unless you want to... show me I'm wrong about what you're good for. Make me forget all about this little disappointment? My memory always gets so fuzzy when I'm reviewing my employees'... *performance*."

Nicole tried to back away, but there was nowhere to go. Ravi had their foot firmly planted on the base of the chair to keep her from rolling away. "I... I mean..." she stammered, "That... that can't be... good for performance reviews..."

"Why do you think I had to hire a talented secretary like you, Miss Doyle? I need someone to keep track of this kind of thing. —So! Miss Talented Secretary, are you going to show me why I hired you? Or do I need to find another pretty set of lips to remind me what my employees are *worth?*"

Nicole was already getting a little flustered at the game, breathing heavier in anticipation, pupils darting hungrily between Ravi's eyes and lips. She really loved being teased and bossed around a bit like this. And Ravi had to admit, this was... kind of fun. They just hoped they could keep up the act until she was satisfied.

They continued with their little performance: "If you're ready to show me what good you are, you can start by reminding me what kind of coffee I had this afternoon."

"How... how should I...?"

Ravi brought their lips within an inch of Nicole's and let their subtly coffee scented breath mingle with the warmth and sweetness of her own. "Figure it out."

Nicole's act continued right on into the shape of her kiss. She was pretending to hesitate, to take a tentative first taste of Ravi's lower lip with her eyes wide open, looking into theirs, pleading for mercy, eager for some sign of approval.

She never wore lipstick.

It was a nostalgic taste on their lips.

Lots of fun reckless evenings tasted like this.

They wrapped a firm set of fingers around the back of her neck and held her still while they returned her kiss, with all the hesitation of a wolf devouring a deer. Her lips tasted like a lifetime of danger. Her tongue tasted like honey and green tea. They pulled away licking their lips with an intimidating grin and challenged her for a report on her findings: "Well?"

"I um. I need more... um. Evidence...?"

"Then get it. I didn't hire you to hold your hand all day, Miss Doyle—"

She interrupted their teasing chiding to bring her lips back to theirs for a *thorough* taste test that lasted longer than Ravi could hold their breath. The shock of it and her persistence sent rushing wave after wave of salacious warmth through their body. God, were they really getting wet for this? Why did that feel so embarrassing?

When they pulled away with a little gasp for air, she gravely reported that she didn't actually drink coffee. "I can't tell. I'm sorry Mx. Beausoleil—"

"—Sir."

"Sir! I'm sorry sir. Maybe you should... find someone else... I don't think I can do this. I have... I told you, I have someone—"

"—Well, call this a test, then, Miss Doyle."

"A test?"

"Mhm. How can you possibly know how strong your love is if you don't... put a little weight on the rope once in a while, mm? Call it... a *safety test.*"

Nicole shivered a little at Ravi's playful words. She broke character to inform them that they were giving her little goosebumps. "Lucky I don't have a boss like you for real, Rav, gods. I wouldn't last."

Ravi brushed her cheek with their fingertips and informed her they would be heartbroken if they couldn't make her happy enough to win out over some skeezy boss. "Tell me my hands are a little more talented than that."

"Mhm! Yup! Yeah. Hands. Lips. Tongue. —And that smile of yours, gods. I could never betray that smile, Rav, I promise."

They grinned at her and brought their teasing fingers down to the playful ends of the ribbon encircling her throat to tug the whole thing undone until it was hanging loose on her neck, revealing the top button of her blouse so Ravi could start working their way down the seam. "So Miss Doyle? Ready to show me how strong your love *really* is?"

She held her breath as button after button failed her, until at last, on the second last one down, she took hold of their wrists and insisted, deeply in character, "This is the only time."

"Of course. Just a test, right? I'm sure you'll pass with *flying colors.* —Oh, Miss Doyle, Miss Doyle, Miss Doyle..." Ravi shook their head in mock disappointment as they untucked and opened her shirt to reveal the soft, tempting skin underneath, "Lingerie to the office. Really? Do I need to speak to HR about your attire?"

"...Should I... Should I take it off?"

Ravi nodded sagely and confirmed, "That would be best."

"Yes sir. Sorry sir." Then she dutifully unhooked the easy clasp between her breasts to fully reveal her bountiful chest for them. She was still looking into their eyes, unwavering, desperate for some sign of approval, but they refused to give her anything more than a cold coy grin that said Miss Doyle still had a long way to go to make things right.

When they ducked down to take a teasing taste of her delectable pink areola, she reminded them: "Just once. Okay? I... —Mmm... Gods I love how you do that Rav... —Sir! Sir, I'm putting my foot down. This... this can be the only time. O... Okay? Are you listening?"

A sweet trail of saliva dangled between the sharp tip of Miss Doyle's nipple and Ravi's tongue when they pulled away from her and shot her with a hungry grin that should have done absolutely nothing to assure her that they understood her perfectly. —And the cooing squeal she let out when they put a little love bite on her chest made it pretty clear she understood *them* perfectly.

They were eager to strip her bare and bury themself in her, especially after their lackluster performance earlier. If she was into this, they had to take advantage of that, before their mind started wandering into the misery of their real job again.

But their ambitions were stopped short when Nicole grabbed their eagerly prying hands and broke out of her character to tell them this wasn't how she wanted to play: "Tell me what to do."

"I want you to let me eat you up."

"No," she said firmly, truly putting her foot down now. "You're the *boss*, Ravi. You don't work, you delegate. You *supervise*. And if you start groping me and leaving marks, you're going to have an HR disaster on your hands. —Now stand up straight like you've got some spine and tell me what to do. —Sir."

"...I... Okay, but Miss Doyle *just said* she won't even get on her knees for me... Isn't that the whole point of this game...?"

Nicole showed off a wolfy grin while she dropped out of the chair and onto the floor, on her knees, ruining her beautiful stockings just for Mx. Beausoleil's approval. Her hands were folded shyly in her lap, waiting for Ravi to tell her where to put them.

"Don't make me beg, sir," she pleaded with them.

"Oh come on, Nikki, you sound so sweet when you beg."

"Please just tell me what you want so we can put all this behind us."

"What I want..."

"Anything."

"And you're *sure* I can't just bury my face between your thighs until

I pass out, Nix?"

"Nope. You're not allowed. De-le-gate," she added, with a tidy clap on each syllable.

Ravi took a deep breath and looked at the ceiling for a moment to collect themself. Putting what they wanted in words was *not* their forte. Quietly working towards their goals, keeping everything in their control, that was their comfort zone. Even on the *rare* occasion that they let Nicole have her way with them, they just trusted her to do what felt good for them. They'd already done the hard work of teaching her how to treat them – manually – and by now their embarrassing writhing whimpers and moans were enough to guide her.

But there was an extra layer of complication here: Nicole wanted Miss Doyle to be *disgraced.* Not yanked around by a beautiful leather collar or held down struggling or tied up in pretty red rope. Not cherished. —Degraded. Exploited. *Used.* —And there was something very different between the love in, say, using a goddess's throat at her giddy insistence as a cock sleeve for their strap, versus the cold cruelty in taking away her dignity and humanity to use her as some kind of tool for their own base gratification.

And... the fact that they were already feeling a little sadistically *high* on the idea was... troubling. That *meant* something about them. That meant they might be on the verge of awakening something *dangerous.* That meant that Nicole might be about to draw something dangerous out of them that could never be sealed away again.

They drew their tongue over their own canines and toyed with the idea of unapologetically being that kind of cold cruel *carnivore.*

When they returned their gaze to Miss Doyle's pleading eyes, they felt the temptation of it already worming its way into their blood, putting an uneasy warmth there.

Too late now, wasn't it? In for a penny.

They lackadaisically leaned back on their desk and provoked her to come to them. "My belt's a little too tight," they said plainly. "Fix that."

"Yes sir," she said with a nod, then she crawled over to them and drew her fingers up their thighs before settling on the clasp of their belt. It came loose with a satisfying clatter. Then she dutifully waited for more 'delegation', with a look in her eyes pretending at hoping this was as far as it would go.

"Keep going," they said.

"Sir?"

"You're really going to make me hold your hand every step of the way, huh? They really didn't teach you to suck off a clit for the prestige of it at that fancy school of yours?"

"No sir. What do I do?"

"Undo that button. —With your teeth. Zipper too."

She brought her face to their crotch, and made a little show of trying to hide it when she took in a deep taste of the scent of them, before she dutifully did exactly as they asked. And then, again, forced them to carry on guiding her:

"Jesus Miss Doyle, just take them off already. I'm very *patiently* waiting for you to show off what that expensive tongue of yours can do, not stare at my crotch all day. —And frankly, after all this hassle, you'd better be a damn prodigy if you want to bring in a single cent for that useless lay-about lover of yours."

"Yes sir," she replied.

She took her sweet time with it, but by the time their pants and boxers were around their shins, she had her cheek pressed warm against their inner thigh staring apprehensively at their apparently very intimidating bush.

"Lick, Miss Doyle. Lick it. Staring doesn't do anything for me."

The hungry look in her eyes when she asked, "Where?" was intoxicating, watching her drink in the scent of them with heavy breaths like she was flush drunk. Why did she have to tease them like this?

They gestured ambiguously at their cunt and reminded her what sure felt obvious, "My cunt. Lick my fucking cunt. Godsake."

Nicole shot them with a disapproving out-of-character glare, then put on a stupid grin and did exactly as they asked: Dumbly dragged her tongue over their cunt in the most uninspiring way possible, like she was licking a fucking stamp, like she was *afraid* of it. Missed their clit entirely, and didn't do a damn thing to lap up the uncontrollable wetness that had been slickening their hole since this whole ordeal started. Useless.

"How was that, sir?"

"Terrible."

"Oh no… Am I going to get a bad grade on my performance review?"

Ravi smirked at the stupid premise. They really hoped they were done with that part of the game. They wanted her in them already. "Yeah Miss Doyle. Needs work."

Nicole pretended to fret over it. The look on her face was so pathetic it made Ravi's heart ache. Puppy dog eyes and quivering pouty lower lip and hands together in a pleading prayer and everything else to look naïve and desperate for them. It was cute. God she was cute. "I need this job so badly, sir. They didn't teach me any of this in school. Please."

Ravi joked with her: "God, there's no hope for this generation." But Nicole didn't laugh. She was still pretending to be desperately begging for guidance. "So much for prodigal talent. Fine. Your mouth is for me now. A little clit sucking machine. And there are only two things your mouth is good for: Painting my clit with your tongue until it's soaked in your sweet saliva, and sucking that lovely sheen right off."

Nicole nodded along like she was taking mental notes. "Then what?"

"Then you do it again."

"Okay. …When do I stop?"

"You don't, Miss Mouth. This is your job now. Until your knees bleed. Get to it."

"Yes sir," she said grimly, then obediently dipped her lips to Ravi's clit and did exactly as they asked: Painted them dripping wet, licked them clean, and sucked their clit until it was stiff and swollen and so pristine and bare to the air that they could feel every molecule of Nicole's breath as it passed between her hungry lips.

"Good… Good girl…" Ravi was pretty sure that's what a boss was supposed to say in this situation.

"Thank you, sir."

"I didn't say you could stop to talk, Miss Mouth."

Nicole let a flash of an out-of-character grin escape before she dutifully went back to her job.

The sight of her on her knees like that, dressed so professionally, acting so subservient, so compliant, it felt so so wrong. Exploitation in the worst possible way. Pretend, but even pretend it sent a dark sadistic nerve-stroking rush through Ravi with every heavy breath as their body started building up to something big.

And then they spotted something that took a small bit of their guilt away: Nicole had her hand down her skirt, well hidden between her thighs, while she was performing her corporate duties for Ravi's approval.

She was enjoying this.

A *lot*, it looked like, from how fervently she was rocking her hips and grinding herself into her fingers. Ravi wished they could get a better look. Or a taste. But it was all hidden under her 'work attire'. So instead they closed their eyes and tried to satisfy their craven desires in their mind alone. And it was a heavenly vision – pushing her to the floor and ripping all her clothes off and pinning her down to ravage her, to force rough fingers inside her, to bite her neck and mark her for her lover to see how unfaithful she'd been, to own her completely... — To have her *back*, late for work again on *purpose*, knowing exactly what she'd have to do to make up for it...

God it was so unprofessional.

They were a better boss than that.

But the guilt just fed into the rush.

They gripped the edge of their desk firmly and tried to control their breath to keep from letting her push them over the edge but god it wasn't working at all.

"That's... that's good, Miss Doyle..."

She pulled away from them with a disappointed look and told them pleadingly, "You're not done yet, sir."

"I get the idea... You can keep your job..."

"Mm... but what about... a raise?"

"Getting cocky..."

"I haven't even shown you everything my prodigal tongue can do, Mx. Beausoleil. You don't know what you're paying for. —And since this is the only time, why don't you... put me to use properly...?"

Ravi gave her a quizzical look. What exactly did she have in mind...?

"Something Ravi would never ask me for," she led them on. "Something... *degrading*...?"

"What, you want to suck on my toes Miss Doyle? That doesn't do it for me."

"Mm... something a little... more up your alley," she teased them, then she coldly broke protocol to glide a teasing finger down their cunt and around to their sensitive asshole to give them a tantalizing hint of a preview.

"...No that's..."

"Use me, sir. I'm already on my knees for you. I'll do anything for this job. Anything."

Ravi had never ever asked her to do that. And they absolutely never *would*. But they weren't Ravi right now, were they? They were depraved sadistic exploitative boss Mx. Beausoleil, and Miss Doyle was nothing more to them than a mouth right now, a set of lips and tongue to put where they wanted. —And it was something they'd secretly always... wanted to try... After all, she already treated their ass so nice when she fucked them, but god, there was something very different about this. Fingers and toys were nothing compared to the depraved intimacy of her tongue.

"Just tell me what to do, sir," she reminded them, still gliding her finger teasingly over their eager asshole.

They took in the eagerness to please in her eyes, noted her hand still working over her own pussy for all the fun this was for her, and decided there was no harm in this. It was just pretend. It didn't count. They continued in their role: "...You're not done yet, Miss Mouth." Then they turned around and faced their desk, leaning forward and arching their back to give her a better view of her new assignment. "Your tongue has a new job. Get to work."

"Sir?"

"What?"

She kissed their ass cheek with a little lick, then teased them in a singsong rhythm, "Tell–me–what–to–do–boss," punctuating each word with a little nip at their sensitive flesh.

"...Lick... lick the sex off my asshole, Miss Mouth. That's all you're good for now."

"...Yes sir," she replied with a smile in her voice.

Ravi sighed and clenched their fists and pinched their lower lip between their teeth at the very first firm circle she took around the twitchy rim of their hole. That felt way better than it had any right to. And in only a few seconds, once she'd truly licked off every drop of wayward cunt slick that coated their asshole, she was sliding her tongue over them like a dumb hungry dog.

But that wasn't enough. That was just teasing.

"Stop fucking around... Get right in there, you slut..."

She bit their ass a bit and chided them. "Don't call me a slut. I'll be your mouth today, but I'm not like those other girls, sir. I have a lover waiting for me—"

"—*Shut up* about your lover already and put your expensive ass-licking tongue to use, Miss Mouth."

Nicole slid her free hand between Ravi's thighs to press firm fingers into their clit to hold them securely in place, then she did exactly as Mx. Beausoleil asked. The sensation of that warm wet instrument of hers slipping past the first tense ring of their asshole was enough to send a shudder through their whole body. And the way she swirled it around inside them, stroking every happy nerve she could reach, it was so much. They couldn't move but to press themself into her, not that they needed to the way she was eagerly pulling them into herself by their cunt.

Ravi rolled their crotch against her fingers desperately but she wasn't doing what they wanted and they were sick of being teased by this useless secretary who couldn't fucking figure out what to do with them. They darted a hand between their thighs and guided her fingers to their dripping cunt. "Fuck me, you useless—*fuuuuck*..." She started firmly pistoning her fingers into their cunt in symphony with her tongue slipping in and out of their asshole. "*Oh*. That's... Fuck. Good... good... girl... Mm...fffuu..."

They clutched desperately for anything to hold onto on their desk, sending notebooks and papers scattering to the floor in their fever. They shook their head and bit their tongue and held their breath but nothing was going to stop what was coming.

They collapsed pathetically flat on the surface of the desk, pressing their face into the wood of it, leaving a little pool of drool there while their body shook with wave after wave of uncontrollable pleasure. — And their dutiful desperate-to-please Miss Mouth refused to let up on them.

But despite her fervor, they could feel something change in her rhythm, even in the throes of their orgasmic madness. She was distracted. Breathing heavy. Moaning to herself between staggered assaults on their cunt and asshole. She was cumming for them too. Just from serving them. Just from being *used*.

Their mind went blank with pleasure at the thought of her

depravity. And the thought of the darkness they'd awoken in her. The corruption. This was sick and they couldn't stop cumming for her, from the sick filth of it all.

When she was done with her professional *demonstration*, she was resting her cheek on their ass cheek and breathing heavy breaths on their asshole that sent little shockwaves of pleasure with every caress of the air.

When they finally caught their breath, Mx. Beausoleil teasingly provided their final review of her performance: "That was... prodigal... Miss Doyle... Tell your useless lover you'll be getting a raise on your very first day... I'm sure they'll be delighted to hear how *valuable* you are..."

She sighed at them and replied with an exhausted barely-in-character, "Yes sir..."

"I hope you're planning to be on time tomorrow..."

She pulled her face away from them, but not before leaving them with a teasing bite, and informed them with a pathetic excuse: "The buses are really unreliable, you know."

"Mm... well I'm sure you'll make it up to the company if it happens again..."

"Yes. Sir," she replied with a satisfied smile in her voice.

Ravi turned to face her and take in the glowing beauty in her eyes. They did up their pants nice and professional, then collapsed to their knees in front of her and let gentle fingers slip past her ears to draw her to them for a deep kiss, to taste themself on her. It was as intoxicating as always, to know they were lingering on the tongue of a *goddess*.

She happily wrapped her own fingers around the back of their neck and held them there to taste the lingering hint of coffee on their tongue. "Arabica dark roast," she reported with a knowing grin when she was done.

"Good girl."

She gave Ravi a proud dozy grin. "I was so so good, wasn't I?" Then she took their hand and slipped it down under her slick wet lingerie and pleaded with them in a breathy whisper, "Fuck me? I earned it, right?"

They replied with a playful grin, "No HR complaints, Miss Doyle?"

"Game's over, Rav. Do whatever you want with me. —As long as whatever you want includes wearing that suit and fucking me stupid over your desk, please and thank you very much."

The following week, Ravi sat down and divided up their work into a dozen smaller bits and asked Miriam to find them some minions.

And they made sure to correct every one of them who thought to call them Miss Beausoleil:

"*Mx.* Beausoleil. —Or if it's easier, just 'sir' is fine," they always added with a playful grin, and a subtle clench of their thighs.

They never had to look at another stupid form again.

—Thanks Nikki. Unorthodox mentorship, but it sure got the job done.

Then, at last, a couple weeks later, the project had finally moved the three fucking inches forward Ravi needed, and they finally got an email from Miriam asking what resources they'd need to move forward on the research part.

Subject matter experts, they replied. A lot of them.

At last, after way the hell too long, they were going to get some answers.

A sickness by another name

❀

(Afternoon, Tuesday, 12th September)

Twelve probably-poached scientists in a room at last, including Ravi and Carrie – though Ravi sure felt like an imposter of a scientist these days.

They arrived a bit late to the tenth-floor conference room, that had a lovely floor-to-ceiling view of the whole river, to find the ten strangers around a large table engaged in a heated debate about the merits of the project. Turned out a few of them were fully aware that the 'science' that informed the underlying theory they were about to use to try to create immortal semi-biological photonic ceramic brains was a little bogus – though, somehow, a few of them saw some merit in it.

Ravi got seated quietly to watch in awe at the passion on display here. It had been so long since they saw anything like this, so long since they last attended a conference, a meeting of the minds, a forum for heated debate about anything so scientifically contentious.

And from the look on the faces of each and every one of the others in the room, they got the feeling each of them was suffering from the same hunger, after withering to nothing at the company, having their talents wasted, kept silent and pointless in their cages.

Ravi wasn't 100% sure these people would all be loyal to the cause, so they had to warm them up a bit first. And the best way they could think to do that was introduce a false premise to the project:

"It's being kept very quiet," they said in a conspiratorial tone, "but there's a reason for this project that isn't in the documentation. The epidemic of these inexplicable sarcoid cysts – the tar, they call it out there – is getting worse."

Terrance Paul, who had been cagily glaring at Carrie the whole time, spoke up first about that: "Sarcoid cysts are the last thing I want to be thinking about – sorry, what was your name?"

"Ravi." —An unknown name at the office.

"Ravi, the last time I worked on that stuff, my whole shop got shut down and my research got bought up by this glorious tech company of ours and burned to ash. Suffice to say, I'm just a *little* bitter about it."

A few of the others nodded along, with similar stories.

The looks of recognition and suspicion that made waves around the circular table were telling. This might be a hard sell.

Ravi continued trying to justify the secretive focus of the project: "The company is ready to move on to Phase 2 of their treatment solution for the illness."

One of the others scoffed – a 'subject matter expert' in robotics, pilfered from a university halfway across the country. "And your proposed solution is <u>this</u>?" she challenged them, dismissively jabbing at the fraudulent project's dossier in front of her. "*Immortality?* Ortiz is living in a fantasy world. I can't believe we're indulging this."

Another spoke up to defend the idea – a cybernetics expert this one. "Miss Ortiz's ambitions for the Singularity are the only projects worth chasing around here. —Or would you rather keep your head down to keep on with the latest greatest walking talking automated killing machines?"

"They're saving lives—!"

"Don't spout that propaganda at me. You psychopath…"

The robotics expert, who was presumably responsible for some of the autonomous robotics research that was being deployed in InThetics' military tech, stood up in a furious huff and slammed her palms down on the table. "You're playing <u>God</u>—"

Ravi stood up and raised their hands up in a plea for peace. "Please. Take it offline. Or to the parking lot. I don't care. I have a project to finish here—"

"—This is impossible," the robotics expert reminded them. "It doesn't even make sense. You're planning to imprint a whole consciousness into a hunk of clay? We can't even get a damn rat's brain working in a whole data center full of supercomputers."

Ravi sighed. "The sarcoid cysts," they said, to return to their real reason for bringing everyone here. "You've all had some... *experience* with the disease, I think. Research? Research that didn't quite get where it was supposed to go? Research that maybe *brought you* to InThetics?"

Again the scientists exchanged uneasy glances around the table, but they at last turned to Ravi with a chorus of nods and affirmatives.

"Above all else, this project *must* be a solution to that problem, before the disease becomes so endemic that humanity's very survival is threatened. So, in confidence, I'd like to collate the results of your old research – what you remember of it, anyways, before it was tragically cut short in its prime."

A medical researcher piped up to dismiss the ridiculous premise. "It's not contagious," he assured them. "The cause may be unknown, but the rate of infection is *steady*. The number of infections plateaued two years ago, around ten million."

"Miriam is concerned it'll get worse."

"That's just paranoia. There's no evidence—"

"—She doesn't need evidence. She needs solutions."

The medical researcher flopped back in his chair and let out a little huff of a sigh, resigned to the authority of the all-powerful owner of the company who held his leash. Apparently this wasn't the first time he'd been roped in to deal with some overly ambitious thoroughly misguided project of Miriam's.

A materials scientist, who had been very quiet until now, piped up with a quiet contention: "It shouldn't be cured. It should be cultivated. Transferred to some lesser species—"

The robotics expert interrupted again, "I'm truly in a room full egotistical maniacs, aren't I? 'Lesser species'? You want to pass on some of the worst pain humanity's ever faced to something else? Just let it be! We don't deserve to play God with this stuff. Even the treatment is too much – just prolonging the suffering. If this stuff is supposed to kill you, let it! I can't believe anyone would choose a lifetime of pain over a quick death. Nothing good will come from any of this, I swear—"

Ravi scowled bitterly at the woman before they stood up again and unbuttoned their shirt, revealing the binder underneath and tugging their right sleeve off to let it hang loose, exposing their shoulder for the little crowd. Then they shifted the straps of their binder so they could show off the wincing pain of the blackening cysts there.

The room went silent for a few heavy seconds before the robotics expert abashedly told Ravi to put their shirt back on. "I don't want to see that..."

"Neither do I," they confirmed while they put their shirt back together. "Neither does Miriam," they lied. InThetics definitely had no interest in putting an end to this disease. —And the company would surely be overjoyed if that materials expert were to get his wish. A farm built for suffering, an endless supply of relatively guilt-free tar to make their precious Saffron out of. There'd be no market for life-long treatments that way, but Ravi sure wanted to believe that even the most evil company in the world could see the value in ending the use of humans in their horrifying tar harvest. Sadly, as far as Ravi could tell, there was no hope of that any time soon, since no progress had ever been made 'transferring' the illness to a 'lesser species'.

"So, can we focus?" they continued. "I need it all. Everything you know about the tar, every piece of research InThetics seized from you, every dangerous decision that brought you here." And to reaffirm the false premise of the lofty endeavor, they quickly added, "—We need everything we can get to make sure whatever comes out of this project isn't going to be affected by this disease."

Terrance chimed in again for the first time in a while to bitterly ask, "Why doesn't InThetics just dig up the old research on their own? They couldn't have really destroyed it. ...Could they?"

"Whatever wasn't destroyed was redacted by the government," Ravi explained.

They folded their hands on the table and shot a grave glare around the table, lingering briefly on the difficult gaze of each member of the reluctant impromptu coalition, to impart the seriousness of what they were about to say: "There is no other research into this happening right now. It's all being suppressed, by forces unknown, though we could all probably guess. The people at this table? We're the last testament to a decade of work trying to figure this thing out. We <u>can't</u> let that be lost forever. —Not when the success of this project depends on it."

The medical researcher scoffed miserably. "Maybe they should've thought of that before they destroyed it all."

"Maybe they should've," Ravi confirmed. "Hopefully it's a lesson learned. All I know is we need to move forward and correct that mistake as best we can. So how about it? Will you help me move forward? Help this company move forward? Help the *field* move forward?"

The room was filled with a symphony of uneasy, discordant rhythms – fingers and heels tapping, pens clicking, teeth grinding. But at last, Ravi got an affirmative out of everyone in the room, accompanied by a few grumbled variations on, "Not like we have a choice."

And that was absolutely correct. Ravi was ready to use the full authority of Miriam Ortiz's misguided ambition to twist these arms.

Luckily it didn't come to that.

At the bar after work, Carrie punctuated every other drink with a hearty clap on their good shoulder to remind them how good they did on this.

"Had my doubts," she admitted.

"I bet. Me too."

"Should've known. Should've known you could do it, Ravi. Day one you walked into my lab I knew you were something special. Just keep proving me right over and over, hey hun? Unbelievable." She paused to take a swig of her drink. There was something uneasy in her, despite the roaring success of the meeting, and it came out in her next question: "What next?"

Ravi's empty gaze drifted to the far wall of the room. They rolled their fingers on the table for a few bars before they realized they truly had no idea what came next.

If this turned up something incendiary enough, they could just report it to the media. InThetics would be ruined. Everything would change. The grim harvest would stop, patents would unlock, research would start again, a cure could be pursued properly. It might not be overnight, but eventually. Eventually things would get better. Not in time to save Ravi, but that wasn't what this was about. This was bigger.

And if not…

They shook their head to get that disappointing possibility out, but it wouldn't go.

If not? If they got nothing the media could use?

They'd have to resort to some kind of desperate plan that they couldn't quite find the courage to embrace just yet.

But it would have to be something… incendiary.

They couldn't let this go on, and they'd stop it themself with their own bare hands if they had to.

No matter the cost.

Okay, In My Defense, Those Raspberries Really Did Look Good Enough to Die For, and I Was Pretty Sure I Had Better Gloves

A sigil, shifting subtly, lines and characters forming and unforming like a tangle of strange worms, had wriggled its way into every one of Felicity's dreams for the last few weeks.

Until one afternoon when – alone in her bedroom, in the middle of a restless nap, while she was wrestling with toothy faceless mirrors or something – she saw the sigil again, appearing with a crack and a flash before it leapt forward and bound her body in ribbons hard as glass, with a glimpse of a brilliant dagger-toothed grin and a sound that shook her bones.

She shot up in bed in a panic and desperately clutched at her chest to make sure she was still alive.

Her fingers disturbed something dangling from her neck.

The virgin chime of that useless Silver Bell pierced the still air of the room and reverberated through her mind, sparking her imagination and realigning disconnected thoughts and memories until she had tears in her eyes for being so arrogant.

Danica. The Barghest. The Black Dog. The Grinning Dagger. The shifting sigil that Felicity knew was the only thing she had left in her possession to defend herself against the beast. She was the only one who could stop that... *monster.*

And the finale of that bitter vision: The whole purpose of the Bell: Danica leaving Ravi behind, next next Friday. Two weeks. Just as that misguided contract promised.

In a rush, Felicity threw some semblance of an outfit on, stuffed a whole bunch of critical items in a bag, and impatiently mashed the buttons on the elevator until she could dash out to her car.

The highway was a blur of hours – silence in the cabin except for the strained roaring engine and her frustrated swears at the trucks and cowards who wouldn't get out of her way – and, piercing it all, the delicate chime of that Silver Bell that sang out with every hard sudden brake that slammed her chest painfully into the seatbelt.

Her mind was anything but silent, though, tearing her apart and drawing tears out of her eyes with every merciless tooth and claw.

—*You _stupid_ piece of shit. You fucking arrogant _asshole_. Who could be so... so... naïve? You knew _exactly_ what she was and you _still_ trusted her??*

Amy's fire escape was way more rickety than should be legal. Felicity stumbled on the stairs twice, nearly dropping her bag and losing her balance in her fury.

No one was home when she broke in, so all she could do was wait.

And while she waited, she started putting up dozens of iron nails and four-leaf clovers and every other ward she had stuffed into her hefty bag.

She was standing on the couch, nailing a horseshoe to the wall, mid-swing with the hammer, when a set of keys jingled outside the front door.

She lackadaisically tossed the hammer on the couch and stepped right up to the front door, clutching the safety of that personalized iron-inked sigil of banishment in her pocket.

When Danica flipped the light on, she let out a sharp little yelp of surprise to see Felicity glaring at her.

Amy poked her head around Danica's shoulder and raised a pair of shocked eyebrows at her. "Felicity? How did you—?"

"Your screen's loose," she said, gesturing at the violated window she crawled through when the back door refused to open. "Should get that fixed."

Felicity took an aggressive stride to get right up in Danica's space before Amy or Danica could ask any more questions, then she lifted her iron necklace away from her chest and shook it gently back and forth to draw out the haunting chime of the Silver Bell for Danica.

"You're done," Felicity told her firmly, barely holding back her rage. "You know the deal. Pack your shit and—Hey!—"

Danica interrupted her mid-sentence by suddenly grasping Felicity's blouse firmly in both hands while glancing over her shoulder to tersely and sheepishly tell Amy she would be right back.

Felicity didn't even have enough time to try to shove the iron sigil into Danica's chest before the room disappeared.

The next second was nearly impossible for Felicity to find the right words for, but when she inevitably took a stab at it, she best-effort described it as feeling something like being violently checked through a hundred layers of chaotically misshapen gelatinous electric ice that shoved each of her organs in wildly different directions with every shocking breakthrough.

When the two of them landed on the other side of that mess, she was struck by the worst, sharpest, most blinding migraine of her life, and the second Danica released her, she immediately fell to her knees to empty her highway-starved stomach on the dirt of the floor of the forest that this wicked faerie had just dragged her to through that God-forgotten hell.

"Sorry!" the shameless pretender cried out pathetically. "Oh my gods, Fleece, I'm so sorry. Are you okay?"

Felicity tried to spit the bitter bile out before she answered that she was very much not okay. "What the fuck Danica…"

The beast crouched in front of Felicity with a show of dire concern in her eyes, fingers outstretched but restrained from actually touching Felicity – probably out of the very justified fear that Felicity was ready to bite any one of those fingers right off if she tried.

Fake concern.

Lies.

All part of her little game.

Felicity would never be taken in by this monster again.

At last, when Felicity regained control of her twitchy guts, she glared at Danica with a cruel fire in her eyes. "You. Will. Leav— Mmph!!—"

Again Danica interrupted her, this time by darting out her hand to cover Felicity's mouth and snuff out her words.

"Hold on! Please," she pleaded with Felicity, who was desperately trying to twist herself free from Danica's grasp, but the monster had her other hand wrapped around the back of Felicity's head to hold her still, and Danica was far too strong for Felicity to pry herself free.

But at least she managed to get her teeth in the meat of Danica's hand and bite her hard enough to get a wincing hiss of pain out of her. Unfortunately, even after Felicity could taste the faerie's sweet filthy blood trickling into her mouth, Danica refused to pull away.

She spoke through a bitter painful wince at Felicity's attack: "Fleece. Please. Please calm down. If you get rid of me now, I can't do *anything* to help." She peered deep into Felicity's eyes with aching sincerity – a pathetic simpering puppy – when she assured Felicity that she wasn't going to stop her from doing what she needed to do to keep Amy safe. "You can banish me if you want to. That's the deal and I'll stick to it, I promise. But can we… just… talk first? Please. I need to know what happens."

Felicity glared at her bitterly, but it sure didn't seem like there was a real choice here. Danica was just going to keep silencing her until she got her way. What a miserable loophole. Can't 'command' someone to do something if you can't even *speak.*

She relaxed her jaw to release Danica's hand, then spit the nasty blood on the forest floor next to the former contents of her stomach when the wretched cheater withdrew her hand.

Danica hissed at herself in pain while she examined her bloody hand, cradling it with a woeful look on her face. "Gods you weren't kidding, you really do bite…"

"Your throat's next if you keep cheating."

Felicity stood up and dusted her hands and knees off, then took a moment to scan the depths of the dark, vast, untamed wilderness around the two of them. It was hot and humid here. The air smelled of peat and decay. And as much as Felicity normally loved being taken camping by big strong outdoorsy women – women who *weren't* threatening her life – she wasn't exactly an outdoorsy person herself. She wouldn't be getting out of here alive on her own, that was for sure.

"Holding me hostage, I guess? That your game now?"

"I just want to talk," Danica repeated, as if that were reason enough to imprison Felicity in an impenetrable living dungeon.

"…Oh my God. You're actually planning to drag me back through that… *hell* again, aren't you?"

"Um. It'd… it'd be a *long* walk…" she answered sheepishly. "…Sorry. I panicked."

"Great. Some cowardly faerie monster panics at the very *thought* of being held accountable for her actions and I end up in the middle of nowhere, left to die if I don't play nice. Very mature, *Danica.* Jeezus Christopher, how the hell was I so *stupid* that I thought I could trust you... Fine. Let's *talk* then, to your *heart's content*, so I can get back to getting rid of you properly."

"...What happens?"

Felicity, sarcastic and bitter, held up the Bell again and shook it aggressively to make it ring out to demonstrate what she *thought* was pretty fucking obvious: "You break your promise. In two weeks, you leave. And you *break her heart* doing it. You show the whole world how much of a cold unfeeling monster you are, just like you always were."

"No. No that's... Come on, it's just not possible. The deal... Gods' sake, you're holding the leash! You're supposed to stop it *before* it happens."

"...Sorry, what?"

"The only way I'd ever leave is if you sent me away, Fleece. And you could only send me away if I hurt her. And that's not *possible*. It was supposed to be a self-sealing hole – an unfulfillable prophecy. Like, if I was going to hurt her, you'd come get rid of me – and since I would be gotten rid of *before* I could hurt her, I wouldn't be able to hurt her anymore, so you *couldn't* come get rid of me. —See? Hurting her would make it impossible to hurt her. The paradox of it would break the universe. —The whole thing was supposed to keep her safe from me, for gods' sake... Ughhh, I *hate* this foresight stuff... —I *told* you! I <u>*warned*</u> you!"

Felicity's hands dropped to her sides in awe. "You were using me."

"...Sort of?" she said with half a grin and a sheepish shrug. "—For something you wanted! We both want this! To keep her safe!"

Felicity turned away from Danica to bury her face in her hands and groan at herself. Danica was trying to... what, to exploit... *causality paradoxes?*

She turned back and laughed pathetically at herself, then verbally jabbed at Danica, "I thought *I* was the arrogant one. You're trying to play the whole universe? Trying to spite your... *gods*, whatever they are?"

"Okay, to be fair, it's *been* working."

"Or you just never had a chance to hurt her until now!"

"...Or... that."

Felicity scowled at Danica in a silent fury for a few tense breaths before she closed her eyes and clicked her tongue. "God I hate you so much. How do you get in my head <u>*every time*</u>?"

"...I'm really cute?"

"Joke time is over, Danica. You screwed this up real bad. I thought you were making that deal to look out for your own interests, but if you were *actually* trying to keep *her* safe then obviously it was going to backfire and get her hurt. You said you're smart. You said you're good at this. What happened to that? Lying about your skills there? Miss 'I Can't Lie'."

"...Okay, to be fair, *statistically*, I *am* good at this—" She looked away and rubbed her forearm awkwardly. "—But uh, *lately*, not so much..."

"No kidding. So. What's the plan here?"

"I don't know... It wasn't supposed to go like this. The original contract I had in mind was just about hurting her, and there wasn't going to be any of this... *clairvoyance* nonsense. But it was fine, I figured – adding your stuff. I didn't think I'd ever *leave*. I *want* to stay here. I want to stay with her." She looked at Felicity with pleading eyes and begged to know, "Why do I leave? Can you see it?"

"Nope. But I don't need to think too hard to guess. I bet it's because you're a selfish coward. —Because that's what you *do*. You leave and leave and leave, and you leave a wake of misfortunate everywhere you go. I looked into it, Danica Llewellyn Doyle. Everyone you spend more than a couple months with, they all get screwed over after you leave. You. *Leave*. It's what you do. —And she's afraid of it, you know. She's not stupid. She's afraid it's coming, that you're going to just... get bored and fuck off. That's why I put it in there. God, she's always been afraid of you. 'Love'. What bullshit. You're so obvious. I thought I could... *control* you, keep you good, but that was so... *so* arrogant."

Danica's eyes fell at Felicity's admonishment, which was... not at all what she was expecting here, especially after how monstrously this once-terrifying demonic Black Dog was treating her.

"I wouldn't, though," she sulked. "I'm not planning to leave. I'm serious. I <u>would</u> <u>not</u> leave."

"Well *apparently*—"

"—No. No, you're... seeing it wrong or something. You're getting tricked. I *won't* leave. I have to fix things first. —I *have to*. I have to fix this! I have to keep her safe! Why would I *leave?*"

"Are you really going to make me keep listing this stuff off? Cowardly? Selfish—?"

"Stop. Stop, okay, just... ask me. Ask! I can't lie! It's in the deal! The

Bell rang! I have to answer every question until you're satisfied now – just *ask!* I'm *not* going to leave!"

"I don't want to know. I don't want to pity you. I just want you to get out of her life—"

"—You want me to <u>leave</u> so I <u>don't leave</u>?? You want to keep me from breaking her heart by breaking her heart? Are you insane? Are you listening to yourself? Gods' sake Felicity, you drove the whole way here and you didn't take a single second to think about what you were doing, did you? It's you! It's *you*, Fleece. It has to be. *You're* the one making me leave! I would never go. I would never, not until it's fixed, I would *never—*"

Felicity clicked her tongue. Some nerve, blaming her for this. But… if Danica was right…

She clenched her teeth and took a breath to silently curse at herself. Her curiosity was getting the better of her again.

Danica was so…

"…You keep saying that. 'Fixed'. What's broken?"

Danica's eyes went wide with surprise at Felicity's interest. She straightened her posture and folded her hands together, seemingly both to put on an air of sincerity as much as to have something to fiddle with while she admitted to her shameful behavior.

"My cousins—"

"—The fae."

"Yes. The fae—"

Danica went on to explain some weird convoluted stuff about how she was being 'tortured by Amy's suffering', and how her cousins were devoting themselves to ruining Amy's life for *some reason.*

Felicity idly mumbled something to herself when she mentioned that: "*Your human will suffer…*"

Danica's eyes went wide and scared when she told Felicity to repeat herself.

"…Sorry, nothing. Go ahead. I just… remembered… something… Song lyrics… Or something…"

Danica raised a very skeptical eyebrow at Felicity for a few long silent seconds, but she eventually relented and went back to her explanation.

It sounded like Danica thought all of that 'torture' directed at Amy culminated in some horrible disaster at the warehouse.

Felicity put her hand out and demanded Danica stop to confirm the extravagant number she just said: "130k?? How big was that shelf??"

"Big."

"Jeezus. No kidding..."

"...That's not... all of it," Danica continued. "She lost her job at the warehouse—"

"—Yeah I bet!"

"And she took another job – a job she *really* shouldn't have taken."

Felicity scoffed. "Oh I see how it is. When *I* say she should have a better job—"

"It's at InThetics."

"That tech company? *Seriously?* That's amazing! What's wrong with that? —Don't tell me it's just some fancy *InThetics* warehouse now..."

"Research. It's a great job. It's an *amazing* job, on paper. But InThetics is... kind of... *evil*. Kind of extremely evil, actually, as far as we can tell. But she's still working there, to pay off that debt – and for... other reasons. Dangerous reasons. And I won't leave her alone to deal with all that. She needs someone supporting her. Someone keeping her safe. I'm the only one who can do that now. Get it? I made this mess. And it's too big for a normal person to handle now. *I* have to fix it."

"Wow. This is... *quite* the turnaround, Danica. What happened to the whole 'it's not my job to fix her' thing?"

"This is... Come on, Fleece, this is completely different. I *made* this mess."

"Sure but she made the choice to work there. She chose this path to deal with her problems. —Unless you used your sketchy manipulation tricks on her too?"

"I would never do that. —Not... not to her."

"Perfectly fine doing it to me."

"I *never* manipulated your mind. I just put a *little* squeeze on you so you'd *listen to me*, that's it."

Felicity gestured dramatically at the impossible jungle around them in a silent exasperated demonstration of how wrong Danica was. If being held hostage in the wilderness wasn't manipulation,

Felicity sure couldn't imagine what else was.

Danica looked around and let out a little sigh of defeat. "...Are you going to behave if I take you back?"

"Oh my God. *'Behave'*? And you're not trying to manipulate me? Are *you* even listening to yourself?"

Danica grimaced at herself and looked away. She closed her eyes and took a deep breath, then gathered herself to face Felicity again and offered her hand out. "Where do you want to go?"

For a few tense seconds, Felicity stared incredulously at Danica's hand – some grand showy gesture of a peace offering – but as stupid as it was to do it, she obviously didn't have any choice here. She uneasily reached out to take Danica's hand and told her to take the two of them to that book café.

Danica offered her other arm to welcome Felicity in for an embrace and explained that it'd be a lot smoother if Danica didn't have to *drag* her the whole way.

She reluctantly accepted.

For a monster, Danica was *remarkably* warm and soft. Felicity saw why Amy found this so appealing.

And sure enough, safe in Danica's tight embrace, the instantaneous journey to the back alley behind the book café felt a lot less violating than that first hurried leap into the jungle. No migraine, and after a few unpleasant gags, she was even able to swallow down the miserable sensation in her guts trying to double her over to retch the *nothing* in her stomach onto the pavement.

"Better?" Danica asked, hopeful.

"Still terrible. We're *walking* back to the apartment, I hope."

"...Well, *you are*, at least. Sounds like I might never be going back, depending on how this goes."

"Good point! Nothing stopping me now, huh?"

"Nothing at all," Danica lamented with an uneasy smile, while she took a full step back and folded her hands behind her back to show she really really *really* wasn't going to do anything.

Felicity crossed her arms and gave Danica a stern staredown for a few long seconds. When she finished her assessment, she cursed at her own stupidity.

"You are going to *actually* drive me to madness, Dani... Let's go," she

said, directing Danica towards the front entrance of the café. "You're
buying my coffee. And a sandwich. And the fanciest bottle of water on
the shelf."

You Think the Fates Ever Played Cat's Cradle?

(Evening, Friday, 29th September)

While the monster took care of ordering, Felicity got set up at a small table in a quiet corner at the back of the building, surrounded on three sides by bookshelves, lit up by warm incandescent light. She folded her hands on the table and fiddled with her thumbs uneasily for a few seconds before she switched her pose to bring her palms to her eyes and growl at herself.

Danica was right. *Again.* If Felicity decided to banish her, it *would* be a self-fulfilling prophecy thing, wouldn't it? According to what Felicity saw in the Bell's vision, Danica was definitely going to leave in two weeks, for some reason she couldn't see. And, really, whether it was banishment or just packing up and leaving on her own, it didn't matter much. The monster would be gone soon. Felicity would just have to let it play out on its own, or else she'd end up being a pawn in some convoluted scheme of the universe.

Which, annoyingly, meant that no matter how tonight went, Felicity wasn't going to be able to get rid of the demonic Black Dog in Amy's bed at all before then, no matter how badly she thought she wanted to – unless she could find some way to change the fate of the universe.

Foresight stuff really *was* absolute bullshit.

When Danica came up behind her and set the food and drinks on the table, Felicity immediately opened the expensive artisanal bottle of water and drank half of it in one go to get the wretched bilious taste out of her mouth.

She eyed the sandwich uneasily. She was wolfishly hungry, but this sure didn't feel like the time to eat, not while she had so much to sort out with the beast across the table.

"You know Dani," she grumbled at Danica again while she opened up her sandwich to inspect the quality of its toppings, "I've had some shitty friends in my life but I don't think anyone's ever made me feel as gross as you do. I can't believe I keep letting you drag me over to your side like this."

"I'm just lucky you've got a big stupid heart, Fleece."

"You're insulting the person who's got your leash in her hand, huh?"

"Right. Sorry."

Felicity returned the top of the sandwich to its place, then slouched forward to rest her elbows on the table and steeple her fingers in front of her chin. She had a very important unanswered question, and now that she was resigned to talking to this monster, she might as well take advantage of all the knowledge that was on offer here.

"Last time, you said *something* can change fate. Explain."

"Ah. Right. I did. Say that. Didn't I. Right… Okay, listen: Before I get into it, I really have to get it right in your head here, Fleece: The fae are *built* to make everything in the universe worse."

"No kidding."

"…Yeah, I guess you don't need convincing. So, as you… *probably* guessed, it's us. The fae are the only things in the universe that can change the path of fate, that can shift the worldlines of the stuff of the cosmos around. —But! But. We don't know where the new path leads, no idea what'll change long-term. So, sure, I can do *something* to mess with the trajectory of your path, or Amy's, or anyone's, really, but the consequences of that? No way to know. And like I just said, we're here to make things worse, so, you know, *pretty good chance* it'll make things worse, for *someone*."

"…And… *how* do you change fate?"

Danica took a quick scan of the room over Felicity's shoulder before clapping her hands gently and producing a sheet of paper with a little singsong ta-da – the enchanted paper that held the terms and signatures for the little deal between the two of them that created that annoyingly prophetic Silver Bell.

"…Contracts?" Felicity asked, to state the obvious answer.

"*Contracts*. Games. Faerie mischief. Anything that looks like magic, basically. If it breaks the rules, the fabric of the universe has to be flexible, or *it'll* break."

"So when you teleported us—"

"—It's not teleporting."

"...<u>So</u> when you *not-teleported* us, that changed fate?"

"Um. ...Hm. Did it...?" Danica gave it a few long seconds of consideration. She closed her eyes, then tentatively probed the air like she was trying to remember the shape of something. At last, she replied with a scrunched-up brow, "You know what, I don't actually know... I don't normally think about that. Probably?"

"You can't even tell you're doing it?"

"Can you tell you're processing oxygen out of the air?"

"With enough science stuff I could tell."

"Yeah. But you wouldn't bother unless someone challenged you on it, right? So, it's about the same, I think. Just, part of being fae. Natural and unquestioned. Like breathing."

Felicity tapped the pads of her index fingers together in a pensive rhythm while she stared Danica down, trying to figure out what exactly to do with this information. There had to be *something* to this, some trick that she couldn't quite plot out, some way to weaponize Danica's power, to focus it and direct it towards some specific purpose...

Then she realized the answer was pretty obvious and already right there on the table in front of her:

The contract.

If Felicity wanted to change what was coming, all she needed to do was come up with some new deal that fixed everything.

Or... made it worse, as the fae were doomed to do, apparently.

She stared at the document deep in contemplation for a while before she idly asked, "What makes the fae so special anyways?"

"Mm... It's our *purpose*, I guess – to put on a good show, to make the universe dance in chaos and misery. And to help with our *noble* mission, we're free from the pesky confines of the boring old 'deterministic causality' that you're all stuck with. Gift of the gods."

"Hell of a gift."

"You'd think. But all their gifts come with a cost," Danica said, tapping the contract for emphasis.

"...You always call them 'nameless'?"

"Yeah. I mean, maybe they have names, I don't know. We sure don't know them. We just have the First Pacts. The rules. But their signatures on those pacts? Their true names? They're *unknowable*, even to us – just like my true name is to you."

Felicity pulled the iron-inked sigil out of her pocket and showed it off to taunt Danica and prove how wrong she was.

"Oh that. Yeah, sorry Fleece, I know you put a lot of work into figuring that signature out, but it's uh… *expired*, I guess, is the best way to think of it."

"…Why were you freaking out about it, then?"

She shrugged with a stupid grin. "Bluffing?"

Felicity stared at her, dumbfounded for a few seconds, before, in a growling fury, she crumpled up the spell and threw it at Danica's face.

"Hey, come on," she said, effortlessly deflecting the not-so-enchanted paper without a thought, then scowled at Felicity and retorted defensively: "You were bluffing too."

"Oh yeah? And how would you know that?"

"Well first of all, that's not a banishing spell. It's an extremely poorly worded *invoice*."

"…What?"

"Fae society, as much as you could call a bunch of monsters trying to cheat each other out of everything they own a society, runs on debts and favor. That looks like fragments of a strongly worded overdue notice. —Which is kind of an odd thing for <u>you</u> to know *anything* about, isn't it?"

"Oh. So…"

Danica crossed her arms and sternly asked, "Did you steal my mail, Felicity?"

"…Okay well, hold on, let's take a second to define… like… what *is* stealing? You know?"

Danica sat up straight in her chair, gritted her teeth in a fury, and tossed her fists at her sides as she jabbed at Felicity: "It <u>*was*</u> you! Gods, Fleece! I was supposed to get that letter a whole month earlier! —Holy *hell*, you caused me so much trouble!! I could've missed a <u>very</u> important court date because of your sticky little fingers, you cretin! —Oh my gods… I could've *done something*—"

"Well excuse me—"

"—You are *very much* not excused! That's super fucked up! —Gods, <u>you</u>… You have a *lot* of nerve calling <u>me</u> a monster, Fleece, seriously."

"…Sorry," Felicity offered a sheepish apology. "I didn't… know…"

"*Thief*. <u>Forger</u>. —You want to know why I knew you were bluffing? Because that little *mockery* of a signature you're so proud of cobbling together there is *worthless*. I can't be bound with my *name* or my *signature*. I can only be bound with my *averit* – with the sealed will of my true name – and you can't *have* my averit. It's in a certain miserable witch's possession, and I don't think she'd trade it away for all the knowledge in the world. I'm kind of a big deal back home and she knows it."

Felicity took a few seconds to let that settle in, and she sure didn't like where it landed in her head.

"So... you *knew* then. You knew the whole time I was there." Why was that so annoying? Why was that so *freaking* annoying...? Her eyes popped wide open when she realized. "—You... you just let me *think* I was in control, didn't you? So... so I'd let my guard down...? So I'd agree to that *stupid* deal? So you could *use* me? ...Oh my <u>God</u> Danica! Fuck off, I can't call you a monster! I sure as hell can! You're just... the <u>worst</u>! How do you get me <u>every</u> <u>time</u>!?"

She shot Felicity with a cruelly cute and disarming little smile before she tried to explain, as kindly as a dagger-grinning wolf comforting the bloody bones of its latest meal: "I *have* been messing with humans for thousands of years. You're sharp, Fleece – and you've caused me no end of trouble, I swear – but you've still got a *bit* of catching up to do."

Felicity scoffed at that. "Whatever, Danica, you're not going to make me feel bad about causing a murderous beast trouble. —And I think you'll find I'm the one holding the leash here, so I'd say you're the one with a bit of catching up to do, monster."

"Are you?" she asked with a teasing smile, showing off those impossibly sharp teeth of hers.

"I could banish you in a second, Dog. Don't test me—"

"—Could you?"

"I could! What did I just say about testing me??"

"You don't, though, do you? In your vision. Not yet. So, why? Worried it'd break Amy's heart? Feeling merciful enough to let me say goodbye? Or maybe it's not even *you* at all that makes me leave, hey Fleece?"

Felicity bit her tongue and scowled at the monster, but she didn't reply.

"That collar of yours must be made of silk and suede Felicity, how comfy it is that you don't even feel it. I'm not leaving for two weeks. We're *both* on someone's leash until then."

"…You're surprisingly chill about that."

Danica let her gaze wander to the titles of the books on the shelves around them. She was wearing a tired grin, dreamy. It looked like she was ticking off a list in her head: *Read it. Read it. Read it…*

She said 'all the books' before, the first time the two of them were there. Did she really…?

Felicity hesitated to ask, "You *want* to leave, don't you?"

She answered with a little scoff, "I never want to leave. That's the problem. But I was supposed to. I was supposed to crawl back on my hands and knees begging them not to hurt *my human* anymore."

She heaved a withering sigh with the weight of centuries stitched into it before she turned to Felicity and tiredly admitted defeat, to someone, somewhere: "I didn't want to let them win. You get it, don't you? You and Amy, you've both got the same spite in you, I love it. I wish we could've been friends, Fleece. You get it. I would've done anything to win. I thought I could." She scoffed at herself and bitterly added, "Gods, I can't believe I screwed this up so badly again. I was supposed to stick around and protect her from them forever. I was supposed to make everything right this time. I was supposed to *save humanity* this time. That was the plan. But now there's no one in the world who can help… No one who can fix everything I ruined… — Damn it, I'm never even going to pay *Amy* back. You have any idea how much it aches to have unpaid debt as a faerie, Fleece? It's *awful.* I can't even compare it. It hurts a part of me you don't even *have.*"

"You owe her money or something?"

"I owe her more than a thousand and one kindnesses that she *refuses* to let me pay back. It's infuriating."

"Why are you supposed to leave then?"

"Lucrative job offer back in the Faelands," she replied, in that way that Felicity had started to pick up meant she was using some vague metaphor to cheat the truth.

"What, and they were holding Amy hostage to make you take it?"

"No. It was never about *her*. This is a sentence," Danica said, gesturing at her chest. "I'm supposed to suffer in this prison. Instead, I keep oh-so-cleverly finding ways to have fun anyways."

Felicity scoffed at the revelation. "Color me surprised: Danica Doyle, the great and treacherous Black Dog, finding ways to cheat out of her responsibilities."

"Well, they find ways to cheat me right back. —You know the Black Death?"

Felicity replied sarcastically, "I've heard of it, yes." What a stupid question. Her whole career was the archaeology of books. Obviously she'd consumed dozens of texts on the Plague.

"That was my fault," Danica confessed, cold, detached.

"Your fault."

"Well. My fault for having fun. My family decided to punish me to balance the scales."

"By killing millions of people? How the hell is that worth a little fun?"

Danica laughed at herself. "I'm kind of broken, Felicity. I've got a big soft spot in my heart for humans. My family doesn't have the same curse."

"Empathy's a curse, huh. Spoken like a true demon."

"It is for us. Our lives don't end—<u>can't</u> end. Year after year of unforgettable mourning after mourning piling up for the rest of time? It's a curse. I wouldn't trade it for anything, but they sure know how to use it against me. And they keep... doing it. Centuries of wars and famines and plagues, just to spite me. Just for me..."

Felicity rolled her eyes at the selfishness of what Danica was admitting to here. What a monster. Truly. "Sounds like you should probably stop making them use it against you then, huh!"

"...Would you?"

"Would I? What, would I suffer to save the people I love? Let the bad guys win? Be a martyr? Give up?"

Danica nodded solemnly.

Was she really asking?

"...Forever? That's the deal?"

"Forever."

"That's a long time."

"It's a long time. But I thought, maybe it's long enough that I can still win, you know? Maybe I can find a way to wear them down, fix it all, make it better, pay back all the horrible things I've done. Protect you. If I give up, if I let them win, there's no hope left."

"And how's that going?"

"...Bad."

Felicity couldn't keep her eyes on Danica's forlorn face anymore. She felt all that manipulative sympathy growing in her again.

She started idly searching for familiar titles on the bookshelf behind the beast while she thought of how to answer that trick of a question.

At last, she let out a sigh of defeat before she chided the miserable faerie: "Danica I don't know what you're thinking coming to me for life advice here, but this sounds... *pretty obvious*. If you being here is hurting the *entirety of humanity* – hell, even if you being here is only hurting *Amy* – that's... enough."

"Mm..."

"...You don't get to talk about this much, huh?"

Danica shook her head sadly.

Felicity stared at her inedible sandwich for a few long moments of silence while she thought about the weight of Danica's question. Could *she* give up? *Forever?*

Well, it didn't really matter what Felicity could or couldn't do. What mattered was what Danica *had* to do.

"...You have to go, Dani."

"Mm."

"For Amy."

"Mm..."

"—For humanity! For everyone. It's the only way, isn't it? The only way to... to make things right – to stop it getting worse at least. You know that. You obviously know that, why do you need *me* to say it?"

"Because I'm a monster, Felicity. And it's been so long since someone with a good heart had me on a leash." She scoffed at herself. "Hope you'll forgive me for leaving her behind like this."

"...It's for the best."

"It is."

"I can't... hold that against you..."

"You really can't."

"I won't."

"Thanks."

"...So. What happens now?"

"Oh, I don't know. I'll pack my things, I guess. Hail a ride back home. Say goodbye to everyone. —Or maybe it's better to just disappear. Should I just go? I should probably just go. Easier for everyone, isn't it? Goodbyes suck..."

"You're just going to *go*? Just... like that? After everything? —Wait, but you said... You said your cousins... They'll *stop* torturing her when you go, right?"

Danica shrugged. "That wasn't an explicit part of the new contract. I mean, they wouldn't have any *particular* reason to bother Amy after I'm gone, but, you know, who could say? They're kind of vindicative and cruel for no reason. It would be a pretty good final shard of glass to drive into my heart. —Why? Does it matter? I'm leaving in two weeks no matter what, and there's not really anyone else in the universe that could stand in their way. Can't do anything about it now, can we? Fate's sealed."

"No... No, come on... Don't do this..."

"Do what?"

"...Amy's going to die if you leave... isn't she..."

Danica shook her head and sadly stated a plain obvious fact: "Everyone dies."

"...On God, Danica, on Christ, on Mary, I swear if you're just... screwing with me again..."

"—You want a perfect solution? I leave, she lives, everyone's happy? I can't give you that. I'm sorry."

Felicity gritted her teeth and cut into her palms with her fingernails for a few tense seconds before she asked something she knew she'd regret before she even parted her lips: "...Can you trade for it?"

Not to Brag, but It's Damn Fine Print

(*Late Evening, Friday, 29th September*)

Now, Nicole wasn't exactly *proud* of manipulating Felicity. Like, first of all, it felt way too easy. She was such an open book, and anyone with as much love in their eyes as Felicity had in hers for Ravi was always pretty easy to catch her claws on. But Felicity was also pretty smart, and there was definitely something dangerous about negotiating with her that was kind of thrilling. It had been ages since Nicole had felt such a rush, such a fear, trying to work someone over. Since Angie, really, though Felicity wasn't quite on the old witch's level. But after spending most of a postgrad thesis on researching old texts with such meticulous passion, she sure had a pretty huge advantage over every other person Nicole had been forced to swindle this time around.

But second of all, she was such a sweetheart under all that *Felicity* that Nicole couldn't help feeling a little guilty, so she was going to be *extremely* careful to make sure the terms of the contract were going to be *safe*, even more than usual. It wouldn't do any good to save Ravi and lose Felicity in the process. Those two, they'd need each other.

And it was pretty obvious that if Nicole presented Felicity with the facts – some of them anyways – that after she left, Ravi would be in danger – that of course Felicity would immediately jump to the question of how to save her best friend.

It was also pretty obvious that if Nicole presented Felicity with the facts – that she could use Nicole to manipulate the fate of the universe – she'd immediately get tunnel-visioned on that as the only answer.

Which was good, because it was, but Nicole couldn't possibly have convinced Felicity of that with a straightforward discussion.

It sure would've been nice if that first 'using Felicity to keep Ravi safe forever' trick had worked out, but Nicole sure wouldn't waste a chance at taking a second try at it.

While Nicole waved her hands over the stack of pages of the

contract to set up the technical preamble, she mulled over what she'd have to offer, what she'd have to take. The trick to making these things safe was to make them *hurt*. If Nicole could think of something that would destroy Felicity's heart and soul without killing her or ruining her body, then Felicity might be able to find a way to make the best of the fallout after Nicole was gone.

But what could possibly break her like that? Destroying her research maybe? She'd give that up for Ravi. Easily. Too easily. It had to hurt more. The more it hurt now, up front, the less it would hurt later.

Nicole sighed to herself while she reviewed the careful interlocking definitions and fae legalese for holes.

Half of that sigh was for the realization that this was soon to be the nine-to-five of the rest of her eternal life – reviewing her cousins' contracts for holes that could destroy humanity.

The other half was because she knew there was something else this contract would need to be truly safe: She'd need to crush her *own* heart and soul. After all, this deal was as much for her as it was for Felicity, even though she couldn't exactly tell Felicity that. —And more importantly, it was for *Ravi*. She couldn't risk some unforeseen catastrophe hitting them later. Everything needed to balance out – *today*.

Felicity startled Nicole from her troubled musing to probe at her in annoyance: "Hey. Hello? Dani? You've been working on that thing for like twenty minutes now without a word. Am I not getting a say in this or... like... what's happening here?"

"You will. Be patient. I'm setting things up so we can start. Takes a lot of *precise* definitions to make one of these safe. Safer. And... I haven't actually... done this in a long time – a proper trade. I'm trying to be careful. It's more complicated when you're making the universe create things from nothing. And the world's a lot more... complex now. Harder to account for complications."

"And... what exactly are we *creating?*"

"What you asked for. The things you need to protect Amy."

"I don't just get to steal your powers?"

"Usually kills humans to do that. I kind of want you to live through this. Don't you?"

"...Alright. I'll trust the expert."

"Thanks," Nicole replied. She tried to give Felicity a pleasant smile but it sure didn't feel like it was coming out right. This was miserable work. Miserable, important work.

"God I can't believe this is the only way to keep Amy safe," Felicity grumbled to herself, well loud enough for Nicole to hear.

Amy. Amy Amy *Amy*. Gods Nicole was sick of using the wrong name. Sick right down to the marrow of her bones. She couldn't believe she'd been lowered like this for so long, forced to be so cruel to her own lover, to erase them behind their back. Just once she wanted to celebrate their name for Felicity, to defend them, to reveal them for who they were: Ravi Beausoleil, strong, talented, resourceful, unshakably *good* in everything they did. Amy was just some childish fantasy, a dead body Ravi put on to make it easy, and the whole thing sat sick in Nicole's stomach every time Felicity came around.

And what a miserable situation to leave the two of them in. Ravi's great protector was never going to know the true name of the person she was swearing to protect, and Ravi would never be known by the person they loved most in the world.

But what could Nicole do? She never actually *promised*, but Ravi still trusted her to keep their secret safe, to the bitter end. If she lost that trust? It would crush her. It would... it would crush her heart... and... her soul...

...

Oh gods <u>*damn it*</u>.

"What's with the face there Dani?" Felicity asked, as Nicole was bitterly putting the finishing touches on the meat of the trade.

"What's wrong with my face?"

"You look like someone just crushed your toe with a slab of concrete."

"...I don't like doing this stuff anymore, Fleece."

"You seemed pretty happy about it last time."

Nicole put on a big fake smile for Felicity to show off, "I'm a good actor."

Felicity clearly didn't like the truth of that statement, because she looked away in bitter disgust when she realized she'd been tricked again. Poor thing.

After filling in the final details on the last page, Nicole quickly scanned the document before handing it to Felicity for review.

She'd love it of course, Nicole had no doubts.

Though she was stuck on the first section of the document with a creased brow, muttering the words to herself. Looked like she was trying to make sense of one of the closed loops from how she was frantically flipping between pages in the lengthy glossary.

"Danica what is this... None of these words mean anything if you define them like this..."

"Which words?"

"You're defining... ownership in terms of personhood, and personhood in terms of consciousness, and consciousness as something a person owns... It's... circular."

Nicole peered over the top of the page to see what Felicity was looking at, and then assured her that was the only way to define things safely. "It's a loop! A complete loop. No ambiguity that way."

Nicole was sympathetic to Felicity's confusion, though. Fae legalese was dense, and almost impossible to read, for a human anyways. It was barely English at all from all the interjections and novel definitions of even the simplest words.

Felicity clicked her tongue at Nicole's assurance, but after flipping through the definitions again, she eventually conceded that the premise kind of made sense. "Reminds me of this stupid math course I had to take in first year, though. All those tricky proofs built on a shaky foundation of empty promises that somehow turned into these... unshakeable facts of the universe that make all that physics and chemistry stuff work."

"Trust me, you don't want a contract with weak definitions."

"Yeah. And I guess if half the language is defined in the contract itself..."

"It's safer. You don't want to mess with the ambiguity of the English language. It's too powerful."

From the look on her face, Felicity clearly still wasn't super confident in what the preamble meant, but with a huff and a shrug, she finally turned to the first page of the actual trade.

Her jaw dropped at the first item on offer.

"What's this?" she asked, stunned. "I don't want money."

"You sure do! Amy's got that debt to pay off. You know, the one that's entirely my fault? This can pay it off right away. And that's *exactly* what you're going to do with it after I leave, right?"

"Okay but this is... Why is it so *much?* I couldn't spend all this in ten lifetimes... Jeezus..."

"So don't. Just spend it to keep her safe. That's the whole point, right?"

"...Right."

"You'll use it to make sure she's healthy?"

"Yes. Of course. ...Is she sick?—"

"—And you'll give her a free ride wherever she wants to go, right? Whatever she wants to do? School, travel, a nice house – *whatever* – you can give her the life she wants, *no strings*, right? I mean you couldn't exactly hold it over her head if you lost just a little pittance of that vast fortune, could you? —And that's what I was going to do, as best I could anyways. Maybe I don't have a fortune to spend but I was still going to help her, to help her get to the life she really wants. You can't let me leave that unfinished."

"Ah I see, this is about your grand legacy."

"It's about her."

"Sure..." Felicity was barely able to keep up barbs with Nicole. She was too busy staring dumbfounded at the number on the page. Looked like she was trying to count the zeroes with confidence.

Then she scrunched her brow at the caveat under the sum:

"What's this...? No investing?"

"Yeah. You'd ruin the economy injecting all that into it."

"So your genius solution to that is that anything I invest in is going to crash?"

"You wouldn't be that stupid, right? —Look there's something else to doing it like this. It becomes less valuable in the trade if it's defined with a curse. Makes it so your side of the trade won't be as devastating as it would be if it was just put up against a huge pile of normal cash."

"Right. ...And what exactly am I giving you in return for this generous gift?"

"Patience. Just keep reading, you'll get there."

Felicity shook herself from her bewilderment at the first item and moved on to the next thing:

"A ward against the fae?"

"You can't keep the fae away with piles of money, sadly. It's gotta be strong enough to keep every one of my cousins away from her, and whatever this thing is going to be, it'll keep them far enough away that they'll never be able to hurt her again."

"And exactly what kind of 'thing' are we talking about here? I thought iron was the best ward against the fae, and apparently that doesn't even work on all of you monsters."

"Yeah. It sure *was* the best thing. But just for you, we'll get the universe to make something even better."

"...Okay but what?"

Nicole shrugged. "No idea. This kind of thing you want to leave vague. Like, if I was too specific, if I said it was something like... I don't know, a sword that killed any faerie within a hundred yards, there's definitely going to be a catch on it that I can't think of."

"That sounds pretty good to me though. Can't I just have that?"

"Okay well you can't kill faeries so right away there's something broken about it. Trust me, this way – specific *intent*, vague *details* – this way, the universe can't find a way to weasel out of it. Whatever it makes will do *exactly* what it's supposed to do – just, maybe not in the way you'd expect it to. Maybe in a way that sucks actually, but it'll *work*."

Felicity flipped through a few pages of caveats and exclusions under that particular item.

"You're pretty familiar with this, huh? You warded off a lot of faeries before?"

Nicole laughed uneasily and replied that she'd seen a lot of contracts and seen a lot of them go wrong in ways that ended up screwing over the fae party. "This is just... everything I remember about that, turned around to screw over the fae on purpose."

"Including you."

"Yeah. If it can stop *me*, it can stop anyone."

"That's very noble of you."

"...Yeah. 'Noble'. I'm sure my cousins will be *delighted* I'm bringing something like this into the universe."

"That's the price of protecting the people you love."

Nicole painted her glare with a chill darkness when she gravely retorted: "You have no idea what it costs."

—*Though by the end of this, she might.*

"And what's the 'curse' on this one?"

"I just told you. Whatever it is, it'll even ward me off."

"...Shouldn't that make it *more* valuable to me?"

"Does it?"

Felicity didn't respond. She just tapped on the paper pensively while she considered that easy question.

"You know," Nicole poked at her, "*somehow* I keep prying open the locks on your supposedly well-guarded sympathy there Fleece."

"You're a monster is how."

"No. It's because you know I make Amy happy."

"...Somehow."

"And when I'm gone, what's that going to do to her?"

Felicity didn't respond.

So Nicole carried on: "Hey look, maybe against all odds and past performance I'm reading it wrong, but I don't think you really want me to leave her behind. Why else would you be here tonight? Isn't that the whole reason you drove out here? You want me to stay. You want me to be with her. And something that defies that? Something that keeps me away forever? That's a curse for you too."

—*For all of us...*

Again Felicity didn't have a response. She just stared at the details of the contentious bargaining chip for a few long, heavy seconds before she flipped over the page, apparently expecting to find more on offer, but she was clearly disappointed to see that was it. The rest of the trade was just... the cost.

And what exactly *was* a massive cursed fortune and an impervious ward against all the fae worth?

Even Nicole didn't want to think about the answer.

And Felicity was clearly on the same page.

"No," she said plainly, abruptly returning the first couple dozen pages to the stack and tossing the loose package at Nicole in a chaotic flurry of flying paper.

Nicole calmly reassembled the document with a wave of her hand and slid it back across the table. "*Read it* first, Felicity. Gods."

"No! No. <u>No</u>! Nothing would make me give Amy up. That's the whole freaking point—!"

Nicole opened the deal back to the offending page to point Felicity's attention to it, "If you would *read it*, you'd see it's just her name."

"Okay well I'm not stupid enough to give someone's name over to a faerie! That's rule number one!"

"It's not her *name* name, it's just your *memory* of her name. —Read it for gods' sake!"

Felicity huffed and grumbled about it, but at last she picked the contract back up to begrudgingly look over the carefully crafted language Nicole used for the heavy ask.

"...Still know her, remember her... Never again call her any derivative of her 'old name'...? 'Scrubbed'...? What does that mean?"

"Her name won't be in your brain anymore."

"...To take effect the moment you leave...?"

"Oh yeah, I don't want to be here when all that goes down."

"...This is... ridiculous. Why is this even worth so much? All that money and some super powerful magic ward? It's just... It's just the *sound* of her name, isn't it?"

"Right."

"Nothing else changes."

"Correct. You'll call her whatever new thing she asks you to and it'll feel just as true."

"Okay but that'll be super weird for her, won't it?"

"Oh, yeah, I'm counting on it being super awkward for both of you. You'll suffer. She'll suffer, which will make you suffer more. It's perfect."

"I'm sorry, you *want* to make her suffer now?"

"No. But this is the only way to make *you* suffer properly, so, you know, cost of business. But don't worry, you two are tight, you'll figure it out. You can even tell her it was my fault."

"Okay but that doesn't... *Why* is this worth so much?" she asked, incredulous, whacking the page with the back of her hand.

"Because it <u>hurts</u>. That's the <u>point</u>. I told you, the fae are agents of <u>suffering</u>. There's always a cost, always pain that has to be extracted from these deals, a tax on the euphoria. And the more tax you pay up front – the more this deal hurts *now* – the less it can do to surprise you *later*."

Felicity let herself fall back in her seat to read over the proposed sacrifice over and over again, flipping back and forth between what Nicole was offering and what Felicity was supposed to give up for it – between the offer of a complete package of everything Felicity needed to keep Amy safe forever, and that precious name, the name she'd always known her beloved crush of a best friend by, the name that meant everything to her.

"It feels like a trick…"

"Yes? It is? Fleece, sweetie, I feel like we're not communicating here."

"I'm <u>not</u> your sweetie. And that's not… I mean it's… How do I put it…? It's like it's both too much *and* too little. I mean Jeezus Dani, you can't just take my soul or something?"

"You know, human souls are worth a lot less than you might think." —Seeing as they don't exist, as far as Nicole could tell, beyond some playful metaphors anyways.

"What about… like… a decade off my lifespan?"

"What would I do with ten years of a human's life, Fleece? I'm leaving."

"Firstborn?"

"…Sorry, are you…" Nicole stopped herself for a second, and shot Felicity with the most incredulous glare before she twirled her hand in the air and sarcastically summarized the offer in a dramatic tone: "The *devoted lesbian* is offering the *naïve faerie* her firstborn child! Will the clever ploy succeed?"

"It's called *in vitro* Danica!"

Nicole scoffed at her, "Right! Right, sorry. Well, unfortunately for you, I'm not one of those child-eating faeries."

"…You *eat them??* "

"What did you think we did?"

"I don't know! Slave labor??"

"…Oh, dear, sweet Felicity."

"I'm going to throw this damn plate at you if you keep talking to me like that, I swear on all your nameless gods."

Felicity pressed the heels of her palms into her closed-tight eyes for a few long seconds. This really was getting to her. Nicole was right about this one: It was the perfect knife to twist and twist away at her. —At both of them.

Without moving, she pleaded for some alternative, quiet and desperate: "There's nothing else? *Nothing?*"

"Nothing else I want."

"You really are a monster."

"Just like you always wanted me to be."

Felicity scrunched up her nose and grimaced bitterly at that with a dismissive click of her tongue.

The false silence that fell over the room was heavy. Cutlery clattered at other tables. Conversations tittered. The espresso machine roared. Everything around the two of them was so mundane. This wasn't really the right stage for such a grand negotiation, but it's where Felicity wanted to go. How could Nicole complain now?

She was the first to speak to break the silence. Felicity clearly needed a push here: "You really think it's too much, don't you?"

"You're such a prick Danica."

"You want me to sweeten the deal, then?"

"No! I don't want to trade *anything* for her name! This is sick!"

"Ah. I get it. Feels guilty?"

Felicity sneered at Nicole. "You know exactly what you're doing. You know how much she... Jeezus Dani you're sick... Making me choose between her safety and happiness, and my... my *everything*. I can't betray everything between the two of us like this. It's so... so *tawdry*."

Nicole put her hands out on the table, fingers splayed, in a humble entreaty: "Come on, Fleece. Don't feel bad. Look, I know it feels tough, but I have just the trick to make it feel better. —For now, anyways. I've done this so many times, and it's *remarkably* easy to take that uneasy feeling away: Everyone has a price. We just have to find yours. —Or you can let me twist up that pretty little heart of yours to make you a little more *acquiescent*, if you want. That works too," Nicole added with a sharp-toothed grin and a little flash of cunning in her eyes, the kind of monstrous look she knew Felicity absolutely hated. Might as well play it up now. Nothing to lose. And nothing to hide.

Felicity scrunched up her face at Nicole's entirely accurate assessment of human nature, and chose to completely ignore that last generous offer there. It would be the ultimate kindness in a situation like this to take the choice out of her hands, after all. That's definitely the most painful part of it, and Nicole knew it: The choice.

"'Everyone has a price'? That's... that's disgusting. You really believe that, don't you?"

"It's a belief backed by a *robust* body of evidence."

"I bet..." She shook her head disapprovingly and tried to assure Nicole, "No. No I can't accept that. There's definitely someone out there with enough dignity to refuse your devilish little tricks."

"Well, the question is what would you rather be, then? That one exception to the rule? With the iron conviction to be better than any person before you? Flawless? Perfect? Uncorruptible? *Impossible?* Or are you willing to be just human enough to sell out when the price is right? Because that'll be a lot easier on your conscience at the end of the day I think."

"Will it?"

"Or you can refuse to sell for any price, and then you get nothing at all. —And then Amy's left at the mercy of her cruel fate."

Felicity scowled bitterly at Nicole, because she was right, and Felicity always seemed to hate that for some reason. She scowled and scowled until at last she was content enough – that she'd proven some point of her conviction through the gesture – that she was willing to concede and submit to the flaws of her humanity. "Fine. But I'm not cheap, Dani. I'm a princess and you're going to make me feel like one with whatever you're offering here. —And you're going to make it hurt worse than anything in my life to say no."

Nicole grinned proudly, and assured Felicity that wouldn't be a problem. "I'm good at this."

You Can Do Better Than That

(Night, Friday, 29th September)

'I'm good at this,' said the arrogant beast, before she immediately went on to throw useless offer after useless offer at Felicity for the entire walk back to Amy's apartment.

Seriously, if all the money in the world wasn't enough, what was left on the table? That's kind of the thing with money: It buys basically anything else. Practically a cheat code for free happiness. You want fame? You want prestige? You want some semblance of love? It's all easy enough to pay *someone* to hook you up with all of it, eventually.

And she didn't want any of that anyways.

...Well. Okay, the... the love thing... might be nice...

But it didn't matter whether it came from some magic trade or from a vast fortune, there's no way *trading* for love would feel right.

Felicity was surprised actually that Danica never once offered love, though. That seemed like a pretty common bargaining chip.

No resurrecting the dead either?

Immortality?

She asked about it, and Danica gave her a grim staredown before she insisted that Felicity didn't want to go there. "Trust me."

But as much as Felicity was getting kind of sick of the tricky Dog insisting she was worth trusting on this stuff, and as much as it sat wretched in her guts to do it, she had to accept that there was no one better qualified to speak on the pitfalls of faerie trading than Danica.

When the two of them finally got back, Dani hesitated at the door to Amy's unit.

"Well?" Felicity challenged her to open up with an impatient gesture at the lock.

"I don't suppose I can convince you to take all that warding stuff down," she said with a cute smile that was clearly supposed to be disarming.

Felicity raised an incredulous eyebrow at that and asked with a hint of smug superiority to rub it in that she might have won some kind of victory here: "What, it really works?"

"Oh get over yourself. It's just going to be agitating. Itchy. And I can't exactly explain to Amy why I want it all taken down."

"But *I* can, can't I? Now that the Bell rang."

Danica lowered her eyes from Felicity's to let out a little huff of a sigh before she asked, "Could you hold off? For now? Until I'm gone? I don't know what she'll do once she figures out the rest of my secrets."

"…'The <u>rest</u> of your secrets'?" she asked, curious, suspicious. Then she realized, and her eyes went wide, her hands dropping lifeless to her sides. "Oh… my God… You… you *teleported* in front of her!"

"Okay I keep saying this and no one is listening: It's not teleportation. But yeah. It's not the first time she's seen it."

"So she already knows!?"

"A little. She found out some stuff a couple months ago."

"What the hell Danica! You've been acting like it's a big secret! — Why do you do this to me??? Can you stop for once!? Holy Jeezus Christopher I'm going to lose my mind!"

"It *is* a secret, though. Mostly. She doesn't know I'm fae, just that I have some magic tricks. But if she found out what I can *really* do?" Danica waved around the unfinished contract for emphasis before making it disappear in a small burst of glitter. "I don't know what happens after that, Fleece. And I don't want to find out. Not with her. Not her."

"What, you think she's going to force you into some weird contract?"

"I think she'll always wonder what would've happened if she did, you know? That's just… how she is, I think. Wants quick solutions to big problems. Wants to fix the world. And I'm pretty sure she'd always wonder if she could've done something with an all-powerful wish-granting faerie in her bed. She'd always wonder if there was some ultimate sacrifice she could've made to make everything right."

"…Could she?"

—Wait. Could… you? <u>Everything</u>? Jeezus are you really being so small-minded here?

Danica laughed at the idea, though. "No. No, trust me, I've tried." Her eyes sunk, and that grim smile returned to her lips. "Honestly, I've never been able to save even one person like this, with some careful mostly-benevolently crafted deal. But hey, hundredth time's the charm, right?"

"...You've... tried to save a hundred people with this crap?"

"Oh. Uh. No. Definitely... *way* way more. Sorry, didn't want to oversell it there."

"You didn't want to oversell how terrible you are at this," Felicity flatly echoed.

"Gods you're rude. I meant I didn't want to oversell how desperately I've been trying to make things... better. I mean hell, Felicity, you already think I'm some horrible monster. I don't think anything I say or do will ever convince you I'm not. What's a little bragging going to accomplish?

"And... Gods, I mean, you're right, right? Really. You're right. You've always been right. If I wasn't a monster, I'd actually be able to save someone for once, wouldn't I? I wanted to believe it for so long, but maybe it's time to just accept it. Maybe there are just some unkillable things in my heart... But, you know, can't say I didn't try." Danica interrupted herself with a scoff, then added with some obviously false hope in her voice, "No point giving up now, though, hey? In for a penny, right?"

The two of them jumped with a start when the door opened.

Amy gave the two of them an impatient scowl when she sarcastically welcomed the two of them home: "Heyyy, what a surprise: The two most important women in my life arguing right in front of my door. What a gift."

"Hey Ames," Felicity greeted her sheepishly.

"Fleece. Care to tell me a bit about all the junk you nailed to my walls? Because I have a damage deposit that I'm not getting back with a hundred holes in the drywall. —And maybe while you're at it, you can explain why you attacked my girlfriend so viciously that you both *phased out of existence* and left me here all night worrying? You two can't answer your phones or what? I love that you're bonding or whatever but holy fuck guys..."

Felicity patted herself down and realized she'd left her phone at home in her rush out the door, and gave Amy a pleading apology for it.

—Brilliant work, Felicity... Make her worry all night...

Though that didn't excuse Danica. But she already had some poor explanation ready. She pulled her phone out of her bra and, with a sheepish apologetic shrug, held it out to show off that it had been powered down all night. "Sorry. I turned it off when you and me were out before. Wanted to give you my *undivided* attention," she added with a romantic grin.

"Great. All accounted for. Well-excused. You two coming in or what?"

As they entered the apartment, Felicity gleefully noted to herself that Danica's posture shrunk the second she crossed the threshold – from her usual cheerful overbearing confidence to a slouchy unease, while she looked around at all the 'junk' on the walls.

Truly Felicity had done a great job ruining the apartment for her. Proud moment. The first true victory in this stupid little war of theirs.

Amy got herself set up reclined on the far corner of the couch with an arm slung over the back and a leg curled up on the cushion, with a look in her eyes that implored Felicity to explain herself.

So she tried:

"Uh. So. I was… having nightmares… about evil spirits attacking you…"

"Mmm."

"And I thought… You know, you'd probably be stubborn about it, so, so you know, as a surprise…"

"Mhm."

"They're… they're… wards…? Good luck charms."

"Mm."

"…I'll take them down."

"Great. Thanks. You staying the night?"

"…Is that okay?"

"Oh, *more* than okay. You're filling all the holes in tomorrow, yeah?"

"…Right. Yes. I'll fill the holes in tomorrow. —And I'll repaint it. …Sorry."

"Hey no problem! Just making sure you haven't totally lost your mind."

Felicity glared at Danica and sarcastically replied, "Not yet."

Amy looked back and forth between the two of them with a

discerning glare. At last, she chided Dani: "You told me it was too dangerous to do that with a person."

"...I uh... panicked?"

Amy crossed her arms and raised a judgmental eyebrow at her.

Danica tried to defend herself, "Okay listen no one has ever died—"

"—I sure fucking hope not! —And how are you even allowed to do that in front of her, huh? What happened to 'not making it obvious'?"

Felicity got the feeling this was about to get kind of *domestic*, so she quietly retrieved her hammer and slinked away to start prying the iron nails and trinkets out of the drywall in the kitchen.

She was standing on the counter working on the stuff hidden above the cabinets when Amy was done chewing Danica out for endangering Felicity's life.

Felicity's dear fuming friend rounded the corner of the kitchen and leaned against the wall with impatiently crossed arms to give her the same disappointed glare as Danica had been enduring.

"What do you know?" she asked plainly.

Felicity got caught in Amy's eyes. What a tumultuous chimera of emotion was swirling in there. Worry. Rage. Desperation. Hope. What was she supposed to do? Danica had pleaded so earnestly for her to keep quiet.

"...Not... much?" she replied, crawling down from the counter to meet Amy on her level. —Well, okay, half a foot beneath her, as always.

"Not much," Amy echoed incredulously.

"Okay, fine, I know... a lot. —But I can't talk about it. Sorry. I... promised."

"You can't talk about it! Really? That's a very *convenient* excuse around here!" she said, pointedly loud enough to serve as a verbal jab at Danica.

Danica shouted back from the other room, "You promised to be cool about this!"

Amy clicked her tongue at that, but she didn't respond, so Felicity continued trying to explain herself:

"Look, I'm still... figuring things out, okay? So yes, I know she can do that... teleporty thing. —And trust me, you do not want to let her do that to you. I still feel queasy thinking about it. And I know she hates these... *things*," she said, holding up her growing handful of iron nails and gesturing at the other trinkets she'd already set aside on the counter. "And I'm just... I'm trying to... I... —Jeezus Ames, I'm scared for you, okay? This is *scary*. How can you... *know* all this about her and just... just... *pretend* everything is normal?" Felicity looked her in the eye and implored with her to understand, "Do *you* even know what kind of monster she is?"

What little kindness and patience was hidden there drained out of Amy's face in an instant. "Don't... talk about her like that."

Felicity shook her head and glowered at her deluded friend, "You really don't see how crazy this is, do you? You're seduced. You're totally seduced—"

Amy stood up straight and slammed her palm into the wall, rattling the plates in the cupboard and rumbling the concrete foundation of the apartment in her fury when she demanded Felicity's silence with a single word: "Enough."

Felicity curled her nails into her palms and gritted her teeth bitterly, but she couldn't bring herself to defy Amy's command.

She continued in a bitter, incredulous rage: "Seduced. I'm *seduced*. What's wrong with you? Of course I'm 'seduced' by the woman I love. God, if anyone's crazy obsessed with her, it's you. You've been like this since day one. For no reason. I'm sick of it. I'm sick of it, Felicity! It's enough! You be nice to her or... or I don't... want you here. Period. You understand? This *hurts* me. You will be fucking nice to her. You will apologize to her for being so shitty. And you will make a goddamn effort to be friends with this woman. I don't care what kind of 'monster' you think she is. You will be good to her. Or you can just... just... stay away – from both of us.

"I love you, Fleece. I never want to lose you. But I don't want this toxic *bullshit* in my life. I'm happy. I've never *been* this happy. And you will not take this away from me with your paranoid jealous *fuckery*. You understand? I don't need you to protect me. I can take care of myself. What I need is a friend who's *happy for me* when I've got something good in my life, not a psycho who's going to break into my apartment and try to *sabotage* me and my girlfriend."

"...Yes ma'am."

Amy glared at her for a few more tense seconds, but after that, all the tension dropped out of her shoulders before she opened her arms to welcome Felicity in for a hug. "God, you look like such a scorned little puppy... Come here, godsake..."

She *felt* like a scorned little puppy.

Amy's embrace was nice, despite all the pity in it.

But her body wasn't soft. Not like Danica's. She was... solid. Strong. Safe.

She could take care of herself, couldn't she? She'd been taking care of herself for a long time.

So what was even the point of Felicity, then?

She buried her face in Amy's shoulder and tried her best not to have a little breakdown. This wasn't the time. Amy had no idea what was coming. And no matter how tough and strong and capable she was, Felicity was the only one in the world who could save her from the disaster that was waiting for her after Danica left.

"You can't just magic all these holes away?" Felicity lamented, on the thirtieth or fortieth one, well into the afternoon. Amy was out on some errands, and taking a well-deserved break from the two of them. Danica was keeping Felicity company while she patched up the walls.

"Doesn't work like that," Danica assured her.

"Useless magic then, huh? Can't even do basic home improvements."

"Correct."

"What's it like?"

"What's what like?"

"This... I don't know, this life. You have all this power 'to change the fabric of the universe' and you can't even use it without cursing yourself."

Danica laughed at herself. "It sucks. I make the best of it, though. There's a lot here that makes me happy. I have to hold on to that. ...Well. *Had to.* I guess. Not gonna matter soon."

"...Think of anything to sate my pathetic human greed yet?"

"Car that never needs to be refueled?"

"You mean an electric car? I think the cash can cover that, Danica."

"...Fine, car that never needs to be... what, 'topped up'?"

"Perpetually running on fumes? Oh, won't even start?"

"...You're too sharp for this stuff Fleece."

"I'm not getting swindled by some basic monkey's paw stuff. You have any idea how many stories I've read about genies and sprites and wishes gone awry? —About *you?*"

"...Too many."

"Too many. Keep going."

"Understand any language? You like words."

"And put my lovely translator out of work?"

"Come on Fleece..."

"...Okay... What's the catch there? I can't see that one."

"Probably... lose the ability to *speak* any language? That feels about ironically devastating enough."

"Ah great. Yeah."

"Not worth it?"

"No it's not worth it! Jeezus..."

Danica crossed her arms and dropped her chin to hum to herself. She'd been stuck on this all last night and all day today. Apparently Felicity was a little harder to seduce than a typical human. What an honor.

"Famous?"

"No."

"...Respected in your field?"

"I don't even want to know the catch on that one."

"What about that project you're working on? What if it was just... *done*. Perfect. Guaranteed to last forever, just like you want it to. —You have any idea how impossible *forever* is? That's usually reserved for the fae alone."

"Don't tease me."

"Oh ho? You like that one?"

"I like my *research*. I like... *making it* perfect. Chasing that impossible 'forever'. You think I don't know how hard it is? Backups and recovery and redundancy are all a *huge* part of the project, and I've got it all covered. —Well... okay, I'll have it covered eventually. We're getting there. And what good is it to me if that's all done *for me?*"

"Felicity Aurelia Vicente, I had no idea you were so humble about the grand success of your work. I thought you had some ego invested in this thing."

"I do. I have ego invested in the *work*. It's the *philosophy* of it more than the final product. A legacy of scholars pursuing the humblest of stories. So what good is it if it's all done? No one would ever care about it again."

"What if it's perfect *and* guaranteed to be a hit with the rest of humanity forever?"

"...No. —Come on, do better."

"Gods Fleece you're a tough nut to crack..."

"None of this garbage is worth Amy's *name*, Danica. None of this is worth everything that name means to me. None of this is worth my *dignity*. Do better."

"Okay but we're on a tight schedule here. Can you at least try to meet me halfway with this? Try to get a *little* psyched up? You really don't have *anything* you want badly enough to make this worth it?"

Felicity sighed and dropped the spatula in the spackle bucket to take a break and sit down with Danica to take this haggling process seriously.

"Keep going," she said, waving her hand dismissively for Danica to continue. "What else have you got?"

"Give me a hand here. Nothing's coming close? I'm usually pretty good at this part, you know."

"I don't know Dani it's all... *close*. But nothing's so amazing that whatever catch is worth it. Languages. Cool. Useless if I can't talk about what I read. Respected in my field? Amazing. People work decades for that. I don't want the quality of my field *diminished* to my lowly novice level by some cursed magic crap. My project. Of course I want to see it... perfect. Not with just a snap of your fingers, though. There's no satisfaction in that."

"*Any* language is big, Fleece. You've never found a book your translator can't handle?"

Felicity reflected on the pain of not being able to translate the page out of that Witch's book. The kind of information in a book like that, something so valuable to a Witch that she'd spend tens of thousands on it and threaten Felicity's life for it?

"...A couple."

"Doesn't the curiosity eat you up?"

"...Like I said, it's useless if I can't—"

"—Oh!" Danica shouted and clapped with a sudden rush of stupid giddy inspiration. "Oh, I know! You'll love this: You like to gamble?"

"Gamble?"

"Nine out of ten. Good odds, right?"

"Nine out of ten what?"

"Books. What are we talking about here? Nine out of ten books, no catch, just touch a book – any piece of it, in any condition – and you'll know every word, you can tell the world, and you can understand everything – *everything:* The context, the history, the world it was read and written in, the author's *intent*, the marginalia and the brilliant thoughts it sparked in every reader who ever touched it. —<u>Everything</u>."

"...And number ten?"

"Feels the same. Feels like you got it all. Like it's just as good as the other nine. But it's all fake. You're wrong. About all of it. And you'll never know. Ever."

Felicity's interest was finally sparking. That was something. That was something... big.

"...Nine out of ten..."

"Good, right? *So* in your favor."

Felicity shook her head. "What good does it do to just tell people what's in these books? I'd sound insane if it's a language no one could translate yet."

"Hm... what if... it came with all the evidence you need to prove it?"

"What, it just materializes out of thin air?"

"The universe provides," Danica said clapping her hands together in a praying gesture.

"That's... Okay, what about the wrong book?"

"Bad evidence that looks good. Everyone will believe it. Even though it's wrong."

"That sounds... kind of dangerous."

"Oh come on, plenty of people believe hoaxes and stuff. How's this different?"

"Hm..."

The knowledge Felicity could bring into the world with something like that... Finding and curating the perfect collection of ten books wouldn't be easy. —A life's work, honestly. But this was a chance at *nine* anthropologically complete Rosetta Stones that could change history forever – that could connect humanity to its past in a way we've never been able to before and may never be able to again – nine of *those*, and one 'harmless' Voynich Manuscript style hoax of a sham.

She had to admit, it was... pretty good.

But did it *hurt*?

The betterment of the world *and* keeping Amy safe from whatever Danica's vile kin had in mind, up on a scale against the sound of Amy's name – the sound of Amy's name and Felicity's pride.

Too much. Too little.

This could change everything. Forever.

And... some things are bigger than individuals, aren't they? Bigger than a little *discomfort* figuring out a new way to talk to Amy.

And... wasn't it fair? After asking Danica to sacrifice her own pride and happiness for the world? For Amy?

There was no way she could let herself be outdone by a heartless monster, right?

"...Nine out of ten...?"

Danica teased Felicity with a smug look on her face and a singsong tone in her voice: "Hmm~? Good? It's good! Right?"

"...Let me sit on it."

All the proud confidence in Danica's face drained away. She crossed her arms with a little huff. "Time sensitive here, Fleece. We've got thirteen days to fix this."

"I know! I know, okay. Just. Give me some time. —Wednesday! Wednesday night. Okay? Four days. —And... I don't know, try to come up with something better while you're waiting."

Danica coldly replied to confirm, "Four days. Wednesday night. Give me your address, I'll save you the trip."

Felicity shot her a snide grin and taunted her, "Cute trick, Dani, but I'm not giving you my whole damn apartment just because you ask for it."

"...Just write it down, smartass."

Danica didn't just visit Felicity on Wednesday. She intruded on the privacy of her precious apartment every night to make some bold new offer.

Sunday night, it was an offer of an enchanted map that would always lead her to the nearest archaeological treasure trove – though never by the fastest route, and occasionally through hazards that no human should be able to survive.

Danica waved her hand dismissively while she enumerated some examples: "Radiation sites, deep water cave dives, active war zones—"

Felicity shook her head. "No good if I die *en route*, Dani."

"What! You won't die!"

Felicity responded flat and incredulous: "I won't die. In the explicitly *deadly* pitfalls."

"You're smart, right? You could figure it out. Just because it's deadly to a human doesn't mean it's deadly to a human with a cool safety suit or whatever."

It was tempting, but Felicity said no. Anything that might threaten her life wouldn't be worth it, and Danica should know better. What good would it do if Felicity succumbed to temptation and died chasing down some precious drowned and forgotten tome? Who'd protect Amy then?

Monday night was just, the ability to fly.

"I have that. It's called airplanes."

"Okay but imagine, flying without all the airport nonsense."

"Just get my own plane? With the money? Are you forgetting the money thing again, Dani?"

Danica grumbled something about people usually loving the flying thing – until it killed them.

"No deadly stuff! Danica! What is so hard about this for you??"

"You wouldn't die! You're smarter than that!"

"Oh my God Danica please stop..."

"...Okay what about invisibility? People love that one."

"Mhm. Lovely. Built in blindness too yeah?"

"What... makes you say that...?" she asked anxiously.

"Light has to hit your eyes to see, Danica. If you're invisible, light can't hit your eyes."

"Super strength?"

"Are you actually spending all day coming up with these terrible offers? This is the best you can do?"

"Hey, super strength is really cool!"

"Yeah, sure, super cool – until I start breaking all my stuff all the time. —Or until I accidentally punch someone right to death and spend the rest of my life in prison?"

Danica groaned at Felicity for being so difficult and then disappeared for the night in a little burst of ethereal glitter. —Before suddenly reappearing an hour later to startle Felicity near to death with a triumphant shout of, *"Camouflage!"* like she'd finally solved the puzzle, right when Felicity was changing into her nightshirt.

"Jeezus Danica! Can you not message me before you show up like this?? You peeping Tom. Holy hell, my heart... I almost died... —And seriously, <u>where</u> are you getting these stupid ideas? Comic books?"

"...So... is that a no?"

"That's a no."

She looked genuinely crestfallen when she disappeared again, actually for the rest of the night this time.

҈

Tuesday night, she came back with something actually interesting.

"Always know when someone's lying?"

Felicity genuinely considered that for a few moments. At least knowing if Amy was lying would be nice.

Though, what are you even supposed to do with that information? Other than be kind of hurt how often it happened. Not like she could press Amy on it without being a prick about it. You can't extract the truth just because you know someone's lying. And, like Danica, a lot of people get away with not-quite-lying by couching the truth.

She shook her head no. "That one's too messy."

"Could do a nine out of ten thing again?"

"Even ten out of ten wouldn't feel great."

"Okay, how about the other way? Always be able to lie convincingly to anyone?"

"I'm already great at that."

"Ego."

"Look, your whole 'the universe provides' thing," she started, adding heavy bitter air quotes around the words, "is the most dangerous part of these trades, right? If I can tell lies like truth, then I bet part of that is going to be shifting the world around to support the lie, yeah? Or ruining people's minds?"

Danica reluctantly nodded to confirm the theory.

"—Yeah I thought so. I'd have to be so careful to always actually tell the truth that I couldn't even take advantage of the power, or else I'd be risking breaking the whole of reality by saying something stupid like two plus two is fish. Might as well never say anything again."

"I'd define it a little more carefully than that Fleece—"

"—Not risking it. The fake book thing is bad enough. —And while we're talking about it, add something in there that promises reality *isn't* going to be fundamentally altered by whatever 'evidence' supports that tenth book, hey?"

"Yes ma'am," Danica said with a dutiful salute.

Felicity caught a hint of a smug grin shaping the monster's lips. She was up to something again.

"What are you scheming, Dog?"

"Do you always have to assume—"

"—Barghest. Grinning Dagger. Black Dog. Ruiner of the lives and minds of countless innocents."

Danica rolled her eyes and tried to assure Felicity, "I'm not like that anymore..."

"I've seen how you much you're enjoying all this."

"...That's just... reflexive. Fae nature. I can control it. —I <u>do</u> control it."

"I'll believe it when you stop showing off those monstrous teeth of yours every time you think you're winning."

Danica dropped the grin and gave Felicity a stone-faced glare while she silently altered the terms of the contract with a bored wave of her hand. Then the stack of paper disappeared before Felicity could even confirm the changes, and Danica left her alone in the silence of her apartment with a perfunctory, "Tomorrow night. Be ready."

Unfortunately, tomorrow night rolled around, and nothing else Danica had on offer – after, as far as Felicity could tell, she'd spent that entire final day drawing inspiration out of video games, fantasy novels, and cartoons – was anything more impressive than dollar store ring pops compared to that Faustian nine out of ten gamble of a lifetime.

Felicity, on the other hand, had been spending the week: 1. Skipping work at the university; 2. Waiting in turmoil debating the worth of her pride; and 3. Reading over dozens of ancient collections of fairytales and folklore – specifically, the ones where the humans won. And they won with the greatest anti-faerie artillery in humanity's armory: Loopholes. There were *always* loopholes in those stories. The fae were tricky, but, at their best, humans were just as clever. And not to brag, but Felicity was *pretty* clever herself. Definitely more clever than a handful of maybe-fictional medieval paupers and princesses, right? She'd definitely proven that this week, deflecting every one of Danica's sketchy offers.

And if she could do that, she could find the loophole that got her out of the worst part of that contract after she signed it, find some way to trick Amy's name out of the deal – later. For now, the most important part was keeping her safe, and no matter much she turned it over in her head, she always ended up settling on the grim truth of it: This deal was the only way she could be sure that Danica leaving Amy behind wouldn't end up killing her.

But Jeezus did it hurt to pen her name on the line.

—*Well played, demon...*

The moment the duplicated contract landed in Felicity's hands, she felt the weight of a new set of keys in her pocket – keys and a note that pointed to a nearby address that turned out to be, after a short drive after Danica left, a well-ventilated storage locker full to bursting with stacks of vacuum-sealed cash, and an inventory of other equally well-stocked storage lockers around the city that the same set of keys would open for her.

In the very same moment as the keys appeared for Felicity, a mysterious note appeared for Danica. When Felicity peered at it curiously, there was something familiar about the words, written in the same language as Virgil's partial translations, and penned in the same humming golden ink.

After Danica finished reading it over, she let the page drop to the table and miserably collapsed back in her seat, staring vacantly at the ceiling for a few long silent seconds before Felicity had to ask what the deal was.

The beast took a while to even acknowledge Felicity's voice, and when she finally did, she could only acknowledge it with a hideous cackle that devolved into something just shy of piteous sobbing.

She hid her eyes with the heels of her palms while she lamented her very nature: "I'm so gods damn stupid..." before she numbly explained that the all-powerful fae ward was apparently already here, just waiting to be picked up, she said, gesturing at the note, which presumably contained an address just like Felicity's did. "—And it looks like I'll be the delivery girl."

Even a Mithril Sword and Shield Don't Help Much in a Skydiving Kind of Situation

(Early Evening, Friday, 6th October)

Nicole was practically standing on her toes with apprehension at the threshold of Ravi's bedroom door. She had been practically standing on her toes with apprehension at the threshold of Ravi's bedroom door for what felt like an hour, with a tightly curled fist threatening and retreating from the task of knocking on the door, and her tongue pinched painfully between her pointy canines until she could taste the sting of the iron in her blood.

She couldn't keep pretending everything was fine.

She had to tell them, right?

She had to prepare them for what was coming.

She was running out of time.

Just... open the door, Nicole.

Open the door.

Reach out.

Move your arm.

Come on.

Stop chewing the damn blood out of your tongue Nicole and *move your arm.*

But when she *tried* to move her arm to knock on the door, she stumbled with a little head rush and had to catch herself on the frame.

Was the hallway always so... cramped...?

And why was her head swimming...? Fever...?

...And what was that awful *grinding* sound?

And that <u>pounding</u>? That oppressive hurried rhythm that swelled the darkness at the edge of her vision until she could barely see her fingers waving in front of her face…?

Why were her **lungs**… so… <u>tight</u>…?

Drowning…?? **Was she**… drowning ???

In a stupid panic, she pathetically clawed at the air in front of her as if getting it out of her way could possibly help. And then in a last desperate effort, she clawed at her throat. —To free herself. —To let *anything* in—

…Oh.

She was holding her breath.

She was crouched on her heels in front of Ravi's bedroom door curled into herself and clawing at her throat for air because she was… holding her breath.

Right. Yeah. That would do it.

She exhaled deeply for a rush of embarrassed relief and took a few steady breaths to recover and let the carbon dioxide balance out with the oxygen in her blood again.

Gods, that was an old, old habit. A habit from long before oxygen or carbon dioxide had names. When she first got *confined* to this beautiful body of hers for her exile, she did everything she could to test its limits, to escape its inescapable agonies, to cheat the game.

This body was never supposed to be a permanent abode. It was a tool she used as a faerie, to seduce, to manipulate. It was a tool she spent thousands of years perfecting. The pain made it convincing. It was useful to bleed like a human. She was the only one of her cousins who had such a brilliant plan. What better way to understand the weakness of the human heart than to put one in your chest?

After she'd got stuck in it, she discovered that there was one easy way to turn it off when the pain flared up like a raging hearth: Smother the embers. Still her lungs. Drown in darkness. Awaken a while later. Troubles still there. Smoldering. Often worse. But gone for a while at least. But that was fine, just do it again, and again, for weeks, months. All Earthly things must pass eventually. She figured she could wait out anything. She even spent some whole winters like that, sick of the cold and the hunger and the loss and the loneliness and the damn frostbite, just suffocating herself until the sun warmed the hills again in the spring and the promise of life couldn't possibly be betrayed by the surprise of some spiteful tactless frost again.

If she just could spend this one last week drowning herself in darkness too, it'd be so much easier. But there wouldn't be any vernal sun coming to relieve her after this one.

But Ravi deserved better than that, didn't they?

Felicity's words echoed in her head:

—They're afraid of you. Afraid you'll leave. Because that's what you do.

But she didn't *want* to leave. Gods, she *never* wanted to leave. Sometimes she just *had to* leave, before her friends or lovers got hurt, before *she* got hurt, before one more layer of agony got added to the eternal ache in her cursed heart. She had to leave when things got complicated. She had to leave when she got found out. She had to leave when she was careless. And she was... *so* careless. Henry was right. —*Felicity* was right: It's what she did. She left. She had to.

She swayed subtly in the hallway while she turned over her thoughts.

...Why was her head swimm—? Oh. Right. Right. Breathing.

—<u>*Breathe*</u> *Nicole.*

Bleh. If she kept this up, she really would pass out.

She clapped her cheeks sharply a few times to psyche herself up. *Time to do it.* Time to do the horrible painful thing. Time to do the horrible painful thing to the person she wanted more than anything to protect from pain, that she wanted so badly to never hurt that she even risked messing with a dangerous faerie trade to use Felicity to exploit the tricky causal rules of the universe to protect them forever – twice.

Time to... to...

Vision... fading...?

<u>Breathe</u>.

Nicole.

Breathe. Gods damn.

...

...She closed her eyes.

She held her breath one last time.

And then she knocked on the door.

...Wait, *why* was she knocking on the door? This was her room too. For one last week, at least. She could just go in.

...Actually, why was the door even closed in the first place?

Nicole knocked again when she realized she hadn't heard a reply yet. "Ravi?"

Nothing.

She cracked the door open to peer inside. The room was dark. There was a muffled whisper of tinny music coming from a pair of cheap earbuds. Ravi was lying in the dark completely buried under the covers with the volume loud enough that it was probably going to make their ears bleed if they kept at it.

Nicole uneasily approached the bed and... kind of... knocked? on the comforter.

Ravi came to life with a start and a swear like a spooked cat, clawing the covers off themself in a panic.

"Nicole! Hi! Hello." They pulled their earbuds out, which unmuffled the sound and filled the air with even louder extremely tinny music. Something punk from their teenage years it sounded like. Kittle Skisses, wasn't it? Was the music always that crunchy? Or were the shitty little speakers causing all that distortion?

"Hi hello," Nicole echoed playfully.

She was expecting a smile, but instead Ravi just looked away uneasily. Nicole was apparently not supposed to be seeing them in this state.

"...You okay?" she asked.

"Yup!"

"...Lying in the dark?"

"Mhm! Just a regular Friday night in the Beausoleil household."

"Not *this* Beausoleil household," Nicole reminded them with a little teasing smirk. "Feeling nostalgic for your old bedroom or something?"

"...Something like that."

It didn't take much probing before Ravi gave in and confessed they were trying to avoid thinking about that dossier of theirs – the one with all the scientists' collated research on the sarcoid cysts and InThetics' dark harvest.

"Is it done??" Nicole asked, absolutely failing to hide her elation at the possibility. It would be so amazing if she could see all Ravi's hard work come to a good end before she left. She knew Ravi was almost finished. The two of them had been happily celebrating Ravi's progress last Friday when Felicity decided to ruin their date night with that dramatic breaking-and-entering stunt of hers. She'd forgotten all about it in the chaos of the past week. She suddenly felt a little guilty, that she'd managed to push all Ravi's hard work out of her head just so she could have room in there to sulk about having to leave.

Ravi nodded that they were in fact done, and gestured at a thick folder on their desk – a physical copy of the final draft of the digital compilation of all their research.

"That's amazing!! Ravi!!!" She eagerly reached over to bring the pile of documents to her lap and started flipping through with a huge grin on – a grin that faded with every page when she was reminded exactly how grim the subject matter of the report was. This was the most miserable thing she could imagine to be excited about – but it *was* exciting.

There was a lot of information to take in all at once. Most of it was in there to confirm what the two of them had already figured out: InThetics was harvesting the tar out of people and using it to make their Saffron products. The details, though, the facts – meticulous, specific, with verified research reports that detailed every step of the process – they all made the ludicrous conspiracy theory a little more grounded.

One heading in the table of contents jumped out at Nicole:

" 'Faerie Tears'?" she asked idly, flipping to the page to scan the summary. This wasn't in the last draft Ravi showed her.

"Mm. It's what they use to catalyze the reaction." Ravi sat up and snuggled in next to Nicole to observe the document beside her while they explained, gently pointing at the words and diagrams on the page for emphasis whenever they mentioned something written there. "One of the material science guys was on this. —He was actually doing contract work *for* InThetics right before he got poached, unlike the others. Everyone else was doing their own independent things before InThetics just shut them down. His team, though, they were told to figure out some stabilizing agent for the tar. I guess when the gunk comes out of your body fresh on its own, it just sort of... deteriorates after a few hours. Or more like... disintegrates? InThetics handed them a few proprietary black-box substances to mess with and told them to figure out which one of them would work best. The result of all that was figuring out they can put a few drops of these Faerie Tears in the extraction vials before they hand them out to the nurses to make it shelf stable basically forever. Also makes it behave nicely with that sparking extrusion process on the production floor."

Nicole looked over the diagrams that explained the cycle the various substances went through. From Ravi's notes and references, it looked like research and development for every fractional step of the process was handled by different teams with no communication with each other. The whole system was designed blind and piecewise, but... *coordinated* by Miriam Ortiz's guiding hands, hands that somehow seemed to know exactly how those pieces *should* fit together before they were even given form. And somehow those hands knew that raw tar was <u>supposed to</u> turn into a stabilization of tar and 'Faerie Tears', which was <u>supposed to</u> turn into the processed tar in that pool at the factory, which was <u>supposed to</u> turn into that proprietary Saffron thread when exposed to electricity in some particular way Nicole couldn't make sense of the words for.

...Which meant that the stuff in Ravi's shoulder was different from the stuff in the vials? And way different from the final product. No wonder it felt so much stronger once it was out of them, then. Purified? Enhanced? Altered, at least.

Angie's 'iron and malice and greed', refined into some super substance so dangerous that the universe decided it was the best ward against the fae – a ward strong enough to keep even Nicole away – a ward worthy of the demands of Nicole's ill-advised contract with Felicity.

And exactly how was she supposed to get something like *that* in Ravi's hands before she left?

Worries for another day. —Tuesday, specifically, according to the note's half-detailed instructions.

For today, that mystery fluid was troubling her mind. It was a *little* too aptly named in the documentation, considering the fae-aching side effects of the final product...

"...Why 'Faerie Tears'?"

"Because it's *magic*," they replied as a joke, twinkling their fingers like a spell. Then they explained in earnest: "Apparently it's got an otherworldly consistency to it. Very thin. Almost invisible in air. Behaves like a supercritical fluid in a stupidly wide range of temperatures and atmospheric conditions, including just... *sitting in a glass*. And apparently the only way to know if it's there is to just know it's there. The only smell is a very very faint hint of chemical sweetness. It's generally unreactive. Litmus tests don't work. Molecular composition unknown and untested, by InThetics' strict instructions – proprietary, black-box stuff, like I said.

"Wish I could get my hands on some," they lamented miserably. "No idea where InThetics makes it, though. It's even harder to find any details about *it* than their Saffron tech – and unlike their oh-so-versatile Saffron thread, this seems to be the *only thing* this stuff is used for. —And from how they prep those extraction vials, it sounds like the stuff just *disappears* when it's exposed to anything but the vacuum inside the tube. It's really like a sick little magic trick. Practically a scientific fairytale."

"...Do chemists normally just do science on 'black-box' substances like this? Shouldn't you know what you're messing with?"

"I wouldn't. But apparently you do whatever science you're told to when InThetics is funding half your department – until they pull all the funding and tell you you're working in their basement as a 'subject matter expert' for the rest of your life."

Nicole skimmed through the rest of the documentation quickly while she thought how exactly to ask the impossible: "How did Miriam know about all this? You said she's not a scientist."

Ravi shook their head sadly, "I have no idea. Maybe it came to her in a vision or something? —I know you can't tell me, but if there's really magic in the world, maybe it's like... clairvoyance or something? Wish granting genie kind of thing?"

"...What kind of wish are you thinking?"

Ravi tentatively plucked the documentation from Nicole's hands and flipped through it themself to a few particular pages while they chewed on the answer. "Wealth? Maybe? Like, a *crazy* amount of wealth. The monopoly they have on this stuff is practically supernatural. —Or... maybe... the Singularity? Miriam won't shut up about it."

"The Singularity..." Nicole echoed idly. She'd heard Ravi mention it before when talking about Miriam's rambling rants at work. Something about—

"Man and machine becoming indistinguishable," they summarized again, to remind her the answer to her unasked question. "Becoming *singular*."

"Right. Like some kind of... manchine..."

Ravi tried to stifle a laugh while they corrected her silly portmanteau: "*Cyborg*. But sure, a manchine. Some people think it's the key to ending suffering forever, the first step to a golden utopia. That's Miriam's vision for it if you can ignore all the greedy manipulative marketing bullshit. But *some people* also forget that machines break all the time, so it's a little... naïve." Ravi glared at the words on the page again, not really reading them. "But with every new generation, every new breakthrough, this Saffron stuff gets stronger and stronger, more resilient, more adaptable. It sounds like it can even be sort of... *self-repairing* if you feed it more Saffron – seasoned over and over like a cast iron pan. Maybe she thinks it'll get to a point that it'll never break. And if we *could* tie ourselves into a machine that would really truly never break, forever – or at least, a machine that has some unlimited capacity to recover from damage, given enough... seasoning material... then that's it, that's immortality, for real."

Nicole gave that sentiment a few seconds of grim consideration. A body that can break and heal without limit. That was a painfully familiar curse. "That's definitely... *one* way to live forever." Then she asked idly, "Would that even be a human anymore?"

Ravi grinned at her and reminded her that it wouldn't fit her special criteria: "Immortal things can't be human, so decreed Nicole Doyle – the ancient magical not-a-human – in this very apartment."

"...So she decreed, so it must be..."

Immortality. At the cost of... humanity.

It occurred to Nicole that there was something uncomfortably familiar about this. The process in Ravi's documentation, a process in service of Miriam's vision for the Singularity, it was describing something impossible, something that would be extremely dangerous to wish for, something that would be extremely dangerous to *trade* for: The 'means to become immortal'.

A very, *very* flawed means to become immortal.

So flawed, in fact, that it might even fit the grim whimsy of a gods-crafted curse.

And considering how damaging this stuff was to the fae, it might even be a curse that was meant to be just as miserable to the faerie who penned the words in that foolish contract as it was to the greedy misguided human who agreed to it.

Nicole shuddered uncomfortably when she turned it over in her head.

Did prodigal visionary tech leader Miriam Ortiz know about the fae too, then? Or was she truly just an untrained tech savant with enough vision and drive to make something impossible like this real without a hint of magic?

If Nicole had more time, she could figure it out. Track Miriam down, seduce her, get all the information she needed out of her. Maybe she could even find some way to undo it. Track the contract down, rip it out of the gods' Archive of the Pacts Eternal, shred it in the Aether just like she did the first time she saved humanity from extinction – though this was... definitively *not* extinction, wasn't it? Instead it was just... an eternal plague on humanity and the fae. A plague on them both worse even than agriculture and industry.

But it was too late.

And Ravi was on the verge of fixing it anyways, about to destroy the whole depraved operation when they revealed all this stuff to the media.

Henry was right, she could just sit this out, let it run its course. It wouldn't stick.

Nicole nodded to herself subtly while she tried to keep focused on the bright future that she was leaving all this behind to protect.

But she noticed something a little troubling about the whole scene in the bedroom there: Ravi, on the verge of destroying this grand evil, wasn't smiling. Instead, they were apprehensively thumbing through the pages of the game-changing report like it was covered in corrosive slime.

Why exactly *were* they hiding in the dark in here when there was so much to celebrate? Why were they leaning into Nicole like they were hoping to fall inside her and disappear?

At last, they opened the document to the references section, where dozens and dozens of redacted documents were listed. Dozens of documents, and dozens of... names – familiar and unfamiliar names. Some of them were the scientists Ravi found at InThetics, some of them they'd never managed to track down. Truly disappeared, they figured. —Maybe even by the very government body that thought all that research was dangerous enough to black it out and bury it in the first place.

They stared at the page with dead eyes for a long time before they let out a pathetic whimper, "Tell me I can do this."

"What? Of course you can! You've been working on this for months—"

They miserably pointed to a few of the unaccounted-for names in the document and explained: "These ones. —You know, I tried. I tried so hard but I never found them. And… the others, the ones safe and sound working at InThetics now, they're afraid what that means – disappearing like that. Completely disappearing. These were colleagues, working in the same trenches, and we'll just… never see them again." Ravi turned to look Nicole in the eye with a deadly earnest look of defeat, "They all asked me to leave their names out of this. Every one of them."

"So just leave them out? That seems reasonable. There's power in a name, Ravi, you shouldn't just give it out—"

"—Yes. There's power in it. The power to keep them safe. If the world knows who they are, they can't just disappear without anyone noticing. It's one thing for some near-anonymous scientist to disappear. It's one thing for some near-anonymous scientist to disappear in a community of scientists who are already afraid of the real risks of getting in too deep. The public isn't watching. —But if the public *is* watching, it's safe! Right? It has to be safer to be known than to be kept secret in the dark. No one would notice something secret in the dark going missing.

"I… I *get* why they're afraid, Nikki, I get it. —But we have to put our names on this. All this stuff is just conspiratorial speculation without references, without named and indexed accountability of the truth of it. —But there's more to it than just credibility. You get it? If we leave our names out, there's nothing keeping us safe." Ravi looked down at the document and grimaced at it. "You can't kill a name that everyone knows. They can't erase us unless we *let ourselves* be erased."

Nicole noted that the name Ravi had put on the document for themself was wrong, and pointed it out to them.

"…I never changed it," they admitted shamefully, as if Nicole didn't know from all the mail that came in from banks and government bodies. "Amaira's the label on the body they'll come for. It's what I need to show the world, to keep me safe."

Nicole took a few moments to consider Ravi's assessment of the situation with a scowl.

Most of her own life had been spent carefully guarding her true name. There <u>was</u> safety in it. She knew that really, really well. And it was one of the cruelest terms of her exile, that she had to be terrifyingly honest about it here, to speak the sound of it for humans to understand, to put it on every official document that verified her 'humanity' enough for her to live among humans. The only safety she had was keeping her middle name safe, but even that part of her name was required for some official records with the various governments she'd lived under – especially in the last century. It was a compulsion here, to answer the question of her name truthfully when she couldn't protect it with clever omissions and half-truths and deflection. *Paperwork* didn't like deflection.

She'd been living anxious and dangerously exposed like that for six centuries. To think Ravi was so determined to expose themself to the same danger by exposing their name so carelessly like that. —To expose so many of their colleagues to that danger.

Their philosophy was wrong. Naïve. Childish. Something only a short-lived mortal could come up with.

Gods, this wasn't something Nicole had ever thought she'd need to worry about. She always thought Ravi would be sharp enough to see how reckless it'd be to be anything but anonymous in all this. That had always been the plan.

Being identified was what made their original research so dangerous in the first place, being found out. Being identified was what got them poached – it was what got all of these scientists poached. If any of them could've just done their work quietly, under the radar, in the shadows, then maybe some of it would've been able to avoid InThetics' ire long enough to fix any of this.

It was a sharp painful prick in her mind when she realized: For all her careful planning, putting together that contract with Felicity to keep Ravi safe – from their illness, from their misfortune, from her malicious family – there was one thing she hadn't accounted for: Keeping them safe from themself. And someone like Ravi who was convinced they weren't going to live long anyways wasn't going to have any real investment in keeping themself safe from anything if they thought sacrificing themself could make the world better.

Ravi was self-destructive by their nature.

Ravi was resigned to the mercy of the eternal void that waited to consume them at the end of it all.

Ravi was ready to die for this.

"...Ravi I really don't think this is a good idea. Can't you just be anonymous? Please? —At least you."

"That's not fair to the others..."

"So, all of you."

"...Nicole can you... —I need you to push me here..."

"I'm not going to push you into shark-infested water!"

"...You know, sharks are way less dangerous than you think—"

Nicole crossed her arms and spoke stern and bitter at Ravi to make it very clear why this wasn't acceptable: "We promised to do this safely. I promised to keep you safe. —I can't *keep you safe* if you're going to be so reckless. This isn't fair to me—"

"—This isn't *about you!* This is about *humanity.* And the only way this makes any difference to humanity is if the media takes it seriously – and the only way the media takes it seriously is if every person in that list of names there is alive to back it up—"

"—Oh fuck off Ravi... Can you *listen to me?* There's got to be some other way—!"

"—There *isn't,*" they insisted, sounding twice as bitter and helpless as she was feeling. "Nicole why are you being like this..." they pleaded with her. "You're supposed to be—"

"—Supposed to be <u>what</u>?? What, I'm supposed to just let you kill yourself over this?"

"I'm not!"

"You are!"

"For fucksake Nicole!" they shouted, standing up in a fury. They shoved the dangerous dossier into her chest defiantly and scolded her: "I don't fucking need this!"

It looked like they wanted an apology or something, but Nicole was absolutely not about to back down on this.

But the moment she opened her mouth to continue protesting, Ravi swore at her again and stormed out of the room.

The thunderous slamming of the front door of the apartment put a cold shiver in Nicole's shoulders that matched the subtle vibrations that shook the whole building.

In the silence of the empty room, in Ravi's suddenly very cold and very lonely and very *unwelcoming* bedroom, Nicole gritted her teeth at that dangerous pile of Ravi's research before she tossed it all on the bed and stormed out of the apartment herself – though she didn't know exactly where she was supposed to go.

On the elevator down to the lobby, she felt hopeless and claustrophobic in a way she hadn't at any point in this lifetime, struggling her very best to keep herself breathing steadily.

She expected this from her family. Eviscerating her by destroying the people she loved most.

Ravi was never supposed to be *family*. Not like that.

In the depths of her bitter fury, she sought out the only person she could talk to about this kind of thing anymore, to plead with Henry for some guidance – and maybe some magic liquor that might erase it all, but he never delivered on that.

He also didn't deliver on any helpful guidance this time. He just reminded her of his sage advice so long ago: Let it go. Let them go. Let it run its course. It wasn't her business.

Useless old man.

Ravi didn't return that evening, no matter how long Nicole waited up for them. It seemed like Ravi wasn't even *reading* her messages pleading for reason.

At last, shortly after 1AM, Ravi messaged her. Without answering a single one of her messages, they told her they were staying at some unnamed friend's place for the night.

The words on the screen were peppered with the usual mistakes and embellishments that accompanied a night of heavy drinking.

…At least they were safe. It was a weight off her heart. But she still couldn't find sleep. Not that night. Not the night after. Her mind was a fuzzy mess by the time Ravi finally decided to return, late Sunday night. But Nicole still didn't have an apology for them.

The bitterness in their eyes still hadn't run out, even after two whole nights of cruel, cold shoulder silence.

And it was joined now by something new she'd never seen there before: Suspicion, and fear.

Come on, Does This Island Seriously Have to Sink Into the Sea Before Anyone Listens to the Damn Oracle?

(Late Morning, Saturday, 7th October)

"I warned you," Felicity chided Amy, being as sympathetic as she could, though it felt kind of hard to convey that sympathy over the phone like this. Plus it was kind of hard to *feel* sympathetic when she was so right from the very beginning and Amy had been so stubbornly refusing to listen. "Just dump her! Dump her and get her out of your heart already, she's poison."

"Would you stop... She's never been like this..."

"Are you kidding me?? She's <u>always</u> been like this! Selfish and manipulative and controlling. —She's a monster! Just using you for her own satisfaction! —Jeezus Amy and you still have no idea, do you? What she's hiding. You'd leave that beast in a second if you knew. — I'll do it myself! If you won't. I'll get rid of her—"

Amy turned the camera of her phone away to try to hide her bitter disgust, but Felicity caught a glimpse of her sneer before it disappeared out of frame. Not that she needed to; it was pretty obvious in her words: "Fucksake Felicity, I didn't call you for more of this overprotective bullshit... I'm not dumping her over some little tiff."

Amy hadn't gone into details about that 'little tiff', but Felicity wasn't stupid. She could tell this was something huge. A trust-shattering betrayal. She was certain this is what triggered the Bell to ring – though the timing was a little off...

Felicity continued on trying to convince her dear naïve friend to see reason: "Some little *tiff*? Amy. Jeezus. Forget the <u>tiff</u>. You're sleeping with a *literal monster*. She's <u>fae</u>. —I told you! I warned you. You've been seduced. All she cares about is milking the misery out of humanity. Tricking us. Making us suffer. And she's just doing it to you! She doesn't care! She told me herself – told me *everything*. —She's killed people, Amy! Lots! Lots of people! She's just... just some... heartless *demon!*"

Amy went silent for a few long seconds. Felicity could hear some pensive tapping sounds on the other side of the line. At last, still off-camera, Amy asked, apparently deciding to very rudely ignore the direness of everything Felicity just said: "And why exactly did she tell you all that? Did something happen?"

"...Something's *about to* happen," Felicity confessed.

Though she didn't want to confess... *too much.* She had *maybe* done a few things worthy of Amy's ire there, after all – including signing a couple contracts with the very monster she was in the middle of calling out.

"What?" Amy asked.

"...Can you just get rid of her? Please? Just forget about her! You're going to get hurt."

Amy returned the camera to her face to scowl coldly at Felicity. "You're really not going to tell me?"

Felicity glared at the ceiling for a few seconds before she closed her eyes and decided to bite the bullet: "Fine. *Fine.* —She's leaving."

"She's not leaving," Amy replied, absolutely confident in that statement, sarcastic rolled eyes coloring her words.

"She is. She's leaving you. —Forever. —So leave her first! You don't deserve to get hurt over a horrible monster like her."

"Christ you're such a prick sometimes Fleece... I don't need this from you. —Can you *please* just drop all this protective jealous paranoid bullshit and tell me what actually happened? Did you threaten her or something? She's been acting weird since you broke in last week and I *swear* if you did something..."

Felicity hesitated to answer that truthfully, but she was at her limit. If it meant Amy hated her for what she did – hated her for trying to keep her safe – then whatever, Amy could hate her.

"You bet I threatened her after I found out what she was planning to do! She promised not to hurt you! She said she was going to keep you safe! And now she's doing *this* to you!? —I'm coming over. I told her. I <u>warned</u> her. I'm wrapping her in iron chains and throwing the damn monster in the river. She's done—"

"—No. You're not doing *anything* to hurt her. I just want to know why she's being so weird all of a sudden. —And it's *you*. It's you? You're doing this to her? Trying to scare her? Trying to hold secrets over her head? —And <u>she's</u> the monster?"

Felicity gritted her teeth bitterly. *Danica*. She was right: There had only ever been two ways this was going to go: Amy would believe the truth of Felicity's story and fall apart, or she'd think Felicity was a raving jealous lunatic. —Except Danica conveniently left out the *third* option: Both. —And somehow this felt like exactly the kind of bullshit that slippery monster would pull on her way out the door. One last trick, to spite her, to bait her, to ruin everything. Amy would probably go home now to find some loving tender pretender of a lover, full of fake remorse and apology and some devil's smile ready to smooth everything over, just to prove Felicity oh-so-wrong, to make a villain out of her.

That *bitch*. If Amy wasn't protecting her – if it wouldn't just make things worse – she'd be there in a second to burn the vile faerie's flesh just like she deserved with all the cruel cold iron Felicity could track down, to torture her for every second up to the very moment she decided to oh-so-mercifully banish herself.

But there was nothing left that Felicity could do now that wasn't going to just dig herself deeper into Amy's bad books. The painful truth wasn't going to work, not until Amy felt the sting of it for real, not until Danica revealed herself for the pretender she was and broke Amy's heart for good.

Once Danica was gone, she'd have a chance to make things right again, but for today...

"...I can't do anything to help you if you're going to be like this, Ames."

"Well then I guess you can't help me."

"...Okay. ...I'm... I'm sorry. ...Just... take care of yourself, Amy. You don't deserve this."

There was a long uncomfortable silence while that miserable and very obvious truth hung in the air – and apparently that miserable and very obvious truth was also pretty damn pointless, since Amy was clearly not ready to deal with *any* kind of truth right now.

The screen went dark and the call disconnected with a perfunctory and wholly inappropriately cheerful jingle.

That was it. There was nothing Felicity could do now. Until that monster left, she'd just have to wait and pray that Amy had the strength to get through all the pain of this on her own.

—*Good luck, Ames…*

We Never Had All the Time in the World, but We Can Still Make a World Full of Time With What We've Got, Right?

(Before Work, Monday, 9th October)

Ravi hadn't felt like saying much of anything to Nicole since they got back the night before, after two long, bitter nights and days of coldly ignoring her while they tried to put themself together, hiding out on Carrie's couch all weekend.

Little things came out, though. Habits.

Love you.

Goodnight.

Good morning.

You hungry?

Cold words. Obligatory words. But an apology didn't feel right. They weren't sorry. They were angry. They were betrayed. And Nicole didn't seem to have any intention to apologize for any of that herself.

But it still felt very generous that she was having breakfast with them, even if it was a miserable stale cutlery clattering affair.

—*She said she was going to keep you safe.*

Ravi couldn't get over Felicity's bizarre rhetoric. Was she seriously trying to turn such an earnest and loving sentiment into something sinister? Of course Nicole was trying to protect them. And they'd do the same for her. —Nicole was just wrong. That's all. She was wrong, and Ravi was right. They were going to be fine. If only she could just... understand that. If she could just fucking *listen*.

But whatever, even if Nicole <u>was</u> right about how dangerous their plan was, it shouldn't *matter*. They'd already made it clear to her that their life wasn't important. They'd made it crystal fucking clear to her that they weren't planning to stick around forever. They weren't *capable* of sticking around forever. A painful death was coming for them – soon. A few years in bitter agony at the mercy of their illness, or a few months until it ended at the mercy of some mysterious government spooks disappearing them to the bottom of the lake or to some weird torture prison – it didn't matter, did it? At least if they did the right thing here, they could die having *done* something, they could take it in their own hands, leave the world on their own terms – leave it *better* – leave it *good*.

They peered into Nicole's eyes over breakfast. She was cold and distant. The usual glimmer there was... glimmerless. And there was a fleeting moment of doubt in their mind. Had it ever been there? It was hard to remember details like that about her sometimes. They knew she smelled of summer, but whenever Ravi had spent any time wandering even the greenest park alone this past summer, the green and the flowers and the warmth all smelled grey and cold and stale compared to her. They knew she tasted like ambrosial honey, but even a whole spoonful of honey never tasted quite as sweet as *her*. And they knew her irises shone like gemstones sometimes – sapphire and turquoise and emerald all at once that shimmered like she'd found a way to trap the sun in them even in the greyest sky – but they'd never seen a gem in any store or museum display that seemed to catch the light quite so perfectly.

She made the memory of all those things more beautiful. But none of those things could possibly do anything to remind them of her. The world without her, without her magic, it could only ever be a disappointing facsimile of her.

...If she *did* leave, would they forget? Was that part of the charm? Was that just how faeries worked?

They shook their head of the idea. Fae. Some fae *monster?* Her? Ridiculous. —And whatever, what did it matter anyways if it was true? Not like they could ask. They promised never to ask again. What good would it do to hold some suspicion like that in their head? She was some kind of magic they couldn't understand, and Felicity was bitter, and jealous, and trying to abuse their vulnerable state. She'd have said anything to turn them against Nicole. Anything.

She'd even accuse Nicole of being some murderous manipulative monster.

Of course she would.

God, had she ever said anything else?

...Had she... always known? Somehow? Somehow, from the very moment she met Nicole again in their apartment back last December, did she know?

Had Ravi been blind to it the whole time?

How stupid were they? Pretty stupid sometimes, right?

And Fleece was a lot of really frustrating things sometimes, but *she* wasn't stupid.

Could they really ignore her about something like this?

But they knew Nicole wouldn't leave. She wouldn't. Felicity was just... playing on their fears. God, they never should've told her about Nicole's *nomadic* tendencies, about their drunken anxieties. Stupid of them. They didn't even believe any of that. It just rattled around in the darkness of their mind sometimes. But it was obviously wrong. Nicole said it, over and over, with every glance, every kiss, every loving word: She wanted to spend the rest of Ravi's short miserable little life together with them, no matter what. Of course she wanted to protect them. Of course she wanted to milk every minute of joy out of this thing. Of course she wanted more minutes than they could possibly promise.

They wanted that too.

Ravi gave her a sad smile and finally, after two whole days and nights of it, they broke the heavy silence between the two of them: "I really wanted to spend the rest of my life with you, you know."

"I know."

"Let me? Even if it's short. Even if it's... shorter. —God though Nicole you're worrying over nothing! It's better this way, I'm telling you. I'm right. You have to see that. Why can't you just trust me?"

"I know how dangerous a name is, Ravi. You're wrong to treat it so... lightly. But I'm not going to keep asking you. You'll do whatever you want, I know that, I can't stop you, and I guess I really can't protect you from yourself, no matter how much that hurts." Nicole lowered her gaze to stare at her plate, jabbing her fork into it in a pensive rhythm. After a few bars, she asked them for a compromise: "—But... can you... wait? Maybe...? Not long. I just want... some time. Before... before I have to worry about losing you."

"...How long?"

"Just one week? Please? —I know. I know it's... selfish. I'm sorry. I'm selfish. I am. I know that. But it's not that much to ask, is it? Just one last week?"

Ravi gritted their teeth uneasily. They knew how long a week could be with this woman. She had a way of stretching it out. And they were pretty sure if they let her have her way of it, she could probably even make it last a whole ten thousand days if she wanted. —And they might just let her. They were kind of stupid that way.

"And if I give you a week, will you stop sulking about it?"

"Would *you*? If I gave you a week before you knew I was planning to throw myself in the river?"

"...Fair enough. But I still think you're making a big fuss for no reason."

"I know Ravi Bee. And I hope you're right." Nicole let out a little huff of a sigh, then she conceded on at least some part of it: "This is good of you, Ravi. You're doing something good. And I believe in you, in what you want to do. It's amazing. I just wish it wasn't so... dangerous. I wish there was some better way."

"Well if I can think of one in the next week I promise I'll do it."

Nicole shot them a sad smile, but a little sparkle returned to her eyes when she said a soft thank you.

A week.

Yeah. What would a week matter? It had already taken this long. For Nicole? They could give her a week to prepare for this. A week to have her peace of mind. And maybe it'd even be enough time for her to come around on it.

After breakfast, Ravi got ready for work. It felt ridiculous that they were still going to the office after all this, but they had to keep up appearances, look normal, do their job, no matter how pointless it was.

With a soft forehead-press and a kiss at the door, they told Nicole the two of them would have a little celebratory dinner after they were done their shift. "Anywhere you like. It's my last week alive, so pick somewhere nice," they added as a joke, which managed to get a half a cheerful scoff out of her and a promise she'd pick the best place in town.

It felt a little forced, but they had her blessing now, and they knew with that, with her behind them, they could go ahead with this – even if it meant betraying the trust of the other scientists. It was for their own good though, all of them. Ravi would keep all of them safe. No one else was going to.

That Could've Gone Worse,
but It'll Take a While to
Imagine How

(Afternoon, Tuesday, 10th October)

Nicole had spent the better part of an hour sitting in the living room with her eyes closed, remotely probing the depths of the InThetics facility with the other end of her Aethereal Tether in search of that precious treasure she failed to secure for Ravi months ago – the alpha prototype of that miraculous pain suppressor, their freedom from a life of torture and agony at the mercy of this unjust illness of theirs.

She still hadn't told Ravi what was coming – that she was leaving – that she was leaving them in Felicity's dutiful care.

She had to laugh at herself for her stupid request. A week. One last deception for the road, huh? Make them promise to put it off until after she left.

It was all she could do though, for herself. It was selfish, it was so selfish and so horrible of her to do it, but she'd remember them for the rest of her eternal life, remember their final goodbye, and it would be nice if she could remember them with at least half a hope that they saved themself after she left, that they found a way to live a long happy life in a world free of the illness they'd been enduring all these years. She could even convince herself that maybe, somehow, all of this would end up producing a real cure. Ravi would release the research anonymously, InThetics would be ruined, and a cure would come of it all. They'd live until they were withered and dry, free of pain, and they'd get the happy ending she imagined for them.

A little fairytale to tell herself between poring over her cousins' miserable contracts forever.

Unfortunately, for that fairytale to even have a chance at coming true, she had one miserable little task left to take care of before she left: Nabbing that wretched bit of Saffron tech from InThetics – the impossible ward Felicity's contract promised her, strong enough to keep even the toughest faerie away from Ravi as long as they kept it on them.

The note was kind of vague about the specific item to recover from the facility, but she knew right away when she saw the job that there was no better candidate than that prototype pain suppressor – the very piece of Saffron tech the two of them had been hunting down months ago on the night they stumbled upon that sinister pool of tar.

It was part of the fairytale. She may never be able to cure them before she left, but at least she could do this. It would never be enough to pay them back. Nothing ever could be. But it might ease the eternal ache of her own of her debt to them, just a little.

Her remote bumbling search finally stumbled on a section of the building labelled 'Cybernetics Testing Lab'. It was mercifully unpopulated today, as expected from the careful instructions in the note that came out of that deal with Felicity – instructions which included a time and a date and a very stern assurance that she would be doing this whether she wanted to or not.

—The universe provides – sometimes, apparently, via unwilling outsourced couriers.

She had to laugh at herself when she realized the two of them had truly been on the exact opposite side of the facility's basement last time.

Luckily, the instructions in the grimly assertive note didn't specifically say she had to be *in* the building, and she didn't have any desire to go back there herself ever again, so she was hoping this remote pickup strategy would pay off. She especially didn't want to actually touch the suppressor itself, or get anywhere near it, honestly. It was apparently *designed* to ward her off, after all. Guaranteed to be worse than anything Felicity could track down in her books. It was probably going to be even worse than that older Saffron tech – like Carrie's old Saffron Green hand. And that stuff was already absolutely bone-shakingly terrifying whenever she was in close proximity to it. Her instincts said it was more dangerous than anything she'd ever touched – worse than iron, worse than the tar, worse even than that wretched blade her dad used to brutally amputate every grand and beautiful tendrilous ribbon of her glorious wings – and she absolutely did not want to test those instincts.

Unfortunately, when she managed to find the room that contained the alpha prototypes – all neatly sealed in labelled plastic bags, each identifying a specific experiment number with a summary of minor variations in the design, and conveniently ranked by efficacy – she found that she couldn't actually... touch any of them with that Aethereal Tether of hers. In fact, her vision of the room scrambled in a chaotic staticky mess as soon as she reached out to grasp the top ranked unit with the Tether. She summoned the distant end of it back to see what happened and found it was singed and frayed.

And... that... wasn't... *possible*. Niede's scrap of Aethereal Tether existed beyond the material plane. It broke the rules. It tugged and twisted and crocheted the fabric of reality to do what it did. Maybe in the Aether it could fray, if Nicole wasn't careful with it, if it got caught on the craggy monsters there – leaving scraps behind for someone like Henry to come along and collect to cobble together a much, much shittier Aethereal Tether, like the one she'd twisted into wool and left dangling uselessly from her left hand, waiting ever-so-patiently for the day she would need it, as he promised – but nothing in <u>this world</u> should be able to do anything to it.

She took the end of the frayed Tether between her finger and thumb and twisted it back into a cohesive strand, but the vision it gave her was fuzzy now. An imperfect repair. She had no idea how to fix something like this, *or* how to sever it to make a clean cut, so she was kind of stuck with the miserably compromised strand until she could convince Niede to repair it.

—*Because <u>that</u> was possible.*

She scoffed at the idea that Niede would even dignify a request like that with a 'no'.

Nicole spooled up the Tether to start folding it into complicated shapes between her fingers while she considered what her next move was here.

She couldn't remotely pull the thing through the Aether.

And she wasn't about to go back to the terrifying facility herself. The miasma that filled every hall of that building was insufferable.

And even if she *did* go back, she definitely couldn't just... *touch* the device considering how destructive it seemed to be. If it did all that damage to the Tether, she didn't want to imagine what it could do to her.

No one else could do this though. And she had a very, very limited window to pull this together. —And if she was plumbing the depths of her motivations here, if she was being honest with herself, she *wanted* to do this alone. She *needed* to do it alone. If she asked for help, if someone else did it, it wouldn't do anything to ease her conscience, to whittle away her debt. Plus, if she asked for help, she'd just owe *someone else* a favor. The last thing she wanted to do on her way out the door of her exile here was ask for yet another favor she couldn't possibly repay.

So what was left?

She couldn't go back.

She couldn't touch it.

But... when she thought about it, neither of those things was true.

She was the daughter of the self-proclaimed king of the fae, wasn't she? That meant something. That meant she was one of the most powerful beings in the universe. She was practically a god in the eyes of a human, and an adept prodigal princess in the eyes of the fae, and she *could* do anything. What kind of pathetic god could be beaten down by the fear of a little pain?

She looked at the empty box she had prepared on the coffee table, the box that was meant to contain and safely seal away the pain suppressor once she pulled it through to Ravi's apartment. She'd adorned it with a note and a warning not to open it until Saturday, until she was gone – though she wasn't planning to tell them that she would be gone by Saturday.

She could imagine Ravi's reaction and she didn't want to deal with it, cowardly as that might be. She wanted every moment she had left with them to be filled with fun and smiles and a celebration of them, of their love. —And fighting over Nicole trying to protect them again definitely wasn't going to be fun and smiles.

Her nails dug into her palms until the pain made her teeth clench.

She could do anything, gods damn it. Fear be damned.

∿

It came back in an instant – the intense malaise this facility suffocated her with the last time she was here with Ravi. It was worse, honestly, even though she had dropped herself 'safely' on the other side of the glass of the room that held the target of her daring heist.

She rested her palm on the window. The heat coming out of the room was intense. Not real heat though. This was heat that crawled through her, that felt like sickening nauseating tendrils that slithered and caressed her primordial essence, the essence that had constantly yearned to stretch itself out of this constraining body of hers for centuries. But when she felt the touch of that malevolent heat, she had no desire to stretch herself out of her body. She only wanted to curl up and hide – though it felt like there was nowhere to go to escape it.

She hesitated. She wilted. She quivered in fear.

—Nicole Doyle, you are not going to be deterred by a little fancy human tech, no matter how terrifying it feels. You've beaten iron, for gods' sake. This is just... scarier iron. It's fine.

She took a deep breath, which only served to make her cough pathetically from the ache in the depths of her lungs from the unpleasant taste of the air here. Then, with a hastily constructed sense of reckless abandon, she pulled herself into the room.

Her knees shook while she took uncertain steps towards the shelf with the bagged-up prototypes, until she froze, shaky hand outstretched just a meter away. The skin of her fingertips felt like it was burning away when she pushed them beyond that impossible threshold.

These things were in bags, though. It should be fine. No matter how close she got to the tar, or to the cysts in Ravi's shoulder, it never hurt without touching them directly.

This Saffron stuff might be a little different, a little more intense, but it had to follow the rules, right?

And the contract! The note! It had to be possible. She *had* to be able to do this. The universe provides. Always. No matter how agonizing it might be.

But no amount of reassuring herself was enough to make the pain of moving closer bearable.

...Was this *really* possible? Did she miss some weird... loophole in the instructions? Some trick to exploit that she just couldn't think of?

She backed off and retreated to the other side of the glass to reassess her strategy and try to regain some composure. While her mind crunched away on the possibilities, she tried to calm her shaky hands by massaging alternating palms with her fingers and thumbs.

It didn't help.

A meter. She could find something long enough to pick it up, right?

And then. What? Carry it home like that? Slung over her shoulder, burning her back the whole way with its bitter heat? Or could she get it through the Aether? The Tether didn't work, but if it was touching something mundane and Earth-born, maybe it would behave a little better?

After a bit of searching, she managed to track down a janitorial closet, which conveniently had exactly the tool she was looking for: A broom and a dustpan with a long handle and a deep rectangular bucket to it – definitely more than a meter long. It might even be enough to shield her from some of the heat.

She returned to the miserable room and approached again, broom and dustpan outstretched fearfully towards the shelf like she was approaching a terrifying scorpion on a kitchen counter.

But even like this, carefully inching the head of the broom and dustpan closer and closer, the oppressive feeling radiating off the device on the shelf was growing more and more unbearable. —Which didn't make a lot of sense, considering that the slithering heat was previously increasing only as she moved her *flesh* beyond that one-meter threshold.

It didn't make a lot of sense, until suddenly it made an excruciating amount of sense.

As soon as the first bristle of the broom touched the bag containing the pain suppressor, a crackling chain of red and white lightning arced off the device, along the broom handle, and directly into Nicole's right hand, burning her primordial essence with a pain she imagined could only be matched by submerging her ever-healing mortal flesh in molten iron for an hour – but squeezing the whole hour of suffering into one single moment of agony.

She dropped the broom and the dustpan in an instant and staggered backwards with a scream that curdled into a whining groan, clutching her wrist as if she could possibly choke it right off her body, but it wouldn't go. In the throes of that blinding pain, she slammed her back into the glass wall behind her, putting a tall crack in it and lighting up the room with an ominously silent red light of an alarm.

So much for being discreet.

The tears welling up in her eyes made it hard to see exactly what the damage was, but when she could finally see it, she was horrified to find her fingers and palm had turned as black and matte as coal.

And it wasn't healing at all. She could feel it. Not like the iron burns she'd learned to recover from. This was... different – closer to the way touching Ravi's sores nettled up her nerves, leaving her in miserable agony for days afterwards, but worse. Far worse. This was... gods, was it... eternal...? It felt like it was echoing back from every moment in the rest of the infinite collection of moments that would make up her life. No amount of wildly writhing the path of her endless worldline around seemed to free her of it.

She curled her afflicted hand into a painful fist to test how bad it was – and it was *bad*. She desperately wanted to dissolve her material form just to free herself from it, but there was no way to do that now, not until her exile was over. The universe wouldn't let her, no matter how hard she willed it. And she was suddenly filled with a desperate, anxious longing like she'd never felt before for the end of the exile that refused to let her flail away from this agony.

With bitter ire, she glared at the shelf as she slid her back down the wall, until she was seated, curled up pathetically, clutching her wrist, holding back tears and stifling groans of pain into hisses.

This explained why exactly the stuff had always felt so awful to her, explained why she was always so uneasy around InThetics prosthetics, around Carrie. Gods, if she had ever accidentally bumped into someone... She didn't want to think about it.

Red lights flashed behind her in the hallway. A muffled alarm. Shouts. Footsteps.

She didn't look.

It didn't matter.

She had only one thing to focus on now.

Her eyes glanced uneasily between her marred fingers, the foreboding shelf, and the discarded, useless broom.

— *...In for a penny, right Rav?*

Yeah. Too late to back down now. If she was ruined anyways, she might as well go for broke. The rest of the pain of her task couldn't possibly be worse than this. Two broken bones don't hurt any worse than one, from miserable experience.

And she was out of time.

She returned to her feet and steeled herself for the ordeal that was ahead of her.

—*For Ravi.*

It turned out the thing *could* travel through the Aether, as long as it wasn't *directly* touching and destroying her Tether – the end of which had very frustratingly been burned right off the finger it was tied to when that Saffron-tech pain suppressor charred her right hand.

Losing that familiar extradimensional connection to the universe had left her terrified and trapped in that horrible torturously hot little sample room, frantic and rushed and one-handed, messily trying to retie what was left of it to a finger on her left hand with her *teeth* while the security guards tried to break down the door she'd barred.

She tried. But the knot came loose and the Tether slipped out of her grasp – and at the worst possible time: Halfway home, in the brilliantly overcast-grey static void of the Aether, in the middle of a crown of terrifying black living glass crags.

There was no time to catch it. She had to leave it behind, to be lost forever somewhere in the Aether.

In a blind panic, a fraction of a second before getting snatched up in the Aetherean creatures' horrible spines, she was stuck using the only thing she had left to get out of there:

That… incredibly shitty… patchwork… three-stranded Aethereal *Twine*…

—Gods damn it, Henry…

The knotty Twine was practically blind, <u>and</u> she was stuck clumsily trying to manipulate the shitty thing with her *offhand* in a desperate attempt to get back home home home home home now now *now now* now Nicole <u>*now*</u>—

The landing in Ravi's apartment had been pretty rough because of it. —Though it might *also* have been because she was in blinding, mind-blanking pain from the lightning and heat coming off the miserable little ward in its clumsy dustpan carriage.

Frankly she counted herself lucky she could even find the apartment at all. Traveling through the Aether on blind vibes alone was *not* a winning strategy.

She probably… shouldn't do it again…

It had only taken a second to get back to the living room from the facility, but even in such a short period of time, her entire right hand was made black with ruin from holding the suppressor in the dustpan. The char had even crawled up the veins in her wrist in the timelapse pattern of a chaotic lightning storm.

But she'd pulled it off! —And even managed to get the horrible thing in the gift box, right next to that note she wrote explaining that it was a surprise, with instructions for Ravi to leave it alone until Nicole said so. There was no way she could wrap it as pretty as she was hoping to, but at least she could throw a fancy silk cloth over it – kind of askew, but good enough. She left it there on the coffee table, and made some distance with breathless staggered steps back.

Unfortunately, even when she wasn't unbearably close to it, the thing still worked as a pretty damn good ward, exactly as advertised. The oppressive heat coming off of it, even in the box, continued pushing Nicole back until she bumped up against the front door of the apartment with a gasp of surprise. Despite her best efforts to endure it gracefully, it was making her head fuzzy. Words were scrambling in her head like ice in a deep frier. And the pain in her hand was a blaring fire alarm on top of all that.

So, in that state, she couldn't quite put together what was happening when she was shoved stumbling to the ground by the door opening behind her. And she couldn't make sense of the look in Ravi's eyes when they saw her, dazed and disfigured on the floor.

They had been so angry.

And she was so scared.

Desperate and flailing in pain, she scrambled away from them before they could touch her, and, in her confusion, she made the extremely bad decision to reach out with her offhand and that nearly-blind knotty Twine to clumsily drag herself to the only safe place she knew in that state.

She expected to find herself in the back alley of the Serpent's Fang.

She did *not* expect to find herself screaming at a *new* pain, caught by the ankle halfway to her destination on something sharp and painful.

The crown of crags was waiting for her.

Gods she was stupid.

Like an animal in a trap, she writhed and wailed and did everything she could to free herself from the spiny grasp of the black, glassy creature that suddenly had her calf snared in its thick thorny tendril. The perfect Tether she just lost would've made this easy, but the Twine? She could barely put any weight on in before she felt it stretch uneasily.

She was far too stupid in far too many different kinds of pain to realize how pointless it was to struggle. In a growing panic, she watched as the monster swelled, inch by inch, constricting around her, hard as obsidian, sharpening itself and snaking its crawling extradimensional branches further and further up past her knee – until in a moment of excruciating clarity she remembered that she had a few more dimensions to move around in here herself than on Earth or the Faelands. All she needed to do to slip her leg free was move her corporeal body a *little* alterwise – if she could just remember how. It had been a *long* time since her childhood adventures here.

It took a few bitter, jaw-clenched attempts at it – all while the thing cut up the meat of her calf and thigh worse with every failed jerk – but she finally managed to twist her body away properly, letting the extradimensional messy of obsidian tendrils slip harmlessly through the flesh of her leg like a knife through smoke. As soon as she was free, she desperately tugged on her barely-not-useless Twine to finish her delirious ill-conceived dive through the Aether.

In a tumbling grunting clamor, like she'd just been hit by a bus and launched a few lanes, she landed hard on the steel lid of the dumpster behind the bar with a thunderous pigeon-scattering **THOOM** that reverberated for a few seconds in the quiet alley.

Her leg was a bloody mess, but her hand still hurt so bad that she couldn't even feel the lingering burn of the cuts that Aether-born monster's thorns left in her leg, or the damage that *extremely* professional landing of hers just did to her bones.

Silent tears streamed down her cheeks uncontrollably until at last she cracked from the weight of it all and heaved a few painful sobs.

She almost got stuck.

In the Aether.

Forever.

She curled into herself and let the sobbing terror shake itself out of her until she was empty.

Once her fearful tears were finally dry and the only thing left shattering her thoughts was the pain in her hand, she rolled her body off the dumpster and limped on the partly-healed meat of her leg through the back door of the Serpent's Fang to get herself settled in a dark lonely corner, to quietly nurse her entirely-<u>not</u>-healed hand and try to let herself grow acclimated to the exquisite new mind-scrambling agony of it in peace.

When she flopped down in the booth, she felt something jabbing into her back. In all the chaos, she hadn't even noticed it, but it seemed like the guards had managed to smash open the glass wall in that room and stick her with a couple taser barbs right before she disappeared.

She yanked them out by the cables with a bloody hiss and tossed them dripping red on the other end of the table.

She needed to talk to Henry. He'd been around for a long time, and he'd seen a lot of things no one was ever supposed to see, in a lot of places no one was ever supposed to be. He was the one who gave her all the trash about Ravi's illness before, about InThetics' business, about scary faerie contracts. It all came together in the end, far too late, but it still came together. And if all that came together, then there might still be more secrets to dig out of that pile of garbage. And, despite his cagey responses before, he wasn't bound to the truth the way she was. He might actually know what those secrets meant. He might have always known. And that meant there was still a chance he might know what to do about this impossible burn.

Her bra was buzzing relentlessly with messages from Ravi. She couldn't bear to look. And her head was absolutely not clear enough to answer. The truth might be dangerous, and she hadn't figured out a way to not-quite-lie about this yet. But she realized she should probably do something to tell them she was okay, so she just sent the buzzing phone itself back to the apartment... *somewhere.* She could barely aim right now, but it felt like it made it. Ravi would find it. They'd figure it out.

When Henry eventually noticed Nicole silently enduring her pain in the darkness, he casually sauntered over to offer her a drink.

When he saw her hand, though, he stopped short and took a step back.

Nicole grimaced and tried to speak lightheartedly, but her voice was coming out way more cracked and pathetic than she was hoping. "That bad, huh?"

"Danica..."

"Something... *gold* tonight, Henry. —And bubbly. —And... just for fun, can you call me 'Nicole' tonight?" She couldn't talk to Ravi right now, which meant the precious hearth and home of her good name was off limits. But maybe Henry could stand in a little, get a little fire going for her, even if he *had* always looked at her with that same millennia-old reverence and fear in his eyes, a fear and reverence that he never quite seemed to shake no matter how long or convincingly she pretended at weakness and humanity.

It would be nice if she could be remembered for this instead, though – for this sacrifice – for something other than the vile accomplishments of her father's Danica – for something other than the malice and menace in that murderous old Black Dog's teeth.

After all, this? What she just did? How thoroughly she'd just *lost?* It sure didn't feel like something that ancient beast could be capable of. Her father's proud prodigal princess Danica Llewellyn Doyle would never accept a loss like this. Only Ravi's concessional lovesick Nicole could be that stupid.

Henry didn't move until Nicole repeated his name to shake him from his stupor.

When he returned with her drink as requested, the look of dire concern wasn't gone from his face, but at least he managed to find the courage to approach the table and sit across from her to get a closer look at her fun new disfiguration.

He was absolutely bewildered by what he saw, which wasn't at all what Nicole was hoping to find.

"So," she started, playfully disappointed, "I'm guessing from the look on your face that you've never seen this before."

He raised his eyebrows and shook his head slightly with a little huff of a sigh. "No. I certainly have not."

"Cool. Well. Guess I'm still out here on the cutting edge of stumbling into new ways for the fae to suffer."

"What did this?"

Nicole laughed and tried to think of how to explain it simply. A wave of pain shook her when she shook herself, forcing that laugh to cut short into a wincing hiss.

"What did this…" she echoed. "Well, if you ask Angie, she'd tell you it's something the humans are making out of 'iron and malice and greed'. The universe seems to be convinced it's a ward strong enough to scare off anything fae. I sure hope it's right after all this. —Seems like it's *probably* right."

"I thought iron wasn't a problem for someone like you."

"Yeah. You're right. I'm a badass superstar. Daddy's wretched prodigy. But as you can see, we're apparently living in a world with something just a tad worse than iron."

"What is it?" he asked again, uncomfortably cradling his own fist in his hand.

"Ah I see, looking out for yourself, huh?"

"Excuse me if I want to spare myself from *that*," he said, nodding grimly at Nicole's blackened hand.

Nicole briefly explained what InThetics was doing, to Henry's stunned silence. He shook his head when she got to the part about the prosthetics and the Saffron, confirming that he too always felt uncomfortable near those artificial augmentations.

"Well, now you know: Keep your distance."

"Thanks for the tip."

Nicole sighed, still clutching her wrist miserably. "I was really hoping you might know what to do about it."

Henry shook his head and regretfully informed her that he had no idea.

Nicole glared at her hand, and curled it into a tight, agonizing fist. She closed her eyes and calmed her breathing to really take in just the *singular sensation* of the pain. Even the curse of her achy empathetic heart wasn't this bad. *That* pain swelled over time, and it echoed back softly, like the tide of a rising ocean lapping further and further up the shore of her eternal being. She could feel it growing, feel it taking her over. She had been feeling it swell for centuries, even before her exile. Her unfortunate fascination with humans went back a long, long time. But she could feel that she would grow accustomed to it as it grew, as her heart swelled with the pain of mourning every person she loved and lost. It would ruin her, but she would find a way to go on somehow, ruined, though she had no idea how.

This pain, though, it was different. It wasn't going to swell. No, it would spark up suddenly, randomly, over and over again, for eternity – a cruel torture that would break her every time it returned. She would never get used to it. It wouldn't let her. This was going to be the legacy of her exile, wasn't it? Centuries of finding ways to carry on through tragedy and heartache, feeling strong, feeling spiteful and powerful, feeling like she won, and in the end it was going to be *this* that broke her?

"It's echoing back..." she said sadly. "All the way back from the end of my eternity, I can feel it echoing back, forever. This never heals..."

Henry gave her a shrug of a smile and apologized. "Sorry my dear, I can't feel eternity like you do. But it certainly sounds miserable."

She looked at him curiously. "You're really not fae, then."

He didn't reply, or smile, or do anything to acknowledge her. That was a question Nicole was never getting an answer to.

The devastating reality of her misery was setting in for her. It would never heal. It would *never* heal. Ever. It was maddening to accept it. Nothing was meant to last forever. Nothing but the gods and the fae themselves. The fae don't suffer injuries like this. Even the weakest of her cousins could recover from the blade of an iron knife with enough centuries to rest and heal.

The closest she could imagine was what her dad did to her wings, but that was the magic of the gods, that seal on her back. Of course it could break the rules. And even that didn't... *hurt* anymore. It didn't *keep hurting*. It was just a bitter loss she'd learned to put up with.

But she couldn't imagine even the cruelest of the gods unleashing this unreasonable poison on the fae. They promised the fae true immortality, the gift of eternity and a world that never dies – a trade, in exchange for their eternal servitude, for their tireless efforts to extract misery from each other and the human race.

How could the gods promise immortality and then put something in the universe that had the power to do... *this?*

Gods, what would even be the point of putting this kind of curse in the world? If humans kept using this stuff, if every human had access to this technology, as the ambitious Miriam Ortiz dreamed they would, then none of her cousins would ever be able to approach the human race again. And then the fae couldn't even serve the gods properly anymore, couldn't even keep up their end of the bargain. And then what? What would the gods do once they made humanity and the fae useless to them?

She didn't want to think about it, and tried to push it to the bottom of her mind – but she sure had a long time ahead of her to try to avoid it, spending the rest of her life on Niede's leash, and it wasn't going to stay down forever.

The only way she could figure for it to fit into the gods' plans was the promise that Ravi's exposé would dismantle the whole production process once they released it. Long before the entirety of the human race was blessed with the tech, Miriam's pursuit of this fae-poison immortality would fail.

It had to fail.

Nicole suddenly realized, seeing Henry's uneasy gaze on her blackened hand, that once Ravi put that pain suppressor on, they'd be a huge danger to him – assuming it was just as dangerous to whatever he was as it was to her.

She explained why exactly she'd done this to herself, and that the next time he saw Ravi, they'd probably be extremely dangerous.

He lowered his eyes to the table and considered the gravity of that.

"You've unleashed something dark on us, Nicole."

She shook her head. "It was coming anyways. At least now you know what it'll do," she assured him, holding up her ruined hand for emphasis. "And if we're lucky, Ravi's going to stop it before it gets bad enough to cause real problems."

"Well that's all well and good, but it's going to be heartbreaking barring dear Mx. Beausoleil from the bar. I'll miss them."

"You and me both."

The old man tapped his fingers on the table for a few seconds before he ventured to confirm, "You're leaving soon, then."

"Yeah. On Friday – so foretold that stupid Bell."

"I see. 'Something bubbly'. To celebrate?"

She lethargically cheered, "To freedom," raising her glass in the air with her remaining good hand before downing the whole thing in a single throw.

When she returned the empty glass to the table, she asked playfully, "You'll visit me in my new prison cell, won't you?"

"You couldn't keep me away if you wanted to."

"What a good liar you are," she said with a smile. Then she offered her good hand to Henry to catch him in a handshake. "It's been good, old man. I'll miss you."

"Oh stop."

Nicole's eyes fell to the table after that show of a cheerful farewell. She stared at her empty glass wistfully, rotating it back and forth while she turned something over in her mind.

"Don't suppose you might leave the alarm off tonight, maybe do a very bad job checking that everyone left the building before you lock up."

"Can't go home?"

She glanced at her blackened hand. How was she supposed to explain this to Ravi? She needed more time to figure it out.

So much for milking every moment of joy out of these last few days. Gods... The universe couldn't even give her that, could it? Cruel.

"Never slept in a bar before," she said, hopeful.

"Well, I suppose a terrifying Black Dog is a fine substitute for an alarm for one night."

She grimaced at herself. That was a cold reminder she didn't need to hear, especially after she specifically asked him to call her by her good name. But still, she thanked Henry for his mercy without quite thanking him with just a silent nod. Then she asked for another bubbly drink – and to keep them coming until the lights went out.

It was the last time she'd get a chance, after all, to enjoy the fruits of tens of thousands of years of her beloved humanity's passion for turning rot into life.

See Ya

(Late Afternoon, Tuesday, 10th October)

"Nicole? Are you okay?"

She looked like a scared animal, sprawled out on the floor after Ravi had accidentally knocked her to the floor with the door. Her shifty pupils were so wide open that Ravi could barely see the blue and green of her irises. Face flush. Breathing short. —And her right hand. Jesus. What the hell happened? Did she dip it in lava or something? It looked like she couldn't even put any weight on it from the way she was leaning on her elbow every time she shuffled away from them.

"Nikki. Calm down. Come here. You're okay."

They tried to crouch down and approach her with calm words and open arms, but she dashed and scrambled away with desperate gasps and pleas for them to stay back every time they reached out to put a soothing hand on her: "No! Nono_no_. Don't. —Don't _touch_ me!!"

And that was it. In a final desperate scramble, she turned all her fearful attention to scowling at her left hand while she clumsily gestured with it in the air, and then she disappeared, leaving Ravi alone in the hauntingly silent apartment.

There were a couple thin trails of blood on the carpet where she'd just been.

They crawled forward to inspect the stains, but there wasn't much to learn from them other than that Nicole was definitely bleeding right before she disappeared on them, which meant she only just got hurt. She healed really fast normally. Part of her magic. Couldn't have been more than a minute or two ago that she got cut.

What the hell was going on?

They fired off a message to her phone asking if she was okay, but considering the state of panic she was in, they didn't really expect a response immediately. While they waited, they cautiously scouted out all the rooms in the apartment to make sure there wasn't some attacker hiding and waiting to jump out and stab them too. The only thing they found out of place was a mysterious box on the coffee table with a sheet of pretty patterned silk messily draped over it and a nicely handwritten note from Nicole insisting that they not open the box until Saturday.

That message they sent went unread. —And the next one. —And the next and the next and... Ten minutes later, they noticed that every time they sent a message, there was now a buzzing sound coming from somewhere in the apartment.

After a bit of hot and cold with themself and a dozen test messages, they managed to track the sound down to a corner of their bedroom, under a pile of Nicole's clothes – her phone. Abandoned. She must have sent it back home for some reason.

Which meant... what? That she was alive, at least. And... that she didn't want to talk to Ravi? To even read their messages?

They stared at the screen miserably, reading the echoes of their increasingly desperate messages in the locked phone's notification feed, unread. Not even glanced at.

When the screen timed out and went black again, they caught a glimpse of themself in the reflection.

That look in her eyes when she left.

She was afraid of them.

Why?

No, more importantly, what on Earth could possibly do that much damage to her? Who on Earth... could possibly...?

...What did Felicity say? 'Wrap her in iron and drop her in the river'?

Ravi dialed her up in a frantic fury, expecting to hear some maniacal laughter and a triumphant shout over splashing river water that she'd finally done away with 'the monster'.

But Felicity had no idea what Ravi was talking about. Instead, she used this crisis as yet more evidence that Nicole was a sketchy untrustworthy monster and that Ravi needed to dump her immediately. They, instead, immediately disconnected the call.

Nicole and they had planned to spend every night of this, Ravi's supposed last week alive before they released their exposé to the world, doing something exciting. Tonight was supposed to be Nicole's turn to surprise Ravi. And this was... definitely a surprise.

What the hell had she done to herself?

There wasn't any point worrying about it, though.

That didn't mean they weren't worrying about it, obviously, but at least they could remind themself that there was no one on Earth more capable of taking care of herself than a crazy powerful magic being who could slip away from trouble to anywhere she wanted.

Which meant, of course, that she didn't want to be *there*.

...She'd come home when she was ready.

Right?

Obviously.

She'd come home.

Soon.

Soon as she was done freaking out.

Alone.

Scared.

Of Ravi.

Why? Why?? What had they done to make her feel anything but safe here? There was nowhere else in the world she could feel safer. Right?

They realized with a cold sense of morbid dread that they had definitely done *something*. The two of them had never had a fight like that before.

But it was just a little tiff. —Wasn't it?

...Oh fuck. Fuck fuck fuck, was it <u>little</u>? Was it a *little* tiff?

Fuck! Why had they made such a big deal about her trying to look out for them?? Why would they push her away like that?

—*And what happens when you push people away, Ravi?*

Not even just *push*, though.

They swore at her.

They shouted at her.

They disappeared for two whole nights and days and gave her a cruel bitter cold shoulder even after they came back.

She didn't deserve all that. She could never deserve all that.

How could they hurt her like that?

—*And what happens when you hurt someone you love, Ravi?*

What happens when they finally see how awful you are?

They leave. They leave, Ravi, you know that...

There are patterns...

They shook their head to get the stupid thought out of their head. Nicole wouldn't leave. Not over... some... little tiff.

Felicity was such a fucking miserable excuse of a friend, putting this kind of doubt in them.

—And then you pushed her away too, didn't you?

And what happens...

...Ravi didn't get much sleep that night, staring at the still silence of Nicole's phone. They set it perfectly square on her cold pillow. It must've been hours of that in the dark, waiting and waiting on some response from her that was apparently never coming, until sleep stole them.

In the morning, the phone was hidden under a folded-up sheet of paper.

A note, from Nicole. It was messily written, like she'd done it with her left hand. Which meant her right hand was still messed up...?

I NEED SOME TIME.

N

Nicole had figured out a way to send Ravi a one-way text message. That would almost be cute if it weren't extremely frustrating.

She really was afraid of them.

Well, if she could leave a note, surely she could retrieve it. They tried writing a response on the back, like passing a note around at school.

Are you okay?
Where are you?
How much time?
Please come home.

Unfortunately, the note was still exactly where they left it, even hours later.

This was supposed to be a regular working Wednesday for Ravi. They were supposed to be pretending everything was normal, at least for one more week, for Nicole, since they weren't allowed to release all that stuff about InThetics' evil schemes yet, but they couldn't bring themself to pretend today. They needed to catch Nicole the very moment she came home, to make sure she knew she was safe, to apologize for scaring her, to plead with her for forgiveness for being such a monster to her, to promise never to do it again.

They stared bitterly at the mystery box on the table. There was some connection, they were sure of it. But Nicole's note specifically said not to open it yet. And the last thing they wanted to do right now was break her trust any more than they clearly already had.

Instead, they hid it in the corner of the living room to get it out of their mind and free up the table for them to fuss with the random papers and pens and coasters and hair clips there while they very calmly and very rationally tried to come up with explanations.

—*She's **dying** and she's **afraid to see you**.*

...<u>Rational</u>. Ravi. Rational. Calm.

What the hell can hurt a faerie?

—*No. Not faerie. Not monster. Not evil. Don't let Felicity get in your head, Ravi...*

But whatever Nicole was, they knew one thing for sure: She healed fast. Even the deepest cuts they left in her back in their passion with their short little nails, and their darkest love bites on her neck and chest and thighs, they always disappeared way faster than they did on any lover they'd ever had before.

And yeah, that burn on her hand was clearly a little more serious than a night of rough play in bed, but after a whole night to recover? That should've been enough, right? She should at least be able to write with it.

One of the pens on the table refused to line up with the others no matter how hard they tried. Their shaky fingers kept nudging it out of place. Eventually they just grabbed the whole bunch in a fist and tossed them to the floor with a furious, "Fuck! Fuck you. <u>Fuck you</u>! You stupid <u>fucker</u>. Fuck you..."

She loved when they doted on her, didn't she? She loved when they treated her like a princess, when they cooked for her, when they treated her to whole decadent hedonistic days in bed. She loved it. She had even learned how to just bask in the joy of it with a grateful smile – *without* insisting she would pay them back for every kindness.

But there was that time when she was really sick, the only time, poisoned from that little misadventure in InThetics' factory floor. She didn't want to be fussed over then. She wanted to hide like a hurt animal, wanted to lick her own wounds. She probably only didn't run then because she didn't have the energy or clarity of mind to do it.

Despite everything they did to make this a home for her, this still wasn't the place she felt safe running to when she was hurt.

And then Ravi made it even worse by shouting at her on Friday, when she was scared for them. When she needed them to comfort her, they shouted and swore and made her feel anything but safe.

"Come back," they pleaded quietly, to no one. "It's safe here, I'm sorry, just come back…"

After sulking pointlessly about it for a while, they glared at the mess of the pens they made. If she came back now, there's no way that would feel… safe.

They tidied the pens away properly in a drawer, then hid the mess of all the random notes and half-finished crossword puzzles and remotes on the table somewhere out of sight, and then for good measure they scrubbed the table's surface until it sparkled.

There. Clean. Safe.

…Except… now that they were looking… The whole apartment still had all those cracks in the paint everywhere… Was that safe? That wasn't safe…

God, Felicity really half-assed that paint job, huh?

They dug out some sandpaper and the leftover spackle and paint to smooth out the cracks in the walls and ceiling that slacker had missed in her not-quite-best-effort repair job last week.

They opened the windows to let the fumes out and the autumn air in. It was almost nice. It would have been nice, if the apartment wasn't so bitterly empty. The smell and the crispness of the air, it reminded them of… Well, it was around this time last year, wasn't it? When she moved in? When she screwed her way into their life and their heart with that smile and that eternal summer of hers and all the charm in her eyes and the playful joy in every word that danced off her tongue.

She made this place a home.

She made it safe.

…They tackled the bathroom next. Got it even cleaner than it had been when they moved in. Sparkling. Acrid with chemical cleaners that also demanded the window be pried open.

They replaced the gasket in the showerhead. No more leaks. They replaced the flickering lightbulb just outside their front door, the bulb that had been messed up since before they started living there and that the superintendent clearly never intended to fix. They tidied up the spaghetti mess of cables behind the TV.

The bookshelf in their bedroom got every book arranged by color. The medicine cabinet got every bottle arranged by height. The condiments in the fridge were given the same treatment – color first, then height. Not even the grease-caked stainless steel in the kitchen could escape. By the time they were done scrubbing it with vinegar and polishing it with baking soda, it glistened with a mirror finish.

They peered at their warped reflection there.

Safe.

It was safe.

It had to be safe for her.

It took them the whole day, past the setting of the sun, but they'd done it: Everything was clean. Everything was fixed. Everything was right. Even the bed was perfectly made for the first time in... god, years, wasn't it? Their bedroom looked like a hotel.

But even all that wasn't enough to draw her back to their arms.

They spent the night on the couch, afraid to disturb the bed from its pristine condition.

Thursday morning's sun dragged them out of the bitter lonely bed they'd made for themself. When they checked their room, there was no sign she'd been there.

They stared at her note with dead eyes over breakfast – pancakes, obviously, in case she came home – lonely pancakes – her plate growing colder and colder and colder across from them on the table, until it felt like it would be the greater insult to feed her something so stale than nothing at all. They stared at the note with dead eyes and crinkled the edges of the paper with tight kneading fists while their own plate went cold.

—How much time, Nicole?

They had never wanted to drink themself blind so badly, never felt a more desperate ache for a whole pack of throat-charring smokes, never felt more longing for the cold grasping embrace of the river's relentless current. But they couldn't. They couldn't be anything but perfect for her when she came back. They had to show her they were good, that they were safe, that they would mean it when they told her it would be different, that they'd never do it again.

The only thing they could think to do was get wired on coffee and watch old familiar shows on repeat to numb their mind, though that didn't do as good a job as they hoped, since those familiar shows kept reminding them of dozens of cute and passionate conversations with Nicole, on that couch, in her arms, *about* those familiar shows.

Friday's sun was rising by the time they finally drifted off to sleep on the couch, fully clothed, full of darkness and doubt.

It was late in the afternoon when a timid knock at the apartment's front door startled Ravi from miserable half-asleep dreams.

They cursed at themself for their messy hair and sleep-wrinkled clothes on their scrambled rush to let her in. Good job Ravi. What good is a pristine home when the only other person living there looks like a depraved lunatic?

Hand on the doorknob, they glanced in the mirror by the front door to confirm their hair looked terrible. They caught sight of the keys hanging on the wall there. Empty hooks, except for the one for the apartment's basement storage. Nicole must've had her set on her. So. Why? Why was she knocking on the front door of her own home?

When Ravi threw the door open, they found her standing there stiff and small and wilted like she never was.

Her right hand was hidden in the sleeve of a ridiculously oversized black knit sweater she was wearing over her dress – <u>not</u> a part of her regular wardrobe.

That wasn't a good sign.

"Nicole! Oh my god, where have you—Are you okay?"

She didn't answer. But she did let out a huge breath that she'd apparently been holding in for a while from the color in her cheeks, so she could say—so she could nearly *whimper*, "Hi Ravi… Can I come in?"

"Of course you can come in! What kind of question is that? This is your home, Nicole. You can… you can always…" Ravi trailed off as the significance of her uncertain request hit them.

Nicole wasn't coming home.

She was visiting.

And visitors don't stay.

As Nicole crossed the threshold into the apartment, Ravi noted that she seemed kind of… wrong? Where was sun in her eyes? The warmth in her cheeks? The bounce in her step? Where was the woman who smiled and laughed and brightened every corner of the apartment and every moment of Ravi's life? This couldn't be Nicole, could it? How could she change so much in just a few days?

The maybe-doppelganger marveled at the apartment, like she was truly entering again for the first time.

It felt like they ought to be giving her a tour of all the fabulous new safety features.

...Oh. Oh god... It didn't look like *home* anymore, did it?

What had Ravi done?

—You hurt her is what you did. You scared her. You monster. How the fuck did you think cleaning the damn apartment would fix that?

Nicole glared bitterly at that mystery box of hers when she got to the edge of the living room, then grimly directed Ravi to lead the way to their bedroom instead.

They realized they hadn't returned the box to where they found it. Stupid stupid stupid. It must've looked like they were throwing a tantrum or something, hiding it in the corner just to spite her. Or maybe...

"I didn't open it," they tried to explain. "I didn't, I swear. I was just cleaning."

She scoffed at their excuse and assured them it didn't matter anymore, though she didn't explain why.

She instructed Ravi to sit in their desk chair.

She stood in the doorway.

Right hand hidden.

This felt so wrong.

She was looking around the spotless room in silent awe, pausing on the window for a few seconds. Ravi had done a great job tidying up. Even the dead and yellowed plants on the windowsill were culled and pruned. The green ones, the ones Nicole showed them how to take care of properly, were the only ones left.

This silent treatment felt like some kind of punishment.

They suddenly remembered they had something for her, and dug her phone and that one-way note out of their pocket to hand them over to her, stupidly telling her what she obviously already knew: "You forgot these."

She glanced at the words Ravi had written on the other side of the note, but apparently there was something wrong with their questions, because instead of answering any of them, she just set it silently on the dresser by the door, along with her neglected phone, before she froze in place to stare silently at the dresser's surface, which was – because of Ravi's brainless cleaning spree – bare of its familiar knickknacks now.

It almost looked like she was considering just leaving without another word.

They couldn't let her. They had to say something. They had to fix this.

They crushed their palm between their finger and thumb to distract themself from the bitter taste of their apology: "Sorry. That I yelled at you. —And sorry that I forgot to apologize. And that I cold shouldered you like that. You didn't deserve all that. I won't do anything like that again. I promise."

After absorbing their words for a few seconds, Nicole turned back to face them. The tired melancholy in her eyes had melted away into a look of pity, and for a moment, they had some hope that it was enough, that they'd fixed it all with such a small gesture.

Then she scoffed at it, at their sincere apology, like it was nothing, and their heart sunk into their guts.

But she gave their heart a hard whiplash snap when she apologized right back: "I'm so sorry, Ravi. I shouldn't have left you like this… I really did just need some time to figure something out. And I couldn't… talk to you about it. Not honestly. Not yet. But it wasn't your fault, I promise."

Ravi felt a little bitter at that. They glanced around the pristine bedroom and suddenly wondered why they'd wasted all that effort. She couldn't have just told them that in the first place?

"It really wasn't… I didn't fuck up?"

"Mm… Maybe you could've been a *little* gentler with me before…"

"Sorry. I'm sorry. Like I said, I won't do it again—"

"—Stop. Please. This is going to be hard enough without you feeling guilty for no reason."

"This?"

Her eyes went shifty as they always did when she was preparing a not-quite-lie, and she held her breath while she chewed on the details, but she seemed to give up on that effort to answer with a question: "How much did Felicity tell you?"

"What makes you think I talked to her?" Ravi challenged her bitterly.

"Who else would you talk to?"

Ravi clicked their tongue a bit at those miserably true words.

Nicole asked them again to tell her what Felicity told them.

"Just the same jealous insane bullshit she always says Nicole I don't care…"

"Can you be… a little more specific?"

Ravi sighed short with impatience, glanced at Nicole's pleading eyes for a moment, then glared at their own hands while they crushed their palm again to squeeze the answer out of themself: "She said… you're some… evil faerie monster thing… And she said you're… leaving."

There was a breath of relief in Nicole's voice when she, unbelievably, complimented Felicity: "Gods she's such a good girl, isn't she? So reliable. I really love her."

Ravi scoffed at that, "The only thing she's reliable for anymore is toxic vitriol. I'm done with her."

"She's the best friend you're ever going to have, Ravi. I hope you keep her around."

After that insane bit of advice, Nicole took a deep breath, put her left hand in front of her lips like a one-handed prayer, and told Ravi she was finally breaking the seal on that box of questions they had about her true nature: "You can guess now."

"…No."

"…What? What do you mean no?"

"I mean no! You said never. I promised never."

"Okay, well, now I'm saying now. So if you would kindly—"

"—No."

"Please don't be stubborn… I came here to talk to you about this, and I can't talk about any of this properly until you guess. —Just guess! You already know the truth!"

Ravi clenched their teeth and bitterly swore to god that this was the stupidest shit. With absolutely incredulous conviction, they verbally jabbed at her: "Fine. Fine! She's right, then? Is that it? That's what you're saying? Felicity fucking Vicente figured it out before I did? You're really just some... evil faerie monster?"

As soon as they said the words, Nicole's posture changed, like every bone in her body just lost a coat of lead – though her right hand remained hidden hanging numb and heavy at her side. A faint pulse of light rippled through her, leaving her skin looking brighter and her hair more vibrant. Her lips glistened and her eyes shimmered in pearlescence in a way they never had before. And the way she was standing – so tall with her shoulders flexed – gave Ravi the sense that she was carrying the weight of the memory of grand unseeable wings on her back. She truly looked... fae. Like the stories. An elegant faerie princess. The whole time, she was hiding this from them? All because... because, god, it really *did* make it 'obvious', didn't it?

She was a faerie. Pretending to be human. And damn poorly.

And letting the disguise finally fall away for Ravi seemed to let a wave of relief course through her and put a grateful grin on her face that even managed to hide the misery there for a few seconds.

But only for a few seconds.

Once the warm gratitude drained out of her face, a cold grim resignation returned, and she shot Ravi with a sparking left-handed finger gun to let them know they finally won some game they gave up playing long ago, with a lethargically singsong, *"Ding-ding."*

The impact of that imaginary bullet struck Ravi silent for a few seconds while their mind was trying to decide whether it was worse that Felicity was <u>right</u>, or that *Felicity* was right.

"No," they finally said in cold defiance of the truth. "No, she's just... She's jealous, Nicole. She's fucking *deranged* about it! —About *you!*"

"Oh she is *so* deranged about keeping you safe, Ravi. You have no idea how much work she put into figuring me out. And she's pretty smart, you know. I promise you can trust her on this one."

"No. Nicole, come on. You're not a monster. —You're not *evil!*"

"Mm... You might change your mind about that in a sec, Ravi Bee."

Nicole then went on to do her very best to convince Ravi she was one of the most vile demonic figures in human history, torturing vulnerable people for thousands of years with devilish offers that betrayed their most desperate desires – greed, ambition, hunger – even just... loving familial devotion. She ruined people. For fun.

"Like I told you before, I can't let you get it in your head I'm some darling angel just because I'm wearing a pretty face now. That's part of the trick," she added sadly. "Back then, I was a creature they were afraid to name in the dark. —You might've heard of me actually. I'm in a lot of stories," she added with a hint of shameful pride. "When they were too afraid to say my name, they called me the Black Dog. The beast that appears in the darkest depths of your despair to slither a silver tongue in your ear and promise you—"

"—Stop."

—Godsake, is this *what Felicity was so incensed about? What the hell does any of this bullshit matter?*

"What? It's true. You need to know—"

"—I don't! Actually! Is the thing!"

Nicole crossed her arms and quirked a disapproving eyebrow at them. "Mx. Scientist here doesn't want to face the truth, huh?"

"It's not the truth! It's stories! It's old, *old* stories, Nicole. That's not who you are. That's like... like... the history of the atomic model. Who cares? I don't care if we used to think the world was made of fire and water and earth and air. I don't care about fucking raisins in a muffin. I don't care about impossibly perfectly circular orbits. That's not what atoms are. We know better now. That's just what they were, before we understood them. —And you, Nicole, you're <u>not</u> who you were. You're who you <u>are</u>."

"I haven't changed..."

"Oh fuck off you haven't changed... Then ruin me. Go on. Slither that fucking silver tongue of yours in my ear and ruin me if you're such a horrible monster."

Nicole's gaze darted about Ravi's determined face. Her lips tightened and curled as she clenched her teeth bitterly. Then, with her left fist firm and determined at her side, she took slow steps to stand towering and terrifying in front of Ravi while they sat helpless in their chair.

She reached her fingers out to caress their cheek and spoke their name in that same way she did when she first revealed her magic tricks to them months ago in that very room – with the same warmth, the same power, and the same swelling delirium: "*Ravi Beausoleil*, you shouldn't play with forces you don't understand."

A rush of fever pulsed through them and left them leaning

pathetically into her palm, like all their breath and blood suddenly came surrogate from the warmth of her touch alone.

She wasn't speaking anymore, but somehow her words were swirling around in their head anyways:

*Don't. **Play**. With. Me.*

   ***Fear**. Me.*

      ***Run**.*

But even if they wanted to do what she commanded, there was nowhere to run from her now. They couldn't even look away from the soft vortex of the warm summer storm in her eyes. She had them trapped in her, trying to scare them with nothing more than a loving smile, a tender caress, and warm words of warning.

It felt like bad roleplay.

If she was ever any good at this, she'd sure lost her touch.

The thought of how bad she was at this game made them crack a smile with a dozy laugh that managed to clear their head enough to defy her, and remind her: "I'm a scientist Nicole. Playing with forces I don't understand until I understand them is my *job*. And I've played with you plenty long enough to know you're not *evil*."

Nicole's act faltered for a second, a twitch in her smile, a wrinkle in the corner of her eyes.

They were frozen like that for some uncountable uncertain feverish breaths, staring into each other's eyes like a pair of statues sculpted with no other purpose in mind but to be frozen forever lost in each other's gaze.

With every intimidating rise and fall of Nicole's chest, waves of wildly inappropriate warmth and affection mixed in with the rapid pulsing adrenaline coursing through Ravi's blood. They could show her. They knew they could win this. They feverishly wanted to fight her, to bite her and tease her and torture her until she gave up and admitted how wrong she was. They wanted to leap out of their chair and push her up against the wall and hold her wrists over her head and show her how stupid she was being until she begged for mercy and admitted she was lying like she never could. They wanted to cherish her stupid until she gave up this embarrassingly bad act and admitted she was the good person Ravi always knew she was.

They were boiling over, with a toothy menacing grin on, breathing heavy with righteous furious passion to prove her wrong, when she finally withdrew her hand from Ravi's cheek to press her curled fingers bashfully into her own cheek and titter at them with a stupid grin on. "Gods... You're really... something else, Ravi..."

Their sober senses returned to them, but the warmth of Nicole's 'demonic' touch lingered on their cheek, and the fire of that desperate desire to make her admit she was wrong lingered in the heat of their adrenalized blood.

She slumped her shoulders and turned to flop her butt down on the bed, curling her back to rest her cheek on the fist of her good hand with her elbow planted on her knee. She had a look of absolute consternation on her face as she looked them over, trying to puzzle something out from them, just from the shape of their face, while she tried to figure out what to say next to convince Ravi of her ridiculous lie.

When Ravi tried to get out of the chair to sit next to her, she pointed at them and told them to stay in their seat. Apparently, she was planning to stay in control of this whole interaction.

At last, she shook her head and insisted Ravi didn't understand. "Maybe I'm not that *thing* in the stories anymore, Ravi, but I'm not better now. I'm not."

They scoffed at that. "Okay Miss Travels The World Literally Making Lives Better."

Nicole shook her head and scoffed at them. "Felicity didn't tell you, then? —That I'm responsible for hundreds of years of human suffering since I got exiled here?"

"...That's... hard to swallow, Nikki."

"It's my punishment, for being happy in this body, on Earth, when I'm supposed to be miserable. My family doesn't like that, so they have a habit of throwing a little disaster at humanity to make me suffer – plagues, wars, famines."

"They can do that?"

"My dad is—*was*—he was a monster. He could write up a clever contract with a human to do whatever he wanted. And even the biggest war starts with just one ambitious misguided person having just a *little* too much power. He knew that. He used that. Often."

"...Contracts...? Because... you're a faerie? What, like in Sleeping Beauty or Rumpelstiltskin or whatever?"

Nicole closed her eyes with a stupid grin and dropped her head with a little laugh. "Yes Ravi. Like in Sleeping Beauty or Rumpelstiltskin or whatever. They're cursed trades. It's what we live for. It's how we ruin humans. Too-good-to-be-true once-in-a-lifetime offers. —What exactly did Felicity tell you? It sounds like you didn't get as much as I was hoping."

"I hung up."

"What? What do you mean you hung up? You heard the words 'evil faerie monster' and ended the call?"

"That's about how it went, yeah." But even if Ravi had heard more, they wouldn't have believed a word of it. Nicole would have to do her own dirty work if she wanted to convince them about all this.

Nicole shook her head at that and continued trying in vain to explain why she was still an evil monster actually:

"Guess I'll fill in the blanks for you, then. I've got all the blood of millions of people on my hands," she said, offering up her perfectly clean and innocent left palm for Ravi to inspect. "Everything I do now, it's just… trying to pay that back. It's always been. But it's never enough. And it only gets worse the longer I try. They always come for me. They always come to punish me. Because I'm just too stupid drunk in love with you, with all this. Gods, it's awful when it's awful, but it feels so gods damn good to be here when it's good. It's like… poison. It's ambrosial poison – humanity. And… I… I have to, Ravi… I… can't…" The words got stuck in her throat. She looked at the ceiling to avoid looking at Ravi and swallowed hard a few times before she let out a stuttered little breath and said what she needed to say: "I can't keep letting them do this to you."

"Come on Nikki… How can you possibly feel responsible for all that? Your *family* did all that stuff. It's not your fault they did something so shitty."

"I could've stopped it," Nicole coldly insisted. "If I just played along, did what they wanted, suffered properly, I could've stopped it."

"So?? They could've stopped it too!"

"They don't even see how it's *wrong*, Ravi.

"Gods, I wish I could explain it right, how small a human life is in the eyes of an eternal being. —How still you are. —How impossibly sharp and sudden and *gone*. Less than a blink, less than a flash – less than the spark of a single broken synapse, firing once and dying to be lost and forgotten in the memory of a lifetime with no end. I fell in love with that, with the magic of it, the beauty of the ephemeral. But you're nothing to *them*. Guilt-free cattle to be farmed for the sick *joy* of your misery. We feed the gods with your suffering. That's your purpose, Ravi. —And for the rest of them, for my family, destroying a million lives just to *try* to make me shed a single tear? It's like brushing dust off a table to watch it dance for a moment in the sunlight. It's a giggle to them. A silly pun of a joke. And then nothing.

"They don't ache for mortals. They can't. But I do. And I knew. I knew it was wrong, the whole time. I knew what I was doing to you. To the world. —I'm a monster. I'm a <u>monster</u>, Ravi. You have to understand that, I'm <u>still</u>... I've always been..." she trailed off, the pointless remorse in her eyes saying loud and clear that she thought she'd said enough to make her point.

But what a stupid fucking point.

Ravi turned away and mashed their palms into their cheeks in silent frustration, struggling to find the words for this.

They were a *punchline?* Their misery was a *joke?*

They had to laugh to themself about it. It felt like they should be upset about that, but really, what did it matter? Did it change anything? Eternity, dust, nothingness – it was all too big for them, too small. But it had always been like that. After all, what else had Ravi ever been but a little joke of a chemical engine built to know and fear and speed along the inevitable entropic heat death of the universe?

At least now they knew they were making someone smile about how stupid it all was.

And as much as Nicole was trying to convince Ravi they were nothing to the fae, it sure felt like the fae were just as *nothing* to Ravi. There was nothing to fear in them. It was just a different name for the same cruel unknowable godlike force of nature that they'd *always* served as a mere speck of a human, right? They already knew how small a human life is. You don't study the fabric of the universe and walk away from that feeling big. So what did it matter whose indifference was shoving them around: Whether it was the cold formulaic unknowable machinations of the universe; or the relentless heartless cruelty of the fae? It was all above them anyways, all impossible to change, impossible to question.

All of it was just the rules of a game they couldn't opt out of without giving up. And they were far, *far* too spiteful to give up now.

It was nice that Nicole didn't want humans to suffer, but how could she possibly feel guilty about her family just... enforcing the rules? From her explanation, it sure sounded like they'd all be trying to make humans suffer regardless of how much it made Nicole ache.

They dared to glance at Nicole, to take in a moment of her sadness and her shame, and it cut them to the core, ripped nerves out by the root and put some violently furied fire in the hollowed out channels.

How could she get it so wrong? How could she get it so wrong for *so long?*

"You're not a monster for wanting to live a good life," they told her firmly, very poorly containing their fury. "Being *tortured by your family* doesn't make you *evil.* How the hell did you get all this in your head? Felicity is wrong. Okay? Don't listen to her. She doesn't see it. She doesn't see what you do. —What you <u>do</u>, Nicole? *Nicole* Doyle. You have never had anything but love in your heart since the day you shoved your way into my life. You love people. You love life. You love being happy and making people happy. There's nothing wrong with any of that. That's not evil, that's human. —You are not evil."

Ravi stared deep in Nicole's doubting eyes, imploring her to believe them – and failing. They offered their hands out, trying to invite her to take them in hers while they pleaded with her, "You are a good person. You're a good person Nicole say it. Say it like it's true. You know it is. You have to know."

She didn't take their hands, though, and she refused to admit the truth of it. Instead, she just scoffed at the idea and turned away from Ravi's imploring gaze.

After a few breaths to collect herself, she continued trying her very best to make a show of how uncaring and cruel she'd been to *Ravi* specifically:

"They've been torturing you Ravi, just to get at me. And gods it works. All your mistakes? Your clumsiness at work? Your endless parade of misfortune? That was for me. You lost your job because of me. You blew up that chem lab *because of me.* Gods, I'm starting to think even this *illness* is just to spite me now. Do you understand? You did nothing wrong. You didn't deserve any of it. I got too close to you and they saw how happy you made me and that was it for you. Fate sealed. Destined to be nothing to them but a tool to make me hurt. But I could've stopped it any time. *Any time.* Just by playing along, by doing what they told me to do. I could've saved you, and instead I let you... I let all this... Gods I'm so sorry Ravi..."

They couldn't help rolling their eyes at this stupid pity party Nicole was trying to invite them to, because all that sure sounded like a load of shit. Ravi could take responsibility for their own fuckups. They didn't need her trying to excuse everything that had gone wrong in their life with this nonsense. They especially didn't need her trying to take the blame for them being *sick*. Selfish. Stupid. Arrogant. What was wrong with her?

"...And what exactly did they tell you to do? —To 'save me'."

"Leave."

"Leave," Ravi echoed bitterly.

"Yeah. Leave. Forever. Turns out they want me to come home now – you know, since I keep having such an *uproariously* good time over here," she added sarcastically. "Seems like they've got some new torture planned for me. An eternity of paperwork. —Can you imagine?" she asked with a wildly inappropriate playful smile.

Ravi grimaced and turned away. Was Nicole really trying to joke about this?

"This is so stupid... What did you even do to deserve all this?"

"I broke a contract."

"That's it??"

"Oh, no, it was very <u>very</u> bad to do that. This isn't like... 'court litigation' kind of contract breaking. I *physically* broke the original copy of a gods-blessed Eternal Pact and undid all the magic in it. We're not supposed to do that. Makes the gods mad. —In fact, as it turns out, it makes the gods mad enough to obliterate a good solid slice of the whole endless plane of the Faelands. —Who knew?" she added with a little shrug and a bitter grin. "I sure didn't!"

"Why would you do that?"

"Ah... it's... not important..."

"You got exiled for it and it's not important??"

"—<u>And</u> had my wings torn off, thank you!" she added. "Not just *any* faerie gets their wings destroyed, Ravi. It's a very special honor. You gotta be *real* broken to get that kind of treatment."

"...That's... awful... They don't grow back?"

"Not like this. They're sealed by the gods now. My dad always does a very *thorough* job of this special treatment of his."

"A seal... Those tattoos on your back?"

"Yeah. At least they're pretty, right?"

"Can we... break the seal?"

"I appreciate the sentiment, Ravi Bee, but 'we' can't do anything. I'm leaving, and I won't be allowed to see a human ever again for as long as I live."

"Would you stop already? You aren't leaving. What's even the point in leaving now?"

"I have to stop them from hurting you."

"Let them hurt me! I don't give a shit. You think I'd let them use me to hurt you—?"

"Gods Ravi, stop. It's not just about you. Okay? I'm sorry. But it's not about you. I know it hurts, but this is bigger than you. This is for humanity. For everyone."

"Come on Nicole this is so stupid... You really think you leaving is going to stop all of humanity's suffering forever? We're *very* good at making each other miserable. Pretty sure we'll be at it a long time after you're gone. —So stay! You make people happy here. Lots of people. You can't do that if you're gone. You have to see that."

Nicole looked down at her feet hanging off the side of the bed and kicked them in the air idly for a few seconds of quiet thought before she reluctantly explained, "...Look, Ravi, it wasn't just about the contract. My dad got it in his head at some point that humans are some kind of poison to the fae. He went a little crazy. And, maybe on purpose maybe not, he made a contract that would've killed all of you if it went wrong, a contract that put just a little too much power in the hands of the wrong person. That's the contract I broke. But I'm not being punished because I broke the rules, I'm being punished because of *why* I broke the rules – for you. For humanity. Out of a love for you that, to him, sure looked a lot like poison. All of this was supposed to break me, break my heart so badly that I'd never love another human again, cure me of my sympathy by making it hurt so bad I couldn't even look at you again without feeling bitter and angry and spiteful. He wanted me to feel like he does again. He wanted me to be his precious vile little heartless prodigy again. I was supposed to break, and then beg, and then come crawling back – perfect, loyal, *cured*."

She lifted her head and gave Ravi an intense look before she continued, "I made him promise to never do it again – to never let *anyone* do it again. But he's gone now. If I don't go back, there's no one left who's going to be good enough to take over for him, to stop every other stupid crazy faerie from doing something just as bad. —And while I'm still here messing around *pleasuring myself* for the hedonistic joy of it all, they're going to keep trying to do worse and worse things to me, to make me suffer, to cure me of my poison – and I don't know about you, but I don't think there's a huge line between 'wars and famines and diseases that kill millions of people' and 'extinction events'. If they keep trying to ruin me, it's going to escalate eventually, and someone has to stop that. —I mean gods, what was the point of all this if I let humanity suffer anyways? If I let you just die off horribly? Huh? Hundreds of years of this for *nothing??* To lose everyone anyways??"

She clenched her left hand into a tight fist and dropped it firmly on her thigh while she bitterly explained, "I thought I could keep you safe from here, but I'm so powerless now. I'm so weak. I traded too much of myself away, Ravi. I let myself get crushed and crippled under the weight of a hundred thousand mountains of debt. —You get it? There's no point trying to fight them from this side anymore. I have nothing left to fight with," she said, wincingly raising her sleeve-obscured right hand in the air as a cryptic demonstration. "So: I leave, you stop suffering, humanity survives, everyone's happy."

"Fuck off 'everyone's happy'... There has to be a better way than this, Nicole. You can't let them win like this."

"*I'm* winning," she boomed at them. "I <u>win</u> this way. You stay safe. That's all that matters to me. That's everything. —And they're just *handing* it to me. I <u>win</u>."

Ravi clicked their tongue at that and muttered, "Sour grapes..."

"Excuse me?"

"You obviously don't want to leave..."

"I want to leave *a whole lot more* than I want to lose everything I love!"

Ravi was furious and shaking and desperate for any alternative, but nothing was coming. They couldn't just keep sitting down for this, though, shaking themself to pieces with *barely* contained rage.

In a furious huff, they launched themself out of their chair, leaving it spinning behind them. They stood before her, staring down at her, bitter, pleading, silent, but they lost to their frustration and had to storm out of the room before they started shouting at her for being so ridiculous and selfish and *giving up.*

Nicole Doyle didn't give up.

They couldn't let her degrade herself like that.

So what if it meant disaster after disaster would hit humanity forever? Who could give a shit about that?? It was going to happen anyways! How could she not see that?? That this was some stupid *obvious* trick her family was playing on her?? All it would do is take away her ability to try to make the world a better place! All it would do is take all the power out of her hands and leave her feeling helpless and guilty forever while humanity drove *itself* to extinction.

This had the scent of Felicity's meddling all over it. Why else would Nicole suddenly decide to do this? After *centuries*. Why else would she be acting weird? It only started after Felicity assaulted her, after Felicity *threatened* her, used her secrets against her, twisted her guilt into these *asinine* plans of action.

They slammed their fist into the hallway wall, trying to get their frustration out as violence before it turned into a sobbing breakdown at how powerless they were to stop her.

You can't tie down someone who can just... disappear.

Not without a whole net of iron chains or something, apparently.

Maybe Ravi could keep her in a bottle? Was she that kind of faerie?

...No. She was leaving. Forever. To save humanity, so she believed.

And that sure sounded familiar, they bitterly scoffed at themself.

It cut them to admit it, but... she'd given them the same privilege, hadn't she? The freedom to die for what they believed in, no matter how pointless she thought it was.

They couldn't turn around after all that and tell her she wasn't allowed to make the same sacrifice, no matter how pointless they thought it was.

Fuck.

Maybe she'd give them a week too.

And maybe they could figure out how to stretch a week out too using whatever magic she had used to warp their reality for so long.

They found her thoughtfully thumbing through the wardrobe in her section of their closet. She idly informed them, when she noticed they'd returned, that it was a shame she'd never be able to wear any of this again.

"Donate it for me, okay? Nice big clothes are hard to find, you know."

Ravi couldn't imagine another human in the world dressing like Nicole. The idea that some mere *human* could wear something touched by someone as beautiful and enchanted as her, it felt tawdry.

They didn't promise.

They didn't return to their chair, instead opting to stoically lean back against their dresser drawers while they said their bitter goodbyes.

"I really can't stop you, huh?"

"Gods I wish you could, though. You have no idea."

"When?"

"Today. Now. Now, actually..."

"Now?? Jesus Nicole, what the fuck?? Give me more than that!"

"...I couldn't. I can't. I'm sorry. I wasn't... even planning to... I only came back because you deserve to know, after everything you've given me. You earned an honest goodbye. Gods, though, I wish I was strong enough to look you in the eye and tell you I never want to see you again, but it's such a lie. I can't give you more time. I can't let you stop me. And I'm so weak to you, Rav. I don't know if I can..."

"...I just... A week? A week, Nicole. Give me one week to say goodbye properly. It's fair. It's only fair! You have to—"

"—I'm leaving today. It's set. It's happening. I can't change it anymore."

"...Just one night then. One night? What's one night!"

"I can't. I can't, Ravi. I can't let you—"

"—I'll let you go," they insisted, taking a step towards her, which only got her to take a step back away from them. "I'll let you leave, I promise. I just want one more night. Please. To hold you. To... to show you..."

With her beautiful bottom lip pierced wincingly between her impossibly sharp teeth, she considered it for a second, and for a second Ravi thought they might have won, they might have at least stretched the seconds between 'now' and her bitter exit from their life out for a few hours.

But she shook her head sadly, put her left hand out to insist they keep away, and made her way past them to the hall, leaving Ravi behind to sulk.

They stared bitterly at their desk. It was pricking their mind that something was in there. Something that could keep her.

Their mind flashed with realization when they remembered what it was. They threw the drawer open and snatched that promise she made, the promise she signed, the contract they made so long ago, and dashed out of the room to challenge her.

"You promised," they said in a desperate last attempt to keep her. "You promised." They held up the stupid little note and reminded her, "You said you wouldn't leave until you were sick of me. —You signed it! You signed it, right there: Nicole Doyle. You can't break this, Miss Faerie, you'll piss off the gods—"

She barely gave the note a glance before she gave Ravi a sad smile and told them the truth of it at last: "Sorry Ravi Bee, but that's not my true name."

"…What? What's that supposed to mean?"

"It's just a little fantasy. A trick. The first trick I played on you. The first trick any good faerie plays on their victims. That's not my true name. You fell for it."

They flipped the note around and glared at it bitterly. *Nicole Doyle.* It shimmered in blue on the page. Magic. Magic, wasn't it? Her magic. It *was* true. It had to be. Who else had she ever been? What other name could possibly be hers? The name that shitty old woman used to torture her? The name bitter jealous Felicity used on her? The name she'd suffered under for who knows how many centuries of guilt and unrealized redemption?

That name was *dead.*

"It's true to me. Doesn't that count for anything?"

A hint of a nostalgic smile shaped her lips, but she wouldn't accept the truth of it. "Doesn't matter anyways, Rav. All it says is I don't *have to* leave. Nothing about being forced to *stay.*"

They reread the note a few times while she *particularly* perfectly tied up her boots and tentatively tapped the toes to adjust the fit, though they couldn't imagine why she'd need boots where she was going.

Their arm fell to their side in bitter defeat.

What a stupid loophole.

That was it then.

There was only one thing left to ask for:

"A kiss then," they begged her. "Just a kiss."

She bit her lip again looking them over, considering it, seriously considering it, but she still shook her head no. "I can't."

"For me?"

"Stop. Stop. Please. Don't make me regret coming back here. I just... I wanted to say goodbye with your blessing, Ravi, with a smile. I want to remember you like that. Can't you give me that?"

"...Why? Why should I smile? This isn't what love looks like, Nikki. Tricks and secrets. You won't even listen to me. Was it real? Any of it? Was Felicity really right the whole time? You were just using me until you were done with me?"

"Please stop."

"If you love me, show me. Show me. I don't want to remember you like this. I don't want my last memory of you forever to be the sight of your back turned away and a cold goodbye. I want to remember what you've given me. I want to remember the warmth of your love."

"You have my love! How can you even question that after everything—?"

"So show me!"

"I've *been* showing you! Godsake Ravi, if you can't believe it after everything I've given you, everything I'm giving up for <u>you</u>, then there's nothing a *kiss* is going to prove now."

Ravi scoffed at that and told her, bitterly, "A human would understand..."

"Well I'm not fucking human! I think I've made that pretty damn clear! Godsake why is this so hard for you to understand, Ravi? You're <u>poison</u> to me. Not that tar in your shoulder, <u>you</u>. Even worse than the 'all the evils of the world corrupting the purity of the fae' poison my dad thinks all humans are. Even worse than my own poison that keeps twisting me *stupid* thinking I can fix everything if I just keep making things worse. No, you're special, Ravi. You're more like a... 'stay here and fuck the world' kind of poison when I've got you in me. I knew that the first time I tasted you on my lips. And I've selfishly been lapping you up for months. I'm an idiot for staying. And it's been amazing being your idiot, but I have to stop.

"Do you get it? I would *die* to lick the venom off your lips if I could die. I'm so fucking stupid for you that I would fuck the whole fucking world just to taste you for just one more day. —I've <u>been</u>. I <u>am</u>. I'm too stupid and too weak and too broken now to get away from you. And I would let you hold me here forever if you asked. So please, please just <u>stop</u> asking. *I can't do this* without you."

She glared at them with bleary red eyes and flushed cheeks, her left hand clenched in a bitter fist, her ruined right hand still hidden in her sleeve and idle at her side. She glared at them pleading, silently begging them again to leave her with the memory a smile.

But they couldn't give her that.

And so she left them with the bitter last memory of a cold goodbye and her back turning away from them, forever.

The finality of the heart-shattering click of the latch on the door handle felt like a bullet through their brain.

That was it.

After everything.

Nicole was gone.

Forever.

To save the world *from herself.*

So fucking stupid...

It wasn't even a minute later before their cheeks were hot with tears, before their chest was aching from the heaving sobs, before they could barely keep their retching stomach inside their body.

They had woken up every day since Nicole disappeared in fear thinking they'd ruined everything, that they'd taken every sense of safety out of her home. And they'd been ready to do anything to make it better. But to find out it had nothing to do with them? To find out they had been pointless and powerless the whole time? They had no control over this at all and it was a shrapnel bomb going off in their guts again and again. The most important person in their life was just ripped out of their arms forever, and it wasn't even their fault this time.

But it turned out forever was a lot shorter than they imagined, because it wasn't even five minutes later that there was a slow, faint knocking at the door, that grew louder and louder with every rap until it sounded like someone trying to escape a pack of wolves.

Ravi wiped their face and hurried to the door.

It opened to a pair of enchanting, blood-shot, gemstone eyes. It opened to tender fingertips that shot through space like shooting stars to trace lines across their cheek, until those tender fingertips found a home behind their ear. It opened to a strong loving arm that drew them in, that held them still, that lifted their lips to hers.

Ravi melted in her grasp. They wanted so badly to put their arms around her, but they were poison – and not the kind they always worried they were, not the kind that hurt her, not the kind that made her sick for days. No, they were some irresistible temptuous poison to her, and they had no intention of abusing that, no intention of poisoning her anymore. Keeping her forever would be too cruel. They only wanted to remember her. Remember her love. And what a sweet gift of a memory goodbye she was offering them. They wanted more, they wanted *forever*, but all they could do now was let her take what she wanted from them, to let her give them what she could, and find some way to cherish it until the day they died.

When she'd taken her fill, Nicole affectionately nuzzled her cheek against Ravi's and whispered, promised, "I love you," in their ear.

"I know," Ravi promised her right back. "I'm sorry. I knew. I knew I swear." And they did. They knew. Even though it felt like Nicole was ripping their heart out and running off with it, dragging the rest of their guts along with it, they knew Nicole wasn't doing any of this *to* them. —*For* them. It was for them. It was obviously for them, as bitter as that sat in what was left of their heart after she tore it out.

And yeah, it hurt – bad – but it was Nicole. They trusted Nicole. She would only do what was best, what was right. And if this was her best, then they knew it must be worth hurting for. They knew this must come from a love that was bigger than the two of them. She would never hurt them, not for nothing.

They didn't need a kiss. Of course they knew they were loved. They'd always known. They would never doubt it. They just wanted to hear it, to feel it on their lips, one last time.

Ravi whispered, "Thank you."

Nicole pressed her forehead into Ravi's with her eyes closed. She stayed there long enough for someone's tears to run down Ravi's cheek.

Then she pulled away, just barely, just enough to give Ravi a chance to get lost in her eyes one last time. She took what Ravi was sure would be their last kiss from them. A kiss that was a hundred kisses. A kiss that was the deepest ocean and the wildest rapids and the most thunderous of storms.

She took Ravi's poison kiss. Like an idiot. And for one more night, like an idiot, she said fuck the world, and the two of them got lost in each other, carefully, tenderly, insatiably, trying to make eternity out of the hours before dawn. Nicole refused to explain the unbearable injury on her right hand. And Ravi took every effort to keep her safe from pain while they refused to let sleep take her, or themself. A cruel poison crept into their own mind the longer they held her, the longer they savored her, cherished her: If they could just keep her here, steal her, hold her captive in the chains of their toxic touch, forever—

Saturday's sun was old when Ravi woke.

Nicole was gone.

She'd left a note at their bedroom door.

One last gift:

I'LL KEEP YOU FOREVER.
NIKKI

❦ *Part V* ❦

It Kind of Sounds Like Bullshit, but Sometimes Goodbye Really Is Just the Start of Something New, Isn't It?

Ravi felt a little too numb to open the mystery box Nicole left them. Every time they went to lift the silk cloth off, the weight of it felt impossible.

She'd taken everything she owned when she left in secret that morning – everything except those clothes she asked Ravi to donate. Every other sign she'd ever lived in their apartment was gone, except the intoxicating aroma of *her* in their bed that made them want to never wash those love-stained sheets ever again.

At least she left behind all the gifts she'd given Ravi.

Neglected plants.

Memories.

Handmade pottery.

A lovely knit blanket.

Memories.

The beautiful stitchwork on their jacket.

Memories.

Memories memories memories memories memori—

—Oh, and that impossibly delicious homemade achaar.

But they could never eat any of that again, could they? She put so much of herself in it. They'd be eating *her*. And then she'd be gone. Really truly gone.

There was also that one last going away gift of hers: Whatever miserable treasure was in this foreboding mystery box – some gift she thought would soothe their pain after losing her forever. But what could possibly wrap that wound?

There was a connection between that grave injury on her hand and whatever was in the box, they were sure of it. And it was a connection they very much were not ready to pull the cloth off of.

But if she really did hurt herself getting this for them, then it was the least they could do. They had to at least *look* at it.

With a heavy sigh, they finally set the heavy silk aside and peered into the little gift box.

Inside was a clear perfunctory plastic bag with a strange little piece of tech in it – a shiny plain inch-wide titanium-oxide-white ceramic square that was far heavier and more solid than it deserved to be for its size, with a few equally white filaments growing out of each of the four edges – filaments Ravi recognized right away as ill-gotten Saffron thread from the reddish shimmer. The bag was labelled with the InThetics logo and a table of indecipherable numerical details about a trial experiment of some sort – though one number was very easy to understand: Efficacy: 99.998%.

They removed it from the bag and immediately felt a... hum? to it. Was that right? A buzzing, almost. Static charge maybe? A persistent subtly pulsing static charge? That didn't make sense... The sensation lingered for as long as they held it, crawling up their arm and slow-dancing around their tar-infected shoulder.

The design looked familiar.

The prototype pain suppressor, wasn't it? From Lexy's prettified schematics.

When they tentatively brought the thing closer to one of their half-dark cysts, the long Saffron filaments reacted, curling and writhing and *reaching out*, seemingly seeking the very source of their pain.

Unsettling.

What crazy tech. It felt too early by a hundred years.

They could practically hear the cloying advertisements already: *Saffron White™: Ahead By a Century* – backed by a trendy take on a little Tragically Hip riff.

Before any of the eager strands of Saffron could touch them, they pulled the thing away from their sores and set it on the table, relieving themself of that strange fuzzy hum.

This. This vile monstrosity made of the concentrated suffering of millions of people.

This.

For Nicole's hand.

Fucking hell of a goodbye gift.

And a real <u>shit</u> trade, frankly.

There's something to be said for taking the price tag off your gifts. They had to spare a little appreciation for the misguided sentiment of it, but how the hell could they possibly use it? Knowing what it cost. What it cost her. What it cost the world. What it was going to cost *them* for the rest of their short little life.

—You're owed this, Ravi. You suffered for this. You're <u>in</u> this. You deserve something for everything you've lost. You deserve—

A buzz on their phone interrupted their moral calculus.

For a second their heart fluttered with hope, but it was dashed into the dirt when they saw it was just their brave little knight, The *Golden* Dame Felicity Aurelia Vicente.

Not what they wanted to read right now.

Or ever.

Why hadn't they blocked her already?

—Just block her. Don't read it just—

👑 *The Golden Fleece* 👑

Is she gone? >

                        < oh fuck off

Wait did I get the right number?
It's Felicity
Please tell me you still know me >

                    what is it about fuck off
                 < you're struggling with fleece

Oh thank God it's you
Jeezus my heart almost stopped >

                    is it the fuck or the off
                 < is the oh throwing you

Okay I get it I get it
But can you answer my question first?
It's kind of important
Because if she didn't leave, then I'm
having the craziest seizure or something
and I should probably go to the hospital >

she left this morning
thanks for that
< you absolute bitch

Wow!
Wow
Okay I know you're angry and sad
And all that stuff
But that's still kind of harsh >

< don't contact me again

Wait
This morning?
Not yesterday?
Because it was really really really
supposed to be yesterday
For reasons that will be difficult to
explain
But I definitely have to explain it if
she didn't
She didn't, did she?
I bet she just left
I knew she'd do this to you I KNEW it
Hello?
Don't do this
Answer me please it's important >

Ravi couldn't deal with this. Not today. But it still took a solid thirty uneasy seconds of hovering their finger over the block button before, at last, they pressed it and whisked away every one of Felicity's messages to whatever dark corner of their phone unwanted people disappeared to.

They cracked a beer out of the fridge and sipped at it for a long time, leaning against the window sill in the living room, staring at that bitter gift of Nicole's on the coffee table, trying to remember what it meant to die, what it meant for a boat to float, what it meant for a human to be human, occasionally swearing at themself, occasionally swearing at Nicole, *frequently* swearing at Felicity.

How could Nicole honestly tell them to keep Felicity around after everything that little gremlin did to them? That she did to *Nicole?* Even if everything she'd done had been done out some twisted sense of white knight concern for Ravi, that didn't make it even *close* to okay. And anyways they never asked for it. They never would've asked. Sure as hell, they never wanted to be *anyone's* concern. But especially not hers. Before, it had been out of some hope of sparing her the burden of worrying about them. They'd had a lot of worrying shit going on for a long time. But now? Godsake, they hadn't seen 'concern' manifest as something so toxic since their dad tried to 'cure' them.

Talk about human poison.

An email pinged their phone. Felicity. Obviously.

"Hey you. Sorry how all this turned out. I know it sucks. But it's **really** important we talk. Life or death kind of thing. Please call me."

'Hey you'? What kind of greeting was that? Was she really trying to be cute right now?

Ravi obviously didn't answer, or call. Instead they grabbed their beautifully embroidered jacket, cherished the feel of the fabric in their hands for a few somber seconds, then slipped it on as magically near-painlessly as always and made their way out the door to go for a walk to get their head together.

By the third unread unsolicited email, they turned their phone off entirely.

They tried their best to find something to feel good about in all this. Nicole didn't want them to hurt. She even gave them a whole night of warm memories to keep. Just, remember *that*. So many good times, right? That joy of hers so infectious that it spread to their lips, day after day, month after month, since the moment she crashed back into their life. That love of hers like they'd never had, of all of them, through and through, making even their worst feel worthy. That love for her like they'd never felt before, like they'd never feel again.

But there was one way they could feel it forever, wasn't there? If they could just keep her like that in their head. Holy. Hallowed. Frozen. Perfect. *Forever*. Until they died, anyways.

Wasn't it better that way? To pretend? To *feel* loved? To give up and give in to the soothing sedation of memories painted pink by desperately lonely nostalgia? Wasn't that better than being completely honest and naked and known and *still* abandoned by the person they loved more than anything in the world?

Nicole had really poisoned their mind with all that 'you deserve to be known' bullshit, hadn't she?

Hypocrite.

She wouldn't even let them put their damn name on the most important paper they were ever going to publish.

Her cruel words echoed in their mind:

"That's not my true name."

They slammed their fist into a passing tree in the little wood by the river while they stumbled along the rain-slicked dirt paths there.

There was no one to hide their eyes from, but still they lowered their head in shame.

Couldn't they smile for her? Why did they have to cry? Weak. Pathetic.

—*Man the fuck up, Ravi, you owe her this. You promised.*

But they couldn't do it. Instead they leaned back and collapsed all their weight into the trunk of a thick oak. They stared overhead at the barren branches that cut pretty black cracks in the bright overcast sky, and while they stared and ached, they absolutely failed her – failed to stifle their croaky heaving sobs while they wished she could be there with them again, like she'd been there with them so many times before, and so many times more in their stupid naïve fantasies.

Why the fuck did they think it was a good idea today to go to the park the two of them always walked around in? Idiot.

When their tears ran out, they dried their cheeks and found themself numb again, staring down at the mercilessly steady flow of the river with a sick longing they'd felt many times before but never quite managed to give in to.

—*What's the point of you now, Ravi? Everyone you love is gone. It all turns to nothing in the end. Why wait?*

October.

The water would be cold now.

Maybe it was even cold enough to shock them out the moment they dove in.

It wouldn't hurt. Not for long. Drowning is supposed to be one of the most terrifying experiences but it's over fast – especially if they managed to hit their head on a rock in the current.

They let their back slide down the trunk of the tree until they were sitting on their ass with their thighs pressed hard into their chest, their chin resting on their folded arms.

They couldn't pay her back.

They couldn't ever pay her back now.

And they sure as shit couldn't keep *her* forever.

Maybe they could write a stupid little story for Felicity's book preservation project.

Once upon a time there was a horrible heartless murderous beast who fell in love with humanity and spent the rest of her eternal life trying to make it better. And she wasn't a monster.

...But then they'd have to convince Felicity something so pathetic and stupid was worth saving. Felt like a bit of a hard sell. —Though it sounded at least a *little* more profound than a journal full of decades of records of clouds.

Felicity didn't believe in the endless void that waits more patient than a hungry star to swallow us all. She believed in eternity. In something bigger even than the universe itself.

Maybe they could too.

They got up and dusted the wet dirt off their backside before turning away from the water. The poor hungry river would have to wait, yet again. They weren't done yet.

The Trouble With Nihilism Is You Have to Craft Your Own Meaning, and There's Not Really an Artisan's Guild for That Kind of Thing

(Morning, Tuesday, 24th October)

"We can't publish this."

"What? Of course you can—"

"—Unverifiable. Slanderous. Incomprehensible *technojargon*. And even if it weren't, there's not even a story here." Notably absent from the end of the editor's assessment was the *apology*. Apparently it was Ravi's fault the guy couldn't understand the significance of what was in his hands.

They were feverishly looking up the publication's details on the internet while they were on their burner phone 'negotiating' with the editor.

"...Aw come <u>on</u>, man. Are you serious? Just because there's InThetics ads all over your site—?"

"That's irrelevant."

"I bet. —You know what, that's fine. That's fine! I'll just find some other journalist with enough fucking *dignity*—"

"—*Amaira Beausoleil, discredited scientist, spreading slanderous rumors about former employer, trial date to be decided.*"

"Godsake you <u>fucking</u> bootlicker, they're *poisoning* people. —They're *farming* us! You seriously won't take this on?"

"Listen to me. Listen very carefully: Bury this. Let it die. Or you'll be the one in the dirt."

"That a threat? *Editor of top paper in country threatens innocent whistleblower?*"

"Good luck."

"Do you have <u>any idea</u> what this cost—!?"

The call clicked off with a pleasant chime before Ravi could finish. They crushed the phone bitterly in their hand until the cheap seams creaked in protest, staring at the 'Anonymous' number and the flashing 'Disconnected' message until the screen idly faded to black on them.

It was just one editor. There were others.

But when they checked, every other 'respectable' platform and publication in the country was also tainted with cloying advertisements for the latest InThetics AugMe™ tech:

The Human Touch™
More Human than Human™ with Saffron White™
Coming Soon[††]

Some of them even had sickly-saccharine articles about the company's performative tax-dodging philanthropy, and none of them said a damn word about its world-fucking military industry or the stranglehold it held over medical research and development in Canada. The most critical article any of them had published about the company was about a missed profit goal a few years ago that made some indignant shareholders *extra* indignant.

The less notable publications they reached out to had teams too small to verify any of Ravi's claims, and lawyers too fucking impotent to take on InThetics' litigation team if things got messy.

Fuck, by the time they were done calling around, it felt like they'd be *lucky* to get a single word of complaint against InThetics published in a goddamn anarchist *zine*.

So. No. Not one of them had any idea what it cost Ravi, and not one of them was willing to foot the bill for whatever it *might* cost to do what needed to be done.

Nicole would be delighted to know Ravi never even had an option to sacrifice themself to all the deadly teeth in a tank full of hungry sharks, since apparently some ambitious dentist had already filed off every sharp serrated tooth in the whole fucking pack.

It was dead in their hands.

Months of work for nothing.

What was the point? They sold their soul to InThetics for *nothing*. They shoved Nicole away for <u>nothing</u>. They were living for absolutely fucking <u>nothing</u> good at <u>fucking</u> all, weren't they?

—*What's the <u>fucking</u> point of you now, Ravi?*

You Said It Wrong

(Late Night, Friday, 17th November)

What's-Her-Name had her hungry claws in Ravi again. They hoped it would be enough to get their mind off things. To move forward. But it tore them up to feel so wanted and so forgotten at the same time. It tore them up to *be forgetting*.

She called them the wrong name. She had always called them the wrong name. She didn't know. When she whispered in their ear to take their pants off. When she growled at them to roll over, or demanded they tell her they wanted it, whatever 'it' was – which usually ended up being true. She certainly delivered.

But Ravi didn't want to be loved by the wrong name anymore. They didn't even want to be *fucked* by the wrong name anymore. Every syllable felt wrong – poison dripping off the sharp tip of What's-Her-Name's deft tongue. That slick blade was ripping the silk out of a tapestry they'd spent years crafting and months learning from a self-proclaimed expert how to fall in love with.

—And holy hell why was their brain being so fucking twee about all this? God, maybe it was a mercy to have it all torn apart – just, letting What's-Her-Name go nuts untangling all the bright amber and honey threads that pierced their aching heart to the weave, threads that sewed *belonging* into a name that had always meant being alone.

No. No, they weren't here to be untangled. They were here for the drinks, and the human contact, and to be forgetting.

But not to be forgotten.

Not anymore.

After weeks of letting her chew them up, they broke. Just one strand too many torn out by her careless canines, one finally unforgivable syllable on that warm tongue. That night – in the temple of What's-Her-Name's tequila-flavored bedroom, with that lewd knee of hers between their thighs that trapped them and forced them to listen to that vile, spine-tingling whisper in their ear, paired with that hungry, toothy, loveless kiss on their neck that always managed to steal a stifled gasp from their lungs – that was the last time they would stand to be known wrong.

Ravi pried What's-Her-Name off of them with a talon grip on her throat, keeping her on the edge of coughing, silencing her attempts at voicing those forbidden 'Am's, 'Ai's, and 'Ra's in her pleas for freedom. She tried to pull Ravi's wrist away, clawed at their fingers, but Ravi wasn't letting go, not until they were known right.

"That's not my name," they said in a cold, commanding voice – a voice they had never heard from themself before, spoken by whatever seething soul was moving their hands. That possessor used their grip on the pleading woman's throat to force her into a submissive position on the bed, below them, *where she belonged.*

"My name is Ravi," they taught her. "Say it. *Raw-vee.*"

They let What's-Her-Name have enough breath to speak, hoarse, voiceless.

"*Ravi,*" she whispered. There was a sick smile on her face. She was loving this. "*Fuck this is hot Amaira don't stop...*"

They growled, "*Ravi,*" and squeezed the powerless woman's throat until her veins showed, even in the dim voyeuristic street light peering through the blinds.

She clutched Ravi's arm for mercy and nodded emphatically until they let her speak again. With her first breath, she desperately repeated Ravi's name in earnest – still with that fucking smile.

"This isn't a game. You're going to say it right from now on. You're going to call me by the right name, and you're going to let me worship you like a fucking goddess until you can't speak anymore – and when you can't speak anymore, you'd still better be crying the right fucking name in your head." Ravi kept her terrified gaze while they descended on her with bared teeth sharp and hostile, halting a hair from her quivering, giddy lips to snarl at her, "*Understand?*"

She understood.

Ravi took a real kiss out of this woman who had never seen them as anything more than an attractive piece of meat. They forced her beneath them every time she tried to move, held her hostage in their deference, bound her with ritual commands. This pretty, precious, pathetic little *social scientist* didn't stand a chance against Ravi's calloused, world-hardened, venerating hands.

They kept her captive, taught her the full depth of *Ravi's* adoration, and pushed her to the end of a hundred ecstasies until they had what they wanted – an answer to their prayers, oral evidence of her absolute unequivocal adoration of them – of *Ravi*.

She was still pawing at them pathetically for a comforting embrace when she finally remembered how to talk.

"Jesus Christ, Am—R—Ravi. *Ravi*. I didn't know you were so fffucking... —That was *intense*."

Nestled into their mock lover's arms, warm on a facsimile of affection, they heard their own voice escaping their throat: "Tell me you love me," almost pleading, afraid to ruin it with a command.

They needed it to sound right when they heard it.

It didn't.

Where There's a
Spiteful Bitter Will,
You Might Be Lucky
Enough to Find a Way

"I'm so sorry. It's gone and I can't figure out how to get it back. —I thought I could cheat it! I thought—"

"—You thought you could outsmart a faerie who's been outsmarting humans for thousands of years."

The malaise in Ravi had been dragging them around like a morphinic zombie for weeks, but at least they could still pull out a sarcastic little jab for Felicity when she earned it.

Forty minutes ago, Ravi had opened the front door to a timid knock to find Felicity on her knees in the hallway practically kissing the filthy carpet begging for mercy.

They slammed the door on her. They were far too busy getting ready for a fun night in with ~~Val~~—What's-Her-Name to waste any time on whatever nonsense Felicity was about to drop on them.

But after listening for half an hour to Felicity's harried struggle climbing the fire escape and her relentless tapping on the damn window and her pathetic pleading through the glass for another chance, they did eventually give up and open the kitchen door to let her in from the cold.

With a grumble, they cancelled their date.

The two of them caught each other up over a pot of coffee.

Ravi dutifully reported that yes Nicole was gone. Really gone. For real. And yes, on a Saturday morning, not a Friday evening, Ravi confirmed at last – which seemed to trouble Felicity a lot more than she could properly explain. Something to do with the threads of fate and Nicole being a lying cheat.

They also explained that Nicole had left them a gift. Felicity nodded like she already knew, though she was quite curious about it. They were wearing it on their wrist as a bracelet now. She peered at it for a long time, asking questions about it until she was confident that she understood exactly what it was and explained it for them – that it was a lot more significant than they could've imagined. Apparently, it wasn't just a piece of impossible futuristic tech. It was also a protective ward. —A real one, not like the horseshoes and clovers and all that other stuff Felicity had been using to antagonize Nicole before.

Good thing their sentimental ass had been stupid enough to figure out a way to keep it with them. The Saffron threads refused to stay knotted with each other, so they'd twisted the impossibly thin filaments coming out of the little porcelain chip into some nice wool. From that, they finger knitted a shitty white cuff of a bracelet. And since then, they'd been wearing it on their wrist everywhere, looking like a weird useless watch.

They figured maybe if they pretended to like it long enough, they'd stop being pissed off about it.

It had not been working.

But they had, after all that time, almost gotten used to the dull ticklish hum of it on their flesh.

The chip did nothing to ease their pain tied down there but, apparently, according to Felicity, it had probably at least been keeping them safe from supernatural predators.

And then from Felicity's accounting of the *rest* of her horrible trade with Nicole, it seemed that Nikki had also left a couple *more* shitty gifts that she hadn't warned Ravi about at all.

Like for example, this shit with their name.

Which brings us back to Felicity's groveling, standing with her hands together in a prayer for forgiveness in front of Ravi, who was fuming on the couch with their arms crossed.

"Okay, in my defense—" Felicity said, only to be cut short by Ravi before she could embarrass herself:

"—Stop. I don't care. Just. Vee. You can call me Vee."

"Vee. Okay. That's cute."

"Thanks," they replied lethargically. "Picked it myself." The words were an echo of a bitter old introduction to a hateful manipulative old witch of a woman. They cringed to imagine that Felicity too probably thought that abandoning the first and most precious gift one gets in life is a bit blasphemous. She loved her mom so much. She loved her own name. Though she also seemed to glow whenever Ravi used her playful nickname, oh blessed Golden Fleece.

"—And keep the fucking money," they added bitterly. "Jesus Christ…"

"I promised, though," she whined.

"Well bad news, Fleece: You're breaking your promise. Deal with it."

After pouting about it for a few seconds, she gave Ravi a sad little salute and tried to give them a dutiful affirmative: "Yes m… mmm…? …Mmm??" Felicity's eyes filled with a hint of panic when she couldn't open her mouth to finish the word. "What the fuck?? Yes 'boss'? Yes 'sir'? Yes mmmm<u>mmm</u>…!"

"…Ma'am."

"…Wh… *what?*" Felicity looked terrified, like Ravi was a cat that just *barked* at her.

—Fucksake Nicole…

"—Fine. Sir. Just call me sir. Fuck. Who cares." Then Ravi, too, was hit with a little panic before they challenged Felicity: "Hey, 'Felicity has such cool clothes. I like her fit.'"

"…Not sure where that's coming from but, thank you? That's sweet of you."

"Say it about me."

"Uh. Fishing for compliments?"

"Just do it."

"Vee has cool clothes?"

"And…"

"I like…"

"Mhm."

"I like… h… hhhhuh…? —The hell…? This again? —I like… *Vee's* fit?" Ravi heaved a bitter sigh. "Their. Fit. You like their fit."

"…Their fit. Is cool."

"Great. Great! Glad we got all that out and fucking sorted."

"You're…?"

"'Non-binary' is fine. Yes."

"No… No way. But she… That's how *she* called you. —When she was mad, she... she... *forgot*... —Jeezus. Come on, Vee, *I told her off for it.* —Are you serious? This whole time? How long??"

Ravi looked away bitterly. Had Nicole really done something so goddamn cruel to them on her way out the door? So much for all that 'leaving them with some happy memories' bullshit. Fuck. They glanced at that curse of an enchanted cuff of theirs and gritted their teeth. *Fuck* happy memories. This was a *betrayal.* A deep cut of a betrayal. She didn't deserve an ounce of mercy for this. So fucking selfish.

"Why didn't you tell me?" Felicity pleaded with them, clearly heartbroken. "Why?? Why did you... —Why was she worth it?? A fucking stranger? Twenty-three years Vee! Twenty-three *years.* Didn't I fucking earn it?? —*Lola* forgive me but on *Jesus Christ* and *Mary* why can't you ever fucking talk to me!?"

Ravi gestured at Felicity's whole frustrated situation and lethargically told her, "This. This is why."

"No. No nonono, you don't get to use this as an excuse, Vee. I'm only pissed because you think you can't trust me! What did you think I was going to do?? Disown you? Spit in your face? You think I'm some prudish bigot or something? Do I really come off like that? Because if I do then I seriously have to start wearing a whole fucking mosaic of pride pins on my chest to fix my heinous image, Jeezus..."

"You want some of the ones off my jacket?" they offered as a bad attempt at a joke.

"Oh my God. That yellow one? It's that yellow one isn't it. With the purple. Oh I'm so fucking *stupid.* It was right there the whole time, wasn't it?"

Ravi nodded with an attempt at a supportive grin. She really should've put it together a lot sooner, shouldn't she? She really had just been... blinding herself to it the whole time. Ravi probably could've gotten away with it forever if it weren't for Nicole's meddling.

"Jeezus, I thought that was all just... like... solidarity? You know? 'Dykes united' or whatever? You've got the lesbian one too, right? And the rainbow one and the trans one and... and... —Well how was I supposed to know??"

"Truly there were no clues at all," Ravi replied with a smirk, bumping out their flat bound chest for her and tipping their head to the side to show off their androgynous undercut.

"...This doesn't change anything," she said, serious, stern.

"It should."

"No. —I mean. Yes. —I mean it *has to*. —But I... still... You're <u>still</u>..."

"I'm <u>not</u> still her. That's the <u>point</u>. That was the fucking point, Felicity. I can't live like that anymore. I can't. But I didn't... —I don't know. I'm sorry. I just didn't want to lose you too. You always looked at me like I was worth something, like you wanted me around. And I needed that. There was no one else left. God, I've just... I've lost a lot of people, Fleece – *over this* – and I've been *real* lonely for a long time. I couldn't lose you too. If I just pretended, I thought—"

She charged up to them and interrupted them to jab their chest a few times to punctuate a bitter admonishment: "Selfish! —Stupid too! What's wrong with you??"

"I was scared!"

"Jeezus. —*I'm* the bad friend??"

"No. No, you're... You're an asshole sometimes Fleece but... Nicole was right. You're probably the best friend I'll ever have. I never deserved you. Sorry for being such a prick to you."

"...She said that?"

"She had nothing in her heart but love and respect for you. Right to the very end. She left for you. I'm sure of it. She changed after you pushed her. For you. A *stranger*. I wasn't worth it I guess."

"Oh stop it. She left to save you, Vee, not because I was riding her."

"I didn't want to be saved. I never wanted to be saved. Not by her or you or anyone else." Ravi crushed their bicep in a talon grip and gritted their teeth while they bitterly added, "She didn't even ask. You know? Isn't that insane? How do you pretend to love someone for so long and then make such a stupid *selfish* choice without even *asking*? Like I didn't even matter. —You were right. The whole time. I really was nothing to her in the end. Just... the flash of a mortal life in the eyes of the eternal. Worth less consideration than the errant spark of a single fucking disconnected synapse." Ravi turned their dead eyes to Felicity and told her plainly, "I told her <u>because</u> she was a stranger. She didn't matter, I thought. Then suddenly she just... *did*. —But that has nothing to do with how important you are to me. It never has."

Felicity curled her knuckles white and clenched her jaw until it creaked before she let out an exasperated swear: "Fuck! Fuck. I can't believe you're making me stand up for *her* but that is the stupidest thing you've <u>ever</u> said about her. She worked so hard on this stupid trade. —And she hated it. It was so obvious the whole time we were drawing it up. She hates this stuff. It's like some weird trauma for her or something I don't know I didn't ask. But she did it anyways, for you. And only for you. She left for *humanity* but she did all this extra stuff for <u>you</u>. And you're being super cruel to say she didn't think about you before she left. You can say she was pushy about it, that she should've asked, and yeah she definitely should've talked to you about it, but you can't say you didn't matter to her. That's more naïve than letting a faerie queen sleep on your couch for free."

"...I think she was a princess actually."

"She sure was."

"God... I can't believe I can never tell her how fucked up all this was."

Felicity went silent. When Ravi turned to see what was wrong, they found her lip pinched gently between her teeth while she peered into their eyes for something, like she was looking in the eyes of a wounded animal on the side of the road for a sign of life. After a few seconds of searching, she bit down hard and cursed at herself before she uneasily asked:

"Do you... want to?"

"I want to chew her damn ear off is what I want. Instead I'm stuck with all this bitterness and these *shitty* fucking gifts until the day I kick the bucket." Ravi scoffed at a thought. "I swear I'll have her name on my lips when I die. And a whole mouthful of swears. What a piece of work."

Felicity turned her head away slightly to let her eyes dart about the room, trying to sort her thoughts into a tidy enough pile to show them off.

After a few seconds, she got caught on a thought stupid enough to make her laugh at herself and smile sadly before she corrected herself, "No... Of course you do..."

"What?"

She turned to them with a grim look in her eyes before she challenged them to be honest: "It won't be easy. Or cheap. But there's a way – a Witch's guide to all things fae. So, say it like you mean it, Vee: Do you want to find her?"